# Summer of the Second Coming

by
## Colin Hayward

*Dedicated to:*

*Linda Hayward*

*Marcia Ranger*

*Paul Comacchio*

*Tony Hayward*

*Jeannette Mallay*

*and*

*Nigel Leith*

## Also by this Author

*Other Times Other Places*

*Dark Enough to Dance*

Title: Summer of the Second Coming

ISBN 978-0-9737685-1-0

Published by:

**Molten Ice**
Publishing

cjhmoltenice@gmail.com

Cover Photo: Colin Hayward
Photo of the author: Tony Hayward

# Summer of the
# Second Coming

by
## Colin Hayward

**ONTARIO ARTS COUNCIL**
**CONSEIL DES ARTS DE L'ONTARIO**

an Ontario government agency
un organisme du gouvernement de l'Ontario

*Special thanks to the Ontario Arts Council for supporting the writing of this book with a Professional Writer's Work-in-Progress Award.*

# About the Author

Colin Hayward at the helm of the *Stars and Stripes*, America's Cup contender out of San Diego.

When not travelling with his wife, Linda, Colin lives among birches and evergreens near Sudbury, Ontario. Author of two previous books, *Other Times Other Places* and *Dark Enough to Dance*. Colin has published many travel articles and short stories. In a long career, he has worked in theatre, directed the Technical Theatre Programme at Cambrian College and spent much of his leisure time sailing and scuba diving around the world.

If you have any comments,
Colin can be reached at
cjhmoltenice@gmail.com

# Summer of the
# Second Coming

*"Therefore be ye also ready:
for in such an hour as ye think not,
the Son of man cometh."*

~ *Matthew 24:44*

# Part One:
# Northern Ontario, Canada, 1989

## The Persistence of Vision

Messy people live in an ever-changing landscape stratified according to the immutable laws of sedimentology. Because of this, books and bills are much easier to locate than neat people would have us believe. Professor Arthur Whitehead had been known to explain to skeptical visitors that all he has to do is calculate the era, say last Wednesday, when he consulted a certain book or received the gas bill and, following sound geological principles, excavate to the required stratum.

With a comfortable creak, the professor leaned back in his swivel chair and surveyed the piles of paper that silted his desk, cluttered the windowsill and overflowed in stalagmite piles onto the faded Persian carpet that his wife had insisted would add a touch of color to his study.

A warm breeze seeped through the window, rippling through the papers and ruffling the tentacles of white hair that fringed the professor's alabaster dome.

The professor lifted his heavily thatched eyebrows and surveyed the bookshelves that completely obscured two of the walls. He rubbed his substantial nose as if expecting the genie of inspiration to appear but no such luck. He needed a precise date to locate the correct stratum; the precise date would be in his field notes. But his field notebook was precisely what he was looking for. Trapped in a mathematical strange loop, he sighed and, with a less musical creak, left his swivel chair and padded to the door of his study.

"Lydia!" he called. No answer.

While the professor is waiting, head cocked slightly to one side, perhaps we can peek back into his study. Anything missing? Check the outlet under the window. Two plugs running to the desk lamp and an IBM follow-the-bouncing-ball typewriter, already old in 1989. No line running to a surge protector whose non-existence does not connect to a computer terminal.

It is tempting to leap to the conclusion that computers arrived too late in the career of Arthur Whitehead for him to adjust to the neocomplexities that they would have introduced to his life. But inductive logic is a slippery tool and can lead us to infer that the not-yet-known is true based on the already-known. Alternate, and less seemingly likely conclusions are also possible. In fact, as Max Planck discovered in 1900, the continuity we think we perceive in the external world does not exist in the fundamental processes of nature.

So why is there no computer? The presence of a mug of sharpened pencils and a sheaf of papers grey with calculations on the relatively clear patch of desk in front of the professor's chair would seem to indicate that the professor still crunched numbers by hand. Why?

Far from being computer-phobic, the professor had eagerly embraced this new tool when it appeared, persisting even though the constantly refreshing images on the screen sometimes made him nauseous. For three months he immersed himself in the intricacies of computer languages: Fortran, Basic, APL, COBOL, Pascal, and Algol.

Then an odd thing happened. At first he began to get headaches. Eventually the headaches disappeared, but the computer-generated characters on his screen began to dance in the most disconcerting way. Calculations on things as disparate as zircon radiation decay and his latest pay increase invariably produced the same answer: 165321062533. Since the computer was not connected to anything but a 120-volt AC power source, and Tim Berners-Lee did not yet have the World Wide Web online, Arthur could not be dealing with a virus. Even so, he checked with his colleagues. None of them had noticed the magic number.

Laboriously he began to repeat the calculations by hand, or with a pocket calculator. The results were within the parameters that he had expected. He would return to the computer and go through the program again only to learn that 165321062533 seemed to be the answer to everything. He took the number and, with his pocket calculator, applied the sieve of Eratosthenes, convinced that it must be a prime number, but when he divided by 11, he got a whole number: 15,029,187,503. Arthur was intrigued by the fact that the new number had eleven digits. As a result, he began researching numerology to see if the number '11' had any special significance. The most interesting finding from this avenue of research was that numerologists were an odd lot. He did learn that 11 was a master number, big in Biblical applications, indications of the 'light bearer' – Lucifer, an indication of the end of days, the rapture and the second coming. None of this information seemed to shed much light on the number itself. When he asked Lydia if the number eleven had any significance for her, she considered for a moment and then said, "Spinal Tap."

"Spinal Tap?" he asked, wondering if she was being merely playful.

"They had an amp that went up to eleven."

"Ah." After a moment's thought, he told her. "Afraid it doesn't help any more than the sunspot cycles."

"Like the huge one in March?" she asked. "The one that knocked out all the power in the Québec grid?"

Arthur nodded. For the next twelve hours he calculated everything from the cube root of the beluga population in the St. Lawrence River to the value of pi at 165321062533 decimal places. Not until the computer flashed up a screen full of machine language happy faces and the message, 'Abort, Retry, Fail?' did he finally pick up the machine, and yell, "Fail!" as he hurled it through his study window. When it hit the gentle ripples of Lake Ramsey, it made a satisfying splash before slowly sinking with a dying gurgle.

After he had calmed down with the aid of a couple of stiff scotches, the professor humbly decided that the problem was not in the stars, but in himself. He was suffering from the VDTs and suspected that his failure to get any answer out of the computer, other than 165321062533, was related to his problem with moving images.

The vast majority of us may grumble about the exorbitant prices of movies, but when we are seated in the darkened theatre, popcorn on lap, feet firmly glued to the sticky patch on the floor, it never occurs to us to complain that half the time we are staring at a blank screen waiting for the next still frame to come up.

There is no record of how well the thirty-three customers enjoyed the twenty-minute showing of the first commercial pictures on December 28th, 1895, but five-year-old Arthur Whitehead made no secret of his reaction to *Bambi* over half a century later. He screamed in terror and was quickly removed from the theatre by his embarrassed mother.

For some reason, little Arthur had seen only a confusion of still images, each followed by a terrifying black nothingness that recurred forty-eight times a second so that the boy felt he was sinking into the abyss.

"Don't worry," Walter Schwartzkopf, his sad, grey stepfather had offered. "God is in the gaps. Perhaps that is what you are looking at." The child's face became serious as he thought about this. After a few moments, he shook his head. Arthur's stepfather, a physicist, had had no experience with children before marrying the boy's mother when Arthur had been a two-year-old. As a result, he tended to talk to the boy as if he were a short, uninformed colleague. The boy, for his part, tried to adopt an adult seriousness to live up to the grownup world his stepfather invited him to join. Now Walter was stalling by puffing on his pipe. Eventually he nodded to himself, pointed the stem at his son, and cautioned, "None of us actually perceives reality directly, only our own interaction with it. The act of perception changes whatever we perceive. Whatever it was before, it has become something else. If you think about it, Arthur, your ability to see the blackness when the shutter is down in the projector is undoubtedly a more accurate perception than that of the rest of us, because that is what actually happens. In fact, your brain, it seems, refuses to be tricked. That, my boy, makes you special." Privately, however, Arthur's stepfather was appalled that little Arthur seemed to lack the protective illusion granted to the rest of us. After all, humankind cannot bear very much reality. Five-year-old Arthur understood little of this but some instinct told him that his secret would be dangerous to share with anyone else.

Three days later, over breakfast, the boy asked, "What is light?"

Arthur's stepfather had begun researching the idea of after-imaging shortly after his son's first and last trip to the movies. Now he sipped his coffee thoughtfully before replying, "It depends on who is looking at it. Remember I said that looking at something can change it? Well, we know light is energy that appears in measurable wavelengths, but it also appears as particles called photons. If we are looking for a wave, we'll see a wave. If we are looking for a particle, we'll see a particle.

But we never observe both at the same time." He stopped, hoping his explanation had sufficed but the boy was still staring at him expectantly. "We see the world because of light. Even the Bible tells us the earth 'was without form and void' before God said, 'Let there be light.' Nothing is visible until light strikes it. You might as well say that, without light, nothing would exist. By the same token, without any sentient being to perceive the light, perhaps the light would not exist either."

At the time, the idea impressed five-year-old Arthur. Not until years later did he learn that his stepfather had not unveiled the idea at that moment; that it could be traced back at least as far as Bishop Berkeley's famous '*esse est percipi, esse est percipere*.'

"But why does everybody except me see light when it's not there?" Arthur persisted.

His stepfather began slowly. After all the boy may be bright, he reminded himself, but he is only five: "Ah, yes. Well, a film is made up of twenty-four still pictures projected each second on a screen." Arthur nodded. "In order to proceed from one image to the next without blurring our perception, a gate comes down while the sprocket moves another frame into place. The gate lifts and reveals the new still image. Then it comes down again and goes up again, so we see each individual image twice. Apparently a flicker rate of forty-eight is about right, since we only retain a single positive image for a brief time in our brains. That's why some people call movies 'the flicks.'"

He paused, permitting himself a rare smile, but the boy was still staring at him intently. So he continued, "This after-image had been noticed by the ancient Egyptians but nobody had ever studied it scientifically until a Scottish physician called Peter Mark Roget noticed the spokes on the turning wheels of a moving carriage through the slats of a window blind. He saw that, except for the spokes in the vertical position, they appeared to curve downward. He wrote a scientific paper on it, which he presented in 1824. He speculated that the illusion was caused by the brain retaining an after-image and attaching that image to a new one on the other side of the slat. Since the wheel had moved forward, the two images taken together gave the illusion that the spokes were curved. Look." He diagrammed, from memory, the sketch in the original paper. "See?" The boy nodded slowly, feeling that when he thought about it later, the idea would become clear.

Warming to his topic now, Arthur's stepfather went on: "Well, then several other people realized that they could make apparently moving images from still ones by putting a blank space between them, and relying on our brains to create the movement. There are some later theories too. Max Wertheimer, for instance, doubted the idea of positive after-images and posited a phi phenomenon which..."

But by this time, the boy's attention had been captured by the picture on the Quaker Oats box of a Quaker holding up a Quaker Oats box with a Quaker holding up a Quaker Oats box with a Quaker... Suddenly, the boy understood the idea of infinity.

When his parents bought their first television set, Arthur tried to watch but felt dizzy at the sight of Lucille Ball's face undergoing a smeary metamorphosis every thirtieth of a second. After that he retired to his room to read whenever the set was on. It never occurred to him to complain about the flickering of his bedside lamp as the alternating current pulsed at sixty hertz. He naturally assumed that artificial light was an imperfect substitute for sunlight, and that everyone else was so used to it, that no one even mentioned it.

At university, Arthur studied geology, thinking it the most immovable version of reality he could find. But of course, rocks shudder and shake, subduct, liquefy and flow in perilous pyroclastic splendor. Even the solid ground beneath his feet was suspect. By his third year, he finally summoned enough courage to confide his peculiar view of the electric age to the university physician who had, in turn, sent him to a neurologist. The elderly specialist performed a wide variety of arcane tests, only desisting when Arthur's health insurance company hinted that whatever ailment he thought he had could be paid for by one of their rivals in the field. Eventually the specialist had theorized that Arthur's brain had become hardwired at an incredibly early age. He explained that, just as people blind from birth are unable to sort out images if their sight is restored in adulthood and frequently commit suicide as a result, so Arthur lacked the ability to process still images into moving pictures. Therefore, he was condemned to shun the media images that were defining North American culture.

The bleak diagnosis did not cheer Arthur, but the neurologist was delighted and subsequently published several learned papers on 'Patient X's Syndrome.' Unfortunately, Arthur's anonymity did not survive for long. Within a couple of weeks, a shifty-looking man in a coffee-stained suit turned up and, introducing himself as a member of the fourth estate, proceeded to quiz him on his unique condition. Arthur slammed the door on the man's foot thinking that was the end of the interview.

It was not. A few days later, Arthur was lined up at the 'Eight Items Only' lane of his local supermarket behind a lady writing out a check on a Hong Kong account and two other people whose heaped grocery carts indicated that they believed that 8 represented an infinite number. In fact it does, Arthur thought idly, if you look at it sideways.

His eyes settled on the magazine rack. What he saw made him blanche with surprise and embarrassment. On the front page of *The World News Enquirer* the headline screamed, "MAN SEES ALIENS IN MOVIE IMAGES." In slightly smaller letters, "EMINENT SCIENTIST SAYS CASE ONE IN A MILLION." Underneath was a grainy picture of Arthur seated at his kitchen table, no doubt shot through the window of his basement apartment, and a carefully garbled account of the old neurologist's theory.

Feeling suddenly exposed, Arthur dropped his tomatoes and pound of burger and left. "Perhaps Balzac was right," he muttered bitterly as he scuffed through the crowded parking lot trying to calm down. Honoré de Balzac had suspected that the act of photography removed one of the finite number of spectral layers of self. By the time he found his car, Arthur had managed to comfort himself with the thought that Balzac had also believed that the quality of his writing depended on a high sperm count and that an orgasm at the wrong time could ruin a masterpiece. We all have our blind spots, Arthur noted. Look at Pythagoras. Marvellous at mathematics but forbade his followers to eat beans in case they farted out their souls. After all, my father taught me that external reality is forever unreachable. We experience only our own singular interaction with it. The fact that my own perception is markedly different from most others does not invalidate it.

Arthur's conclusion that his troubles with computers were directly linked to his inability to watch still images disguised as movies or pixelated constructs disguised as videos may not be correct. For instance, it fails to explain the answer: 165321062533.

Nevertheless, the die (or the computer in this case) had been cast.

From now on any computing could be safely left to Lydia.

Arthur called his wife's name again. A muffled acknowledgment came from the direction of the basement. He opened the door and called down the stairs: "I can't find my field notes."

"And I can't find my new diagonal," Lydia countered from the nether depths.

"What the Hell's a diagonal," the professor muttered to himself and then remembered that it was something to do with the eyepiece on the Newtonian telescope Lydia was building. "When did I use them last?" he pursued.

No immediate reply, just a rhythmic tap-tap-tap-shit, tap-tap-tap-shit. She must be hammering the bits together, Arthur surmised. Resigned, he picked his way down the detritus that littered the cellar steps, a mixture of winter implements on their way to the basement for the summer and summer implements that could now be safely moved to the patio. Here they would probably linger in landing limbo until the seasons changed, victims of an incomplete subduction.

"How's my little Galileo?" asked Arthur, carefully skirting Bart's tricycle. Child of the professor's previous marriage, Bartholomew was twenty-seven now and lived on the west coast, but the tricycle remained, a fossil record of his childhood.

Lydia looked up and gave him a warm smile. It had been fifteen years since she had been Arthur's brightest (and only female) graduate student but, except for a few fault lines sketched around the eyes and an almost imperceptible concession to gravity in her nether region, she had retained her smooth-skinned good looks. Today her long hair was done up in a complicated bun. "The telescope will be ready in time for Stellafane – if I can find my diagonal," she told him.

Stellafane was not until August. A group of amateur astronomers gathered on a hilltop in Vermont once a year to examine each other's homemade telescopes by day and to listen to talks by invisible experts by night. The experts were invisible because of the astronomers' collective horror of artificial light pollution. Latecomers sometimes drove into trees or over tents because they could not put on their headlights, but such accidents happened only rarely. After the talks, the crowd dispersed as people felt their way to the telescopes and either took turns gazing at Messier objects or cursed the clouds and drank too much. Arthur and Lydia would not have dreamed of missing Stellafane.

"Looks as if it's almost ready," Arthur encouraged after a careful examination of the octagonal tube. Straightening up, he added, "I'm going into the field on Wednesday. Can't find my notes."

Lydia's green-brown eyes sparkled with amusement. "In the field." The sign decorated most of the office doors in the geology department at this time of year and could mean that the occupant was shivering in a tent on Baffin Island or using a hand lens to examine the gems on the G-strings of strippers at Solid Gold. "If my telescope is finished, I'll come with you and field test it," she announced.

"That would be nice," he said with genuine pleasure, "but I still need my notes."

Lydia calculated for a moment. "Eleven days ago," she said at last.

"Just before I received the thin sections from Sri Lanka," the professor remembered. "Must be under the padded envelope and that green book of abstracts I was wading through."

"Good luck," she called after him.

Arthur found his notes easily. Just a case of knowing where to dig.

## The Numbers Game

"Curious," commented Dr. Mahinda Rapasinghe, visiting professor from the Institute of Fundamental Studies in Sri Lanka.

"What's curious?" asked Arthur keeping his eyes on the road ahead.

"That cemetery that we have just been passing. It has a letterbox."

Arthur nodded. He too had wondered about the mailbox at the entrance to the French Catholic cemetery when he had moved to

Sudbury. Box for dead letters? Or perhaps even in death you couldn't escape junk mail.

OPEN IMMEDIATELY.
YOU MAY HAVE WON
A ONCE-IN-A-LIFETIME TRIP TO PURGATORY.

"French letters?" Arthur offered. The dark little man next to him frowned in puzzlement. "It's a French-Canadian graveyard," Arthur explained lamely.

"Ah, and did you notice the statue with the fur coat. That too is a French custom?"

Arthur chuckled. "You mean the poured marble Jesus covered in caterpillars?"

Mahinda smiled but remained silent. Canadians had many odd customs and he was not sure if it was polite to ask about them.

On the car radio the one o'clock time signal beeped after ten seconds of silence so that Canadians strung out in a thin line across a continent could synchronize their watches. The CBC news followed: In Houston, Texas, a man drowned at a pool party for lifeguards; Sudbury's City Council had just passed a resolution that would change the names of all its playgrounds to Leisure Activity Centers; In Newfoundland, yet another Catholic priest had been charged with sexually molesting young boys, bringing the total to eleven so far; Results of a seven-year study revealed that unemployment for a prolonged period of time can lead to clinical depression.

Summertime news even though the official solstice was some days away. The seriousness of Canadians declines in direct proportion to the rise in temperature so that stories about people dying in numbers too big for sympathy rarely reappeared before the chilly evenings of September to remind them that their annual ice age is approaching.

"Turn here," Dr. Mahinda Rapasinghe urged Arthur.

"Here?" echoed Arthur, puzzled.

"Right, left." Mahinda agreed.

Realizing that there was no right turn, Arthur eased his rusty Land Rover into the left turn lane and waited for the traffic to clear. "Are you sure you got the directions right?" Arthur asked politely.

"Oh yes, my fine bugger," said Mahinda confidently. "It is right here."

"Right, here?"

"There." Mahinda pointed at the small plaza across the street.

Arthur turned left. "That's a Miracle Mart. We can't eat there," he protested.

"Eating place too. You will see."

"The donut shop? For lunch?"

"No, no. Around the side." Arthur shrugged and drove cautiously through the parking lot, past the bedding store and Singer Sewing Center. Threading his way between a shimmering snake of shopping carts and a suicidal toddler, Arthur turned the corner. Dr. Rapasinghe clapped his hands in delight. "It is still here!" he cried excitedly.

"The chip wagon?"

"Yes, yes. Park here. Best chips in the world. Gunatilaka told me about it." Arthur nodded, remembering the visit of Professor Rapasinghe's colleague, four years earlier.

"You didn't tell me we were lunching alfresco," Arthur protested mildly. Actually, the fumes coming from the chip wagon smelled marvellous.

"Alfresco? No, no, Arthur. Chips and hot dogs. No alfrescos. Come, I am paying."

As Arthur stared at the windowless brick wall in front of the car, a question occurred: "Doesn't Buddhism forbid the killing of animals?"

"Oh, yes, very much so," agreed Mahinda, an impish smile creasing his brown face, "but not eating meat, oh no."

"So who slaughters animals for meat in Sri Lanka?" Arthur pursued.

"Oh, the Muslims. They have very strict rules about it." He paused and considered. "In fact the Qur'an has very strict rules about everything, even the direction of passing wind."

"Farting?" asked Arthur, incredulous.

"So I believe. One is obliged to fart downwind. I don't know what you do if there is no breeze. Bottle it until later perhaps. That would account for the tales of evil djinns being released after centuries. Come, let's eat."

The nose is the most primitive, and at the same time the most direct of our senses. Unlike the eyes and the ears, which infer the outside world from waveforms, the olfactory glands actually sample molecules of the thing itself. So, following their noses, Arthur and Mahinda each ordered a hotdog, chips and a Coke – much more typically Canadian fare than moose steaks or pemmican.

"What are hotdogs made of?" Mahinda asked innocently as he popped the last charred knob into his mouth.

"No one knows," Arthur confessed, "and no one is eager to find out."

"And Coca-Cola?"

"It's a secret."

Mystical Western foods, Mahinda told himself. Perhaps such things keep their skin pale, he speculated. He looked at the back of his own hand. Had it been getting lighter since his arrival here in the North?

"It's all fixed," said Arthur, suddenly businesslike. "We'll be gone for three days. Should be enough time to gather samples."

"We will find some shatter cones?" Mahinda inquired.

Sipping their Cokes, the two men lapsed into geology talk which, like the jargon of any field, is intentionally incomprehensible to the layman.

They were, in fact, talking about the formation of the Sudbury Basin, an enormous hole in the Precambrian shield, north of the city. This hole, an elliptical ring 60 kilometers by 27 kilometers, is the reason that Sudbury is the largest producer of nickel on the planet as well as supplying a large portion of the world's copper, zinc, lead, silver and gold. While the multinational mining companies cheerfully rip the various ores out of the bones of ancient rock and take everything else for granite, hardrock geologists, like Professor Whitehead, examine endless core samples and thin sections to determine what caused the Sudbury Basin and the rich metal ore deposits that surround it.

Before 1966, everyone more or less agreed to call it a massive volcanic event (endogenesis). But then a Professor R. S. Dietz proposed the Astrobleme Theory (exogenesis) noting that the area was littered with shatter cones, a phenomenon created by high impact. Therefore, he concluded, the huge hole was caused by an enormous meteor.

Hence Dr. Rapasinghe's inquiry about shatter cones.

Professor Whitehead, a confirmed exogenecist, had promised to take his colleague out into the field to a place near Onaping where the Sri Lankan could collect samples to take back to his own country. Oddly enough, much of the rock that makes up the island of Sri Lanka is of the same type and age as the local rock, but it has been rotting away for ages under the assault of the tropical climate.

"My wife, Lydia, will be coming with us," Arthur announced when the two scholars switched back into comprehensible English.

"Your wife? Wonderful. Such a charming lady," Mahinda beamed, wondering privately if the three of them would be sharing the same tent.

"She is bringing her telescope, so she'll probably be up all night," Arthur added.

"Ah." Only the two men then. One can never be too sure with Westerners. Mahinda leaned over and confided, "I too am getting married."

"Well, congratulations," said Arthur, pumping the little man's hand with rather too much vigor. "Someone back home, is it?"

"Oh, my goodness, yes." Mahinda cringed at the thought of marrying one of the Canadian amazons.

For form's sake, Arthur asked, "What's her name?"

Mahinda looked puzzled. "Her name?" he repeated. "Surely I am not knowing that yet. Before I came here, I said to myself, "Mahinda, you are thirty-seven years old. It is time to take a wife." He shrugged. "So I asked my parents to find one for me. Look. This arrived yesterday."

He reached into an inner pocket, pulled out a neatly folded section of the *Columbo Sunday Observer*, and handed it to his startled companion. The paper was folded open at the 'Marriage Proposals.' Arthur scanned down the Bridegrooms until he reached an advertisement circled in pencil.

"Govi Buddhist parents seek fair, attractive educated partner below 128 years for their eldest son, 37 years, height 5'3", professor employed at Sri Lankan Institute. Send particulars with horoscope ..."

"The 128 is a misprint," Mahinda pointed out. "Should read only 28."

Arthur nodded and chewed meditatively on his antepenultimate chip. "And does it work?" he asked. "Placing an ad, I mean."

"Oh, generally, yes. Of course, Canadians do not arrange marriages, so you do not need such things. Alternate universes, perhaps," Mahinda replied with a smile.

Arthur popped in the last chip and sucked the salt off his fingers before replying. "Perhaps," he mused. "But an alternate universe to yours would still bear many similarities. Take your marriage column. We have something similar called 'Companions Wanted.' Look." Grabbing yesterday's Sudbury Star out of the back seat, he rummaged through the classifieds until he located the column and handed it to Mahinda who read it with growing wonder.

"What do you think?" asked Arthur after a few minutes.

"That there are a large number of lonely Canadian males who are 5'10" and enjoy candle light dinners and walking in the rain."

Arthur was impressed and asked, "Anything else?"

Mahinda shrugged. "Discreet encounters in the afternoon are for adultery?" he guessed, too embarrassed to mention the many homosexual ads.

"That's right."

Mahinda put down the paper and risked one final question: "What please is a 'herpes man'?"

Arthur laughed as he started the car and put it in reverse. "Someone with a sexual disease looking for a partner with the same disease to mingle microbes with," he told his Sinhalese friend.

"I see," said Mahinda, although he did not see at all. "Look. Would you mind if we stopped over there." He pointed to the corner of the parking lot.

"Sure," Arthur agreed, wondering why his colleague would be interested in paintings rendered on velvet.

After wandering through the thicket of velvet Elvises, vague landscapes, bleeding Sacred Hearts and unicorns, Mahinda selected a Virgin Mary in the traditional blue housecoat sporting an apparently radioactive halo. "$29.95," said Mahinda picking it up. "What do you think?"

"Why do you want to buy it?" asked Arthur evasively.

"Souvenir of your French folk art," Mahinda replied.

"But it isn't," Arthur protested. "All this stuff is painted in a factory in Ciudad Juàrez, Mexico. Lydia and I were there once. They turn them out in ten to fifteen minutes. Something like 20,000 a week. A semitrailer full of velvet paintings leaves for Canada at least once a month. What made you think they were French Canadian?"

"My landlady has three of them," said Mahinda, looking disappointed as he put the Virgin back on her easel. Still, there was something haunting about the gaunt face that secretly impressed even Arthur.

"I see you're a connoisseur, sir," said the chubby lady in tight shorts toasting herself in her plastic chair. "You have a kind face," she flattered, "so I'll let you have it for twenty dollars only." She shook her head. "Perhaps we don't eat tonight but..."

Mahinda could not pass up such a bargain and comforted himself with the thought that not eating might do the lady some good. Arthur shook his head as the woman wrapped the painting in brown paper and string.

"If you really want native art, we'll go to Manitoulin Island and you can have a look at the Ojibway crafts. Much more attractive than... than this stuff." Arthur shuddered and led Mahinda gently back to the car.

"How are you getting along with crunching the numbers on those samples I analyzed?" Arthur said as he nosed the car out into the traffic.

"I'm afraid not very well," Mahinda confessed uneasily. "The computers seem to have become ill with a virus. Anything I call up gives me the same answer."

"What's that?" asked Arthur, a sense of foreboding rising in him.

"The number 165321062533."

"My God!" Arthur exclaimed. "I abandoned computers years ago because all I could get was that number."

"Ah, did you realize what the number meant?" inquired Mahinda.

"No… At first I thought it must be one of those exceedingly rare high prime numbers. But I applied the sieve of Eratosthenes and found it wasn't," said Arthur, hardly daring to ask, "Did you find out what the damn number meant?"

"Oh yes, but it was not I that discovered the solution. Oh no. I tried all kinds of things with no solution forthcoming. Not until late one night when one of the cleaning women came into my office did I discover the beginning of the solution. I asked her to look at the screen and tell me what she saw. Fascinating. A good Buddhist woman, she saw it right away."

"What was it?" Arthur demanded, ready to stop the car and beat the answer out of his companion.

"Oh, a date."

"A date? What do you mean a date?"

"The last four numbers – 2533. I should have seen it myself. This is the year 2533 in the Buddhist calendar. Working backwards, 06 is this month, June 21 must be the day… You know that woman had been cleaning my office for six years and…"

This time Arthur did stop the car, screeching to a halt and causing a chorus of horns to doppler past. "What are the first four numbers," he asked through gritted teeth.

"Ah yes, simple, really. The time. It took me a couple of hours before I realized it was the time stated in a military fashion. 1653, isn't it?"

"June 21 at 4:53 p.m. That's it? It still doesn't mean anything." Arthur started the car.

Mahinda smiled seraphically. "Oh, yes. The time is of greatest importance. For months, I consulted railway timetables, airplane arrival times, decaying protons, phases of the moon. I had no success. And then I come here and poof."

"Poof?"

"Poof. It was on the radio, your Canadian Broadcasting Corporation. The summer solstice arrives on Saturday at precisely 4:53 p.m. local time, isn't it?"

"The longest day," murmured Arthur.

"The longest day," agreed Mahinda.

After a long silence, Arthur said, "But what does it mean?"

"The magic number? Perhaps we'll find out on the solstice."

"We'll be in the field on the solstice, camped up Highway 144, near the Arctic Watershed."

## The Plague Year

At first few noticed them, clusters of eggs shrouded in silky strands. The snow melted, the rivers rose, the trees budded, then they emerged in their billions: tent caterpillars in the worst cycle in centuries.

Tree trunks writhed with them; furry caterpillars snapped under foot; cars skidded on them; roads were sanded as if for mid-winter. Visitors to the woods dared not stand still for they crawled up legs, dropped into hair on gossamer skeins. Black curtains of them hung from hydro wires.

And there was the sound, a constant whispering, as millions of mandibles crunched, chewed, cut and carved every green leaf in sight, leaving deciduous trees bare as January.

Then came the flies to land on the eyes, to crawl across cradles and barbecue tables, to buzz around beaches, infest forested reaches.

Called *Sarcophaga aldrichi*, big blue flies with reddish brown eyes laid their eggs in the living caterpillars so their young on hatching could suckle a stranger.

And the black flies rose in clouds from the running streams, the mosquitoes hummed over standing water.

The hills were alive with the sounds of springtime.

People scratched their heads, backs, bums and privates and put up road signs warning of maddened mammals being driven from the bush: 'Deer Crossing', or a triangle with the picture of a moose.

*Springtime, oh Springtime, the only pretty ringtime....*
*A car skids on caterpillar slime.*
*Act of God chirps the priest.*

*A transport jackknifes spilling toxic waste.*
*Act of God mumbles the Ministry of the Environment.*

*Caterpillars clog the eaves in the heavy spring rains*
*and bring down the ceiling.*
*Act of God intones the insurance agent.*

*A moose charges a car carrying two children*
*forcibly removed from their mother.*
*Act of God sobs the social worker.*

And God smiled and muttered to himself, "You ain't seen nothin' yet. Remember the Egyptians?"

A nanosecond later, or earlier since no one observed it, He devised a plan. "Everything is for a purpose, so why this sudden interest in entomology?" the Big Guy asked himself. "*Insha Allah*, the Muslims would say and think no more about it. But the people in this part of the planet tend to be Christian, the few who still believe anything. How about the Scientologists?" He asked Himself and laughed until the tears ran down his hairy cheeks. "No, they'll never do. And the ordinary mortals will need a reason. I need a convergence that they can twist into sense." He rubbed his forelegs together and sucked meditatively on a Black Hole looking for inspiration. "*Gott wurfelt nicht,*" he quoted with a chuckle, "God does not play dice."

"A prophet," he murmured at last. "Haven't had a successful one in centuries. Last one was Mohammed. Tough these days now that they've got mass media, global village and experts on everything from parenting to particle physics. Prophets were easier in days of donkeys and camels. Mmm. A motorcycle? *Deus ex Machina*?" God grinned broadly to himself and sucked a stream of high-test gravity.

"A visionary turning point," He said, warming to the idea, "maybe even with a scientific basis, obeying the laws of this-and-that. Not like that Saint What-his-name on the road to Damascus. Nobody would fall for that old trick these days. Something so complex that intellectuals could argue about it but so simple that even TV reporters could understand it. With a touch of nostalgia for the good old days, too, of course. Ah, the Golden Age!"

But what was His golden age, He mused. Ah, before the sects came along, before hysterical teenage girls had visions of Him dressed as the Virgin Mary, before Moses with his carefully carved tablets, Jain, Zoroaster and that radical Essene preacher. Back when Gods were everywhere, except in the empty Americas. Before He had outlived them all and had only himself for company.

Then he remembered the erratic, a boulder of gneiss striped pink and white that he had watched in its slow wanderings over the eons until it had found its final resting place after the last ice age.

"Upon this rock, I will kill my birch," He said, feeling particularly pleased with himself.

"There!" he boomed, and a flash of lightning cleaved a silver birch, forking it over the boulder at the place where two roads meet: rail for transport and tarmac for travel.

Piece of cake, if you're omnipotent.

## Rocky Road

Millions of years were to pass before the rock saw the light of day, and even then its surfacing was temporary. Beginning life in the underworld as a simple granite pluton, it already had been cooked and squeezed by volcanic activity and continental shifts, until it had metamorphosed into pink and black layers, before the hot mantle cooled and the short-lived radioactive elements died and disappeared from the earth.

For eons it lay trapped beneath hundreds of meters of the green stone spewed by volcanoes, lay trapped like one of Michelangelo's prisoners. With infinite slowness, the gneiss was exposed, as the winds and weather eroded the green stone. One Arctic night it reached the surface but its exposure did not last.

The continental crust thickened again as the Hudsonian erogeny once more coated it with volcanic green stone until it sank out of sight. Or rather out of the possibility of perception, for there was no life form to observe it.

Except, of course, the Deities and, of them, only God actually perceived it while the rest squabbled over suzerainty in case evolution turned up anything remotely intelligent.

Early life forms were anything but promising. Single celled creatures groped blindly through the primordial soup, reproducing themselves by splitting into two, and two again thereby gaining immortality but not intelligence.

And God created Sex, and with it death. After all, without death, his creatures would never evolve.

Eons later, God was impressed that the obscure tribes who had chosen to worship Him alone seemed to be aware of this progression. In their creation myth, the earliest birth is through bifurcation as woman is made from man's rib. Later, so the story went, the humans, perhaps realizing that there was no possibility of progress in such a method of reproduction, got themselves kicked out of amoeba heaven so that they could produce creatures like, but distinctly separate from, themselves. The price was death, and further myths were required to remove the sting from extinction.

When humans entered the race, they immediately split into groups and began choosing Deities, real and imagined, to help with the crops, to keep the fractious in line and generally as a make-work project for the world's second oldest, least useful profession – the priesthood.

Tired of the plethora of rituals and annoyed by the constant groveling that became known as prayer, God forsook the rabble that roamed the earth and looked again for the pink-and-black stripes that had once caught his eye.

There it was, uncovered again, an outcrop of gneiss peeping through the earth, far in the north, at a place that in this timeline would one day be called Wager Bay.

The ice began to thicken again and flow south at a stately glacial pace, scraping and compressing the rock beneath it. When it reached the outcrop, the ice began to pressure it so that, after no more than a century or two, a jagged boulder snapped off and was carried south being smoothed and rounded as it went.

Some ten thousand years later, the ice deposited the rock almost exactly on the great continental watershed. As the earth began to warm, the ice, most common rock in the universe, became molten.

God glanced at his pet rock sitting like a present on the Precambrian shield, polished smooth by the ice. The shield slowly rebounded as the weight was removed, so that the beaches on Hudson's Bay became suspended in air. Eventually the country where the boulder of gneiss had come to rest became known as Canada, a native word which originally meant small village but came to mean the-vast-area-north-of-the-United-States-where-almost-nobody-lives.

Canada came into being with a gradually accretive formation of the different territories as they reluctantly joined between 1867 and 1949. Forever after, Québec, like the outer electron of a copper atom, threatened electric separation.

God peered at his rock and nodded with satisfaction and, for the sake of future geologists that would pass this way, He boomed, "Have a Gneiss Day!"

# Part Two:
# San Isidro, California, 1958

## Not Your Average Joe

For the second coming, God decided to reverse polarity. The gospels had featured Virgin Mary and Harlot Mary. The virgin had got all the good press in zero B.C. Time for the obverse.

God looked around and found just the woman he was looking for: a young hooker eking out a living on the dusty streets of San Isidro, California, within taco-heaving distance of the Mexican border. Maria Magdelana had that look that had lately become so prized by fashion designers, heroine chic, but, unlike most runway models, she achieved the look honestly. And, like her predecessor, she had that great hair, black and rich, cascading down to her thighs.

God moistened his mandibles as He looked through his planetary disguise collection. White bull? No, he had used that. He sighed. Europa had known how to have a good time. A swan? Ah, Leda. What a coupling. Michelangelo Buonarotti had made them a pretty good likeness. Shower of gold? Too tacky. No, no, something contemporary, something irresistible. He reached in and pulled out the white glitter suit and sideburns. "Treat me like a foooooool but love me....," he crooned setting up enough of a pressure wave to cause a local star to go supernova.

160,000 light years away, on a mountain top near La Serena, Chile, a group of astronomers that included Ian Shelton from the University of Toronto stood out in the cold night air and looked with awe at the first supernova visible to the naked eye since the time of Kepler.

Ignoring the scientific interpretation, one of the local porters ran back to his small shack and reported to his neighbors that God had sent a sign to them. Both hypotheses were true.

The bar was almost empty when God walked in out of the night sky, but all eyes followed him as the black light over the deserted stage picked out his white suit. The bartender went on wiping the same piece of bar with his cloth. Maria, who had just shot up in the bathroom marked *Senoritas*, watched open-mouthed as the most beautiful man she had ever seen flicked on the sound console so the JBLs and began to hum. Maria gasped as He pushed up the sliders on the small lighting board and his suit came alive with many colors. He picked up a guitar and launched into "Treat Me Like a Fool."

"*Madre de dios*," muttered Maria reflexively. "It is Elvis." Of course, we know it is not really Elvis, but God. What we cannot know is that we are not watching God taking on the form of Elvis, but God taking on the form of Jesse Garon, Elvis' twin brother who had been still-born. Elvis considered his dead brother an almost constant companion throughout his life. God would have said, had anyone been listening, that He couldn't argue with Elvis' claim that "Jesse had a way better voice than me." A more potent reason for disguising himself as Jesse was that, unlike Elvis, the boy had never experienced life on earth. The danger of letting people see him as the real Elvis could alter the future by cluttering the timeline of the King. People would still see Elvis when the Big Guy appeared but, since he was actually channelling Jesse, a being who had never been born, the time line since January 8th, 1935, the day Elvis was born, would not have been affected. Which name would the Big Guy use? Elvis? You bet.

That night Maria's shabby room was transformed into Graceland as Maria's Elvis flew her to the moon and she conceived among the stars.

The bar? It became a shrine to the King of Rock and Roll. Nine months later, on an air mattress in the back of a garage, Eddie was born. Joe, the towering, greybearded mechanic who owned the garage, had let Maria live in the back room for the past three months. For her part, Maria could see that the big man really liked her so, of course, she treated him like shit. Joe hung in, trading kindness for cruelty because he knew that, at his age and with the beer belly and the various scars he had collected over the years, he did not deserve such delicate beauty. To him, Maria was a gift from God. Joe was even looking forward to the birth of her baby. He had always liked kids, but had never had any. Maria's baby was his last chance.

"How're you feeling?" he asked, gently mopping Maria's brow with his pony tail.

"Jesus, it's hot," she said, irritated at his concern. Wrinkling her nose, she sniffed the mingled smells that filled the windowless back room, smells of oil, exhaust and her own sour sweat.

Katya, the Russian woman who was a professional waitress at the bar where Maria had met the King and an amateur midwife, cleaned off the large baby and handed him to Maria saying, "He is the biggest baby I have ever seen. Must be thirteen pounds."

"Lucky my cunt has been well greased," said Maria, reluctantly taking the heavy creature. She had just closed her eyes again when a hot rain began to fall, a shower of gold. "God dammit!" yelled Maria, tossing the baby into the air. "The fucker's pissing on me."

God watched the trajectory of His son until Joe snaked out a huge hand and caught the child inches from the concrete floor.

"Welcome to the world," Joe told the child. "You are made of star stuff."

"Take it away!" ordered Maria. Not surprisingly pissing on his mother, even reflexively, had an adverse effect on the bonding process. For two weeks, Maria refused to see the child. Eventually she relented, and Joe brought the big baby to her. "I'm going to call him Jesus," she announced. "Hey soos," she said, trying out the Spanish name. "Yeah."

Joe nodded. She was the mother, it was her call, he told himself. Joe liked the little guy, but there were things about him that made the big man uneasy. Babies were not supposed to be able to focus at this age, but Joe observed the boy looking around him with intelligent eyes as if he understood what was going on. But when he heard the baby whisper his name, he felt a shiver up his spine. He tried to get the child to repeat it, but the little elver gave him a Mona Lisa smile and fell asleep.

"He's really strong," Joe told her. "Know what he did? Killed a snake with his bare hands. I found it in his crib."

"Yeah, he's superman," said the skeptical madonna.

"You want to hold him, maybe, you know, put him to the breast."

"You fucking old pervert ... No, I don't want to hold him." She lit a cigarette and her tone softened as she approached him. "Mind looking after him for a little while longer, Joe?" she asked, stroking his curly, grey hair and playing affectionately with his ponytail. "Just 'til I get on my feet, you know."

"Sure, I don't mind." And he really didn't. Despite the uneasiness he felt about the child, he was fascinated and watched the boy by the hour, devising little games.

Maria ground her crotch against his leg. "Put that thing back in its crib," she said hoarsely. "Momma wants you to fuck her right now."

Joe hurriedly put the boy to bed. After all, this was the only payment he was ever likely to get for being a baby sitter.

That night Maria disappeared, as Joe suspected she might, leaving him holding the baby. She went back to the only life she knew. She even had some luck. For a while, she posed for porno magazines and was paid better than hooker wages.

Some of the magazines made their way into Mexico. Pedro, one of the artists for the velvet painting factory in Ciudad Juàrez, was flipping through a copy in his room when he came across a picture of Maria clad in leathers with cutouts for breasts and crotch. "*Madre de Dios!*" he exclaimed and climaxed himself in a new record time. Afterwards, more calmly, he looked closely at the picture, now flecked with semen. The face, he noted, was of someone who has suffered.

"*Madre de Dios!*" he repeated, this time in a reverent whisper.

The next day, he covered the blank, black velvet with a head-and-shoulders painting of Maria as the Madonna. When he was finished, he admired his own work before giving it to the jobber who came to collect the paintings. Someone will be moved by her, he told himself. But there was something disturbing about the painting, and it sat in the warehouse for years. Rediscovered during a routine inventory, the painting of the Blessed Virgin was shipped to Canada where Mahinda would eventually buy it from a summer street dealer.

The child, now a sturdy five-year-old, would sometimes spin like a whirling dervish and yell out phrases Joe did not understand, phrases like '*In principio erat verbum*' and 'reality is just a hypothesis commonly agreed upon', '*je suis le tenebreux, le veuve, l'inconsol...*', 'a hundred by the heliometer', 'levity is the opposite of gravity' and '*sabbadanam dhammadanam jinati.*' Turning and turning and turning and turning....

Because of his strange gyrations, Joe renamed the child Eddie. Not until five years later did Joe realize that the word for a whirlpool was spelt with a 'y' not an 'ie.' By then, of course, the name had stuck.

Although he himself had no time for religion, Joe insisted on Eddie going to church. To Joe's surprise, his stepson enjoyed the mass and even became an altar boy. And the boy had a wonderful soprano voice. Only natural, thought Joe, considering who his father was. In fact, his mother was no slouch as a singer either, but rarely committed the act. At Christmas midnight mass, Eddie would sing *Panis Angelicus* in a boy soprano voice so achingly pure that Joe would get a lump in his throat, and tears would stream down his weathered cheeks.

By the time he reached puberty, Eddie was bigger than Joe, almost seven feet and 283 pounds of muscle. People would comment on how much he looked like his father, but what did they know.

At sixteen, Joe gave him his own motorcycle, a rebuilt Goldwing, and took him riding up through Big Sur. Just around dusk, on the winding mountain roads south of Monterey, the fog began to close in so that visibility was only a few feet through the glowing shroud that surrounded them. Eddie pulled up beside Joe and grinned at him before cranking his throttle wide. Within seconds his taillights had disappeared.

"Crazy bastard!" Joe yelled, and with a laugh he gunned the big Harley under him. Leaning into the rock away from the yawning gap to his left, Joe let out a rebel yell. Suddenly the road ahead of him was filled with an old school bus, its color blending with the mist. Joe swerved left, lightly brushed the fender of the bus, and rode out into thin air. Sounds of rushing air, crashing surf far below and somewhere, faintly, a choir singing an ethereal Amazing Grace *a capella*.

On the bus, no one perceived the biker and the bike arcing into space. Bishop Berkeley (*esse est percipi, esse est percipere*) would have claimed that Joe's ultimate ride never happened because no one had noticed it. God knew better. To himself he quoted the classic refutation: "Hallo, my name is God and I'm always around in the quad..."

With a jolt, the bus driver came wide awake. Seeing things, he told himself. To make himself more alert, he raised his voice with the Full Gospel Heavenly Choir he was bringing back from a day outing to Redwood City. His fine baritone rose: "...'twas grace that taught my heart to fear and grace my fears relieved, how precious did that grace appear, the hour I first believed."

# Part Three:
# Northern Ontario, Canada, 1989

## The Wages of Sin

When he got ready for his regular Friday night outing, Alphonse checked to see that the back door was locked, the stove off, his mother's cats had enough food and water. Before leaving, he straightened his tie in the hall mirror. At the door, averting his eyes from the picture of Jesus exposing a palpitating heart wreathed in thorns, he nevertheless dipped his well-manicured fingers into the font by the front door to bless himself. Empty. Of course, he had run out of holy water shortly after his mother finally passed away. Still, it was a habit that died hard, and he flushed at the thought of what his mother would have said.

When he opened the door of his subcompact, a wave of hot air leapt at him like a breath of Hellfire. Alphonse rolled down the window, stepped back and waited, looking idly at the cloudless sky. 7:30 pm and the sun was still high. Ah yes, he remembered that the radio announcer had said that tomorrow would be the longest day of the year. With a sigh, Alphonse reluctantly collapsed his long, thin frame onto the driver's seat, and once again wished that he had not let his mother and the salesman bully him into buying such an uncomfortable machine.

The few remaining leaves hung limp on the trees as he drove around Capreol's circular one-way system, an innovation introduced by Mayor Marzetti after a mayoral convention in Calgary. He passed the CN Station, turned left onto the main street past the boarded-up Rialto, the Chinese greasy spoon, Marzetti Sporting Goods, the fire hall, Marzetti's IGA and crossed the railroad tracks.

Veering left past the library and liquor store, he sniffed at the sight of the local Catholic church where the priest had expressed disgust when he had confessed his sins. Since his mother's death, Alphonse had stopped attending, preferring the anonymity of St. Gabriel Lalemant in the city where Père Jean-Pièrre Abélard was much more forgiving. Soon he was heading out past the drive-in at a sedate pace that would see him in Sudbury in a little more than half an hour. Alphonse, always a careful driver, was especially cautious on Friday nights because a single slip could mean the difference between Heaven and Hell.

He parked behind the tavern that was almost directly across the street from the old flour mill that gave the district its name. The mill that had lain derelict for years was now a seldom-visited museum with a few exhibits meant to celebrate French-Canadian culture. Turning it into a museum had been a hasty afterthought of the city council who, embarrassed by an unsuccessful attempt to blow up its sturdy silos, had instead installed a few quilts and wooden ploughshares and painted the pitted silos a bilious yellow.

The tavern, too, was old, but Alphonse liked it because everyone spoke French, but nobody knew him. Almost every Friday night he dropped in here, found a seat by himself, and drank precisely three beers. As he poured the first of the evening, he inhaled and smiled. Alphonse loved the unique smell, a mixture of stale beer, cigarettes and vinegar from the large jars of pickled sausages called 'horse cocks.'

Tonight he managed a seat near the window. He listened to the conversations around him, sometimes smiling at something that was said, sometimes shaking his head at some sad tale. As always, Alphonse, a tall, thin man, balding, early forties, sat by himself wrapped in his cloak of loneliness. After two beers, he looked at the wavy purple glass of the window and moved his head slowly back and forth. The silos rippled, dancing together and apart like two women beckoning to him. Hurriedly he finished his last beer and walked out to his car.

His tie loose now, Alphonse cut across York Street and passed the old bakery where he worked as a bookkeeper. The bakery specialized in hosts and these bread coins, transcendental currency, were shipped throughout North America to end their careers glued to the hard palates of the faithful.

Up the Elm Street hill past the courthouse and now the usually staid Alphonse began to tingle with excitement. Carefully averting his eyes from the old house with the veranda, he parked up the street in the supermarket lot and walked briskly back down the hill. Outside the old house with the veranda, he stopped as if he had lost something. His excitement at a peak, he felt in his pockets in an elaborate mime, while he carefully checked that no one was watching. When he was satisfied that he was unobserved, he darted up a path beside the house and rang the bell.

Madame Souci answered the door herself. She was very large woman of a certain age who exuded both sensuality and the exotic odor of frangipani. In her left hand, her cigarette in an impossibly long holder described a fragile infinity in smoke, her right she held out to be kissed. Alphonse bowed and touched the plump offering with his thin lips.

"Come in, John," Madame Souci invited with a wink. "We were just talking about you."

Alphonse took on the look of a cornered rabbit. "Me?" he said.

She nodded, shepherding him into the large living room. The room was gloomy, lit by two low-wattage lamps their, salmon-colored shades tinting the faces with flattering light. The heavy curtains were drawn. "Lisa was telling us about your adventures in South America."

Alphonse blushed. "It was a long time ago," he mumbled, trying to remember exactly what lies he had told her about his mental trips across the wilds of Patagonia. He took solace in the fact that he had only been trying to paint himself a more interesting persona.

Madame sighed. "Ah, time. The years rush by so fast. Why, only yesterday I was ..." She stopped, a catch in her voice, unable to say the word 'beautiful.'

"Time speeds up as we slow down." A male voice out of the darkness in a far corner of the room.

"Yes, yes, that's it," cried Madame. "When we are young we are impatient for it to pass ... and then ..."

"It begins to race away behind us," said Alphonse, relieved to abandon South America. His eyes had become accustomed to the relative darkness. Now he could make out the man in the corner, a small figure completely bald, and yet the face looked young.

"If time were related to altitude," the man went on, "we would begin life at sea level where it would move the fastest, and throughout our lives we would constantly move to higher ground. The most prime real estate would be at the top of Everest."

Surreptitiously, Alphonse looked at his watch. He did not have a lot of time. He caught Lisa's eye. Nodding, she rose and disappeared through the archway into the hall.

For the next few minutes, he waited anxiously for the time to pass, while the man in the corner rambled on about Einstein's thought experiments and the relationship of acceleration to gravity. "In fact," the man droned on, "time dilates in a more intense gravitational potential. Therefore, we would age more slowly, or fractionally so, if we lived at the top of Everest rather than at sea level. In a city like Sudbury that crouches on top of vast deposits of heavy metals, the population should be aging at an accelerating rate." Madame had fallen asleep propped in her chair in an attitude of rapt attention.

Time has stopped, Alphonse was theorizing when Nana, the old crone who washed Madame's laundry, beckoned him from the archway.

"Will you excuse me?" Alphonse said, springing to his feet.

"Of course, Monsieur John, of course. It is time," said Madame.

Silently, Alphonse mounted the carpeted stairs and entered the second door on his right, carefully closing it behind him. The familiar smell of incense wafted smokily from an ornate silver censer hanging above the bed. Standing motionless on a chair silhouetted before the only light in the room was Lisa, her hands clasped prayerfully before her, her gaze fixed on nothing. She was dressed in the familiar blue and white robes of the Madonna.

Alphonse, feeling his member stiffen, rushed towards her and dropped to his knees. "*Ave Maria, plena gratia...,*" he began.

"Silence," she ordered. "You have not made a votive offering." Ashamed, he crossed himself, rose and went to the dresser. There, he counted out the money and lit a candle. "We are all born naked," she reminded him.

Hurriedly, he undressed but took the time to fold his clothes before piling them in the corner. Returning, he stood before her, head bowed, penis erect, holding the candle.

Lisa did not smile at his brown socks as she descended awkwardly from the chair and stood before him. Reaching out, she took the candle from him and tipped a few drops of hot wax on his penis. Alphonse panted heavily and began to mutter a prayer in French. "*En Englais,*" Lisa said harshly. "English is so much better for the sinning." She dropped some more wax on his quivering member, expertly blending it until Alphonse was standing with a fully formed candle thrust out before him. With a deft movement, Lisa inserted a wick. Alphonse looked down in amazement as she lit his candle and said, "Now close your eyes and say one 'Hail Mary' while I give you absolution."

"Hail Mary, full of grace, the Lord…"

While he prayed, she massaged the hardening wax on his member. As Alphonse reached "pray for us sinners now and at the hour of our death" Lisa squeezed so that he screamed a last "Amen!" as his semen spurted skyward snuffing out his candle. Knees sagging with ecstasy, he gave thanks to the virgin before him.

"Go with God," Lisa told him as he was leaving, slivers of wax faintly rattling in his underwear. Alphonse risked a final peek before he closed the door. Lisa was counting the money on the dresser.

"*Mon Dieu,*" he whispered to himself as he descended the stairs. Lisa had suddenly appeared at Madame Souci's only three weeks before. She was older than he usually liked them and spoke French with some kind of accent, but there was no one like her. "English is better for the sinning." He grinned as he reached the bottom of the stairs.

## Sin Tax

When he left Madame's establishment, Alphonse carried with him the weight of a mortal sin. For at least the next fifteen minutes, he knew that his soul was in the greatest danger. Even an act as simple as crossing the street was fraught with peril. A single wrong step could mean eternal damnation. Naturally, he walked with great care, hovered with intense concentration on the brink of the sidewalk, and looked both ways before hurrying across. As he reached the other side, a car, tires shrieking, turned the corner and screamed past him leaving a trail of foul-smelling exhaust. Alphonse shook his fist but could not see the driver because of the heavily-tinted windows. Nevertheless he had no doubt of the driver's identity even if the car had not left behind the tell-tale odor of sulphur.

Folded into his car, Alphonse draped his rosary over the rearview mirror, put on the emergency flashers and drove ever so slowly down the street. Past the bus depot he turned north. Some drivers honked impatiently; others looked at him oddly as they passed. Some even pointed and laughed, but he did not see them, so intent was he on the road ahead.

Time seemed to pass so slowly. Alphonse remembered the man at Madame's. Perhaps time was slower here because it was subjected to the deep gravitational pull down the many mines that dot the landscape. This slower time might be leaching up to the surface.

As he sat in his overheated vehicle at a stoplight on a deserted street, there seemed to be no time at all. Intuitively Alphonse had grasped Leibnitz's claim that there is no time without actual change. But then the light did change, Leibnitz's calculating rival Newton took over, and the car inched forward.

Half an hour later, bathed in sweat, Alphonse pulled his car into the deserted parking lot of St. Gabriel Lalemant. Inside, time had been passing slowly for Père Jean-Pièrre Abélard, waiting in the tiny cubicle of the confessional. Nobody comes, nobody goes. Nothing happens. It's awful. The time for confession officially ended twenty minutes ago but Père Jean-Pièrre was still waiting for Alphonse, as he waited every Saturday. Alphonse's confession was a highlight of his week.

Père Jean-Pièrre's main source of pleasure was his pride in having maintained his celibacy intact after more than twenty-five years in the priesthood. Of course, onanism was another matter, but he found his Friday night orgy at Alphonse's seamy tales put him in the right frame of mind for the early mass on Sunday ... *Domine non sum dignus...* he would say as he elevated the host, feeling a delicious humility at the thought of Alphonse's latest escapade.

The outer door creaked. Steps on the flagstones. Someone entered the other side of the confessional and knelt facing the darkened mesh between himself and the priest. Alphonse, waiting for Père Jean-Pièrre to pull him back from the jaws of Hell once again. The priest flexed his fingers and raised his cassock.

The preliminaries over, Alphonse launched into tonight's tale about offering his candle to the Madonna. Père Jean-Pièrre was open mouthed with shock and delight. As Alphonse began the Hail Mary and the wick was about to be lit, the priest grabbed his own candle and offered it up to the Blessed Mother. Suddenly there was a wild groaning, and Alphonse thought he had gone too far.

"Are you all right, Father?" he asked. No reply. Realizing he had not yet received absolution and was still teetering on the slippery slope to the underworld, he shouted, "Father, are you all right?"

Finally a hoarse voice, seeming very far away said, "Yes, my son," and offered absolution and a penance of ten Hail Marys. A wave of relief engulfed Alphonse. Saved from damnation for another week, he left the confessional and knelt in a pew to say his penance. Eyes screwed tightly closed, Alphonse tried to feel the uplifting presence of the Virgin Mother but, try as he might, the serene face he brought to mind kept metamorphosing into the face of Lisa.

Père Jean-Pièrre took a hearty swig of scotch and sighed as it warmed his innards. He too would never be able to think of the Blessed Virgin Mary in the old way again. Getting too old for such difficult confessions, he told himself gloomily, but despite his attempt at piety, a sly smile began to crease his face. Alphonse had outdone himself this week.

Half an hour later, Père Jean-Pièrre peered out of the curtained confessional. The darkened church was deserted. He got unsteadily to his feet and rounded the corner to lock the front door.

The priest gave a startled cry as he stepped into the vestibule. Alphonse, standing still as a statue, was silently reading the notices on the bulletin board. "You almost gave me a heart attack, Alphonse," the priest chided.

"Pardon, Father, I was only reading about the Blessed Virgin Mary appearing in Timmins."

Père Jean-Pièrre chuckled. "Timmins. I used to think it the most Godforsaken town on the planet, but not now, eh? Not with the Virgin Mother appearing on the walls of donut shops."

Alphonse, not sure what to make of the old priest's remark, merely nodded.

"Why don't you sign up for the bus trip? There are a few seats left. We're leaving Wednesday. Early. Should be a grand trip. And when you think that the Lord will probably knock off a week or two of purgatory time for those that make the pilgrimage, it's a bargain."

Alphonse considered the offer seriously for a few moments. Since his mother's death, he had suspected that he might find himself stuck in purgatory for a long, long time. "I think I will, Father," he decided. The bakery owed him a few days vacation anyway.

"That's the spirit," said the Father, squeezing his arm. "You can sit with me. Timmins. The Lord surely works in mysterious ways, Alphonse."

"Amen."

## Upon This Rock

"We turn off just before we reach the railroad track," Whitehead yelled above the roar of the wind through the open windows of the old Land Rover. "Some of the best shatter cones you'll find anywhere." In the nest made out of the camping gear in the back seat, Lydia looked up from her book for a moment, thought of replying, thought of reminding her husband that today is the longest day of the year, that today would inspire sacred rites throughout the hemisphere, then sighed and turned the page, smiling to herself. Time for Arthur Whitehead crept forever in millennia.

A few minutes later, Arthur turned off the road. "We're almost exactly at the latitude of the North American Watershed," he told Mahinda. "You might say that, for rivers, it's all downhill from here," he added in great good humor. Arthur always felt free whenever he could get out in the field.

Mahinda hung on grimly, smiling the special smile of the deeply mystified, as Arthur dropped the Land Rover into four wheel drive and careened up a winding track over the smooth rock of the Precambrian shield. The Rover shrieked as Arthur dropped a gear and bulled its way through a swamp, scattering tall cattails. "The trees are alive, isn't it?" noted Mahinda.

"Never seen anything like it," Arthur said, a note of wonder in his voice. The birches, scrub maples, alders and poplars appeared out of focus until the car neared the stand of trees ahead. Up close, Arthur and Mahinda could see that the trees were mummified by transparent grey shrouds. Inside writhed billions and billions of furry black tent caterpillars, devouring every leaf in the landscape.

Arthur stopped the car and shut off the engine. "Hear it?" he asked.

"What?" asked Lydia.

"Listen."

The trio sat in silence for a moment. The pinging of the car, buzzing of blackflies, and then, slowly, a pervasive, menacing noise surrounded them. "It sounds like a scratchy record after the song has ended," whispered Lydia.

Arthur nodded. "What is it?" asked Mahinda.

"The sound of a million mandibles chewing," Arthur replied.

"Disgusting," said Lydia with a shudder.

"Don't worry, love," Arthur assured her as he started the Land Rover.

"No trees where we're going. Just good old granite. Hold on, though. I'm going to take the next section pretty fast. Oh, and you might want to roll up the windows."

They did so quickly as Arthur stamped on the accelerator and the car lurched forward into the trees. Sudden grey darkness. Headlights and wipers on but Arthur could barely see. "Left, Arthur, left!" Lydia urged, totally unnerved by the web that had wrapped up their car, trapping thousands of twitching black commas and question marks against the windows. The Rover began to slow, all four wheels spinning on shredded black corpses and green entrails. Desperately, Arthur dropped into four-wheel low gear, and the Rover lumbered forward and into the sunlight.

"Made it," he announced triumphantly. "Thank God," said Lydia fervently.

Half a mile on, the vehicle rose onto a smooth rocky crest dominated by a single erratic. Arthur stopped the car. "We're here," he told the others.

Mahinda opened the front passenger door but it bounced back almost trapping his foot. Arthur applied his shoulder and opened the door on the driver's side. It, too, immediately slammed shut.

"The webbing of the tent caterpillars," said Lydia beginning to feel the tell-tale signs of claustrophobia. "It's all over the car. We're stuck in here. My God, Arthur, do something!"

"There's a lock knife in my pack," he told her. "Pass it over." Lydia found the knife and handed it to him. "Mahinda. Give me a hand with this door. Now heave." Both men pushed the door open far enough so that Arthur could use his free hand to cut the caterpillar silk that shrouded the car. With a whispering, tearing sound, it parted, and he tumbled out and landed flat on his back. With a broad grin, he propped himself up and said, "Never know what you're going to run into out in the field."

Lydia and Mahinda scrambled out and looked around. The old Land Rover had stopped on a bare rocky outcrop overlooking the intersection of road and rail far below. The eye was immediately drawn to the erratic perched impossibly on the edge of a precipitous cliff. On top of it was a dead silver birch, sundered by lightning so that its trunk, riven into three curved struts, spread out against the cloudless sky. The dead branches supported a shining silver canopy that, as if by design, shaded a flat expanse of rock perfect for their tent.

"Gneiss," observed Mahinda.

"Nice? It's absolutely beautiful," said Lydia. "Almost seems, I don't know, ... magical."

"Good spot to camp," Arthur offered prosaically, looking up from the rear of the Rover where he was busily cutting away the matted web to get out the gear.

An hour later, the camp set up in the shade of the curious canopy, the two men left in search of shatter cones. As they disappeared from view, Lydia was drawn to the erratic. Carried down eons ago by glaciers and left here, she told herself. She circled it, letting her hand rest lightly on its rough skin. Feeling more than a touch of acrophobia, she carefully looked over the edge of the outcrop. Below, toy cars slowed for the sharp curve that leads into the railroad crossing. She knew that several people had been killed at the spot below her, drivers who learned too late that the crossing was right in front of them. From here, she could see why the Department of Transport had never straightened out the curve: they would have to move millions of tons of granite.

Drawing a deep breath, she stepped back and looked up at the shattered birch and its canopy. The huge tree must have grown out of a few handfuls of earth that lodged in cracks weathered in the erratic. From where she stood, the tree seemed to be cradling the sun in the skeins of silk that wove together its outstretched arms.

Stepping back, Lydia peered closely at the canopy. Its grey webbing enfolded the branches in abstract patterns that seemed to flow as she moved. "A trick of the light," she told herself just as the sun, bleeding through, kissed the Tropic of Cancer far to the south at precisely 4:53 p.m. local time.

About to turn away to set up the cooking stove, Lydia noticed something strange. There were no caterpillars in the birch's silk canopy. After a few moments she shrugged, dismissing the mystery, and turned to the more pedestrian task of filling the fuel tank on the camp stove.

The breeze up here kept the black flies and mosquitoes to a minimum so that soon Lydia was able to relax in one of the folding chairs they had brought, pour herself a glass of chilled white wine and read *A Brief History of Time*. Again.

From time to time, she checked the time. From time to time, she strolled over to the erratic and looked down on the silent cars weaving along the route below. The men would be gone for hours, swapping geologoi and arguing about meteors, volcanoes, astroblemes, seismic events. Opening her book again, she settled back to enjoy the magical solitude.

### Second Coming

Like Jesus before him, Eddie's history after the death of Joseph was murky before thirty. When he had eventually realized that Joe was not behind him, Eddie had turned around and ridden slowly back along the winding road until he saw the skid marks. Dismounting in the twilight, he looked over the edge and saw far below the mangled wreckage of Joe's bike. No sign of Joe himself. It cost Eddie over two hours and several heart-stopping moments to find a way down. Standing by the twisted handlebars of Joe's machine, he looked up. There were streaks of blood on the rocks above him but no sign of a body. Eddie stood and puzzled over the possibilities: either Joe was dead and his body has been taken by some large local predator, or Joe was alive but living in one of an almost infinite number of alternate universes like Schrodinger's cat before the observer opened the box. Like Schrodinger's cat, all timelines would be possible until the observer, Eddie in this case, identified one as the current reality.

God could have pointed out a third possibility, that Joe, like Joseph the stepfather in the first messiah story, had simply faded away, his part in the story fulfilled. But, as usual, God kept his own counsel.

How Joe would have wanted to go, Eddie murmured to himself, his tears glistening in the westering sun. After observing two minutes of silence watching a condor circling, Eddie began to climb back up the cliff. By the time he reached his bike and kicked it into life, the stars had prickled the sky. As Eddie swung out on to the deserted mountain road, a meteor streaked across the heavens.

God knows what the future holds, Eddie told himself. Only in a strictly cause-and-effect universe, mused God. When every event spawns an infinite possibility of futures, Gods cannot be expected to watch every little sparrow fall.

Eddie spent the next few years looking for his mother, Maria, and supporting himself with odd jobs. A rumor had led him to San Isidro on the Mexican border where he found work as an attendant at the parking lot that had replaced the Macdonald's Restaurant where a crazed gunman had opened fire a few years before. There, he heard that his mother had fled an open arrest warrant for carving up a cop who had tried to rape her. Eddie had tracked down the cop, an officer named Brutus Maggiore. When Eddie passed the word that he wanted to meet Brutus, to ask him to drop the warrant against his mother, he got back the message to meet him outside a junkyard near the border. Eddie turned up early, just after dark. The street was deserted. The two nearest streetlamps were out. Eddie parked his bike around a corner and walked into the darkness until he was standing opposite the junkyard gate. At that moment, the gate opened, and a huge black-and-tan dog, trailing a heavy chain, leapt through. Without making a sound, the dog sprang at Eddie, knocking him back and ripping open his cheek. The dog bounced off the wall behind him and came at him again. Eddie, realizing he was fighting for his life, grabbed the dog in a headlock and smashed its head into the wall until the creature went limp. Out cold Eddie decided, and dropped the dog to the sidewalk. Slowly, he walked back to his bike, clutching the flap of his cheek to his face and, with difficulty, rode to the local hospital. The doctor who sewed him up told him he was lucky. Not a sentiment shared by Eddie. When he got back to his hotel room, he found a letter slipped under the door. "The bitch headed for Canada," it said, "suggest you do the same." Sounded like as good a plan as any. The next day, Eddie headed north.

Less than a month later on his thirty-first birthday, running late, Eddie was burning up Highway 144 towards some place called Timmins to make a delivery.

Eddie knew that his day might be ruined if he stopped but, as a Catholic, at least in memory, he just could not pass a dead nun on the side of the road. With a sigh, he cranked on the anchors of his custom Harley chopper. A cloud of dust and rattle of stones hung in the air as he shut his machine down. Then, nothing disturbed the silence except the pinging of the hot engine and the atonal whine of eager insects.

Eddie sighed again, took off his red bandana and wiped the sweat from his armpits. "Shouldna worn my leathers in this heat," he muttered to himself as he dismounted. But who would have thought it would be this hot in Canada. Even in June. Although he would never admit it to the good citizens here, Eddie had expected snow as soon as he crossed the border and had even considered packing mitts and a fur hat in his panniers.

His riding boots raised little puffs of dust as he scuffed back along the soft shoulder past a sign that read '*Accotement mou.*' Probably an Indian name for this patch of swamp and rock, he guessed.

About fifty yards back down the road, he spotted the skinny white ankles and black oxfords poking out of a habit now covered with a fine film of light brown dust.

It had been the ankles really that had made him stop, and now he peered at them in fascination. As a boy he had thought the nuns who taught him at St. Jude's had run around on wheels concealed under their long black habits. It had been years before he had learned that they had ankles, but he had never seen them. Like many of the tenets of Catholic doctrine trumpeted in the Baltimore Catechism, he had taken nuns' ankles on faith. Finally, here was proof.

Running late, Eddie reminded himself and checked his watch: 4:53 p.m. eastern daylight time. At that instant, the sun was kissing the Tropic of Cancer. The moment of summer solstice had arrived. Tonight would be the shortest of the year in the northern hemisphere. It would also be the moment that the universe would be forever changed. Tonight Eddie, God's rough beast, would appear. This time the firmament would present an occultation of Venus rather than a Star of Bethlehem.

Eddie was totally ignorant of this magic time and could not possibly guess what a midsummer night's dream awaited him, what a revelation awaited all mankind.

He leaned over, waving in vain at the cloud of black flies that had chosen him for lunch. The nun was half-sprawled in the dry, weed-choked ditch, and Eddie was forced to climb down to get a good look at her. The face framed in a starched white wimple was smooth and serene. What few lines it held seemed to have been etched by laughter. She seemed peaceful with even the ghostly hint of a secret smile and... and something about her reminded him oddly of Joe, the man who had raised him.

Eddie straightened up, feeling the miles of traveling in the muscles of his back, and wondered what to do. After a few minutes, he bent down again and looked carefully without touching (she is a nun after all) for signs of injury. None visible. He did notice a rosary clasped tightly in her left hand. Eddie stood up again and slapped again at the cloud of black flies buzzing around his head. How did she end up in this godforsaken place called *Accotement mou*? And, more important, what was he going to do about it? Maybe he could flag down a car and someone else would take care of it. As long as the cops didn't get interested in him, he'd be O.K. Yeah, flag down a car. But he hadn't seen one in almost an hour. "Doesn't anybody live up here?" Eddie demanded loudly to a seemingly uncaring universe.

For the next hour or so, Eddie stood on the side of the road sweating, batting with an increasing sense of futility at the flies, and waving frantically at the few cars that roared past. No one stopped. Eddie guessed correctly that his appearance was against him. He was not sure that he himself would have picked up a huge guy standing in the middle of nowhere dressed in black leathers, long hair tied in a ponytail, and a livid scar running from the left eye to disappear in his heavy black beard.

"Why don't I just leave her here for somebody else to find?" Eddie demanded angrily. Let somebody else find her, somebody who isn't carrying a couple of keys of cocaine in his gas tank. Already he was going to be late for his delivery, and the guys he was working for didn't believe in sick leave.

He walked back and bent over the nun again. "Look," he explained reasonably, "I got to leave. Nobody's gonna stop if I stand out here for a week, y'know?" The ghostly, beatific smile seemed to mock him, so with mounting irritation he shouted, "This ain't even my country! I got no idea who you even call to pick up a dead nun!"

A slight breeze had sprung up, raising dust devils on the side of the road and blowing away the halo of flies around his head. Eddie caught a whiff of what he at first assumed was the sweet smell of decay. Under the circumstances, an understandable mistake. Then he identified it: church incense. Immediately his mind skipped back along a rosary of years until he saw little Eddie Magdalena, an immaculate cassock and starched surplice over his scruffy jeans and running shoes, singing 'Panis Angelicus' so achingly high and pure that old Father O'Rourke had unashamedly wept into a large white handkerchief.

Other memories tumbled in – leaving the confessional with a soul so clean that he would not have cared if a truck whacked him on the way home because then he would go straight to heaven, swinging the censer in the procession and inhaling the mysterious mixture so hard he almost hyperventilated, trying to catch a glimpse of God flying down from the stained glass window behind the altar into the tabernacle during the solemn ringing of the Sanctus. Gradually, after his voice changed, Eddie had drifted down a different road. No longer able to move people to tears with his voice, Eddie had eventually been relieved of cassock and surplice, after Father O'Rourke had caught him lifting his weekly 'salary' out of the collection plates.

Eddie leaned back on the edge of the ditch and sighed. The old nun had him. As the breeze stirred the weeds in front of her face, Eddie had the uncanny feeling that she was winking at him. If only something about her did not remind him of Joe.

"O.K., you win," he told her. "I'll go find a phone. Somebody around here must have noticed they're one nun short by now."

Eddie walked back to his bike and dug out the map of Ontario he had picked up back in Niagara Falls. He was on Highway 144 heading north. Only one town was listed on the entire highway before it petered out in Timmins, a place called Gogama. He estimated that he must not be more than twenty to twenty-five miles south of it. There must be a phone there and a gas station. Eddie folded the map, put it away and kicked the chopper into crackling life.

Just over twenty minutes later, Eddie wheeled up to the pumps at the gas bar/greasy spoon that seemed to be all there was of Gogama. A screen door slammed and Eddie turned to see a teenage boy heading in his direction from the restaurant. "Some gas?" the boy asked politely.

"I'll put it in myself," said Eddie, grabbing the hose and switching on the pump.

"It's not supposed to be a self-serve," complained the boy. He took a couple of paces back as Eddie stared hard at him. "But I guess it's O.K.," he conceded with a shrug.

Eddie smiled, which made him look slightly less menacing, so that the kid relaxed, leant up against the pump and scratched his crotch. Eddie wondered if the kid had crabs. "Nice bike," the teenager commented.

"Yeah," agreed Eddie who was not in the mood for a lot of questions about his machine. He turned his attention to the digital readout and was surprised at how fast the numbers were mounting. "Jesus, you got small gallons here," he grumbled.

"They're liters," replied the kid complacently. And fucking expensive, thought Eddie but said nothing.

When the tank was full, Eddie asked, "You take American money?"

"Sure," said the kid, standing up and holding out his hand a little too eagerly."

Eddie held out a twenty and growled, "Don't forget the exchange, kid." The kid looked hurt and sulked back inside. Eddie shrugged. Maybe the bastard wasn't on the make, but he doubted if Canadians were any different from Mexicans when it came to separating Americans from their dollars. Eddie parked his bike next to a pickup in front of the restaurant, collected his change and went inside.

He grabbed a stool at the end of the formica-topped counter. As he lowered his weight, it gave a tired pneumatic squish. Apart from two old men in truckers' hats nursing coffees at a table by the window, the place was empty. One of them was speaking French and gesturing at the pickup outside. The screen door banged, and the teenager slouched behind the counter like he was only looking after the place as a favor to somebody.

"You want somethin," challenged the kid.

Eddie glanced up at the menu spelled out in blue plastic letters on a white grid that advertised Pepsi. "Burger with the works, fries and coffee," he ordered.

As he munched his way through supper, Eddie mulled over his problem. Already he was running behind schedule. Maybe he'd better put a call through to the man in Detroit and explain that his bike had broken down and he couldn't make the drop until tomorrow. Yeah, he'd better do that. But who to call about the nun?

"Hey," he called to the kid who was reading a comic book. The French Canadians had left. "You got a convent around here?" The kid stared at him open-mouthed. "You know, like a nunnery," Eddie elaborated.

The kid shook his head. "Ain't nothin' around here 'cept rocks and trees. That's why I'm moving to Sudbury first chance I get."

"Got a phone book?"

"Yeah," the kid conceded, "but you'll have to use the pay phone outside."

Eddie nodded and paid for his meal. "Better give me some change. How much is a call here?"

"A quarter for a local call, but from here almost everything's long distance."

Eddie handed him five Canadian dollars. "Give me some quarters."

"Ain't got that much in the till," objected the kid.

Eddie lost his patience. Leaning over the counter, he grabbed the kid by the shirt and said quietly, "Listen, motherfucker, don't jerk me around. You give me the quarters you got and make up the rest in nickels and dimes. Got it?"

The color drained from beneath the kid's tan. "O.K., just leggo my shirt." Eddie let go. Just as he was about to exit the front door, Eddie thought of something and turned back to the kid. "I'm guessing this area's called *Accotement mou*, right?"

The kid looked like a deer in the headlights as he stuttered, "It's no place. The signs just mean 'soft shoulder.'

"Soft shoulder?" Eddie thought about it for a couple of seconds and then started to laugh. A few seconds later, when he thought it was safe, the kid joined in. "Good one, amigo," said Eddie. Shaking his head, he let the screen door slam behind him. "*Accotement mou*. I guess I need to learn more French."

Sweating in the booth outside, Eddie went through the yellow pages until he came to churches. 'See also '*Églises*' it told him, but he ignored that instruction and located the Roman Catholic listings. No listing for Gogama. After eliminating all the churches with French sounding names, he picked one at random and dropped in a quarter. A tinny female voice told him, "*Le numéro composé est un numéro inter-urban...*" and he hung up. Jesus, even the operators speak French up here. He'd thought Canadians all talked American. He wiped the sweat off his palms and called the operator for help. Maybe some of them spoke English, too. She did, with a French accent, and put him through to the church in some place called Foleyet.

"Hallo, Father Short here," replied a thin, reedy voice with an English accent.

"Oh, hi, Father. I've got a problem you might be able to help me with," Eddie began.

"To whom am I speaking?" demanded the voice.

Snotty, English bastard, thought Eddie but said, "Look, that doesn't matter. I'm just wondering if anybody around here has lost a nun."

"Lost a nun?" whined the incredulous voice.

"Yeah, nun dressed in one of those old-style habits where you can't see their ankles." Eddie was not sure he was explaining himself very well so added, "Well, actually she's... well, she's an ex-nun. You know, she's passed away."

The line crackled with static for a few moments while the priest on the other end pondered this revelation. Finally, the voice came on again, indignant, "Is this some kind of joke? Because if it is, it's in very poor taste."

"No, no," Eddie hastily reassured him. "I was riding by and I found her. Swear to God! I just want to see she gets buried in hallowed ground. I mean I can't just leave her there."

"And where is this deceased nun you claim to have found?" demanded the squeaky voice.

Eddie detected the heavy sarcasm but kept his cool. "About twenty or so miles south of a place called Gogama."

"Ah, not my parish, I'm afraid," declared the priest and hung up.

Eddie slammed down the receiver and, instead of biting chunks out of the booth, contented himself with kicking in one of the panels and cursing the English asshole in Foleyet. The phone rang, startling him into silence. When he picked it up, the operator demanded another seventy cents. Eddie plopped in the extra coins and then asked if she could put him through to the nearest undertaker. "It's an emergency," he added darkly.

Sounding sympathetic, the operator made the necessary connections and put him through to the Jerry Stack Funeral Home in Sudbury, which she assured him was the largest in the area. Maybe she thinks

I want to report a Jumbo Jet crash, thought Eddie glumly.

The phone rang three times, and then the earpiece was flooded with Mantovani Strings. After a couple of seconds, an unctuous male voice-over recited:

*When you call in time of grief*
*For loved ones lost to death the thief*
*We'll strive to comfort at your side*
*If you will brief on hold abide.*

This doggerel was followed by the warblings of a heavenly choir out of some old Bing Crosby movie. Thirty seconds later, a soothing female voice asked, "May we help?"

"Yeah. Put me through to the undertaker. I got a pickup for him," said Eddie.

"Mr. Stack, Jr., sir?"

"Sure." Getting somewhere at last, he thought, as he swatted a mosquito to a red blot on the glass.

"Yours in your hour of need. How may we be of service?" It was the same voice that recited the poem. Maybe he thought it gave the joint some class. Probably got it out of the *Undertaker's Almanac*.

Eddie decided to get straight to the point. "I'd like you to pick up a ... a corpse and see that she's properly buried," he said.

"I see. Is the deceased a relative, Mr. ... ah ..."

"No. She's a nun. Up Highway 144. Better hurry, though, I don't know how long she's been there, and it's hot as Hell up here."

"Perhaps if you gave me your name and the name of the deceased," pursued the unctuous voice.

"I don't know who she is!" yelled Eddie. "I was just cruisin' by. Look, I've wasted enough time already. Can you pick her up?"

"I'm afraid we need a death certificate first, sir," said the voice getting a little snappish now. "We cannot accept anyone not officially deceased. I suggest you call the police and leave the matter with them. Goodbye."

"Nobody gives a shit!" railed Eddie as he slammed down the receiver again. What did they expect him to do? Put her on his bike, buy a shovel and bury her himself?

## Messiah Ex Machina

"Nobody really knows what the Virgin Mary looks like anyway," said Thomas LaRue, the sober skeptic.

"Of course we do," objected Alphonse, working on his fourth beer since leaving Timmins, and trying desperately not to compromise the holy hollow feeling he had felt when he had stood before the image on the outside wall of the donut shop. "She looks exactly like that face we saw on the wall up in Timmins."

"Oh, you've seen her before?" asked doubting Thomas.

Alphonse's face flushed in shame as his mind filled with the image of Lisa, and his member stiffened. A victim of mind over member. Nobody noticed in the darkened school bus rumbling south along Highway 144. "Only in pictures," he admitted.

Sitting alone at the back of the bus, Judy Legrand had only signed up for this trip so that she would not be tempted to spend yet another night at Sudbury Downs, the local harness racing track. During her last confession, Père Jean-Pièrre had hinted that she might have a gambling addiction only to be told, "What I've got is a ten bell losing streak, Father. Nothing a lottery win can't fix. I make good money. What I do with it is my business."

Judy was Head of Security at the local college and did make good money but lately many of her staff had been reduced to tears by her efforts to instill some discipline in their ranks. So many complaints, not just from her staff but even from the faculty, had landed at Human Resources that, just last week, the president had called her in for a chat. President Geoffrey Banbury had waited for weeks before confronting her. Although he would not have admitted as much, he was intimidated by this tall woman with a sharp tongue.

"Is this about the complaints?" Judy had challenged as soon as she entered his fourth floor office.

"Well, yes. I just think you need to build a better rapport with your staff and the faculty," he said. Judy said nothing, just stared at him. "Please take a seat, Judy," he had urged but she ignored the offer. Banbury sought refuge behind his imposing desk.

"If they can't take the heat, they should damn well get out of the kitchen," Judy had barked.

"Just use a little tact, Judy. That's all we're asking."

"Oh I do, Jeff, I really do. For instance, I've never mentioned to anybody that your long driveway out on Lake Wanapitae is kept snow free all winter by the college's snow plow equipment."

"Look, Judy, it's imperative that I get in even on the snowiest of days."

"Yes, of course. That's why I haven't pointed it out to the board of regents."

Banbury sighed, and, making a mental note to get an outside company to plow his driveway next winter, said, "Well, Judy just try not to be so heavy-handed in future and we'll say no more about it."

"Certainly, Jeff." Her face cracked into a wintry smile. "I'll see to that."

At the front of the bus, sitting behind the driver, Claude Bissonette, the better to monitor his driving, were the Dionne quadruplets: Annette, Émilie, Cécile and Yvonne. Born on May 28, 1935, exactly one year after the Dionne quints, the girls had been named after the famous five by their mother who hoped, naively as it turned out, that some of the wealth that was being lavished on the babies of Corbeil, a mere seventy miles down the highway from Sudbury, might descend like manna on her own offspring.

When Mme Dionne was interviewed by a local reporter, she had explained that since she already had one little girl, eighteen-month-old Marie, who shared a name with one of the quints, she had decided to give her quadruplets the rest of their names. She even had her husband put up a sign on their modest house behind the flour mill silos stating 'Home of the Dionnes: Marie, Annette, Émilie, Yvonne, and Cécile.'

Occasionally a couple who had missed the turning to Corbeil would turn up at the Sudbury Dionne's house. Mother would charge them a quarter each to see her babies. M. Dionne, who spoke no English, would skulk in the kitchen, drinking beer with his friend the mailman, while mother led the couple upstairs to the 'nursery.' If anyone objected that one of the babies was much bigger than the others, Mme Dionne would say, "She can sure eat, that one. I think Marie will be a giant."

At school, *École Jeanne d'Arc*, the Sudbury Dionne sisters had been cruelly teased. Marie eventually found acceptance by flouting the rules, smoking cigarettes in the washroom and even cursing the Dominican brothers who ran the school. Brother Simon, not as simple as he looked, had taken a liking to her and befriended her in a decidedly unbrotherly way. Despite his vow of poverty, not to mention chastity, he found enough money to keep Marie in cigarettes and candy.

The younger quintuplets had withered under the bullying of the other children and kept to themselves. A tight four-cornered clique, they had found refuge in piety and assisting their mother in decorating the altar, ironing the priest's garments, and serving him supper. The parish priest of Notre Dame in those days was Père Francis. A kindly old man, he would sit the girls down around the fireplace after they had finished the supper dishes and tell them stories out of Butler's *Lives of the Saints*. Night after night they would listen enthralled, as the wind howled in the chimney and rattled the window panes, to stories of holy martyrdom, virgin transformations, and spontaneous eruptions of the stigmata.

No one was surprised that the four sisters became sisters, grey nuns whose vocation was to bully Sudbury's sick into health as nurses at St. Joseph's Hospital, a large ramshackle brick building surmounted by a neon cross and helipad on the shores of beautiful Lake Ramsey. Among themselves, they would never mention Marie. The summer that Marie had turned fourteen, she and her friends had gone to the fair that arrived every summer where it set up on a strip of vacant land off Notre Dame. There, so the story goes, she had met a roustabout and joined Conklin's traveling carnival.

"Do you think we saw the virgin today, sisters?" asked Alphonse.

"God works in mysterious ways," Annette told him.

"His wonders to perform," Émilie finished the thought.

"We went all that way to see a waterstain from the air conditioner," said Thomas.

"Ah, your faith was stronger when you were in for that hernia operation, Thomas," said Yvonne caustically. The other sisters nodded primly and fingered their rosaries. Thomas blushed; Alphonse tried not to laugh.

Cécile, long considered the holiest of the quadruplets, was about to say something when the singing from the back was drowned out by the roar of a large motorcycle as it edged up beside the bus. Everyone crowded to the windows on the left side and looked out.

"It's one of those Hell's Bikers," said someone.

"Hell's Angels," Judy corrected. "Nice bike."

"His girlfriend looks like a nun," said Père Jean-Pièrre.

A collective gasp from the quadruplets. "She looks like..." began Émilie.

"Don't mention her name," Annette warned.

"She has come back as a child of God," Cécile said in wonder.

The biker gave them a clenched fist salute as the bus slowed for the tight turn before the rail crossing. Cranking the throttle, Eddie pulled the front wheel off the ground and roared down the side of the bus. The passengers crowded to the front.

"He'll never make it," said Alphonse.

"*Mon Dieu! Mon Dieu!*" chorused the sisters as the roar of the bike was swallowed by the diesel rumble of the freight train approaching the crossing. Before it ground to a halt, the bus nudged the rear of the motor cycle bouncing it into the path of the locomotive. The passengers streamed off the bus just in time to watch as the Harley became airborne. Almost immediately, its gas tank exploded. A thick cloud of cocaine smoke enveloped the witnesses and, as it dissipated, they watched in awe as Eddie and the oldest quintuplet climbed away towards the few stars that littered the clear moonlit sky.

"*Mon Dieu!*" whispered Cécile, crossing herself.

"*Mon Dieu, Mon Dieu!*" chorused her sisters, crossing themselves in turn. "*C'est un miracle.*"

## '...Gonna Push the Clouds Away'

How did Eddie end up tangling with a freight train? If we rewind the bobbin of time, an earlier Eddie comes into focus as he looks, once more, for a dead nun.

She proved much harder to locate than Eddie had expected. For one thing, there were several signs reading *Accotement mou*. At the first place he stopped, there was no sign of her. Maybe someone else had picked her up after all, and his dilemma had been solved. Curiously, the idea did not make him happy. After carefully scrutinizing the lie of the land, he realized that, although similar, it was not the same arrangement of scrubby trees, rock and swamp as the spot where he had found the corpse. With a sigh almost of relief, Eddie resumed the search.

After nearly an hour of cruising the same two-mile stretch, he finally located the tell-tale oxfords and white ankles. So much for step one. The rest of his plan was rather vague. Eddie climbed down into the ditch. "I'm back," he said, squatting down beside her and involuntarily squeezing out a loud, rattling fart. "*Mea culpa*," he apologized automatically and then chuckled at the absurdity of apologizing to a dead nun.

It was getting late, but the sun seemed reluctant to set although its rays were shifting to the long end of the spectrum and casting a red glow over the rugged landscape. Mosquitoes were taking over from the black flies for the night shift, mosquitoes so formidable that they were fabled in the songs of the native Cree and the tall tales of Northern Ontario fishermen. They came in waves, gleefully using Eddie's tender city skin as a landing pad and his blood for refueling before takeoff. Eddie got up and cursed and flailed at them, then shook his fist at the red ball of sun which still hovered in the west.

Step two of Eddie's original plan called for darkness but, unknown to him, Eddie had chosen the longest day of the year to stumble across a dead nun and revive his Catholic heritage.

The sun had already come as far north as it dared, and sparked celebrations in Russia, in Finland and in England, all building bonfires and honoring John the Baptist. While other places in the Northern Hemisphere celebrated the summer solstice with ancient rites, Eddie performed a lumbering dance of frustration.

"Smoke!" he cried suddenly with the force of revelation. He had seen it in some movie. Smoke kept bugs away. Unwilling to risk lighting a fire, he did the next best thing. He lit the huge hash joint he had rolled as soon as he crossed the border and had been saving for an emergency. It helped. Whether it was the smoke or they were getting too stoned to fly straight, the mosquitoes seemed confused.

By the time he roached the joint, Eddie was feeling a fine buzz and decided to proceed immediately to step two despite the continued presence of the waning sun. Moving with utmost deliberation, he stepped delicately over the prostrate black form and gently lifted her in his arms. She seemed to weigh nothing. He carried her to his machine and carefully propped her on the seat so she was leaning back against the sissy bars. "It's O.K., Sister," he whispered to her, as he jacked one of her legs over the saddle and, flipping down the rear footpegs, placed one black oxford on each. She smiled at him, and he smiled back, an awkward grin that made him look boyish except for the scar. The grin got stuck. Try as he might to wipe it off, it kept coming back, so that eventually he learned to live with it, going about his toils as cheerfully as St. Francis of Assisi setting up a bird feeder.

When he had finished hooking the nun to the sissy bar and footpegs with rubber bungee cords, Eddie stepped back to admire his handiwork. "And now, folks," he announced grandly to the assembled mosquitoes, "as soon as she's revved up, another episode of the Flying Nun." He giggled, toppled over into the ditch, and laughed until his guts ached. He only managed to stop by imitating the whiskey tones of Father O'Rourke in the confessional: "That'll cost you three Hail Marys and a Glory Be, so it will, boy. And don't you go touchin' yerself there agin."

Time for step three, he told himself, and paused, trying to remember where they were going. I'll make up my mind on the way, he decided. He clambered out of the ditch, mounted and kicked the Harley into life. Spraying gravel and weaving dangerously on the soft shoulder, he set off south, a decision dictated by the direction his machine had been pointed, and one that could easily prove fatal.

"Comfortable, Sister?" he yelled over his shoulder, as he redlined the tachometer and shifted up with a squeal of rubber. No answer came.

Eddie cranked up the speed, enjoying the cooling breeze on his face and the landscape scudding past on both sides of the deserted highway. After the first couple of bends, he adjusted to carrying the extra weight and dared to lean deeper towards the tarmac. Periodically he raced through rock cuts, slabs of sheer rock that threw the thunder of his engine back, so that he laughed at the sheer sound of power. Once he had to dodge a skunk meandering across the road at the bottom of a hill. The bike set up an alarming wobble but, within a few seconds, Eddie had it under control and was accelerating again. He cocked one mirror in so that he could check on the Sister from time to time. She seemed to smile back at him like someone feeling equal doses of terror and exhilaration on a roller coaster ride.

"Don't worry, Sister, enjoy the now," he yelled over his shoulder. "Eddie Magdalena is in control!" She nodded, and Eddie's scalp prickled with fear until he figured it must have been caused by a bump in the road. "Don't do that to me, Sister," he chided, relieved. "You almost had us back in the ditch." The sun finally set with a red flare of protest and, minute by minute, the light leeched from the landscape until the Harley's headlight appeared, fingering the road ahead.

Eddie risked another glance in his rearview mirror, but all he could see was the pale, moonlit glow of her face hovering in space behind him. The sight triggered scenes of his Catholic childhood which chased one another through his head. Maybe I would have been a priest if things had turned out different, he thought to himself. "Bless me, Father Eddie, for I have sinned...," Listening to the guilty mutter of his parishioners' petty sins. Deciding whether they were mortal or venial. Maybe the Vatican sent you a sliding scale or even a full list with an absolute cutoff point.

Doing without sex though, what about that? Not that his sex life had been a garden of earthly delights, at least in the last few years. About all he'd got lately was a tumble with whores when he was flush and not too pissed.

The weather had become suddenly chilly with the darkness, and Eddie looked up to see that the moon and stars had winked off. Must have clouded over, he told himself. Gradually, the impression grew on him that he and the dead Sister were sitting still, and the landscape flaring up in his high beam was coming at him like a video game. Crazy, he murmured, but the eerie feeling persisted so that he began to search for an antidote and came up with the image of little Eddie Magdalena in his immaculate white surplice singing so high and clear that the ladies wept at the beauty of his voice.

He began to sing, "*Panis Angelicus, fit panis hominum ...*"

After the first couple of words, he was aware of a pure soprano swelling his baritone offering, and he knew she was singing with him. At first, the voice at his back frightened him, but in only a few moments, he accepted his part in the strange duet and opened up the big engine rumbling under him. Singing at the top of his lungs, he came up behind a yellow school bus. An eerie light ahead as he pulled out beside it. Faces stared down at him and his passenger from darkened rectangles. Eddie waved and sang louder. The nun responded ... *Panis Angelicus* ... Ahead, the great light in the sky was growing, bouncing off the bellies of the clouds. Buoyed by the audience, Eddie sketched a sign of the cross and ripped open the throttle as he pulled the front wheel of his Harley off the ground. As he cut in front of the bus, a huge yellow-and-black checkered warning sign flashed past. Too late he saw the tight curve into the rail crossing. Kicking down a gear and pulling on his brakes, he veered left away from a sheer wall of rock. The nun leaned forward against his back. In his ears, a blaring loud enough for the last trumpet. Bells rang, lights flashed, tires screamed. The Harley just might have made it, but behind him, Claude was standing on the brake pedal too. Mesmerized by the glowing taillight growing in front of him, Claude was cursing the mechanic who had failed to replace the brake shoes on his bus. "*Mon Dieu*," he muttered and frantically steered to the right, but a giant's toupée of caterpillars, the only ones in the area that were still alive, exploded into green slime beneath his left front tire. "Jesus," whispered Claude, as the grill of his bus pushed the Harley into the path of the freight engine.

An immense force hit the back of the bike. Eddie and the Sister were flying through the air. In less than a second, the rear of the Harley's gas tank exploded in a jet of flame and smoke that increased the bike's velocity exponentially. Riding the world's biggest freebased cocaine high, Eddie heard the nun croak something in Latin. *Per ardua ad astra?*

Indifferent as God, the diesel locomotive rumbled on through the crossing, pulling its mile-long freight towards Onaping Falls.

The bus slewed across the road and halted. Instinctively, Claude opened the door. Quadrophonic gasp from the quadruplets as they watched the Harley soaring into the firmament. In a collective intake of breath, the people of the bus inhaled the cloud of cocaine fumes rocketing away from the Harley. More than one of them was convinced the smell was of church incense.

After bike, rider and passenger had disappeared into the darkness of the shortest night in the northern hemisphere, the passengers stared frozen, their silence underscored by the bass rumbling of laden freight cars coursing east. As the last container car disappeared into the night, there was a moment of silence as Claude turned off the bus engine and the headlights died. Another general intake of air, cacophony of voices, and rattle of rosaries, as the witnesses stampeded into the night to follow the flight path. Across the tracks, they stumbled into the edge of the bush and were stopped by a cliff towering above them. Claude, who had the best night vision, looked up and could just make out a huge erratic apparently teetering at the top. From this angle it appeared as a black hole in the brightness of the night sky, a black hole that had swallowed up every trace of the bike and its riders.

The ragged clouds had blown away. Nine upturned faces stared at the fragments of the indifferent universe visible beyond the bright steel-blue glare of the full moon that had just emerged from the cloud cover.

"They have vanished," Père Jean-Pièrre whispered just as a bright flash of light flooded the distant landscape for a few nanoseconds.

"*Mon Dieu*," muttered Annette. She and her three sisters made the sign of the cross.

"They're probably lying dead in the bush somewhere," said doubting Thomas.

"No, no," insisted Émilie, remembering a religious painting of the ascension. "I saw them. They rose like Jesus up to heaven."

"Yes, yes, I saw them too," said Yvonne, usually the timid one.

"And the Sister?" Annette said softly, turning to her sisters.

"Marie," came back the whispered chorus.

"Marie?" asked Claude.

"Their older sister, the fifth quintuplet," explained Père Jean-Pièrre.

"What do you think happened to the two of them?" asked Alphonse, sniffing the air as if for traces of the pair. Like the others, he felt his senses had become unusually keen. Definitely altar incense. Were the sisters right?

"We have witnessed a miracle," Cécile murmured in awe. "It is the only explanation."

With that, she and her three sisters knelt as one. "It would be a miracle all right," agreed Thomas cynically, "if they survived."

They all stared up again towards the moon. Père Jean-Pièrre was the first to break out of his reverie. He looked at his small flock and said to Alphonse, "We have to do something."

"The nun was their sister Marie?" said Alphonse, unable to rid himself of the image of the nun's habit rippling in the wind as she rose towards the heavens.

"Or somebody who looked like her," said Thomas.

Despite himself, Alphonse was reminded of Lisa and blushed with shame in the darkness as his votive candle began to glow.

"Well, we can't just stand here all night," said Judy impatiently. "Let's do something."

"Phone the police," said Claude. "It's their job."

"Nearest detachment's in Chelmsford. So is the nearest phone," Judy pointed out. "Let's go and find them."

"I should stay with the bus," said Claude quickly.

"We will all go," said Père Jean-Pièrre, turning to Claude. Then, watching the four tiny, geriatric sisters helping each other up, he added, "Perhaps the Dionne sisters should stay on the bus, in case someone comes."

"We are not staying behind," Émilie said in a determined voice.

"No, we are coming with you," affirmed Cécile. The others nodded.

"We don't even have a flashlight," said Alphonse gloomily.

"We'll use the lamp of the poor," said Père Jean-Pière, cheerfully. "I never saw such a moon for light."

He was so positive that, within minutes, there was general agreement. They got back on the bus and, with the lights out, Claude drove slowly down the deserted road until they saw a track gleaming as the moon emerged from the clouds, a track that seemed to lead up to the top of the cliff.

Shivering with anticipation and the cool air of the evening, the pilgrims got off the bus and began their climb.

## Fly Me to the Moon

"What time was the actual solstice?" asked Arthur, leaning back contentedly in his lawn chair and sipping a twelve-year-old single malt.

"1653 local time. 4:53 p.m.," said Mahinda, consulting his watch as if the answer resided there. "Almost eight hours ago now."

"Mmmm. So much for the numerical prophecy," snorted Arthur, looking up at the few stars that had become visible despite the moonlight. "The universe still seems to be unfolding as it should."

"We do not know that," protested Mahinda, his dark features all but invisible in the steel blue light of the full moon that had just risen in the east. To preserve Lydia's night vision, they were sitting in darkness made visible only by the pale light reflected from the moon.

"We arrived here about that time," Lydia pointed out as she set up her telescope with sure fingers. "Anything might have happened since then. We might be the last three people left on earth."

"True," said Arthur feeling the first glow of the scotch blot out the unfortunate demise of the rest of the human species.

"Besides, the witching hour is midnight, always," Lydia added mischievously, "four minutes after the occultation of Venus begins."

"Venus meets Diana," mused Arthur, "Lust colliding with chastity ... What time is it anyway," he asked Mahinda. Arthur himself never wore a watch when he was 'in-the-field,' reasoning that he was on geological time.

"11:13 p.m.," said Mahinda, after consulting the glow from the radioactive hands on his clunky dive watch.

A thought suddenly struck Arthur. "Why are there sixty seconds in a minute, sixty minutes in an hour anyway?"

"No one knows, I believe," said Mahinda, "although some speculate that Babylonian mathematics depended on base sixty."

"I read that it had something to do with the ancient Egyptians' 360-day year. That also accounts for the degrees in a circle."

"So we measure time and space in minutes and seconds," said Arthur, "at least since John Harrison invented the first reliable sea-going chronometer."

"Didn't he invent the water closet also?" said Mahinda, dredging up a faint memory.

"No, that was Queen Elizabeth I's godson, John Harington," said Lydia who loved all things Elizabethan. "He published details of it in a book called *The Metamorphosis of Ajax*. That's why the English still sometimes call the toilet, the jakes."

"And we call it the John. Your mind does dart into some strange places, dear," said Arthur who really did love Lydia's frequent flights of erudition. "John Harrison appears somewhat later in the historical timeline, the eighteenth century. Anyway, he perfected a clock called H-4, which was accurate to within ... "

And so they whiled away the early hours of nascent summer talking of time while Venus rushed through space towards its occultation.

"The same dull round, even of a universe, soon becomes a mill of complicated wheels," quoted Lydia after a lull in the conversation.

"But surely the universe is still in red shift mode," Arthur objected.

"Red shift?" asked Mahinda.

"Expanding. Moving apart. Red are the long waves in the visible spectrum. According to the most accepted theory, the universe will eventually stop, fall back on itself, blue shifting, and then repeat the process."

With that non-sequitur, the conversation lapsed until Arthur asked her, "Looking for M31?"

"Wouldn't see it with all this light from the full moon, Dear," she told him. "No, I'm not looking for a galaxy at all." While she spoke, she was attaching a new Barlow and fiddling with the eyepiece of her Newtonian telescope. "Looking for the moon."

"Hmm," sighed Mahinda, barely paying attention. He had seen shatter cones that afternoon and was mentally reviewing a paper he would present to the Institute of Fundamental Studies when he got back to Sri Lanka.

"Should be easy to find," observed Arthur. "Anyway, I thought astronomers hardly ever looked at the moon."

"Except on Midsummer's Eve," said Lydia. "Tonight's occultation is quite rare because it is a grazing occultation."

"Ah ... that makes all the difference," said Arthur, not having the slightest idea what she was talking about.

He was rescued by Mahinda who asked, "What is an occultation?"

"Ah," said Lydia, sounding pleased. "An occultation occurs when the moon passes in front of a celestial object, in this case the planet Venus. In effect, we will see the eclipse of the planet."

While she was giving this explanation, Lydia was bent over looking through her box of lenses. The movement had caused her shirt to open slightly, revealing the white curvature of the two moons nestled inside. Mahinda, transfixed by the vision of loveliness, had not listened to a word. "And ... and a gravid occultation?" he asked quickly, as she began to straighten up.

She smiled, stood up and stretched, much to Mahinda's disappointment. "Grazing, not gravid," she chided gently. "If a planet lines up with the moon's equator, it can disappear for about an hour. But if it just grazes one of the poles, it can disappear and reappear several times behind the irregular topography of the moon." She turned to Arthur who, used to the sight of his wife's bosoms, had followed the explanation rather better than Mahinda.

"Only once in a blue moon," Arthur said, and husband and wife smiled at each other.

"That's why I've been in such a rush to finish my telescope," she told him. "This will be its maiden flight," she added, casually mixing metaphors.

Arthur nodded. "I'm sure we'll see something extraordinary," he said.

You don't know the half of it, thought God, who was naturally focusing on his pet rock and the various convergences that would shortly be centerd there. No one had yet noticed the sudden absence of mosquitos and blackflies in this vicinity. Even the caterpillars, apart from the small contingent crossing the road near the rail crossing, had cocooned at exactly 16:53 eastern daylight time. Not surprising, He supposed. These bipeds tend to shy away from nothingness. And yet, how many times a day do they ask the question, "Why did God make the mosquito?" The very simple answer is that He had restricted Himself, more or less, to stirring the primordial soup, not serving it. Evolution had taken care of that. Nietzsche had not been entirely wrong in claiming that God had created the universe and then died. Like the *Artibatirae*, the *Cynocephali* and the flesh-eating *Epiphagi* with eyes on their shoulders, monsters who had once lurked around the edges of medieval maps, almost all of the other deities had winked out one by one, as the terra incognita, both physical and intellectual, had shrunk. Individually and in groups, the doomed deities had suffered the death of self-doubt, brought on as the inhabitants of this outpost of the universe ceased to believe in them. A few persisted, shrunk into pockets of ever-diminishing belief in out-of-the way places.

When Lydia had located the moon with her small spotting scope, she began to center its reflection in her telescope's concave parabola, a mirror that she had polished and silvered herself. "Want to have a look?" she asked the others when she had fine-tuned the focus.

"I see it," said Mahinda excitedly as he took the first turn at the eyepiece. "It is grazing the south pole."

"Actually the north pole, or northern limb. The image is reversed, of course. It is wonderful, isn't it?" said Lydia.

"Oh, my goodness, yes... but the moon is moving too," said Mahinda.

Lydia gently pushed him aside and refocused the reflector of her Newtonian. "There," she said. "Want a look, Arthur?"

"Of course." He stepped up and stooped over the eyepiece. "Really quite remarkable the way Venus skips in and out of the lunar landscape." Suddenly a flash in the eyepiece temporarily blinded him in one eye.

"Christ! What in Hell was that?" yelped Arthur, jumping back. The others were looking open-mouthed at a bright shooting star; trouble was, this one was coming up towards them, not down. For a second, Mahinda felt he was looking through a lens and seeing the image upside down. Arthur, too, felt disoriented, as if deprived of a local vertical. Lydia gazed in wonder as the heaven-tracking meteor streaked upwards and past them with a whooshing exhalation, trailing a knife blade of flame. As they craned their heads back, the flame seemed to slow. When it appeared to reach the moon, although falling far short of the 11.2 kilometers per second needed for earth escape velocity, the fireball seemed to stop and hesitate, as if about to set the disc aflame.

For an instant, the Harley with its passengers had occluded both the moon and Venus before beginning its inevitable descent. Eddie's clothing was falling away in smoking shreds, but the nun's habit somehow remained intact.

"What goes up...," muttered Eddie in the moment of weightlessness at their apogee. His scrotum shrank, and his fingers welded to the handgrips. And then, that sinking feeling as Eddie began to feel the embrace of earth's gravity well.

Thank God for my laws of physics, said the Creator, as He happily watched the most exciting event of these few moments in this universe. "Let the bike go," the nun crooned in Eddie's ear. "It is finished."

So are we, thought Eddie but, with an act of pure will, he released the solidity and apparent safety of the bike and let it fall away.

**"Into thy hands ..."**

Yes, God nodded, yes. Now spread your arms and legs and trust her, He said silently. Eddie did so. The nun clung to him and seemed to swell as her habit billowed out like a sail. Yes, yes, said God, as He watched the bike fall away until its superior mass built up a terminal velocity of 76 meters per second. Eddie and the nun slowed to 56 meters per second, the speed of a sky diver before opening his chute, and then to 45, 40, 33 and counting. Yes, yes, said God, Galileo knew that his different weights would not have reached the ground together if he had ever dropped them from the top of the Leaning Tower. But it made a good story.

And then Eddie relaxed, began to enjoy the ride.

The twelve spectators on the ground watched the flaming star streak across the firmament and disappear. Only the three camped on the top of the cliff saw something detach from it, blotting out an ever-expanding circle of starscape as if the universe was being devoured by a ravenous black hole.

Gradually illuminated by the brilliant moon, and trailing clouds of smoking glory, the now-naked Eddie swept down in the arms of the nun.

"My God," whispered Lydia, "it looks like... like an angel carrying a naked giant."

"Like Michaelangelo's Pieta," said Arthur.

"Siva," added Mahinda.

An explosion and searing flash of light somewhere behind them made the trio turn towards the funeral pyre that once was a gleaming Harley. So none of them saw the two ghostly figures land softly in the dense web woven into the riven birch that topped the erratic towering over their campsite.

## Modern Magi

"What is it?" asked Arthur, putting an arm around his wife's shoulder and drawing her close.

"I don't know," she told him. "It came in like a meteor, but from the wrong direction." For some moments all three academics watched the small bush burning in the distance until it flickered and went out.

In common with most other mammals, Arthur possessed the survival instinct that signals when we are being watched, perhaps by a predator. He turned to see the figure of a woman dressed in what he took to be dark flowing robes. Her face pale but visible in the bright moonlight, she smiled at him, and his momentary fear disappeared. "Who are you?" he asked softly.

Instead of answering, she pointed up to the dense web that topped the gneiss erratic. Arthur looked up at the dark strands and thought he detected movement.

Mahinda and Lydia turned at Arthur's question but saw nothing. Mahinda tensed with apprehension, but Lydia knew that Arthur's brain was wired in such a way that he could see things no one else could. Into an alternate universe? She ruled nothing out. "What do you see?" she asked Arthur.

"A woman in dark robes, over there." He pointed to an empty space beside the erratic, a space that stretched on to the dark undulations of the pre-Cambrian hills on the horizon. Without thinking, Mahinda moved behind the other two. This was not his country or his culture, he told himself.

"Is she saying anything?" Lydia asked calmly.

"Ah, you don't see her then," Arthur said matter-of-factly. "I wondered if you would. Do you see anything, Mahinda?"

"Nothing, absolutely nothing," he said quickly, "but I feel a definite chill."

"She's pointing up at that tangle of caterpillar silk," Arthur informed the others.

"The canopy that extends between the three parts of the birch tree up there?"

"Birth tree?" Mahinda's uneasiness had intensified.

"How can we get up there?" Lydia looked up at the three pillars of living wood glowing luminous under the dark skein of silken strands.

Before he could answer, the woman in robes extended her hand towards Arthur who took it. Sensation of soft, cool flesh. She led him to the north side of the erratic, next to the dizzying drop to the crossing below. There, she placed his hand on the rock. Arthur ran his hands over the rough surface. At head height he felt an indentation, then another above it, then another.

Lydia, who had watched in wonder as Arthur followed his own outstretched hand and began to fondle the striated rock, came up and stood beside him. Mahinda, terrified by the enigmas piling one on top of another, hung back ready to bolt for the dubious safety of the tent and chanted quietly under his breath. "There are footholds leading to the top," Arthur told Lydia, "but they only begin here." He indicated a spot almost two meters from the ground beneath their feet. "I'll have to find some way to get up there. Neither you or Mahinda is strong enough to lift me that high."

"I'll go," said Lydia, surprising herself.

Careful to make no mention of her acrophobia, Arthur said, "I'll lift you, but be careful." He turned back to Mahinda and called him to come and help. When he turned around again, the woman in robes had become invisible even to him.

With Mahinda's help, he lifted Lydia and placed her foot in the first indentation. Feeling light-headed, Lydia reached up and found that the footholds were at almost regular intervals. Cautiously, she climbed away from the men. "Be careful," pleaded Arthur unnecessarily.

"Don't look down." Lydia repeated the phrase over and over to herself, until she was calm enough to release one hand and slide it up the curved face of the rock feeling for the next indentation. She found it but was unable to move. Looking up, she fastened on Venus now well clear of the moon. Sing, she told herself. Faltering at first but gradually more confident, she began to sing, "There's a lady who's told all that glitters is gold and she's buying a stairway to heaven ..." Behind her, a faint, pure soprano voice joined her. Arthur's vision, she told herself. After a moment of frozen hesitation, Lydia relaxed and began to sing again. Her fear had disappeared, replaced by an inexplicable feeling of ... she searched for the word ... Exaltation. Midsummer Night's Eve; everything is possible. Even my fear of heights is, not gone, but manageable. She laughed. *Exultato jubilato* ... for thou art always beside me ... As she reached the top and steadied herself by holding on to one of the three birch columns that was the tree, she was too short of breath to continue singing, but even her inhalations were matched by an invisible other. The moon, a few visible stars and the flickering of myriad fireflies were the only illumination, but Lydia's vision was well adapted to the darkness. Before her she could see a mass of tent caterpillar silk suspended from the three corners of the birch, but no tell-tale squiggling commas to indicate the tiny creators of the sagging canopy. Something was weighing it down. Holding her breath, she could hear ragged and irregular breathing coming from the grey mass in front of her.

Eddie had awakened to find himself alone, blind, deaf, and totally immobilized. A moment of panic was followed by a calm such as he had never ever experienced before. For some time, Eddie reviewed the possible explanations for his current state of being or non-being. At first he naturally drew on his past, the church of childhood. Was this purgatory? Was he trapped in a cocoon waiting to become a caterpillar, waiting to assume a totally new kind of existence? Did he have to remain here like this for half an eternity working off the indenture of past sins before moving on to his reward? Half an eternity. But, of course, eternity was no more divisible than zero. The thought surprised him. Until now, he had always been too busy just scuffling a living to indulge in abstract thought. What had Jesus dreamed between crucifixion and resurrection?

And then an inward smile as Eddie heard a muffled breathing not his own. I am not in Hell then, he told himself, because Hell is unrelieved loneliness. God nodded. Eddie was learning his part. Like any good director, God knew that the most crucial skill is casting.

Lydia put out a hand and touched the cocooning web, expecting it to feel sticky as such strands usually do, but these skeins were smooth and soft. She tried to tear a hole in the web, but it was much stronger and more elastic than she had anticipated. She called down to the others, unseen below the curve of the rock: "I'm going to need a knife."

"Just give us a minute," came back Arthur's voice. As she watched, he emerged below her, crossed to the old Land Rover, and started the engine without turning on the lights. Well trained, she thought to herself. With Mahinda directing, he backed the vehicle up to the erratic and cut the engine. Sounds of soft shoes on a metallic surface, followed by grunts as the men ascended the rock, first Arthur and then Mahinda. Only Arthur glowed in the moonlight.

"Someone's trapped inside here," she said before they could catch their breath. "I heard breathing."

Arthur nodded. Pulling a well-worn lock knife from a leather holster on his belt, he opened it and set to work carefully cutting away the strands. Lydia, suppressing the urge to tell him to be careful, watched intently as the taut strands separated. Within minutes, Eddie's face appeared, the scar a pale river in the moonlight, eyes closed as if in sleep. Slowly the eyes opened, and he smiled at his rescuers.

"Jesus," breathed Arthur.

"Are you all right?" asked Lydia.

"I think so," said Eddie. "Won't know until I can move the rest of my equipment."

"What happened to you?"

"You know, I don't remember anything after passing the bus, same kind that killed Joe," Eddie replied.

"Joe?"

"Another time, another life," he told her, then suddenly added, "Careful around there" looking down as Arthur, with Mahinda's help, uncovered the more private parts of Eddie's anatomy.

"Don't worry," Arthur reassured him. "I left my hard rock hammer down below."

My God, he's totally naked, Lydia noted silently, trying unsuccessfully not to stare at the erect uncircumcised penis that arose like a ghostly maypole, as Arthur and Mahinda released it. She smiled as the two men jumped back in surprise. And he's huge, a giant of a man, Lydia mused.

As Mahinda and Arthur helped Eddie to his feet, Arthur asked, "Are you all right?"

"Nothing seems to be broken," said Eddie, but he was glad of their support.

"You don't even have a scratch," observed Lydia. "It's miraculous."

"Mmmm," said Arthur. "Speaking of miracles, do you know anything about a woman in long robes?"

Eddie suddenly remembered. "The dead nun? Yeah. Where is she?" Mahinda shivered, but Arthur was merely puzzled. "Dead?"

Eddie laughed, and it was a deep melodious sound. "Well, I thought she was dead when I picked her up, but then she started to sing. Maybe she ate some weed that paralyzed her."

"She was down below," Lydia told him, "but I'm afraid only my husband can see her."

"I'm the husband," said Arthur, shaking Eddie's hand. "Got a strangely hardwired brain. And this is my wife, Lydia, and my colleague Professor Mahinda Rapasinghe."

Mahinda nodded before asking, "Are you, by chance, the answer to the number 165321062533?"

"What?"

"Where were you at exactly 4:53 local time? It's important," said Arthur, scientific curiosity overriding concern.

"How the fuck should I know," protested Eddie. "Wait a minute. That's about the time I picked up the nun. Couldn't swear to the exact minute though. No, no, not true. For some reason I checked my watch and it was 4:53. Hey, what's with that?"

Lydia caught herself staring at Eddie's private parts again. "Hold still," she told him. As he did so, she removed the white sweater she had tied loosely around her shoulders in case she began to feel cold viewing the night skies. With a deft flick, she fashioned it into a loincloth.

"Jesus," said Arthur.

"Does look a bit like his pictures," added Lydia, "especially with his hair long like that." Eddie laughed, and the others joined in, even Mahinda.

Eddie had rarely felt more alive. Happens, he tells himself, when you cheat death. "Upon this rock...," he intoned for their amusement."... you can build your church, but later," said Arthur, trying to appear the practical one. "Right now, though, we've got to get you down."

And so it came to pass that the nine bus people stumbled on to the moonlit plateau in time to witness the descent of Eddie. Making fervent signs of the cross, the nine newcomers dropped to their knees at the sight.

"Christ!" complained Arthur, as he guided Eddie's feet on to the Rover's roof, hoping the big man would not go through it. He looked up at Lydia and asked suspiciously, "You didn't invite these people, did you?"

Lydia was holding Eddie's left arm, Mahinda the other shoulder. Arthur, on the ground now, guided Eddie's legs. Still groggy and weak, Eddie was glad of the help. "They're probably lost," she said.

Carefully, his rescuers released him, and Eddie managed to stand without the Land Rover's roof caving in. Père Jean-Pièrre looked up and saw a halo of cool ethereal light playing about Eddie's head amid the flickering fireflies and, not realizing the full moon was providing the halo, said, "Sweet Jesus! You've come back to us."

Suddenly Claude, the bus driver, jumped up and began to caper dangerously close to the drop off. "I'm healed," he cried over and over. "I'm healed! I'm healed!"

The remaining eight kneeling figures gasped. The stiff left leg that had plagued Claude ever since an ancient accident suddenly seemed perfectly fine.

"The arthritis has gone from my hands," said Annette, holding them up and flexing her fingers for all to see.

"Mine too," chorused her sisters. "It's a miracle."

Arthur helped Eddie off the hood and, lunging, he managed to grab Claude before he disappeared down the cliff. "Who the Hell are you people?" he asked in exasperation. They ignored him and began to approach Eddie. Only doubting Thomas LaRue held back, telling himself there must be a scientific explanation for all of this. The rapt expressions on the faces of the others reminded Lydia of the pilgrims she had once seen at Fatima, burning offerings of wax legs, wax arms, even waxen ears.

"Who are you?" Arthur demanded again.

Père Jean-Pièrre was the first to tear his attention from the huge figure towering above them. "There was an accident," he said. "We came in search of survivors."

"An accident," Mahinda repeated. Like Thomas, Mahinda was hoping for a logical explanation for the night's mysteries.

"Our bus ... that is to say the train, yes, the train, hit the motorcycle and … and … and …"

"It exploded right before our eyes," said Judy.

"The bush is still burning over there where they landed," said Claude, pointing.

"A burning bush," whispered Émilie with fervent misunderstanding.

"I am Père Jean-Pièrre, and these people are my parishioners," the priest explained, a look of wonder on his face, "but, please, who are you?"

"Eddie Magdalena," said Eddie, adding, "I come from a long way from here," meaning California, but his remark was naturally misinterpreted by everyone present.

Père Jean-Pièrre nodded. "Yes, from the heavens." There were murmurs of agreement.

"He's an alien," whispered Judy to herself.

Alphonse was the first to ask himself the question: am I witnessing the second coming? But the conviction spread like wildfire through the tiny throng of pilgrims.

"We have been waiting such a long time," said Annette, fervently crossing herself.

Just then, the first long blood-red rays found their way over the low Precambrian hills, the bare bones of the earth, and painted Eddie's pale skin a startling crimson, so that he took on the appearance of an avenging angel. The Dionne quadruplets dropped to their knees again, closed their eyes tight, and began a desperate muttering of prayers of salvation.

"Holy Mary, Mother of God," they began in whispered French. Alphonse and several of the other bus passengers cowered in fear. Arthur and Lydia had been standing behind Eddie so they did not see the apparition before them, but Mahinda was not so lucky.

"Siva," he murmured and even considered taking flight down the trail.

What the Hell is going on, Eddie wondered. The dead nun? And now these people are speaking French and I can understand it like it was American. He sighed, trying to make some sense of what was happening. "Look," he said holding up his right hand, "I'm sure there's some kind of reasonable explanation for all this."

"No," said Mahinda, surprising himself by his own vehemence. "Oh, my goodness, no, I'm afraid there is not."

Silence. Suddenly Judy realized that she had brought a camera with her. She reached in her pocket and, holding it above the heads of the others, flashed three quick pictures of the scene in front of her. For a few moments there was confusion, as the strobe flash temporarily blinded all of them. Lydia, outraged at the assault of photons on her optic nerves, cursed and groped towards the perpetrator. "Give me that!" she demanded, but Judy backed away and disappeared. Lydia listened to her scrambling down the hill towards the road. "Bitch!" Lydia yelled after her.

When she reached the road, Judy thought briefly of taking the school bus, but Claude, of course, had the keys. She began to walk towards the city. A few minutes later, she flagged down a truck and climbed aboard. "Where you headed, ma'am?" asked the wizened old driver.

"Sudbury," she said.

The driver told her. "Gotta dump a load."

"Of what?" asked Judy, trying not to breathe through her nose. "*Merde*," said the driver delicately. "Twenty-four hour service, me," he told her proudly. "Garage in Gogama had its septic back up. Turds floating into the restaurant, eh."

A honey wagon, Judy told herself. I had to get a ride in a honey wagon. She comforted herself with the thought that these pictures of the alien will be worth a fortune. "You going anywhere's near the TV station on Frood Road?" she asked him.

"Sure," he said. "I live in the Donovan. But first I got to dump in the lagoon just south of Chelmsford. Won't take too long."

Judy thought for a moment and then said, "Look. I'm in a real hurry here. Got to report an accident. Now if you can drive me in to the TV station first, it's worth a hundred bucks to you." She waited, but the old man did not say anything. "What do you think?" she said at last.

"You really need to get there that much, I'll take you," the man said slowly. "You can keep your money though. Wouldn't be right for me to take advantage."

"That's really nice of you," she told him. No wonder you're still shoveling shit, she observed silently to herself.

By the time the old man dropped her off at the TV station, the rosy-fingered dawn had already brightened to amber. Through the glass doors she could see the reception desk. Empty. She knocked frantically, but no one came. Nathan, the overnight technician, was sleeping on the couch in studio A. Only two things would wake him: the chiming alarm that only cut in when the network feed went down and the clank of pails when the cleaning staff arrived.

Finally, dispirited, Judy sat on the cold step, leaned back against the doors, pulled her coat around her and prepared for a long wait. "Thought they ran twenty-four hours a day," she muttered to herself.

She awoke after what seemed like mere seconds. Someone was shaking her gently by the shoulder. "You are lost?" asked the elderly woman standing over her.

"I have to see one of the news people, you know ..." She thought for a moment trying to remember the names of the local news anchors. "Ah, Tamara Ishenko or that guy who's on with her ..."

"Scott Turnbull," said the woman.

For the first time, Judy noticed the woman was wearing some kind of cleaning lady uniform. "Yeah, that's the one."

The woman shrugged. "No one is here now," she said with a sigh, "only Nathan."

"Nathan?"

"The night operator. He looks after the equipment."

Judy brightened. "Could I speak to him? It's urgent. Biggest story ever."

The old woman shrugged again. "I could lose my job."

"Look," said Judy, desperation in her voice, "I've only got ..." She checked her wallet. Just over a hundred dollars, "twenty bucks, but it's yours if you let me in to talk to this guy."

The woman patted her shoulder kindly. "Keep your money," she told Judy. "I'll find Nathan and send him to the door. He will talk to you."

"Thanks," said Judy, stepping aside as the woman unlocked the door and ushered her inside.

## Now and Then

Lydia shook her head and turned back to a scene that could have been an illustration out of a child's Bible: the people of the bus were standing in a respectful semicircle around Eddie. Arthur was at Eddie's right hand, Mahinda at his left. Behind Eddie, a faint shadow, a deeper darkness. Lydia could just make out the outline of the shadowy figure by looking at it obliquely, a trick known by astronomers to activate the maximum number of working rods in the eye. She watched Eddie turn towards the shade but, when she blinked, it had disappeared.

"You survived," Eddie said to the nun.

She smiled. "I have become incapable of death," she told him in a voice both soft and ancient.

"So how about telling me what I'm doing here," Eddie asked with more than a touch of exasperation in his voice.

"The second coming," she told him simply. "Your arrival has been foretold."

Eddie shook his head. "You've got me confused with someone else."

"No. You are the son of Maria Magdalena. Your stepfather was Joseph. There is no mistake."

"But ... but ..." The others were watching him as he seemed to mutter to himself.

"You see her too," whispered Arthur.

Eddie glanced at Arthur. "You mean no one else does?"

"Can any of you see the woman in the robes?" Arthur asked the pilgrims, pointing in her direction.

Some of the bus people began nervously fingering rosaries. "There's nothing there," sniffed Thomas, doubtfully.

"Perhaps a faint shadow," said Père Jean-Pièrre slowly.

"Yes," agreed Cécile.

"She was our sister," Annette blurted out.

"The long lost Marie?" said Père Jean-Pièrre.

"She was riding with him," added Émilie.

The other sisters nodded agreement.

"But now none of you can see her?" asked Lydia. Fear in the eyes of some; others shook their heads.

"God is in the gaps?" asked Arthur slowly.

"The gaps? In the fossil records?" Eddie laughed. "Only old dyed-in-the-wool creationists spout that stuff anymore."

"My stepfather told me that 'God is in the gaps' when he learned that I have an abnormal response to flicker rate. In fact, unlike everyone else, I can see the nothingness between so-called moving images."

"Ah," said Eddie, surprised that he actually knew what Arthur was talking about. "So that's why none of the others can see her." Eddie shook his head, delighted and somewhat in awe of the vast array of insights floating around in his head. "Anything else?"

How about the true cause of the Sudbury Basin, Arthur whispered to himself. Just as he was beginning to smile at the very idea, an intense prick of light appeared on the horizon, a light so bright he had to look away. All the vegetation burned off the surrounding hills in a moment.

With a deafening, crackling roar trailing it, the gigantic meteor parted the air around it, as it arced in towards the earth. Covering his ears and peering through slitted eyes, Arthur saw rock turn molten, before the earth heaved under him, as the enormous impact of the meteor's mass gored a basin-shaped wound in the earth. Hundreds of thousands of tons of shattered rock erupted skywards. A millisecond later, as if the meteor had hit a geological artery, fiery magna spurted from the gash in the earth. Overhead, the dawning sun had disappeared.

"Oh, my God," Arthur managed, as he fell to the ground.

"Arthur, are you all right?" He felt the hands of Lydia and Mahinda lift him into a sitting position. When he opened his eyes, the low rays of the fresh sun were shining on him. The lush spring vegetation had returned; the landscape was intact. He looked across at Eddie who smiled at him and nodded. Arthur gripped Mahinda's sleeve tightly. "I know how it happened," he told him.

"What?" asked his friend, obvious concern on his face.

"The event," Arthur said.

"I think we should get you to the hospital," Lydia told him. "You were out for over a minute."

Shaking his head, Arthur struggled to his feet. He looked around and saw that everyone was staring at him. "I have to make some field notes," he said and headed unsteadily for the tent. Admitting to himself that he did feel a little light-headed, even euphoric, he accepted Lydia's arm around him as he stumbled over the rough ground. "I saw it," he whispered to her. "We were both right. We were both right. Do you realize what that means?"

"Sure. Just let's get to the tent and get you some rest. There'll be plenty of time to ..."

"There!" he said, suddenly stopping and shouting back to Mahinda. The sun had illuminated a solitary rock, just as its rays slid around the erratic. "There's your proof, Mahinda."

Mahinda hurried over and peered at the rock. Protruding from a nearby rock face was a strange conical shape, with feathery striations. Mahinda reached out to touch it and quickly drew his hand away. This shatter cone was still hot.

Only later did Lydia ask Eddie, "Did you cause that?"

Eddie looked at her and said, "Guess I don't know my own strength yet. I'm really sorry."

"Just try to be more careful," Lydia said, "for all our sakes."

## Meet the Media

"Answer your goddamn phone!" The command was accompanied by a sharp elbow to Marc's ribs that finally convinced him that the ringing was not in his dream. Flailing wildly, he knocked over a glass before locating the receiver and picking it up. "Hallo?"

"Marc, Nathan here..."

"Nathan?"

"At the station, the night man."

"Oh yeah, Nathan." Oh, yeah. The pencil-necked geek who babysits the network feeds over night.

"Sorry to wake you, but according to the roster, you're on call, and do I have a story for you."

"It's my birthday, dammit! My birthday, and I'm the guy on call." He risked a peek at the woman who had been sleeping beside him. And last night began to trickle back into his memory reservoir. She had been amazing. Her blonde hair covered one eye. The other eye was watching him, amused. Must be a dye job with that brown skin, Marc mused. Sure gives her an exotic look, though. Older than she looked in the dim light at the Townehouse last night but still a good looking woman. Something odd about her accent. Not French. That would be normal around here. A trace of Spanish? He wanted to know more about her, but last night she had made it clear that her past was her own. "What time is it?" he asked Nathan.

"I know it's real early but ... Look, why don't I put the lady on the line, the one who brought in the story."

"Sure."

During the pause, he leaned over and whispered, "Why don't you get us some coffee, Leah?"

"It's Lisa, asshole," she said and added more gently, "I don't do coffee. I'm a professional, proud of my work. You wouldn't ask a ... a doctor to get coffee, would you?"

"Not even instant?"

Shaking her head, Lisa checked his travel alarm and said, "I still owe you forty-five minutes. Coffee's not the only way to get your heart beating this time of day." With that, she disappeared under the covers and he felt her hot tongue on his penis.

"*Mon Dieu!*"

At that moment, Judy came on the line. "Hi, Mr. Baptiste. I watch the news at six all the time and I like your stuff and..." On she rambled. For once, he was not annoyed by the fact that the person on the other end could not get to the point. He tried with only partial success to keep his breathing under control and threw in the odd all-purpose grunt that he hoped sounded like approval or sympathy. "... Are you O.K., Mr. Baptiste?" The ejaculation had caught him by surprise.

"Oh, just a cramp near my leg," he panted, as Lisa, with a faint smile, ran her tongue over her lips before hopping lightly out of bed, gathering up her clothes and heading for the bathroom. "... so then you went up the hill to look for survivors."

"Yeah. And when we got there we saw this alien and ..."

"Alien?" Now he really was annoyed. "You woke me at this hour for a story about aliens?"

There was a short silence and then, "But I got pictures ..."

Pictures? Of an alien. Suddenly he was listening. After all, this was the slow season for news. Any luck, and a couple of grainy shots of flying saucers, and he just might go national, get some real exposure. "You really got pictures?" he asked slowly.

"Yeah," Judy confirmed. "Where are they?"

"Right here in my camera," she told him.

"Look, don't move 'til I get there, O.K.," he said, excited now for a different reason. "I should be no more than fifteen minutes."

"Oh, I'll be here," said Judy.

"Great. See you then." He hung up just as Lisa emerged from the bathroom looking neat and fresh in a skimpy black latex top over tight leopard-skin print pants and stiletto heels.

"Take care," she said.

"The... ah, the money?" said Marc.

"Your friends paid me last night. Happy Birthday, I hope you liked the way I waxed your candle," she said with an enigmatic smile.

"Oh, yeah," he sighed. "You are a true superstar."

"Any time you want a repeat performance," Lisa said, handing him a card and kissing him on the cheek.

As the front door closed, Marc looked at the card and read, "Madame Souci's. Everything for the adventurous gentleman," followed by a phone number.

Marc laughed. God, everybody wants to be called a professional these days, he mused as he headed for the bathroom, but Lisa, now she's the real thing. Me? I wanted to be a drummer. Ended up beating the bushes for news. And what am I doing now? Hunting down aliens on my birthday to further the cause of free speech. *Tabernacle!*

Stopping only to pick up a large coffee at the Tim Hortons Drive-thru, he reached the station at 6:28 a.m. Judy was sitting on the couch in the lobby when he let himself in. She was well over six feet, wearing Doc Martins and sporting both a buzz cut and, he guessed, a permanent scowl. Gotta hand it to skinny little Nathan who, not the least bit deterred by the woman's size, was trying to make small talk, hoping he might get lucky. Good luck, Nate, thought Marc.

After introductions, he asked, "Mind if we wind the film out and get it processed?"

Judy's eyes narrowed. "What's it worth to you?"

"Nothing 'til we see if there's anything usable on the film," Mark told her before turning to Nate and asking, "Did you line me up a cameraman?"

"Camera? No, I didn't know you'd need one."

"Isn't this still a TV station? Get Jules. Tell him, I'll pick him up in ten."

"But Jules isn't on call," Nathan objected, "Debbie is."

The troll. He didn't want to spend a large chunk of the day with the troll, listening to her complain about how the heavy Betamax and battery packs are cutting into her fat shoulder. "Call Jules. Tell him, I'll owe him one." Nathan nodded and disappeared. Marc turned his attention back to Judy. "Look. Why don't you wind the film out of your camera and leave it with Nathan. He'll see it's developed. Anything usable, we'll pay you."

"How do I know that?" said Judy.

"Because if we use it without your permission, you can sue our asses off."

Judy weighed this information for a moment, before fishing out her camera and hitting the auto rewind button. "O.K.," she said over the whine of the tiny servo motor, "but you try to fuck with me, Mr. Baptiste, and you'll be sorry."

This is getting better and better. His twenty-seventh birthday too.

"Any people on here, besides aliens?" he asked.

"What? Yeah, why?"

"Of course, you got releases from all of them."

"Releases?"

"Never mind. Let's get going," he said briskly as Nathan came hurrying back.

"Jules says to pick him up on the way," said Nathan eagerly.

"He got equipment?"

"Yeah. Even says his batteries are charged."

He handed Judy's camera to Nathan and said, "Give her a receipt."

"A receipt?"

"Yeah, just get a chunk of station letterhead and write down that she gave you the camera with the alien pics." Nathan wandered away.

"Now, let's get out of here before this story disappears," Marc said to Judy.

"But the receipt ..."

"By the time Nathan finds any paper, it'll be Christmas. Besides, I'm not so sure he can write. Come on. We've got to pick up Jules." He left without looking back. After a second of indecision, Judy followed.

Jules was waiting on his front step when Marc pulled in to his driveway. He was a native Ojibway from Manitoulin Island who wore his raven hair in two pigtails. Never one to say much, he just nodded in Marc's direction, slung the gear in the back of the Pathfinder and squeezed his very large self into the back seat.

"Morning, Jules." Jules nodded in the rearview mirror, and his face creased in a melancholy smile. On the way, Marc got Judy to tell her story again.

## First Contact

Constable Kim Gauthier was only thirty-eight minutes from the end of her twelve-hour shift when she came across the abandoned school bus. Stolen, she guessed, as she ran the plate number by her dispatcher. No report on it yet. Didn't necessarily mean anything. The owners, Northern Bus Lines, may not have discovered the theft yet. Alerting dispatch again, she got out of her cruiser and approached the bus. The crunching of her shoes on the gravel was not the only sound disturbing the early morning silence. Somewhere above her faint sounds of ... of what? She stopped and listened intently. People singing? Maybe some campers who belonged to the bus. First, though, she decided to check the bus.

The door was open as if whoever left the bus here expected to be right back. Nothing much on the bus ... a picture of the sacred heart dangling from the rearview, a rosary dropped by Émilie and an old Polaroid camera and four pictures: two of a group posing in front of a Tim Hortons, two of a wall with some kind of stain on it. She put the pictures back on the seat and tried to make sense of what she had found. Louder now, the singing distracted her. Ducking down, she peered through the window.

*   *   *

"Aliens."

"Not aliens, there's only one."

"O.K. Only one alien. How did he arrive?"

"He fell from the sky."

"You saw him?"

"Yeah, I saw him. Wasn't wearing nothing but a goddam loin cloth."

Story was just getting better and better. "Like Ghandi?"

"Like Jesus," she told him, exasperated.

"Jesus?"

"Sure. You'll see," she told him confidently.

Marc looked in the rearview mirror at Jules. As usual, it was impossible to know what he was thinking about this alien chase. Marc was sure this would be a huge waste of time … but he'd been wrong before.

"This is it," said Judy, excited. Marc nodded and pulled his Pathfinder on to the shoulder opposite the empty school bus and the blue-and-white cop car. As he got out, he spotted Constable Kim Gauthier and waved. She had been about to start up the hill when she had heard his vehicle and stopped on a rock above the road. My God, some women just looked good in uniform. They knew each other slightly from a couple of accidents he had covered.

He scrambled up the hill and held out his hand. "Marc Baptiste from News at Six," he said in case she did not remember him. "We've met a couple of times …"

"Sure, I remember. What brings you here? The singing?"

Marc finally stopped and listened and heard the voices. "Actually, I heard there was an alien."

Constable Gauthier laughed. "That's all I need. My shift was finished fifteen minutes ago."

Jules finally reached them with his gear. He was alone. "Where is the woman?" Marc asked him, exasperated.

"Wouldn't get out of the car."

"Why not?"

Jules shrugged. The three of them stood still for a while peering up the hill, as the singing got louder. Eventually, Père Jean-Pièrre appeared, beaming and singing at the top of his lungs, the rest of his flock straggling along behind him, singing a ragged counterpoint. Suddenly Kim recognized the song as *Hosannah*. "Jesus, they're singing *Jesus Christ Superstar*," she said.

"The only hymn they all knew," explained Père Jean-Pièrre, as he came up to them. "We don't sing much at Saint Gabriel Lalemant."

The singing petered out as the pilgrims gathered around the constable and Marc. Jules handed Marc a microphone, backed off and shouldered the heavy camera. "Rolling," he said quietly, as three more people appeared, and finally a bearded giant silhouetted against the blue sky, clad only in a loincloth. For long moments, Marc could not think of anything to say, before finally blurting out, "Jesus Christ!"

"Looks just like his pictures," whispered Kim.

"Christ, he's big," Marc said, before turning to Jules and saying, "Cut! I'd better get some background. The guy sure doesn't look like an alien to me. What do you think, Jules?" Jules shrugged. As usual, Jules was about as free with words as a miser is with money. "Give me five minutes."

Walking over to Père Jean-Pièrre, he asked in French, "Who is the big guy, Father?"

"Me, I believe he just might be Jesus himself, come back to save the world," Père Jean-Pièrre said. Marc looked back up the hill. Eddie had stopped and was sitting on a rock, a small erratic too insignificant to have interested God much. The others, all except Alphonse, had drifted off and were standing in a small group whispering to each other and gesturing up the hill at Eddie. Behind Eddie, Lydia was standing protectively. Arthur was showing Mahinda yet another shatter cone. Alphonse sidled into the shade of a scrubby birch tree, trying not to be noticed.

"I heard he was an alien," Marc tells the priest.

"Alien? Who told you that?"

"Woman who came to the station. Name of Judy something."

"Hah! You can't believe anything that damn woman tells you." He seized Marc's arm and added, "Believe me, this is the real thing, the second coming we have waited for for two thousand years. He came into the world naked as a newborn."

"He fell from the sky," Annette offered.

"Trailing clouds of glory," her sister, Émilie, elaborated. "In a great ball of fire," added Cécile.

"So he's not an alien?"

"Alien?" said Claude Bisonnette, the bus driver. "He is coming from heaven. We all saw him."

"Where were you when he fell?" asked Marc, trying to make some sense out of what he was hearing.

"We were on the bus."

"That school bus down below?"

"Yes, of course," Annette broke in, impatiently. "The motorcycle had just passed with our sister on the back."

"Sister?"

"Marie," said Cécile, shaking her head at his stupidity. And then they were all talking at once. Marc stepped away from the small crowd and glanced up the hill at Eddie. Certainly an impressive-looking guy, but the second coming?

"What do you think?" he called across to Alphonse.

"Me? … I don't think anything." Don't get involved, Alphonse was cautioning himself. Whatever you do, don't get caught on camera. All you need is Madame recognizing you, or even Lisa. He started sweating at the thought, despite a cool morning breeze.

"Maybe I'd better talk to the big guy," Marc said, turning back to the priest. "What's his name, Father?"

"Eddie Magdalena."

Marc carefully repeated the name, then, motioning to Jules to follow, he moved up the rocky track. Lydia intercepted him. "He's been through a lot," she told him. "You wouldn't even be here if that witch hadn't taken those pictures."

"Then you tell me what happened," Marc challenged her. So she did. "Just five minutes with him," Marc bargained. Lydia looked at Eddie who shrugged his broad shoulders and nodded.

"O.K.," she agreed reluctantly and stood aside.

Here goes, thought Marc. Interview on the Mount. "Marc Baptiste, News at Six," he said, holding out his hand. The big man rose and they shook hands. "Mind if we do an interview?"

"Uh, no, I guess not." Eddie glanced around until he caught Lydia's eye. Already he had come to trust her, but she had no advice on this one. She shrugged and favored him with a sympathetic smile. He was on his own. Eddie glanced around the other smiling faces of the small crowd and felt them waiting for him to say something significant. What? That he picked up a dead nun? That she had saved his ass after the collision with the freight train? That he had been smuggling cocaine? That he was high on marijuana at the time?

Eddie cleared his throat, stalling for time, as Marc turned to Jules.

Jules nodded and held up three fingers, two …

Eddie's panic rose as each finger disappeared into Jules' fist. At two, he felt a warm, celestial calmness overcome him. Marc watched as the troubled, hunted look faded from Eddie's face, morphing into a look of serene certainty.

God, too, had been watching as Jules began the silent countdown. At two fingers, He decided, not for the first time, to break his own rule of non-intervention. He whispered instructions to the holy, ghostly spirit that the nun had become.

Only Arthur, glancing around just in time, saw what was happening. As Jules' second finger, the fuck-you finger, disappeared, Arthur caught a shimmer of movement to the right of Eddie. Careful not to look at the spot directly so as to activate the rods in his eyes, a technique Lydia had taught him to limn the shape of dimly-perceived objects, he saw the sketch of a hooded figure approach Eddie, bend down, kiss him lightly on the mouth and dissolve into him. Arthur gasped. Only Lydia caught Arthur's surprise and realized that something special had just happened.

One. The final finger went down. Jules pointed at Marc.

"I'm standing here on a hill north of Sudbury, Canada, very near the continental watershed. Something amazing has happened here, seconds before dawn on this, the longest day of the year. About a dozen people witnessed a ball of fire streaking in from the sky. Apparently when they went to investigate, they found this man totally unharmed. Miraculous? That's not even the beginning …"

While Marc was speaking, Jules zoomed in past him to pick up a headshot of Eddie. A strong face … and look at the piercing eyes. Jules had a knack for recognizing when the camera loved a face, and it loved the face that was filling his frame. As Marc finished his intro, Jules pulled out to get a two-shot.

"… Tell us in your own words, Mister Magdalena, what exactly happened."

"I have passed through the fiery furnace and arrived here naked as a newborn babe," Eddie said softly.

"But where did you come from?"

"My home is far from here, but I have come as has been foretold."

"Foretold?"

Jules dropped to a crouch a few feet below Eddie so that he was shooting up at a slight angle. Slowly, carefully, he tightened the shot to eliminate Marc's image and let the powerful figure of Eddie dominate the screen. The sun backlighting the big man's shining black hair made for a stunning shot and Jules, uncharacteristically, caught his breath. Black hair, light brown skin, he could be a brother. Except for the beard.

Eddie turned his gaze directly into the camera and said slowly, "165321062533. It is a human number." With a mysterious smile, he rose. With a broad gesture, he said, "Talk to these beautiful people. They will tell you true." With that, he turned his back on the camera and the crowd and walked up the hill until he disappeared from sight. "Get the crowd! Get the crowd!" Marc hissed at Jules. In a well-practiced move, Marc crossed behind the cameraman, grabbed his heavy belt and guided him slowly backwards through the crowd. Everyone was staring at the spot where Eddie had disappeared. Some were praying, some quietly weeping.

What the Hell was that all about, Marc asked himself. Aloud, he asked Jules, "Does that number mean anything to you?"

"Oh, I think I can help you with that," said Mahinda, stepping forward.

While Mahinda explained the significance of the number to Marc, Lydia pulled Arthur aside and asked, "What are we going to do with him?"

"Him? You mean with Eddie?" Arthur asked. She nodded. "Well, there's a cop here. Why don't we let her handle it."

"Why don't we ask him if he wants to stay with us?" asked Lydia, adding, "After all, you're the only one who can see the shadowy figure with him."

Arthur, who deferred to his wife in most things, thought about the possibility for a few moments, before saying, "As long as it's just for a few days."

Lydia reached up and kissed him on the cheek. "Deal," she said.

## The Multitudes

The story of Eddie Magdalena's arrival might have spiked for a day or two before disappearing, to be archived with stories like 'The Face on Mars', 'I was probed by Aliens', and 'Man born with Three Penises' had it not been for the number. Millions of people around the planet had puzzled over the number and how it had arrived on their screens. After Marc had edited his video, the explanation of the significance of the number played prominently. The shots on Judy's camera? Worthless. Every picture had turned out to be uniformly black. Act of God, many asserted. More likely, the woman had left the lens cap on, Marc guessed. Judy, of course, accused him of stealing the images, but he just smiled and told her, "I don't need your pics. The number will sell this story." She had threatened a lawsuit and stomped out of the station. Marc was proved right, though. It was because of the number that the story exploded around the planet.

"The Second Coming?" "Eddie Arrival Foretold" "Ready for the Rapture?" shouted the headlines. I'm sure some of you still remember them. So many aircraft filled with members of the media began to land at the Sudbury Airport, that takeoffs of the Ministry of Natural Resources' firefighting water bombers were sometimes delayed. More media were clogging highways 17 and 69, the main arteries leading into the city from the south, east and west. Local hotels had filled quickly, and so latecoming members of the fourth estate were forced to rent every trailer and Winnebago within a two hundred kilometer radius and drive them into Sudbury to park next to their mobile satellite uplink trucks.

It had not taken long for the media to discover that Eddie Magdalena was staying at the Whiteheads' house overlooking Lake Ramsey. Ramsey Lake Road was soon lined with parked vehicles, all the way past the university. The parking lots at the boat launch and Science North were full.

And not just the media were swarming in thicker than black flies. Hundreds of pilgrims and sightseers were arriving too, only to find that there were no rooms at the inns and that the restaurants were running out of food. Some people had set out to walk the 450 kilometers north from Toronto. A few dragged homemade crosses. Some even flagellated themselves as they crunched along the gravel at the side of the highway. Canadian tourism was suddenly booming. The Ontario Provincial Police and the Sudbury Regional Police were put on full alert, and all leave was canceled.

The Cortina tour boat that runs on Lake Ramsay during the summer was full for every trip. The captain had altered his usual route to approach within 100 meters of Arthur's back deck. This was as close as he dared because of the rocky reef reaching out in the shallows near the shore. By the second day, three houseboats were anchored off the point where Arthur and Lydia lived. Powerful lenses probed every line and shadow. Not surprisingly, all the curtains were drawn tight, even at midday, in the Whiteheads' house. Calls to the house went unanswered.

"This is crazy," said Arthur, as he peeked out of one of the windows facing the road and saw reporters trampling Lydia's flowerbeds. "You told them he wasn't here. So what do they want now?"

The heat in the gloom of the house was oppressive. Should have sprung for air conditioning, thought Lydia, but who knew this was going to happen.

Within an hour after Lydia's frantic call about the swarming reporters, the Sudbury Regional Police had set up a cordon around the house to keep the media at a distance of one hundred meters. As the first twelve-hour shift was coming to an end, though, there was an ominous rap on the front door.

"I'll get it," offered Arthur. "It is probably Mahinda." And he was right, but Mahinda was not alone. Arthur recognized Larry Sawchuk, Sudbury Regional Police Chief, standing beside Mahinda. Behind the chief were two of his officers.

"May we come in, professor?" asked the chief.

"Certainly," said Arthur, anxious to close the door on the shouts and camera flashes emanating from the far side of the yellow police tape. As he shut the door behind Mahinda and the three policemen, Arthur pointed to a table in the hall. "Just leave the luggage there," he said to Mahinda, adding, "What's the big square thing wrapped in paper?"

"My painting, isn't it?"

"Painting?"

"Of the Christian Madonna on velvet."

"Ah." Arthur remembered. "Well, your room is all made up. First on the left. We'll bring your bags up later."

Mahinda flashed a tired smile. "Thank you so much," he told the Chief and his men. "I will be safer here."

Lydia appeared as Mahinda mounted the stairs and waved to him. "Thanks for getting him here," she told the Chief. "Apparently, the reporters tracked him down and never stopped knocking on his landlady's door."

"No problem, I assure you, Mrs. Whitehead," the Chief said smoothly. "But we do have a problem out there." He gestured vaguely towards the mob outside. "I can't keep my people here much longer. We were short of manpower even before this … this incident happened and now …"

"But we can't have them invading the house," cried Lydia. "What do you suggest we do?

"I can leave twenty men here until morning. As you know, if you've been watching the news, Parliament has been recalled by the P.M., and we have requested that they send an RCMP detachment to take over the perimeter until the problem, ah … resolves itself."

"And if they don't vote for that?"

"Several churches have offered to provide the manpower to form a perimeter and …"

"No!" said Lydia and Arthur in unison.

"Eddie doesn't want anything to do with religious factions, as he puts it," said Lydia.

A pause. "I'm sure the RCMP will respond," said the Chief. "It really is a federal matter after all." He backed towards the door flanked by his men. "If there's anything more I can do …"

"Yes, yes," said Arthur, jumping in to forestall a more vigorous reply from his wife. "Thanks for all you've done for us. This has been trying for us all."

At the door, the Chief stopped, straightened his hat and turned back to Arthur. "There is one thing, if you don't mind."

"What?" asked Lydia suspiciously.

The Chief was suddenly diffident. "It's just … Well, you see, we've all seen the video. I wondered if we could meet the man himself."

"Hello, Chief Sawchuk." A rich, baritone voice from the shadows at the far end of the hallway. "I understand you are a great disciple of Taras Chevchenko. I, too, love his poetry."

Eddie advanced into the light and began to utter softly, in flawless Ukrainian, lines from Taras Chevchenko's 'I was Thirteen.'

*But not for long the sun serene*
*Not long in bliss I prayed*
*It turned into a ball of fire*
*And set the world ablaze.*

Lydia and Arthur were mesmerized by the Slavic sonorities. Tears were glistening in the corners of Chief Sawchuk's eyes. When Eddie finished, the Chief reached for his hand and said, "It was as if Taras himself had come back to life. *Spasybi. Spasybi.*"

The other policemen looked decidedly uncomfortable, but Eddie and the Chief ignored them. "Thank you for understanding how difficult it has been for these people," Eddie told the Chief, "and for realizing how much we needed your help."

"It is nothing, nothing. Mrs. Whitehead, we will stay until the RCMP arrive. You have my word."

Just as the sun was going down, there was a new commotion in front of the house. The RCMP had arrived and were taking up positions around the property. "Come and see this," Lydia called.

Arthur, Mahinda and Eddie appeared beside Lydia at the French windows overlooking the lake. "There." They looked where she was pointing. An RCMP launch was slowly cruising past the point. On deck, a female officer in working blues was saluting them as the launch pulled up alongside one of the moored houseboats. "Always get their man," said Arthur.

"Oh, yes," Mahinda agreed. "Oh, yes."

The sun was finally beginning to filter out of the western sky, as they went back into the house. Lydia stooped and pulled back one of the curtains. "There's an RCMP truck at the end of the driveway," she told the others. "Must be some sort of command post."

Arthur drew back one of the other curtains. "Looks like most of the mob is leaving," he noted in surprise. "Any of your doing?" he asked Eddie.

"No, no. Not me," Eddie protested. "Must be a higher power."

Lydia laughed and added, "Yes. Mosquitoes. They come out at this time of day."

"And people say that mosquitoes are useless creatures."

## We Stand on Guard for Thee

In the evening, as the sun still stubbornly shined on, Eddie told the others honestly about his past, about Joe, about the little he could remember of his mother, of his father Elvis and of the metamorphosis he had felt taking place within him since his decision to pick up the dead nun.

"Then you are the Messiah?" asked Lydia, a note of wonder in her voice.

After a slight hesitation, Eddie said slowly, "I guess that's what's happening. Not something I ever wanted, even in my wildest dreams. I mean, look what happened to the last guy."

"Jesus? Yeah, not a promising ending," said Arthur.

"Not all prophets are sacrificed," Mahinda pointed out, "and the magic number refers to the birth of the Lord Buddha, not the Jesus. Don't forget that Lord Buddha died a natural death ... or, at worst, an accidental poisoning."

"Didn't Buddha say that to achieve enlightenment you must give up all attachments?" asked Lydia.

"Yes," Mahinda agreed.

"And that believing in a god was one such attachment?"

"Well, yes," Mahinda admitted uneasily.

"So the number, or maybe we should call it the prophecy, because that's what it is, refers to the one religious leader that doesn't believe in a god," said Arthur, looking genuinely puzzled.

"What about L. Ron Hubbard?" Lydia asked mischievously, but the others ignored her.

Mahinda sighed and said, "The position of the various forms of Buddhism differ greatly on the existence of a god or gods. In Sri Lanka, for instance, there are many gods, mostly borrowed from the Hindus but, in some ways, you can equate them with the Christian saints.

"O.K.," pursued Arthur, "but what do the traditional texts say?"

"Do you know the story about the three questions?" Mahinda asked.

Lydia glanced at her husband who shrugged. "Not unless you told it to us," she said.

Mahinda nodded. "One morning as the Lord Buddha entered a village, he was approached by a man who asked, 'Does God exist?'

"'No, he does not,' Buddha replied.

"That afternoon another man asked, 'Does God exist?' The Buddha looked at him carefully and replied, 'Yes. Of that there can be no doubt.'

"In the evening, a third man approached and again asked the same question, 'Does God exist?' The Buddha closed his eyes and said not a word. The man, too, closed his eyes. For some time, both men sat in silence. Eventually, the third man touched Buddha's feet, bowed low to pay his respects and whispered, 'You are the first man who has ever answered my question.'

"That night, just as the Buddha was falling asleep, Ananda, the Buddha's constant companion, said to him, 'You must answer a question for me or I will not be able to sleep.'

The Buddha smiled and nodded for him to continue. 'Today three men came to you and asked the same questions, but to each you gave a different answer. None of them heard what you told the other two, but I was present for all of them, and I am troubled.'

"'I was not talking to you, Ananda," said the Buddha quietly. "You did not even ask a question of me, so none of my answers was for you. The first man was a believer, a theist. I told him god does not exist because I wanted to free him of his idea of God, an idea he had not experienced. Otherwise he would not have asked me the question. And all such religious ideas are barriers to the truth.

"The second man was an atheist whose belief in the non-existence of god was likewise a barrier to the truth, so I told him, 'Yes, there is undoubtedly a god.'

"The third man, the agnostic, was the right inquirer. He had no belief, so I kept silent, and that was my message for him: be silent and know. He also became silent and was finally overwhelmed with joy when he understood my answer." Mahinda stopped, smiled and put his hands together in a *wai*.

Lydia smiled in turn and returned the wai before looking over at the couch where Eddie had been sitting clad in one of Arthur's robes. Eddie was asleep. Putting her fingers to her lips, she ushered the others out of the room, found a comforter and a pillow in a cupboard and made the big man comfortable. After tucking him in, she kissed him on the forehead. Straightening up, she whispered, "Get all the sleep you can. This is just the beginning."

Turning out the lights, she stood for a moment looking out at the finger of moonlight on the still water of the lake, before sighing and making her way upstairs.

## Sunday Morning Coming Down

On Saturday night, Père Jean-Pièrre waited in vain until after ten o'clock, but Alphonse did not appear. When at last he wearily made his rounds, dousing the lights in the church and locking up, he thought nostalgically of the string of Saturday nights that had ended here. Alphonse will never be back with the same tales. Père Jean-Pièrre guessed that Alphonse's trips to the whorehouse had stopped, that he had even refilled the holy water font inside his front door.

The next morning the church was crammed with worshippers. Despite the close quarters, when a murmur passed through the crowd, people squeezed back to admit a path down the center aisle for the four quintuplets. People touched the hems of the sisters' Sunday dresses, as the women passed nervously down the aisle towards the altar. Seats were found for them. Outside, the crowd was spilling into the street, and police had arrived to direct traffic.

Père Jean-Pièrre needed a couple of gulps of courage before he sneaked in through the sacristy. The mass proceeded over an electric buzz. When the time for his sermon came, Père Jean-Pièrre mounted the steps to the elevated pulpit and, staring at the sea of upturned faces, quietly dropped the sermon he had written for today and launched on a journey that he hoped would lead towards the light.

"Let me welcome our usual parishioners …" He smiled down at the four quintuplets and nodded to Alphonse who was wearing a new suit and slouching against the wall under a window to his right. Thomas LaRue and Claude Bisonnette were sitting behind the four sisters. Standing at the back, hesitant to join the others, was Judy. "… and the faithful who have made this journey here from so many parts of the world to bear witness at this special time." He paused, not sure what to say next. "Look, I am a simple priest, not a very good one at that perhaps. There have been times when I doubted, times when I sat here alone in the dark and wondered whether I had really had a call, or had become a priest only to please my mother, God rest her soul. But just before dawn on the day of the summer solstice, my doubts disappeared in a purifying fire. Together with eleven other people, many of whom are here today, I witnessed a flame plunging from a starry sky, and my Lord appearing on a mountaintop." He held his arms on high and shouted, "Hallellujah! The Lord is risen! Hallelujah! The Lord is come. And we are all witnesses."

A mighty roar went up in the crowd and spread beyond the walls to ripple through the throngs outside, and swell down side streets and through the town.

Three hours later, the crowds had gone. The streets were deserted, except for a single black car with heavily tinted windows. Inside the church, only Père Jean-Pièrre and the others who had been there that fateful night remained. Judy, at first, hovered uncertainly near the doors, until Père Jean-Pièrre motioned her to join the others. In a whisper, she apologized for her actions on the mount. The others, led by Père Jean-Pièrre, welcomed her back to the fold.

Outside, the door of the black car opened into the shimmering heat of the day. A heavyset man stepped out, surveyed the street, and then opened the rear door and stepped aside. A tall, thin figure clad in black emerged, crossed the deserted street, and slipped like a wraith through the wide church doors into the gloom inside.

Père Jean-Pièrre and the others had been waiting for him in a small knot next to the altar. Only Alphonse hung back in the shadows of the confessional. All eyes were on the man in black striding up the center aisle. The face was gaunt and old, but the eyes were sharp. "Père Jean-Pièrre?" the man asked in a voice that did not sound as if it had been used for a long time.

"Yes," said Père Jean-Pièrre stepping forward.

"I am Cardinal Bertelli, the pope's *Legatus a latere*." With a bow so slight as to be almost imaginary, he held out his hand and Père Jean-Pièrre kissed the large ring. The pope's personal legate had arrived.

"Welcome to our humble parish," Père Jean-Pièrre told him. "When your secretary phoned, I must confess I thought it was someone playing a joke."

The archbishop nodded. "These are parlous times. It is well not to trust too much." He looked over the group. Before leaving Rome, he had learned all he could about the pilgrims who had been witness to that night. He had even pored over Marc's footage in an attempt to memorize their faces. His sharp eyes spied Alphonse lurking in the shadows. That was the one who would prove most useful.

"No matter," said the nuncio briskly. "I trust the rest of you can be ready to leave in the morning."

A ragged chorus of assent. "It is not every day we have the opportunity to meet the Holy Father himself," said Père Jean-Pièrre.

"We are all excited. But … well, some of us do not have passports. What are we to do about that?"

"It is all arranged. You have no need to worry." The nuncio permitted himself a wintry smile. "The Holy Father wishes to see you and I am here to make the meeting happen. Please pack. We will be leaving early tomorrow morning."

"Where would you like us to meet you, Your Eminence?" asked the priest.

"Here. The minibus will pick you up at 8 a.m. Please be on time." He looked at his watch. "I am afraid I have other duties to attend to, so I will say my goodbyes until tomorrow."

Annette, Émilie, Cécile and Yvonne insisted on kissing the Cardinal's ring, and then held each other as the black figure strode down the aisle, his shoes echoing on the stone floor until the front doors were thrown open by the Cardinal's driver, admitting a brilliant shaft of light that swallowed them both.

## By the Dawn's Early Light

When Eddie padded barefoot out on to the deck just before dawn that same Sunday morning, the anchored houseboats had disappeared. How many cities have a lake in the middle of downtown, Eddie wondered, as he stared out at the morning-still waters. The others were still sleeping after the long conversations that had eaten away the few hours of darkness.

Arthur arrived just as the sun was rising and handed Eddie a coffee. Both men leaned on the railing and watched the low mist drifting over the surface of the lake slowly disappear, as the sun burned it away. Even in this first week of summer, there was a slight chill in the air at this early hour.

"Beautiful spot," said Eddie, warming his hands around the coffee mug.

"Yeah. Lydia's father helped us buy it. Too expensive for a lowly professor." Off to the left at the end of the lake, Eddie could make out the A-frame building that was the Sudbury Yacht Club. Behind it, masked by a hill, he could just see the tips of the masts through the trees, and to the right the gleaming silver snowflake that was Science North. "So, where do we go from here?"

"We?"

"Well, Lydia and I are involved now, I mean we were there. By the way, do you realize how many people witnessed your descent from the heavens?"

Eddie nodded. "Twelve."

"Coincidence?"

Eddie sighed. "Who knows …" He laughed. "Does that make one of them the Judas?"

Arthur was not to be put off. "You haven't answered my question."

"I was hoping it would all go away and I could, you know, disappear. I never realized what a great thing anonymity is."

"It's not going to go away. At some point you're going to have to face them, give them some words of wisdom. You know, stuff like 'the meek will inherit the earth.'"

"I thought that was the Greeks."

"Only in the Monty Python version."

"Ah." Eddie finished his coffee.

"Another?"

"Sure." But as Arthur reached for Eddie's cup, Eddie took his wrist and said, a note of desperation in his voice, "You know, I've only done this once before. Giving a speech, I mean. I need to try it out."

"Your performance on the hill was magnificent. You'll be fine," Arthur reassured him. But Eddie did not look convinced. "Look, give it a shot. I'll be your audience."

"Yeah? O.K., I could start by telling them that God really did create the earth and the heavens in 4004 B.C."

"Good start," Arthur said with a laugh. "If you can convince an old geologist of that, I'll be totally impressed."

"Because of the fossils dating back millennia?"

"Of course."

"What if I told you that Bishop Ussher was right, that the earth really was created on the night of October 23rd, 4004."

When he saw the serious look in Eddie's eye, Arthur sat down. "O.K. Convince me."

For a few moments, Eddie paced, then stopped, looking out over the lake. Arthur felt a thrill of revelation, as he saw the darkling shadow of the nun melt into the big man. As he turned back to face Arthur, Eddie seemed to have grown. Their eyes met, and Arthur was a little taken aback by the intensity he saw in Eddie.

In a rumbling baritone, Eddie began: "In the beginning, God created the heavens and the earth. And the earth was without form and void and darkness was upon the face of the deep. And the spirit of God moved upon the face of the waters. It is the night of October 23rd, 4004, a date close to the autumnal equinox and the beginning of the Jewish New Year at that time. Bishop Ussher worked it all out brilliantly early in the seventeenth century. The church liked his theory so much, it was incorporated into the authorized Bible of 1701, and believed by almost everybody. And his methods were very clever. He used the lineages in the Hebrew Bible and cross-referenced them with known dates like the death of King Nebuchadnezzar II. He originally came up with the date at 4000 B.C., but then realized that Dionysius Exiguus, the guy who invented the Anno Domini numbering system, had missed the birth of Christ by 4 years.

"Not exactly a scientific process, you'll object." Arthur flinched, as this was exactly what he had been thinking. "You know the great astronomer, Johannes Kepler?"

"Sure," agreed Arthur warily, "but not as well as Lydia, of course. Oh, hallo, darling."

Walking out on the deck, cradling a mug of coffee, Lydia asked, "Kepler?"

"You know his *Tabulae Rodolphinae*?"

"Kepler's Rudolphine Tables?" She turned to Arthur. "He used Tycho Brahe's observations and his own discovery of the fact that planets have elliptical orbits to predict the positions of the planets against so-called fixed stars."

"Bishop Ussher used Kepler's figures. So there was certainly science involved."

"But what about the fossil records?" Arthur, playing his trump card.

"Ah, yes, the fossil records. Child's play, really. God's idea of a cosmic joke maybe. As you know, hundreds of fossils tell us of animals, such as the dinosaurs, that no one on earth has ever seen. Consider this. What if the fossil records are based not on animals that once roamed the earth, but on animals that had evolved to a dead end on any of the billions of other planets in the universe?"

"But why?"

Eddie smiled. "To give a respectably long provenance to the planet? God works in mysterious ways, remember?"

Arthur's jaw dropped. "So the Creationists are right?"

"He's pulling your leg, Arthur," Lydia said.

"You told me to try to convince you, remember? Sorry, Arthur. How did I do?"

"Goddammit! You had me going," said Arthur. "For a second, there, my whole career seemed a waste of time."

"Maybe you're right, Arthur, believing seems to be an easier bet than not believing."

"Yeah, well, my brain doesn't work too well on only one cup of caffeine. I need another coffee," said Arthur. "Want one?"

"This is the last of the coffee," said Lydia, holding up her cup. "I'll make a fresh pot."

"Sure?"

"Yes, I think I'll make it a bit stronger."

"Good idea."

When she had gone, Eddie said, "You know, Arthur, maybe I need some kind of agent."

"To do what?"

"If I'm going to go out there and face them, I need somebody to help me make a plan."

Arthur looked at him for a moment before saying slowly, "You could do worse than Lydia, much worse. She already has more than a nodding acquaintance with the cosmos. Luckily, she's not too busy at the moment."

"You think she'd do it?"

"You're the most interesting thing that has dropped into her life for some time. I think she might."

"I'll ask her. But what am I gonna tell the people outside?"

"No idea," admitted Arthur, then, smiling, he added. "Hey, maybe you could change your name to Jesus, say that this was the …"

"I wouldn't have to change it."

"Seriously?"

"That was what my mother named me. You know 'Jesus' pronounced the Mexican way, 'Heysoos.'"

Arthur shook his head in amazement. "Wait 'til the press gets hold of that."

"I think I need to go out to the gate, talk to all those poor sons of bitches who have come here from all over, tell them … tell them …"

"It will come to you. You just about convinced me that creationism was true. I watched when you talked to that TV guy, remember? You had no idea what you would say then either. And then the hooded figure just melted into you, and you spoke. I saw the same thing happen this time."

"You saw that? I forgot that you could see her too."

So Arthur smiled and said, "Seems my father was right. God is in the gaps."

"Or at least the Holy Ghost," Eddie said quietly. He looked at Arthur carefully for a few moments before adding, "Deep down, though, you don't really believe there is a God, do you, Arthur?"

"For quite a while I thought I didn't," Arthur confirmed. "Then, somewhere around my thirties, I decided I was an agnostic. You know, the third guy in Mahinda's tale."

"Not an atheist?"

"No, I could never achieve that level of certainty. I work at the university, and there are quite a few atheists there, of course, many of them quite as self-righteous and priggish as any born-again Baptist. In the end, somewhere around my fiftieth birthday, I decided to believe in a higher being."

"You decided?"

"Well, let's just say that I decided to put my chips on Pascal's wager. You know the philosopher, Blaise Pascal?"

"Wrote *Pensées*, right? Goddam! You know, I still don't know how all this shit got into my head."

"I'd say your dead nun is pretty widely read," said Arthur.

"Catholic tastes, too."

"A pun is a pistol let off in the ear, not a feather to tickle the intellect." The voice was Lydia's. Both men turned to find her standing in the half-opened glass door, burdened by a tray. "Toasted crumpets and fresh coffee," she said, putting down the tray and joining them under the parasol at the table.

"Ah, sweetheart, I was just talking about Pascal's wager and the extent of my … my religious fervor. Mind you, my usual take on religions, a plague on all their houses, has taken a sharp upturn with Eddie's fall from the skies. Anyway, Pascal felt that to believe in God was a win-win situation. If He exists, you bet the right hand. If He doesn't, what have you lost? Therefore, the logical person believes in God."

Lydia nodded, "Pascal thought you could will belief. I'm not sure that's true."

"Oh, it is, it is. Look at the rush to believe in fairies in the nineteenth century, the amazing number of superstitions practiced. On a bet, L. Ron Hubbard even invented a religion that thousands of people still flock to."

"Then you must believe in an afterlife too," Eddie said with a sly smile.

"No, I wouldn't go that far," Arthur conceded. "But, like belief in a God, it's a win-win situation."

"How so?"

"Well, if you believe in an afterlife, you won't be disappointed."

"But … Oh, yes. I see what you mean. If there is no afterlife, there is no consciousness after death …"

"And, therefore, no chance to be disappointed," added Lydia.

"Damn! Caught in a logical cleft stick," Arthur conceded with a chuckle.

Eddie smiled at Arthur as he poured himself another coffee and said, "You know, Arthur, Pascal also said that men never do evil so completely and cheerfully as when they do it from religious convictions."

"Well, he was sure right about that."

Lydia turned to Eddie. "Through all that talk last night, you never told us whether you believe in God."

Eddie sighed. "You know, I never really thought much about it, until I got smacked in the ass by that locomotive."

"Act of God?" asked Arthur, with a wry smile.

"I guess." Eddie got up and began to pace. "You know I didn't ask for any of this. Even, you know, these amazing things I seem to know since my … my low earth orbit with the sister. It's like, well, not exactly hearing her voice but … how can I explain it … Eddie the high school dropout suddenly owns a wealth of knowledge and a sense of … of purpose. Up 'til now I've just been scuffling a living, not always legally, as I told you last night. Now I have this presence inside me. Be still and know. The dead nun is part of me now. I've spent most of my life as a loner but not any longer." He sighed and grinned at Arthur. "Sounds crazy, huh?"

"Being inhabited by the Holy Ghost? No crazier than me seeing the gaps in the cosmos," Arthur told him.

"And, just like you, the apostles received the Holy Ghost at Pentecost. If anything, it authenticates who you are," said Lydia.

"Who I am? I'm still trying to get a handle that. Who was it said that reality is only the result of a lot of agreement? I thought I knew who I was, but since the nun …"

They sat in silence for a while, enjoying the peace, and the warming rays of the sun. Arthur broke the silence. Turning to Eddie, he asked, "Then I take it there is only one God."

"Oh, yeah, I'm sure of that now," Eddie replied, getting up and stretching.

"Whatever happened to polytheism? There used to be gods for everything. The Romans had *penates*, their household gods. The Greeks had a dozen gods. Even the Old Testament mentions other gods …"

"India still has thirty-three million gods at last count," Lydia pointed out.

"What can I tell you? Most of the other gods faded away over the ages as people stopped believing in them. Many of them got to be saints or angels in the monotheist religions that spread around the globe."

"So would you say that the Christian trinity is a relic of polytheism?" Lydia asked seriously.

Eddie waited for a moment, but nothing came to him. "Could be, I guess," he said lamely.

Lydia smiled, "Oh, I think polytheism is rampant, but only locally. Look at India."

Eddie leaned on the railing and gazed out over the still waters of the lake. "Hinduism. Now there's a special case." He frowned as if waiting for some cue and then went on, "Ah, Bhakti, that's it, the devotion of Hindus to God and the gods. Hentotheism. That's what it's called." Eddie shook his head, surprised at mouthing such erudition. "Holy Fuck! Hentotheism. I actually know what the Hell the word means, Arthur."

"Not a term I've ever encountered," Arthur admitted. "What does it mean?"

Eddie opened his mouth, but at first nothing came out. "Shit!" he said and then suddenly laughed. "Apparently it's belief in one supreme deity, without denying other gods that may be worshipped as well. Christ, I don't know if my muse missed her cue or is just playing with my head. Anyway, Hinduism will not be a problem. It is the three monotheisms, all springing from the same book, that worry me."

"Jews, Christians and Muslims?" said Arthur.

"Yeah. The people of Abraham. People of the book."

"What about Buddhists?" The voice startled them, and they all turned towards the patio doors where Mahinda was standing.

"I don't know." The ghostly whisper in his head remained silent, and Eddie admitted again, "Right now, I just don't know."

Mahinda smiled and said, "The magic number contained a Buddhist date only."

"Yes," said Lydia, starting to gather up the coffee cups, "but right now we have something more urgent to do. We need to get out of here, get some food and some clothes big enough to fit you, Eddie. God knows, you look like the Incredible Hulk about to burst out of Arthur's hand-me-downs."

Ah yes, God knew indeed and savoured the fact that even He did not know what exactly would happen next. His laugh, though, was loud enough to fracture a diamond when Eddie asked Lydia, "Can I make one request, Lydia? I've always wanted one of those black Harley T-shirts. Do you think you could find one in this town?"

Lydia laughed, in turn, "Yeah, this town even has a Harley dealership on Long Lake Road. I'll get a couple in XXL."

"Can't get them today," said Arthur. "Everything's shut on Sunday."

Just then, the telephone rang inside the house. "Nobody knows this number," said Lydia. "I delisted it yesterday."

By the third ring, Arthur rushed inside and snatched up the phone. The others followed. After a moment, the worried look on Arthur's face faded away. "It's O.K. It's Père Jean-Pièrre. Wants to talk to you." He handed the receiver to Eddie.

Père Jean-Pièrre told him about the legate's visit and the summons to Rome. "We're leaving tomorrow morning. I gave him Lydia's new home number. I hope that's O.K."

"Yeah, don't worry about it," said Eddie. "I've been wondering how to get the message out. Making first contact with the Vatican is probably a good thing. If we can convince the pope, I think we might convince the rest of the people of the book. Call us from Rome and give us a number where we can reach you. *Via con Dios*, Jean-Pièrre."

The second phone call came in early in the afternoon from Rome.

A voice identifying himself as Luigi Fuseli, the pope's valet, asked politely to speak to Eddie Magdalena. Lydia passed Eddie the phone. When Luigi was sure he was talking to Eddie, he announced that Pope Urban IX would like to speak to him.

"Of course," agreed Eddie. As he waited for the pope to come on the line, Eddie searched his memory for information about this pontiff. Urban IX had been elected only a few weeks ago. A pope for the poor, he was originally from Argentina where he had got into trouble with the civil authorities, and even the Vatican, for practicing liberation theology in his work with the downtrodden.

Both fell into Spanish as they talked. The pope told Eddie that, after his audience with nine of the witnesses to Eddie's arrival, he would be moving down to Castel Gandolfo, his summer residence. He wondered if Eddie could make a secret visit. "Many of my cardinals consider you the AntiChrist," he explained, but at Castel Gandolfo, we should be able to keep the press and the dissenters in my own church from learning about our meeting. Eddie readily agreed.

"Wonderful," said Urban. "When can we expect you?"

Eddie realized he would have to consult with the others. "Give me a couple of hours, and I'll call back with a date, Your Holiness."

Over the next hour, Eddie, Lydia, Arthur and Mahinda discussed this secret meeting with the pope over a late lunch.

"I think you should get out your message here first," said Lydia. "After all, thousands of people have come here to hear you."

"And that includes the media," added Arthur.

Eddie saw the wisdom of their advice. "You're right. But it has to be no later than next weekend. I have to call the pope back, and give him a date. I'd like to get there on Monday, July 3rd."

"What about putting the Big Reveal on Saturday?" asked Eddie.

"Doesn't give us much time. I'll see what I can arrange," promised Lydia.

"Saturday is July 1st. That's Canada Day," said Arthur.

"That's right," said Lydia. "It's Canada Day. There'll be a big fireworks display at Science North on the night of July first. Better arrange the

Big Reveal for Sunday."

"O.K. then. Sunday." said Eddie. "I can still get to Rome on Monday."

Lydia said, "Right. I'll call Liz." She decided to use the phone upstairs.

Half an hour later, she was back. "I've got good news. I've set up your first public rally at the Jim Gordon Amphitheater for Sunday, July second. It gives us exactly one week to get ready."

"Well, done, my love," said Arthur, rising and giving her a hug.

"How'd you manage that, and on a Sunday, too?" asked Eddie, truly impressed.

"It helps to know the mayor," Lydia said.

"Ah, yes, of course." Arthur explained to the others, "Lydia and Liz have been friends since they were undergraduates together. They were both taking, God help us, a B.A. in philosophy and English. That is, before Lydia literally saw the light and switched into the sciences for her post grad."

"Liz is setting up a committee and thinks we may be able to get a grant to cover the rental fees, sets, lighting," said Lydia. "She was hesitant, at first. But I pointed out that the city council must already have security and traffic flow planned for the Canada Day event anyway. They can use much the same security plan the next day. What do you think, Eddie?

Eddie, looking suddenly boyish, said, "Could we have fireworks, too?"

Lydia laughed. "Of course. I'll ask Liz if her budget will cover it."

"Terrific!" said Arthur.

"Oh, I also called that reporter, Marc Baptiste, because we're going to need someone to deal with the media. He jumped at the chance. He's bringing his cameraman, Jules, with him. As he says, 'Jules is a genius with a camera, and can provide muscle if needed.'"

"So July second it is," said Eddie. "I'm going to call Pope Urban IX and confirm that I'll see him on Monday, the third. Could someone book me a flight to Rome leaving Sunday night or early Monday morning?"

"I'll pass it on to Marc," said Lydia.

Arthur rose, walked into the kitchen and circled Sunday, July second, with a magic marker. For a moment he stared at the date and then smiled and wrote next to it: *The Big Reveal.*

# Part Four:
# Rome, 1962

### Seems Like Only Yesterday

Père Jean-Pièrre looked at the glowing dial of his alarm clock and sighed. Less than four hours before he had to be up to catch the flight to Rome. Returning to the Eternal City would take him back to the time when he had come within a hair's breadth of abandoning his faith and the priesthood itself. He had been fresh out of the seminary when Cardinal Raoul Dupuis had asked him to come to Rome as one of his aids at the Second Vatican Council in 1962.

The cardinal, a kindly old man, had said to him when they arrived, "You will find that Rome is a Catholic city with a pagan heart. There won't be much happening for the next few weeks so get to know the city. But don't let the pagan heart seduce you, Jean-Pièrre."

"Of course," he had told the cardinal with naive certainty.

"My staff have arranged you a room at the Domus Romana Sacerdotalis. It is a residence for visiting clergy on Via della Traspontina, within sight of the Dome of St. Peter."

Jean-Pièrre found his room a little spartan and the idea of an eleven o'clock curfew irritating but he loved the location. From the terrace, he could see the Castel Sant'Angelo on the near bank of the Tiber and, if he craned his neck the other way, the Dome of St. Peter. He knew he was lucky to be staying in such a handy location as the eternal city was already absolutely full of visiting clergy for the opening of Vatican II coming up in October.

So when Jean-Pièrre was not running errands or doing research for his cardinal, he would don civilian clothes and wander through the city. One day he would visit the Castel Sant'Angelo and explore the banks of the Tiber; on another, he would seek out the thirteen Egyptian obelisks that dotted the city, smiling at the fact that many of them were surmounted by a cross to counteract the pagan hieroglyphic messages along the sides. He found himself drawn to the pagan center of the city. One day after visiting the Pantheon yet again to watch the shaft of light coming through the opening in the middle of the dome and slowly traversing the walls, he decided to walk over to Piazza Navone, his favorite square in all of Rome.

There he had seated himself at Ai Tre Tartufi, one of the outdoor cafes that line the two longest sides of the square. Just as he was finishing his lunch, a pretty woman wearing a large-brimmed white hat, had seated herself at the table beside him and ordered a Tartufo bianco, a white chocolate and ice cream dish that was a speciality of the house. Before she had arrived, Jean-Pièrre had been marvelling at the beauty of the marble figures in Bernini's famous *Fontana dei Quattro Fiumi*, fountain of the four rivers. Now she became the focus of his complete attention. Surreptitiously, he watched as she removed her hat, and tousled her long dark hair. Jean-Pièrre, felt light-headed when he detected the faint scent of her perfume. He was sure he had never been so close to such beauty. When she had finished her ice cream, she ordered an espresso before rummaging around in her purse, pulling out her cigarettes. She caught his eye and asked him, in French, if he had a light. Before Jean-Pièrre had been able to confess that he did not smoke, the white-coated waiter had materialized beside her with a bullet-shaped lighter. Something like rage seemed to well up in Jean-Pièrre at the realization that he had missed his chance to talk to her. The strength and the absurdity of his anger surprised and confused him.

But then his luck changed. The woman began to thumb through her Michelin Red Guide and then to look at the Bernini fountain. She turned, catching his eye again. Embarrassed that she had caught him staring at her, he had looked away. "Excuse me, do you know what piazza this is?" she asked him in English flavoured with a delightful Parisian accent.

"Piazza Navone," he said, hoping she could not hear his heart thumping. "And that," he added in French, pointing to the elegant fountain in front of them, "is the famous *Fontana dei Quattro Fiumi* by Bernini. Wonderful, isn't it?"

She smiled at him, "You speak French."

"Montreal French," he told her apologetically.

"I've always liked the way Montrealers speak French," she told him as her espresso arrived. "Now tell me about the fountain. It is magnificent!"

"As you can see, mademoiselle..."

"My name is Héloïse, Héloïse Garlande."

"Héloïse? But that is marvellous," Jean-Pièrre said with delight. He stood and sketched an awkward bow. "Allow me to present myself. I am Jean-Pièrre Abélard."

Héloïse laughed in turn. "Then we are famous lovers?"

Jean-Pièrre blushed and, flustered by her beauty, stuttered a reply,

"Oh, yes, yes, of course. The famous lovers."

"And the fountain?"

"Ah, it is by Bernini. If I remember rightly, the four rivers are the Nile, the Danube, the Ganges and the Plata. The pope of the time had commissioned a fountain to surround the Egyptian Obelisk you see there in the center. Bernini's enemies had conspired to cut him out of the bidding but Bernini had outsmarted them all. In a window, probably right over there, Bernini installed a large maquette of his design. When the pope went past, the window was open and, glancing up, the Holy Father fell in love with Bernini's design. So this beauty was born." He pointed to the travertine figures in the tumbling waters surrounding the soaring obelisk as if he had designed it himself.

"You should be a tour guide."

Jean-Pièrre blushed again. "No, no. It's just that I arrived a couple of weeks ago and have been wandering around Rome ever since."

"You are with a tour?"

"No, no, I am living here now," he said proudly.

"Me, I only just arrived yesterday. I have only three more days here."

They had talked for quite a while but not once had Jean-Pièrre told her that he was a priest. Héloïse told him that she worked at Galignani, the oldest English bookstore in Paris. Père Jean-Pièrre, not surprisingly, was somewhat more vague about his profession, only hinting that he had a job with the Québec provincial government.

He excused himself with the thought that the French were famously anticlerical and he was loathe to lose her company.

By the time they parted, they had agreed to meet that evening at a restaurant he had eaten at a few times. "It's called Antonetta's and it's just north of here on Via dei Portoghesi. May I?" he asked, pointing to her guidebook. She handed it to him and he wrote the name of the restaurant and the street on the inside of the back cover and handed it back. "Just show this to the cab driver," he told her.

She kissed him lightly on the cheek and he watched her walk away, feeling aroused, and at the same time guilty. Sins of omission are as serious as sins of commission, said a voice in his head.

With grave misgivings but elated all the same, he left the piazza and hailed a cab. At the Castel Sant'Angelo, he paid off the taxi as his residence was only a two minute walk up the Via della Conciliazione. At the Domus Romana, he showered in tepid water, dressed carefully in his light summer suit and left quickly feeling that any priest who saw him bounding down the steps could tell that he was about to break his vows just by looking at him.

Rushing out as if pursued by demons, Jean-Pièrre walked up Via della Traspontina to Via della Conciliazione and turned towards the taxi stand in Vatican Square. "Via dei Portoghesi," he told the driver. In the side mirror, he could see the Basilica of St. Peter receding into the distance as he settled into the backseat. As the cab passed a *tabacchi*, he told the driver to stop and wait while he hurried into the cluttered little shop and bought a Zippo lighter. He waited impatiently while the man behind the counter filled the lighter with fluid and rushed back to his cab.

Five minutes later, the driver dropped him outside Sant'Antonio dei Portoghesi Church. As he paid the fare, the narrow street filled with the strains of the organ in the church. Père Jean-Pièrre recognized Cesar Franck's Chorale Number 3 in A minor, one of his favorite pieces. For a few moments he stopped to listen but found he was shaking with nerves. What was he doing? Should he just turn around and walk away? Should he tell her he was a priest? But just then he saw her sitting at an outdoor table. Attracted by the music, she had seen him and was waving. He waved back and walked down the cobblestone street to greet her.

She rose and kissed him on both cheeks. All his doubts melted and he sat down beside her.

"Have you been waiting long?" he asked.

"Just long enough to order a *vino della casa*."

"Is it good?"

"Taste it for yourself," she offered and held out her glass to him.

Until that point, it was the most intimate exchange Jean-Pièrre had ever experienced with a woman but, determined to pass himself off as a man with some veneer of urbanity, he put his hand over hers and sipped the wine. "*Bellissimo!*" he told her. "We will need some more." He caught the waiter's eye and ordered a carafe. "Do you like the music?"

"What a wonderful place to hear an organ playing. Did you arrange it just for us?

"Yes, of course. I set it up this afternoon."

For the next two hours they drank the white house wine as they progressed from the *antipasto misto*, in this case a plate of grilled vegetables, through the *secondo piatta*, small portions of the *pasta alla puttanesca*, and then the excellent *saltimbocca alla romana* while they exchanged the stories of their lives. Jean-Pièrre's autobiography was necessarily truncated and omitted any reference to his vocation.

Jean-Pièrre found his nerves disappearing as the wine began to flow. Only once when a piety of priests passed by did he feel the edges of panic. He caught one of the priests looking in his direction and picked up a handy menu to hide his face.

After the meal, the waiter offered them a glass of *amaro* liqueur 'to help with the digestion.' He set three tiny glasses on the table and filled them with practised flair. "To love," he saluted them, drank the contents of his own glass in one gulp and was gone.

"To Abélard and Héloïse," she said before sipping her liqueur. "Oh, it is very bitter."

"Yes," agreed Jean-Pièrre. "In fact, *amaro* means bitter in Italian."

"Ah, and you speak Italian too?"

"Only a little. I am learning."

"Ah." She pulled out her cigarettes and selected one.

Jean-Pièrre produced his lighter with a flourish and lit it for her. This must be love, he thought as he watched her blow a stream of smoke into the night air.

That night, he walked her back to her hotel through the deserted streets lit brightly by a gibbous moon. When they reached the steps, she took his hand and led him behind one of the large columns that flanked the main entrance. They kissed in the shadows. After arranging to meet again the next day, she tripped lightly through the door with a last wave and a warm smile.

Almost giddy with pleasure, Jean-Pièrre walked to the taxi stand beside the Pantheon and picked up a cab. As soon as he climbed into the back seat, a wave of guilt came over him as he gave the driver his address. His mind conjured up a series of unanswerable questions. Had he entered the priesthood to please his mother and his aunts or was his really a true vocation? A shy boy, he had had almost no experience with girls. Until Héloïse.

As he paid the driver, he looked at his watch. Almost midnight. Too late for the curfew. "*Merde*," he muttered, realizing that he would have a difficult time talking his way in to the priestly residence.

For the next three days, whenever the cardinal did not require his services, he spent the time with Héloïse. He had decided that he would not tell her he was a priest until he was sure one way or the other about his vocation.

On the night Héloïse had to leave, Jean-Pièrre went with her to the Rome Termini. As they hurried towards platform five, the speaker announced that her train was boarding. They embraced passionately. There were tears in her eyes as she took her suitcase from him and hurried towards the train. After a few steps, Héloïse stopped and turned to him. "Oh, you will need my address." Reaching into her purse, she pulled out a business card that listed her as an assistant manager at *la Librairie Galignani*. "I have written my home address on the back.

I'm still waiting for a telephone to be installed. I will be counting the days, Jean-Pièrre," she said handing him the card.

"Me too," he answered fervently. Less than an hour ago, during their last supper together, Jean-Pièrre had crossed the Rubicon by promising that he would see her in Paris as soon as he could get away from Rome.

"*Je t'aime*," she said and blew him a kiss.

"*Moi non plus*," he said in return but already she was hurrying towards the Paris train. He watched as the clack of her high heels carried her to the second class carriage. Jean-Pièrre waited until the train pulled away.

"As beautiful as an angel," said a rasping, heavily-accented voice behind him.

Startled, Jean-Pièrre turned to find a very short man with a prominent nose looking up at him. The man wore an old trench coat that almost reached the ground. His eyes were obscured by a battered pair of dark glasses.

"What?" Jean-Pièrre said, startled and not a little repulsed by this ill-favored apparition.

"The lady," the little man said. "The devil could not have come up with a better temptation, don't you think?"

"Who the Hell are you?" demanded Jean-Pièrre of the little man who reminded him of the crafty commedia character, *Pulcinella*.

The man emitted a rattling laugh and, with a slight bow, said, "I am Father Tito di Belmonte."

Jean-Pièrre's recognized the name and immediately felt afraid. Tito di Belmonte was famous everywhere in Rome for having the '*iettatore*', the evil eye, like his great-uncle Cardinal Granito di Belmonte. The old cardinal had been so feared that no one had dared oppose his choice during papal elections.

"I am ..."

"Yes, yes," Father Tito muttered impatiently, "I know who you are. Come Father Abélard, I need a drink and we need to talk." Without waiting for a reply, he walked away at a surprisingly brisk pace.

Jean-Pièrre, his heart sinking, stood frozen for a few seconds before deciding to follow. The little man did not slacken his pace or look back. When they exited the station, he turned right. Jean-Pièrre followed him a few paces behind. At one point he looked at his watch and realized he was going to miss curfew again. After the trouble he had got into last time, he thought for a flickering moment of abandoning this procession of two but something told him, if he did, the decision might haunt him for the rest of his life.

Turning a corner, Jean-Pièrre stopped. The little man had vanished. Jean-Pièrre advanced warily until he found a dimly lit basement bar. Peering in the window, he saw the little man sitting at a table in an alcove. The only light in the dark alcove was from a candle stuck in a wax-encrusted Chianti bottle. Jean-Pièrre descended the stone steps and went in. Father Tito pushed out a chair and gestured him to sit. "Have you ever tried absinthe?" he asked Jean-Pièrre.

"No, it is banned in my country and ..." Father Tito held up a hand, silencing him, before waving two fingers at the bartender. "Don't worry about the curfew. I will see to that."

Feeling distinctly uneasy, Jean-Pièrre looked around and saw that the shabby bar was almost deserted. The only other patron, an old man wearing a cloth cap, sat at the bar reading a copy of *L'Osservatore Romano*. The bartender, a cloth draped over his left arm, brought a loaded tray to their table. They watched in silence as the bartender placed a balloon reservoir glass before each of them. In the middle of the table, he stood a small silver fountain with two tiny spigots, a bowl of sugar cubes and two ornate slotted spoons. Jean-Pièrre felt as if he were participating in a religious rite as he watched the bartender take up one of the slotted spoons and fit it across the top of his glass. A notch in the handle prevented the spoon from slipping. After setting up the other glass, he dropped a single sugar cube in the bowl of each spoon and carefully poured the viscous green absinthe over the sugar cube until he had filled the balloon in the bottom of each glass. "To ease the bitterness," Father Tito explained in a whisper. Finally with a slight bow, the bartender left as quietly as he had come.

"What's the silver samovar thing for?" asked Jean-Pièrre.

"Absinthe is usually drunk with cold water." Father Tito placed his glass under one of the tiny spigots and released a trickle of water over the crumbling cube. The absinthe which had been glowing bright green by the light of the candle immediately turned cloudy and dull. As Jean-Pièrre copied the process, Father Tito sipped his absinthe and smacked his lips noisily.

"Not for nothing is absinthe called *La fée verte*. The muse of artists everywhere," he said holding up his glass as if to toast. "Absinthe is banned in Italy, of course, but not in Vatican City."

Cautiously, Jean-Pièrre sipped his own drink and, to his surprise, found he liked the bittersweet taste. The candle in the bottle had burned down and was flinging photons out in irregular bursts. Jean-Pièrre had just plucked up enough courage to ask what this meeting was about when Father Tito reached over, pinched out the guttering candle and removed his dark glasses. Jean-Pièrre, now looking at a hunched silhouette, let out an involuntary gasp of alarm. Father Tito's eyes had taken on an eerie glow in the semi-darkness. "I'm sorry," said Jean-Pièrre. "It's just that..."

Father Tito's rasping laugh. "It's all right. I am used to such reactions. Everyone thinks I have the evil eye, the *'iettatore'*, like my great uncle, *l'Innominato.*"

"*L'Innominato?*"

"The one who is not to be named. But since he is long dead now, we can call him Cardinal Granito di Belmonte. I do not think he had the true evil eye. More likely he, like myself, suffered from congenital achromatopsia. It means I am a monochromat and can only see in black and white. And, like the wolf, my eyes glow in the dark as you can see." He gave a small growl and laughed as Jean-Pièrre flinched and spilled a few drops of his absinthe on the table.

When he had recovered his composure Jean-Pièrre laughed too. The small joke had put him at ease for the first time since they had met. And he was getting use to the glow of the man's eyes. "But surely you did not lead me here to tell me about your eyes," he ventured.

"No, no, of course not. I have been following you and your... your paramour for the past two nights."

"Why?" Jean-Pièrre asked indignantly.

"Because your boss, Cardinal Dupuis, asked me to. Now, before you get too pissed off, he asked me because a couple of priests had reported seeing you in street clothes at Antonetta's with a beautiful girl."

Jean-Pièrre thought back to his first night with Héloïse and the posse of priests that had passed by. A couple of them had probably been from his residence near the Vatican. Not that he needed to keep their tryst secret any more. Taking a deep breath, he said, "I have decided to give up the priesthood and move to Paris to be with her."

For several moments, Father Tito stared at him, a most unnerving experience. Then he sighed, pulled out a notebook and flipped through the pages. Even in the low light, Jean-Pièrre could see pages of neat notes in Italian. "How much do you know about this lady?" he asked slowly.

Jean-Pièrre shrugged. "Enough."

"Ah, then you know that Héloïse Garlande is married."

"That's a lie," Jean-Pièrre told him, furious.

"True enough. She was married until a few weeks ago when her divorce from Paul Garlande was finalized. But, as we both know, according to Mother Church, she is still married to her husband."

"I don't believe it," said Jean-Pièrre, feeling on the verge of tears.

"Why do you think she was here in Rome? A woman travelling alone."

"She's a free spirit. Anyway, she is in love with me. Nothing can change that."

"I believe in your country, they call it a summer romance."

"This is crazy," said Jean-Pièrre, starting to rise from the table.

Father Tito's hand snaked out and caught his wrist in a surprisingly strong grip. "Wait. Consider this. If you run away now, you will be damned for all time." Paralyzed by indecision, Jean-Pièrre stood hunched over the table and then, feeling defeated, he subsided back into his chair. Father Tito regarded him for a moment before adding in a voice that was almost inaudible. "The divorce was over adultery. She had been unfaithful to her husband with a man called..." He consulted his notebook.

"I don't care what his name was," Jean-Pièrre said bitterly, dropping his head into his hands, unable to look into those eyes. He sat there for some time, a weight in his chest making it difficult for him to get his breath.

Father Tito sat back and lit a cheroot while he waited for the young priest to compose himself. Finally, when Jean-Pièrre's breathing sounded more regular, Father Tito said gently, "I have told nothing of this to the cardinal." He waited for a reply but none came. "He need never know, Père Jean-Pièrre."

At the familiar phrase, Jean-Pièrre looked up. "Maybe I am not meant to be a priest anyway," he said.

"There you are wrong. The cardinal says great things about your dedication. He is sure that you have a true vocation. He called on me. Why me? Because I am the *'canus dominae'*, the hound of God." Father Tito waited for a few moments before adding ominously, "And I have never been known to fail."

The eerie glow of Father Tito's stare seemed to Père Jean-Pièrre to penetrate his very soul and was ready to scourge out the black stains of sin found there. "Bless me Father for I have sinned." Père Jean-Pièrre began, tears slowly rolling down his cheeks.

Father Tito gently put his hand on Jean-Pièrre's arm and said in a hoarse whisper, "In Latin, my son, the language of Mother Church."

Father Jean-Pièrre nodded and resumed, "*Deus meus, ex toto corde me paénitet ac dóleo de omnibus quae male egi et de bono quod omísi, quia peccándo offéndi te, summe bonum ac dignum qui super ómnia diligáris. Fírmiter propóno, adiuvánte grátia tua, me paeniténtiam ágere, de cétero non peccatúrum peccatíque occasiónes fugitúrum. Per mérita passiónis Salvatóris nostri Iesu Christi, Dómine, miserére. Amen.*"

When Jean-Pièrre had lapsed into silence, his confessor murmured, "*Ego te absolvo*," and it was as if a weight had been lifted from Jean-Pièrre's shoulders.

Two hours and several glasses of absinthe later, the two men found a cab and, true to his word, Father Tito di Belmonte talked their way past the concierge and even enlisted the man's aid to deposit a very drunk Père Jean-Pièrre onto his bed. The green fairy filled his mind with absinthe dreams; some terrifying (Héloïse making love to a faceless man while he was suspended in a cobweb above the bed unable to move as a large black spider eyed him with bad intent); some reassuring (A large bearded man with a scar takes him by the hand and leads him to the door of St. John Lateran).

When Père Jean-Pièrre was awakened the next morning by the maid, he found a note on his bedside table.

> "*I am curator of the relics in the Sancta Sanctorum.*
> *If you want to talk again, come to the Lateran Palace.*
> *Next door to St. John's Lateran Church.*
> *I'm there most days.*"
>
> *Father Tito*

Despite his night of dreams strange enough for an opium eater, and a vicious hangover, Père Jean-Pièrre dressed in his priestly garb and made his way to St. John's Lateran Basilica thinking to pray there for guidance before looking for Father Tito across the road at the Lateran Palace.

As he passed through the baroque facade of white marble into the cool interior, he stopped and held his breath, overcome by the beauty of the place. After genuflecting to the main altar, he wandered down the nave and turned into the Lancellotti Chapel famed for its pure white light admitted by the plain windows set into the small cupola above it. There he knelt at one of the simple wooden prie-dieus.

He closed his eyes, but a vision of the fine line of Héloïse's cheek as she sipped amaro after their meal together loomed behind his lids. Married? Divorced? An adulterer? How fitting then that their time together had begun and ended with a bitter draught, *amaro* at the restaurant and then the even-more-bitter absinthe that accompanied Father Tito's revelations. Sins of omission. Each of them had been holding back a dark secret. After a long pause, he muttered a perfunctory *Pater Noster*, got up, and brushed off his knees.

On his way out, he stopped for a moment before the inscription '*Mater et Caput*' that indicated that this was the mother and the head of all the churches in Rome and of '*omnium urbis et orbis*', of all the cities and the world. His eyes moved up to the Keys of St. Peter.

"The first Christian church in Rome, authorized by the Emperor Constantine himself," said a rasping voice behind him. Jean-Pièrre turned to find Father Tito di Belmonte. "See that gothic baldachine above the high altar?" Without waiting for a reply he added, "That's where you'll find the heads of St. Peter and St. Paul. Time has not been kind to them I'm afraid. How are you feeling today?"

"Less than wonderful."

"Ah, yes. And you just tried to pray and all you could think of was your lover. I'll..."

"Look, I don't feel like talking right now, so if you don't mind Father,"

"But I do mind, Père Jean-Pièrre. Your vocation lies in the balance. Come." He took Jean-Pièrre's arm and led him out of the church, across the road and into the Lateran Palace.

"The Scala Sancta," he said pointing at the twenty-eight marble steps, now sheathed in wood, that led up to the Sancta Sanctorum in the Lateran Palace. "These are the steps that Our Savior ascended to be judged by Pontius Pilate. There is no holier staircase in all of Christendom. I did not give you your penance last night. Here, you must mount the Scala Sancta. On your knees."

Père Jean-Pièrre looked up at the twenty-eight steps of the Holy Staircase and thought that, in his current condition, he might die before reaching the top. Above him, shuffling on their knees from step to step were five women and one old man. He looked around but Tito had disappeared up one of the flights of stairs on either side of this one reserved for penitents.

Vaguely embarrassed by the idea of such public display of humility, he nevertheless got down on his knees, pulled out his rosary and began a litany of muttered prayers. By the eighth step, he began to notice patches of fresh blood on the steps ahead of him and, looking up, he saw a middle-aged woman dressed in a threadbare coat despite the summer heat shuffling painfully up to the next step. With a soft moan she settled down to her devotions. He wished he had the woman's uncomplicated faith.

It seemed to take him forever to reach the top but finally he did and dragged himself across the floor to sit for a time and look at his aching knees. Red and raw. The old man he had seen earlier turned to him and said breathlessly in American English, "Done it. Made all twenty-eight fucking steps. Worth it though. You know Pius VII decreed nine years off from purgatory for every damned step. Pope Pius X, not to be outdone, added a plenary indulgence if you go to confession and communion first. So it's a good deal when you think about it."

Père Jean-Pièrre smiled at him and asked, "Then it was worth it?"

"Sure was. Although it wasn't for me. No, no. I'll take my lumps in the afterlife. I did it for my wife. Promised Audrey before she died."

Père Jean-Pièrre was silent for a few moments, trying to assess his own feelings. The headache had gone and he felt cleansed by the penance he had just accomplished. "Good for you. Me, I'll have to skip the plenary indulgence," he told the American. "I haven't been to communion in a while."

The old man looked puzzled as Père Jean-Pièrre got to his feet and held out a hand. The American took his hand gratefully and allowed himself to be hauled to his feet. "Next time don't forget the communion," he told Jean-Pièrre.

Père Jean-Pièrre laughed in surprise. "Oh, I don't think there'll be a next time," he said. "Not unless I get a new set of knees."

"I know what you mean," the American agreed as they parted.

Turning his back on the Scala Sancta, Père Jean-Pièrre peered into the Sancta Sanctorum, the Holy of Holies, through a small window with a heavy wrought-iron grill. The Holy of Holies, also called the Chapel of St. Lawrence, was surprisingly small and plain. Over the altar in gold letters carved into the black marble was the famous inscription: *NON EST IN TOTO SANCTIOR ORBE LOCUS*, there is nowhere in the world holier than this place.

Someone tapped him lightly on the shoulder, startling him. He turned to see Father Tito di Belmonte eyeing him. "It is true," the older priest said. "Rome is the center of the catholic universe and here we are at the center of Rome. Ready for the grand tour?"

"What? Of the relics? Yes, of course. When?"

"Why, now of course."

Père Jean-Pièrre was impressed when Father Tito led him down a side passage to the right, through an open door with a massive medieval lock and into the Sancta Sanctorum, the former Pope's Chapel that was seldom open to the public. Two visiting priests were admiring the altar but Tito ignored them and pointed out the gothic tabernacles that held a piece of the table of the last supper and the *Acheiropoeton*, the picture of Christ made without hands by St. Luke. "It has been painted over and badly restored so many times but underneath there somewhere we believe is the image of our Lord that St. Luke began to paint. It was finished by angels, and finished off by restorers." When Father Tito laughed harshly at his own little joke, the two priests turned to see who was disturbing the pious peace. On recognizing Father Tito, they hurried away. As they passed him, Père Jean-Pièrre glimpsed one of them making the old pagan sign against the evil eye.

Over the next few weeks, Father Tito took Père Jean-Pièrre on a tour of the countless relics that permeated the churches, monasteries and convents of Christian Rome. A veritable forest of splinters from the True Cross. "Are all these really parts of the cross?" Père Jean-Pièrre asked at one point.

"You ask because there is enough sacred wood in Rome alone to fill St. Peter's. But why could not our all powerful Savior make them all part of the true cross if he chose? In 345, Cyrillus of Jerusalem preached in his catechesis at the newly rediscovered hill of Golgotha that Our Savior was crucified there and that there his cross had been splintered into fragments filling the whole world with his presence.

"Still not convinced? Then remember that there is such a thing as a relic *a contactu*. Any ordinary piece of wood such as any of these, or these." Father Tito began pulling out drawer after drawer of ancient wood fragments much to the alarm of a monk working nearby. "If only one piece of wood in each drawer were from the True Cross, the others would have absorbed the healing powers of this one piece just by touching it."

"Ah," said Père Jean-Pièrre, deciding not to ask about the many fragments of the Holy Lance that had pierced the side of the Christ.

Or the various relics *ex ossibus*, of blessed bones, *ex carne*, of the saintly flesh, *ex pilis*, of holy hair, or even *ex vestibus*, of Godly garments.

"Come. Let me show you how reliquaries are made to house the holy relics," said Father Tito. They were in the Pauline Ossuary, a non-descript building on the same piazza as the Pantheon and Père Jean-Pièrre could see its impressive dome from a window as they proceeded along a corridor lined with pre-Raphaelite paintings.

"Of course, not all so-called relics are accepted by Mother Church," said Father Tito as they walked, their footsteps echoing on the marble floor. "There was a jar said to contain a sigh of the Holy Ghost which we rejected and, my favorite, a feather from the partridge of Saint Nicholas of Tolentino. One of the Vatican's zoologists identified it as a grouse feather. Not even the right bird."

"Saint Nicholas of Tolentino?" asked Père Jean-Pièrre, mystified.

"Ah yes, the tale is not known to everyone although there is a painting of the miracle by someone or other. Saint Nicholas had apparently been sick and when he had begun to recover was brought a roasted partridge to build his strength. Actually in the painting there are two partridges, but no matter. Anyway, the cook seems not to have known that St. Nicholas was a vegetarian. When the saint was presented with the dish, he brought the bird back to life and it flew away. What do you think? I doubt St. Nicholas botched the reincarnation and accidentally used grouse feathers. So you see what we have to put up with."

They turned into another room lined floor to ceiling with glass fronted cupboards crammed with all manner of bones, vials, and dusty jars. At a workbench, an old monk was working with a jeweller's loupe screwed into his eye. He was contemplating a tiny fragment of bone. "Fresh from the catacombs?" Father Tito asked.

"Yes. We think it is part of a metacarpal of St. Judy of Ravenna."

Turning to Père Jean-Pièrre, Father Tito said, "Much of our work comes from the catacombs these days. There are so many Christians from Roman times buried around the city that it gives us an almost inexhaustible supply of relics. Add to that bones of the blessed who are about to jump the candelabrum and…"

"Jump the candelabrum?"

"About to be elevated to sainthood," Father Tito explained.

Père Jean-Pièrre nodded as he watched the old monk carefully glue the bone fragment to a red satin base. Next he trimmed the printed name 'St. Judy of Ravenna' and glued the paper below the bone. Then he took his tweezers, positioned a small glass bubble over the relic and snapped a gilt metal ring around it to hold it in place. "There," he said, holding up the finished piece to Père Jean-Pièrre who regarded it with awe.

"What happens to it now?" he asked.

"Oh, it will go to a monastery in Ravenna to please the faithful," Father Tito said.

"Do you sell them?"

Father Tito roared with laughter and even the old monk managed a smile. "Sell them? Of course not. We only charge for the certificate of authenticity. Sell a relic? No, no. That would be simony, would it not?"

"Yes, of course," said Père Jean-Pièrre, keeping his objections about sharp practice to himself.

Father Tito slipped on his sunglasses, a mirrored pair today. "Let's get some lunch and then I'll take you back to the Sancta Sanctorum. I've talked to your boss, Cardinal Raoul Dupuis, and he has agreed to let you work with me for three days a week, if you agree."

Over the past few days, Père Jean-Pièrre, grateful to the man who had literally saved his vocation, had begun to grow accustomed to the idiosyncrasies of his mentor and knew he would learn much working with him. Besides his Cardinal was still waiting for the real work of Vatican II to begin and would not really need him until the end of September, so he eagerly agreed to become the sorcerer's apprentice.

"Good," said Father Tito, clapping him on the back. "And when we get back to the Lateran Palace, I'll show you the most precious relic of all. Come on." He turned and headed briskly for the stairs.

"The most precious relic of all?" asked Père Jean-Pièrre scurrying to keep up.

"And certainly the most dangerous to even talk about." Father Tito's voice had dropped to a hoarse whisper. "In 1900, Pope Leo XIII issued

Decree Number 37A. It forbade anyone from talking, commenting or writing about this relic on pain of excommunication."

"What is it?" asked Père Jean-Pièrre, growing alarmed. After all it would not do to be cast into the outer darkness just after his vocation had been rescued.

"If I tell you, we could both be excommunicated," Father Tito said solemnly. "Eight years ago, there was a special session of the Supreme Congregation of the Holy Office to reconsider the matter. The discussion to lift the excommunication was debated for hours. In the end, the petition was not only rejected but the level of excommunication was raised from *speciali* to *specialissimo*. Catholics would now be called upon to shun anyone speaking against the edict."

"And you want to get us excommunicated?"

"No, no. I have a kind of dispensation because of my work with relics. And now that you are to become my assistant, it will apply to you also."

"Really?"

"I pledge on my soul," said Father Tito with a grim smile. Out in the piazza, he hailed a cab. Père Jean-Pièrre flinched when the older man told the cabbie to take them to Antonetta's restaurant. Tito turned to him and said, "At this time in the afternoon, we should have the place to ourselves. No self respecting Italian would eat at this time of day. I know what you're thinking but look on it as a kind of exorcism to celebrate your renewed vocation."

But all Jean-Pièrre could think of was his first night there with Héloïse.

# Santissimo Prepuzio
## Canticles I-VIII

When he arrived at Antonetta's with Father Tito, Père Jean-Pièrre could not help looking over at the table he had shared with Héloïse on that first night full of promise. Today it was unoccupied as the late afternoon sun was streaming in under the awning and baking the row of tables closest to the street. "*Bonjour tristesse*," Father Tito said as Jean-Pièrre passed 'their' table on the way into the cooler confines of the inner restaurant. As Father Tito had predicted, the inside of the place was deserted. Father Tito chose a table in a dark corner well away from the bar and the prying eyes and ears of waiters.

Over their late lunch, Father Tito stuck to gossip about the approaching Vatican II and news of Scott Carpenter's recent triple orbit of the earth. "You see, Jean-Pièrre, we can thank Pope Paul V for finally finishing Saint Peter's but perhaps he should not have excommunicated Galileo."

Père Jean-Pièrre smiled dutifully and hoped that the older man would produce the promised taste of the forbidden fruit. Finally, after the waiter had cleared the table and brought them their espressos, Father Tito glanced around to make sure they were truly alone. Satisfied, he lit a cheroot and began his remarkable tale.

"We have Saint Helena to thank for the relic that now resides in our own Sancta Sanctorum, well, part of it anyway."

"The mother of Constantine?" asked Père Jean-Pièrre.

"Yes, of course. I presume they teach you about Emperor Constantine in Canada, my son?"

"I was schooled by Jesuits, Father," Père Jean-Pièrre told him and, ignoring the crooked smile that crept across Father Tito's face, he went on, "In 313, Constantine was in Rome facing a much larger army but saw the flaming cross in the sky with the inscription '*In hoc signo vinces*.' He won the battle and his rival was drowned in the Tiber. It led to Constantine becoming emperor and making Christianity the state religion even though he might not even have been a Christian himself."

Father Tito raised his eyebrows in surprise. "Then you know that Constantine called the Council of Nicaea two years later to settle the divinity of the Christ. In other words was Jesus part of the Godhead or merely the flesh-and-blood Son of God? All but two of the bishops voted for Jesus' divinity and the Holy Trinity was born.

"Next thing you know, Constantine's mother was off on a shopping trip to the Holy Land even though she was in her late seventies. She returned to Rome with ships full of relics. Most of these relics can still be found, as you know, in Santa Croce in Gerusalemme, the church she founded in 320 and still one of the ugliest in Rome."

Père Jean-Pièrre nodded. "We saw the first piece of the true cross there and the *titulus crucis*, even a few thorns from the Savior's crown."

"Yes, yes, but Santa Croce did not get the *praeputium*," said Father Tito, his eyes glowing eerily.

"*Praeputium?*" asked Père Jean-Pièrre as it was not a Latin word he had run across in all his years of study.

Father Tito reached out and grabbed Père Jean-Pièrre by the sleeve.

"The words that we are forbidden to voice, the *santissimo prepuzio!*"

Père Jean-Pièrre gasped. The savior's foreskin? The prepuce of Jesus? But, despite Father Tito's claim that they shared a dispensation from Pope Leo's edict, he could not utter the word in any language. "You mean the... the…"

"Yes, I see you are afraid of mentioning the Savior's *prepuzio*. Quite understandable but, as I told you, we two have a rare dispensation because of our work."

Père Jean-Pièrre nodded. "*Et verbum caro factus est.*"

Father Tito cackled until he began to cough, leaning so far back in his chair that Père Jean-Pièrre thought he might fall and crack his head on the wall behind him. "Precisely, Jean-Pièrre! The word was made flesh. Pope Leo suggested that priests involved in the Feast of the Circumcision refer to the venerated object as a '*reliquia*' as it is enclosed in an ornate reliquary."

"A *reliquia*," repeated Père Jean-Pièrre. Yes, that was a word he would have no trouble uttering.

"Or even a *cosa*," added Father Tito, regarding the discomfort of his younger companion with grim humor.

Referring to the world's holiest relic as a 'thing' seemed almost as blasphemous as calling it *un cazzo*, a penis. "I think I'll refer to it as a *reliquia* then Father. Until I get used to the idea of our dispensation."

"I understand, of course. Now, go find that lazy waiter and tell him to get us two more coffees…. and perhaps some biscotti, eh?"

When they were settled again and the waiter had gone, Father Tito launched into his tale.

## Canticle I

On the eighth day, Joseph fetched the local rabbi and led him into the cave where the Christ child lay. There, with a knife of the sharpest flint, the mohel circumcised the child as was the law. The old Hebrew woman that had assisted the rabbi took the tiny piece of flesh and preserved it in an alabaster jar filled with old oil of nard. The woman's son was a dealer in unguents of all sorts and she gave the jar to him for safekeeping saying, "Do not sell this jar of nard, even though someone should offer you three hundred denari for it." The dealer promised his mother he would never sell the precious ointment and put it on the top shelf of his tiny shop where the years covered it with a patina of dust and it was gradually forgotten.

## Canticle II

And it came to pass that one day, an older woman but still a woman of great beauty came to him and pointed to a shelf in the dark shadows near the ceiling. "I have little money but I would buy that small jar of oil of nard," she said. To the dealer, who had grown old in his turn and dim of sight, the woman's voice sounded like that of a seraphim and, forgetting his mother's entreaty, he sold the jar to the woman that very day. That night, Jesus was in Bethany, in the house of Simon the leper. And there came unto him a woman having an alabaster jar of very precious ointment which she stroked into his long hair as he sat at meat so that he would be soothed. Judas grabbed the woman's arm and said, "What purpose is this waste? For this ointment might have been sold for much and the money given to the poor." And Jesus said, "Why trouble ye this woman for she hath wrought a good deed." And Mary, His mother, took the woman with the alabaster jar into the kitchen and bade her eat for she was hungry. Then the woman, Mary Magdalena for it was she, gave her the jar and said, "Take this jar for it contains all that will remain of your Son on this earth."

And Mother Mary knew that the woman referred to the flesh of her Son and so she stoppered the jar again and hid it in a niche in a terra cotta wall no more than a few hundred paces from the Temple Mount. She understood that someone of great piety, beloved of the Lord, would someday discover it. And there it stayed sealed in its jar of alabaster, undisturbed and miraculously preserved by the oil of nard for more than three centuries until Constantine's mother, the holy Helena already in her late seventies, visited Palestine in 326. There she discovered a cornucopia of relics which she had shipped to Rome, to Cyprus and to Constantinople. Early one morning, one of her priests came to her and showed her an alabaster jar now dirty and covered with moss. "We believe it contains the prepuce of our Holy Savior," he told her.

Excited, she dictated a note to her son, the emperor, with instructions to her scribe to see that it was shipped off to Constantinople on the next ship.

When the ship arrived in Constantinople, two sailors discovered that the jar had been fractured during the voyage and the remaining oil had leaked out. Fortunately, Helena's note had survived, although stained and smelling of nard. "What shall we do?" one of the sailors asked the other, a man with only one eye. "Put it in this," said the other, tossing him a fine leather pouch. And so, being careful not to touch the holy flesh, they transferred it into the pouch. When the emperor read the note from his mother, he ordered a fine reliquary to be made to house the most holy item in all of Christendom. But before the reliquary was even begun, Constantine died.

### Canticle III

By the time Pope Leo III crowned Charlemagne Holy Roman Emperor in Aix-la-Chapelle on Christmas Day, 800, the veneration of relics had spread across Europe. After the coronation, Charlemagne presented the pope with a priceless gift in a container that belied its worth. "It is the sacred *praeputium* of the Holy Savior, your Holiness," the pious emperor told the pope. "While I was praying in the Holy Sepulchre that stands over the tomb of Our Lord, an angel descended and placed this insignificant pouch before me. Suddenly a small boy appeared and told me he was the Christ Child himself and that this small gift was of his true flesh and true blood. For many moments I was stunned, your Holiness, but when I had recovered my senses, I contemplated the gift before me. With more trepidation than I have ever felt in battle, I opened the sack and found the *praeputium* inside, miraculously preserved. I give it to you today to take to Rome, the center of the church's authority."

The day of Charlemagne's magnificent coronation had been long and the newly minted Holy Roman Emperor was probably too tired after the ceremony to remember that the pouch had actually arrived as a gift from the Empress Irene in Constantinople to celebrate his elevation. Pope Leo III promised this most holy of relics would be kept in the Sancta Sanctorum in the Lateran Palace. Word soon spread that the Savior's *praeputium* had been presented to the Pope by Charlemagne in a simple leather purse. As a result, purses copied from the original became highly sought after throughout Christendom. In 1070, the *praeputium* was included in the inventory of all the relics held at the Lateran Palace.

## Canticle IV

In 1204 the knights of the fourth Crusade successfully laid siege to Constantinople, the richest city in the world. The sacking and looting, murder and mayhem, reached breathtaking depths of depravity when they breached the city walls. The looting went on for days and included the largest collection of holy relics ever assembled. Within a few years, these relics were spread across Europe until, it seemed, even the least prince, the lowliest church or abbey, had at least one relic to show a pious public. No less than eighteen monasteries and churches claimed to have the prepuce of our Savior in their keeping.

But in the 14th century, during the Babylonian Captivity when the papacy moved to Avignon, St. Bridget of Sweden recounted her vision of the Virgin's appearance. The Blessed Virgin assured her that the tiny fragment of holy flesh residing in the Sancta Sanctorum at the Lateran Palace was indeed the true *santissimo prepuzio*.

And there it remained until 1527. During the night of May 5th of that year the frightened few who guarded the walls of Rome could see cooking fires pricking the darkness in every direction. The army of the Holy Roman Emperor, Charles V, commanded by the Duke of Bourbon, an army 34,000 strong, had finally reached the eternal city. The Duke had little choice but to attack Rome as he had been unable to pay his troops for months. His army, led by the mutinous German protestant mercenaries, the *Landsknechte*, had already looted and plundered their way down the peninsula. Now it was Rome's turn.

When the morning of May 6th dawned, a heavy fog shrouded the walls. "The Romans will all be dead before nightfall," Francz predicted to his constant companion, the giant Randulf. They had been friends since their days growing up in the back alleys of Cologne. They wore the colorful uniforms of the *Landsknechte*, slashed doublets, flat caps and each carried a *zweihänder*, a two-handed broadsword. Francz was even a *Doppelsöldner*, a soldier on double-pay, or would have been if there had been any pay, because of his superior talents as a warrior. Having Randulf at his side had helped his reputation for ruthlessness over the past eighteen years and now, once again, Francz and the small band of mercenaries loyal to him lined up in the front ranks ready for the command.

Over the past few days, Pope Clement VII had pleaded desperately for men to man the walls but he had only been able to raise 8,000 ill-equipped militia to augment his own superbly trained Swiss Guards. The results were inevitable. Within an hour and a half, the siege ladders and the sappers managed to breach the wall and Francz and Randulf fought their way through the gap at the Duke's side. At the sight of the Duke in his distinctive white cloak, a small group of militia on a nearby rooftop opened fire with their notoriously inaccurate arquebuses. The last to fire was Benvenuto Cellini. The duke fell dead, blood staining his broad chest.

The invading army soon overwhelmed the militia and pushed back the Swiss Guards. Following one of the dead duke's captains, Francz and Randulf found themselves on the steps of St. Peter's where 189 of Pope Clement's Swiss Guard made a last stand to enable the pope to escape down the Passetto di Borgo, a secret corridor that links Vatican City to the Castel Sant'Angelo to this day. The Swiss fought well and death claimed men on both sides. With a roar, Randulf charged into a knot of pikemen, only to be cut down by an ill timed swing of a broadsword from one of his own companions that caught him on the follow through. He went down with blood spurting from a deep cut in his left thigh.

Ripping a strip from his own doublet, Francz bandaged Randulf's wound. "Wait by that column," he told Randulf. Charging back into the fray, he penetrated the wall of pikes and wielded his *zweihänder* with consummate skill until no less than three Swiss Guards lay at his feet but a fourth managed to stab him in the back just below his shoulder. In fury, he swung around instinctively and beheaded the man. The few remaining guards now broke and ran. Only 42 of the original troop of 189 Swiss Guards survived that day but they had held off the invaders long enough for the pope to make his escape.

By noon, the battle was over and the looting began in earnest. After washing their wounds in a fountain, the two friends let themselves be propelled by the crowd until they found themselves outside the Lateran Palace. As they entered, one *Landsknecht* told them, "Most of the gold and silver has gone."

"What's left?" asked Francz. "Nothing but shit! Shit and relics."

Francz nodded. What good are relics to a protestant, he thought.

Still, he nudged Randulf. "Come on. We'll find something."

An hour later, they emerged from the Sancta Sanctorum with a broken chalice of gold, the jewel settings now empty and scratched by whatever blade had pried the gems out, and an insignificant silver reliquary. Later in the afternoon, they found a stale loaf of bread behind a looted bakery and, after they had eaten, and Francz had tended to the makeshift bandage wrapping his companion's wound, they had curled up in a corner of St. John Lateran Basilica and slept fitfully beneath their cloaks.

At dawn, they woke to find that the army of the emperor had

disintegrated into a leaderless rabble and armed gangs were patrolling the streets. The smell of death filled the air. Any citizens of Rome who could still do so had left the city and were hiding in the hills east and north of the city. "Let's get out of the city," Randulf said his voice weak, "before we join the dead." Francz nodded worried about his friend's increasing pallor. Wordlessly, he helped his friend up. Randulf gasped involuntarily and swayed unsteadily on his feet. Francz checked Randulf's bandage, the strip of cloth was saturated with blood and was beginning to smell of decay. "Can you walk?" Francz asked.

Randulf nodded and touched his *zweihänder* with his left hand as it hung in the sheath at his back. Francz tended his own wound which was not bleeding anymore and seemed to be healing. "Let's head north," Randulf said, "away from the stink of Catholics." Francz and Randulf left and, picking their way around piles of corpses and drunken soldiers, they eventually found their way to the Via Flaminea. Randulf had already pulled out his broadsword and was using it as a crutch.

At first the road north was almost empty but by the time darkness fell, they came across a rag-tag encampment of Roman refugees. Francz sat Randulf behind a tree and, taking the gold chalice went off in the darkness to barter for food. But his distinctive doublet revealed him as one of the ruthless mercenaries and a group of men challenged him. Drawing his sword, he killed two of the men and the others scattered but he came away hungry and empty handed. When he returned to find Randulf, the big man was sleeping and Francz covered him with his cloak.

The next day they left the road and followed a track into the valley of the Treja River. Eventually, Randulf could go no farther so they spent the night next to the river. When Francz awoke, he found his friend lying dead beside him. With his broadsword, he dug a shallow grave and interred Randulf after saying a prayer. Before he set out alone, he pried the silver reliquary open with his dagger and was puzzled by its contents, a small silk bag. There was a parchment scroll but Francz was unable to read its message. Inside the silk sack he discovered a round of ancient skin. Curious he balanced it on the point of his knife and held it up to the sun. A relic. Had to be. And suddenly, he realized what it was: the holy prepuce. The most precious relic of all. As a protestant, he had been taught to despise such things but he knew it might be worth a fortune to a catholic buyer.

The next day he spotted a small village perched on a pinnacle of rock above him and, realizing that if he did not get some food he too would die here, he began to climb the rocks. As he reached the only gate to the village, several villagers confronted him suspiciously. He offered the one who seemed to be in charge the gold chalice. Eagerly the man took it and, with gestures, demanded his broadsword. Francz knowing he did not have the strength to fight them all, handed it over and they locked him in a drafty room made of rough-hewn stone. Some kind of storehouse, Francz guessed. A middle-aged woman came after an hour of so and fed him a bowl of gruel with some hard bread and, even more welcome, a flagon of water that he drained quickly. He thanked her and she smiled shyly as she left.

When he had eaten, he carefully pulled the silver reliquary from inside his doublet and by the light of the moon shining through the bars of his improvised prison, he dug a small hole in the hard earth and buried it. When he was finished, he scattered straw from the pallet that served as his mattress and lay down to sleep but the pain from his wound kept him awake.

Over the next few weeks he grew stronger. Sometimes he was invited out to attend church in the small chapel above his cell and, eventually, the townsfolk warmed to the stranger and let him have the run of the village. He might have stayed but there was talk that officials from Rome would be visiting to see the stranger. The night before the visitors were to arrive, Francz stole a set of clothes off a line and, discarding what was left of his rotting *Landsknecht* uniform, he dressed as a peasant. When he tried to return to his cell to retrieve the hidden reliquary, he saw that the woman who brought him food was heading the same way. Reluctantly he turned towards the gate. Perhaps he might return for the relic some day but tonight he must quit the village.

The next thing we know of him is that he ended up in Rome, sick and dying, and was picked up by the hospitallers. In his final days at the Santo Spirito Hospital, Francz told his story to his confessor. The young priests asked eagerly, 'What is the name of the village where the *santissimo prepuzio* lies?' But Francz had never learned its name so the holy prepuce lay buried for yet another thirty years.

## Canticle V

In the year 1557, the summer solstice occurred on Saturday, June 12th just after midnight according to the Julian Calendar, though few, including old Bastiano, were aware of such niceties of the earth's rotation. As the sun rose over the Treja Valley, he drove his five sheep through the gate into the village of Calcata and up the steep passage towards the piazza in front of the church. Bastiano had been thinking of the prices he would get for his small flock at the market in the piazza when the ram leading the four ewes abruptly stopped before a pair of ancient wooden doors. Bastiano cursed the animal but still it stood its ground and stared at the doors. "It is only a storeroom," he reasoned with the stubborn creature. The ewes stood stupidly behind their leader. With a sigh, Bastiano walked up to the ram and looked him in the eye. The ram stared back and, even when Bastiano beat its back with his staff, the stubborn creature refused to move.

Shaking his head in frustration, Bastiano stood in front of the ram and cursed. Bastiano was not a violent man. He crouched down before the ram and tried to reason with him but the ram only stared unblinking at him. Bastiano was unnerved. "*Il malocchio,*" he whispered to himself and made the sign against the evil eye before hurrying away up the hill to find the priest.

When he returned half an hour later with Father Bandolino, the sheep were still standing in the exact position he had left them. "You see, Father," Bastiano explained as they approached the flock, "my ram has been seized by a demon."

Father Bandolino was not a man to jump to conclusions so he said nothing but observed the still flock.

"They just stopped before this door for no reason?" he asked Bastiano.

"Yes, yes, Father."

Father Bandolino thought for a few minutes. Bastiano relaxed a little now that he had passed the problem on to someone in authority.

"Perhaps we should look in the store room, my son," the priest said to the older man. Bastiano shrugged, disappointed. He had wanted to see the priest casting out the demons.

With difficulty, the two men pushed back the creaking doors and peered inside. Dust hung in the shafts of light coming through the window where Francz had once looked out over the valley below. Father Bandolino went inside but Bastiano hung back. After a few minutes of poking around, the priest stood next to the window and watched where the shafts of light illuminated rhomboids on the dirt floor. There. A tiny glint from something in the floor. The dirt had been trampled by some hoofed creatures. Borrowing Bastiano's staff, the priest had carefully dug around the object until he unearthed a silver reliquary, now almost black with oxidation except for the corner that had been exposed. After carefully cleaning it with a handful of straw, Father Bandolino opened the reliquary. Inside was a small white silk pouch with a parchment note in Latin: '*Praeputium Iesu Christe*.' With shaking hands, he closed the reliquary and hurried out into the bright day. "Bastiano! Your ram has found the holiest relic in Christendom."

Bastiano crossed himself, adding the sign against the evil eye for good measure. The priest hurried off to the nearby town of Stabbia where Flaminio Anguillara and his wife, Maddalena Strozzi, lived in local splendor. Bastiano watched him go. As Bastiano closed the doors to the storeroom, the ram decided that it was time to go to market and, much to the wonder of old Bastiano, began to lead the quartet of ewes up the hill. For a few moments, Bastiano was too startled to move but as the sheep rounded the corner and the clatter of their hooves began to fade, he roused himself and hobbled after them muttering '*Agnus Dei*' to himself over and over, '*Agnus Dei*.'

Like Bastiano, Father Bandolino's first instinct when he had uncovered the reliquary was to pass it on to a higher authority, and that authority lay in the nearby town of Stabbia, now called Faleria. An hour later, sweating from the heat of this first day of summer, the priest arrived in the Piazza Colleggiata and passed under one of the two archways into Anguillara Castle. When he was shown into the lofty hall, he sat down next to the empty fireplace and tried to regain his breath.

Soon he was joined by the beautiful Maddalena Strozzi, wife of Flaminio Anguillara, the head of the most influential family in the district of Viterbo. When she entered the hall, the priest, trembling at Maddalena's beauty, rose to his feet and bowed. Maddalena had been the subject of several paintings by the great Raphael and the priest had even heard the rumor that one of the great master's paintings had been of Maddalena Strozzi nude. The very thought made the priest's knees weak. Curious to see this new discovery, Lucrezia Orsini, widow of the former patriarch, Giovanni Batista Anguillera, had accompanied her.

"Now what do you have for us, Father Bardolino?" she asked.

"I believe we have found the Lateran *prepuzio*, m'Lady, the most holy relic in the world." he told her and held out the box-shaped silver reliquary.

Taking it gently from his hand, the old matriarch, Lucrezia Orsini examined it closely before saying, "It certainly looks to be of great age." She passed it to Maddalena Strozzi who lifted the lid and plucked out the single silk sack. Noting the tiny scroll attached to it with a faded red ribbon, she crossed to a window and read aloud the inscription, "*Praeputium Iesu Christe*." With a sharp cry of surprise, she crossed herself. The priest and the matriarch hastily did likewise.

"What shall we do?" asked Lucrezia.

"Perhaps we should open it," ventured Maddalena, closing the reliquary and handing it back to the priest who took it reluctantly.

"If you please, m'Lady," Father Bandolino said, handing it back.

Maddalena, a woman known far and wide for her adventurous spirit, took it. Carefully she plucked out the little sack and grasped the faded ribbon. As soon as she began to pull on it, she declared, "My hand has gone numb."

The priest took a couple of steps back. Maddalena tried again and, as before, her hand lost all feeling and, with a gasp, she pulled it back. "Be careful, my dear," Lucrezia warned. "Perhaps there is a spell on it."

The priest nodded. After a few moments of hesitation, he said, "Perhaps we need someone of consummate purity," adding hastily as he detected the frown gathering on Maddalena's face, "I mean a child perhaps, a virgin pure in the eyes of our Lord."

Maddalena smiled and nodded. Lucrezia said, "Why not my youngest daughter?"

"Yes, of course." She looked at the manservant standing by the doors. "Bring in Clarice."

When seven-year-old Clarice was led into the room, Maddalena, without explanation, handed her the small sack, saying, "Open this sack for us, my child."

Clarice opened it without experiencing any ill effects and tipped the contents into her hand. The adults all peered at it. "What is it?" asked Clarice staring at the small circle of ancient skin in her palm.

"The holiest relic of Christendom," the priest said without going into detail about such a delicate part of the male anatomy. "Holy Mother Church has been searching for it for thirty years, ever since it was plundered from the Sancta Sanctorum in Rome."

With a beatific smile, Clarice said, "It feels... It feels alive."

Maddalena, fearing for the child's safety, scooped up an empty pewter bowl from a nearby table and urged Clarice, "Put it in here."

Clarice placed it into the bowl and immediately the ancient sacred flesh began to issue forth a perfumed mist that soon pervaded the palace. Within minutes, servants and family members began to filter into the hall until soon there was a crowd of at least forty people, some weeping, some making the signs of the cross and one or two even making signs to ward off evil spirits.

For two days, the miraculous mist expanded until it blanketed the whole of Stabbia. Father Bandolino proclaimed the discovery a miracle and led a procession back to Calcata to place the *santissimo prepuzio* in the Anguillara family chapel. Word spread and soon pilgrims were coming up the Via Flaminia and Via Cassia from Rome. The Sisterhood of St. Ursula made a nocturnal visit, walking in procession from the nearby village of Mazzano carrying torches and candles to light away the darkness. At the church door, they pleaded for entrance and, when Father Bandolino let them in, they proceeded up the aisle of the tiny chapel singing the praises of this last corporeal remnant of their Lord and Savior.

The church was soon filled with stars. Father Bandolino, filled with the holy spirit, climbed up the campanile and tolled the single bell to announce the miracle. Soon the church was so full of the faithful that some climbed on the roof and tore holes to see the event below.

The next day, Maddalena Strozzi set out for Rome to bring the news to Pope Paul IV that the *santissimo prepuzio* had been found.

## Canticle VI

The village of Calcata is perched on a spire of volcanic tufo and well off the beaten track but that did not stop hundreds of devout pilgrims from making their way to the chapel to pay their homage to the *santissimo prepuzio*. Almost two years later, two canons from St. John's Lateran were sent by the pope to recover what one of them referred to delicately as the '*particula recisa*' and return it to the Sancta Sanctorum where it belonged. The priest eagerly took them into the church where the relic lay. One of them, Canon Pipinello decided he needed a closer look. He picked up the delicate *cosa* and, much to the horror of Father Bandolino, began to stretch it. 'To test the flexibility, you understand,' he told the other two men. Suddenly the ancient skin broke into two pieces. Immediately his hand went numb and froze into a claw. Outside a terrific thunderstorm began to shake the building.

"We must put it back in its sack and return it to its place on the altar," Father Bandolino shouted over the crashing of thunder. Hastily Pipinello complied and the storm ceased as suddenly as it had begun.

When the canons reported their experience to the pope, Paul made one of his last decisions before he died that July: the *santissimo prepuzio* must stay in Calcata.

Pope Benedict XIII, one of the Avignon antipopes, had the chapel enlarged into the piazza and had a sculpture in relief of the Sacred circumcision carved above the altar. In return he requested the tiny fragment of foreskin that Pipinello had accidentally severed. Finally a fragment, un *pezzino di prepuzio*, returned to the Sancta Sanctorum in the Lateran Palace for the first time since the sacking of Rome.

## Canticle VII

Later popes conferred indulgences on the faithful who traveled to Calcata to venerate the *santissimo prepuzio*. In 1723, Bishop Cybo, one of the world's greatest collectors of relics, visited Calcata and was shocked to find the Savior's *prepuzio* enclosed in such a plain silver reliquary. He had a gold, jewel-encrusted one made featuring two angels and presented it to the church. In return, he asked for and received, a tiny speck of the *santissimo prepuzio*, a portion containing so few messianic molecules as to be almost invisible. The *prepuzio*, rather fittingly perhaps, had become a trinity with the third part later crowning Bishop Cybo's relic collection in Rome's Church of Santa Maria degli Angeli, a church designed by none other than Michaelangelo Buonarotti.

## Canticle VIII

The Reformation and the Counter Reformation came and went destroying in their wake the false foreskins that dotted the religious landscape of Europe so that eventually only one remained (albeit in three pieces). Nevertheless, on the first day of every new year, the Feast of the Circumcision, the golden reliquary containing the sacred foreskin was paraded in the piazza outside the Church of SS. Cornelius and Cyprian in Calcata. Even when Pope Leo XIII, exasperated by a supposed reappearance of another holy foreskin in Charroux, promulgated his Decree Number 37A, forbidding any mention in speech or in writing of the *santissimo prepuzio* on pain of excommunication, the priests in Calcata continued their annual procession, but in silence.

On Saturday, May 15th, 1954, a special session of the Supreme Sacred Congregation of the Holy Office was convened to lift the papal decree banning mention in any form of the *santissimo prepuzio*. After a full day of heated discussion the sacred body came up with these conclusions:

1. That the Calcata Holy Prepuce alone is the true one supported by the highest references.

2. The petition is rejected.

3. The Apostolic See reserves the right to excommunicate whosoever shall write or speak of the Holy Prepuce without permission.

4. The excommunication will no longer be *speciali* but *specialissimo*. That is, perpetrators will now be classed as the more severe 'infamous persons to be avoided.' The session closed with a singing of Psalm twenty-five.

And so it was that when Father Tito related the history of the Holy Foreskin to Père Jean-Pièrre just before Vatican II began, the 'trinity' of fragments of the true *prepuzio* resided – in descending order of size: in Calcata Vecchia, in the Sancta Sanctorum, and in Santa Maria degli Angeli. All were blanketed in an unholy silence decreed and policed by the Vatican.

Could things get any worse for the veneration of the tripartite *Santissimo Prepuzio*?

Oh, yes.

# Part Five:
# Rome, 1989

## *la città eterna*

The four sisters had been disappointed that the plane to Rome was a regular Alitalia flight, but they did enjoy travelling business class for their maiden flight. For a while they had gossiped about Judy.

"Do you think something happened to her?" asked Cécile.

Her sister Annette shrugged. "Who knows what's in her mind, that one."

"But she didn't say anything at the church."

"I don't think she ever intended to come," said Cécile.

"She scares me sometimes," admitted Yvonne. "So loud."

"And don't forget those pictures she took of Jesus," said Annette.

"You mean of Eddie. Pictures of Eddie," corrected Cécile.

"On the television, they said his real name is Jesus."

"Yes, yes, Cécile, but everybody calls him Eddie," chided Annette impatiently. "Anyway that woman Lydia was pretty mad."

"I don't blame her. I heard Judy tried to sell them to the TV station," said Yvonne who had never liked the tall woman.

"Père Jean-Pièrre forgave her though."

"He forgives everybody," Cécile said sharply, bringing an end to the conversation.

Alitalia flight 847 landed on time at 1625 hours and, with a speed that almost seemed miraculous, Cardinal Bertelli whisked them through customs and out to three identical black Mercedes SUVs for their trip into the city.

At that time in the afternoon, traffic was moving at a snail's pace once they got into the city. In the leading SUV, Père Jean-Pièrre, sitting behind the driver, sighed as he looked out through the heavily tinted windows at the Colliseum gliding past on his left. "My God," thought Père Jean-Pièrre, "how long has it been?" Decades now since he had worked in Rome. Père Jean-Pièrre remembered with affection his three years working with Father Tito on the famous collection of relics in the Sancta Sanctorum of the Lateran Palace. But this in turn triggered bittersweet memories of his days with Héloïse. That such beauty could hide such a treacherous heart.

The papal legate, sitting in the passenger seat next to the driver, said without turning, "Welcome back to the eternal city, Père Jean-Pièrre. I doubt you will find it has changed much."

Momentarily taken aback, Père Jean-Pièrre caught the cardinal's eye in the rearview mirror and said, "It is always good to be back at the heart of the church." Of course, Cardinal Bertelli would have researched every one of them, especially him. Still the legate's assertion made Père Jean-Pièrre uneasy. What else did he know?

"So you worked here, Father?" asked Alphonse, who was seated beside him.

"Oh, yes. A long time ago," conceded Père Jean-Pièrre, hoping to change the subject.

"Yes, Père Jean-Pièrre came here with the Bishop of Montreal during Vatican II and ended up working most of the time at the Lateran Palace for... how long was it?" says the papal legate.

"Nearly three years," admitted Père Jean-Pièrre.

"You were responsible for cataloguing the relics, were you not, Father?"

"Yes, yes, I was, your grace,"

"Weren't you working with that old rogue, Father Tito di Belmonte?"

"Yes, yes, I was," Père Jean-Pièrre conceded.

"I have not seen him myself for at least a couple of years. He keeps to himself these days. Have you managed to keep in touch?"

"We corresponded for years but gradually less and less. You know how it is. But when I knew I was returning to Rome, I called him. The number was disconnected and I feared the worst."

"That he had died?"

"Yes."

"My spies tell me that he is still alive but has grown frail with age," Cardinal Bertelli told him with a note of satisfaction in his voice.

"Is he at the same address?" asked Père Jean-Pièrre.

"I had heard that he had moved in with his sister who was looking after him but I've no idea where she lives."

"If I have the time, I'd like to look him up while I am here."

"Of course, of course. You must have lots to catch up on, the two of you." The black Mercedes SUVs turned on to Via dei Condotti, the street famous for its fashion houses. Soon they began to slow down until the trio of SUVs glided to a halt within 100 meters of the Piazza dei Spagna. "Ah, here we are," Cardinal Bertelli announced. "Leave your luggage for the porters."

Shepherding his small flock on to the sidewalk, he commanded them to wait and disappeared through an ancient door marked by a discreet brass plaque proclaiming in English the 'Inn at the Spanish Steps.' The Dionne sisters were twittering excitedly about the displays of haute couture fashions and designer luggage in the windows across the narrow street. Claude, the bus driver, was telling Alphonse and Thomas, "Sure glad I don't have to drive a bus around here. Did you see the traffic? Crazy." Walking to the corner, Père Jean-Pièrre looked out at the Piazza di Spagna with its famous Fontana dell Barcaccia, Bernini's Old Boat Fountain. Good to be back, on the whole, he told himself but something was making his mind uneasy and it was some minutes before he realized what it was. They were here to meet His Holiness so why were they staying so far from the Vatican? Just then he heard his name being called by Alphonse. Coming," he said and joined the group where the Cardinal was passing out keys.

"You are actually staying next door," he told them, "at the View of the Spanish Steps, one of the best hotels in all of Rome." He led them off in the direction of the square but, within a few paces, he turned down a small covered arcade that led to a quaint shop with the simple name 'Prada' over its lintel. Beside it was an ancient but ornate elevator. "Be careful to close the outer door," the cardinal cautioned, "or the elevator will not come down from the upper floors. The elevator was tiny enough that it took three trips to take all nine people up to the fourth floor.

"Your luggage is already here," the cardinal told them as he pointed to a series of suitcases lined up in the hallway outside the rooftop terrace. At that time of day, the duck canvas awnings were fully extended to keep the late afternoon sun from baking the tables. "The staff will be bringing up a meal in about half and hour so you can eat out on the terrace. Relax for the rest of this evening. Get over your jet lag. You have tomorrow to wander around Rome. I will be back to pick you up at 7:30 a.m. on Wednesday morning for our two audiences with *il Papa*, the general audience around 10:30 and later our private audience. I will leave my private number with Père Jean-Pièrre. Any questions? No? Then I must be off to report to the pope that you have arrived." With that, he turned to the outer door and was gone.

After the meal, Père Jean-Pièrre retreated to his room. On the table beside his bed was a large envelope with his name on it. Opening it, he found that it was stuffed with cash. He counted 15,000 lira in large denominations. It looked like a fortune but Père Jean-Pièrre guessed that the exchange rate probably was almost as bad as it had been in the sixties. With the money was a small card with the Vatican crown and crossed keys logo above the papal legate's name, address and telephone number. On the back in a spiky script, a handwritten note said, "The money is for your expenses while you are here. Please accept it with our blessings. Cardinal Bertelli."

Père Jean-Pièrre moved to his hotel window, opened it wide and gazed out at the broad sweep of the Spanish Steps climbing from the Piazza di Spagna below him up to the Trinità dei Monte Church. Only a few people were sitting on the famous steps. The calèche drivers were gathered on the shady side of the cobble-stoned square gossiping, playing cards and waiting for customers. The view from his window was certainly one of the most prized vistas in Rome.

Yes, somebody had thought this out well. The accommodations were certainly luxurious and their little party was occupying all the rooms here on the fourth floor, which could only be accessed by a creaky elevator or a steep climb up the stairs that circled it. At the top, a narrow hallway and a locked door that guarded the privacy of the occupants of the fourth floor. To avoid the fearsome paparazzi? Perhaps.

Suddenly realizing how tired he was, Père Jean-Pièrre closed the window, unpacked his bag and lay down under the soft duvet to catch up on some much-needed sleep.

# Part Six:
# Northern Ontario

## You've Got Mail

"Here, take these up to your room and try them on," said Lydia when she had finished extracting the pins and price tags off the pile of clothing on the dining room table.

"Thanks, Lydia," said Eddie as he scooped up the pile.

"And the shoes," added Lydia, putting another box on top of the pile Eddie was carrying so that now only his eyes were visible.

At the bottom of the stairs Eddie said, "I don't know when I'll be able to pay you back."

"Don't worry about it."

"Oh, but I do," Eddie replied and headed up the stairs to his room.

"Prophets never carry money," Arthur observed to Lydia. "That's why they always wear those loose robes with no pockets."

"God, I'm exhausted," said Lydia, flopping heavily into an armchair.

"It's not easy finding stuff for anybody as big as Eddie."

"I'll bet. Have any trouble getting through the mob?"

"I'm sure the Land Rover will be on the news."

"Maybe I should have washed it."

"Anyway the RCMP opened a lane for me and I kept the windows rolled up. It must be scary being famous, being hounded by the paparazzi."

Upstairs Eddie was dressing. The shadowy figure of Marie was sitting on the bed watching him with solemn amusement. When he zipped up his new black Levi jeans and pulled on one of his new Harley T-shirts, he sat next to her to put on his black runners with the Nike swoosh on the sides and said, "So who am I, the Messiah, the AntiChrist, Kellog Albran, L. Ron Cupboard? I really need to know." The sister's shadowy figure gradually resolved into a tiny tornado which rose before him, slowly settled on his lap and began to glow.

"O.K., O.K. The tongue of flames. I get it, I get it. A pentacostal pun? Come on, what I need is a job description."

Her voice surrounded him: "You are Eddie Magdalena, son of God. I am here to help you and I will provide any knowledge you need but the path is your own."

"Miracles?"

"Are everywhere. And, yes, you will have any powers He deems necessary."

Eddie thought for a moment. "Walking on water?"

"Molten ice? Only if it's frozen. Otherwise I'd stick to the shallow end," she told him solemnly.

"Was that a joke?" asked Eddie surprised.

"A feeble one," she acknowledged.

"You are full of surprises. Good deadpan delivery though. By the way, what should I call you? The Holy Spirit is a bit of a mouthful."

"My name is Marie. I was the older sister of the quadruplets before my transformation."

"Marie, then." Eddie hesitated before finally asking, "And what am I here for?"

"Like all the people on this planet, you will have to find the answer for yourself. I can only say that your Father is fascinated by this world and all the people in it and is wondering how they will react to you."

"He's wondering? You mean He doesn't know?"

But the flames faded and were gone.

At the bottom of the stairs, Eddie halted while Lydia inspected him. "The clothes seem to fit," she said. "I'm not sure about the Harley T-shirt. Looks a little tight." Eddie shrugged. "O.K. The size of your arms, though, make you look a little scary, that's all." Not to mention the scar, but she didn't mention that. She looked at Arthur for confirmation, but he was staring at a spot halfway up the stairs. "What is it?"

"What? Oh, she's on the stairs." He took a tentative step forward and, as he did so, the grey shade dissolved into a mist, swirled around

Eddie and then disappeared. "Like some osmotic process," Arthur said. "It's amazing."

"And only you can see it," said Lydia.

"Only me and Eddie. Did you see the subtle change, the sudden… what?… self-assurance, the balance in Eddie?"

Eddie smiled. "Now you don't look scary at all," Lydia told him. And it was true.

"I've been thinking," said Eddie slowly. "I told Arthur earlier that I needed someone to be my manager, agent, whatever you want to call it. He said you might be interested."

Lydia laughed. "Me?"

"Seems to me you've been acting as my manager anyway."

"And I haven't had this much fun in a while. Of course, I'll be your manager. Thanks for the vote of confidence, Eddie."

"Thank you," Eddie said and, bending down, gave her a careful hug. "That would be great. Arthur did point out that you knew your way around the stars."

"Right now, I need to contact Liz. I want the Big Reveal to be the biggest thing this town has ever seen," said Lydia. Just as she was about to head for the study at the back of the house, the doorbell chimed. "Get that will you, Arthur."

Arthur nodded. At the door was an RCMP constable toting a large sack.

"Today's mail, sir," he said and dropped the sack on to the step.

"Christ!" said Arthur.

"Some are addressed to him, too," the constable said. Giving a smart salute, he turned and headed back down the path. Eddie shouldered the bag and took it into the lounge. He pulled out a couple of handsful of letters and spread them across the large coffee table in front of the couch. The three of them began to go through them and a few minutes later Mahinda joined them.

"You seem to be very popular, my fine bugger," he said.

For the next couple of hours, the three men scanned their way through hundreds of letters and postcards. Gradually they agreed to sort the mail into piles: letters of support, hate mail, appeals for money, prayers of supplication, religious skeptics and atheists, letters containing money in various currencies and a miscellaneous pile for those letters that were too bizarre to make out the reasons for writing.

The three of them were just taking a break when Lydia came in. "Quite a haul," she said, "but I am not surprised. I read through the ones that arrived yesterday. I'd say more than half of the messages believe you are the Messiah. The next largest vote seems to be that you are the AntiChrist. A surprising number of death threats from people of a wide spectrum of religions. Some of those are unbelievably nasty."

"Yeah, we got a lot of those today too," said Arthur.

"Lots of media requests, of course," added Lydia. "Marc and Jules are dealing with them. Oh and everyone's agreed to use your title, Arthur."

"The Big Reveal?"

"The Big Reveal."

### Eddie the AntiChrist?

When the chief and his deputy arrived, Marc led them through to the dining room where they joined Arthur, Jules, Lydia and Mahinda.

"The media has done a one-eighty on Eddie because of that journalist in San Diego," Marc explained as the newcomers claimed seats around the table. "She's managed to dig up some of Eddie's past. Some of it true. Some of it pure speculation. Like her false claim that he had fled to Canada because there was a string of warrants out for him in the States."

"They're calling him the AntiChrist now," Lydia said, slapping the copy of *Newsweek* down on the coffee table. "Seems they've been digging. Apparently being born in the back of a garage to a sex worker doesn't have the same ring to it as the Biblical nativity story."

"We've checked on Eddie's past, of course," the chief told her. "He's had a few minor run-ins with the law but that was when he was a teenager. He seems to be clean now." He smiled. "We could find no evidence for the rumor that he was carrying cocaine when his motorcycle was hit by the locomotive. In fact, there's no sign of the wrecked motorcycle and no sign of even a scratch on the locomotive."

"So maybe it never happened," suggested Mahinda. "Maybe he really did just fall from the sky."

"Maybe," said Lydia, "but right now, we need to make sure Eddie is protected from those who would like nothing better than to see him dead."

"Is it true that his mother was a prostitute?" the deputy chief asked. In the silence that follows, he immediately regretted letting his curiosity get the better of his professionalism.

"Sure," said Marc after a short pause. "Eddie's made no secret of it to any of us. But he was hoping to save the revelations for Sunday."

"Ah, yes. I also wanted to talk to you about that. I think we should put the rally in Bell Park off for a week," said Chief Sawchuk, casting a withering glance at his second-in-command. "It would give us more time to organize Eddie's protection."

"I know it's very short notice, Chief Sawchuk," said Lydia, "but surely you've been working on security for Canada Day anyway. Couldn't you just extend the plans you have already made?"

"It's a little more complicated than that," said the Chief. "The security for the Big Reveal will be a combined forces operation. We'll have to liaise with the RCMP and that will take some time."

"Considering the crowds that have flooded the city, Chief, I don't think anyone would object to the Big Reveal on July 2nd.

"I've already got hold of Bob Ivey," offered Arthur. "He's got the pyro contract for the July first display. He doesn't seem to think there would be a problem leaving the barges in place and reloading the pyro for the next day." Lydia nodded. "Chief, Eddie will be leaving the country by Monday, July 3rd."

The chief's deputy said cautiously, "It would get rid of the crowd that is paralyzing the city a week earlier, Chief."

Over the next hour or so Chief Sawchuk came around and finally admitted that a week's delay would have been costly. "Fact is that neither our force nor the RCMP can commit to continuing security after the

Big Reveal. Sorry, but that's the economics of it. I was going to suggest you hire a private security firm for the additional week. But with Eddie's presentation on July 1st, you won't need private security until after the Big Reveal, if at all. Anyway, for future reference, you might try Halo Security. They're based in Toronto," he told the gathering. "When the pope came to Toronto five years ago, they provide his security detail." He handed a card to Lydia.

"Thanks," she told him and tucked the card into her purse.

"Fine," said Chief Sawchuk, rising. "I'll inform the RCMP that we're now committed to the Big Reveal on July 2nd. You have my private number?"

"Yes, Chief. Thanks," she told him as she led him and his deputy to the front door. When they were gone she started making phone calls while Arthur heated the frozen pizzas.

After the late supper dishes had been cleared, Arthur, Lydia, Mahinda, Marc, and Jules gathered around the dining room table again. Lydia pulled out the card for Halo Security and tossed it on the table. "Do we go with them?" she asked.

"No," said Mahinda. "The police are offering security for the Big Reveal. After that, Eddie is going to Rome to meet with the pope."

"You're right," said Lydia. "We won't need private security."

Eddie came down from his room to join them. "Just been reading the death threats," he said. "Most seem to be from people who consider themselves Christians. There are also a couple of *fatwas* from Muslim imams, one in Pakistan and one in Egypt. The AntiChrist label, no surprise, seems to spring from the Christian tradition. So here I am," he dropped his voice to a menacing base note, "Eddie the AntiChrist."

Arthur shook his head. "I guess this AntiChrist thing was inevitable. The media is full of it. Eddie's being compared to David Koresh, leader of the Branch Dravidians and Jim Jones who gave the phrase, 'drinking the Kool-Aid' a whole new meaning. Others have compared Eddie to King Juan Carlos, Sun Myung Moon and even JFK."

"JFK?" Lydia looked puzzled.

"Apparently he won the democratic convention in 1956 with 666 votes." Marc and Lydia laughed.

"It's not really funny," Arthur said. "Marc and Jules have passed over more than 327 death threats to the police already."

"Actually the messiah list is pretty funny," said Eddie. "My favorite is one Marc told me about yesterday. A Canadian connection. Tell them what you told me, Marc."

"Yeah, well, the Québec papers and TV are full of talk that Eddie is Ontario's very own false prophet. Seems that Québec has their own, a guy called Claude Vorilhon. He had been a French racing car driver but changed his name to Raël after some…. *extraterrestre*… How do you say it in English?"

He looked around. "Extraterrestrial," said Arthur.

"Alien," guessed Lydia.

"No such word in Ojibway," muttered Jules. "We're not that crazy."

Shaking his head, Marc resumed, "Anyway some alien came to earth and told this guy He was the Messiah."

"The alien was the Messiah?" asked Arthur.

"Yeah."

"When was this?"

"Back in '73."

"So is this guy still around?"

"Claude Vorilhon? Oh yeah. He has followers in Québec, the States and now he's in Japan."

"Look, could we move on," said Lydia. "Time is very short."

The mood instantly became more somber. "I've talked to the mayor's people," said Lydia. "Liz would like nothing better than to have her city back. It's going to be tight to be ready by Sunday but I'm sure we can pull it off." Eddie smiled but said nothing.

"Might be tight for the rest of Eddie's disciples to get back from Rome," said Arthur.

"Ah yes. They're in Rome," said Mahinda.

"I wonder why the pope would risk a meeting with someone who is being called the AntiChrist," mused Arthur.

"For now it's enough that the pope is willing to take us seriously,"

Eddie told him, a hint of irritation in his voice. "Through him, I think we can approach the Jews and Muslims. Pope Urban is scheduled to meet Muslim and Jewish leaders in Jerusalem soon after my meeting with him at his summer residence. I'm hoping we might be able to invite ourselves along."

"Oh, I forgot these," said Marc, pulling two airline tickets out of his briefcase and sliding them across the table to Eddie. "The redeye flight out of Toronto, leaving Sunday night. Will get you in Monday morning."

"Thanks, Marc," said Eddie, scooping up the tickets, "but why two?"

"I thought you might want to take one of us with you."

"And the tickets are first class."

"It's all I could get at such short notice."

"Thanks, Marc."

"What about the chief's idea of moving the Big Reveal back a week?" asked Lydia.

"It was never going to happen." Eddie gestured out towards the lake and the city beyond. "The media is here now. The people are here now. Even the chief was relieved when you held firm." Eddie put his arm around Lydia's shoulders and added, "You are amazing Lydia. And it's only just beginning, people. We do live in interesting times." Eddie rose and stretched. "Unless you really need me, I'm going out on the deck to get some air."

## Paddling Your Own Canoe

So much to do; so little time to the Big Reveal. The informal meeting lasted well into the night.

"So Eddie will be leaving for Rome almost as soon as the Big Reveal is over. Trouble is he has never had a passport. Still doesn't."

"Then how's he getting to Italy?" asked Marc.

Lydia smiled and looked at Arthur who said, "The day after Eddie arrived, I was talking to him and found out he doesn't have a passport..."

"He'd never had one," interjected Lydia.

"So I told Lydia and she got on to our local MP. He contacted the American Embassy. Eddie's passport should arrive by courier tomorrow."

Lydia nodded in response to the polite applause and said, "I'd like to turn the floor over to Marc. I could use a drink. Anyone else?"

They made their orders and Lydia headed for the bar fridge with Jules in tow while Marc went through his researches with the others. When Lydia and Jules came back in with drinks and bowls of finger food, Marc was just finishing up. "…so I just called Chief Sawchuk. He says he'll be closing all the roads around Lake Ramsey by noon on the Sunday of the Big Reveal so we'll have to be on site as soon as the sun is up. There's a lot of preparation in a fairly short time." Mark Baptiste pointed out the police roadblocks on the large topographical map of the area that was now spread across the living room wall. "And I've been assured that there will be two trailers on site for the sole use of Eddie and his people."

"Just like movie stars," observed Mahinda.

The city council had already put out appeals for help from people with skills in trades as various as accounting, traffic and crowd control, health and safety, catering and portapotties. Oh, and motorcycles, of course. Eddie had been missing his ride ever since the destruction of his motorcycle so finally Lydia arranged to lease a Harley Fatboy from Sudbury Harley on Long Lake Road. "The Fatboy is already in a locked box at the Yacht Club. Eddie will be the only person with the combinations to the locks. He can pick up the Harley anytime he needs it. For the Big Reveal, the police will provide an escort from the yacht club, along the walkway in front of Science North and right up to the Jim Gordon Amphitheater.

"How's Eddie going to get to the Yacht Club?" asked Marc.

"I suppose we could sneak him out under a blanket in the back of the Land Rover," suggested Lydia.

"Be like trying to sneak out a horse in a hamster cage," said Arthur. "No, no. There is an easier way. I've been teaching him how to paddle my canoe. In fact, he'd getting pretty good at it. Easiest thing would be for him to paddle over to the yacht club."

"Sometimes you are too brilliant for words, dear," said Lydia, putting her arm around his shoulders.

After the meeting ended just after one in the morning, Lydia went out to the darkened deck. "Eddie's gone!" she cried, a note of panic in her voice. "He's gone!"

The tiny waves on the lake returned undulating reflections of Science North but for as far as she could see the only boat in sight was the RCMP cruiser slowly drifting past a couple of hundred meters ahead of her.

## Father, Son, and Holy Ghost

From observing the RCMP launch on previous nights, Eddie knew that the crew changeover happened around ten o'clock. Sure enough, at 9:50, the launch began to head up the lake towards the boat ramp. As soon as the launch was out of sight, Eddie walked out on to the dock, untied the painter on Arthur's canoe and quietly pushed off. Using the J-stroke that Arthur had taught him, he pulled silently away from the dock and turned towards the silhouette of Science North looming in the distance. Such a relief to be alone at last.

Ten minutes later, he rounded the headland where the yacht club was located and turned into the basin where all the sailboats were docked. He slipped the canoe in between two 'Sirius 21' sailboats. When he had tied up the canoe, he picked his way past the Sudbury Yacht Club's headquarters to a large plywood box behind it. There he opened the two combination locks and walked the Harley out of its hiding place. When the Harley roared to life, Eddie hoped that no one was out on the Whiteheads' deck because the Harley could be heard at least that far away on the still night air. He quickly dropped the bike into gear, rode up to the gate, opened the last combination lock and proceeded slowly down the gravel drive until he reached Ramsey Lake Road. If he turned left now, he could be back at Arthur's house in a few minutes, but he turned right.

Half an hour later, after leaving the sleeping town behind, Eddie really opened up the bike as he turned north on Highway 144 towards the continental watershed. "Feels good!" The ancient voice behind him made him laugh.

"You know where we're headed?" asked Eddie.

"Oh yes," she told him and began to hum a tune that Eddie couldn't quite place.

"What is that?" he asked.

"'All You Need is Love.'"

"The Beatles, of course." And soon they were singing at the top of their voices as the wind raced by. Could do with some of that fine B.C. bud, thought Eddie.

"On the way back." His companion whispered the promise into his ear.

As they approached the railroad crossing, Eddie pulled off the road and parked the Harley. Feeling an edge of excitement, he began the steep trek up to the erratic. With only a waning sliver of moon, he relied on the dimmer light of the stars. When he and his companion were just below the clearing where he had been discovered, they could see a faint light above them. The pale erratic came into view with the faint white glow of the tripartite birch reaching for the sky above it. In front of the erratic was a plain round wooden table with three Shaker chairs. A single candle glowed in the middle of the table.

For a few moments, Eddie took in the scene, feeling more nervous excitement than he ever had before in his life. And then, seemingly coming from the erratic itself, the opening guitar licks of a traditional twelve-bar blues as Elvis in a glowing white suit backed by four sidereal sidemen sporting wings worthy of Raphael, slowly materialized and began to rock 'Big Boss Man.'

As the last chords faded away, Elvis tossed his guitar to the bass player and said, "Hi, son. Good to meet in the flesh at last."

"Wow!" Eddie cried out in wonder. "What an amazing fucking entrance."

"Thank you. Thank you very much. Not one of Elvis's best known but I kinda like the title," God remarked with a smile.

"Of course," said Eddie realizing that the story Joe had told him about his birth was true. "I loved your band…" What the Hell did you call him, Elvis? God? Dad? "… Dad."

"I thought the wings were a nice touch. Actually I used four of the angels on the Ponte degli Angeli in Rome as templates," God confessed as the band gradually faded away into the night. "Anyway, I figured you'd have some questions by now, son." He gestured towards the three chairs. "So why don't we make ourselves comfortable."

They sat. Only then did Eddie notice a sleek machine next to the seat occupied by Elvis. God grinned that crooked smile that Elvis had made famous. "It's a replicator," he explained. "They're well on the way to inventing such a thing on this planet. Pretty imaginative, these people. Soon they'll have replicators. 3D printers. Not to mention personal devices to talk or text to each other anywhere in the world. Fascinating people. Too bad they use so much of their ingenuity fucking each other over, often in my name." He turned to the Holy Spirit, "How's he taking it, Marie?" he asked her.

Marie looked at Eddie. "He'll be fine. Right now, he's terrified but that will change."

"I sure hope so," said Eddie.

"Nervous about the Big Reveal, huh. You'll be good, Son, you'll be just fine," said God in the soothing southern tones of the King of Rock and Roll. "Now let's have some food and drink."

The replicator started to hum and flashed a complicated series of colors before announcing, "Dinner is served." Then the strange device yawned wide open revealing what looked like a Victorian railway station. A railway line snaked out and circled the table and then a perfectly formed replica of the Flying Scotsman chugged out complete with a tiny uniformed crew. Eddie laughed in surprise and delight as the train stopped before each of them and unloaded a sandwich and a glass of wine. When the freight had been delivered, the tiny train driver tooted the whistle and the train chugged back to the station followed by the rail line. "Well done!" he told God.

"It was nothing," God acknowledged, meaning it.

Eddie took a bite of the sandwich. God was looking at him expectantly.

"It's good," Eddie said, "Divine."

"Heavenly," Marie concurred.

"Elvis's favorite," revealed the Big Guy. "Deep fried banana, bacon and peanut butter sandwiches. I've been partial to these ever since I dressed up to meet your mother."

"And the wine?"

"What? Oh, AB negative."

"You mean…."

"*Hic est sanguis meus*," God intoned and then looked up with a broad smile catching Eddie looking alarmed with the wine glass frozen half way to his lips. "Don't worry, it's not my blood. Just a fine bottle of Chateau Diablo laid down in Avignon during the Spanish Inquisition.

Looking relieved, Eddie tasted it. "Fucking amazing stuff!"

"Thank you. Thank you very much. Piece of cake if you're omnipotent," agreed God modestly.

After the meal, a couple of tiny horses pulling tiny carts trotted out of the replicator followed by a band of Victorian street sweepers and within less than a minute, the table was spotless again, except for a fresh bottle of wine.

God leaned back, relaxed and permitted himself a loud burp followed by an even louder fart. He laughed as the others covered their ears. "You know there are few things more satisfying than a really good fart and yet unless I take some human shape I can never get it right. William Blake wrote, 'Then old Nobodaddy aloft/ Farted and belched and coughed' but he didn't realize that God has to become flesh to get a good one going." God leaned towards Eddie and said, "Hey, you know who used to break me up? Le Petomane. He used to fill the Moulin Rouge years ago. People flocked to the place to watch him fart the Marseillaise." God sighed. "I miss him."

"Wouldn't he be in heaven?" Eddie asked.

"With all that talent. I would have given him a free pass to heaven, if we had one. Now you see why I rarely read my press."

"There's no heaven?"

"Oh, there are dozens of heavens. Most of them are boring."

Eddie asked, "No Hell either, of course."

"Well, artists and archbishops have been much more creative in imagining Hell. Just take a look at Dante, Milton, Breugel and all those medieval torture pictures commissioned by the church and painted by 'Anon.' But is there a real one? Afraid not."

"The power of prayer?" God sat still for a moment looking at his son. Suddenly the two of them broke into raucous laughter. Only the Holy Spirit remained silent.

"They thank me for touchdowns," God added and roared again. "Oh, fuck, this body's going to piss itself if I don't stop this."

"But the power of prayer can work wonders," Marie whispered when the other two had calmed down.

"True enough," the Big Guy acknowledged, "true enough."

"You answered the prayers of the faithful when Peter was imprisoned and saved Elisha when the Syrians had surrounded the town of Dotham. And what about the promised land. When..."

"Yes, yes." God turned to Eddie. "I was a lot more active in those days. Must be getting old." He leaned over and put his arm around Eddie's shoulder. Eddie felt a shiver of divine pleasure course through him at the Lord's touch. "Right now you're getting a lot of bad press about your past. I expected that. As any press agent will tell you, there is no such thing as bad publicity."

Eddie shook his head gloomily. "A lot of them think I'm the AntiChrist."

"Many will come around after your message at the Big Reveal."

"What message?"

"Pretty much the same one Jesus gave: love your neighbor, look after the planet, look after the poor and disadvantaged and, above all ignore anybody, priest, rabbi or imam, who uses my name as a prod to do evil unto others."

During the ensuing silence, God poured them each another glass of wine and said, "The truth is that each of us, and I include myself, is ultimately alone in this vast universe. Scares the Hell out of people. Can't blame them for passing the burden on to the Big Guy upstairs. If it helps to cry prayers into the darkness, if it comforts people in times of grief, times of broken dreams, to talk to God, what's the harm? Prayers do help a lot of people. So if I don't listen, who cares? It's only when some bastards call on me for frivolous things like fixing the World Cup, or murderous schemes like killing their neighbors because they are different that I get really pissed. That's one of the reasons most of the time I don't listen."

For a few moments, God sat gazing up at his stars. When he resumed, there were tears in his eyes. "I should have listened to Jesus though," he said, his voice hoarse. "'Why hast thou forsaken me?' Remember?" Eddie nodded.

"I should have stepped in earlier rather than letting them torture him to death. Instead I agonized for three days before resurrecting him. Then, at least, the Christians on this world would not have a torture device as their sacred symbol. Yeah, Yeah, I know, the three days dead was the point. Christians." He sighed. "Still, I don't do resurrections very often." He noticed the look of horror on Eddie's face. "Hey, don't worry. No crucifixions these days."

"That makes me feel a lot better," said Eddie.

"Hey, don't worry, Eddie. I'm on top of this one. Really paying close attention. Watch. The Big Guy looked up at the birch above them. Sounds of bird song. Eddie stood up and saw three birds perched on a branch right above them.

"White-throated sparrows," Marie, told him. "Beautiful song."

"I thought they only sang during the day?"

"That's right," said the Big Guy.

One by one the sparrows stopped singing and fell to earth, landing with small thumps beside the table. "They're dead," said Eddie, appalled.

"Just trying to show you, I am on the job, Son. You know, watching every little sparrow fall." As Eddie watched, the three tiny bodies faded away. "Hey, Son, lighten up. Just playin' with you. Seriously though, I've already decided to make an appearance in Jerusalem, shake things up."

"You're sure I'm going to Jerusalem?"

"Well, sure, if things work out right."

"But you don't really know. You just said you blew it with Jesus and if Jesus failed..."

"No, no," God interrupted. "He didn't fail. He taught many people the wisdom of suppressing the darkness at the heart of the human soul, to 'turn the other cheek.' In fact the religions of the world have given mankind a sense of community like no other institutions. Their artists have created works of transcendental beauty. Their compassionate have given hope and *caritas* to many of the world's poor. Their shared beliefs have given a place of refuge from the vast emptiness of the universe." He paused before adding, "But many of their priests, their imams and their rabbis, are filled with cognitive dissonance, preaching peace but making war on infidels, atheists and other believers. Look at the treatment of the Cathars, the Huguenots, the Falung Gong, the killing of infidels and innocents by mobs of otherwise warm and hospitable people. Some sects even dedicate themselves to banning music and dancing, squeezing all the joys from life and worship. And they do it in My name. Creating a nasty, vicious, vindictive God that is really a window into their own dark souls. None of them, of course, even think about the fact that their religious practices are dictated by an accident of geography. Where you were born almost always dictates your religion. "You know, William Blake put it best:

*I went to the Garden of Love,*
*And saw what I never had seen;*
*A Chapel was built in the midst,*
*Where I used to play on the green.*

*And the gates of this Chapel were shut,*
*And 'Thou shalt not' writ over the door;*
*So I turned to the Garden of Love*
*That so many sweet flowers bore.*

*And I saw it was filled with graves,*
*And tombstones where flowers should be;*
*And Priests in black gowns were walking their rounds,*
*And binding with briars my joys & desires."*

"Still, if everyone stopped believing tomorrow, would the earth be a better place?" asked Eddie.

God chuckled. "I must confess I have not found creatures on any other planet to be nearly as fascinating as mankind. That's why I have kept an eye on them since they evolved into truly sentient beings. And you know what are the two most impressive qualities about these people? They will die for each other is one. And the fact that people can laugh is the other. Humor is such an amazing thing, I'm in the process of spreading it across the universe. I can't get enough. Hey, have you heard this one? If life gives you melons, you might be dyslexic." Eddie groaned. "Don't like that one? Here, this one's timely: The past, the present and the future walked into a bar. Things got pretty tense."

This time, Eddie managed a smile and said, "Maybe Lydia was wrong about puns."

"Ah, she quoted Charles Lamb at you," observed the Big Guy.

"You mean 'A pun is a pistol let off in the ear, not a feather to tickle the intellect'?"

God nodded. "Yeah. Hey, have you heard the one about the rabbi, the imam, and the priest going into a bar. The bartender looks up and says, 'What is this some kind of joke?'"

For most of the next hour, they swapped jokes until finally Eddie got serious again and asked, "So how do I fit into the grand scheme of things?"

"The Bible promises a second coming. You're it."

"You mean this is a prelude to the end of the world, the four horsemen of the apocalypse, the last judgment."

God and the Holy Spirit laughed at this idea. "No, son. Don't believe everything you read. The earth has a long time left to it. The future of these peoples is not so clear. Ever since they discovered the tiny secret I leave on all inhabited planets as a kind of intelligence test, they have been able to call down nuclear destruction on themselves. So far the creatures on eighty-nine other planets have destroyed themselves but not on this one. I need you to tell them they're on the right path, that loving your neighbor beats killing him."

"But Jesus pointed that out," Eddie protested.

"And you are his second coming. Hey, your mama even named you

Jesus, remember. You are made of the same star stuff as Jesus Christ, boy. Even the same DNA." God rose and says, "Mankind needs a reminder. Come on, time to move on." The others followed as the Big Guy led the way briskly down the track to the road. Eddie stopped for a moment and looked back. The furniture and the replicator had gone.

When they reached the road below, Eddie was surprised to find a huge black car of classic vintage pulled up behind his Harley. "Elvis's favorite car, the Stutz Blackhawk III," God said, "Don't you love the spare built into the trunk like that?"

"But it's only got two seats."

"Ah, Marie won't mind sitting on the little jump seat in the back. Not like she weighs anything. Come on, get in."

"What about the Harley?" Eddie objected, alarmed.

"Don't worry, son. It'll be back in its lock box next time you need it."

Eddie felt the brush of cool lips on his cheek. When he looked around, he saw Marie perched on the jump seat. Eddie smiled at her and slid onto the smooth Italian leather passenger seat hoping his shoes would not get dust all over the lambs-wool floor mat. Through the windshield, he watched as God took out his enormous handkerchief and flicked an invisible speck of dust off the Rolls-style grille as he crossed to the driver's side. Eddie took in the gold-plated appointments and the burled wood on the dash as the Big Guy turned the key. The 425 horse V8 growled to life and then settled back into a rumbling heartbeat.

"Nice lookin' machine, huh?" said God.

"Beautiful. Is this the car Elvis bought out from under Frank Sinatra's nose?"

"No. That was the first prototype. But this was his favorite. Here." He handed Eddie his watch, a Hamilton Ventura with an arrowhead shaped face. "First battery operated watch," God told him. "Elvis wore this one in *Blue Hawaii* and liked it so much he kept it."

"What do you want me to do with it?"

A soft voice behind him. "He wants you to time it 0-60."

"Really?"

"Humor me," God said. "Now when the second hand reaches twelve. Just yell 'Go!'"

"O.K.," said Eddie, noticing that he had just over five seconds left. "On twelve," God repeated.

"O.K. Three..... two...... one...... Go!"

God dropped the big machine into gear and pushed the pedal to the floor. Eddie was wondering how Marie was making out in the back as he was pressed back into his seat. God let out a rebel yell and started counting, ".....55. 60."

"Jesus!" said Eddie.

"Would have loved this," finished the Big Guy. "Just under ten seconds," said Eddie.

"About right. Company claims it'll do it in 8.4. But that's on a straightaway, we had two curves."

For a while, they all sat back enjoying the ride along the deserted highway. "Look over there to the east," said the Big Guy. Eddie and Marie looked out at the dark sky to their right and, suddenly, a searing flash of light appeared and vanished all in the space of less than a second. "About .35 of a degree lower and it would have taken out Sault Ste Marie," God told them cheerfully and then began to sing "Catch a falling star and put it in your pocket, save it for a rainy day." in a flawless imitation of Elvis singing like Perry Como to entertain his mother who loved the old crooners.

When He had finished, the Big Guy began to reminisce. "You know every single culture on this planet had at least one God despite the fact that there really isn't much evidence lying around. One of the professors at Laurentian University in Sudbury here even invented the Koren helmet that uses electrical stimuli to give you a religious experience. He claims that humankind is hardwired for religious belief. Still, he may be able to prove belief but can he prove there is such a thing as a God? Many have tried. Aristotle popularized the Prime Mover. You know, if the universe started with a bang somebody had to light the fuse. The Prime Mover." He holds up a hand. "I'll plead guilty there. Notice the opening chapters of Genesis unfurl the local universe in a manner not unlike the scientific theory. But then,

164

the big bang theory was hatched by scientists born in the Christian tradition so we shouldn't be surprised." God's face lit up with a smile. "That reminds me. I've got a surprise for you, Eddie. Reach into the glove compartment and see what you can find."

Eddie found a stack of eight tracks. "Find the one by Don Maclean and shove it into the, I kid you not, Lear Jet Eight Track Player, the very first cassette player. The King, of course, had to have one." *American Pie* began to blare out of the speakers and when Don Maclean came to the extro, all three of them joined in and sang, "*And the three men I admire most / the Father, Son and the Holy Ghost / They caught the last train for the coast / The day the music died.*"

When, at God's bidding, Eddie opened the glove compartment to change the tape, he asked, "What's this?" as he pulled out a pack of what look like cigarettes and a lighter.

God laughed. "Thought you might like some Thai stick. For your meditative moments. Might help with the Big Reveal."

"Really?" said Eddie, delighted.

"Really. Thanks, Big Guy, for answering my prayers."

"Oh yeah. Thanks."

"Well, light the damned thing and pass it around." said the Big Guy before breaking into *Don't Bogart that Joint my Friend*.

Eddie nodded and hefted the lighter. "Real gold?" he asked.

"Yeah. Colonel Parker gave it to him. Used to hold it backstage while Elvis was performing. Only bulge the King wanted in those tight pants was the one he came by naturally."

"Naturally." Eddie sparked up the joint, took a deep hit and passed it to the Big Guy.

"Good stuff," said the Big Guy approvingly. "And, unlike booze, it's not addictive either. I can't take all the credit. Lot's of dedicated human hybridizing involved."

"Uh huh," grunted Eddie, feeling an unbidden euphoric smile spread across his face.

The Thai stick was strong enough that when Eddie put out the joint, there was still a fairly large roach remaining. Picking up the cigarette pack, he took a close look at it intending to put the roach in it. Only then did he notice the quotations on the outside of the package. First was George Washington's note to his gardener at Mount Vernon, 1794: 'Make the most of the Indian hemp seed, and sow it everywhere!' Eddie recognized this quotation and many of the others but the one that really caught his eye was the last one stated by Harry Anslinger, Commissioner of the U.S. Bureau of Narcotics for over thirty years: "...the primary reason to outlaw marijuana is its effect on the degenerate races."

"Yeah, the prohibition of pot was, and still is, a racist law." the Big Guy remarked. "Seems those black jazz musicians were just having too much fun." All three of them were quiet for a while. Eddie felt as if he was looking from on high at the blue marble below. "Remember, Bishop Berkeley?" God asked suddenly.

"*Esse est percipi, esse est percipere?*"

"'To be is to perceive. To be is to be perceived.' Yeah. Certainly a unique take on perceiving the universe. You know, if a tree falls in the forest and nobody perceives it, did it really fall?" Eddie nodded, looking out of the window. Just as they topped a hill, the towering silhouette of a white pine came crashing down next to the road. "Jesus!" he cried, involuntarily.

"Imagine if it were true though. Everytime anyone closed their eyes and covered their ears, the entire universe would cease to exist until you reached out and touched it. People would be recreating the universe every time they blinked."

Eddie tried it but the tire and wind noise spoiled the illusion. Disappointed, Eddie opened his eyes. "Any interesting revelation?" God asked.

"I could still perceive the world around me, the feeling of the seat, of movement."

"The dope didn't help?"

"Dope's fine," said Eddie, "a very mellow high. And when I open my eyes..."

"What?"

"I can see God."

"I liked my jokes better. Anyway, the reason I brought up the old bishop was to introduce Ronald Knox, the guy who refuted the bishop's philosophy."

"The priest?"

"That's the one. He mentally moved the tree from the forest into the quadrangle outside his room. Remember what he said?"

Eddie nodded and the trinity began to chant.

*There was a young man who said God*
*Must find it exceedingly odd*
*To think that the tree*
*Should continue to be*
*When there's no one about in the quad.*

Reply:

*Dear Sir: Your astonishment's odd;*
*I am always about in the quad.*
*And that's why the tree*
*Will continue to be*
*Since observed by, Yours faithfully, God.*

"See? That's what I'm up to when I'm not watching every damn sparrow fall."

Less than two hours later, with the sun beginning to paint streaks into the eastern sky, God stopped the car in a crackle of gravel. They had reached the Sudbury Yacht Club. "You just dropping me here?" asked Eddie, tempted to take a walk around the back of the A-frame clubhouse to check to see if his bike really was in its hideaway.

"No, no. I've lined up a treat. Worked great last time we used it." The Holy Spirit whispered, "Walking on the water."

"Yeah. Remember what a great hit it was when Jesus did it?"

She nodded. "Took Jesus a long time to get the hang of it, though."

"True enough so let's get started," said God.

"I'm going to walk on water?" Eddie was excited by the idea.

"Yeah. Not as easy as it looks," God warned him.

Eddie looked over to where the sailboats were tied up to their slips. He could just make out Arthur's canoe. Beyond the small bay lay the ghostly snowflake that was the Science North building. There were a few lights on. Cleaners, he told himself. "Let's do it on the lake side," Eddie suggested, thinking that the last thing he wanted was the cleaning staff reporting on some crazy guy skidding across the water.

"Sure. Water's usually calm at this time of day," God observed.

"I've seen this trick on TV," Eddie told him.

"Yeah, makes a pretty easy illusion. I bet the water was a little choppy."

"I don't remember."

"You need the chop to break up the outlines of the plexiglass ramp that's just under the surface." The Big Guy saw that Eddie was a little disappointed and added, "But we don't need no stinkin' ramps."

"All right! Let's do it!" said Eddie, trying to psych himself up. God nodded and led the way down to the gravel shore. "Do I have to take my shoes off?"

"Up to you but I'd leave them on. Water's pretty cold up here even at this time of year. Here, hold on to my hand. Marie, take the other one."

If Eddie had grown up in Canada, he would have compared what followed to his first time walking on ice with skates. But he had never skated in his life and this was molten ice. He would have fallen without support. "My God, it's slippery," he complained.

"You expected something else? The coefficient of friction is effectively zero. No, no, Eddie. The secret is to really believe you can do it."

"O.K.," said Eddie not sounding totally convinced.

"Remember when Jesus did it during the storm on Lake Galilee? He calmed the waters around the boat and called to Peter to join him. Peter did all right until he thought about it and began to lose his nerve. That's when he started sinking."

"Yeah, yeah, O.K., O.K." Eddie could feel his own lack of nerve beginning to make him testy.

"Practice and confidence. Piece of cake," said the Big Guy. "Practice and confidence."

"I have faith in you," Marie told him.

"That helps," Eddie told her with no hint of irony.

"Look. Tell you what I'll do," offered the Big Guy. "Now everybody in these parts already knows how to walk on water. Six months from now, no problem. So watch this." Suddenly there was a chill in the air. Eddie looked around and, by the dawn's early light, he could see frost forming on the trees and delicate traceries of ice forming along the shore. As he watched, fascinated, the ice spread in long crystals until, in less than a minute, a sheet of solid ice had formed in front of him.

"Fucking amazing!" he said. "Is it safe?"

"Sure," said the Big Guy. "Give it a shot, son."

Gingerly Eddie stepped on to the ice. He soon adjusted to the slippery surface and, as he gained confidence, managed a pirouette. His tiny audience applauded politely then God said, "In the next thirty seconds the ice will melt. Remember. Confidence. Don't want you pulling a Peter."

"Wait just for a minute," Eddie protested as the solid surface under his feet began to turn molten. "I don't think I'm ready."

"What?" asked the Big Guy. "I can't hear you over the sound of ice melting."

"I know you can do it, Eddie." The ancient voice of Marie and, at that instant, he knew he would be all right. Don't look down at your feet, he thought to himself. In the next few seconds the last of the ice melted as the air began to warm to the temperature of a summer morning in late June just before true dawn. I can do this, Eddie repeated over and over in his head as he took a couple of tentative steps. Even more slippery than ice, he observed as he corrected a slight lurch. Walking a little flat-footed and feeling his way with each step, he found his confidence growing. "I can do this," he finally said aloud.

"This is my Son with whom I am well pleased," said God with a grin.

Eddie laughed and, elated by his success so far, tried another pirouette and ended up skidding on his ass. God shook his head and said, "*Ecce homo!*" pointing at Eddie. Marie was more sympathetic. She appeared at Eddie's side and helped him up.

Eddie was about to thank her when the strains of the *Skater's Waltz* begin to play softly in the morning air. Without a word, Marie raised her arms and the two began to dance across the water.

God winked at them as they passed, knowing that he was not the only audience. Down the lake standing on the patio with good, light-gathering, hi-powered binoculars, Lydia too was watching. "So that's where he went," she said to herself, pleased that she had resisted calling 911 when she had found that he was missing. A voice behind, startled her. Arthur.

"What are you looking at?" he asked.

"Eddie," she answered. "He seems to be walking on water. "No, no, not walking. Dancing."

"Let me see." Lydia handed him the binoculars. "Ah, yes. I see him. He is actually dancing with the dead nun."

"A *danse macabre*?"

"Well if it is, they seem to be enjoying themselves. Holy Crap! Elvis is watching them too."

Without even thinking, Lydia snatched the binoculars back and said, "Oh my God, you're right. Looks to me as if Elvis and Eddie are having a little Father and Son time."

# Part Seven:
# Vatican City

## Il Papa

Pope Urban IX rose at 6:30, his usual time, knelt beside his narrow bed and muttered a short prayer exhorting God to give him the strength and the wisdom to get through this day. Only forty days in office, and already he felt the full weight of the church upon his shoulders. And now the two meetings scheduled for today could change the course of Catholicism forever.

Levering himself up, he shuffled into his bathroom, produced the papal penis, and stood over the pristine bowl waiting. And waiting. Finally, thank the Lord, a tiny trickle of urine. The old man sighed. When the trickle petered out, he shook his uncircumcised member a couple of times smiling at the memory of his late father's adage: three shakes is a mortal sin.

Just as he was finishing his morning ablutions, a discreet knock. "I have laid out your clothes, Your Holiness." The soft voice of Urban's devoted valet, Luigi Fuselli, drifted through the closed door.

"Thank you, Luigi," Urban called.

"Certainly, your holiness." Luigi said and departed as silently as he had come.

At precisely 7 a.m. the pope appeared in his private chapel dressed in his traditional white cassock and *zucchetto*, his matching skullcap. On his feet, the same scruffy sandals that he had worn to minister to the poor and powerless of São Paulo. Among themselves many of the cardinals had begun to refer to him as the peasant pope. Unusually, the eight benches of the small chapel were full today, mostly with the people who worked in and around the papal apartments, the people that the pope called his Vatican family. The rest of the congregation was made up of Vatican gardeners in their work overalls and sanitation workers in their safety vests. Urban knew that a faction of the college of cardinals was unhappy at this break with tradition but the presence of this, his little Vatican family, gave him joy. Before the mass, he quietly had a few words with each of them before approaching the modest altar and saying mass before the statue of a crucified, golden Christ.

As the pope made his way out of the chapel, one of the gardeners, a giant named Vico, suddenly grabbed the pope's hand, fell to his knees and began to plant wet kisses on the papal ring. "*Grazie! Mille grazie!* Holy Father," the big man boomed. Urban was startled but only for a moment. Quickly, he held up a hand to ward off the people rushing to his aid and said, "No harm, no harm." Gently, he gestured for the big man to rise and said to him, "We should be thanking you, Vico. We are fortunate you have come to us to take care of our gardens." Vico had only been on the job for a few days but did his work cheerfully – not to mention with great strength. Vico's mother, a tiny woman from the pope's own village, had begged the pope to find a job for her son. "He is over thirty now and he has never worked," she told him. "It is because of the Down's but he would be a good worker and strong, if he only had the chance." How did you turn down an appeal like that, Urban had asked himself. "Bless you, Vico," Urban told him. The big man's round face broke out in a broad smile while his eyes welled with tears as Urban squeezed his hand. "Go with God, my son," he told Vico as they parted. Two nuns who worked in the laundry, approached shyly. Each tentatively curtsied and kissed Urban's ring. As the taller one straightened up, she whispered, "We too would like to thank you, Holy Father, for recognizing that we, the invisible ones, also deserve a seat at God's table."

The pope, recognizing the accent, replied in Spanish, "*Via con Dios, mi hermosas,*" at which point the shorter nun burst into tears and was led away by her companion.

On the way out of the chapel, Urban signalled his personal secretary, Monsignor Georgio Ballasteros, to accompany him to the privacy of his study. When they were seated, the pope asked, "Well, Georgio. What can you tell me about the people I am meeting today?"

Pulling a sheaf of papers from his briefcase, he laid them before the pontiff. "We were expecting nine of the people who witnessed the appearance of the man many are calling the Messiah but only eight have made the trip. I have had a brief biography of each of them prepared. There are pictures too."

Urban nodded and scanned the papers quickly. "All Catholics," he observed.

"Yes. The other three who were there are not, your holiness."

"The other three?" The secretary produced another sheaf of papers with pictures and short bios culled from the media and the Vatican's own sources.

"Ah, yes. The geology professor and his wife and the visiting professor from Sri Lanka. Dr. Mahinda Rapasinghe is a Buddhist no doubt."

"Yes, your holiness. He was the one who figured out the computer message foretelling Eddie's arrival."

"Really?" He peered closely at the picture of Mahinda. "I would have liked to have talked to him."

Sensing a criticism, the monsignor jumped in a little too forcefully: "Time was of the essence, your holiness. Your *legatus missus*, Cardinal Bertelli, reached the people you will see today during Sunday mass. Eddie Magdalena is staying in the house of Dr. Arthur and Lydia Whitehead. So is Dr. Mahinda Rapasinghe. The paparazzi is besieging the place so it was impossible to reach them."

"Yes, yes, of course. We should be grateful that the good cardinal was able to bring so many. Convey to him our humble thanks."

The monsignor relaxed and assured the pope that he would pass the papal blessings on to Cardinal Bertelli. For a few minutes, the pope pored over the papers before dropping them on the table. "Do you not think it curious that exactly twelve people witnessed this miracle?"

"It strikes me as more than a coincidence, Holy Father."

Urban nodded, crossed towards the window of his study and, without pulling back the curtain too far, looked out. Below him, crowds were just beginning to filter into Vatican Square, getting ready for his regular Wednesday audience. "And what am I to tell the faithful this morning?" Monsignor Ballasteros, who had worked with Pope Urban since he had been a simple bishop, recognized a rhetorical question and made no reply.

"The piazza is already filling up," said Urban, "and we have not yet eaten breakfast."

While the monsignor was gathering up his papers and putting them back into the briefcase, Pope Urban asked, "Do you think there is a chance that Eddie Magdalena is the Messiah, Georgio?"

"I really don't know," the monsignor confessed.

"Many are calling him the AntiChrist," Urban pointed out.

"Yes, Your Holiness."

"But we should not forget that many of my predecessors were accused of being the AntiChrist also."

"Yes, Your Holiness," said the monsignor slowly, uneasy at the direction that the pope was taking.

"John warns us that the AntiChrist shall come, even now are there many AntiChrists; whereby we know that it is the last time." Urban sighed and said, "Come on. I need an espresso." He opened the door of his study for the monsignor. "With the kind of day this might be, perhaps I'll have two."

At breakfast Pope Urban IX and the monsignor were joined by the some of his 'family' at the single long table in his dining room. The talk, as it had been for days, was of Eddie's appearance from the heavens and the possibility that he really did represent the second coming. "Would that mean the end of the world is at hand?" asked Sister Marfa who spent her life cleaning and polishing the papal apartments.

Cardinal Xavier Buffone, the famously blunt Prefect of the Pontifical Household, told her, "There have been hundreds of so-called Messiahs, sister. He's just another one. If you should live long enough, you will no doubt see several more such pariahs."

Sister Marfa lowered her eyes and bit her lip. Seeing this, the Holy Father, patted her arm and said "I am sure that your prayers and those of your sisters, will keep the end times at bay."

"Yes, Holy Father," she said just loud enough for Urban to catch it. He looked over at Cardinal Buffone who was still eating with great relish as befits a man of such impressive bulk. An able administrator, Urban conceded, but with an unfortunate tendency to bully those working for him. Eventually I will have to replace him.

When Sister Marfa had left the table, Pope Urban caught Cardinal

Buffone's eye as he was wiping his lips after the morning meal. "My dear cardinal," he said, "you do not place any stock in the fact that the arrival of Eddie Magdalena was predicted across the world?"

"On the computers? Instruments of the devil. I've heard that you can make them say anything. Perhaps he is clever enough to have arranged the numbers himself and then make sure he was there to fulfill the prediction. No, no, Holy Father, this man is a charlatan like all the others."

"What proof would make you change your mind?" asked the pope.

"One would have to resort to sophistry to prove such a falsehood," said the cardinal with a short humorless laugh.

"But there were twelve witnesses there," countered the Holy Father.

"Gullible fools," snorted Cardinal Buffone. "The eight people that you are seeing today were on their way back from some place called Timmins. Apparently, their priest had arranged a bus trip to see the stain on a coffee shop wall. The stain was said to resemble the Blessed Mother. Such false apparitions are damaging to the church." He shook his head in disgust. "From Cardinal Bertelli's reports, these people seem to be simple people of the faith. But you will be able to judge for yourself, Holy Father. They will be here for their private audience this afternoon."

"We seem to be missing one of the Catholics, Cardinal Buffone," chided the pope.

"Yes, Your Holiness. She did not turn up with the others."

"So that would be..." The pope flipped through the files on the table. "Ah, the scoop tram operator."

"Yes, Your Holiness. A woman named Judy Legrand. Bertelli's notes hinted that she might be a 'sister of Sappho.'"

"Ah, a lesbian. As the world calls them these days. Nevertheless that fact would hardly disqualify her as one beloved by our Lord and Savior."

"Of course not, Your Holiness."

"And the others are, you said, 'simple people of faith'?"

"Yes."

"Like the shepherds." Buffone said nothing. "So are the three non-Catholics cast as the magi, do you think?"

Again Buffone did not reply but, instead, looked ostentatiously at his watch, a Vacheron Constantin Skeleton of which he was inordinately proud. "We have just over an hour before your last Wednesday audience of the season, Your Holiness. Already St. Peter's Square is filling up," he told the pope and rose from his chair.

The pope nodded and smiled kindly at the cardinal. "Xavier, if this truly is the second coming of our Savior," he said, "what will become of the role of Mother Church?"

The cardinal leaned forward and said with great emphasis, "Mother Church must be protected at all costs, Holy Father. At all costs."

Slowly the pope rose followed by the others. With his faithful valet, Luigi at his side he made his way along the corridor back to his study.

"I don't think I was the candidate that the good cardinal wanted in this office," he told Luigi."

"There is a group of them, Your Holiness. They call themselves the Gang of Four," he told the Holy Father.

"And Cardinal Buffone is one of them?"

"Yes, Holy Father. Two of the other three are also cardinals."

The pope nodded and sat down at his desk. "The other two? Wait. Let me guess." For a second he looked heavenward before counting on his fingers. "Cardinal Achille Silvestrini and... perhaps Cardinal Guisseppe Sardi."

"Very good, Your Holiness, but Cardinal Guisseppe Sardi is not one of them. The third cardinal is Cardinal Alois Schicklgruber."

"Schicklgruber?" He thought for a moment and added, "Not too surprising. And who is the final conspirator?"

"The *Praepositus Generalis*, Reverend Father Tomaso del Sarto, Your Holiness."

For a moment, the pope sat back, stunned. "The Black Pope," he said finally.

"Yes, your holiness. The Superior General of the Society of Jesus."

"A man of great learning, great intellect."

"A man who will bear watching, Your Holiness."

"Oh, yes." He smiled. "At least I know I can always count on you, Luigi.

"To the gates of heaven and beyond, Your Holiness."

## The Gang of Four

As Pope Urban awaited the clandestine visit of eight of the witnesses to Eddie's arrival, another secret meeting was about to take place in the oddest of the seven ancient basilicas in the eternal city, Santa Croce in Gerusalemme. Established originally as a chapel by St. Helena, the indefatigable mother of the Emperor Constantine, its name states that this church is actually, miraculously, in Jerusalem, not in Rome.

In the fourth century, the ever-resourceful St. Helena had a small chapel built to house relics of the Passion of the Christ that she had collected in the Holy Land. But her most brilliant idea had involved not the precious relics themselves but the soil from the Holy Land that had been used as ballast by the Roman triremes on the journey back to Rome. She had ordered that this Holy Dirt, reputedly dug from Golgotha itself, should be strewn across the floor of her chapel so that pilgrims who could not make it to Jerusalem could walk on the same sand as their Savior. Over the centuries, a full-blown basilica had grown up around the modest chapel. Still later, the basilica became embedded within the Domus Sessoriana, a Cistercian monastery that also takes in visitors to Rome.

The meeting in the Chapel of St. Helena was scheduled for ten o'clock. Cardinal Schicklgruber was early as usual. He had been about to descend the shallow flight of stairs to the right of the high altar when he heard the distinct sound of women's voices drifting up from the chapel below. Furious, the pocket cardinal retreated into the shadows. The chapel was supposed to have been out-of-bounds today. A few minutes later, he watched as a small group of elderly ladies emerged from the top of the stairs speaking American English. The cardinal reflected bitterly on the fact that women were even allowed into the chapel. Up until a century ago, they were forbidden to enter lest they drip unclean bodily fluids on the Holy Land. The ban had only been lifted in the nineteenth century when most women started wearing underwear regularly. Yet another example, if more were needed, of the church slipping away from its traditional purity, the cardinal observed to himself.

The tour guide, a Cistercian monk, was the last to emerge. The diminutive cardinal stepped out of hiding and confronted the man who immediately launched into an apology: "Your eminence, the meeting was not until ten o'clock so I thought I had time to conduct a tour for these ladies before..."

Cardinal Schicklgruber cut him off curtly, "Brother Rafael, my orders were explicit were they not."

"Yes, your eminence but..."

"Is the chapel empty now?" Brother Rafael nodded. "Then get these women out of here."

"Yes, yes, Your Eminence." The elderly American ladies, none of whom had more than a couple of words of Italian, had been watching this exchange. Brother Rafael quickly began to shepherd his charges towards the main door of the basilica.

As they departed, the cardinal heard one say to the other, "I forgot to leave my note to St. Helena."

"Shame," said another. "That cardinal sure seems to have got out of the wrong side of the bed this morning, Brother Rafael."

The young monk smiled at her and said, "He was a little upset that I sneaked you ladies in. He has the chapel reserved for the whole day for an important meeting." Suddenly he remembered that the meeting itself was supposed to be secret, and felt a little guilty that he had mentioned it to these ladies. He immediately decided that he would not confess his indiscretion to Cardinal Schicklgruber. After all, in the cardinal's case, there was no right side of the bed.

Cardinal Schicklgruber, still angry at the young monk who had disobeyed his orders, was about to descend the stairs when he spied Cardinal Achille Silvestrini, a fellow member of the Friends of Santa Croce. The aristocratic cardinal, scion of a noble Florentine family, was striding briskly towards him down the middle aisle of the short nave with its procession of mismatched granite columns. Cardinal Schicklgruber watched the tall, thin figure with the aquiline nose that proclaimed his genetic connection to the Medicis. They met before the high altar which stood surrounded by four delicate ionic columns that held aloft the eighteenth century baldacchino. "My dear, Alois," greeted the Cardinal Silvestrini warmly, "Your note said that this meeting was urgent."

"Oh, I assure you that you will find it time well spent, Achille."

"But where are the others?"

"Father Thomas will be a few minutes late. He has to pick up one of his brilliant proteges, a young genius called Dr. Enrico Capelli. He's a genetics professor at the University of Bologna. Cardinal Buffone will not be joining us. He will be looking after the witnesses from Canada who are meeting the pope today."

"We are meeting in St. Helena's Chapel?"

"Yes." Cardinal Schicklgruber's eyes scanned the main church. Only a handful of tourists.

"Too many prying eyes here, Alois. Let's go down."

Taking the plain white staircase to the right of the altar, they descended the few steps to St. Helena's small chapel. Another Cistercian monk greeted them at the outer door. "Ah, Brother Arioso," said Cardinal Silvestrini, "you are looking after us today."

"Yes, Your Excellency," said the young monk, blushing. "And how is Brother Nicola?"

"He is failing fast. We are praying for him night and day."

"Ah. I will add him to my prayers also."

"Thank you, Your Excellency," said Brother Arioso with a bow. Keeping his eyes downcast he led the way to an ornate table and four chairs that had been set up in the middle of the small, gloomy chapel. The room was dominated by a large marble statue of St. Helena in a niche on the wall, a statue that had originally been of Juno but she had been converted to Christianity by the addition of a large wooden cross. Beneath her feet, an area of the floor was covered with plexiglass to protect the earth of Jerusalem from getting soiled by pilgrim traffic.

Small piles of paper, pleas for the intercession of St. Helena, had gathered like so much beached flotsam scattered over the Holy Dirt.

Built at ground level, most of the chapel is underground now. The monk busied himself pouring thimbles of espresso and offering a plate of pastries to the cardinals.

"What are these, Brother Arioso?" Cardinal Silvestrini asked, trying to put the young monk at his ease.

The monk began to blush again and stared at the small pastries made with alternating light and dark rings of dough. "Brother Mario made them in honor of the Canadian pilgrims who are visiting the pope today," he managed. "They are called '*pets de soeurs*,' Your Excellency."

Cardinal Silvestrini threw back his head and laughed, "Nun's farts?" Cardinal Schicklgruber glowered at the young monk.

"I understand it is a French Canadian delicacy," muttered Brother Arioso.

"Well, they look delicious, and they certainly smell heavenly, don't they, Alois?"

The Austrian, appalled at the name, but never having met a pastry he did not like, put a couple of the them on his plate and said, "We are expecting two more, Brother Arioso." Brother Arioso nodded and quietly departed.

In fact, the others had already arrived. Reverend Father Thomas del Sarto, Superior General of the Jesuits, dressed in the traditional black cassock, checked his watch and looked around. "The others probably have not arrived yet." he told his young, slightly-built companion, "so let's have a quick look at the famous relics."

Father Thomas' companion, Doctor Enrico Capelli, appeared to be no more than sixteen but was, in fact, twenty-seven. His black-rimmed glasses with their thick lenses gave him a boyish look of perpetual surprise. "By all means, Father," he agreed enthusiastically.

"Then we must hurry. Cardinal Schicklgruber hates tardiness. Come." Without looking back, Father Thomas, a former all-star linebacker at Notre Dame, led the way briskly through a door to the left of the altar. "The Chapel of the Relics is up here," Father Thomas said, indicating a white staircase that ascended past the stations of the cross. Father del Sarto charged up the staircase until he reached the top where he waited impatiently for the panting professor to reach him before pointing to a brick in the wall that is engraved with the two words *TITVLVS CRVCIS*. "The most famous relic of Santa Croce," Father del Sarto told him. "Not the brick itself, of course but the title from the holy cross. This brick was found behind a wall in 1492, the same year Columbus discovered America." He led the professor to a glass case behind the altar. "Here are all the relics," he told the younger man.

The professor crossed himself at the sight of the holy reliquaries cunningly wrought in gold or silver. After a few moments of staring in frank adoration at the reliquaries, he whispered, "They are not labelled, Reverend Father."

Father del Sarto, who had checked his watch and seen that they were beginning to run late, pointed to the reliquaries one by one and said, "That one contains spikes from the crown of thorns. Those three have relics of the true cross as befits this church and that one is said to contain the finger of Doubting Thomas, though I personally doubt it."

Father del Sarto took the young professor by the shoulder and nudged him gently towards the largest relic, an ancient board made of walnut, the only surviving part of the *titulus crucis*. "This one, I think we can be certain is the actual inscription that Pilate told the scribe to write."

The professor nodded and, quoting from the Gospel of St. John, said, "'And it was written in Hebrew and Greek and Latin.'"

The Superior General smiled down at the professor. "I see you know your Bible. Some have claimed this is a medieval forgery but now we have the essay of Egeria about her travels in the Holy Land in the fourth century. She actually saw it. Later it was smuggled to this church, hidden in the walls during the troubles with the Visigoths and rediscovered in 1492. Pilate certainly would have had a scribe fluent in all three languages. The fact that, not just the Hebrew, but all three languages are written right to left means that the scribe was a Jew as we would expect. The Arabic is almost too faded to read but the other two lines are clear, especially the Latin: *Iesvs Navarenvs Rex Ivdeaorum*."

"Jesus of Nazareth, King of the Jews. INRI." The professor crossed himself again.

"Come. We're running late," Father del Sarto urged. "Alois will be in a bad mood." *But when is he not*, he added to himself.

"But where is the... the..."

"The *santissimo prepuzio?*"

"Yes," said the professor.

"In the Lateran Palace. A short walk from here."

They descended the stairs rapidly and, crossing to the other side of the altar, took the staircase down to the chapel of St. Helena. As they walked, the priest told the young man, "When I was a boy, nobody could even mention the *santissimo prepuzio* on pain of excommunication." The professor looks alarmed until Father del Sarto added, "Don't worry. The ban was lifted at the end of Vatican II."

Below them, Cardinal Schicklgruber, looked up at the sound of their descending footsteps and said, "That must be the black pope and his boy genius now." The Inspector General of the Jesuits is one of the most powerful men in the church and his informal title reflected the prestige of his position. "Well, we are all here at last," said Cardinal Schicklgruber, trying in vain to keep the annoyance out of his voice. Turning to Brother Arioso, he told him, "Now you can retire and seal the door. Stay outside until you hear a knock."

"Yes, Your Excellency." Hurrying out, he closed the door behind him and wound a red ribbon around the door handle, glad to be alone once more. In heavily accented Italian, the American Superior General of the Jesuits introduced his young companion: "This is Dottore Enrico Capelli, Italy's foremost expert in genetics. He is from the University of Bologna. In fact, this is his first visit to Rome. Dottore Capelli is also a faithful follower of all the teachings of Mother Church. Even wears a scapular, don't you Enrico?"

"Yes, Holy Father," Enrico said in a squeak that made him sound even younger than he looked. "I wear the scapular of Our Lady of Mount Carmel."

"Ah, the brown scapular. So you are a lay Carmelite of the third order," said Cardinal Schicklgruber approvingly.

"Buffone will not be here?" asked the black pope who was growing impatient.

"He is conducting the witnesses of the arrival of the AntiChrist to their audience with the Holy Father," Cardinal Schicklgruber explained.

"Then, let us get started," the black pope responded as he seated himself at the table. He indicated to the boy genius that he should sit at his right hand. "Now we all agree that this Eddie Magdalena is at best a charlatan or, at worst, the AntiChrist that has been foretold. He is perhaps the greatest challenge to the church since Martin Luther." At a slight nod of agreement from the two cardinals, he continued, "Buffone tells me that he thinks Urban is leaning towards recognizing this man as the Messiah." He looked to Cardinal Schicklgruber to take over the narrative and poured himself a cup of espresso. The boy genius was following the proceedings with rapt attention.

The pocket cardinal said, "The Holy Father thinks that we are perhaps in the end times and is impressed that Eddie Magdalena's coming was foretold on the... the..." He looked to Enrico for help.

"The number appeared on computer screens across the world. Nobody is sure how that happened. There is a growing interconnectivity of computers around the world happening as we speak but it has not yet developed enough to cause the magic number to appear on so many screens. My theory is that..."

"Yes, thank you, professor," said the pocket cardinal, a clear note of irritation in his voice. "We are looking for your expertise, not your opinions."

The young professor hunched down in his seat and began to wipe his glasses with a handkerchief to cover his confusion. "Of course, Your Excellency," he said at last.

Before the cranky Austrian cardinal could reply, Cardinal Silvestrini jumped in smoothly: "Thank you, professor. You are here because we desperately need your expertise."

"I just meant that..."

"Yes, of course." Silvestrini looked at the two older men. "Now, Thomas if you would explain the plan that the Jesuits have come up with. But please remember that we are poor churchmen who have but a basic grasp of science. And don't worry. Mother Church may have burned Giordano Bruno as a heretic for claiming that the earth moved around the sun, but our view of the contribution of scientists has certainly improved since then. There are rumors that one day we may even pardon Galileo."

The black pope nodded and began, "Actually it was Enrico who came up with the idea so I think we will let him explain it."

"Of course, Holy Father." Enrico turned to the others. "Actually it is Reverend Father del Sarto who deserves most of the credit. He came to me just after the news broke that Eddie Magdalena was the son of a... a woman of the evening. He pointed out to me that most of the media were calling this man, not the Messiah but the AntiChrist." Bishop Schicklgruber let out a loud sigh.

Seeing that the young professor was getting increasingly nervous, the black pope stepped in, "Let me explain, Alois. I called a meeting of my science advisors and asked them if anyone had an idea that would forever discredit this supposed Messiah. One, Father Entwhistle, an Englishman, suggested we should see about extracting DNA from the *santissimo prepuzio*. Then we would need to obtain the DNA from this Eddie Magdalena, not an impossible task, and compare them."

"But what would you expect to find?" asked Cardinal Silvestrini eagerly.

"That this imposter doesn't have the royal jelly, so to speak."

"Ah, so you think that this Eddie Magdalena's DNA would not match that of Our Savior?"

Suddenly getting it, Cardinal Schicklgruber cried excitedly, "Yes, of course. The second coming. The DNA should be identical."

"As it is in identical twins," said the professor, carefully.

"And if there is no match..." said Schicklgruber.

"Then there will be no doubt," added the black pope, "that this man is yet another in a long line of false messiahs."

"And we have a sample of the holy foreskin not too far from here," said Cardinal Silvestrini, "in the Sancta Sanctorum in the Lateran Palace."

"But that is not the only fragment. The rest of it is in the church at Calcata Vecchia, is it not?"

"That piece, I believe was stolen a few years ago," said Silvestrini. "Most people think the Vatican has it but we don't," growled Schicklgruber.

"And there is supposed to be a third tiny fragment collected by Bishop Cybo when he presented a new reliquary to house the *santissimo prepuzio* in the church in Calcata Vecchia," explained the black pope, who had obviously been doing some intensive research.

"But surely that fragment is so tiny as to be almost invisible," said Silvestrini.

"Not almost invisible. It is actually invisible. I have had my people go through Cybo's collection but not a sign of it."

"Then we must rely on the fragment at St. John's Lateran," said Schicklgruber firmly.

"It's not really that easy, Alois," said the Black Pope. "I'll let Professor Capelli explain."

All eyes turn to the nervous young man. "Deoxyribonucleic Acid, or DNA, is present in almost every cell in our bodies. And it is present in nearly all living creatures right down to the bacteria level. DNA controls inheritance of everything from eye color to bone density, to height and body type.

"Most important for our purposes, each person's DNA, except for identical twins, carries a unique sequence of four building blocks: A, T, G, C. We will be analyzing the sequence of the DNA of the *santissimo prepuzio* fragment using a fairly new technique called a polymerase chain reaction, PCR for short. Using PCR we can then compare it to the DNA of Eddie Magdalena provided, of course, we have a sample of his DNA that we can analyze for comparison."

The black pope, looking very pleased with himself, assured the two cardinals, "We are in the process of obtaining the AntiChrist's DNA. If all goes well, the sample should be in Rome within two days."

Cardinal Schicklgruber who had had trouble following the professor's explanation, asked sourly, "So what does all this mean?"

"If the two sequences match, then Eddie Magdalena is the Messiah come back to us," the professor said.

The pocket cardinal's eyes narrowed, his long face taking on a vulpine cast. "But surely that is impossible. There can be no match."

"Don't worry, Alois," Cardinal Silvestrini encouraged. "The chances are one in a billion."

"Oh, far less than that," said the professor. Cardinal Schicklgruber sat back, mollified. "Extracting ancient DNA is fraught with problems. This sample has almost certainly been contaminated through the ages by the various people who have handled it. Bones or teeth would be much easier but we have to work with what we have, soft tissue.

Cardinal Schicklgruber nodded thoughtfully before saying, "Then we have nothing to worry about. Whether through contamination or pure chance, we will have the proof that this man is no more the Messiah than you are, my dear Achille."

Turning to Reverend Father Thomas del Sarto, he said, "Won't somebody miss the piece of the holy *prepuzio*?"

The black pope, smiled and leaned in conspiratorially. "I've arranged to have it removed later tonight. No one will notice as the substitute looks exactly the same in every respect."

"Except for the DNA," added the professor with a high pitched chuckle. The others looked at him as if he were mad. Scientists. Certainly not a trustworthy lot.

"What will you put in its place?" asked Cardinal Silvestrini, intrigued."

A piece of a *preservativo*, suitable aged of course."

"You are using a condom?" asked Cardinal Silvestrini, awestruck.

"I'm sure the church will permit the use of a *preservativo* in these circumstances," Cardinal Schicklgruber observed with the ghost of a wintry smile.

The black pope rose, towering over the two cardinals, and signalled the professor. "The DNA will take some time to analyze but I think it will solve the problem of our latest 'Messiah.' Go with God!" he concluded and headed for the stairs, his boy genius trotting along behind.

"Shame to waste the *pets de soeurs*, Alois," Silvestrini said, taking one and offering the plate to Schicklgruber who nodded and took the last one.

"We must protect Mother Church from her enemies," Schicklgruber told him.

"Of course, of course," said Cardinal Silvestrini. "What did you think of the young professor?"

Schicklgruber shrugged. "I don't think anything about him. If he can do what we ask of him, I will be content."

"A very unworldly boy."

"Mmmm."

"Did Thomas tell you the boy is a vegan?"

"What? No. What does it matter?"

Cardinal Silvestrini rose, brushing the last crumbs from his hands. "Well, when Thomas first mentioned him to me, he was going on about what a wonderfully devout Catholic the boy is. Then he mentioned that the boy is even a vegan as if that too is a Christian virtue. I told him that I have always had a slight reservation against vegans who declare themselves devout Catholics ."

"Why?" Schicklgruber asked as they started up the stairs.

"Transubstantiation."

"Ah, yes. Very clever. Achille. You would make a good pope."

**Public and Private: Two Papal Audiences**

That Wednesday morning Père Jean-Pièrre and the others received early wake-up calls followed by breakfast on the terrace overlooking the Spanish Steps and the chic shops of the Via Condotti. The Dionne sisters were far too excited to eat more than a roll or a piece of toast but Claude Bisonnette and Thomas LaRue consumed more than enough to make up for the sisters' lack of appetite.

Today's ride was a white minibus with the Vatican crown-and-crossed-keys logo on the doors. Cardinal Bertelli, *legatus missus*, apologized for cramming them into such a vehicle and explained, "Parking is almost impossible in Vatican City."

Their driver turned up the Via della Conciliazione and pulled in to a line of taxis dropping off fares in front of the police barriers opposite Via della Traspontina.

"*Mon Dieu! Ah, Mon Dieu!*" from the four sisters as the great dome of St. Peter's loomed into view straight ahead. Père Jean-Pièrre, the only one of the pilgrims familiar with the scene, smiled nostalgically as he got out of the van right in front of the Domus Romana Sacerdotalis, the residence where he had stayed all those years ago during Vatican II. They joined the good-natured crowds flocking down the sidewalks on either side of them although it was only a little after eight in the morning. Pope Urban would not appear for his Wednesday morning audience until 10:30 but his popularity meant that seats would be filled well before then.

When their small flock reached Vatican Square, Cardinal Bertelli stopped and pointed to their right: "See the yellow taxi sign." The others nodded. "Our driver will pick us up there after the Holy Father's private audience this afternoon." The cardinal managed a smile and added, "Welcome to the center of the Catholic world, the Piazza San Pietro." He paused to hand out their blue tickets to the pope's general audience. "Come."

The entire square was ringed with security. "A modern necessity," explained the cardinal as their bags were examined and Alphonse and Thomas LaRue were submitted to pat-downs from security personnel. "These security measures are a result of the attempted assassination of Pope John Paul II here in 1983," the cardinal explained.

Once they were through security, he led them across the cobblestones to the Egyptian Obelisk that marked the center of the square. "The Emperor Caligula brought this obelisk to Rome from Egypt in 37AD packed in lentils to protect it. It was originally placed over there nearer the sacristy. According to legend, this column stood witness to the crucifixion of St. Peter. Pope Sixtus V had it moved here in 1586 to represent the very *omphalos* of the Catholic world. It took nine hundred men to erect the column's 330 tons on this sacred spot. Now look around you. The arms of the church enfold us here in the form of Bernini's colonnade. See how the two sides curve around the piazza like the arms of mother church herself." The pilgrims look around, awestruck. Tears were coursing down the cheeks of all four Dionnes.

A pagan phallus once used to worship the sun god Ra, reflected Père Jean-Pièrre. The last time he was here Cardinal Dupuis had warned him to beware of the pagan heart of Rome but, being young, he had not listened. Instead he had succumbed to Rome's pagan heart, fallen in love with Héloïse and almost lost his vocation. And now here he was back, standing beside this magnificent obelisk, a 25 meter tall monument to paganism in the center of St. Peter's Square. Originally the *pyramidion* at the pinnacle of the obelisk had been topped by a bronze urn rumored to contain the ashes of Julius Caesar. The bronze cross that had replaced the ancient urn only draws attention to the obelisk's pagan origins, Jean-Pièrre mused. "Beautiful, isn't it, ladies," Père Jean-Pièrre said softly.

The sisters nodded in unison and Émilie said, "We have been blessed ever since we met Eddie Magdalena."

"So have I, Émilie. So have I," said Père Jean-Pièrre. Already the arrival of Eddie Magdalena had led to his own unexpected return to Rome and soon he would be having a private audience with the new pope.

Already the weather was getting hot as Cardinal Bertelli led them through the crowds to the seats reserved for them in the second row. Their seats were no more than a couple of meters from the dais that had been set up in front of the main doors of St. Peter's for today's address. "Clever how they've kept paths open through the crowds," Claude said as he took his seat. "I guess the pope will be will be coming in the popemobile."

"Probably," said Père Jean-Pièrre.

The concrete barriers had been set up overnight, cunningly arranged so that none of the crowd would be more than a few feet from His Holiness during his slow drive.

Père Jean-Pièrre looked over to his right, at the windows of the papal apartments visible over Bernini's curving colonnade. "I thought the pope always spoke from up there," said Thomas LaRue.

"He does speak from there on some special occasions, like giving the Angelus on Sundays. He appears at the second window from the right on the top floor," Pierre Jean-Pièrre told him and added quietly,

"We will see the view from up there soon enough."

Overhearing, Yvonne said, "We can hardly wait."

By ten o'clock St. Peter's Square was crammed and a few soaring bars of organ music signaled the arrival of the popemobile, shorn of its bullet-proof glass at the new pope's request. The white vehicle was surrounded by a phalanx of men dressed in black suits. Pairs of Swiss Guards wearing their traditional blue and yellow with small flashes of red (to honor the Medicis) were strung along the pope's route at regular intervals. Today they were wearing their black berets. For the next half an hour, Pope Urban IX waved to the cheering crowds and kissed babies who were presented to him by members of his security detail. Once, he accepted a cage containing two live doves and freed them to the loudest cheers of the morning.

At 10:30, precisely on time, the popemobile drew up to the dais in front of the doors to the basilica and the pope proceeded to the microphone set up before a large upholstered chair.

The pope began his remarks with a general welcome which included mention of several groups such as The Bell Ringers of Cologne Cathedral and the European Union of Catholic Asparagus Growers. In all, over a dozen groups were mentioned that day but not theirs. "He didn't mention us," commented Thomas LaRue, feeling put out.

Cardinal Bertelli, leaned towards him and hissed urgently, "The reason for our visit is not known to anyone. Please keep it to yourself." Thomas mouthed a silent apology.

Next the pope gave the apostolic blessing to those present, to the sick and the suffering and to the oppressed before blessing rosaries, bibles and saint's medals that people were holding up. The sisters held their rosaries above their heads for the blessing before replacing them in their purses with trembling hands.

Since the pope would be delivering his sermon almost entirely in Italian, a young priest approached a second microphone and delivered an English preamble to the pope's sermon omitting any reference to Eddie. When the pope stepped up to his microphone, his homily was about the dire state of the world, an inexhaustible lamentation in nearly any papal reign since the church arose from the deserts of the

Middle East. The audience listened to him in rapt silence.

Père Jean-Pièrre suddenly sat forward as did Cardinal Bertelli when the pope began to talk about an item not covered in the priest's preamble: the possibility that a new Messiah was at hand. Gasps ran through the crowd. Père Jean-Pièrre, realizing that, of their group, only he and Cardinal Bertelli understood Italian, began to translate for the others.

"The most important event of the past few days, not just for our Holy Mother Church but for the entire world, is the arrival of Eddie Magdalena on the summer solstice as had been foretold." Cardinal Bertelli leaned forward, the expression on his face one of shock and surprise. In attendance behind the pope, Cardinal Buffone, looked outraged. Père Jean-Pièrre guessed that the pope had told no one he was about to bring this up here, literally ex-cathedra.

"Over the centuries since the birth of Jesus, there have been many, many Messiahs, all of them false. Many in the media have even called Eddie Magdalena the AntiChrist, a vague term of abuse that has been hurled against many of my predecessors in this very office. But this time, not only has the coming of Eddie Magdalena been predicted around the world, his appearance from the heavens on the shortest night of the year was witnessed by twelve people at the place that was predicted. What does this mean for us? Unlike the world's press, we cannot allow ourselves to rush to judgment. Instead we must talk to this man and to his followers before evaluating this claim that he has come as the Messiah. Then we must consult with the leaders of the other major religions and pray together for guidance."

The pope went on to talk of the grinding poverty, the oppression and the racism still afflicting so many people around our fragile planet but Père Jean-Pièrre stopped translating as the pontiff moved away from the subject of Eddie Magdalena.

Twenty minutes later, Pope Urban IX drew to an end. Sounds of an organ filled the air as Urban began to recite the *Pater Noster* in Latin. The entire crowd recited with him: "*Pater noster, qui es in caelis, sanctificetur nomen tuum. Adveniate regnum tuum...*"

Except for Père Jean-Pièrre, the pilgrims stared around them, puzzled that everyone in the crowd seemed to know the Lord's Prayer in Latin. Noticing their confusion, Père Jean-Pièrre held up his ticket, pointing out that the entire prayer was on the back.

When much of the crowd had cleared and workmen were beginning to dismantle the dais, Cardinal Bertelli told his flock to grab a quick lunch and meet back at the foot of the obelisk at 1:30 p.m. for their private audience at 2:00 p.m. "Even if you are not wearing a watch," Bertelli told them, "you can tell the time by the obelisk itself." He showed them that the huge stone also acted as the gnomon of a sundial. "You'll see the sun's shadow half-way between those two round markers over there." He pointed to the stones marking one and two. "I'll see you then," Bertelli said. "Please, don't be late." With that he hurried off towards the entrance to the apostolic apartments as he was due to lunch with the pope.

Cardinal Bertelli collected the pilgrims under the shadow of the obelisk at precisely 1:30 p.m. Everyone was there, even Alphonse. The cardinal led the way to the huge bronze doors to the right of St. Peter's. They were expected and, passing through the ancient entrance to the Papal Apartments, they proceeded along the curve of the Tuscan pillars designed, Bernini tells us, to represent "the maternal arms of Mother Church". Two Swiss Guardsman came to attention as they passed and saluted them with their partizans. They entered a small antechamber guarded by two more Swiss guards. A plainclothes member of the Vatican Police introduced himself and, pointing to the metal detectors, shrugged apologetically and said in English, "A sign of the times. Welcome to 'Checkpoint Charlie.' When we have determined that you ladies and gentlemen are not devilish terrorists, we will issue your passes. Please do not lose them. They must be turned in when you leave. Enjoy your visit. I understand you are to have an audience with the Holy Father. I envy you."

When they had all been wanded, an attendant handed each of them the prized blue-and-yellow pass embossed with the Vatican seal. A second receptionist called them over. Positioned behind a massive desk, under the scarcely dry portrait of the new pope, he told them that everything was ready for their audience. Turning away, he picked up a telephone and alerted the receptionists at the elevators to expect their party.

As the pilgrims approached the broad Stairs of Pius IX, Cardinal Bertelli warned them to be careful as the steps were not at the usual height. "The steps are wide and exceedingly shallow," he cautioned them. "This is so that we men of the church can negotiate them without lifting our cassocks to prevent us from tripping." At the top, they paused to catch their breath before crossing the cobblestones of the Courtyard of San Damaso to the elevator to the papal apartments. The elevator operator, wearing a dark suit, greeted Cardinal Bertelli and told him that Cardinal Buffone awaited them above.

Sure enough, when they reached the top floor and the mahogany doors of the elevator opened, the great bulk of Cardinal Buffone loomed into view accompanied by Luigi Fuseli. When the introductions had been made, Cardinal Buffone reminded the pilgrims of Vatican protocol: "The pope is never introduced. People are presented to him. Luigi will be conducting you today so please let him see your passes so that he can make the introductions."

Luigi smiled warmly and talked to each one in turn to put the pilgrims at their ease. Whether by accident or design, Luigi reached Père Jean-Pièrre last. Looking over at Cardinal Buffone, he noted that the large cardinal was deep in conversation with Cardinal Bertelli. "This is from a dear friend of yours," he told Père Jean-Pièrre as he handed him an envelope. Père Jean-Pièrre slipped it into an inside pocket wondering what friend would be writing to him. Luigi added, "His Holiness, too, will give you a letter. It is the invitation we talked about. Please deliver it to Eddie Magdalena. And tell him, it is most important that the meeting be kept secret."

"Yes, of course," Père Jean-Pièrre responded, mystified but being careful not to show it.

Cardinal Buffone said goodbye to Bertelli as the elevator arrived for him. Cardinal Bertelli told the party that he would be leaving them in the good hands of Cardinal Buffone. As the elevator doors opened, he reminded them that they would be picked up after the audience, at the taxi stand in Vatican Square.

As the doors closed, Cardinal Buffone told them that he too had a previous engagement and would leave them in the capable hands of Luigi Fuseli. "Don't forget to refer to the pope as either 'Holy Father' or

'Your Holiness.' I'm sure you'll have no trouble recognizing Pope Urban, even though he was only elected a few weeks ago."

"Oh yes, your Honor," Claude Bisonnette assured him.

As Buffone took his leave, he reflected that with these peasants as the so-called witnesses of a second coming, there did not seem to be much to worry about. Already he had Bertelli's report on the background of each one of the pilgrims, a much more detailed report than the one presented to the pope earlier in the morning. No, it was the three non-Catholics that worried him.

Luigi ushered the pilgrims into a spacious room tastefully decorated in browns, yellows and grays under a high paneled ceiling. "As you probably guessed from the bookcases, this is the pope's library. Make yourselves comfortable and I'll let His Holiness know you are here. The long table that often occupied the middle of the room had been replaced today with soft grey armchairs arranged in a circle. The pilgrims were too excited to sit down. Alphonse had wandered over to the pope's desk and was examining the gold clock sitting there. Père Jean-Pièrre was staring at him, willing him not to touch it.

And almost like an apparition, Pope Urban IX appeared in the doorway dressed in his traditional white cassock, his matching white zucchetto, and his worn sandals. Luigi introduced the pilgrims one by one. The women sketched awkward curtsies, the men bowed and each kissed the pope's ring. Pope Urban, speaking in French, put each of them at ease with a few words based on Bertelli's research.

When they were all seated, Luigi opened the door briefly and whispered to someone outside. A few moments later, a nun rolled in a small tea trolley loaded with a silver coffee pot, espresso cups and two plates, one with biscotti, the other with *pets de soeurs*. "Sister Magda created these," the pope said, a twinkle in his eye, "in honor of your visit. I understand they even have a clerical name." The four sisters blushed in unison, but each took one.

"My personal favorite, Your Holiness," said Père Jean-Pièrre as he piled two on his plate and accepted a demitasse of espresso.

"They are especially good," the pope agreed, biting into one with obvious relish.

"Made of the purest of ingredients," risked Père Jean-Pièrre, "and famous for their heavenly aroma, Your Holiness."

"Indeed, Père Jean-Pièrre."

The small refreshments went well with the small talk that the pope expertly managed and soon everyone was contributing to the story of their encounter with Eddie Magdalena.

"None of us knew about the prediction until later," Thomas LaRue pointed out.

"I'm the only one with a computer, Your Holiness," Père Jean-Pièrre explained, "but I just use it for spreadsheets of the parish's finances and to write my sermons. It was a complete surprise to all of us that Eddie's arrival had been foretold."

Judging that now was the time to broach a delicate subject, Pope Urban said, "And yet many are calling him the AntiChrist."

"No, no, Your Holiness," Yvonne protested before stopping, surprised at her own boldness.

"Then you are sure that Eddie is the Messiah?" he asked softly. "Oh, yes, Your Holiness. I have no doubt," she told him.

"I'm sure Your Holiness would have felt the same if you had been there," said her sister, Annette. Much to the pope's surprise, the four sisters crossed themselves in unison.

The pope asked each of the others in turn whether Eddie Magdalena was the AntiChrist. Only Thomas LaRue and Alphonse said they were not sure.

All too soon their hour was over and Luigi appeared at the door to remind the pope that he had a prayer meeting. As the pilgrims departed, the pope drew Père Jean-Pièrre aside, walked him over to his writing desk and pulled out an envelope closed with the papal seal. "The envelope contains an invitation to Eddie Magdalena for a private meeting. I have suggested my summer residence at Castel Gandolfo. I ask him to come to visit me since I cannot travel because of my office and I think we should keep our meeting secret for the time being. The date and time would be up to him, of course. Once again, I am sure you can understand the importance of keeping our meeting secret, Père Jean-Pièrre."

"Yes, yes of course," said Père Jean-Pièrre.

"Then I would like you to deliver our letter to Eddie in person. Would you do that for me, Jean-Pièrre?"

"Of course, Your Holiness. I would be honored."

"Thank you, my son," the pope said warmly and handed him the envelope.

"Of course, Your Holiness, of course."

Pope Urban looked into Père Jean-Pièrre's eyes long enough to make the priest a little uncomfortable as if Urban was searching his soul. "You are a good man, Père Jean-Pièrre. *Grazie.*"

"*Prego.*"

Père Jean-Pièrre tucked the pope's letter into an inside pocket next to the letter that Luigi Fuseli had given him before hurrying to catch up to the others. "*Sono diventato il postino per il Papa,*" he muttered to himself smiling at the thought of being the Vatican mailman.

When he reached the others, they were already boarding the elevator. The operator asked whether they enjoyed their audience with the pope and many voices began to talk at once. So it was not until they stepped out of the elevator where Cardinal Bertelli was waiting for them that Père Jean-Pièrre noticed that Alphonse was missing. He told the cardinal who immediately asked, "Do any of you know where M. Ouimet is?"

"He said he needed to find a toilet," said Claude. "Yes, yes," the sisters agreed.

Looking alarmed, Cardinal Bertelli crossed to the secretaries behind the broad mahogany desk. An urgent conversation in rapid Italian before the nearest secretary picked up the telephone to call security.

Alphonse had meant no harm. He had wandered away looking desperately for a toilet. Stumbling upon the *Scala nobile*, the broad staircase that led down from the Vatican Apartments, he had exited on the third floor and now was looking for someone, anyone, that could direct him to the nearest bathroom. Passing a door, he saw a nun washing the marble floor inside. At his loud "Excuse me" she jumped and let out a small yelp. "Sorry, sister," he said. "Can you tell me where to find a bathroom?"

The old nun backed away holding her mop before her and muttering "*Io non parlo inglese.*"

Alphonse whipped out his phrasebook and looked up 'bathroom.' "*Stanza di bagno,*" he cried triumphantly when he found the phrase.

The nun nodded and, still wary, beckoned him to follow her out into the hallway. She pointed to the end of hall where light was filtering through an open door. "Along there?" said Alphonse impatiently.

"*Si, si! Stanza di bagno. A sinistra,*" she said.

"Thanks a lot, sister," Alphonse told her and hurried off. He found himself walking along the Loggetta of Cardinal Bibbiena between small benches under antique maps of the world on the left and the tall windows on the right that gave a panoramic view over the city. Almost running now, he kept going until he found a door and passed into a large anteroom. "That's it," he said to himself when he spied a heavy wooden door set in the opposite wall. Joy turned to rage as he tried the handle and found that it was locked. Desperate he looked around for a key and saw one lying next to a statue of Cupid standing in a small niche. The key was certainly ancient. He placed the large skeleton key in the brass keyhole and managed to unlock the door after a couple of tries.

The door opened into a large rectangular room with a high barrel-vaulted ceiling. A square stove, replica of a Roman *calderium*, which would have heated Bibbiena's bath and the room itself, was the only furnishing in the room. Alphonse stepped in and gasped. Naked images of nymphs and horny satyrs covered the walls. And there was Apollo sporting a giant penis as he was springing from the bushes. The fact that someone had painted over Apollo's member with crude white paint only emphasized its size. And there were images of the naked Venus admiring herself in the mirror, lying between the legs of Adonis, swimming through crystal waters. Every inch of the room was covered with ribald images from classical mythology. Oh my God, papal porn, thought Alphonse, horrified, not realizing that he had stumbled into the *Stufetta della Bibbiena*, Cardinal Bibbiena's hot room. The paintings had been created by the cardinal's good friend, Raphael.

The room once sported a large ornate bathtub complete with a solid silver tap shaped like a leering satyr but the bathtub had been removed long ago. The nun had indeed directed Alphonse to the nearest bathroom but these days it lacked a bath and it never did have what Alphonse was really looking for, a toilet.

Rushing back out into the airy loggetta, Alphonse looked down the hall to make sure he was alone. No sign of anyone. One of the windows was open. Feeling he had no choice, Alphonse unzipped, pointed his penis out the window and watched as his yellow stream arched into the garden below. Feeling exquisite pleasure at relieving the pent up need for micturation, Alphonse began to hum *Panis Angelicus*. A loud scream coming from his right startled him so much that he jumped back and started spraying a panel on the opposite wall, a panel which was also the work of Raphael. Panicking now but unable to stop his own golden stream, he stumbled back spraying the two closest benches before scoring a bullseye on an ancient map and accidentally flooding the holy land.

"*Merde!*" Alphonse shouted unaware of the irony. He had just managed to stumble back to the window and was squeezing out the final drops when he heard a new sound, running feet accompanied by the sounds of clanking armor. Two Swiss Guards appeared as Alphonse was zipping up and within seconds, he was backed against the far wall with two well-sharpened partizans pointed at his throat.

As Swiss citizens, Swiss Guards tend to be fluent in German, Italian and French so when Alphonse raised his hands and said in French, "I got lost and..." the older guard feinted at Alphonse's chin and told him to be quiet. Alphonse nodded.

Within a minute, two plainclothes Vatican police advanced down the loggetta each carrying a snub-nosed Hechler and a Koch MP-5 submachine gun. As they reached the end of the loggetta, the Swiss Guards moved to each side of Alphonse and stood to attention. Alphonse was frogmarched back to the elevators and escorted down to ground level. Père Jean-Pièrre, the only one of the pilgrims who understood Italian, had been listening to the radio communications and had picked up enough to realize that Alphonse had caused a major problem with Vatican security.

Over the next three hours, Alphonse told his story over and over again, punctuated with frequent apologies. When he had finished, the senior security personnel withdrew to one side and discussed the breach of security in hushed tones. Finally the Captain of the Swiss Guards insisted that they all turn in their Vatican passes and that Père Jean-Pièrre take responsibility for Alphonse. The priest agreed, with some private reservations. After handing in their passes, the pilgrims were escorted back out into St. Peter's Square.

When the pilgrims finally made their way back to the white minivan Cardinal Bertelli said nothing until they were back at their hotel at the Spanish Steps. "I will take my leave of you now," Bertelli said frostily. "You have the next few days to explore the city. On Friday morning you will be leaving so please be ready with all your luggage packed by 6:30 a.m. Enjoy your stay."

Alphonse, eyes brimming with tears of shame, began yet another apology but the cardinal had already turned on his heel and within seconds he was gone.

Annoyed at the taciturn cardinal's lack of forgiveness, and remembering the times he had eagerly awaited Alphonse's colorful confessions, Père Jean-Pièrre put his arm around his parishioner's thin shoulders and said kindly, "The body makes demands on us at the most inconvenient times, Alphonse. Your failure, if such it was, was of the body not of the spirit."

Alphonse nodded but continued to stare abstractly at the traffic on Via Conditti as tears trickled down his cheeks. The sisters gathered around Alphonse and began to make soothing sounds. Too much raw emotion for Thomas LaRue and Claude Bisonnette who shuffled over to the empty elevator shaft. As he pressed the button to call the ancient elevator car, Claude leaned over to Thomas and whispered, "Well, at least Alphonse can't say he has been thrown out of better places."

### Finding Tito

As soon as he closed the door of his room, Père Jean-Pièrre reached into his pocket and fished out the two envelopes entrusted to his care. Putting aside the envelope addressed to Eddie Magdalena, he opened the one addressed to himself. It contained a note in the spidery hand of his old friend Tito, a note written in Italian. As he read, he could almost hear Tito's rasping voice, see his face illuminated by a single guttering candle as they had drunk absinthe together at their first meeting all those years ago.

*Greetings my dear Jean-Pièrre,*

*My spies tell me that you have returned to Rome at last so I have prevailed on my friend Luigi to get this note to you. As you may have heard by now, I have been struck down by a stroke and now must lie here living on scraps of Vatican gossip. There are plots afoot, my friend, aimed to discredit this latest Messiah, this Eddie Magdalena. I must see you, Jean-Pièrre, before you leave. You know you are welcome any time of the day or night. I rarely seem to sleep anymore so come as late as you like. I am staying in my sister Anna's apartment. The address is on the back.*

*Your friend, the old relic,*

*Tito.*

*P.S. You are being watched. Try to make sure that you are not followed.*

Père Jean-Pièrre crossed to the window and gazed down at the crowds on the Spanish Steps. A calèche driver was haggling with a tourist couple about a fare; a man was drinking from the Old Boat fountain. On the steps, lovers embraced. Père Jean-Pièrre smiled to himself. It would be good to see Tito again. Over a quarter of a century and yet the pain was still there whenever he was reminded of Héloïse's betrayal. To push such thoughts away, he had immersed himself in his pastoral work. It had been a lonely life but rewarding too and he had been present to witness the amazing apparition of Eddie Magdalena. And now? A private audience with the pope. Mind you after Alphonse's disastrous bathroom break, they would probably all go down in Vatican lore. Père Jean-Pièrre laughed, surprising himself, at the mental image of Alphonse stumbling around in Bibbiena's *Stufetta* and then pissing out the window.

Lying down on his bed, he re-read the letter before laying it down on the pillow beside his head. Just twenty minutes, he told himself, closing his eyes. He awoke with a start to someone knocking on his door. Groggily, he levered himself to his feet and checked his watch. Almost nine already.

When he opened the door, he found Thomas and Claude. "Have you eaten, Father?" Claude asked.

"No. In fact, I was just having a nap and ..."

"Oh. Well, sorry to disturb, Father," said Thomas preparing to withdraw.

Claude grabbed his arm and said, "But we were wondering if you would like to come out to dinner with the rest of us. We found a great restaurant last night just off the Piazza di Spagna."

"I'd be delighted. Give me ten minutes."

The pilgrims enjoyed their meal at a local trattoria. The sisters got a little tipsy on the red wine and even Alphonse began to cheer up as the evening progressed. By 11:30 they had returned to their rooms in the top floor suite. Père Jean-Pièrre waited for an hour until he was sure all of his charges were safely asleep before he left his room, shoes in hand, and crept out of the suite. On the landing, he remembered to check that the outer door to the lift was closed all the way. Otherwise, the cage wouldn't descend when he returned. Still holding his shoes, he descended the marble stairs that circled the lift. Once on the ground floor, he put on his shoes and headed up Via Conditti. At the first corner, he checked back to see if anyone was following him but admitted to himself that he couldn't really tell.

On the Via del Corso, he flagged down a cab, a battered old Fiat, and gave the driver the address of Tito's sister, Anna. The taxi driver was an attractive blonde. Probably from the north, maybe even Milan, Jean-Pièrre guessed.

The driver nodded to acknowledge that she knew the address. "Not far from the Ostia Station," she said, "near Testaccio."

Testaccio, 'the ugly head,' named after a huge pile of broken amphorae and terra cotta tiles. Rising to over 200 feet, the mound had been created by Emperor Nero in 55 B.C. Sometimes called the Pyramid, it had grown into a working class district with houses and even wine caves built into the Testaccio.

Leaning over the seat, he touched the driver lightly on the arm and said "I know that it sounds crazy but I'm afraid that someone is following me," Jean-Pièrre said. "Can you tell?"

The blonde driver sat up, suddenly interested. "I can lose anyone. I have been driving in Rome for ten years, Father."

The roads were not busy at that time of night so a tail became more obvious. "I think I see him," she said, watching her rear-view mirror. "Three cars back. A black Mercedes."

Jean-Pièrre peered through the rearview window just as his driver made a sudden turn down a narrow side street. Unable to stop himself, he slid off the seat and ended up wedged between the seat and the floor. "He is the only one turning," she told him, her voice tight with excitement. "He's following us all right."

For the next fifteen minutes, they careened around Rome but no matter what evasive manoeuvres the cabbie took, the Mercedes stayed around fifty meters behind. "He doesn't care that we know he is following," the cabbie told him. "Do you know who it is?"

"Someone from the Vatican," he admitted.

She spit out the open window on the driver's side and made the sign against the evil eye. Not a Catholic then, concluded Jean-Pièrre. "He's very good," the cabbie told him, a note of professional admiration in her voice. "O.K. This time we lose him." Flooring the accelerator of the old yellow Fiat, she yelled, "Hold on!" Père Jean-Pièrre was slammed back in his seat and tried to find two matching ends of a seatbelt to wrap around himself. He managed to get buckled in as they flew past the Pantheon and turned left on a narrow street leading towards the Piazza Navone. Looking back, Père Jean-Pièrre saw that the driver had opened up a larger lead on the Mercedes. The street suddenly widened into a deserted piazza with three exits. Père Jean-Pièrre was about to protest when he saw that they were approaching the only alley that was blocked by two bollards when the driver slewed to a halt, pulled an electronic device out of the glove compartment and aimed it at the bollards. Obediently they retracted into the pavement just as the lights of the Mercedes appeared across the piazza. With a laugh, the driver guided the cab over the bollards which automatically rose up behind her. "He won't catch us now," she told him. Behind them, they could hear the honking of a car horn. "It is a police barrier. I borrowed this," she held up the electronic device, "from my brother who is a member of the carabinieri."

"Well done," Père Jean-Pièrre told her.

When he arrived at Anna's address, a shabby three story block of apartments, a bell in the tower of a nearby church rang once. Worried that Tito's sister would not let him in at such an hour, he pressed the button on the intercom. When he received no answer, he called again and finally a sleepy female voice crackled in the speaker. Identifying himself, Père Jean-Pièrre apologized for the hour and told the woman about the note from Tito. "*Si, si,*" she told him, "We have been expecting you." and buzzed open the door into the lobby.

A tiny grey-haired woman with a careworn face opened the door. "Excuse me for calling so late, signora. I am looking for Father Tito di Belmonte," Père Jean-Pièrre told her in Italian.

She nodded and her face lit up in a weary smile. "Welcome, Padre, he has been waiting for you. I am his sister, Anna."

"Yes, of course. Pleased to meet you."

"Come," she said and led the way down a dark hall. At the end, a faint light leaking from an ill-fitting door.

"He is awake?" Père Jean-Pièrre asked.

"Oh, yes," she told him. "He has been looking forward to your visit." She pushed open the door and there was his friend, Tito, lying in bed propped up by pillows. The room was stuffy and had that airless sickroom smell, an unpleasant combination of medicinal and body odors. To Père Jean-Pièrre, his friend appeared to have shrunk to the size of a strangely wrinkled child but the eyes still glowed faintly in the low light.

"My old friend," said Tito and tried vainly to rise until Anna pushed him gently but firmly back on to the pillows.

"It is so good to see you again," Père Jean-Pièrre told him, grasping Tito's thin white hand. The hand was dry and cold in his.

"I will leave you two," said Anna and quietly closed the door as she went.

"Were you followed?" Tito asked immediately.

"I was, by a black Mercedes, but we lost them."

"Ah, this smells of Buffone's doing. But you are sure you lost them." Père Jean-Pièrre told him about the escape, much to Tito's delight.

When Père Jean-Pièrre finished, Tito nodded his satisfaction before saying in a light, more bantering tone, "Your hair is turning grey, but we were all much younger then, Jean-Pièrre." Jean-Pièrre nodded. "Now tell me about this Messiah of yours."

For the next half hour, Jean-Pièrre told Tito about Eddie. "And you think this man is the true Messiah?" Tito asked.

"He is, how shall I say, larger than life. And his coming had been foretold. So do I believe Eddie Magdalena is the Messiah? I have not heard him claim to be. If and when he does..." Père Jean-Pièrre took a deep breath. "Then I will believe that he is the true Messiah. Frankly I still can't believe that I was one of those twelve chosen to be there when He arrived."

The two men were quiet for some time as Tito regained his strength. Anna knocked cautiously and entered with two pills and a glass of water. Père Jean-Pièrre helped the old man sit up until he had taken his pills and then lowered him with infinite care back on to the pillows.

When Anna had departed again, Tito grabbed Jean-Pièrre's hand with surprising strength and said, "The Vatican has not been idle. You may soon have proof one way or the other. Yesterday I heard through my sources that a group of four highly placed churchmen are afraid that Pope Urban might recognize Eddie Magdalena as the Messiah. To prevent that, they are scheming to set up a DNA test. They hope to prove that there is no connection whatsoever between Jesus Christ and this man."

"But how?" asked Jean-Pièrre, mystified.

"By obtaining a sample of Eddie Magdalena's DNA and comparing it to that of the Savior."

"But he ascended into heaven," protested Jean-Pièrre.

"How quickly we forget," chided Tito. "You don't remember the *santissimo prepuzio* in the Lateran Palace?"

"Ah, yes. Of course."

Tito's eyes seemed to flash in the semi-darkness. "Two hours ago I received a phone call from one of my informants. One of the security guards noticed that the *santissimo prepuzio* had disappeared. But when he and his supervisor returned twenty minutes later. It was still there. The supervisor suspended the guard. I think the original was switched."

"But even if they have it, surely they will still need Eddie's DNA for comparison."

"That will not prove too much of a problem. The Vatican, Jean-Pièrre, has a very long reach."

Père Jean-Pièrre nodded, remembering the unexpected appearance of the papal nuncio after he had said mass last Sunday. "They are assuming that the DNA samples would be totally different. But what if they are a perfect match?"

Tito flashed a wan smile. "That would indeed be a miracle, would it not?"

"I remember you reminding me once that God works in mysterious ways."

"All right. Let's assume that they are a perfect match. I am guessing that the information would be buried deep inside the Vatican vaults never to see the light of day. And your man, this Eddie Magdalena, would be in great danger."

"From the Vatican?" asked Père Jean-Pièrre, incredulous.

"From the Gang of Four, three cardinals and the black pope. And they have their supporters inside the College of Cardinals. There are many who think that accepting this Eddie Magdalena as the Messiah would cause the destruction of the Holy Mother Church."

"And what do you think, Tito?"

"I haven't got long so I will not be affected but I think, if handled right, it could lead to a wave of reform that would clean up the corruption that afflicts the modern church."

"You mean like the abuse of children, the corruption in the Vatican Bank, the excesses of the Friends of Santa Croce, nuns dancing with crucifixes?"

"Oh yes. And much more. But there are some Vatican secrets that will never see the light of day," Tito said gravely.

The two men talked so long that dawn was beginning to poke rosy fingers under the blind of the small bedroom window. When Père Jean-Pièrre noticed that the room was getting gradually lighter, he said, "I had better go. I should have breakfast with my parishioners."

They said their farewells and Anna reappeared to accompany Jean-Pièrre to the front door of the apartment but before they reached it, Anna lifted her index finger to her mouth to signal silence. After glancing back down the hallway to make sure Tito's bedroom door was closed, she guided Jean-Pièrre into her tiny kitchen and motioned to him to sit down.

Puzzled, Jean-Pièrre asked what was going on. "Did he tell you about the woman?" Anna said in a harsh whisper.

"The woman?"

"The one you were interested in when you were last in Rome?"

With a start, Jean-Pièrre realized that she was referring to Héloïse. "No, what about her?" he said, louder than he had intended.

"It is the main reason he was so desperate to see you. He has not got long and he needs to confess."

Confess? "Confess what?" asked Père Jean-Pièrre, feeling an unpleasant sense of foreboding creating a knot in his stomach.

Without replying, she told him to wait in the kitchen while she went to talk to Tito. Père Jean-Pièrre pulled out a chair and sat down at the kitchen table, wondering what great crime Tito might have committed that would require a dawn confession. A few minutes later, Anna returned and led him back to Tito's bedroom. The bedside lamp had been turned off, the bright sliver of sunlight had reached the dresser but gave little illumination to the room. Tito was lying motionless, his face a pale blur against the pillows.

"I'll leave you, Father," Anna said quietly and closed the door behind her.

Sitting in the chair next to the bed, Père Jean-Pièrre directed his eyes at the sliver of light moving slowly across the top of the dresser.

For a few seconds he collected himself as dust motes danced in the beam and said a whispered prayer. Then, without turning to Tito, he said, "You wish to make a confession, my son?"

"Yes, Father," said Tito and launched into the ritual response. "Forgive me Father, for I have sinned..." The familiar ritual calmed both men as Tito began his confession: "For all these years, I have carried a sin on my soul that I have never confessed to any priest. At last, I can unburden myself and beg your forgiveness, my friend." Père Jean-Pièrre was tempted to point out that absolution can only come from God but refrained. "When you were here during Vatican II, I lied to you. Oh, I thought it was for your own good but a lie is a lie. I thought I would be forgiven because my lie saved your vocation but now I am not so sure." Père Jean-Pièrre could feel the tension ramping up within him. "I told you that Héloïse had been married and had just got divorced. It was not the truth. She was still single when you two met. I am sorry, Jean-Pièrre."

Jean-Pièrre, caught completely by surprise, rocked in his chair and, when he turned away from the beam of light on the dresser to Tito's face, he saw a dark afterimage superimposed like a black mask across the glowing eyes. Tito was staring at him silently pleading for forgiveness. Mechanically he gave the sacrament of reconciliation before making the sign of the cross. Père Jean-Pièrre rose and, without another word because he did not trust himself to speak, he left the room.

Anna went to say something to him but thought better of it when she saw the look on Père Jean-Pièrre's face. He let himself out.

Out on the street, he slumped against a lamp post and stood staring down the hill at a stray cat scouting for breakfast. After a long while, he realized that he had absolved Tito's sin but assigned him no penance. True the old priest's lie had saved his vocation. Without Tito, he would never have been present at Eddie's coming. Perhaps Tito had deserved no penance. But still, he was filled with bitterness at what might have been as visions of Héloïse crowded the bright eyes of the dying Tito out of his mind. At last he pulled himself together and walked slowly down the hill looking for a cab. The cat watched him go.

## The Train to Paris

Père Jean-Pièrre arrived at the suite overlooking the Spanish Steps just after seven in the morning. Thankfully, no one seemed to have noticed his return. Quietly letting himself into his room, the first thing he noticed was the papal invitation propped against the television. What to do about that?

Sighing, he looked down on the Piazza di Spagna, almost deserted at this hour, as he tried to decide how to proceed from here. First thing would seem to be to call Eddie Magdalena on the unlisted line. In his head, he worked out the time difference. Sudbury was six hours behind which meant that his call would arrive just after one in the morning. Can't wait for a more convenient time, he told himself. He pulled out his wallet and found the piece of paper with the Whiteheads' unlisted number on it. Picking up the phone, he asked the hotel desk to place the call.

The woman on the desk cautioned him that an overseas connection to Canada might take up to two hours. Even though a new optic cable had been laid just a year earlier, it still could not handle more than 40,000 calls at a time. Nothing to be done. Trying to curb his impatience, Jean-Pièrre dragged the armchair over to the window and watched people slowly gathering on the steps below him.

After he had got hold of Eddie, he would breakfast with his charges and tell them that he had been urgently called away. How would they react, he wondered, if he were to tell them the truth, that he was heading to Paris to find the love of his life.

As it turned out, Jean-Pièrre only had to wait twenty minutes for the call to go through because the North American markets had not yet opened so that stock traders were not yet jamming the lines. The phone at the other end was answered after only two rings. "Hullo." The voice of Lydia.

"Ah, Lydia. It's me, Jean-Pièrre. Sorry to call so late, but I need to speak to Eddie. It's urgent."

"Good to hear from you, Père Jean-Pièrre. I'll get him right away."

A minute later, the deep rich tones of Eddie's voice: "Jean-Pièrre. What's so urgent, *mon ami*?"

When Jean-Pièrre told Eddie about the disappearance of the holy foreskin from the Lateran Palace and the scheme of the gang of four to discredit him, Eddie laughed and said, "I'll be sure to co-operate if someone comes looking for a sample of my DNA."

Jean-Pièrre was startled. "But they want to use it to discredit you." Eddie said, "You know, Jean-Pièrre, I think they'll find a match. Then what?"

"I hope you're right." Jean-Pièrre told him, sounding worried. "Now the other thing I called about. I'm catching a train to Paris."

"Paris?"

"It's a long story."

"Don't worry. I've got all night."

# Part Eight:
# Sudbury, Ontario

## Devil in Her Ear

Rev. Father Thomas del Sarto, the Black Pope, placed his call to the Jesuit Provincial Curia in Toronto at eight p.m. Rome time the next evening, two p.m. local time.

"Father Jakob, please," he asked briskly. "This is Father Thomas del Sarto." Instantly, the voice on the other end of the line became more serious.

"Yes, Reverend Father, I will get him. Can you please hold?"

"Yes, of course."

It was so quiet in Father Thomas's study that he could hear the faint mains-hum that is the background *continuo* to urban living everywhere. Idly, he identified the note as G sharp, three semitones lower than the B natural background hum in North America, 466hz versus 392hz. Was this why Americans tended to move faster than Italians? Were they wired to the beat of a faster universe? In his youth, the Black Pope had been an accomplished organist but lately the pressure of work had ...

A voice came on the phone: "Hullo, Reverend Father. Good to hear from you. This is Father Jakob Holtzer."

"Ah, Jakob, good to hear your voice." The two men had met several times in the course of their work. Father Thomas had taken note of Jakob Holtzer. An ambitious man positioned to rise quickly in the order. "Something urgent has come up, Jakob. I have a task for you that requires the utmost secrecy. I can count on your discretion?"

"Yes, of course, Reverend Father," Father Jakob said.

"Good, good. I was sure that I could count on you. Do you have a pen handy?"

"Yes, Reverend Father."

"It concerns this man who claims to be the Messiah, this Eddie Magdalena, or rather the people who witnessed his first appearance. Eight of them have had an audience with Pope Urban yesterday and, I understand, they received a very sympathetic ear."

Being a shrewd player, Father Jakob risked, "I am sorry to hear that, Holy Father."

Jakob's comment confirmed Father Thomas's opinion that he had chosen the right man for this delicate job. "You can imagine, I'm sure, that any indication that Mother Church is leaning towards conferring her legitimacy on this man could be disastrous. Who knows where such a perilous path might lead us."

"Yes, yes. Quite true, Reverend Father," confirmed Father Jakob. "Anyway, as you probably know, there were twelve people present when Magdalena appeared. Three are not Catholics. Eight of the others are here in Rome at the moment. The other one, a woman named Judy Legrand, did not show up. We have made extensive inquiries about her. She has isolated herself from the rest of the group. She is also heavily in debt. So here is what I want you to do, Jakob ..."

\* \* \*

Judy's phone rang just after three the same afternoon. Judy, who had taken the day off, reached out, but her hand stopped, hovering over the receiver. Could be work checking up on her or, worse, one of those goddamn credit agencies. She decided not to answer. As a male voice began to record a voice mail, Judy became more and more interested.

"Good evening, Ms. Legrand. This is Father Jakob Holtzer, S.J. I understand that you were one of the twelve people to witness the appearance of Eddie Magdalena, and that you are a parishioner of St. Gabriel Lalemant. I am wondering if we could meet soon about an urgent matter. I will make sure you are more than adequately compensated for your time. Please call me back at your earliest convenience. I'll be waiting for your call." The message concluded with a number that had a 416 area code.

A call from Toronto. You'll be more than adequately compensated. With her credit cards maxed out, she could do with a little compensation. She was still bitter about that reporter, what the Hell was his name, ah Marc Baptiste, for stealing her photos of Eddie's arrival. They would have been worth a fortune by now. Judy called back twenty minutes later, and the meeting was set for later that afternoon. Father Jakob immediately booked a seat on the four o'clock flight into Sudbury. During the one-hour flight, Father Jakob opened his briefcase and studied the information on Judy Legrand that had been put together by the ultra secret Seventh Bureau run by Opus Dei. The detail he fastened on was Judy's credit card debt: $23,666 at the moment. Thinking back to the biblical thirty pieces of silver, he had hit on the sum of $30,000 U.S. confident that it would be enough to satisfy Ms. Legrand.

And he was right. Judy readily agreed to the priest's proposal, and for the next half hour he drilled her on the tale she was to tell Eddie Magdalena.

Sensing she was as ready as she would ever be, he asked, "Shall we get started, Judy?"

She nodded. He punched a number into the phone and, when it began to ring, handed it to her. Judy, dazzled by the idea of paying off all her debts, never thought to ask how he got the number of the secret line that Lydia had had installed after Eddie had moved in.

When Arthur answered, she identified herself and asked to talk to Eddie. Intrigued, Arthur passed the phone to the big man. With so much riding on this, Judy launched into a long *mea culpa* about the photographs and about the fact that she had 'missed' the flight to Rome. Eddie told her not to worry. Judy looked over at Father Jakob who silently mouthed the word 'Now' and, taking a deep breath, she said, "Look, could I come over? It's important. I have just heard something that I don't want to talk about on the phone. Would that be all right?"

"Sure," said Eddie, not even bothering to check with Arthur and Lydia. "We'll alert the guardians at the gate that you're coming."

Father Jakob nodded with satisfaction. She was in.

"I'll be there in less than an hour," Judy told Eddie. "Thanks." She hung up and wiped her sweaty palms on her track pants.

"Well done," Father Jakob told her. "You have earned the thanks of Mother Church. Here." He handed her four blue plastic bags with the word 'Sterile' printed on them and a small package of individually wrapped swabs. "You'll need these."

As she pocketed them, she asked, "Where will you be?"

"Right here. I'll just watch some television until you get back."

Judy was not sure she liked this idea but, hey, thirty grand U.S. That had to be thirty-five, thirty-six thousand in Canadian funds.

Father Jakob settled down to watch a rerun of *Roseanne*.

As Judy drove over to Lydia's house, she tried to keep calm, but a myriad of butterfly thoughts were flitting through her brain: What about Lydia, the woman who had screamed at her for taking the pictures? Or Eddie? If he turned out to be the Messiah, it wouldn't take a genius to figure out her role. But there was the money. At least she could stop losing sleep over her credit card debts, and even buy that new quad she had been coveting. And all for an hour's work. "Fuck them all!" she shouted aloud as she turned down Ramsey Lake Road.

The door was opened by Eddie himself. "Come on in, Judy," he told her warmly and led the way to the living room. It was deserted. No sounds coming from the rest of the house either. Best of all, no sign of Lydia. Judy started as if Eddie was reading her mind when he said, "The others are out on the deck. I thought you would like a little privacy. Can I get you anything?"

"No, no thanks. Look, let me apologize for taking the pictures."

Eddie laughed. "That's something I'm going to have to get used to. Did you get my good side?" He turned his head to profile the right side of his face, the one without the scar.

"No. Actually none of them turned out," Judy admitted.

Eddie nodded. "Must have been disappointing. Anyway, that's not what you came here to tell me."

Judy launched into the cover story she had rehearsed with Father Jakob. She had accidentally missed the flight to Rome, slept in, but she still wanted to be one of the twelve. "I am asking for forgiveness, I guess," she concluded, a quaver in her voice, and was that a tear in her eye?

Eddie crossed and sat next to her. Putting his arm around her shoulder, he said, "Nothing to forgive. And we'll save you a seat at the Big Reveal. I think your fellow parishioners will be back in time for it too."

Judy actually burst into tears, and Eddie comforted her. When she recovered herself a little, she asked Eddie where the bathroom was. "Need to freshen up? Use the big one upstairs. That's the one I usually use."

She thanked him and ascended the stairs. At the top, she found the bathroom on the right. Closing the door, she turned on the taps before pulling out the bags and the swab kits she had brought. Now, which ones belong to Eddie? She appeared to be in luck. There were two mugs on the counter, one marked in china pencil 'Eddie,' the other marked 'Mahinda.' There was no way she could know that Eddie had marked the mugs after he had got off the phone. Quickly, she pulled on latex gloves and, taking the two toothbrushes out of Eddie's mug, she put them into separate sterile bags. Next, she swabbed the used toothpaste in the bottom of the mug. Her heart was pounding now, as she pawed through the waste basket and removed some hair that matched Eddie's distinctive thick, dark locks. Next to the bathtub, she spotted a white tube sock and tucked it into her pocket. Finally, flushing the toilet, she tucked the packages into her pockets and exited the bathroom. "I hope you found it all right," Eddie told her when she came back down.

"Oh, yes," she said, anxious to leave.

"Then we'll see you on Sunday," Eddie said, as he conducted her to the door.

"You can count on me," she lied.

"Oh, I'm sure of that," Eddie told her and closed the front door, silently thanking Père Jean-Pièrre for his early morning phone call from Rome.

Grinning to himself, he walked back through the house and slid open the door to the deck. Arthur, Lydia and Mahinda all turned their faces eagerly in his direction. "Père Jean-Pièrre was right," he told them. "The game's afoot."

"Great," said Arthur.

"Did you find anything else out about Père Jean-Pièrre's trip to Paris?" Lydia asked.

"Yeah. Something that'll knock your socks off."

"*Cherchez la femme?*" asked Arthur.

"*Cherchez la femme,*" agreed Eddie and proceeded to tell the others about Jean-Pièrre searching for the love of his life.

"But he's a priest," objected Lydia when Eddie was finished.

"Not any more apparently."

"D'you think he'll find her after all this time?" asked Lydia.

"If anybody can find her, I'm sure Jean-Pièrre can."

"My money's on Jean-Pièrre," said Arthur, delighted at the news, "I'm betting he'll find her."

"Amen," agreed Eddie.

# Part Nine: Paris

### *'À Paris il y a une dame'*

Jean-Pièrre packed quickly and checked out of his hotel before the others were stirring. He was leaving behind not only the Spanish Steps but much of his previous life. Yet he felt a weight had been lifted. As he climbed into his cab, he wondered how the others would react to the note he had left. They would be fine, he told himself. As the driver pulled away down the deserted Via Conditti, he did wonder how the maid would react to the neatly folded clerical garb arranged on his bed.

And what about Arthur and the others back in Canada? Eddie had not even seemed surprised when Jean-Pièrre had called to tell him that he was leaving for Paris in search of his long lost love. Jean-Pièrre had hesitated before confessing that he was leaving the priesthood, too, but Eddie's reaction had been reassuring: "The world has always needed lovers more than priests."

And, of course, Héloïse might well be married. He had promised himself that if she did have a husband, or even a lover, he would not approach her.

Late in the afternoon, he arrived at l'Hôtel de l'Orch in Montmartre. Before setting out the next morning, he indulged in a coffee and croissant on the terrace, his mood swinging between optimism and despair at his chances of success.

Jean-Pièrre knew where to start his search: at the bookstore where Héloïse had worked all those years ago. A picture of Héloïse would have been a great help, but he had not owned a camera in those days. Héloïse had had a little Kodak Brownie. Her pictures had included a shot of the two of them in their favorite restaurant, Antonietta's, taken by the waiter. But, as she still had not finished the roll when they parted, he did not have a copy. He had kept her card but, of course, it was still sitting in a bureau drawer in the rectory back in Sudbury. He did remember that the bookstore was called *la Librairie Galignani*, the oldest English language bookstore on the European continent. At the hotel reception desk, a pleasant woman looked up the address of la

Librairie Galignani for him, 224 rue de Rivoli, and instructed him on how to get there by metro.

Just after ten, he found the bookstore located in a long portico featuring upscale shops near the Tuileries Gardens. Not crammed to the rafters with teetering piles of books like the bookstores on the left bank, the Galignani was laid out with narrow aisles that featured large sections of English literature and fine art books. At this time of the day, there were few customers, and it did not take Jean-Pièrre long to locate the manager, a tall stooped man with a morose expression. Jean-Pièrre's explanation that he was looking for a long-lost lover who had worked here once, evinced no spark of romance. When Jean-Pièrre had finished his tale, the manager said without hesitation, "She may have worked here once but not in the five years that I have been here." Jean-Pièrre nodded, but the forlorn look on his face evoked an unwonted sympathy in the manager who added, "Perhaps you should speak to Mme Rimbaud. Wait a moment."

The manager handed over the desk to his assistant and walked back to a small staircase descending into the basement. Jean-Pièrre followed. Standing at the small wooden gate with its 'Private' sign, the manager called softly down the stairs. A young female assistant with half-moon glasses poised near the end of her nose appeared below. "Is Madame Rimbaud down there?" the manager asked.

"Yes, I'll get her." The face disappeared.

"Madame Rimbaud has been here since the flood," the manager told Jean-Pièrre while they waited. "If anyone remembers the woman you are looking for, it would be she."

A minute later, the girl's face reappeared. "Actually she's not here, M. Foucault. I thought she was in the stock room, but I just remembered she's in the English section." With that, she tripped lightly up the stairs, carefully closed the gate at the top and led the way towards the back of the store and the English Section. "That's her," she told Jean-Pièrre.

Ahead of them, they could see a woman with long grey hair arranged in a bun. She was handing books to a young man on one of the ladders to place on the top shelf of the English Section.

"Ah, Mme Rimbaud, I have brought M. Abélard to meet you. He

is seeking a woman he knew many years ago. *Une affaire de la coeur.*" M. Foucault confided, immediately capturing the interest of the other two sales clerks. "She worked here for a time."

"I am hoping desperately that you remember her, Mme Rimbaud," Jean-Pièrre told her. "Her name is Héloïse Garlande."

The young man peered down from the top of the ladder, his shelf stocking forgotten. The female sales clerk waited, hardly daring to breathe, as Mme Rimbaud removed her glasses, letting them dangle on their chain over her ample breasts. For a few endless moments, she hesitated, trying to recall, and then, nodding her head, she said, "Yes, I did know Héloïse. Very bright woman. She left Galignani sometime in the late sixties when she started showing." Seeing the shock in Jean-Pièrre face, she put her hand on his arm. "In those days, things were different, you know? Single women having babies were not treated as kindly as they are today. The father turned up one day and they had a huge fight right here in the English book section.

M. Simon, the manager at that time, gave her her notice on the spot although the argument had not been her fault. Despite M. Simon, she brought in the baby a few months later to show us girls." She smiled at the memory. "A little girl, her skin the color of copper. Perhaps the most beautiful child I have ever seen. The father was an Algerian. They had been married while she was pregnant but apparently he had disappeared two weeks after the baby was born."

Jean-Pièrre felt a glow of hope. "And you didn't stay in touch?"

"No. We had been work friends. You know how it is. I never even knew where she lived."

"Of course." Jean-Pièrre thought for a moment before finally asking, "When was the last time you saw her?"

Mme Rimbaud sighed and looked up as if the date was written on the skylight. "Oh, a long time ago. I met her once near Les Halles, by chance. Her girl would have been about six or seven by then. Quite tall for her age, I would say. Héloïse did say that it was difficult to bring up a child without a father. The child had had some trouble at school because she was Algerian. Some people are still bitter about the Algerians. But to take it out on such a beautiful child." She shook her head at the idea.

"Do you remember the child's name?" asked Jean-Pièrre.

"It was a strange name. Not French. But no, I don't remember it. I am sorry, monsieur."

"No, no, Mme Rimbaud. You have been most helpful," Jean-Pièrre told her, impulsively clasping her hand. "And don't worry about me. I will find her."

As he took his leave, the younger female clerk impulsively hugged him and told him they were sure he would find her.

"*Bonne chance!*" said Mme Rimbaud, a tear in her eye, as Jean-Pièrre shook hands all round. "*Bonne chance, Monsieur Abélard!*"

Crossing the rue de Rivoli, he wandered into the carefully manicured Tuileries Gardens, found a bench with a distant view of the top of the Eiffel Tower, and sat down to consider Mme Rimbaud's revelations about Héloïse. She had a child by an Algerian. And she had still been a single mother when Mme Rimbaud had last met her. Where would he go from here, he wondered. First find a pay phone and look up her last name. If that did not work, he decided that he would search every bookstore on the left bank in the hopes that Héloïse had stayed in the same line of work.

The blue sky had begun to cloud over while he had been sitting on the bench and, when he looked back towards the Louvre, he saw an ominous buildup of nimbus clouds presaging a storm. After a quick look at his map, Jean-Pièrre crossed the Pont Royal to the left bank, where there was a much greater concentration of both bookstores and bars.

He ducked into a tiny bar just as a clap of thunder signaled that the storm had arrived. A few seconds later, the sky opened. The bar was almost empty and smelled heavily of stale beer and cigarettes. The bartender, a cigarette clinging to his bottom lip, was reading *Le Figaro*. Jean-Pièrre looked around and noted a battered pay phone on the wall near the corridor to the washrooms. He asked the bartender for a telephone book. The man looked up, wiped his hands deliberately on his apron and said, "The phone is only for customers."

"*Bière pression*," ordered Jean-Pièrre, "if I can borrow your telephone book."

Without a word, the bartender reached under the copper-topped counter and slapped down a large phone book in front of Jean-Pièrre. "*Merci*," Jean-Pièrre told him and began to flip through the book while the surly bartender drew him a liter of *bière pression*. Ah, Garlande. His index finger traced down the listings. He counted them: thirty-one. This was going to take a while. Only four began with the initial 'H', none with the name Héloïse. He picked up his beer and the phone book and selected a table next to the phone. The bartender was about to protest then just shrugged and said, "You have *jetons*?"

Tokens? He bought a handful of *jetons* and started with the Garlandes preceded by an 'H.' As he went, he copied down the unanswered numbers in his small daytimer. Only one of the H. Garlande numbers answered, but the voice of a young boy told him it was a wrong number. By the time he had finished the entire list, he had eliminated fourteen names, left his hotel number on eight answering machines and had recorded the nine numbers that no one had answered.

Discouraged, he paid for the beer and left. The rain had almost stopped, but the sky was heavy with clouds. For a while, he wandered aimlessly, wishing he'd had the forethought to have copied down a list of the bookstores in the area while he had the telephone book. On a corner near the Seine, he looked up as the clouds parted and a sudden shaft of light illuminated Notre Dame on l'Île de la Cité.

The sight cheered him. He would visit the famed church later in the day. After all, it would be almost a sacrilege to visit Paris without seeing any of the sights. Just then, the traffic on rue de la Bucherie halted to a cacophony of horns. He turned his eyes away from the towers of Notre Dame and noticed a green drinking fountain featuring four caryatids holding up an ornate dome. Behind it, the Dickensian green facade of the most famous bookstore in the world. Above the door, in yellow lettering: *Shakespeare and Company*.

The place looked as if it were just opening, as three or four scruffy youths were moving out bins of books and blue plastic tarps to protect them from the threatening rain. Jean-Pièrre checked his watch, just a couple of minutes after noon. He threaded his way through the stalled traffic and entered. The absolute antithesis to the neat, orderly shelves of la Librairie Galignani. Books in piles, books balanced at an angle along the staircase, books to the ceiling, books on chairs, books on tables, books on windowsills. A young woman, who looked as if she had slept in her clothes, was spreading books on the faded red counterpane of a small, makeshift bed. She caught his puzzled look, favored him with a warm smile and said in English, "The writers who stay here use the beds when the store is closed, monsieur."

"Ah, I see," said Jean-Pièrre, although he was not sure that he did. Would Héloïse work at this kind of bookstore? Probably not, he guessed. "I'm wondering if a woman named Héloïse Garlande works here."

The woman thought for a moment before stopping a young, bearded man carrying a large black cat and asking, "Dimitri. Know anyone around here called ... ah ..."

"Héloïse Garlande," supplied Jean-Pièrre.

Dimitri shook his head. "Never heard the name, but some of us use *noms de plume*, so I'd just look around if I were you."

"Who would know?"

"George, of course," said Dimitri and left with the cat.

"George?"

"The owner, he from whom all blessings flow," said the young woman. "I think he's still upstairs in his apartment. Second floor. Third floor if you're from across the pond."

Jean Pierre thanked her and mounted the narrow stairs. On the second floor he had to jump aside as two young men pulled a third out of a makeshift bed on to the floor. "Get up, you lazy sod," said one. "We're open and George wants you to clean the windows."

The man on the floor pleaded, "I wrote almost all night."

"Time management. That's the answer."

Jean-Pièrre could hear the clacking of typewriters from two different directions. At the top of the stairs, he found a room with an old upright piano nestled in among shelves sagging with books. He wandered towards the windows at the front of the store, past a narrow alcove filled with a manual typewriter, a desk and a stool. A young, bearded writer was banging away furiously. The windows looked out on to the sidewalk in front of the store. Below, a girl singer and a young man with a guitar were entertaining a small crowd. To his right, another flight of stairs. Jean-Pièrre had to stand aside as a man wearing a turtleneck came hurtling down. A cup crashed against the wall just behind the man's head and smashed. "All I said was I think there's a few cockroaches in the crêpes," the man told Jean-Pièrre.

"Is George up there?"

"Yeah, but you might want to give him a few minutes."

Wise advice, Jean-Pièrre decided and spent the next quarter hour looking at the mostly second-hand books. When he had screwed up his courage, he peered up the narrow stairs again. He heard women's laughter coming from the top. Taking a deep breath, he started up. When Jean-Pièrre reached the top of the stairs, he stopped and stared at one of the oddest sights he had ever seen. Before him stood a thin old man with an equally thin goatee. The man's hair was on fire. Two plump young women, one holding a lit candle, were enjoying the spectacle. Before Jean-Pièrre could make a move to help, the old man casually patted out the fire and announced, "Better than going to the barber and paying his outrageous prices. Quicker too."

The man noticed Jean-Pièrre and asked suspiciously, "Who the Hell are you?"

"My name is Jean-Pièrre Abélard. I'm looking for George," said Jean-Pièrre, trying to ignore the acrid smell of burnt hair.

"Are you a writer?"

"No, no. I'm looking for someone and ..."

"If you're not a writer, get out!" the old man roared. "This is a writers' commune, not a missing persons office." To emphasize his point, he picked up a cup and made as if to hurl it at this intruder, but Jean-Pièrre held his ground and even took a step towards the old man.

"Then what about the slogan that I saw on my way up here?" he said in a voice much more calm than he felt. George, for of course it was he, paused and cocked his head to one side as Jean Pierre quoted: "Be not inhospitable to strangers lest they be angels in disguise."

George, his eyes as wide as a child's on Christmas morning, put down the cup, wiped his hand on his pants and held out his hand. "George Whitman."

"Jean-Pièrre Abélard. Pleased to meet you." They shook hands warmly. George turned to the two girls and introduced them as "my spiritual daughters, Edeltraud and Karin. Three years ago they escaped from East Germany. Their father was not so lucky. That's why I have adopted them as my spiritual daughters." Jean-Pièrre nodded and smiled at the girls. Turning to them, George said, "Leave us, children. And tell Sylvia to put a '*Ne pas déranger*' sign at the bottom of the stairs. Oh, and tell her to come up and help me wrestle the Angel Jean-Pièrre. We will probably need her help."

The girls departed and George motioned for Jean-Pièrre to sit at the cluttered breakfast table. "Now, who are you looking for?" he asked.

"A woman called Héloïse Garlande. Many years ago, she worked at la Librairie Galignani. I've just been there. One woman told me she has a daughter, but the woman did not know the daughter's name."

"And who is this woman?"

"The love of my life, and I have not seen her for a quarter of a century."

George's daughter, Sylvia, a pretty young woman with short blonde hair and a ready smile, appeared just as Jean-Pièrre's story reached the goodbye to Héloïse at the Rome Termini. George introduced her, and quickly filled her in on the backstory. When Jean-Pièrre finished his tale, she reached out, grasped Jean-Pièrre's hand in both of hers and pledged, "We will find her."

"How?" George asked.

"We'll get the writers to check all the bookstores on the Left Bank," she told him.

"I can always count on you to have the answer," George told her. "O.K. How many writers do we have on the premises at the moment?"

Sylvie thought for a moment. "Seven. No, another one arrived just a few minutes ago, down on her luck. So, eight."

"All right." George rose and rubbed his hands together, excited by the prospect of yet another adventure. "Get the writers together around the wishing well and we'll set them to work." He turned to Jean-Pièrre. "Pity we don't have a picture. Still, why make it too easy. No challenge in that."

The writers were gathered around the tiny wishing well downstairs with its sign: 'Give what you can, take what you need.'

After introducing Jean-Pièrre and giving the bare bones of his story, George passed out slips of paper with Héloïse's name on them and dispatched the posse of poets and writers to comb the bookstores of Paris.

"Now we just have to wait," he told Jean-Pièrre. The summer sun had set before the writers began to filter back. The looks on their faces as they reported in was enough to tell Jean-Pièrre that they had not been successful. By midnight, when the store was closing, only two writers had not returned. Finally, quiet descended on the Shakespeare Bookstore. The bins had been pulled in, the door locked when the telephone rang loud enough to startle Jean-Pièrre into full wakefulness. Sylvia snatched up the receiver. It was Dimitri. He had located the last bookstore she worked in. The proprietor said Héloïse had quit about five years before to open a flower shop in Place Joachim-du-Bellay. Sylvia listened quietly for another few seconds before hanging up and bursting into tears. One of the woman writers put her arm around Sylvia's shoulders to comfort her. Jean-Pièrre's mind was so flooded with tragic images of Héloïse that he could hardly breathe.

Slowly Sylvia recovered herself, blew her nose and said, "Sorry. When Dimitri told me the name of Héloïse's flower shop, I couldn't help myself." She looked at Jean-Pièrre and whispered, "Her shop is called, *Les Fleurs d'Argenteuil.*"

"Oh my God," said Jean-Pièrre his own eyes welling with tears in turn.

"What does it mean?" asked a bearded writer with a British accent.

"The convent at Argenteuil is where the original Héloïse was sent when she and Abélard were separated forever," Sylvia explained.

And soon there was not a dry eye among the tiny crowd surrounding the wishing well. Sylvia walked around the well and hugged Jean-

Pièrre. Into his ear she whispered, "It's a good sign. It means she is still thinking of you."

Jean-Pièrre nodded, hoping desperately that she was right. Reaching into his pocket, he found a franc coin and tossed it into the well. "For luck," he told her.

"Yes, for luck." Soon people were passing around coins and tossing them into the well, wishing Jean-Pièrre *"Bonne chance!"*

One by one, Sylvia and the writers retreated to their beds, until a pale girl with long straight hair and Jean-Pièrre were the only people left. He learned that her name was Carmen and she was from New York. "Do you know where the flower shop is?" Jean-Pièrre asked her.

"Sure. It's about a twenty minute walk from here. Maybe less. It's across the river on the other side of Notre Dame."

Jean-Pièrre rose and asked, "Could you show me?"

"Yeah, why not?"

"Wait. Won't you be locked out?"

She laughed. "We all know how to get back in," she told him.

"Then let's go."

## La petite fleur d'Argenteuil

Jean-Pièrre and Carmen had crossed on to l'Île de la Cité, past the brightly lit facade of Notre Dame. When they reached the right bank of the Seine, they walked into the tangle of streets of the First Arrondissement. Just when Jean-Pièrre was convinced that they were lost, Carmen led him through a series of columns that opened up into Place Joachim-du-Bellay, a square dominated by the Fontaine des innocents, one of the largest in Paris.

"It should be just along here," Carmen said confidently. "Ah, that's it." She was pointing at a small flower shop two doors down from le Café Coeur Couronné. At this early hour of the morning, the square was almost deserted.

"Thanks so much, Carmen," Jean-Pièrre told her, and embraced her with a heartfelt hug. "You don't know how much this means to me."

"No problem," she told him as they crossed the square and reached the door of Les fleurs d'Argenteuil. Eagerly Jean-Pièrre looked at the opening hours: ten o'clock. God willing, Héloïse would be here in less than nine hours to open her shop.

"Now that we've found it, do you want to come back to the Shakespeare, get some sleep? I'm sure there'll be an empty bed for you."

"Oh, no, no, Carmen. Now I've come this close, I have to stay, don't you see?" Carmen nodded. "You've been wonderful and so have the rest of the people at Shakespeare and Company. Please thank them for me. If things work out, I'll bring Héloïse around to meet you all."

"O.K. We all want to know how the story ends." She grinned. "We're writers, after all."

"I promise."

Carmen kissed him on the cheek and wished him "*Bonne chance!*"

When Carmen had gone, Jean-Pièrre peered through the darkened window and could just make out a few tubs of flowers, a tiny counter with a cooler behind it. Leaning his forehead against the cool glass of the window, he prayed to Jesus that she would take him back. And then, just in case, he invoked Eddie's help. After a while, he retreated across the street and sat on one of the marble steps that surround the Fontaine des innocents. The sound of running water cascading from the fountain into its bowl was soothing. From somewhere, the faint sound of a solo saxophone.

Throughout the night, Jean-Pièrre alternated between hope and despair. Why would she have anything to do with him? Because of Tito's lie, he had abandoned her. But he could have, should have, checked for himself.

She had even written to him three times in the year after they had parted, letters that still lay unopened in the drawer of his desk. If only she would hear him out, he might have a chance. But maybe she had remarried. And the daughter. Had she heard about her mother's Canadian?

Just before six, as the sun was beginning to brighten the square, Jean-Pièrre nodded off. Half an hour later, a *flic* was shaking his shoulder, saying, "You can't stay here, monsieur."

"What? Oh yes. Of course." Getting up Jean-Pièrre realized that he badly needed to pee. "D'you know where I could find a *pissoir*?" he asked the cop.

The cop smiled and directed him to one a couple of blocks away. On his way back to the fountain, he found a cafe open for those going to work at that hour and ordered a couple of crêpes and a café au lait. The coffee helped wake him. Looking out the window, he watched as a man pushing a cart full of vegetables shook his fist, as an old *deux chevaux* bumped through a puddle created by the morning flush of the gutters and splashed him.

When he got back to the square, the cop had gone and the sun had reached Les fleurs d'Argenteuil. Over the next couple of hours, sounds of the city waking up. As the hour approached ten, Jean-Pièrre almost talked himself into leaving, getting a shower and a change of clothes before meeting her.

A slim woman with attractive streaks of grey in her long hair was striding towards the flower shop. Jean-Pièrre felt his eyes well up. He would have recognized her anywhere. Beautiful as ever.

He rose, walked to the edge of the sidewalk and watched. Across the street, she unlocked the front door and went in. Now? He wondered. A few seconds later, she emerged carrying the crank to unroll the green-and-white awning. When she was finished, he promised himself. But then he waited because she was moving the tubs of flowers out on to the sidewalk in front of the windows.

Before he could make himself cross the street, she went back into the shop. "Now!," he told himself and started across, only to be frightened by a loud car horn as a taxi managed to avoid him. Had she seen him through the window?

He launched himself through the door, and for several long moments they both stood in silence staring at each other.

Héloïse was the first to speak, and there was anger in her voice. "What in the Hell are you doing here?"

"I came to Paris to find you, Héloïse."

"Twenty-five years too late."

"You can't imagine how sorry I am. Believe me. If you just give me a chance, I will spend the rest of my life making it up to you."

"*Casse-toi!*"

"You can curse me all you want, but I'm not leaving here until you hear me out."

"I have work to do." She turned away from him and grabbed a box of potted sprigs of lavender to take outside. Jean-Pièrre stood in front of her and seized the other end of the wooden box. For a few moments, an almost comic tug-of-war, until Héloïse released her end and collapsed on to a stool behind the counter. "You broke my heart."

"I know. I broke my own too. You are the only woman I have ever loved," he told her.

With a bitter laugh, she asked, "So what excuse is there?"

Jean-Pièrre held up his hand, crossed to the door and reversed the cardboard sign on the door so that it read '*Fermé*.' He sat on a stool nestled among the plants and saw that she was watching him expectantly.

"When we met in Rome, I was a priest."

Héloïse stared at him wide-eyed for a few moments before asking, "A priest? You were a priest even then?"

"Yes. I was in Rome for Vatican II. When we first met, I thought I had never seen a woman so beautiful. I think I might have fallen in love with you the moment I saw you. I knew our relationship would change if I had told you I was a priest ... so I didn't. By the second day, I was like a moth to a flame. By then, I knew I had found the love of my life. When I promised to meet you in Paris, I was about to tell my bishop that I was leaving the church. Then I met Father Tito di Belmonte, devil in my ear. He had been following us because another priest had reported that I had been seen with a woman. He told me that you had just got divorced. For adultery." Héloïse was about to interrupt when Jean-Pièrre held up his hand and said, "Let me tell you the whole story, then you can ask as many questions as you like."

Héloïse frowned, thought about it, nodded. "Go on."

When he finished by telling her how he had managed to find her,

Héloïse said, "And now you are a priest no longer?"

"Technically I am still a priest until I inform my bishop. I'll do that as soon as I get home."

Héloïse rose and said, "Wait here. I'm going out back to have a cigarette and think about this."

"Sure. I guess I can wait a few more minutes after all this time."

Héloïse disappeared down a narrow hallway. For Jean-Pièrre, the seconds ticked by so slowly that he felt trapped in his own personal purgatory. "Make this right with her and I'll follow you to the mouth of Hell itself," he whispered to a faraway Eddie.

She was calling his name. The narrow hallway led him to a tiny high-walled courtyard filled with flowers. The only furniture, two wrought-iron chairs painted bright yellow, crammed each side of a shabby table. Héloïse gestured to him to sit on the other chair and pulled out her cigarettes. Jean-Pièrre took her lighter from the table and lit it for her. He could tell that she remembered him doing the same thing in Rome.

"You even bought a lighter, although you didn't smoke," she remarked.

"Yes."

"I've been married, you know."

"Yes, to an Algerian. Mme Rimbaud at the bookstore told me."

"And I have a grown daughter, Pannychis. Tall, brown and beautiful. She's become one of the top models of Europe. Working for Versace. She's in New York at the moment. She's the reason I could afford to open this little shop. And, oh yes, I am a divorced woman now."

"And I am an ex-priest. Seems to me a perfect fit."

Héloïse smiled for the first time. When she put out her cigarette, Jean-Pièrre noticed for the first time that the ashtray was a souvenir of Rome.

In a moment, they were both on their feet. A long kiss. Jean-Pièrre had never felt more happiness.

They were interrupted by a series of odd sounds coming from the street. Héloïse asked, "What is that?"

"Let's find out." Jean-Pièrre took her hand and led her to the front of the shop. Through the window, they could see about a dozen people with guitars, kazoos, even a washboard, all staring at George Whitman who had his back to the shop. Someone spotted them and nodded. George gave the downbeat and the ragged band of poets, anarchists and dreamers launched into an enthusiastic version of 'All You Need is Love.'

"It's the gang from Shakespeare and Company," he told her. "Without them, I might never have found you."

As Jean-Pièrre and Héloïse emerged from Les fleurs d'Argenteuil, the band and the crowd that had gathered broke into applause. George, his fire-singed locks as wild as ever, pirouetted and gave Héloïse a full Shakespearean bow before reciting Portia's famous speech about the quality of mercy. More applause as he finished. In the brief moment that followed, he commanded imperiously, "Well, kiss her, for Christ's sake!"

Jean-Pièrre needed no further prompting.

# Part Ten:
# Sudbury, Ontario

## Père Today, Gone Tomorrow

"What we really need is a bigger venue," Lydia told the working group gathered in Mayor Liz Tyler's conference room.

"Way too late for that now," said Bella Bunter, the mayor's affable Events Coordinator.

"We'll manage," Arthur assured her.

"How many TV crews have booked access?" the mayor asked. "Eight. Three US networks, CBC, CTV, BBC, Israeli, and France's Canal+. They'll be selling on their feeds, so we're bound to get worldwide coverage. You'd have to live in North Korea to miss Eddie's Big Reveal."

"We've adjusted the color temperature of the lighting for television," offered Colin Francis, the technical director for the show, "and we're bringing in giant screens so that the majority of the people up on the hillsides and lining Paris Street will feel like they are really there. We'll even have two screens facing Lake Ramsey, so that people on boats beyond the two hundred meter security perimeter can watch live, too."

"Where are we putting the twelve apostles?" asked the mayor.

Her assistant, Penny Farding, consulted her notes and said, "We have them seated on stage."

"I'd rather you didn't refer to us as apostles, Penny," said Lydia.

"Sorry. But it's how you guys are being referred to in the press," Penny replied, a little huffily.

"Anyway, I don't think all twelve will be here. Of the eight that were in Rome, only seven came back. The seven arrived in Sudbury yesterday. Père Jean-Pièrre apparently took a side trip to Paris to find the love of his life. And he found her. He called and told Eddie that he and his love – her name is Héloïse – were landing in New York this morning to meet the woman's daughter."

"Wasn't he the priest?" asked Liz.

"Yes. I'm still trying to get my head around it."

"Wow!" said Penny. "What a story."

"Just have to play it by ear," said the mayor. Leaning over to Lydia, she added, "How did the rehearsal go the other night?"

"That was supposed to be secret," said Lydia. "How did you find out?"

"A couple of the cleaning staff at Science North saw you people about three in the morning."

"Ah. Went well. Eddie will be dynamite," Lydia assured her.

"Good! Good!" The mayor looked around the table and nodded at the chief of police. "Now, Chief Sawchuk, could you say a few words about the security arrangements."

"Sure, Your Worship." He nodded to his constable who got up and set up a flip chart and a projector before switching out the lights, except for a small one illuminating the chief's lectern and the flip chart. For the next forty minutes, the chief went through the RCMP involvement, both uniformed and undercover, through the concentric security rings that would be manned by his own men and the national force. Arthur missed all but the first and last minute of the forty-minute presentation, Lydia's elbow making sure his eyes were open when lights came back on.

As the meeting broke up, Lydia waited until almost everyone had gone before crossing to Liz and asking, "Mind if I use your phone?"

"What? Oh, sure. Use the one in my office. Bella. Can you and Penny see that all these binders and papers are filed?"

"Sure."

"I'll be outside," said Arthur. "I'll meet you at the truck."

"O.K. I just want to phone to see if Père Jean-Pièrre has arrived yet."

"Don't forget, he's not a 'Père' any more."

"That's right. He's found the love of his life."

"I say good for him," said Arthur approvingly. "And her daughter is a famous model. There's a lot more than meets the eye with Jean-Pièrre." With a wave to Liz, he hit the elevator button to take him down to the underground parking lot.

"Useful meeting," Lydia told Liz as they walked down the empty hallway to the mayor's office. "You must be tired."

"I have wondered why Eddie chose this part of the world. Why not Antarctica? All those penguins to impress." Liz stopped to open her office door, and for a moment she stared at Lydia. "You think he's the real thing?"

"Yeah. I'm beginning to think I do," Lydia said slowly.

"Because?"

"A hundred little things but maybe most of all because I swear I got a glimpse of Eddie trying to learn how to walk on water."

Liz gasped. "Really?"

"Oh yeah. He seemed to be getting the hang of it, too. Right now I've got to phone home to see if Jean-Pièrre has arrived from New York with the love of his life and her daughter."

"The famous model?"

"Pannychis? Yeah, that model."

"God, you do have an interesting life." Liz picked up her briefcase and said, "Just turn out the lights when you're done."

Mahinda answered the phone and told her that Jean-Pièrre had arrived with Héloïse and her daughter, Pannychis, but Eddie seemed to have disappeared again.

On the drive back home, Lydia asked Arthur, "Any guesses about where Eddie went tonight again?"

"Learning to levitate?"

"I'm serious, dear."

"Then I think he rides out to that erratic where he first appeared. I'm guessing if we followed him, we'd find him talking to God. And with my X-ray vision, I could tell you if the Holy Ghost is making up a third."

"Hmmm. Yeah. That's what I think, too. Maybe we should ask him."

"He'll tell us when he's ready."

The sun was just setting when they were waved through by the RCMP security detachment at the top of their driveway. Lydia spotted an unfamiliar silver car parked beside the double garage. "It's got New York plates," she said as she manoeuvred past it into the garage.

Jean-Pièrre, dressed in a blue linen shirt and a pair of jeans, sprung up from the couch when they entered and hugged Lydia, before shaking hands with Arthur. He turned to the slim, attractive woman sitting beside him and introduced her: "I'd like you to meet Héloïse Garlande. Twenty-five years ago, we met in Rome and fell in love. As I told you on the phone, I went to Paris to find her."

"Welcome, Héloïse," Lydia told her. "What a pleasant surprise! I am Lydia and this is my husband, Arthur."

Arthur examined this petite woman with an as-yet-unlined face and salt-and-pepper hair braided into a French twist. Smiling, he extended his hand, but Héloïse reached up and kissed him on both cheeks. Caught by surprise, Arthur blushed. "I've heard a great deal about both of you from Jean-Pièrre," Héloïse told Arthur before taking Lydia's hand and saying, "I am so glad to meet you at last."

"Welcome to our house," Lydia told Héloïse, still trying to absorb the idea that Jean-Pièrre was no longer a priest. Turning back to Arthur, she added, "I'd say it's time to open the bar, dear. I don't know about anybody else, but I need a scotch on the rocks." Arthur nodded and padded off to the bar. Lydia led the others over to the sitting area in front of the dormant fireplace and said to Jean-Pièrre, "You have been busy since we last saw you."

Until Arthur arrived with the drinks trolley, Jean-Pièrre told of his audience with Pope Urban. When Arthur was seated, Jean-Pièrre was about to launch into the story of Father Tito's revelation and the trip to Paris, when Arthur said, "Sorry to interrupt, Jean-Pièrre but Mahinda said that you two had arrived with Héloïse's daughter. Maybe she should join us."

"Oh, yes, of course. After the drive, she went to freshen up and then went out on to your deck to enjoy your beautiful view of the lake. I was out there for a while watching the crew setting up the Canada Day fireworks on a barge up near the snowflake building," said Héloïse.

"I'll go and get her."

She crossed to the curtains drawn across the patio doors and disappeared. A strangled cry had them all on their feet, alarmed. Arthur was the first to reach the doors. As he stepped out on to the deck, Héloïse turned to him and said in a voice filled with panic. "She's gone."

Lydia, who had followed Arthur onto the deck, impulsively hugged the smaller woman to her and said, "She'll be all right."

But as she looked over the head of Héloïse, she saw that Arthur had spotted something. With a look of dread on his face, he reached down next to the swim ladder and picked up a wrap. Under it was a pair of sandals.

"Our canoe is missing, too," said Arthur. "D'you think they are together?" asked Lydia.

"Unlikely. Eddie left before the others arrived."

## You Will Meet a Tall Dark Stranger

The sun was dipping towards the horizon when Eddie arrived at the trail up to the erratic. As he started his climb, he heard unfamiliar music softly playing. For a moment he stopped and listened. Above him, Venus, the evening 'star', had already emerged and, as the sun continued to sink below the far horizon, other points of light winked into view. The music seemed to be coming from the stars themselves. The Big Guy had outdone himself tonight. The tension that had been growing inside Eddie all week at the prospect of the Big Reveal tomorrow evening began to ease. Music of the spheres soothing his savage breast? Wouldn't put it past the Big Guy.

As the moonstruck striations of the erratic came into view, Eddie saw what at first he took to be a campfire, but as he got closer, he realized that the flames, bursting forth in mini-explosions, seem to be coming from a bush with purple flowers. A burning bush? The unmistakable voice of God came out of the flames: "Welcome Eddie. Less than forty-eight hours to the Big Reveal."

"Yeah. All week I've been hoping you might let this particular cup pass away from me. Truth is I'm terrified."

"Nothing so concentrates a man's mind than the prospect that he is to be hanged in the morning, eh?"

"Something like that." Eddie paused and looked at the smiling face of the young Elvis wreathed in blossoms of flame. "Can I call you Dad?"

"No!" The sudden, booming voice makes Eddie jump. "Just be thankful I didn't make you take your shoes off. I wouldn't let Moses even approach me on Mount Horeb without taking off his sandals and brushing the dust off his ugly toes. Call me *Jahweh* if you like."

A name that is no name? Was the Big Guy distancing himself in case the Reveal was a bust? The thought revived Eddie's paranoia and he glanced through the flames at Marie, silently appealing for her help. Dressed in her usual grey habit the color of smoke, she appeared even more insubstantial than usual. "Call him Father," she told Eddie softly, "If He is sending you into the arena, He owes you that much."

Feeling that the Big Guy was getting ready to abandon him, Eddie bowed and said, "*Nos morituri te salutamus.*"

"*Aut non,*" came the ritual reply, followed by a crackling sound as some of the thorns exploded in showers of sparks. The smiling face in the fire said, "Marie is right as always. Call me Father. Certainly you are the product of my seed. By the way, the burning bush is a *dictamnus*, not the thorn bush I showed to Moses. Puts out lots of flammable oil at certain times of the year. Burns like a son-of-a-bitch but if you put it out ..." The flame was extinguished immediately. Eddie was disoriented, afraid to move, as his pupils were wide open and he knew there was a huge drop within a few feet of him. The bush flickered to light again and Eddie could see that none of the leaves or purple flowers seemed the least bit singed. His Father and Marie were now sitting on two of the three camp stools arranged around the fire. "Anyway, take a load off." Eddie sat on the third stool. "This time tomorrow you'll be standing alone on that tiny stage holding the world in your hand. Are you ready?"

"He's ready," Marie assured the Big Guy. "And he won't be alone. I'll be with him."

The Big Guy held up a hand in mock surrender. "O.K., O.K. Stop ganging up on Me." He looked over at Eddie. "Hey, I know how nervous you are. That's why I thought we'd just kind of hang out tonight. I mean, we roughed out the Reveal in the last couple of nights. Any new problems?"

Eddie pondered for a few moments, gazing into the flickering flames of the burning bush. Finally he said, "Last night You said there is no heaven."

"That's right. Ashes to ashes; dust to dust. When these creatures die, they become stardust again, at one with the universe." God made an expansive gesture towards the stars above them and then added, more darkly, "Immortality is not all it's cracked up to be. The creatures of this planet have achieved sentience and are gifted with a sense of beauty. Every sunrise is an affirmation of the wonder of the universe. Why can't people see that sunrises are more precious when they are of a finite number? The knowledge of their own coming deaths is what makes people strive, seek, and contemplate the heavens. Perhaps they can never quite achieve an earthly paradise, but, dammit, they are magnificent when they try."

"But what about hope?" pleaded Eddie. "An afterlife gives us that. Hope that the other asshole will get his. Hope that the saint will live happily ever after."

"Everybody ends up playing a harp? That's paradise? If people really wanted that the world would be full of harp players. Millions of women in long skirts and men in penguin suits playing in vast harp orchestras. Imagine the subways at rush hour. And I sure don't want suicide bombers blowing their guts all over some city bus in my name so that they can get into their weird version of Heaven and fuck seventy-two virgins. You know, if I ever did get around to making a heaven for those fundamentalists that commit obscenities in my name, I'll make the virgins ninety-year-old Catholic nuns who will strangle the bastards with their rosaries the moment they try anything."

Eddie laughed politely. "And no Hell?"

"Hell? No. How vindictive would I have to be to create some eternal torture chamber for the wicked?" God sighed and was quiet for a long time before saying, "I suppose there is a kind of afterlife, a kind of last judgment. For most people anyway. I remember the existence of almost every one. They live on in my dream. The truly wicked, I forget. At the moment of death, they become absolutely extinct."

"As if they had never existed." Eddie said almost to himself, nodding slowly. "That might work. Yeah, that might work."

"Of course it will work, Boy," God reassured him, patting his arm. "What these people have to realize is that, if they can work together, they can build their earthly paradise right here. They don't need a pretend paradise up in the sky."

"But Jesus tried and failed."

The normally pleasant face of Elvis darkened in fury and Eddie rose ready to run. God crossed in front of him and started to pace, before stopping next to the erratic and staring down at the valley below where the railroad crossed the high road. He stood there silently for some time. Marie motioned Eddie to sit.

With his back to the others, the Big Guy began: "We need to look back at the Christ and the hopes I had for him. I'd told Abraham that I would look after the Jews, make them my Chosen People. Why? I was looking for a people ready to take the plunge. The eastern Gods were dying one by one and now the Jews were ready to believe in a single God. Me. It took a few plagues, but eventually the Egyptians let my people go. On Mount Sinai, I made a covenant with Moses ..."

"So that explains the burning bush tonight," muttered Eddie.

"Yeah, I know. Kinda corny but I was hoping to keep it light tonight," said God, smiling at the Holy Spirit.

"And Moses led your Chosen People out of Egypt in 1460 B.C.," Eddie reminded him.

"1447 B.C. actually. Exodus was wrong. Anyway, the history of Jerusalem had been a bloody one long before the arrival of the Jews. Still is, come to think of it. In 63 B.C. the Romans added Jerusalem to their empire. At the time, I wondered about my promise to Abraham, my covenant with Moses. Should I give them the strength to throw off the yoke of the Romans? In those days there was no shortage of men who wanted to wear the mantle of the Messiah, eh Marie?"

Marie nodded, remembering the Jewish revolts of that time. "Hezekiah called himself the Messiah. The Romans, as usual, killed them all. Later in Christ's time, Judas the Galilian, Hezekiah's son, tried on the mantle and had some success. He raided the royal armory in Sepphoris and started a guerrilla war declaring that only traitors paid tribute to Rome.

"He even got that Roman puppet Joazar, the high priest, fired, but of course the Romans counterattacked, burning Sepphoris to the ground and crucifying Judas and two thousand of his followers," added Marie.

God, laughing at the memories, said, "And there was that giant, Simon. And Athronges who placed the crown on his own head. And Theudas, the wonder-working prophet who in 44 BC crowned himself Messiah and brought his followers to the Jordan, promising to part the river to reclaim the promised land from Rome. The Romans slaughtered all of them.

"So, of course, sending the Jews yet another mighty warrior like David was no way to beat the Romans or to spread the new monotheism. Instead, I came up with a more radical solution: an olive branch rather than a sword. And to do that, I gave Mary a son."

"*Et verbum caro factum est?*' intoned Eddie.

"And the word was made flesh," the Big Guy translated. "Yes. Covenant fulfilled. Trouble was that Judea was producing Messiahs by the sackful, and I was worried Jesus would get lost in the crowd. After Jesus had grown, I had John the Baptist meet the Messiah and baptize him to seal the deal.

"And, like Judas the Galilean, Jesus told the priests to render to Caesar what was Caesar's. Separation of church and state, always a good idea. Beware theocracies! They always govern with enormous cruelty and stultifying stupidity."

"But unlike Judas the Galilean, Jesus told his followers to turn the other cheek," Eddie said.

"Turn the other cheek. Radical idea. How would that work? Well, as it came to pass, not so fine. When Jesus was brought before Pilate, I underestimated the cleverness of Caiaphas, who forced Pilate's hand." He shook his head at the memory. "Stupid really. What was I thinking, or rather hoping, trying to sell non-violence to the Jews, a people in thrall to the Romans. They are a tough and resourceful desert people, the Jews, but I asked too much of them. When Caiaphas rallied the crowd behind the rebel Barrabas, I could see that this new way of seeing the world would die in that backward place called Judea. For a while, I considered absenting myself, but then Marie, bless her, pointed out that to spread the gospel, it would be necessary to reach the uncircumcised multitudes."

"Some Jews became early Christians and tried to insist that Christians needed to be circumcised to fulfil Abraham's covenant, but I countered by sending in St. Paul. He preached that Jesus had fulfilled the covenant by dying for mankind's sins. Circumcision was no longer necessary, as the covenant had been fulfilled. I know, I know, the theology's a bit tricky, but the future of Christianity depended on the larger world of the gentiles accepting it. Not surprisingly, few were willing to have their foreskins lopped off to qualify.

Eddie nodded agreement and quoted, "For in Christ Jesus neither circumcised or uncircumcised avails anything but a new creation."

"Yeah, that's Paul preaching to the Galatians. Now, even more important was to make Christianity the official religion of the dominant people of the time: the Romans."

"So the people who nailed Him up got to spread the gospel. You know I never thought of that before. It's fucking genius!"

The Big Guy nodded and said modestly, "Thank you, thank you very much" in a perfect imitation of Elvis.

"Or totally crazy," Eddie added, shaking his head. The Big Guy nodded again and favored his Son with an ironic smile. "So you set up Constantine."

"*In hoc signo vincit*? The sign Constantine saw in the sky. Yeah," the Big Guy admitted.

"I've been getting the impression that you never interfere in human affairs," said Eddie.

" Almost never, but I needed the believers. Anyway, Constantine could have ignored the advice."

"In this sign you will conquer? What self-respecting emperor is going to turn that down?"

"The historian Josephus says Constantine hesitated, not sure. So that night I sent the Christ in a dream to tell him to have his soldiers paint their shields with the intertwined Chi/Ro signifying the Christ in Greek. That vision did the trick. In the morning, Constantine drew up his cavalry on a small plain next to the Tiber. The Tiber is not very wide near Rome, and Maxentius, Constantine's rival and his brother-in-law, had built a bridge across the river consisting of two ramps joined in the middle by heavy iron rings that could be removed. The idea was to feign an assault on Constantine's army and then retreat across the bridge. As Constantine's cavalry stormed across, Maxentius' soldiers would pull the rings, and the bridge would collapse taking with it the enemy cavalry. If the trick had worked, and it was a clever one, Christianity would probably never have amounted to more than a small sect."

"Did you know it wouldn't work?" Eddie asked the Big Guy.

"Know? Not really. I mean Constantine's cavalry could have misjudged the charge. Maxentius' troops mighty have proved more loyal. All kinds of variables. I was almost certain though."

"Then you really can't predict the future?" asked Eddie, still not really able to believe it.

"Oh, I can predict much of the future by extrapolating from the vast knowledge I have of the past and present. For instance, I can see that these humans are going to create such a revolution in technology that one day, fairly soon, a huge section of the population will be able to communicate face-to-face from anywhere in the world. But, like everyone else, you're really interested in what is in *your* future. Well, I predict that you will meet a tall dark stranger ...."

Eddie shook his head in frustration. "That's all you got?"

The Big Guy put his arm awkwardly around Eddie's shoulders. "Look, you can do this. If the whole thing comes off the rails, I'll shake things up a little."

"You'll intervene?"

"Only if it's truly necessary. Look for me in Jerusalem."

Eddie got up, walked away a couple of paces and stared up at the ghostly birch that had cushioned his arrival.

Marie looked significantly at the Big Guy. "What?" He hissed. She turned her head towards Eddie, a look of concern on her face. "All right," said the Big Guy and walked over to stand next to Eddie. "Look, Son, I didn't make a clockwork universe. If everything was predestined, I would know how every war, every relationship, every sickness, every game turned out. I would shrivel with boredom. Like you, I need a little unpredictability in my life." He sighed and added, "Otherwise eternity just seems to go on forever."

"Then you don't know how my future is going to turn out," Eddie persisted, a note of alarm in his voice.

"Well, not exactly. The uncertainty principle, you know. But hey, you'll be fine," said the Big Guy in his most soothing voice.

Eddie, who had been shaken by the doubt in the Big Guy's voice, asked bitterly, "I lost count of the death threats. You got a plan for them?"

"There's a plan in place ..."

"Oh, yeah. How reassuring."

"And you'll have me," said Marie softly.

Eddie felt on the verge of weeping. "Yes, Marie, I'll have you." He crossed, leaned down and kissed her gently on the cheek. She grasped his hand and he felt reassured. Tomorrow would be fine. He would have the Holy Spirit.

"And with Marie's help, you can move mountains, my Son."

"He will do you proud," Marie told the Big Guy, flashing him her best Mona Lisa smile.

After a few moments, Eddie said, "So finish your story."

"Ah, the Battle of Milvian Bridge. As he had planned, Maxentius led his troops across the bridge and commanded them to form phalanxes on the far bank. Constantine smiled at his troops, pointed to the *Chi/Ro*, freshly limned on his shield in blood red paint. "*In Hoc Signo Vincit!*" he shouted, the signal for his Gallic cavalry to charge. Maxentius and his men had already crossed the bridge and were still manoeuvring into place when the cavalry struck their lines. When Constantine sent his foot soldiers in after his cavalry, Maxentius and his troops engaged them, but such was the fury of the onslaught that soon panic spread through the Roman ranks and they, together with their mercenaries, crowded back to the bridge, Maxentius among them. But the bridge was never intended to hold so many. The stout metal rings snapped with the sound of thunder and Maxentius, in full armor, plunged into the Tiber and drowned. Those troops who did not drown with him broke and ran, all except Maxentius' most loyal Praetorian Guard. At the instant that the last of the Praetorian Guard was put to the sword, the center of the Roman Empire shifted with the new emperor to Byzantium.

"Christianity became the official religion of the empire and then outlived its fall to become the greatest power in Europe for more than a millennium. In the next millennium, the European explorers, armed with Christian missionaries, spread the gospel around the world."

"So you won. Billions of believers," said Eddie.

The Big Guy was silent for a few moments. Finally, he nodded. "Billions of believers, the life's blood of a deity. Especially if you add in the protestants, the Jews and the Muslims, all people of the book whether they call me God, *Jahweh*, or Allah. And the various religions do a lot of good. Often they tend to the poor, the sick, the lonely and even the mad. The unbelievers don't tend to open soup kitchens, provide rest for weary travelers or give hope where there is none. Religion gives humankind a sense of their place in the universe, provides ceremonies to mark the important stages of life: birth, adulthood, marriage and burial. And the most beautiful cathedrals, mosques, temples, and the religious art and music that fills them, to lift up the spirits of humankind in a way that nothing else does."

"But ..." muttered Eddie.

"But. The priests, pastors, rabbis and imams are always tempted to freeze human thought and punish creativity. Their followers are told they must believe in childish tales like the Ptolemaic universe and not believe in the big bang, evolution or particle physics."

"Even though Galileo proved that the universe did not revolve around the sun."

"Right. And the Catholics still haven't forgiven him for telling the truth, although I predict that they will soon."

"Maybe we're all finally ready to turn the other cheek," Eddie suggested.

"I think so, but it won't be easy. They must be channeled away from warfare which, right now, spurs far too many of their greatest technical innovations."

"Swords to plowshares," observed Eddie skeptically.

"Swords to plowshares exactly. They are developing means of communication that no one dreams of today. Right now, the internet is in its infancy, but over the next twenty-five years these creatures will develop the most incredible web of communication seen on any of my worlds. People in tiny villages in the Himalayas will have communication devices in their pockets, if they have pockets, that they will be able to use to contact almost anyone on the planet. These devices will also be able to access almost the entire sum of human knowledge. Privacy will become a thing of the past, a mixed blessing. But it will mean that there are no secret wars, no silent holocausts. Wars will become small, and local. So you see, it's just possible that in another century or so, swords will be ceremonial, except for extinguishing small wars."

Eddie considered the Big Guy's predictions for a few moments until he remembered something He had said earlier. "You said that you might intervene in Jerusalem. Why Jerusalem? Seems to me that Jesus didn't fare too well there."

"Because Jerusalem is the center of the universe as far as the three religions that make up the people of the book are concerned."

"Jews, Christians and Muslims."

"That's right. And the piece of land most contested by all three is what the Muslims call the Dome of the Rock. To the Christians and Jews, it is the Holy Temple Mount. As the Messiah, you will be expected to go there and proclaim the new covenant with God."

"And how am I getting there?"

"Pope Urban is going to Jerusalem to meet Jewish and Muslim leaders and try to reduce tensions among the people of the book. Ten minutes ago, Jean-Pièrre arrived at the house on Ramsey Lake Road.

As you know, he is carrying a letter to you from Pope Urban inviting you to a secret meeting at his summer residence, Castel Gandolfo. If, and only if, you can persuade the pope that you are the true Messiah, he'll invite you and your apostles to accompany him to Jerusalem. There you will be able to meet the leaders of the other two religions."

"And my job is to tell them what?"

God let out a long sigh. "Look, whenever one of my worlds discovers the atom, the fundamental building block of the universe, I watch for a while to see if they manage to destroy their own civilization by smashing it. More than half can't resist. Earth came close time and again during the Cold War, but humans seem to be clever enough to have pulled back from the brink, at least so far. And I think the human race can keep the lid on the nuclear option at least for the next half century. The real problem that no one is talking about is the explosion of the planet's population. With you recognized as the Messiah, we will have a chance to fix it. But how to do it?" The Big Guy held up his left hand and began to count on his fingers. "One: turn the other cheek. You would think that wars reduce the population but the truth is quite the reverse. Two: educate women and give them absolute equality. The birthrate in poor countries will drop like a stone, just as it has in more developed countries. Three: reduce the gap between rich and poor and people will be more content, happier."

"You couldn't come up with something easier, like water into wine for instance."

"Hey, 'All You Need Is Love.'"

"Doesn't that lead to babies?"

"Improve the lives of women and they'll have fewer babies."

"So birth control is O.K.?"

"Sure. Quality of life over quantity."

"And abortion?"

"Does it improve the lives of women?"

"In most cases, I guess."

The Big Guy stared at him for a few moments. "Look, what does everyone say they want?"

Eddie thought for a moment and then said sarcastically, "All I want for Christmas is world peace."

"Right! That's why Christians celebrate Christmas much more than Easter."

"Santa Claus?"

"I love Santa Claus. Look how altruistic he is. He's bringing a sackful of world peace."

"O.K. So why don't I wear a red suit?"

"Nobody in Asia would recognize you, and we need everybody. No, no, if this world is to flourish, we need to stabilize the population, educate women, raise the standard of living of the poorest, and find alternative energies to power future innovation and stop the planet from warming. Even I'm not sure it will be possible. The priests, the multinationals, the military industrial complex, all kinds of forces will try to stop it. Hell, there are at least three assassins heading this way as we speak. But beginning tomorrow, with Marie's help, I'll do my damnedest to convince people you are the Real Deal. You're the man for the job, Eddie." He turned back towards them and his face was bathed in an ethereal light. Raising his hands to the heavens, He shouted, "This is my Son in whom I am well pleased!" The Voice echoed around the hills in such a huge rumbling that it provoked the evacuation of every mine in the Sudbury area on the assumption that the tremendous noise had come from a major rock burst yet to be located.

"I'll do my damnedest too, Big Guy," said Eddie, rising too. Caught up in the moment, he almost hugged his Father but drew back at the last moment. Marie entered him and his doubts about tomorrow seeped away.

"That's the spirit! That's the spirit! Now let's chill for a bit. I prepared a surprise."

He pointed to an ornate table that Eddie hadn't noticed before probably because it had only just appeared. It was piled with marshmallows. "I just can't get enough of these things," the Big Guy confessed. "Here," he tossed sharpened sticks to Eddie and Marie. "Start toasting."

Eddie took his stick and was about to reach for a marshmallow when the stick turned into a massassauga rattler. "Shit!" cried Eddie, leaping up and dropping the writhing snake.

God laughed until tears were running down his face. Marie leaned towards Eddie and said, "When He did that to Aaron's rod, Aaron nearly punched him."

"I feel like doing the same," Eddie confessed.

"And I'd probably deserve it," admitted the Big Guy cheerfully. "Now, anyone for hot chocolate?"

\* \* \*

Eddie was feeling positive about the Big Reveal when he got back to the yacht club and locked his bike away in its hiding place. A swish of hull over sand as he pushed Arthur's cedar strip canoe out into the lake under the moonlight. The resulting ripple caused the lake's still starscape reflection to undulate gently like a restless universe. Silently, he dipped his paddle into the water and headed for the Whiteheads' place. He was comforted, as always, by the shadowy presence of Marie now sitting on the front thwart. The technicians on the fireworks barge were too busy testing their circuits to notice Eddie's canoe gliding past them. Lights illuminated the crowds waiting for the Canada Day display, but no one seemed to notice a solitary canoe plying through the darkness.

As the Whiteheads' deck came into view, Eddie spotted a tall figure standing there staring back at the canoe. She was illuminated dimly by the light coming through the curtained patio doors. A few more silent strokes and Eddie had no doubt that this was the most perfect woman he had ever seen. Standing like a statue next to the railing wearing nothing but an enigmatic smile, the woman allowed Eddie's canoe to drift in next to the swim ladder before leaning over him and saying in a quiet husky voice, shaded with the accents of Paris. "I have been waiting for you."

Eddie, who could think of nothing to say, offered his hand and she stepped lightly into the boat, expertly keeping her balance as it rocked from side to side. In the bow, Marie did not turn or murmur a word. Eddie was on his own. Quickly, he reached forward and grabbed a cushion, placing it between his legs. Hardly rocking the boat, she knelt before him and he realized that she was almost as tall as he. And then it hit him: she was the tall, dark stranger. Gently her lips brushed his and she whispered, "I am called Pannychis. That's all you need to know for now." Eddie went to tell her his name, but she pushed a finger to his lips. "I came here just to meet you, Eddie." With that, she smiled, starlight sparkling in her eyes, and turned around, easing herself comfortably between his legs. With a quick glance at the deck above them, he pushed off towards the middle of the lake. As the shore lights and the noise of the crowds receded, Eddie noticed that Marie was no longer sitting on the forward thwart and, at the same instant, felt a familiar but indescribable tingling as she dissolved into him.

Soon Eddie shipped the paddle and they drifted to a halt. Eddie put his arms around Pannychis under her small breasts, and they sat there contentedly feeling each other's body heat as the ripples subsided. A still point in a turning universe, the canoe was surrounded by stars. The ripples began to spread again as they explored each other's bodies and finally made love, a most difficult feat in a canoe. In the entire world, only a few Canadians, mostly natives, and a couple of Norwegians had ever mastered this technique. Eddie, trained by Arthur and filled with Marie, had become an expert, one of the first Americans to do so. Many would expect a nun, even a former one, would cover her eyes with her wimple and groan with disapproval, but Marie's transformation into the Holy Spirit had brought her divine wisdom.

"For saints have hands that pilgrims' hands do touch, and palm to palm is holy palmers' kiss," Eddie quoted into Pannychis' ear.

Eddie would need the love of Pannychis in the coming days and so, being at one with Eddie, Marie felt a most un-nunlike thrill of pleasure as the lovers consummated this their newfound love. At precisely that moment, the skies above them filled with bright blossoms of fire.

For the next forty-five minutes, they lay together staring up at the bombs bursting in air. "Does this always happen?" Pannychis asked.

"The fireworks? Only with you, I swear."

"Happy Birthday, Canada." The fireworks above them were spelling out the same message.

"Yeah. Happy Birthday."

Faint sounds of applause in the distance, but soon the lake became quiet again. A chaste kiss, and then Pannychis sat back against Eddie and sighed with pleasure. "Hear that?" whispered Eddie.

"No," Pannychis confessed.

"Listen carefully. It's very faint."

Pannychis sat up and, as she turned her head slightly, she finally heard. "My God," she cried, "It's Leonard Cohen's *Hallelujah*."

"Sung by Marie, but it sure sounds like K.D. Lang, huh?" he told her, and she nodded agreement.

Together they listened: "I remember when I moved in you, / And the Holy Ghost she was moving too / And every single breath we drew was Hallelujah!"

For the rest of the night, the lovers huddled under the grey cloak that Marie had provided and got to know each other. She told him of her difficult childhood, picked on for being a brown-skinned Algerian. Her mother had tended her bruises when she stood up to the bullies and given her the courage to confront them. "Then they stopped when I became the best player on the first woman's ice hockey team in France. I played right wing for the under-eighteen *Patineurs de Paris*. We used to play at the old Piscine Molitor, a swimming pool that had been turned into an ice rink. We were good enough to play in the *Championnat de France du hockey sur glace féminin* four years ago but lost to Grenoble. I scored two goals and was featured in an article for *Paris Match*. I got a call: Could I meet Giancarlo Ferri, a famous designer for Christian Dior. Over the last few years, I have become famous as a model. It has been exciting as Hell, but lately I find I am growing tired of it. And I'm getting old, almost twenty-two."

Eddie talked to her of his own childhood and the discovery of the dead nun, Marie, that had changed his life utterly. Just as dawn began to paint sky and water, Pannychis asked, "Then you really are the Messiah?"

Eddie kissed her and said, "Yes, I'm beginning to believe I am." With a start, he realized that this was the first time he had actually laid claim to the role.

Pannychis looked up at the sound of a motor launch. "We've got company," she said.

"Oh shit! The RCMP. Your mother and the others must be frantic."

Eddie waved to the woman in working blues as the launch came alongside. "We'll head back," he told her.

"You don't make it easy, Eddie."

"Forgive me."

The young constable blushed. Forgive *Him*?

## Papal Plea

When the call came, Lydia snatched up the phone. For a minute she listened, the others staring intently. As her face relaxed, so did everyone else in the room as they realized that the news was good. Finally she said thanks and hung up before announcing, "She's safe. The RCMP patrol boat found her in our canoe." As everyone in the room sighed with relief, she added, "But she was not alone. She was with Eddie." Everyone began to speak at once until Héloïse, the smallest person there, held up her hand to silence them.

"She is my daughter. I will meet them. Lydia, can you supply me with a robe? I believe my daughter left here wearing nothing."

"Of course." Lydia hurried upstairs.

"If the rest of you will be so kind as to give us a few minutes alone on the deck."

"Yes, naturally," said Arthur, as Lydia returned and handed Héloïse a Thai silk robe with a dragon motif. The others all nodded assent, except Mahinda, who had just finished showering in the upstairs bathroom. Hearing the canoe bump into the swim ladder below, he wiped the steam from the bathroom window and was just in time to bear witness to Messiah and maiden stepping out of the canoe. The fairest of them all, Mahinda muttered wistfully and forced himself to turn away as he heard the voice of Héloïse say, "Here, you will need this" as she thrust a robe at her naked daughter.

"*Merci, maman*," she told her mother with a disarming smile.

"And you are Eddie," Héloïse said, turning to the tall man standing next to her daughter. Eddie nodded. For a few moments, Héloïse stared at him curiously. "And I see you have met my daughter."

"Oh, yes, ma'am. She is wonderful. I am sorry I kept her out so late."

"I am Héloïse Garlande, Jean-Pièrre's friend," she said, leaning forward and reaching up on tip-toe to kiss him lightly on both cheeks.

"Wonderful to meet you, madame," Eddie said, meaning it.

"Héloïse, please."

"*Maman*, I need a shower," said Pannychis.

"I'm sure you do. Come, we'll ask Lydia which bathroom to use.

Eddie said, "If you two are going inside, could you ask Jean-Pièrre to come out. He has something he needs to talk to me about."

"Of course," said Héloïse. "I know you will be busy today, but Pannychis and I will be here tonight with Jean-Pièrre."

"I'm glad."

Just then Jean-Pièrre appeared carrying a silver tray with coffee and croissants, and the two men settled themselves at the table under the umbrella. The women took their leave. As soon as they were alone, Jean-Pièrre passed Eddie the envelope with the letter from Pope Urban.

"From the pope," he told Eddie. "The invitation to meet him at his summer residence."

"At Castel Gandolfo?"

"Yes. Pope Urban wants the meeting to be in secret, even from his own people. That's why he wrote the note himself," explained Jean-Pièrre, as Eddie stared at the red papal seal for a moment before snapping the wax and pulling out two sheets of paper. "It's handwritten in Italian," Eddie pointed out, handing the letter to Jean-Pièrre.

"Urban does speak English quite well, but I'm guessing that he doesn't feel comfortable writing in English. Of course, his Spanish is excellent." Jean-Pièrre held up the second page. "Look. There is a translation on the next page signed by Luigi Fuselli. He is the pope's valet. The pope trusts him implicitly." Jean-Pièrre was lost in thought for a brief time before saying, "I'm guessing that he doesn't trust anyone except Luigi. Here." He handed Eddie the English translation.

"Actually, with Marie's help, I think I can make out the Italian, but I guess I'd better stick to the translation," Eddie told him. For the next couple of minutes, Eddie read and reread Luigi's translation. Then he went through the pope's original message. Finally, he looked up and said, "It's an invitation to visit him at his summer residence. Marc's already arranged my flight to Rome. Pope Urban has arranged to have me picked up at the airport. What's new here is that he tells me to bring any of, what he calls, 'the twelve.' Eddie handed the letter back to Jean-Pièrre who went through it while Eddie talked. "What kind of impression did you get from Pope Urban? Can we trust him?"

"Ah, Pope Urban strikes me as an honest and compassionate man. And he seems to be keeping an open mind about whether or not you are the Messiah. Trouble is, he has a lot of enemies in the Vatican, especially a group that Tito calls 'The Gang of Four.' Three cardinals who have allied themselves with the Black Pope. They will do anything to discredit you. If the pope gets in their way, who knows how dangerous it might be for both of you."

A moment of silence and then Eddie said, "Marc got me two tickets to Rome so I could take somebody else." Jean-Pièrre nodded. "Good. I want Pannychis to be with me."

Jean-Pièrre looked at Eddie, puzzled. "But you've just met," he said.

"It's not like you and Héloïse have been lovers forever either."

Only for twenty-five years, thought Jean-Pièrre, but said, "I'll make sure her name is on the second ticket."

"What about his invitation to the other twelve?" said Eddie. "How many should we take?"

"Why not call ourselves 'the apostles'?" said Jean-Pièrre. "That's what everybody else seems to be calling us."

Eddie laughed. "The Apostles. Sounds like a Southern Baptist college football team. It'll do, though."

"Talking of the apostles, did Judy Legrand visit you?"

"She certainly did. Just about cleaned me out of toothbrushes and face cloths."

"So she got your DNA. It will be back in Italy by now. What do think? Will comparing it to the *santissimo prepuzio* fragment from the Lateran Palace provide a perfect match?"

"Yeah. When I asked the Big Guy about it earlier in the week, he just winked. But if it's is a perfect match, what will they do with the information?"

"Hard to say," acknowledged Jean-Pièrre after giving the matter some thought. "Obviously if there is no match, or their scientists are unable to extract the DNA from the *prepuzio*, they will release the results to the press immediately. If the match is perfect, on the other hand, I doubt if it will ever see the light of day."

"I think you're right," admitted Eddie.

"And if that happens, I think all of our lives might be in danger, especially yours and that of Pope Urban," said Jean-Pièrre looking grim.

Eddie nodded. "I'm in your debt, Jean-Pièrre."

"No, quite the reverse. Without the trip to Rome, I would never have met Héloïse again. I owe you for leading me to the love of my life."

"I'll be blushing if you keep this up," said Eddie. "Look, *mon ami*, I've got a big day coming up, and I need to get some sleep."

"Just before you go, we haven't decided how many of the apostles to take," Jean-Pièrre reminded Eddie. "I will come, with Héloïse, of course. Now I've found her, I'm afraid to let her out of my sight. We'll keep in touch with Lydia and Arthur who will be ready to fly to Rome on a moment's notice if we need them. Mahinda and Marc can look after things here. As for the others, I think it might be too dangerous."

Eddie rose, yawning. "Sounds good. Gotta sleep. If I'm not up by two, send somebody to wake me."

"That I will," said Jean-Pièrre. "And I'll get on the arrangements for the meeting with Pope Urban."

"Good man."

Eddie was about to retreat into the house when Jean-Pièrre stopped him. "One more thing. I had quite a bit of time to think on the flight back from Rome, and I came up with an idea." Eddie waited expectantly. "Well, it's about the DNA. I think that we should obtain our own sample. Then we can get it independently tested. That way, we can present our own evidence if the Gang of Four destroy their sample."

"So how do we do that?" asked Eddie intrigued.

"There were actually three parts to the *santissimo prepuzio*. The one at the Lateran Palace seems to have disappeared. And we know that the Gang of Four have it. The tiniest piece belonged to Bishop Cybo. It had been placed in an ornate reliquary in Santa Maria degli Angeli, but no one has seen it for over a century. Our only hope is to find the original fragment that was hidden so long in the tiny village of Calcata Vecchia. Trouble is, it disappeared six years ago. We would have to track it down."

"Actually, you would have to track it down, Jean-Pièrre."

"Me?"

"Well, you and Héloïse, of course."

Jean-Pièrre laughed, looking at Héloïse. "Are you ready for this?" he asked her.

"I wouldn't miss it for the world."

"The four of us will fly into Rome right after the Big Reveal," Eddie said. "You and Héloïse will head for Calcata, and Pannychis and I will take the papal limo to Castel Gandolfo."

"Oh, yes. But how will we stay in touch?"

"Good point," said Lydia. "Arthur and I will fly in to Rome the day after you and set up a sort of command center. We'll stay near our hotel, and you people can check in with us at least once a day."

"Here," said Jean-Pièrre, extracting a card and handing it to Lydia. "The Hotel at the Spanish Steps where we stayed during our papal visit."

The others nodded and commented about how pleasant their stay had been. Lydia handed the card to Marc Baptiste. "Can you book the suite where the others stayed?"

"I'm on it," said Marc, getting up.

"Oh, and two more tickets to Rome."

Marc checked his notes. "Four arriving Monday, two arriving Tuesday?"

"Yes," said Lydia.

"At this point I can probably only get first class," Marc pointed out. "Eddie told me he would rather fly economy."

"That's right. I'd meet more believers there, but it's more important to make this connection with Pope Urban." Eddie stopped and for a moment seemed irresolute. He's consulting with Marie, guessed Arthur. "Yeah, put us in first class if that's the only way to get to Rome on time."

"You got it," said Marc, leaving to find a phone. For a moment, he stopped and turned back. "What's the time difference to Rome?"

"Six hours," Jean-Pièrre told him. "They're six hours ahead of us."

"Marc!" called out Lydia as he reached the door. "Better book the whole suite, then when Jean-Pièrre and Héloïse are finished at Calcata Vecchia, they won't have to worry about where they are going to stay."

"Got it."

"What do you want me to do?" asked Mahinda, feeling left out.

"Ah, Mahinda," said Eddie. "I would like you and Marc and Jules to stay here and keep in touch with the press and the rest of the apostles. Lydia or Arthur will keep in touch from Rome. I'd like you and the other apostles to be ready, so make sure everyone has a suitcase packed."

Eddie stifled yet another yawn and said, "Have we forgotten anything?"

"Well, we do have one problem that might turn out to be trouble," said Jean-Pièrre slowly. "My former parishioners are going to be shocked at me for not only quitting the priesthood, but also for throwing away my vocation over a woman. I'm most worried about the Dionne sisters. They are pretty conservative."

Eddie was suddenly wide awake. "That's right. I doubt if they'll approve of Pannychis either. Could you arrange a meeting with them? How about two o'clock at their place. I'll go upstairs and get some rest."

"Consider it done."

## Sisters

"Where are we going?" Eddie asked Jean-Pièrre, when their car had managed to get through the checkpoint at the top of Arthur's driveway.

"The sisters live in the Flour Mill," Jean-Pièrre told him while checking in his mirror for paparazzi pursuit. So far nothing, but Jean-Pièrre pulled the car on to the shoulder, braked and backed into the Yacht Club Road. Turning off his lights, he waited. "They've got a big ramshackle house on King Street just behind the silos."

"So what are we doing sitting here?" asked Eddie.

"Waiting for the press to clear ... here they come."

They watched as five cars went flying past. "There they go," said Eddie.

They waited a few more minutes in case there were any stragglers.

Only two more cars passed. While they waited, Jean-Pièrre told Eddie about the calls he had made. "I made the easy calls first. Thomas then Claude and finally Alphonse. They were all O.K. with me leaving the priesthood. Surprised, but O.K. with it. The one that surprised me the most was Alphonse. He told me that he understood and that it was hard to live without a woman."

"Ah, Alphonse," said Eddie, smiling. "He would know. You can't have forgotten that he used to visit the whore house on Elm Street most Saturdays." Jean-Pièrre began to blush. "And then he would come to you for confession and you'd masturbate in the confessional." Seeing the startled look on Jean-Pièrre's face, he added. "I can't blame you. Alphonse is right. We all need love and, for a quarter of a century, you really had no one, Jean-Pièrre." Eddie had already figured out that his own mother had been Alphonse's whore du jour, and it was not something he wanted to think about.

"Then my masturbation was not a sin?" Jean-Pièrre asked.

"It hurt no one. You had something to look forward to all week. Not a sin in my universe."

"I never really thought that onanism was a sin anyway," Jean-Pièrre confessed. "You caught me by surprise, though. I felt as if I had violated the sanctity of the confessional."

Eddie said, "I know you would never ever do that, Jean-Pièrre."

"Seems as if the Holy Spirit is keeping you up on things. Anyway, Claude's reaction was the funniest. He didn't seem to mind my leaving the church for Héloïse. He was worried that I'd have to find a job. Even offered to see if he could get me on as a school bus driver. 'Always need drivers,' he told me. Which is true, of course."

"And the sisters."

"Ah, the sisters," repeated Jean-Pièrre as he pulled his car out on to Ramsey Lake Road and headed towards the Flour Mill. "My guess is they are in shock. Annette answered the phone when I called. I just told her it was urgent that we see her and didn't give her a reason."

The Dionne sisters lived in an old brick house with a veranda on King Street. The house was so close to the flour mill silos that the shadows of its twin towers fell across their porch during the winter months. Jean-Pièrre pulled up behind the sisters' old blue van.

Annette answered the door and led them into the large living room. There, she seated them on the couch in front of the TV while she got her sisters out of the kitchen. "Why am I not surprised that the place is immaculate?" asked Eddie.

"For the sisters, cleanliness really is next to godliness," Jean-Pièrre remarked.

The two men stood as Annette led her sisters out of the kitchen. None of the sisters was smiling. A long silence while everyone was seated. And no offer of coffee and cake, Jean-Pièrre noted to himself.

Finally, taking a deep breath, Jean-Pièrre began, "Perhaps I should start. I know you are unhappy with the fact that I am no longer your priest. Let me tell you how that happened and how I found Héloïse after losing her twenty-five years ago because of a lie." The sisters maintained a frosty silence as he launched into his story.

By the time he had finished, Annette, Cécile and Yvonne had softened towards him, but Émilie said, "But Père Jean-Pièrre, or should I say M. Abélard, none of what you say alters the fact that you took an oath to serve God as a priest."

"Yes, Émilie, I did and I tried to be a good priest. But when I learned the truth about the love of my life, I knew I had to find her. I ask you, all of you, to be happy for me."

"He has found love, ladies. There can never be too much love in this world," said Eddie. "And I have fallen in love with Héloïse's daughter, so I have found love too. Neither Jean-Pièrre nor I have hurt anyone by finding someone to love. Quite the reverse. Remember that you have each other to love."

"You are living in sin, both of you," said Émilie.

"For thousands of years, most poor people got together and made families without the benefit of clergy. Even Catholics these days sometimes get divorced, as you know."

"Père Goriot says we should not have anything to do with you," Annette pointed out.

Jean-Pièrre had been replaced by Père Jean-Joachim Goriot, an ancient priest who had thundered against the Antichrist and his dupe, Jean-Pièrre, from the pulpit last Sunday. The Gang of Four had a long reach. "Père Goriot is entitled to his opinion," Jean-Pièrre said, "but you sisters have seen the miraculous events yourselves. I beg you not to leave us now just before the Big Reveal."

The sisters began to whisper among themselves. Finally Annette, their usual spokesperson said, "We cannot promise. We have a lot to think about."

Jean-Pièrre rose and, looking at Eddie, shook his head. "I'm sorry, Eddie. I didn't think that my love for Héloïse might affect the Big Reveal."

Eddie stood too. "It is right, sisters, that you should be careful. We're leaving now. I thank you for stating your misgivings so clearly. Jean-Pièrre and I will still love the four of you no matter what you decide. Let's go, Jean-Pièrre."

The sisters rose, too, in obvious confusion and accompanied the two men to the door. "We are sorry to have caused so much trouble, but really we don't know what to do."

"The car will be here in a couple of hours to take you to Bell Park. It will be driven by Marc Baptiste. If you decide not to come, he will understand. Goodbye, ladies, and God bless."

"They're very upset," Jean-Pièrre said as he backed out of the driveway. "Do you think they'll come?"

Eddie smiled and said, "Oh, I think we can count on them. They are wonderful, those women. We can't do without them."

At the precise moment that Annette closed the front door, the sisters heard the distant bells begin to toll from St. Gabriel Lalemant. At the same time, the sound of the Agnus Dei began drifting down the hall from the living room. The four sisters looked at each other until Cécile asked the others, "Did anyone turn on the television?"

The others shook their heads. "Maybe one of us sat on the remote," suggested Yvonne. "Wouldn't be the first time." The possibility took the edge off their fear, but still they tiptoed tentatively down the hall, unsure of what they would find. At the archway into the living room, they stopped. The heavy curtains had been closed, and the only light in the room issued from the television set. On the screen, a choir of monks arranged before an altar, their faces obscured by their cowls, sang the Agnus Dei. The sisters were familiar with the song asking the lamb of God to forgive the sins of the world and give us peace, because it was traditionally sung at high mass. As the monks intoned the final verse – *Agnus Dei qui tollis peccata mundi / miserare nobis, dona nobis pachem* – they parted to reveal Marie dressed in her nun's habit. A collective gasp from her sisters as Marie walked towards them, until she filled the screen.

"It's been too many years, my sisters. Hallo, Annette. You are looking well. Cécile, are you still knitting baby clothes for the orphans?"

"Yes, of course ... is it really you?"

"It is me, and at the same time more than me. I will try to make it clear as we talk. And it is so good to see you, too, Yvonne and Émilie. And you are all sitting in the same chairs as when *maman* and *papa* were alive. It's good to see that some things never change."

"Your chair is here, too, Marie," said Annette, pointing to a worn armchair that had once been blue.

"I like to think it reminds you of me," said Marie.

"But why did you leave us?" Annette persisted. "Yes, why?" muttered Marie's other sisters.

Instead of replying, Marie walked slowly down the steps from the altar into the empty nave of the unnamed church, the camera tracking with her. As the camera pulled its focus back, an armchair came into view, the only furniture visible in the entire church. It was a clone of the one that sat empty in the Dionnes' livingroom. "I left because of Dad's brother, Uncle Renard. Remember the time we all went camping up at Windy Lake one summer?" The sisters nodded. "Uncle Renard followed me into the woods. I was only seventeen and you girls were even younger. Anyway, he told me that I had grown into a beautiful woman. Then he asked me if I had ever seen a man's private parts. I told him no, but he undid his pants and ..."

"Enough, Marie. After you left, he tried to befriend me, but I told the others and it stopped," said Émilie, obviously distressed by the unpleasant memories.

"And then he got the cancer," said Cécile. "And died two years ago," added Yvonne.

"He told me that if I breathed a word to anyone, he would say I tried to seduce him," said Marie, "and no one would believe me over him, as he was a well-respected electrical engineer. I thought he was right, so I ran. I hitch-hiked west and eventually ended up in Winnipeg, where I lived on the street for over a year before the Grey Nuns there took me in as a novitiate. I will always be grateful to them. In Winnipeg, I became a nun and trained as a nurse. I lived happily there for many years. But even that was not to last.

"For the past couple of years, I worked in the psychiatric ward at the St. Boniface Hospital. There, I had helped treat a patient called Caleb Jackson. He had killed his two children when his wife left him, but had been found not guilty because of his mental state. Well, after nearly three years or so, his psychiatrists pronounced him sane enough to make visits into town, as long as he was accompanied by one of the staff. One afternoon, I was the staff member that went with him. He was a very good looking man, and quite charming, so I didn't mind. We went to the movies to see *Twins*. Just before the movie started, he excused himself to go to the toilet. He was gone for so long, I began to get worried. I was just about to go looking for him when he came back with pop and popcorn for both of us.

"After the movie, it was time to go back to the hospital. I was about to suggest that we get a taxi, but he was already talking to a young couple that had just seen the same movie. I could see that they had succumbed to his charm. "I'm sure Benjamin and Alice, here, wouldn't mind giving us a ride, would you folks?" he said when I mentioned the taxi.

"Not at all," Benjamin said and his wife, Alice, readily agreed. Stupidly, I went along with the arrangement, and soon we were riding in the back seat of their car making small talk. On the way, Caleb suddenly began to talk about the murder of his two kids, as if he were talking about someone else. Alarmed now, I told Benjamin just to drop us at the next light and we'd find our way from there. Benjamin agreed. No way he wanted this man in his car, but before he could brake, Caleb had a knife to his throat. When Alice screamed, he told her to shut up or he'd kill them both. Alice began to cry. Then he instructed Benjamin to get us on the Trans-Canada Highway heading west.

"An hour or so later, Caleb told him to turn off on a small side road and to keep driving until he told them to stop. After about twenty minutes – by that time you could hear a pin drop in the car – Caleb spotted an abandoned barn, and told Benjamin to pull in and park the car so that it could not be seen from the road. Before he would let any of us out of the vehicle, he pulled out a package of those long cable ties and ripped it open with his teeth. Then he told me to put my hands behind my back and he zip-tied them together. He did the same to the two others and told us to walk into the barn. Alice began to cry again and Caleb slapped her. The interior of the barn was quite dark. There, he cut my cable tie, gave me a roll of duct tape and told me to secure Benjamin and Alice to two posts about six or eight feet apart. When I was finished, he tied my hands again and gagged the couple with duct tape. He found almost $200 and a couple of credit cards in Benjamin's wallet and Alice' purse. I was terrified that he would kill both of them and me too, but he didn't. Instead, he led me back to the car and we drove east on the Trans-Canada past Winnipeg. "If anybody ever finds those two bozos, they'll tell the cops that we were headed west," Caleb explained.

When he got too tired to drive, he locked me in the trunk and slept in the car by the side of the road. When he let me out of the trunk and let me go to the bathroom, I asked him where he had got the knife and the other stuff. He laughed and said, "Remember when I got us the popcorn? I slipped out to the hardware store across the street from the movie house."

"For the rest of the trip, he didn't tie me up any more. Instead, he had me take some meds he had stolen from the hospital that made me almost comatose. When he turned north past Sudbury, he made me take a larger dose of some drug. I passed out. It seems that Eddie found me, but I only woke up when I found myself on the back of his motorcycle. I felt ... I felt as if I was a totally new creature. Had I died? I'm still not sure, but somewhere on that ride with Eddie, I had become the Holy Spirit."

"We saw you from the bus," said Yvonne, excitedly.

"Yes."

"Welcome back, Marie," Yvette said.

"What happened to this Caleb?" asked Émilie.

"He was arrested the next day in Timmins. The couple were found a couple of days later, hungry and thirsty but otherwise O.K."

After a few seconds of silence, Cécile asked, "Then Eddie really is the Messiah?"

"Yes he is, my lovely sisters, and he needs you tonight."

"Then we'll be there. Won't we?" said Yvonne. They all agreed.

"All you need is love, my sisters," said Marie and each of them felt a warm embrace from their older sister as the television faded to black.

### The Big Reveal

On the day after Canada Day, crowds once again packed Sudbury's Bell Park. By mid-afternoon the park was so full that the police had closed Paris Street and allowed it to fill with people too. As sunset approached, Bella Bunter, Events Co-ordinator for the city, was getting frantic phone calls from Bill Payette, City Manager, about the phalanxes of portapotties that had been set up on the Paris Street side of the park, well away from Lake Ramsey, and in the two parking lots on the other side of the road. "There aren't enough of them," he told Bella. "They just keep coming. Holy crap! We've got 3,608 units but already the lines are miles long. We've got to get some more. God knows where from, though."

"I'll see what I can do, Bill," she soothed.

"I bet they didn't have this problem at the sermon on the mount."

"I don't think the Bible even mentions the problem, Bill. Don't worry, I'm on it."

"Thanks, Bella."

Over the next couple of hours, her staff made dozens of phone calls, and by five p.m. another 420 battered old portable toilets had arrived by Hercules transport at the Sudbury Airport. A grateful Bill Payette delegated a couple of assistants to find trucks to bring the units in and find a place for them. When the units arrived and were set up, Bill celebrated with a hot dog and a Pepsi from one of the many food trucks lining Paris Street.

On his way back to the venue, Bill stopped at one of the line of vendors doing a brisk business from their booths. "Looking for a souvenir?" asked the young woman manning the booth.

"What have you got?" asked Bill, thinking that maybe something to remember this day would not be a bad idea.

"These are selling well," she told him, pointing to a box of copper medallions. Bill picked one up and looked at it closely. On one side, quite a good likeness of Eddie's head; on the obverse side, the legend 'I have been Eddified.' At only $2.50 a piece, they would make good souvenirs for his staff, so Bill bought a dozen.

The woman put them in a bag and, as she handed it to Bill, she asked, "Wanna T-shirt too? I'll give you a deal."

Bill laughed. "O.K. Let me see them."

She handed him two Ts, one red, one blue. "We're keeping a kind of tally," she explained. "Which would you like?"

The red shirt had Eddie holding a pitchfork and the legend: Eddie the AntiChrist. The blue shirt had a picture of Eddie releasing a dove and said, "Eddie Magdalena, Messiah." On the back: 'I have been Eddified.'

He bought a blue one for his teenage daughter who was convinced of Eddie's divinity and had been vacuuming up information about Eddie as if he were a pop star.

"So which one is selling the best?" he asked.

"Oh, the blue ones. Haven't sold many red ones at all. Funny. I thought we'd sell more. Oh, I did sell a dozen of the AntiChrist shirts to a couple of born-again Baptist pastors from Mississippi."

Bill looked up at the sky. The sun had finally sunk below the horizon. In the red afterlight, a line of noctilucent clouds like streaks of bright angel hair were woven together like a garland just above the horizon.

On stage, Alphonse fidgeted in his chair, listening to the loud rumble of the voices beyond the drop in front of him. Fear was rising in him as the moment approached when the fly man would lift the drop, expose him and the others to the audience and, even more terrifying, to the millions tuning in around the world. The eleven apostles, plus Héloïse Garlande, had been sitting backstage for over an hour now in a row of ornate chairs on a curved riser, elevated four feet above deck level. Leading down in front of them was a series of six broad stairs, each riser marked with glow tape so that they could be negotiated in the dark if necessary.

To no one's surprise, Judy Legrand had not appeared. Instead, despite her promise, she had chosen to spend the evening at Sudbury Downs Racetrack where she was rapidly depleting her windfall by backing a string of losers.

Alphonse had been seated next to the Dionne quadruplets. Safest place for him, thought Jean-Pièrre who sat between Alphonse and Héloïse. Lydia, Arthur and Mahinda came next, and Thomas LaRue and Claude Bisonnette completed the twelve. Thomas and Claude were having a grand time watching the quiet backstage bustle. The apostles had been warned that at some points during the evening, their risers would move both vertically and horizontally. They had been cautioned by the assistant stage manager working stage left not to attempt to stand unless she triggered a green light to indicate it was safe to do so.

"Five minutes," announced that same ASM, a thin woman dressed in black and wearing a one-muff headset. "Next call is for places." Alphonse felt that he could not get his breath. Émilie, seated beside him, grasped his hand and said kindly, "You will be fine, Alphonse."

"Yes, yes, you'll be fine," agreed Cécile before lowering her voice and telling her sisters, "I've never been so excited in my life!"

Alphonse was not the only one feeling overwhelmed by the event that was about to start. Lydia had been clutching Arthur's hand so hard that he had just extricated it because his fingers had gone numb. "Sorry," she whispered. "Oh God, I can't stand the wait."

"Less than five minutes now," Arthur said.

"Look, those mirrors are moving up there." Claude nudged Thomas and pointed to the overhead trusses holding banks of the new Intellibeams that could project beams in multicolored patterns focused through the moving mirrors in the heads of the instruments. Claude had just seen the lighting board operator testing his lighting presets for the show, without striking the lamps.

"Places," the ASM informed them. Everyone sat up straight. A few seconds later, Heather Chandler, the stage manager sitting in the temporary control booth elevated above the final tier of bleachers, alerted the TV technicians in the trucks parked on the verge of Paris Street above the park and then gave the order to take the show up: "Go Cue 3."

The curtain in front of the apostles rose slowly as the banks of moving lights began to flare and sweep across the crowds in patterns resembling the noctilucent clouds that had scratched bright scribbles across the western horizon. Parcans clustered on trusses to the right and left of the stage, warmed the deck and picked out the apostles in flattering flesh-colored light. Alphonse looked like a deer caught in the headlights, but the others handled the startling flood of light well.

Snowhere, a Sudbury band known from coast-to-coast, broke into John Lennon's 'Imagine' as three tight follow-spots came up on their lead singer, Logan Banks.

*Imagine there's no Heaven*
*It's easy if you try*
*No Hell below us*
*Above us only sky*
*Imagine all the people*
*Living for today ...*

No heaven? No Hell? Jean-Pièrre was puzzled – and he was not alone. Above the band, glowing faintly, sur-titles with Lennon's lyrics seemed to hover in space. Many sang along, but there was an undercurrent of confused conversation buzzing through the night.

Mayor Liz Tyler was not happy with the VIP seating she had been assigned. She and many of her council were sitting near the back of the tier of seats, their view of the stage partially blocked by one of the lighting trusses. Turning to Penny Farding, her personal assistant, she asked sourly, "What the Hell happened with the seating?"

Penny shrugged. "I don't know. When I pointed out that we had reserved seats in Row B, the woman led us up here. I guess for some reason they labeled from top to bottom." Liz started to say something but Penny rushed on. "And look over there. She pointed to their right. The premier and his people are jammed in next to the sound mixing board."

At the thought that Premier Peterson had worse seats than she did, Liz smiled. "Somebody's idea of a joke," she suggested, not realizing how right she was. Eddie had told Lydia that he did not want the dignitaries attending to have all the best seats. "Save the front few rows for the disabled and the poor," Eddie had told Lydia.

*Imagine there's no countries*
*It isn't hard to do*
*Nothing to kill or die for*
*And no religion too*
*Imagine all the people*
*Living life in peace ...*

"Fucking hippies ain't got no respect," shouted old Wendell Crudup from the top of the hill, but by that time so many had taken up

Lennon's anthem that few heard his complaint.

*You may say I'm a dreamer*
*But I'm not the only one*
*I hope someday you'll join us*
*And the world will be as one*

Maria Magdalena had waited in line all night to be one of the first into the park. Despite a patdown and a walk through one of the metal detectors, she had been cleared and had managed to get a seat on the center aisle in the third row. Ever since the reporters had dug up Eddie's background and identified her as his mother, Maria had convinced herself that Eddie had followed her up to Canada to take revenge on her for rejecting him all those years ago. An hour before Eddie was due to appear, she had heard chants of "AntiChrist! AntiChrist!" somewhere over to her left, but the voices were soon silenced. Eddie was the AntiChrist, of that she had no doubt. She had given the monster birth but soon she would set things right. Maria, now going by the name Lisa, had originally been afraid of what Eddie might do to her but over the last few days, she had hatched a plan that would get rid of the threat that Eddie posed. She would also go down in history as the destroyer of the AntiChrist. For the Big Reveal, she had worn her long, black hair back from her face in a chignon held up by a single hair stick carved into the shape of an ornate knife. Security personnel rarely look at hair ornaments. Besides the knife was made, not of metal, but of wood, of lignum vitae, the hardest wood in the world, a wood capable of holding an extremely sharp point. Gently she touched her hair and pulled the weapon clear by a few centimeters. Yes, she could feel the handle. She was ready.

*Imagine no possessions I wonder if you can*
*No need for greed or hunger*
*A brotherhood of man*
*Imagine all the people*
*Sharing all the world ...*

"*Mon Dieu! Mon Dieu!*" whispered Alphonse, furtively crossing himself and staring down at his shoes. "*Mon Dieu! Mon Dieu!*"

"What's the matter, Alphonse?" asked Jean-Pièrre. Alphonse shook his head and said nothing.

Mahinda, too, had been staring at the woman with the long, raven hair. "It's the Madonna," he said, suddenly sure.

"The Madonna?" asked Jean-Pièrre, distracted.

"The Madonna in my painting," said Mahinda. "You know, the velvet painting I bought in town."

"Where?" asked Arthur.

"Third row, on the aisle." He was about to point her out but remembered they were on international television.

"Yeah. That's her, all right," agreed Arthur. "I hope she's not here to cause trouble."

Jean-Pièrre turned to Alphonse and whispered, "Is that her? Your Madonna?" Alphonse kept staring at his feet, saying nothing. "Is it?" asked Jean-Pièrre more loudly. After a slight hesitation, Alphonse gave the merest of nods.

*You may say I'm a dreamer*
*But I'm not the only one*
*I hope someday you'll join us*
*And the world will live as one.*

As the musicians' last chords evaporated into the night sky, the crowd erupted into cheers and applause. Slowly, all the lighting faded to black, and slowly, the people in the packed stands, the thousands standing or sitting on the grass slope behind the amphitheater tiers, the thousands watching on the closed circuit screens beyond, the people lining Paris Street above and finally the TV audience in living-rooms, bars, churches, synagogues, temples and mosques across the world, fell silent. Even the TV commentators stopped talking and waited expectantly.

The theatrical blackout lasted so long that the initial darkness visible gradually revealed to the crowd's recovering retinas a sky full of the bright prickle of stars. Above them the new moon, like God himself, cloaked in invisibility. Dominating the far-flung galaxies, the bright orb of Venus with her promise of love.

An awed whisper ran through the crowd as those who grasped the significance passed the message to those who had not.

At the start of the new boardwalk that bordered Lake Ramsey and ran from Science North all the way to the amphitheater, sat Eddie on his motorcycle. Behind him, Marie. Anxious to get going, Eddie was watching the young man with a sparse beard who would give him his cue. The young ASM's expression darkened and he held up a hand as he listened to a voice in his headset.

"Jesus, really?" he said into his mike. For a minute he stood there nodding at the news beaming into his headset.

Finally Eddie said, "What's the problem?"

"Oh, sorry. The cops just took down a guy with an assault rifle up on the hill. They've just identified him as some born-again asshole who's wanted in the States for shooting a doctor at an abortion clinic. A few minutes ago, they got a man disguised in a *niqab* who was wearing a bomb vest underneath it."

"So two down, one to go," said Eddie remembering what the Big Guy had told him.

The techie suddenly pointed at Eddie and said, "It's a go, Eddie. Break a leg!"

Eddie kicked the bike to life and began his slow ride along the boardwalk past the phalanx of police that lined the route. The first cop he passed was Constable Kim Gauthier. She held up her hand as he passed and Eddie gave her a high five. "*Via con Dios,*" he told her, forgetting for a moment that she spoke French not Spanish.

The restless crowd in the park heard the bike roar to life followed by the reaction of the crowd lining Paris Street above the boardwalk. They began to chant, "Eddie! Eddie!" as they heard the Harley getting nearer. A succession of lights picked out the bike in its progress, and Eddie waving to the crowds. Some people were even throwing what looked like dried reeds. Eddie caught one: a dried out palm leaf bent into the shape of a cross. No doubt left over from Easter observances back in March. Over the final two hundred meters, the crowd surged against the police overwhelming the narrow path they were holding open so that Eddie could reach the stage. Hands were reaching out to touch him. Eddie braked to a halt as the crowd, despite the valiant efforts of Chief Sawchuk's men and women, closed the corridor ahead of him.

As the crowd pressed in around him, Eddie felt trapped by a solid wall of flesh, an unfamiliar panic rising in him. Eddie had a real fear that he would be ripped to pieces like Dionysos at the hands of the Maenads. Marie became more visible, a stark silhouette. "Now rev the engine," she instructed him, so Eddie shifted the bike into neutral and cranked the throttle open. The Harley let out a mighty roar. The combination of Marie's shadowy visibility and the full-throated Harley was so electric that the crowd began pushing away from them in terror.

As if on cue, the cops redoubled their efforts and managed to open the lane to the stage again. Eddie dropped the throttle back to idle, but a single slim woman with long dark hair barred his way. Eddie recognized her immediately. "*Madre!*" The word burst out of him, the first time he had ever used it. For an eternal moment, it seemed that the only sound was the atonal throbbing of the Harley under him.

"She means to harm you," whispered Marie.

Eddie nodded. He could see the cold anger glittering in her eyes. Suddenly his mother sprang at him in a fury. "*Bastardo!*" she snarled, as he put up his hands to defend himself.

Screams from the mob surrounding them. A sharp pain in his left palm even before he saw the dark shape of the knife. Blood was running down his wrist. "*Cabrón!*" Instinctively, Eddie pulled back his left hand and tried to parry the knife with his right. A woman possessed, Maria pressed the attack. An instant later, he felt the sting of the knife's point savage his right palm. Eddie let out a gasp.

And then his mother froze and looked around her bewildered. The external world had become grey, insubstantial. "She can't see you now," Marie murmured, and Eddie realized that she had cast her cloak around them. As he watched, two burly cops grabbed his mother. She bit one of them but the other managed to handcuff her. "How are your hands?" asked Marie, as his mother was led away kicking and screaming.

He held them out to her, blood dripping on the gravel. She took his hands in hers and pressed them to her breast for a moment, raising them one at a time and kissing each palm. As she did so, he felt the pain trickle out of them as the blood flow stopped. "They've stopped bleeding, I think," she told Eddie, "but the scars you will carry forever."

"The Big Guy didn't say anything about getting the stigmata," Eddie complained.

"He thought it would lend you an extra touch of authenticity. I couldn't talk him out of it." Somehow he sensed she was smiling.

"What next?"

"You will be safe now."

"You mean the Big Guy was serious about there being three assassins?"

"Yes. But your Father was sure the odds would be heavily in your favor."

"Oh that's reassuring. If he'd been omnipotent, he wouldn't be quoting the odds like a fucking bookie."

The mist blocking the world slipped away. Four cops lined up on each side of his motorcycle. Gingerly, Eddie put his hands back on the handle bar grips and slowly drove into the amphitheater. Behind him, people were fighting over the blood that had been spilled on the grass while others were trying to attack Maria Magdalena, but the Sudbury cops closed around her.

The apostles had risen as one as they saw the melee off to their right but calmed down as Eddie began moving again. Together with the rest of the crowd, they broke into applause as Eddie rode into the house and up a ramp leading onto stage left. "Eddie looks kind of freaked out," Claude told the others, sounding worried.

"Marie is with him. She will take care of him," Yvonne said to her sisters.

"It's true," confirmed Arthur, "and now she's fading into him. Look."

"I have been Eddified!" someone in the front row yelled as Marie melted into Eddie. As Eddie reached the stage, the Snowhere drummer launched into a prolonged drum roll. With a sudden burst of power, Eddie yanked the big bike back into a lumbering wheelie and headed straight for the risers, spurred on by the cheering crowd out front. At a shout of 'For God sake sit down!' from the ASM, the apostles subsided into their seats, some being pulled down by those beside them. Immediately, the risers beneath them rose into the air to reveal a Gothic arch opening into what appeared to be a small chapel. Eddie and his bike disappeared as two heavy oaken doors closed behind them.

Eddie shut down the bike and passed it to a stagehand who wheeled it backstage. "What the fuck was that about?" Eddie asked.

From inside his head came the soothing voice of Marie: "Your mother resented having you. She was lashing out at her own dim future. She blames you for ruining her life. The life of a sex worker is a short one, Eddie. Now put it out of your mind."

"Where will they take her?"

"The holding cells at the station off Paris Street." "I have to see her, talk to her."

"Tomorrow." Eddie closed his eyes and felt her hands stroking his temples. He relaxed in her hands closing his eyes.

From her perch on a stool high up in the fly gallery, Pannychis looked down into the backstage area, her eyes on Eddie. She thought she saw a flicker of shadowy movement in front of him. Must be Marie, she told herself excitedly. When she saw Eddie smile, she laughed to herself. "*Merde*," she whispered fervently to herself. "*Merde*." Eddie looked up into the gloom of the fly tower above and, seeing Pannychis, gave her two thumbs up. Just having her there steadied his nerves.

"Standby on cue 16," came the calm voice of Heather Chandler. Up in the control booth, the lighting board operator's finger hovered over the 'Go' button. On the floor of the house doing a live mix on the mikes, Stephanie Morris fussed with the sliders for her next preset.

"Rachel, check Eddie's makeup." Two makeup ladies led Eddie back to his dressing room. As they renewed Eddie's makeup, a woman in the black uniform of St. John's Ambulance joined them and offered to check Eddie's hands. "They're fine," Eddie assured her, "not even painful any more."

"Go 16. Two minutes forty-five seconds to your next entrance, Eddie. Standby on 17."

"I'll be on my mark," Eddie acknowledged.

Beyond the chapel doors, the lights came up again on Snowhere, as the band broke into 'All You Need is Love.'

> *Love, love, love, love, love, love, love, love, love.*
> *There's nothing you can do that can't be done.*
> *Nothing you can sing that can't be sung.*
> *Nothing you can say but you can learn how to play the game*
> *It's easy.*

Many began to weep with joy, Lydia among them. Raggedly at first, a few voices tentatively lifted to the tune, then more and more, until it seemed the whole world sang.

"Go 17."

As the Beatles' anthem faded away, the oak doors slowly swung open to reveal a haze illuminated by overhead banks of parcans gelled to a full white 5,800 degrees Kelvin, a whiter-than-white snapshot of the universe a millisecond after the big bang. The wall of light was so bright that most people within a hundred meters of the stage were shielding their eyes as Eddie strode out. When he reached his mark at center stage, the oak doors swung closed. Logan Banks tossed him a microphone. As Eddie caught it, Heather called in Cue 22 so that an electronic peal of thunder accompanied by the flash of a stage blinder assaulted the retinas of the audience yet again. The band broke into a reprise of 'All You Need is Love', this time with Eddie's rich baritone taking the lead. As the song faded away, the lights on the band faded with it, until the members were silhouetted in muted red swirls of light against the set wall while the beams of three follow spots, key, fill and back, moved with Eddie as he came downstage towards the audience.

"Welcome!" Eddie shouted to the crowd as he raised his arms to encompass them all. "We are all God's children! Even those of you who have no faith, no belief. God recognizes you whether you recognize him or not. You, too, are God's children and welcome here because, hey, all you need is love."

He stopped, inhaled slowly and said, "Smells like good stuff, but maybe you'd better save it, as it might annoy your neighbors. But don't give up hope, within a few decades, pot will be legal all across North America." Cries of disbelief answered antiphonally by a small chant of "420! 420!" Eddie shook his head, said, "Get high on love, guys," and laughed. Others joined him. As the laughter faded out, Eddie looked suddenly serious.

"Look, I know some of you have never had love, have had a hard life and have even contemplated suicide. Believe me, I've been there. I was born in the back of a garage, an unwanted baby. My mother ..." he shrugged, "... what would we call her now, a prostitute? A whore? A lady of the evening, maybe. A lot of you are wondering about my origins. Well, I'm here to tell you I really am a Son of a Whore." Cheers from the crowd. "And it brings me no shame. When my mother called me a bastard just now, she was telling the truth. My mother's name is Maria Magdalena. She, too, has had a hard life and deserves our sympathy and our forgiveness." A buzz of conversation from those who had witnessed Maria's attack on Eddie. "Maybe I'd better explain for those who missed it. My mother, Maria Magdalena was here tonight, first time I had seen here since I was a baby. She came here to kill me because nothing seems to have gone right for her since she gave birth to me. Maybe I should have tried harder to keep contact, I don't know. Anyway, she deserves our forgiveness. And I have to thank her for giving you yet another sign that I am the Man chosen by God. The *stigmata!*" Not until that point did Eddie hold up his hands and show his palms, provoking an audible gasp from the audience.

Cries of "*Mon Dieu, Mon Dieu!*" from the Dionne sisters behind him and the many French-speaking local people in the crowd. A babel of other languages, predominantly English, surged through the crowd. "All you need is love. For all her faults, my mother gave love to many sad men who were in need of it. For a fee, of course." A ripple of laughter punctuated by gasps of disbelief. "But even if you spend your whole life in church, you'll still be expected to contribute an offering, to give something back to our fellow travelers.

"John Lennon told us to:

*Imagine there's no heaven*
*It's easy if you try*
*No Hell below us*
*Above us only sky*

"There are dozens of heavens and hundreds of Hells. But above us," Eddie gestured towards the night sky, "is only sky. Paradise in The Bible was the Garden of Eden. Where was it? Right here on Earth.

"Imagine, Lennon tells us, that we could live as one right here. Being good to each other, helping the less fortunate, trying to love one another, looking after our planet. Many of you good people already do these things, and the rest of you are capable of it. We are all hardwired to empathize with our fellow travelers, an impulse that is far too easy to suppress under the pressures of false prophets. Gautama Buddha and his earthly prophet, the Dalai Lama, will tell you that religion has no need of temples, no need for complicated philosophy. Our own brain, our own heart is our temple. Our philosophy? The philosophy of kindness. What was true 2,500 years ago is still true for each one of us. If we look at life the way the Dalai Lama does, Lennon's claim that 'all you need is love' doesn't seem so pie-in-the-sky.

"We have gathered here to celebrate life, to find a new spiritual path. Many, maybe even most of you, already belong to a religion. Why? Religions give us a sense of community in the face of a vast, uncaring universe. Religions minister to the sick, the frail, the lonely, and the mad, providing consolation in times of trouble. Religions bring us the ceremonies for our passages through life: baptism, coming-of-age, marriage and death. Atheists do not open soup kitchens, nor gather to celebrate or to mourn the important events of our lives.

"But, like the new moon up there, these same religions have a dark side. Most wars have been triggered by religious strife. And let me tell you that the Big Guy is pissed. Pissed at religious leaders who claim He is on their side. Pissed at those who demonize the others. Pissed at leaders who push us to kill or convert the unbelievers. To kill the kaffirs, the heathens, the heretics, the infidels, the pagans or the atheists, you have to first deny their humanity. Those who believe in a different religion, or even a different sect of the same religion, are suspect. Not surprising, then, that most wars, persecutions, even holocausts can be traced to religions. Not surprising, too, is the fact that many of the brightest, the most compassionate, are turning away from the fools and false prophets who preach only death.

"So should we turn our backs on religions? No. Cherish them for the good they do but refuse to reject those whose beliefs are different from yours. Reject the hatred. Reject anyone who tells you that no unbeliever can be a moral person. And never forget that all religions are man-made."

"But why the Hell listen to me? I haven't been inside a church in many a year. I haven't done anything heroic to deserve your trust."

Eddie was interrupted by shouts from various parts of the audience of "AntiChrist! AntiChrist!"

Eddie grinned, strode downstage and gazed out at the audience. "You, you and you," he said, pointing at three people near the stage that had yelled. "Yes, you, Billy Bob Winkler, and you, Martha Wanker, and you, Abdul Abdul." Not one of these three could summon the courage to look the Messiah in the eye. "Let me tell you, I am not the AntiChrist. No, no, my friends, I'm here not because of anything I have done to deserve your attention. I am here because I was chosen. It was not my will to come before you as Messiah. It was my destiny. My coming was announced on computers across the planet. Like Jesus, I have asked that this cup pass away from me. And like Jesus, I have asked in vain.

"So what does my Father want of us? Does he want us to prepare ourselves for the Last Judgment? No. God loves us all but keeps his own counsel. Know that there will be no last judgment, no bean counters tallying up your lives on sterile balance sheets. Instead, we must find the empathy within us all and use it to help those who have strayed. It will not be easy. But as John F. Kennedy said, 'Man's problems were made by man.' So it's up to us to create the New Jerusalem."

Angry stirrings in some parts of the crowd. "If he keeps this up, Eddie's going to start a riot," Heather, the stage manager, whispered into her head set. "Can somebody make sure to alert Chief Sawchuk?"

"I've got him right here," an unfamiliar voice replied. "He's on it."

"Where do we start?" asked Eddie. "I think we all know the answers to that. Genesis tells us that God said, *"Let us make man in our image, after our likeness: and let them have dominion over the fish of the sea and over the fowl of the air, and over the cattle and over all the earth and over every creeping thing that creepeth upon the earth."* In other words, we are all stewards of the planet. And how are we doing so far? Over ninety percent of the oceans' fish stocks have disappeared in the last one hundred years. Many species have disappeared; more are threatened. We have severely polluted the air, the land and the oceans. So much carbon is being released into the air that we need to fear calamitous climate change.

"Be kind to each other. Love is not quite all you need. You need to have resolve, courage, and a willingness to talk truth to power, whether religious or political.

"And the driving force behind our dwindling resources, our pollution, our wars? Population. The main problem is that there are too damn many of us. Left alone without predators and with abundant resources, any species will grow exponentially until it suffers a severe collapse. Like the Rapa Nui of Easter Island, we are starting to outstrip our resources. If we keep following this path, we will provoke the Four Horsemen to overwhelm us with famine, pestilence, and wars. At the moment that Jesus died, there were exactly 1,179,302 people on the planet. Now, sometime this year, we are expecting the five billionth human to be born. To its credit, the United Nations has recognized the problem and has declared the first World Population Day on July 11th. A good start, but most people will ignore the problem.

"I'm begging all of you to go forth as stewards to help rebuild Eden on this green and pleasant planet. The alternative is too bitter to contemplate. Are you with me?" Mixed reactions, even some booing, but when Eddie asked again, there was a roar that overwhelmed the naysayers.

Eddie nodded and yelled, "I knew I could count on you! So what can we do to stabilize the world population? China tried with its one child policy, but it has been a disaster because of the unnatural gender balance it created. First of all, we've got to educate women everywhere, work to eradicate the many patriarchal societies by showing them that countries with a high degree of education of both sexes prosper. We must work to diminish the growing gap between rich and poor. Saint Ambrose told us that 'you never give to the poor what is yours; you merely return to them what belongs to them. For what you have appropriated was given for the common use of everybody. The land is given to everybody and not only to the rich.' So let's use the amazing creativity God blessed us with to find cleaner forms of energy rather than more efficient weapons. Push your politicians! Together we will build a new Eden.

"Believe me, the universe is full of habitable planets but none so pleasant as this blue marble we call home. Even with its present problems, this earth is a place of wonders, a place of everyday miracles. Tell them Eddie sent you."

Cheers erupted as Eddie motioned to the apostles to come downstage. They did so shyly, and as each arrived, Eddie introduced them. He saved Héloïse until last. "Héloïse has joined us from Paris and brought someone else that I want you to meet." He turned upstage as a spotlight illuminated the entrance of Pannychis. Immediate applause as many recognized the world-famous model, dressed tonight in a shimmering midnight blue dress overlaid with a sprinkling of crystals representing stars. "Meet her daughter, Pannychis Garlande, love of my life!" he announced, kissing her.

When the cheers died down, he held up his hands until the crowd subsided into near silence. "Now, I'd like all of you who are willing to dedicate your lives to striving to make the world a better place to rise." Almost everyone stood. "Now hold out your hands and cup them together." Eddie and Pannychis held out their own cupped hands and, as they did so, Heather called the next cue and all the lights dimmed slowly to a crepuscular glow. A collective intake of breath as people saw flames begin to dance, not only in the hands of Eddie and Pannychis, but also in their own. Some cried out in fear at first, but they were comforted by those beside them. Others dropped to their knees. "You have received the holy spirit," Eddie told them.

"And we have been Eddified," added Pannychis, turning and smiling at Eddie. As she raised her arms, the lights surged to full and the dancing flames disappeared. "Repeat after me, 'I have been Eddified!'

After three full-throated cries of "I have been Eddified!," the crowd shouted a lusty "Amen!" before subsiding into their seats with much good-natured laughter.

"Now the fun part," Eddie offered mysteriously. "Sudbury's finest is going to open a path down to the lake. You have felt the flame of commitment, now we will feel the purity of the waters."

Eddie handed his mike to Pannychis, who added in English and then French, "Please respect each other and don't push, as people could be injured or even killed."

Eddie took back the mike and, holding Pannychis' hand, he walked down the ramp and out into the path opening up before him. The twelve followed him. Behind them, Snowhere broke into Don McLean's *Waters of Babylon.*

As the small group reached the beach, the stage grew dim behind them as the lighting board operator brought up the lights hidden in the trees along the shore, illuminating both the beach and the waters beyond. "This is from the Big Guy," Eddie announced pointing up at the star spangled sky. "He said you people deserved at least this miracle for coming from all over the world to witness The Big Reveal. And not just one of the everyday miracles like sunlight creating wine using water, vines, grapes, time and enzymes. No, no. This one you'll remember from the Bible."

Those who could not see Eddie, Pannychis and the apostles directly, turned their attention to the giant screens set up throughout the park, fed by four onshore cameras and three mounted on the boats 200 meters offshore. At a nod from Eddie, a dozen pools of light came on, and the Apostles moved smoothly into them and waited expectantly.

"Jesus said, 'Suffer the little children to come unto me.' Now, almost 2,000 years later, I ask the children to come forward in groups of twelve and join the apostles you see behind me." With that, he tossed the mike to Lydia, who was occupying one of the pools of light behind him.

Lydia smiled and instructed the parents to lead the excited children to the volunteers in blue T-shirts who had just appeared. The volunteers politely kept order as each gathered a group and led them into the pools of light. A buzz rippled through the crowd: 'What's he doing?' 'Why just the kids?' Mysterious music emanated from the trees along the shore. No one could quite identify the music but, despite the wide spectrum of musical tastes present in the park, each person felt that the music was the most beautiful they had ever heard.

When he was sure he had the attention of all the children, Eddie released Pannychis' hand and stepped out on to the water. At first the crowd did not react, but when a mike picked up a woman screaming, "My God! He's actually walking on the water," there were cries of surprise and delight from the crowd, with many falling to their knees.

"Not as easy as it looks, kids," said Eddie, as he took a few flat-footed steps before spinning around to face the crowds. "You gotta believe, kids. Now come to me as your group is led from the shore." He pointed at Lydia, who handed her mike to someone with a headset and shepherded her group out. At first they slid around comically, but soon learned how to stay upright. Not surprisingly, the Canadian kids mastered the walk first as, almost since birth, they had been skating and walking on frozen water. "That's it," Eddie encouraged. "Just tell yourself that water is only molten ice and you'll be fine." Peals of laughter and good-natured teasing as each new group tested the waters. As each group reached him, Eddie stooped down and congratulated them. Most of the parents lining the shore were weeping tears of joy.

When the first children began to tire, twelve new groups replaced them. This time Pannychis kicked off her stilettos and strode regally across the water to Eddie, holding hands with two of the children. At midnight, fireworks sprang into the sky from positions at Science North. The blossoms of light that spangled the night sky seemed to provide the perfect counterpoint to the music that wafted through the night. Few people noticed that the first pyrotechnic stars exactly matched the arrangement of crystal stars that decorated Pannychis' blue shift. Afterwards, people who were there claimed that there had never been such an incredible display as the one they had witnessed on this magical night. And, of course, no one ever forgot the gigantic pyrotechnic image of Eddie looming above the crowd with his outstretched hands reaching out to everyone. As the fiery face of Eddie faded, a final climactic image streaked across the sky proclaiming,

"The World Has Been Eddified!"

During the fireworks, the apostles had led the final groups back to their parents on the shore and now Eddie, Pannychis and the apostles waved to the crowds as the final fiery images faded away. The pools of light faded away with them and, for a couple of minutes, as the people on the shore waited for their night vision to return, only darkness was visible.

A warm breeze of no more than four knots sprang up in the darkness. Rick Cooper, Commodore of the local yacht club and its most competent sailor, taking the fresh wind as his cue, adjusted the black main and jib of his 30' foot sloop, and sailed slowly in behind Eddie and his entourage. When he hove to a few meters behind Eddie, he flashed a dim light, visible only to Eddie and the others. Eddie instructed the others to join hands and he led them to the stern where, one by one, they boarded the sailboat via the swim ladder. When the lights came up again, Eddie and the others had vanished into the night.

On shore, Snowhere was joined by three local women originally from Jamaica who launched into a soaring version of *Amazing Grace*. Pizzas began to arrive from all over town, and volunteers passed out glasses of red wine that seemed to appear out of nowhere.

"Did this start out as water?" asked several people but, as instructed, the volunteers answered with a mysterious smile and the words, "All wine starts out as water. It drops from the gentle heavens upon the place beneath, producing the finest grapes. It's a yearly miracle. Just taste it." And all agreed, they had never tasted a finer wine.

As some of the good-natured crowd filtered away, reporters throughout the park began doing their wrap-ups before handing off the coverage to the pundits back in studios around the world.

Most of the crowd stayed until dawn.

## Sometimes I Feel Like a Motherless Child

At four in the morning, Eddie and his mother were sitting in Rudy's, a tiny restaurant just off Lasalle Boulevard that advertised modestly, 'We serve almost the best hamburgers in town.' When Eddie had told the apostles that he needed to bail out Maria Magdalena, a few were appalled at the idea. "She'll just try to finish the job," Thomas LaRue warned him.

"A chance I'll have to take," Eddie had said. "What I need to know is where I can take her at this time of night. Somewhere the press won't find us."

"Nothing open at this time of night except Timmy's," Arthur pointed out, "and you'd be recognized in a heartbeat."

"I know a place," Claude, the bus driver, said suddenly. "Rudy's."

"Won't it be closed?" asked Lydia.

"He's a friend of mine," Claude told her. "I'll call and get him out of bed. He won't mind, if I tell him who's coming."

"You sure he won't alert the paparazzi?"

"If you knew Rudy, you wouldn't even ask."

"O.K. Thanks, Claude."

"I'll drive you to the police station to bail her out," offered Arthur, "then I'll drive you and Maria Magdalena to Rudy's."

Two hours later, Arthur had arrived at Rudy's, a restaurant almost invisible from the four-laned Lasalle Boulevard that ran past it. When Eddie and Maria Magdalena got out of the old Land Rover, Arthur told them he would wait in the vehicle, maybe have a nap. An excited Rudy had ushered them into his brightly lit but empty café, sat them at one of the formica-topped tables, poured them a coffee and withdrew behind the counter.

Maria Magdalena glanced sideways at her son before lighting a cigarette. Eddie watched her, thinking how small and fragile she seemed. He had to remind himself that this woman, his own mother, had tried to kill him earlier that night.

After searching for the right words, he finally decided to be blunt. "So why'd you try to kill me tonight?"

"Because I'm a whore, O.K.?" Maria Magdalena said before taking a deep drag on her cigarette. "And I never gave a shit about you or anyone else. I guess I got what I deserved."

"So because you're a whore, I must be the AntiChrist. Is that it?"

"Something like that."

"Don't believe everything you see on TV."

"So you're really the fucking Messiah come back to save us all. Christ! *Metetelo por el culo!*"

Her hateful stare was so intense that he shook his head in disbelief. "Don't start telling me to stick it up my arse. You're my mother for fuck's sake. Now calm down and let's try to move on." For a moment, he was ready to catch her wrist if she tried to fling her coffee at him, but she just looked at him sourly and put out her cigarette. "Look. Let's try to get to know each other even a little."

Maria let out an angry breath and then folded her arms and nodded at him. Taking this as a sign that she might be willing to listen, Eddie said, "I don't remember you from my childhood. How could I? I was still a baby when you disappeared. The only way I even knew what you looked like was from a picture that Joe had in his wallet. I even went looking for you after Joe died. No luck. Don't feel too bad. You weren't the only one who abandoned me. The Big Guy certainly stayed out of touch until that trick he played on me at the solstice. I never asked to be the Messiah. Who would? You any idea how fucking hard it is doing what I have to do? Fuck no! Even now, I'm feeling that I'm making it up as I go along. Oh, I get hints and some encouragement from the Big Guy, but the person I rely on the most is the dead nun I found on the side of the road. She's inside me now. I can feel her. Between her and Pannychis, love of my life, and the apostles who are helping me, I no longer feel that longing for a normal life that comes with being a motherless child. I may not be sure about where I'm going, but now I have people who love me and who will stay with me wherever the road leads."

Eddie stopped. Tears were streaming down his face. Maria lit another cigarette. In the silence that followed, Rudy busied himself making more coffee, embarrassed to be overhearing. For the first time, Marie spoke, whispering into his inner ear: "She has found a spark of love for you after all these years."

"You were conceived on the most wonderful night of my life. My God, he was beautiful. I never knew fucking could be like that. But a baby? I am a whore. I was then and I am now. There's no room in a whore's life for a baby. Over the years, I've wondered what happened to you, but I never looked for you. And now you turn up in the town where I was hiding from the Yankee *federales*. How the Hell did you find me?"

"I could say that God works in mysterious ways, but you already know that after your night with Elvis. Truth is, I wasn't even looking for you. I was driving a shipment of coke up to Timmins."

Maria became visibly more relaxed. Rudy took advantage of the lull to approach and refill their coffees. Then he said, "I'm taking a cup out to the guy waiting in the car." With that, he opened the door and went out into the night. Eddie got a glimpse of the sky just beginning to take on a rosy hue in the east.

"Nice guy," Eddie observed.

"Yeah." Maria pulled her voluminous purse onto the table and said, "Let me see your hands." Eddie thrust them out, palms upward. "They look painful." Eddie said nothing. After rummaging around in her purse, she pulled out a tube of cream, squeezed some into her palm. Eddie noted for the first time that his mother was left-handed. Taking his hands one at a time, she gently massaged the cream into his wounds. It was the first time his mother had ever mothered him, as far as he could remember, and her touch made him shiver with pleasure.

"There," she said and put the tube back in her purse.

"What is it?"

For the first time she smiled. "It's vaginal cream. It's antibiotic." Eddie grinned. "Well, what else did you expect to find in a whore's pocketbook?"

For the first time ever, mother and son laughed comfortably together, their shared laughter weakening the defenses on both sides. They began to talk without the slightest trace of self-censorship, revealing at long last their disparate biographies. Maria told her son about her own childhood. She had been born in Tijuana to a dirt poor family. Her mother took in washing while her father drank and gambled away the few pesos she made. One night he had come home drunk and begun to beat her mother. Unable to bear her mother's screams any longer,

Maria, then a girl of fourteen, grabbed a kitchen knife and slit her father's throat. With the help of two sympathetic neighbors, they had dumped the body in the dry riverbed that runs through the poorer part of Tijuana. The neighbors had collected a few hundred pesos from the poor people that lived in their ramshackle apartment block. The money had got her a guide for a night run across the border to the American side. An hour after reaching San Isidro, she had turned her first trick. "Such easy money," she told him. "And I enjoyed it. Right then, I decided that this was the life for me."

"What did you like about it?" Eddie asked.

She laughed. "The money, of course. And I guess I just found out I liked fucking."

They talked for a long time before they were startled by a sharp rap at the outside door. They looked up as Rudy entered and said, "I'm sorry to disturb you but I have to get ready to open in twenty minutes."

Eddie leapt up and said, "No, no. We should be thanking you, opening up for us in the middle of the night. We owe you big time. If there's anything we can do ..."

Rudy, his round face crimson with unwonted boldness, cleared his throat. "You can give me your blessing, Eddie."

So Rudy became Eddified, and the next morning, he hired a sign company to change the wording on his sign. When customers asked why the word 'almost' had been changed to 'very', he would just say that there was a good reason for that, but no matter how much he was pressed, he never revealed what that reason was.

When Arthur drove back to the house on the lake, he had an extra passenger, Eddie's mother. When they arrived, Lydia welcomed her and told Maria Magdalena that they could use her help. "With Eddie and Pannychis, Jean-Pièrre and Héloïse leaving for Rome in two hours, we're going to be shorthanded, and there is so much to do and so little time."

As Arthur loaded the suitcases into the old Land Rover, Eddie took Lydia aside and thanked her for accepting his mother. She just shrugged and said, "Glad Arthur and I could help. It was actually his idea, you know."

# Part Eleven: Italy

## 'You Can't Run the Church on Hail Marys'

The sun was just about to kiss the horizon when Cardinal Achille Silvestrini made his way out on to the terrace of Cardinal Buffone's latest acquisition, the impressive Villa del Falco near Viterbo, in the hills north of Rome. As he closed the glass doors, the sounds of the gala going on inside were muted. Today he was dressed in a simple black clerical suit over a gilet. His only ornamentation: a gold pectoral cross, but the cross itself was tucked into a pocket of his gilet so that only the gold chain was visible.

Taking a sip of his mineral water, he sat down at one of the tables surrounding an ornate pond. The lilies were closed now but in the dark still water, an occasional glint of gold as the carp came towards him, hoping to be fed. The valley below had already been consumed by the lengthening shadows. Here and there, lights came on in a smattering of cottages. No doubt they are all good Catholics, Silvestrini thought to himself. In another hour or two, the lights would wink out one by one as the occupants went to bed. There are things to be said for living a simple life. He sighed and chided himself for such false humility. Even with all the problems of the last few days, he knew that he would not trade places with any of those who dwelled in the valley below.

Top of mind had been the impression that Eddie had made with the Big Reveal. The media, and therefore most of the hoi polloi, had been duped by the simplest of magic tricks: walking on water and Pentacostal fire. A few commentators had even explained how the water trick was done: plexiglass platforms just under the water's surface made invisible by a little surface chop. Magdalena's crew no doubt installed them in the lake the day before and removed them again before dawn. Others, however, pointed out that the water had been perfectly calm when Eddie and his apostles had stepped out on to the lake. Other pundits had pointed out that at least some of the children would have discovered the ruse. And surely any magician worth his salt could do the Pentacostal tongues of fire illusion.

People are too ready to believe, he felt, and the skeptics, by and large, had been shouted down by the world's media. He had to admit, though, that Magdalena's performance had been very impressive. It would not do to underestimate such a man.

The cardinal's second and more immediate problem was Pope Urban IX. During a clandestine meeting of the gang of four earlier in the afternoon, Cardinal Buffone, his fury barely suppressed, had informed the others that Pope Urban had not only been impressed by Magdalena's performance but had even hinted that he might invite the man to Rome. Cardinal Buffone, in the bluff manner that he was famous for, had told His Holiness that such a thing would be anathema and that appearing to show favor to this Eddie Magdalena might even precipitate a revolt among the cardinals. Apparently Urban had favored the Prefect of the Papal Household with his most beatific smile and had dismissed him with a blessing. Silvestrini had cautioned Buffone to keep his temper. Decisions made in the heat of anger often result in unforeseen results.

"I will wait, Achille," he had said, his jowls shaking with indignation, "but not for long. This pope could bring about the destruction of Mother Church. It is our sacred duty to do everything in our power to prevent him from doing so."

Was the cardinal suggesting that this new pope should meet the same fate as Pope Jean Paul, Silvestrini asked himself. Not a question that should ever be uttered aloud, he decided, and seeing that there was no reasoning with Buffone, he had agreed that this was a matter of great gravity, before changing the subject. "Are you still holding the gathering of the Friends of Santa Croce in Gerusalemme tonight?" he asked.

"What? Yes, of course. I have been looking forward to this for months. Besides, Thomas's boy genius will be the guest of honor. We are making him a member of the Friends of Santa Croce. At some point, I'll get him to tell us about his DNA analysis. Apparently it's going well. I've promised him a reward for his efforts, so I want this to be a night that he'll never forget. You are coming, my dear Achille?"

"Yes, yes of course. But I will have to leave rather early." For a few moments, Cardinal Buffone looked comically crestfallen, but then his plump cheeks creased into a broad smile when Cardinal Silvestrini told him who he was meeting.

"Then, of course you must go, my dear," he had said.

When Cardinal Silvestrini had arrived at the Villa del Falco that evening for the gathering of the Friends of Santa Croce in Gerusalemme, Buffone greeted him at the door with his arm around Enrico Capelli. "You've met our genetic genius before, Achille?"

"Of course, at the meeting in St. Helena's chapel," said Silvestrini. Buffone looked puzzled until Silvestrini added, "You were shepherding Magdalena's supporters around the Vatican Apartments that day."

"Ah, yes, I remember," said Buffone, nodding, but Silvestrini could see that he did not.

Suddenly Cardinal Silvestrini was startled by Enrico Capelli impulsively taking his hand and planting a sloppy kiss on his ring. Suppressing his disgust, Silvestrini smiled down at the smaller man, noted the alcoholic glaze in his eyes and gently removed his hand. "Good to see you again," he said, resisting the urge to wipe his hand on a handkerchief.

"Come, come, come, my friend," Buffone had urged. "The professor has some good news for us. Let's retire to my study and he can tell you about it." A waiter dressed in breeches and a tunic was passing by, and Buffone stopped him. "A drink, Achille? Oh, that's right. You don't indulge in the fruits of the vine." He took a glass of wine himself. The professor traded his empty champagne flute for a full one. The waiter was just about to depart when Buffone said to him, "Could you find Cardinal Schicklgruber and ask him to join us in my study?"

"Of course, Your Eminence."

Once in Buffone's comfortable book-lined study, Buffone said to the professor, "I hope you are enjoying our little soirée, Enrico."

"Yes, oh yes, indeed, Your Eminence, especially the nun who danced for us earlier," he said eagerly, before taking off his glasses and polishing them on the bottom of his tie.

"Ah, Sister Allesandro, our ballerina for God, as she calls herself," said Cardinal Silvestrini. "We all serve God according to our lights, professor. Of course, her talents are a little unusual."

"Is it true, she used to be a lap dancer, Your Eminence?" Enrico asked, his eyes wide behind his thick lenses.

"I haven't made a study of her previous career, professor. Let's just be thankful that she found God and now dances in His honor."

"Oh, yes, of course," said Enrico, blushing. To cover his embarrassment, he gulped his champagne, which caused a fit of coughing.

The boy's genius did not seem to extend to social skills, Silvestrini decided and began to worry about his discretion in other matters. Just then, a light knock on the study door before Cardinal Schicklgruber slipped in.

"Ah, Alois," said Cardinal Buffone, rising. "Please make yourself comfortable. I wanted you to hear about the professor's progress."

"Good, good," said Schicklgruber.

"Tell the cardinals your good news, Enrico."

The professor nodded and began, his confidence growing now that he was on familiar ground: "When we got the fragment of the *santissimo prepuzio*, I was worried because of the size of the sample and the fact that, after all these centuries, it would be severely contaminated with the DNA of the people who handled it, but I must commend my team."

"Your team?" asked the diminutive Cardinal Schicklgruber, his voice dripping with suspicion. "Were you not instructed to carry out this project in the utmost secrecy?"

"Yes, but analyzing DNA samples is quite complicated and I have had to use people to prepare the samples, operate the centrifuges, do the microscope work ..."

"How many?"

Flustered by Schicklgruber's tone, the professor said, "Eight to ten people here and, of course, Professor Gaylord at the University of Arizona in Tucson." Gaylord was the Jesuit priest in charge of the Stuart Observatory at the University of Arizona. The professor laughed a high-pitched nervous whinny and added. "We had to inform Gaylord because he had to authorize the money. This work is very expensive."

"So by now your secret analysis is table talk on the Piazza Navone." Cardinal Schicklgruber shook his head in disgust.

"Now, now, Alois, the professor is doing his best. And in the end we will be spreading the word of his results. You know as well as I do, my friend, that the chances of keeping secrets in the Vatican are next to nothing anyway."

Schicklgruber snorted his derision and sat so far back in his chair that his shoes barely touched the carpet. No wonder his motto is *semper idem*, thought Silvestrini, always the same. After a few moments of tense silence, he realized that the others were looking at him. "All right! Tell us your news, professor. We are waiting," he announced.

Enrico took a deep breath and rushed on. "When Reverend Father Thomas asked me to take charge of the sequencing of the DNA from the *santissimo prepuzio*, I was worried that human contact over the past two millennia would have degraded the sample. This usually means a miscoding of the nucleic acids corrupting C to T or G to A. Normally the best ancient DNA is extracted from teeth or bones. Mummified tissue can often be a problem, but thanks to a relatively new mode of analysis called PCR or Polymerase Chain Reactions, we can now amplify the DNA sample almost indefinitely. The analysis mimics our own processes of DNA replication." When Enrico peered myopically at his small audience, he saw that the reaction of the cardinals ranged from boredom (Cardinal Buffone) to total bewilderment (Cardinal Schicklgruber) to the dawning of understanding (Cardinal Silvestrini). Already the pocket cardinal was beginning to glower at him, so he turned to Silvestrini, where he could see a glimmer of understanding. Wisely, he decided to simplify.

"What I'm saying, Your Eminences, is that by using this new technique, we are almost at the point of working out the unique sequence of the nucleic acids that belonged to our Savior. The condition of the sample is, how shall I say, almost miraculous, given that it is almost 2,000 years old."

"We expected no less," said Silvestrini, smiling, "from our Lord or from you, professor."

"Do you have the DNA for Eddie Magdalena?" asked Cardinal Buffone impatiently.

"It arrived at our lab yesterday. Already I have a team working on it. Since it is a modern sample, we should have no trouble working out the sequence, but it still will be days or even weeks before we will be ready to compare the two."

"You have done well, professor," Cardinal Silvestrini told him.

"The sooner the better, my boy," Cardinal Buffone urged. "The sooner the better." Rising, he asked the others if they had any questions, and when they didn't, he put his arm around the professor's shoulders and began herding his guests back to the party. "I don't have to tell you to keep this to yourselves until we are ready to release the results." The others nodded.

Cardinal Silvestrini had circulated for the next hour after the meeting with the young professor, making sure that his presence had been noted, before slipping out on to the terrace where he now sat. The sun had dipped below the hills almost an hour before. He checked his watch and was about to go in and say his farewells to Cardinal Buffone when he was startled by a burst of sound as someone opened the door behind him. Silvestrini rose, turned towards the doors and saw a disheveled Enrico Capelli staggering towards him, his scapular protruding from his unbuttoned shirt. The cardinal stepped back as two of the dancers in their brilliant white dresses adorned with tiny wings made of real feathers, rushed out and grabbed the professor amid much screaming and laughter. One of the women whispered an apology to Cardinal Silvestrini as they led their willing captive back inside. Smelling a scandal brewing, he peeked into the house and found that most of the lights were emanating from rooms at the top of the curved marble staircase. Familiar with the house, the cardinal quickly found his way out of a side door and descended the steps to his waiting car.

"Where to, Your Eminence?" asked the cardinal's driver.

"L'Eau Vive," he replied.

## L'Eau Vive

Even at the age of sixty-seven, Archbishop Paul Marcinkus' piercing blue eyes still sparkled and, at 6'3", he still looked as if he could handle himself in a fight. Nicknamed '*Il gorilla*' for his size and fearlessness, Marcinkus had acted as unofficial bodyguard to both Pope Paul VI and Pope John Paul II and had saved each of them from assassination attempts: Pope Paul in the Philippines in 1970 and Pope Jean Paul II at Fatima in Portugal in 1981.

The American boy from the wrong side of the tracks in Cicero, Illinois, had managed to ascend from Chicago parish priest to the highest level any American had ever attained in Vatican City, President of the IOR, the Vatican Bank, despite the fact that by his own admission, "My only previous experience was handling the Sunday collection." Marcinkus' career had suffered a severe downturn when Banco Ambrosiano, Italy's biggest privately owned bank, had collapsed in 1982, resulting in the bankruptcy of thousands of investors. The collapse had been largely engineered by Archbishop Marcinkus and the bank's CEO, Roberto Calvi. Calvi ended his banking career abruptly in 1982 when he was found hanging from Blackfriars Bridge in London. Calvi, like Archbishop Marcinkus, had been a member of P2, or *Propaganda Due*, the ultra-secret masonic lodge hidden inside the Vatican. Growing desperate, Roberto Calvi had roamed Europe trying to find allies, but everyone he turned to, including the archbishop, had shunned him.

In the end, Calvi had threatened to name names and thus signed his own death warrant. Perhaps he had forgotten the initiation ceremony into the P2 where he had been told that, should he reveal any of their secrets, he would be found hanging by his neck and be washed by the tides. When he was found hanging from Blackfriars Bridge in London, his body had indeed been 'washed by the tides' that flow up the Thames. The Italian press pointed out that the masonic brothers of P2, known to refer to each other as friars in their ceremonial rites, might just be prime suspects. No one was ever arrested over the death of Calvi.

His former associate, Archbishop Marcinkus, had not been surprised when an Italian court had issued an arrest warrant against him, not over the death of Calvi, but for being an 'accessory to fraudulent bankruptcy' over the collapse of the Banco Ambrosiano. Invoking the Lateran Treaties of 1929, the Italian justices had later cancelled the arrest warrant on the grounds that the archbishop had immunity as a Vatican diplomat. In his own defense, the archbishop pointed out that the next pope, John Paul II, would hardly have promoted him to the post of Pro-President of Vatican City, the third most powerful position in the Vatican, had he not trusted his banker. But the whispers persisted that Marcinkus would have been removed from his office on the morning of September 28th, 1978, had not Pope John Paul so conveniently passed away.

Shortly after his election in 1978, Pope John Paul had been alarmed to receive a list of 121 masons belonging to the P2 lodge operating secretly within the very walls of the Vatican. Moving with great haste, he had discussed with his Head of State, Cardinal Villot, the replacement of several *liberi muratori*, freemasons, holding prominent positions. Marcinkus was to be removed and sent back to Chicago. Some members of the Curia had even organized a lottery about what day he would be fired as Governor of the IOR.

But at 4:45 a.m. on Sunday, September 28th, 1978, everything changed. After only 33 days in office, Pope John Paul was found dead.

The pope had eaten his last supper with two secretaries, Father Diego Lorenzi and Father John Magee. They had had a simple meal of clear soup, veal, and salad. The priests had drunk wine, the pope only water. The pope's death had been discovered by Sister Vincenza. After she had knocked lightly as usual and left his coffee outside the door, she checked back and found the tray still untouched. Shaking, she had ventured into the pope's bedroom and found the lights on and the deceased pope sitting up in bed, some papers clutched in his hand. She had immediately alerted Cardinal Jean-Marie Villot, the pope's Head of State and a *libero muratore*.

When the cardinal had entered the papal bedroom, he was alone. He dispensed with the ancient Vatican tradition of tapping on the pope's forehead three times with a small silver hammer and asking, "*Albino, dormisne?*" Albino, are you sleeping?

Instead, he removed the papers that the pope had been reading. The papers contained two lists: one of the P2 members in the Vatican, the other of those masons who would lose their positions. Top of that list was Archbishop Marcinkus. The papers were never seen again.

Next, instead of calling the pope's personal physician, the cardinal telephoned Dr. Renato Buzzonetti, Deputy Head of the Vatican

Health Service, a man who had not yet met the late pope. After a superficial examination, Buzzonetti declared that the pope had died of a myocardial infarction, even though the pope had had no history of heart problems. When the famous physician Dr. Christian Barnard heard of the diagnosis, he declared that if a doctor had issued such a cause of death with so little evidence in South Africa, he would have been charged with negligence. John Paul's own physician, Dr. Giussepe da Ros, had recently examined him and pronounced him, "*Non sta bene, ma benone,*" Not just well but very well. Buzzonetti estimated the pope's time of death at around 11 p.m., several hours after he had eaten, plenty of time for a slow acting poison to work.

Now the cardinal assumed the role of Camerlengo or chamberlain, taking charge of the papal apartments during the period of *sede vacante* until the election of a new pope. For the time being, he was the most powerful man in the Vatican.

With unseemly haste, Cardinal Villot had telephoned the Signoracci brothers at five a.m. to arrange for the immediate embalming. Next, he ordered every trace of the dead pope to be removed from the papal apartments. Within twelve hours, all personal possessions of Albino Luciani, the late Pope John Paul, were gone, and the body had been embalmed without an autopsy.

A couple of hours before the pope had eaten his last meal, two cardinals, rumored to be Cardinal Buffone and Cardinal Schicklgruber, had given a certain Gino Carboni a tour of the papal apartments, including the Vatican kitchen. When Archbishop Marcinkus had heard that Carboni was in Rome, he guessed that he had been called in by some of the more conservative members of P2 to deal with Albino Luciani. And now, more than a decade later, Carboni was again in Rome. Someone in Propaganda Due had called '*il angelo della morte*' back. The Gang of Four was the archbishop's guess.

If Pope John Paul had not died of 'natural' causes, Marcinkus himself would have been the prime suspect. The whole Curia seemed to know that it was only a matter of time before he would be dismissed as God's Banker. Even more damning, one of the Swiss Guards had seen him early that morning lurking near the papal apartments around the time of the pope's death. It was generally known that the archbishop was not a morning person. Marcinkus then, had had both motive and opportunity. But since the pope's death was from natural causes, no one ever asked him for an alibi. Marcinkus had known of the plot to assassinate the pope but, despite having so much to lose, had backed away when the plotters had asked him to join them. As a member of P2 himself, he could not reveal the plot but wanted no part of it. Instead, he had risen early and taken up a position just outside the papal apartments in order to intercept Carboni and warn him off. But Carboni never appeared, and it was only later that the archbishop learned that the killer, whose preferred weapon was poison, had visited the Vatican kitchens before the pope's last meal.

For the past few years, Archbishop Marcinkus had been fending off criminal inquiries from the other side of the Tiber about his banking practices.

Now another troublesome pope had been elected, a pope who seemed to be almost the reincarnation of the saintly John Paul. Like John Paul, this latest pope, Urban IX, wanted to steer the church back to its intended role as the church of the poor. Not only did Urban want to revisit the birth control ban set out in *Humanae Vitae* that still divided the church, but he was about to perform some major house cleaning.

In 1978, Marcinkus had tried and failed to protect Pope Jean Paul on that fatal evening. Now sixty-seven, he had grown weary of the constant intrigue and wanted only to return to Chicago and live out his life among his own countrymen. But recent events had made that impossible. Once again, he was seeing a plot against a progressive pope, and that was the reason he was meeting Cardinal Silvestrini. He may have grown old, his reputation tarnished by the scandals at the Vatican Bank, but he was still '*il gorilla*', the man who had saved two popes and tried to save a third. Through his contacts back in Chicago, he had learned that Gino Carbone was once more flying into Rome. When his informant had told him the attempt on the pope's life would take place during his upcoming visit to Jerusalem, the archbishop had promised himself that the gorilla would be there to stop it. One last act to burnish his legacy before he retired to Chicago. The archbishop would rather be remembered as the guardian of the papacy than as the banker who had got it into financial trouble. Silvestrini could make sure that '*il gorilla*' was included in the pope's retinue for the trip to Jerusalem.

One of the archbishop's pleasures was eating at L'Eau Vive, a restaurant discreetly tucked away in the heart of pagan Rome on Via Monterone, between the Piazza Navone and the Pantheon. L'Eau Vive's cuisine is French, and its kitchen is run by a cordon bleu chef. Tonight Archbishop Marcinkus was looking forward to trying the trout cooked in whisky.

His server was a girl from Vietnam. Like the rest of the servers, she was wearing her native costume. The young women were all members of the Travailleuses Missionaires de la Conception Immaculée and came from all over the Catholic world to spend a few months in Rome. Marcinkus liked to tell people that he came for the quality of the cuisine but stayed for the pretty Catholic servers.

The trout cooked in whisky was superb. When the archbishop was finished, he sat back, ordered a glass of Camus cognac and lit a Cohiba while he waited for Cardinal Silvestrini.

His contentment was short-lived. He looked up to see, not Silvestrini, but Cardinal Agostino Bertelli. "Anyone but '*il corvo*'," Marcinkus muttered to himself. Tonight, as always, the cardinal was dressed in black, hence his nickname 'The Crow.'

"May I join you, Paul?"

"As long as it's only for a few minutes, Agostino," said Marcinkus, not trying to disguise his irritation. "I'm expecting someone a little later."

"Certainly. I won't take up much of your time," said the cardinal, waving away the waitress when she approached their table.

"I hear you ran into some trouble at the papal apartments when you were squiring around those Canadian pilgrims, Agostino," said the archbishop, a broad smile spreading across his face.

"Peasants," growled the cardinal.

"Did one of them really piss on a Raphael?" Marcinkus pressed.

"I thought you were in a hurry."

The archbishop nodded. "Look, if this is another try to get me on side with your group opposing this pope, then forget about it."

"No, no, Paul. We know that you would like nothing better than to return to Chicago and spend the rest of your career there. We think we can help."

"I don't want your help, Agostino. I'll find my own way back to Chicago. Speaking of which, I hear that Gino Carbone's back in town."

"Gino Carbone?" asked Bertelli, feigning unfamiliarity with the name.

"The guy from Chicago. Last time I saw him was shortly before Pope Jean Paul met his maker. You may not have met the bastard personally, but you sure know of him." The archbishop's voice had been getting louder and Bertelli motioned him to keep it down. Marcinkus nodded and added quietly. "Here's the thing. If Carbone goes anywhere near the pope, I'm not going to stand by and ..."

"This pope is playing with fire. It's not just his intent to revisit the birth control question. He is determined to create more foreign cardinals. Not surprising. He himself is from Argentina. And I have it on good information that he is ready to recognize this Magdalena as the Messiah."

"That's his business. From what I see, this pope is a humble and saintly man. How many of us can claim as much?"

"He is about to destroy the church."

"Look, if Carbone harms this pope he'll have to answer to me."

"But ..."

"Good night, Agostino. Go with God."

Bertelli seemed on the point of saying something, decided against it, and left without another word.

Marcinkus took a deep breath. What did he care if the new pope wanted to drop the prohibition against birth control. Goddammit, for years the Vatican Bank had even owned the Instituto Farmacologico Sereno which made the birth control pill Luteolas. The archbishop's mistress, Sabrina, had been using Luteolas pills for years.

∗   ∗   ∗

Twenty minutes later, Cardinal Silvestrini entered the restaurant. As he passed the sign in French near the front door warning that interviews and the taking of pictures had been prohibited since 1981, he smiled: no wonder the archbishop liked this place so much. As he reached the top of the stairs, he paused a moment beneath the high vaulted ceilings and noted with satisfaction that L'Eau Vive was almost deserted at this hour. He spotted the archbishop sitting at a table tucked in beside the white marble statue of the Virgin.

"Welcome to my unofficial office," Marcinkus said as the cardinal sat down opposite him.

"How are you, my friend? It's been too long."

"Almost a year," said the archbishop. Both men knew that Achille, with his acute sense of the political, had intentionally been avoiding God's Banker ever since his star had begun to dim.

"Yes, I suppose it is," agreed the cardinal with feigned surprise.

The archbishop was certain that Cardinal Silvestrini would not have come to this meeting if he had not promised to make it worth the cardinal's time. A woman dressed in the native costume of Sierra Leone appeared at the table. Silvestrini ordered a bottle of mineral water. When she was gone, Marcinkus leaned over and, putting his big hand on the cardinal's shoulder, said, "It's good to see you again, Achille, it really is." As the archbishop had anticipated, Cardinal Silvestrini could not avoid flinching slightly under his touch.

"You too, Paul. You too," agreed Silvestrini, relaxing only when the big American withdrew his hand.

"So are you going to try to persuade me to join the growing chorus against this upstart pope. I warn you, Cardinal Bertelli was just here. I told him, I'm too old for this cloak-and-dagger stuff."

"Oh, I agree, Paul. I have enough to occupy my time without these intrigues. But all of us have a sacred duty to protect Mother Church."

"Me, I just try to make sure our Mother Church has the money to pursue her works of charity, Achille."

"Of course, of course. As you have famously said, 'You can't run the church on Hail Marys."

Marcinkus laughed loud enough to startle an elderly couple three tables away. "Well, Achille, it's still as true as it ever was." What the archbishop had actually said was "When my workers come to retire, they expect a pension. It's no use my saying to them 'I'll pay 400 Hail Marys" but he had long since given up correcting people. Like 'Play it again, Sam' and 'Alas poor Yorick I knew him well', 'You can't run the church on Hail Marys' had achieved a mythic truth that the original phrase never could.

The two men had never hit it off and now each seemed lost in his own thoughts. The cardinal wanted to ask why Marcinkus had sent him such an urgent invitation but knew he would appear weak if he broached the subject first. Marcinkus, for his part, was enjoying the cardinal's discomfort. He had first met Achille Silvestrini on the third day of his stay in Vatican City and had immediately been put off by the aristocratic air that emanated from the man. The fact that he seemed to have effortlessly climbed the Vatican hierarchy because of his connection to the famous Medicis had not endeared him to the plain-spoken archbishop, either.

The silence was broken by the sound of plates being smashed in the kitchen followed by a shouted '*Basta!*' Marcinkus smiled. "Well, somebody's going to be saying a few *Ave Marias* at confession tomorrow." The cardinal managed a smile which disappeared when the archbishop blindsided him with "What did you think of this Eddie Magdalena's performance?"

"Banal truths and magic tricks," said the cardinal dismissively.

"I thought he came across as quite a charismatic son-of-a-bitch," observed Marcinkus. "Never underestimate your enemy, Achille."

"No, of course, we don't intend to do so."

"And he did perform three things that people are interpreting as miracles." Marcinkus was enjoying the role of devil's advocate.

"Miracles? I saw only two: the walking on water and the tongues of Pentecostal fire. Both are fairly simple illusions, I understand."

Marcinkus laughed lightly. "Well, somehow I don't see either of us hot-footing it across the Tiber, Achille."

"Well, of course, he would have to have had extensive training."

"Do we know that?"

"His background is quite unsavoury and there are mysterious gaps in his life that we know nothing about."

"Ah, just like Jesus, then." Marcinkus sipped his cognac and watched for the cardinal's reaction but Cardinal Silvestrini was too shrewd to rise to such obvious bait.

Marcinkus pushed a little harder. "What about the third so-called miracle, Achille?"

"The third miracle?"

"Yes. I didn't see any mention of it in the media, but the story seems to be just emerging. Trouble is, not many reporters know a damn thing about the cosmos. Seems the astronomer from Science North, sorry I can't remember his name, has just written an article about the woman's dress. Do you remember what she wore?" Silvestrini shrugged, wondering where this was leading. "No, of course not. You take your vow of celibacy much too seriously. But even if you don't have an eye for female pulchritude, you have to admit the woman was absolutely stunning."

"Ah, the American woman, his black companion."

"She's not American, or black, Achille. In fact, she's a combination French and Algerian and is an exquisite golden color."

"What about her?" A note of irritation creeping into the cardinal's voice.

"She was wearing a tight blue dress, surely you remember?" The cardinal made no reaction. Marcinkus sighed and continued: "There was a pattern of jeweled stars stretching across the woman's breasts." A nod of recognition from the cardinal. "Well, this astronomer guy had taken a picture of it – I'm betting a lot of people took the same shot – anyway, when he blew up the picture, he realized that the jewels show a map of the Milky Way. And here's the kicker. He worked out that this particular view of the Milky Way is not the one we see here." The cardinal started to look more interested. "In fact, he worked out that the view would be the starscape as you would see it if you were standing on a planet orbiting around Deneb."

"Deneb?"

"Yeah, Deneb. Brightest star in the constellation Cygnus. You can see it from Earth with the naked eye."

Cardinal Silvestrini was thoughtful for a few moments before asking, "Is this the news you were going to tell me?"

"No, no. I'm just saying no clever illusionist would have known that. It looks like a miracle, whether it is or not."

The cardinal shook his head. "I'll check with our astronomer, Father Roland Brahe, but I'm sure there's some reasonable explanation."

"Seems crazy, huh," said the archbishop, "two senior clerics of the Vatican looking for a rational explanation for a miracle."

The cardinal permitted himself a small frown. "If that is not your news, then please tell me what it is, as I have big day tomorrow."

Just then, the lights dimmed, and the seven servers assembled in the middle of the room. "It'll have to wait, Achille. The ladies are about to sing."

Achille sat back and accepted the interruption with good grace. "I understand the women are Carmelites from all over the world."

"They're not actually nuns, Achille. They're virgins devoted to the Blessed Mother. And I'd say they're chosen for their looks as well as their singing."

The small choir began to hum. After the opening bars, a young black woman in a sparkling sari stepped forward and began to sing Schubert's *Ave Maria*. As she reached '*Ave Maria Mater Dei ora pronobis,*' the rest of the choir joined her in singing the words to the hymn. As the final note faded away, the few diners clapped politely.

The archbishop stood up and applauded loudly enough to make up for the sparse crowd. The soloist smiled at the archbishop. When the applause died down, the archbishop hugged the tiny woman and whispered, "Vili, let's sing 'Danny Boy' together. Remember it?"

Vili nodded. This would be the third time they had sung 'Danny Boy' together. After the first time, she had plucked up her courage and asked the archbishop why he liked the song so much. "My best friend when I was a kid was called Danny. A feisty little guy. He got jumped on his way to school. I'd been waiting to take him home, as some of the little bastards had been picking on him. But I'd been late that day. By the time I'd turned up, he was already bleeding out."

The duo gave a heartbreaking rendition of 'Danny Boy.' There were tears running down the old bishop's cheeks as he acknowledged the applause and placed a chaste kiss on Vili's forehead.

"You have a fine baritone, Paul," Cardinal Silvestrini said as the archbishop resumed his seat.

"O.K." The archbishop looked at his watch and nodded to himself. "Any minute now I am expecting a call from the VIP lounge at Da Vinci Airport. It will tell me that your Eddie Magdalena and his entourage have just landed in Rome."

"They are landing in Rome now?" The cardinal asked in surprise. Why did Marcinkus know this when no one had informed him?

The archbishop's voice took on a hard edge, "*Quid pro quo*, Achille, *quid pro quo*. I'll tell you what they are doing here and exactly who has arrived but, in return, there is something you can do for me."

"What can I do for you, Paul?"

"I want to be on the pope's upcoming trip to Jerusalem."

The cardinal appeared to be considering the request but really knew that he had no choice. But why, he wondered, did Marcinkus want to go to Jerusalem? "I can get Cardinal Buffone to arrange it. It's one of his duties, after all."

"Good. One more thing. I understand that the pope will be taking a helicopter from Castel Gandolfo."

"Yes, I believe so," said the cardinal slowly.

"Well, you know about my problem with the carabinieri. They want to take me in for questioning." The cardinal nodded. "That means I can't get to the pope's summer residence, understand?" The cardinal nodded again. "Then I would like the helicopter to stop at the Vatican Helipad and pick me up on the way to Castel Gandolfo."

"Buffone can arrange it."

"Then we have a deal?"

"We have a deal."

The archbishop showed his delight by putting his arm around the cardinal as he thanked him. The cardinal winced and closed his eyes as 'il gorilla' squeezed his shoulders painfully. When he opened them again, he saw the girl in the Sierra Leone costume approaching their table with a telephone on a long cord.

## In Pursuit of the *Prepuzio*

As Jean-Pièrre and Héloïse stepped out of the arrivals hall at Da Vinci Airport, a black Mercedes screeched to a halt in front of them. The back doors opened and two men in dark suits jumped out and went running into the concourse.

Jean-Pièrre pulled Héloïse behind a pillar, out of sight of the Mercedes. Héloïse looked at him, bewildered, but he just signed to her to be calm.

She nodded and whispered, "What is it?"

"The car licence place. It's got an SCV number. Means it's from the Vatican. I'm guessing they're looking for us."

"But how would they know?"

"The Vatican has the largest secret service in the world, *ma chère*," he said, and led the way into the shadows behind a large Italian family arguing about how many cabs they would need.

No more than five minutes later, the two heavy-set men were back. Jean-Pièrre watched as one of the men gave directions to the driver. The driver pulled out at a much more sedate pace than he had arrived.

Jean-Pièrre nodded to himself as the car disappeared into traffic. "I was wrong. I don't think they are looking for us. Much more likely they're looking for Eddie."

While the family was still arguing, Jean-Pièrre flagged down a taxi and gave Tito's address to the driver. She looks familiar, Jean-Pièrre thought to himself as he caught a glimpse of the driver's profile, but before he could place her, Héloïse said, "Won't they be in bed?"

"No, no. They're expecting us, *ma chère*," Jean-Pièrre said, pulling her close. "Tired?"

"A little. But excited too. This is the first time I've been back in Rome since we met."

Jean-Pièrre squeezed her hand, thinking how lucky he had been in finding her. A couple of minutes later, as they were sitting at a stoplight, Jean-Pièrre suddenly realized who the cabbie was. Leaning forward, he asked, "Do you have a brother in the carabinieri?"

"Yes. But how do you know?" Suspicion in her voice.

"You took me to this same address in the Testaccio a few days ago," he told her. "I was being followed and you lost them."

Looking in the mirror as the light went green, the cabbie cried out when she recognized him. "Padre! Are we being followed again?"

"I don't think so, but keep an eye on your mirrors anyway."

"Don't worry. I'll take care of it. Welcome back to my cab. You've been away, Padre?"

"Yes. A lot has happened. First, I'm no longer a priest."

"Congratulations."

For the next few minutes, he told her of finding the love of his life. "And this is Héloïse," he said proudly.

"But that is so romantic!" she said, delighted. Catching Héloïse's eye in the mirror, she added "My name is Angelica, Héloïse. Welcome to my cab."

"Pleased to meet you, Angelica."

"And I am plain Jean-Pièrre Abélard."

Angelica got it immediately. "Héloïse and Abélard. Don't tell me. Really?"

"Really," said Jean-Pièrre.

Angelica shook her head. "What are the odds?"

"About the same as ending up in the same cab again," said Jean-Pièrre.

"Or walking on water," added Héloïse.

"Walking on water?"

"I'll explain while we're waiting," Héloïse said.

"You're not coming in?" asked Jean-Pièrre.

"No, my love. It will be quicker if you go alone." In reality, she could not bring herself to meet the man who had kept them apart for a quarter of a century.

"Would you mind waiting for me, Angelica? It shouldn't take more than half an hour or so."

Angelica nodded. "There's a cafe around the corner. I'll take Héloïse there. We'll give you one full hour."

"That should be more than enough."

Jean-Pièrre waited until the cab was out of sight before pressing the buzzer.

Anna looked even more care-worn than ever, as she let him in. "I didn't think we would ever see you again, Padre," she told him. "How is he?"

"About the same." She led him into the kitchen, where a grey-bearded priest sat at the table, an espresso sitting before him. When Jean-Pièrre entered, the priest leapt to his feet and held out his hand. "Monsignor Paolo Contadino." he announced. "Pleased to meet you at last, Padre."

"I'm afraid I'm not a priest any more, Monsignor. Just plain Jean-Pièrre Abélard. Pleased to meet you. You are here to see Tito too?"

"Actually, I'm here because Tito asked me to tell you about the disappearance of the *santissimo prepuzio* from Calcata Vecchia some years ago. I was sent there by the Lateran Palace to investigate the theft."

"Ah, then I am very pleased to meet you, Monsignor. Give me a minute while I pay my respects to Tito."

"Of course."

At the sight of Jean-Pièrre, Tito tried a weak smile. "Again, Jean-Pièrre. I am delighted that you have made the time to see me." He slumped back on the pillows, still smiling. Like any priest, Jean-Pièrre had seen many people through their final days and recognized the pallor, the almost translucent skin drawn tight at the temples that indicate that death lurked very near. Jean-Pièrre heard the door close behind him as Anna withdrew.

"Are you in pain, Tito?" he asked.

"Very little." He drew a difficult breath and said, "You found her."

"Yes, I found her. Thanks to you, my friend."

Tito stretched out his hand. Jean-Pièrre took it. "Glad for you," Tito managed, before panting for breath.

Jean-Pièrre told him to save his strength. Over the next few minutes, he told about the finding of Héloïse and finished by saying, "She is waiting for me downstairs. As you may have guessed, I have resigned my post and no longer consider myself a priest."

A cloud passed across the face of Tito but only for a moment. "You deserve your happiness, Jean-Pièrre."

"Thanks to you, Tito. And now I work for this new Messiah."

"Many are becoming believers, I hear. But many in the Vatican are terrified by him. Could the Church survive?"

"Eddie's on the way to a secret meeting with Urban as we speak. I think this pope might recognize Eddie as the Messiah."

"The cardinals will never accept it." A spark of the old ferocity in his eyes.

"Right now the Vatican scientists are comparing Eddie's DNA to that of the *santissimo prepuzio*. If they match, they will have to accept Eddie."

"Never. Never. They will falsify the conclusions, discredit their own scientists. Anything to save Mother Church."

"Exactly. That's why I came back. I need your help again."

"Yes, yes. I owe you a great deal for ... for your forgiveness."

Touched, Jean-Pièrre leaned over and kissed the old priest on the cheek. "You owe me only love, my friend."

"You have it, my son."

"I know, Tito. And right now, you are the only one I can turn to. As I told Anna on the telephone, we are looking for the part of the *santissimo prepuzio* that disappeared from Calcata in 1983. We need it to conduct our own DNA analysis."

"Yes, yes, that's why I sent for my friend, Paolo. I hope he can help you."

"I don't know how to thank you, Tito."

"Hearing my confession was thanks enough, Jean-Pièrre. Now go and talk to Paolo. I'll rest for a while. Come back to say goodbye before you leave."

"But of course, my friend."

When he returned to the kitchen, Anna was just putting a pot of coffee and a plate of homemade *amaretti* on the table for the two men. The men thanked her and took a few moments to sample the coffee and the almond biscuits before Anna withdrew.

"Tito is not faring well," Jean-Pièrre said.

"No. I'm afraid he will not be with us much longer."

"But what a man. And now he has called on you to help me. I take it he told you why we are looking for the *prepuzio*?"

"Yes. I agreed to help because I admire Pope Urban and what he stands for. He even keeps an open mind about Eddie Magdalena. And Tito. Who can deny him anything he asks?"

"Yes."

Jean-Pièrre's impatience was not lost on the monsignor. "Well, let me tell you what I learned when I visited Calcata just after the *prepuzio* disappeared. I had been sent by the Lateran Palace to investigate the theft. I arrived on a Sunday afternoon, the only day that I could be sure that the church would be open. I had been told that most masses were performed at the church in Calcata Nuova these days. When I knocked on the door of Father Don Dario's house in Calcata Nuova, no one answered. As I turned away, I ran into one of the neighbors who asked, 'Are you looking for Bacco, Padre?'

"'I'm looking for Father Don Dario Magnone,' I told him.

"'Yes, of course. But everyone here calls him Bacco, Padre, because he loves the juice of the grape. Right now he will be sleeping it off. He'll be up in a couple of hours.'

"I thanked him and decided to use the time to take the short walk down to Calcata Vecchia and look at the Church of SS Cornelius and Cyprian to see where the holy relic had been kept for so long. Have you seen the church, Jean-Pièrre?"

"No, I haven't, but we intend to be there tomorrow."

"It is a very plain white church, simple glass windows. No bigger than a chapel really. Strange to think that the *santissimo prepuzio* had resided there since 1527. Anyway, the church, as I said, is small and quite dim inside, even on a bright summer day. I found that I had the church all to myself. I walked up to the altar. There, I glanced around to make sure I was alone. Feeling very much the intruder, but serious about my mission, I passed behind the altar and looked up at relief sculptures depicting the holy circumcision. Above the altar I saw a niche with a heavy gold door. The door featured an old-fashioned keyhole. I was thrilled to find that the door was slightly ajar. This had to be the place where the gold reliquary had been kept since Bishop Cybo had donated it in 1723 in return for his tiny piece of the carne vera sacra. That fragment had been placed in the bishop's relics collection in Santa Maria degli Angeli in Rome, but now it has disappeared. Anyway, only darkness was visible through the crack behind the gold door. Now, as you can see, Jean-Pièrre, I do not come from a race of giants. I couldn't reach the gold door to push it all the way open. Looking around for some sort of tool, my eyes lighted on one of the candlesticks. I seized it and tried to insert it into the crack. The candlestick proved to be heavy and unwieldy, and after several attempts I was gasping for breath. For a minute or two, I leaned back on the altar to rest before my next attempt.

"'Maybe a broomstick, Padre.' I don't mind telling you, I let out a yell loud enough to wake the dead. Turning, I found a bearded hippie standing the other side of the altar. 'Sorry, Padre,' the man said. 'You must not have heard me come in.'

"'No, no, my son. Are you one of the parishioners here?' I had already decided that this skinny young man must be one of the *fricchettoni*, the freaks who had moved in when the regular villagers had abandoned the old town in the sixties and moved to Calcata Nuova. When I looked closer, I realized that the man was not nearly as young as I had thought at first. Grey around his temples. A few lines etched by the sun around his eyes.

"Anyway, the man shook his head and said, 'No, no. In fact, I'm a Buddhist. I just come in once a week to clean the church. Here, let me.'

He wedged the broomstick into the crack and heaved. Suddenly the gold door flew open and banged loudly against the wall startling both of us. The space inside was empty except for a few ancient cobwebs. 'What a tangled web we weave, eh Padre?' the young man said in perfectly accented American English.

"'You are American?'

"The man nodded and switched to fluent but accented Italian. He told me that the gold door had been open for weeks, but no one had had the nerve to look inside. 'Bad karma,' he called it. 'Anyway, that old rogue Bacco told the truth about one thing,' he told me. 'He really did remove the relic from here and hide it in a shoebox in his closet.'

"'In a shoebox?' I said. 'Unbelievable!'

"He nodded. 'You'd think he'd take better care of something that the church considers so holy. But then his predecessor was even worse. Father Don Antonio used to sell holy medals with a picture of the reliquary. He even claimed to anyone who bought one that he rubbed each medal on the *prepuzio*. Crazy, huh?"

"'Crazy,' I agreed. That was the moment that I decided to take the young janitor into my confidence. 'I have been sent from the Lateran Palace to investigate the disappearance of the *santissimo prepuzio*,' I confessed.

"The janitor propped his broom against the altar and sat himself down in the front pew. 'And how's that going?' he asked me.

"'Not so well,' I told him. 'I called on Padre Don Dario, but apparently he likes a few drinks after mass.'

"The janitor laughed again and said, "Oh, yes. In fact, he likes a few drinks after anything."

"I introduced myself and sat down beside him. His name was Ben Stilwell. An American from Maine, but he had been living in Rome for years before moving to Calcata in the early seventies. 'I hate to disappoint you, Monsignor,' he told me, 'but everybody in the village knows who took the *prepuzio*. The Vatican. I can hardly blame them. I'm sure they can find a better resting place for the old foreskin than a shoebox.'

"'But the Vatican does not have it, Ben,' I told him. Ben looked at me skeptically, so I said, 'Look, if we had it, why would I be here?'

"Ben thought about that for a moment and then he said, 'Maybe old Bacco was telling the truth. He claimed a young couple dressed in black visited him in the church here on the Sunday before the reliquary disappeared. That part I know is true, because I saw them leaving the church. They were speaking French to each other.'

"'How did you know it was French?' I asked.

"'I'm from Maine, Padre. Lots of Frenchies there. Anyway Bacco said that the couple had wanted a mass said on the next Sunday. Two days later, he found the shoebox missing. He claims the couple must have stolen it.'

"I had taken out my notebook and was making notes. I asked him to describe the couple.

"'A young woman with an older man,' he said. 'The woman was taller than the man. Long, dark hair. Oh, the man's head was shaved. And, as I said, they spoke French.'

"I asked him if he had heard their names, but no such luck. I asked him a few more questions, but it was clear that he had told me everything he knew. We shook hands and I was just about to leave when he told me that there was something I could do for him. You'd never guess what he wanted. This Buddhist wanted me to hear his confession. Well, I agreed, of course. When I was leaving, I brought up the fact that he had told me that he was a Buddhist. 'Only part of me, Padre,' he said, 'only part of me.'

"Two hours later, when I knocked on Father Don Dario's door again, it opened. Don Dario looked alarmed when I identified myself, but he led the way into his untidy living room and offered me a glass of wine.

"Declining the offer, I asked to see the closet where the reliquary had been stored. Without a word, he led the way into his bedroom and showed me the spot on the floor where the shoebox had rested. No clues that I could see. Only an empty space on the floor.

"'Why did you move it from the church in Calcata Vecchia?' I asked him. He got pretty agitated, started to sweat. He almost ran into the kitchen and poured himself a generous glass of Montepulciano. He took a deep draught before telling me that he had moved the *prepuzio* here for safekeeping. 'Unfortunately, the foreigners who occupy the old village now are not to be trusted,' he said. Mind you, the Calcatese regard anyone from more than a kilometer distance as a foreigner.

"Don Dario then led the way to the kitchen table, and we sat down opposite each other. I found myself staring at an electric sacred heart on the wall above the sink that throbbed in a most disconcerting manner. I asked him to tell me about the couple who talked to him about a mass two days before the theft.

"'They were French,' he said, 'From Canada. They wanted a mass to celebrate their anniversary as members of some group or other.'

"I asked for their names, but he had no idea. And suddenly he shouted that they had stolen the *santissimo prepuzio*. He was sure of it.

"'But how would they have known where to find it?' I asked him. He had no idea, so I asked if he had shown them the reliquary.

"'What if I did?' he said. 'But I made them wait outside the bedroom while I brought it out.'

"I was just about to leave, when a thought came to me, and I asked him whether the couple had dedicated the mass to anyone. Unexpectedly, he told me that there had been a dedication, but he couldn't remember for who, after all this time. 'But don't you keep a record of special masses?' I asked, not expecting much.

"Don Dario rose and left the room without a word. I followed him into his untidy office. 'They left a deposit,' Don Dario muttered as he opened his filing cabinet. After a few minutes of shuffling papers, he pulled one out. 'Here it is. M. and Mlle. Riopelle. And the mass ...' He found his glasses and put them on. '... ah, the mass was dedicated to someone called Claude Vorilhon.'

"I did not recognize any of the names, but I recorded them in my notebook. When I made my report at the Lateran Palace, no one made any effort to follow up my leads. Only then did I understand that my visit to Calcata had been nothing more than a pro forma attempt to seem to be taking the theft seriously. Who knows, perhaps the janitor was right and the Vatican does have it."

Jean-Pièrre thanked Monsignor Contadino and glanced at his watch. Already late. "I need to see Tito one last time," he told the monsignor. "Go with God!"

"Go with God, Jean-Pièrre. I will continue to follow the career of your Messiah with interest."

When Jean-Pièrre stepped back into Tito's room to see him, the old man's eyes were closed. Jean-Pièrre sat on the chair next to Tito's bed and leaned over to whisper in the old man's ear. "That was a fine thing you did for me, my friend." Suddenly, Tito opened his eyes. Jean-Pièrre had long since ceased to be troubled by the eerie gleam in his friend's eyes and now noticed for the first time that their power had begun to dim. Feeling a pang of regret, he realized just how much he would miss his old mentor.

"Thanks for introducing me to Paolo. His information will be invaluable in proving that Eddie really is the Messiah."

"The least I could do." Tito's voice came out as a whisper. He reached his hand towards Jean-Pièrre, who took it in both of his. "You have been one of my few friends. Paolo is another. Most ... most people are afraid of *la iettatura*." He gestured towards his eyes. "As a child, I once tried to do away with myself. God forgive me. You see, I had no friends at all. Even my teachers kept their distance. Some even made the sign against the evil eye whenever I came into view. So once, after confession, of course, when my soul was pure, I was tempted to "fall" in front of a bus. Then I would go to heaven and my eyes would be like everyone else's."

"But you didn't."

"Ah, God would not let me."

"I'm going to miss you, Tito. You have been a wonderful friend to me."

"Even though ..." He let the thought trail off.

"Even though you lied to me to save my vocation? Yes. Perhaps it was for the best. I would never have been an apostle of the new Messiah if you had told the truth that day. And now I have a new vocation, and the woman I love. Who could ask for more? And I have you to thank. And God, of course." He stroked Tito's cold, dry hand.

Tito's grip tightened on Jean-Pièrre's hand. "I must beg one last favor, Jean-Pièrre."

Jean-Pièrre knew that Tito was going to ask him to give the Last Rites. He was about to remind Tito that he was not a priest anymore when he realized that since the coming of Eddie, the world had changed. "I will need some olive oil," he said.

"What house in Rome is without olive oil," Tito chided him. "Over there. On the dresser. Anna rubs it on my sores."

Jean-Pièrre got the small bottle and sat back down beside Tito. "I need to hear your confession, of course, to make sure that you are in a state of grace."

"Bless me, Father, for I have sinned ..." The only sins the old man could dredge up since Jean-Pièrre had heard his last confession were of the most venial kind.

When Jean-Pièrre had absolved Tito's sins, he reached for the bottle of olive oil and could not help noticing that it was 'Extra Virgin.' How appropriate. The phrase had popped into his mind before he could stop it.

"Do you remember the words in Latin?" Tito asked. "Latin. I ... I think so."

"I think getting rid of the Latin Mass in Vatican II was a mistake."

Olive oil is the traditional oil for this final sacrament. In Latin it is called *oleum infirmorum*, the oil of the sick. Jean-Pièrre dipped his fingers into the bottle and said the words while inscribing a sign of the cross on Tito's forehead: "*Per istam sanctam unctionem et suam piissimam misericordiam ...*" When he was finished, he gently lifted Tito and held him in his arms.

"Goodbye, old friend. I'll tell Eddie that here goes a man beloved of God."

He lowered Tito back on to the pillow, unable now to hold back the tears. The old man lay still as Jean-Pièrre let himself out.

As he took the stairs down, hurrying to get to the bottom before the timer left him in darkness, he wondered whether the women would still be waiting after all this time. He need not have worried. When he got into the cab, both women could see that he wore a deep sadness in his eyes.

Angelica patted his hand and said, "Héloïse and I have made the arrangements. You will stay with me tonight and tomorrow I will drive you to Calcata myself."

"I was so lucky meeting you," Jean-Pièrre told her.

"Hah! If you had still been a priest, I would have told you to get another damned cab. Now sit back and whisper your love to this wonderful woman. We'll be at my apartment in ten minutes."

## Castel Gandolfo: Day One

The flight carrying Eddie, Pannychis, Jean-Pièrre and Héloïse had touched down a little after midnight in Rome. The two couples parted in the arrivals lounge with Eddie wishing Jean-Pièrre and Héloïse good luck in their quest for the *prepuzio*. Luigi Fuseli was waiting for Eddie and Pannychis in the VIP lounge and hustled them out of the airport and into a waiting Mercedes. "We're heading to the Vatican Heliport," Luigi explained as their car pulled away.

After they cleared the airport, Pannychis noticed that the driver was checking his mirrors frequently. Finally he told Luigi that another vehicle was following them. Luigi looked back and nodded. "All they'll be able to report is that we took a helicopter," he said. A few minutes later, the chase car drove past as Eddie's party was waved through the security gate to the waiting helicopter, an eight-seater Agusta A109.

After a flight of only a few minutes they arrived in the town of Castel Gandolfo, 24 kilometers south of Rome. Transferring to a van, they drove up through the dark deserted streets to the pope's summer residence, the Apostolic Palace perched high atop a ridge overlooking Lake Albano.

"Pope Urban apologizes for not being here to greet you because of the late hour," Luigi told them, "but he will take breakfast with you at seven."

They were shown to their rooms by a nun. Pannychis' room was next to Eddie's. Eddie had barely unpacked before he heard her gentle knock on his door. "I rumpled the bed," she told him as she slipped in.

"Maybe I should have put some pillows under the blanket in case the sister peeks in to protect my virtue."

"Don't worry, I'll take care of that," Eddie said as he led her to a small table under the window. "Look, they laid on a midnight snack," said Eddie pointing to the plate of sandwiches, olives, cheese and a small carafe of the local white wine. "See? Two glasses. Was there a tray in your room?"

"No."

Eddie poured them each a glass of the wine. "I'm liking this pope already," Eddie told her, as they clinked glasses. "To all the poor and dispossessed of the world."

"And to trying to give them a better life," Pannychis added.

When they had finished the wine, Eddie opened the shutters and they stood in the window looking down at the few lights in the town below them and the inky blackness of Lake Albano beyond.

"Beautiful," said Pannychis.

"You know, I think popes make out much better than Messiahs." Pannychis took him by the hand and led the way to the canopy bed.

"I think you might change your mind," she said as she lit the two candles on the side table and, with a practiced gesture, let her robe slide to the floor. The sudden sight of her naked could still make Eddie take in a ragged involuntary breath at her beauty. "In this light, your skin is the color of the finest honey," he told her.

"My mother tells me that my father used to say I was the color of the Sahara sand at dusk," she told him before leaping into bed. Eddie was not far behind.

✳   ✳   ✳

Shortly before six, Pannychis awoke to find that the summer sun was already streaming into the room. "I should go back to my room," she told Eddie.

Eddie nodded agreement and said, "Doesn't it make you feel like we're teenagers sneaking around behind our parents' backs?"

"Well, they do call him '*il Papa*' here."

"Do we have time to ..."

Pannychis kissed him lightly on the lips. "Later, my love."

Luigi Fuseli collected them just before 6:30. He had already been up for over an hour, most of it spent in earnest conversation with Pope Urban over Vatican protocols. The previous day, he and Pope Urban had spent hours going over press clippings, piecing together the biography of this man who would be the Messiah. Now they were wondering how to greet someone who may or may not be the Messiah, someone that the church had been expecting for almost two millennia. "Normally I would instruct them about kissing your ring, Your Holiness, about not initiating conversation, about the traditional deference to the papal office, but now? What if he is the Messiah?"

"Don't worry, Luigi. It is only breakfast and there will be no cardinals present to object. I'll know how to greet him and his companion when they arrive."

"Of course, Your Holiness."

When Luigi led them into the light and airy breakfast room, Pope Urban was standing before a table laden with food. With easy grace, he stepped forward and took the hand of Eddie and then of Pannychis: "We welcome you to our summer place. I'm afraid it is rather grand. In fact, this place is bigger than the whole of Vatican City. Come, come, sit. The coffee is getting cold."

"Looks wonderful, Your Holiness," said Pannychis, favoring him with a smile that sparked a certain shiver in the loins. Even a pope is not immune to the charms of a beautiful woman.

Urban gave her a mischievous look. "I asked the sisters to serve the breakfast and then retire to their prayers. We have the place to ourselves," he said, gesturing at the vaulted ceilings and the windows looking out towards the lake. "Mind you, I'm sure the rumors are growing like ivy outside these walls."

The pope poured coffee for everyone. As he filled Luigi's cup, he said, "My turn to serve for a change, Luigi."

"Yes, Your Holiness," Luigi agreed, not entirely comfortable with this new protocol.

"In Italy they don't usually eat much in the morning," Urban explained to Eddie and Pannychis as he took a roll, some cheese and a handful of olives and placed them on his own plate. "But my spies tell me that you like bacon and scrambled eggs and white toast." Pope Urban paused for effect before adding, "and your favorite cereal is Honey Nut Cheerios, is it not?"

Eddie laughed. "You really do have the biggest spy network in the world."

It was Urban's turn to laugh. "No, no. Luigi and I spent a long time yesterday reading the press about you. One of those puff pieces that the American press like so much was entitled 'How does a Messiah spend his day?' The intrepid reporter wrote that you like to begin the day with a big breakfast of bacon and eggs and Cheerios. I have a wonderful staff, and they managed to find these Cheerios. I must confess I tried them. They are very good, but Luigi tells me we probably have to import them from America."

Eddie wondered whether one of the apostles had been the source of the puff piece. Or it could easily have been Marc Baptiste, as he was in charge of liaison with the press, but that seemed unlikely. "Well, the reporter was right about my choice of breakfast, Your Holiness. Not Pannychis though. She'll probably just have coffee and a croissant."

"Please, when we are alone, call me by my baptismal name, Pablo."

"Sure. And I'm just Eddie. And Pannychis here is the love of my life, Pablo."

Eddie ate a bowl of cereal before lifting the lid off the chafing dish and helping himself to bacon and eggs. Pannychis selected a croissant and a couple of olives. "In my profession, Lent lasts all year," she said, when she saw the pope was watching her. "Great coffee."

"I'm glad you like it. I too, demand good coffee. Pope John-Paul when he was installed in the papal apartments, claimed that there were only two things in short supply at the Vatican: honesty, and a good cup of coffee. With Luigi's help, I have corrected the coffee situation. Honesty may take a little longer. In a way, Eddie, you and I have something in common. Both of us represent a second coming. You, of course, represent the Second Coming of the Messiah. Myself,

I have been accused by many in the Curia of being the second coming of Albino Luciani, Pope John-Paul I." The pope noticed that this frank talk with Eddie was making his valet distinctly uncomfortable and said, "Aren't you leading a prayer circle with the Sodality of the Virgin this morning, Luigi?"

Luigi picked up his cue. "Yes, Your Holiness, perhaps I should leave now."

"Yes, of course. We'll talk later after lunch."

Eddie waited for the valet to leave before saying, "John-Paul. Isn't he the pope that only lasted for thirty-three days?"

"Yes. And there are rumors, as I'm sure you know, that he was murdered."

"Really?" Pannychis had been caught by surprise.

"Yes, my dear Pannychis. To this day, I can't say what the truth is, but his camerlengo certainly acted strangely after the body was found. The main reason we will probably never know the full truth is because Cardinal Villot, the camerlengo I mentioned, ordered the pope's cremation immediately, without an autopsy."

"Why would anyone want to kill a pope?" asked Pannychis.

"Oh, there are many reasons and even more suspects. Pope Jean-Paul wanted the Catholic Church to be restored to its position as the church of the poor. Many in the Curia opposed him. Like Albino, I too am looking for a way to liberalize the edicts of Pope Paul VI expressed in *Humanae Vitae* which crushed the hopes of the majority of Catholics. That encyclical totally divided the church. It decreed that the only birth control methods available to Catholics were the so-called rhythm method or outright abstinence. Many left the church. Others ignored the encyclical or shopped around for a sympathetic priest. I want to give people hope, and I think I have a good chance. When *Humanae Vitae* was put out in 1968, Monsignor Lambruschini, who announced it to the press, stressed that the encyclical was not an infallible document. If it is not infallible, it can be updated. And that is what I intend to do."

"That's one of the main reasons we're here," said Eddie. "When you invited me, I knew that you were the first religious leader I had to visit.

You are one of the few people who is taking the population explosion seriously. I would probably have sought you out first anyway, Pablo. After all, your church was the first to recognize Jesus of Nazareth as the original Messiah. And it doesn't hurt that a quarter of the world's population is Catholic and a third are Christians of some kind or another."

Pablo nodded. "I would like to allow Catholics to use birth control and even, dare I say it, allow my flock to get divorced when they are trapped in loveless marriages. Let me tell you, I had a brother Donato, a good man. He was a mason in La Plata. He and his wife had eleven children. They were very poor, even though Donato worked all the hours God gave, to support his wife and his children. He died of a heart attack when he was only forty-nine. I want to give people like him a better life. Many oppose me in this. Most are worthy men, but some look at how fast Mother Church is growing in Africa and South America and don't want to allow any form of contraception."

"You are a good man, Pablo," Eddie told him. "Allowing Catholics to divorce would be a radical step."

"Let me tell you, Eddie, in 1970 the government of Italy passed law 898, legalizing divorce throughout Italy despite huge opposition from the church. Well, the passage of the law did not deter the Vatican in the least from its vigorous opposition. Eventually, we forced a referendum in 1974. The turnout was around 88%. Almost sixty percent voted to keep the new law. Italy is a Catholic country, and yet the majority of Italian Catholics wanted the freedom to divorce if their marriage broke down. I'm sure the numbers would be even greater today."

"Oh, sure. Trouble is you're going to make as many enemies as Pope John Paul."

Pablo smiled. "Maybe more. But I'm seventy-three, Eddie, so I don't have a lot of time, even if I make no enemies. I think my third goal may be the one that will upset my enemies in the Curia even more than the other two. I would like to allow my priests to marry. We have an awful problem with priests and even bishops molesting children. Right now, we are only just beginning to realize the extent of the problem. I am sure our prohibition against priestly marriage is largely to blame."

"Wow! That is impressive, Pablo. And dangerous."

"A pope cannot be afraid of doing the right thing, Eddie."

"No. Of course not."

"But priests in the early church married, didn't they?" asked Pannychis, fascinated now.

"Oh yes. Before the Council of Nicea in 325 most priests married, but the assembly at Nicea decreed that priests could not marry after ordination. Other bans followed asserting the same thing. The great St. Augustine was not very helpful when he said in his *Confessiones* that there is nothing so likely to draw down the spirit of a man as the caress of a woman."

Eddie sat back and looked at the pope in awe. "Quite an amazing agenda, Your Holiness. What about the ordination of women then?"

"Banned by the Council of Laodicea in 352. I'm sure women will be ordained one day, as they should be, but I don't think we are ready for that yet."

Pope Urban looked at Eddie curiously, as he seemed to slip into a trance for a few seconds. And was that a shadow flitting about near Eddie's shoulder? Eddie nodded as if to himself before saying, "Marie says that the trinity was proclaimed at the Council of Nicea too. So 325 was the year that the church finally recognized the importance of the Holy Spirit." The pope looked understandably puzzled.

"You must tell him about Marie," Pannychis said softly.

"Of course," agreed Eddie, and a moment later an insubstantial figure appeared in the fourth chair at table. "Meet Marie."

Pope Urban's hand twitched before he caught himself on the point of making the *mano cornuto*, the sign against the evil eye. Taking a deep breath, he said, "You are the dead nun that Eddie found on the night of the solstice, no?"

"Yes." Her voice was soft, mellifluent.

"And you are the Holy Spirit?"

"Yes. I was sent by God to help Eddie when he realized the role that he had been cast to play."

Eddie nodded. "The whole idea of becoming the Messiah scared the crap out of me, Pablo. I'm still not totally clear about what God wants of me. One of Marie's jobs is to be my guardian angel. Before I met Pannychis, she was the spirit that kept me from collapsing under the weight of the responsibility. I'm surprised she has appeared so clearly. Sure sign, you are one of God's chosen, Pablo. This is the first time that anyone except Arthur Whitehead has had more than a brief glimpse of the Holy Spirit."

Pope Urban dropped his gaze and folded his hands in prayer as he fervently intoned, "*Veni, Sancti Spiritus, erple tuorum corda fidelium et tui amoris in eis ignem accende.*"

Eddie recognized the prayer to the Holy Spirit, usually said at Pentacost, to invite the Holy Spirit to fill the hearts of the faithful with the fire of Her love. A tiny Pentacostal fire flickered over the cold, leftover sausages for a few moments before disappearing. Eddie smiled. The Big Guy sure had a sense of humor.

Slowly the image of Marie faded back into Eddie, as Pablo finished his prayer. Pablo seemed to Eddie to be a little unsteady as he got to his feet and said, "I need to pray for guidance."

"Yes, Your Holiness," said Eddie, rising in turn.

The pope bowed to Eddie and Pannychis and said, "We'll talk again this afternoon, if you have no objection."

"That would be fine."

"Then I'll send in the sisters to clear the dishes. One of them will show you back to your rooms."

"Don't worry about us. We'll find our own way back," Eddie told him.

"I'm sorry. I feel overwhelmed at the moment." He managed a weak smile. "We have been waiting for You to arrive for nearly two thousand years and yet when You do ... Your revelations make me feel lightheaded."

Instinctively, Pannychis approached the small figure and, to his surprise, wrapped her arms around him. "It's all about love," she whispered to him.

"Yes."

He reached out a hand and Eddie took it, saying simply, "*Dominus vobiscum.*"

"*Et cum spiritu tuo,*" said the pope in a shaky voice.

"*Amen,*" Eddie and Pannychis chorused.

"He'll be O.K.," Eddie assured her when he had gone. "The sight of Marie must have been a helluva shock."

## Calcata Vecchia

Héloïse was first to spot the ancient village perched on the pinnacle of a finger of volcanic tufa. "That's got to be Calcata," she said, pointing off to her right.

"Yes, that's it," agreed Angelica without bothering to look.

"It looks as if the houses just grew out of the rock," said Héloïse. Jean-Pièrre caught a glimpse, before a nearer hill obscured his view. "No wonder they moved the people to a new village. It looks like those houses crammed on top are ready to fall into the valley at any moment."

"The next earthquake is overdue," said Angelica cheerfully.

Five minutes later they pulled into the parking lot in front of the old town. "Now we have to walk. The streets of the old town are too narrow for vehicles," explained Angelica as they got out of her old Fiat taxi.

Jean-Pièrre noted that there were not many cars in the lot and was glad that they had decided to get an early start from Angelica's apartment. Last night, Angelica had insisted that he and Héloïse take her bed, and she would sleep on the couch. "Think of it as your honeymoon," she said to them when they told her they could not take her bed.

"But we're not married," Héloïse told her.

"Does your Messiah know?" Angelica had asked with mock horror.

"Of course."

"Then this is your honeymoon. I often sleep on the couch. It's softer than the bed anyway." Exhausted, they had slept like the dead until

Angelica crept into the bedroom with coffee for them both.

"This gate is the only way into Calcata Vecchia," Angelica told them as they approached a narrow roman archway. Behind it the cobblestoned lane rose towards the village, curving to the left at the top. On the way up, they passed the door where old Bastiano's ram had stopped and refused to move, prompting the rediscovery of the prepuzio. The narrow lane curved again before it opened out into a piazza in front of the little Church of SS Cornelius and Cyprian.

The sun broke through the morning clouds as they reached the middle of the piazza. No more than four people in sight. Héloïse stopped and surveyed the small square with its flaking plaster-on-stone walls and profusion of greenery spilling off a second floor balcony at the narrow end. Two small stalls had been set up. The one selling used books in English and Spanish was tended by a rotund, bearded man dressed in a tie-dyed T-shirt. Across the piazza, a woman dressed in black latex despite the heat was reading a book and sitting in front of a stall stocked with tourist trinkets and postcards. "More cats than people," Héloïse remarked after spotting at least half a dozen.

"Calcata is famous for its cats – if it's famous for anything," Angelica observed.

Jean-Pièrre was looking back at the small church of Santi Cornelio e Cipriano. "So that's where the *prepuzio* was hidden for all those years," he said. The church was plain, with a rough plaster facade that had once been white. Above the narrow door and just under the peaked roof was a simple clock where time had stopped at 6:30. Above and to either side of the door, two unadorned, oblong windows. Could pass for a protestant church, Jean-Pièrre thought to himself.

"But I like these," said Angelica, pointing at three clumsy thrones carved out of the native tufo, the volcanic rock that made up the spire of rock under their feet. "Here. Come on, Héloïse."

She scuffled around in her purse, pulled out a camera and handed it to Jean-Pièrre. "Take our picture," she ordered and led the way to the thrones. She sat in one, Héloïse in another. Both were dwarfed by the seats.

"Smile." Jean-Pièrre took two pictures to be sure.

When Angelica retrieved her camera, she announced. "I need to pee. Come on, Héloïse. There's a bar down that alley." Jean-Pièrre blushed. He couldn't recall any woman making such an announcement in front of him when he had been a priest.

Héloïse kissed Jean-Pièrre's cheek and said, "We'll be back in a minute."

"No, no. Take your time. There's no hurry. I'll be in the church."

Jean-Pièrre was surprised that the church was open even though it was not Sunday. Nothing worth stealing any more, Jean-Pièrre concluded. Inside, the air was cooler. For a few moments, he stood looking down the aisle at the altar. Without thinking, he crossed himself and then walked down to the altar, and looked at the golden door where the relic had once resided. The door was closed now.

Feeling strange, he genuflected in front of the altar and then walked back towards the windows above the small choir loft. To his left was a simple wooden confessional, and he could not resist pulling aside the red velvet curtain and sitting on the small bench between the two grilled windows. When he closed the curtain and sat in the half light, he was overwhelmed with memories of his life as a priest. Even the smells were the same: furniture polish mixed with a tinge of incense. It had been in his own confessional in St. Gabriel Lalemant on that fateful Saturday night, that this adventure had begun. God only knew where it would end. He sat back and thought of Eddie.

He could not have said how long he had sat there lost in his reveries when he heard someone kneel on the altar side of the confessional. Opening the grille to apologize to the parishioner, he saw as if through a glass darkly, Héloïse. "When I couldn't see you, I thought you'd be in here," she told him. She had put on a beret to enter the church and looked fetchingly French, Jean-Pièrre thought.

"Part of my old life. That's all. You're my life now."

Héloïse blew a kiss through the grille. "*Je t'aime.*"

"*Moi aussi.*"

Suddenly a shout from the door that startled them both. "Where are my lovers?" They smiled at each other: Angelica.

The three of them spent the rest of the day exploring the charming village. Some of the boutiques, and even a few of the dwellings, occupied ancient caves. The fricchettoni, mostly artists and musicians who had begun to move into the deserted village in the sixties, had transformed the place. Twisted lanes, lookouts that leaned out over the 150-meter drop into the Valley of the River Treja below, narrow passageways, wrought-iron balconies, large pots of herbs, masks in windows, and cats and kittens everywhere.

They asked the few people they met about the mysterious couple who had ordered a mass two days before the disappearance of the reliquary. The inhabitants mostly just shrugged and didn't seem to want to talk about it. One woman said, "The Vatican took it. Everyone knows that. The church will steal anything that's not nailed down."

By late afternoon, tired and discouraged, they stopped at one of the restaurants for drinks and a late lunch. The place was almost empty but the proprietor, a man of about forty with a shock of prematurely white hair and two days' growth, greeted them as if he had been expecting them. When they had finished their meals, Angelica ordered three more Peroni beers. The owner brought the drinks and sat down with them. "Rocky," he said, holding out his hand. Over the next hour, he told them about the early days in the late sixties when the word had spread that there was a village here for the taking. "Lot of work to make this place over. And the fucking bureaucrats!" He turned to Angelica. "Only in Italy, yes?"

Angelica laughed. "Where else?"

Héloïse gave him a smile that would melt marble and, putting her hand on his, told him, "We came here to try to find out who stole the relic six years ago. So far, everybody thinks the Vatican has it, but they don't."

"I thought the Vatican had it, too," Rocky said.

"If the Vatican had it, Rocky, they wouldn't have sent a man here to look for it."

Rocky thought for a moment. "Yeah, I heard about him from Ben."

Jean-Pièrre said, "Don Dario says that a young couple was here just before it disappeared. He is sure they took it."

"Bacco? I wouldn't trust anything he says."

"This time he might be right. The Vatican investigator found out that there really was a couple here. Don Dario had a record of the mass they paid for."

Rocky suddenly looked troubled. "A couple. Dressed all in black? He was bald?"

"That's them," Héloïse told him.

"I saw them coming out of the passage that leads down to Semiramis' place."

"Semiramis?"

"Some call her 'la Strega.' In inglese?"

"The witch," Jean-Pièrre told him. Héloïse's eyes went wide.

"Semiramis is a good person, signora. Just..." he shrugged, "she has her ways."

Half an hour later, armed with Rocky's detailed directions, Jean-Pièrre and Héloïse left on their search. Angelica had begged off. "She wants to stay and flirt with Rocky," Héloïse told Jean-Pièrre as they walked through the village.

"Ah." Jean-Pièrre pulled her to him and kissed her on the cheek. "I seem to have missed a lot during my years as a priest."

"But you're catching up just fine."

The door to Semiramis' place was hidden at the end of a dark passage that sloped down into the volcanic rock. To their right, a rough-hewn hole in the wall covered with a wrought-iron grille admitted enough light to see that the door was of a strange construction. Neither of them had ever seen the like outside the enchanted village of Calcata Vecchia. Made of heavy wood studded with iron, the door was a conventional but narrow rectangle at the top and bottom, but the middle curved out on both sides.

"Why would anyone build such a door?" Jean-Pièrre mused aloud.

"Maybe it's the only way to get the furniture in and out," said Héloïse. "Or to get the fat donkeys in and out. In medieval times, Biblical times too, barn animals were the only central heating available. Ready?"

"As I'll ever be."

Jean-Pièrre nodded resolutely, took a deep breath and rapped loudly on the door. A vague shuffling sound behind the door. He waited impatiently for a few seconds and was just about to knock again when the door began to creak open. Jean-Pièrre remembered that Rocky had told them the witch was a recluse.

A tiny woman in her sixties wearing a moth-eaten grey cardigan the color of the native rock stood before them. Her hair, hanging over one shoulder in a thick braid, was black and wiry with a white streak on the left side of her head. Her other shoulder was occupied by a black-and-white magpie.

"No room! No room!" shrieked the bird in English, puzzling Jean-Pièrre.

"No, no, Deneb. Where are your manners?" Semiramis scolded in an unfamiliar Italian dialect. "These are the people we have been expecting. Come in." Expecting? thought Jean-Pièrre as he took Héloïse by the hand and stepped inside. A cave opened up before them roughly divided into two rooms. The remains of ancient stalactites and stalagmites told them that they had entered a limestone cavern. Each room was lit by a small grilled window. Electrical wires were hung carelessly along the wall. The back room seemed to serve as a bedroom, as there was a small canopy bed. By the looks of it, the old canopy overlaid with a large sheet of plastic served a practical purpose. On a perch up in the shadowy recesses above the bed sat a pair of owls, their eyes closed at the moment in a diurnal doze. A few droppings and owl pellets decorated the plastic sheet. Jean-Pièrre guessed that the curtain masking the corner opposite the bed contained a bathroom.

The floors of the entire cave were covered with overlapping Persian carpets from which, in odd places, stalagmites poked up. Four of the stalagmites had been sawn off at the same height and supported an antique table top with traces of gilt on its edges. Half of the improvised table held a very large short-wave radio housed in a wooden cabinet that looked to Jean-Pièrre as if it were old enough to have been constructed by Marconi himself. The display was glowing, and whispered language crackling with static came from its speaker. Semiramis must eat her meals at the table listening to the outside world on her radio, as there was a wooden chair placed in front of the table and a place set.

Semiramis led them into what passed for the living room and invited them to sit on a bench under the window. When they did so, she dragged over the only chair and introduced herself, adding, "You must have some tea after your journey." Springing out of her chair, she crossed to the corner that served as her kitchen where there were a few improvised shelves along the wall. The top shelf held a few cans, packages of dried pasta, a loaf. One of the wires on the wall above snaked down and powered her tiny refrigerator. Another powered an old hotplate. Sitting on a wooden box next to the counter was a silver oil-burning samovar, lovingly polished. After she had lit the oil burner, she pulled out a stove pipe from behind the samovar and, with practiced ease, she slotted it over the hole at the top of the samovar and poked the other end out the window into the open air. "The smoke is bad for Castor and Pollux," she explained flicking her hand towards the pair of owls. "It doesn't bother Deneb, of course, but then, he's a city bird."

Jean-Pièrre was having trouble understanding her and guessed that she was speaking Calcatese, the local dialect. With a struggle, he began to translate for Héloïse, but as soon as he did, Semiramis stopped buttering the bread and looked at them with sudden suspicion.

"The signora does not speak Italian?" she asked. "Then you are not from the Vatican?"

"So that's who you were expecting," said Jean-Pièrre. "I speak Italian but Héloïse has only a few words."

"English then, signora?" said Semiramis effortlessly making the switch. Jean Pierre was surprised not just at how good her English was, but even more so by the fact that her accent was North American.

"Yes, thank you, Semiramis. English is fine."

"I thought you were from the Vatican, looking for the *prepuzio* that was stolen, like that man who turned up in Calcata a few years ago."

"Ah, Monsignor Paulo Contadino. I have met him, but Héloïse and I are not from the church at all." He glanced at the old shortwave. "Have you heard of Eddie Magdalena, Semiramis?"

"The new Messiah? The one who walks on water?"

"Yes. We were sent by Him."

Semiramis cocked her head to one side and stared at Jean-Pièrre and Héloïse while she absorbed this information. Eventually her expression softened, and she reached up and brushed Deneb gently off her shoulder. With an indignant squawk, the magpie fluttered up to a perch hung near the ceiling between two small stalactites. "From the Messiah?" She patted down her hair with a coquettish gesture. "Why would He be interested in poor Semiramis, I wonder."

"Because you seem to hold the key to the puzzle."

"The Messiah needs our help to find the *prepuzio*," she told Deneb who received this news in silence.

When Semiramis had distributed the glasses of tea and the slices of buttered bread with a thin scrape of Nutella, she sat down opposite the couple, sipped her tea and said, still in English, "If I help you, perhaps this Messiah could do something for me."

"Perhaps."

"I have this pain in my side here." She reached down and massaged her abdomen. "And sometimes I think I can feel a lump. Some nights I cannot sleep at all and just stay awake and watch Castor and Pollux hunt the mice. Do you think, signore, he could make me whole again?"

Jean-Pièrre's heart went out to the old woman. "Yes, yes, Semiramis. I am sure he can."

Héloïse reached out and held the woman's hand for a moment. "Eddie will help you."

Semiramis smiled for the first time and said, "Why are you looking for the foreskin? What good is it to you?"

Jean-Pièrre told her about the DNA sequencing being undertaken secretly by the Vatican, and about their need to duplicate the results in case the Vatican suppressed their findings.

Semiramis nodded her understanding before continuing. "When the war ended I found myself in a refugee camp in Poland run by the Red Cross. I was only nineteen. Because we were gypsies, my family had been rounded up by the Nazis in Cracow in 1943. I had been sleeping at a friend's house, so I escaped. I never saw any of them again." Jean-Pièrre suppressed his impatience, realizing that Semiramis had to tell her story in her own way.

"After a few months, I was adopted by a Canadian couple. They were strict Calvinists who owned a small farm near Prince Albert in Saskatchewan." That explained the accent, noted Jean-Pièrre.

"When I wasn't going to school, I spent so many of my waking hours working on the farm that sometimes I wondered whether my parents had wanted a girl or a farmhand. Oh, I was fed and clothed all right, but I was never allowed to go into Prince Albert except to school. Even so, I managed to fall in love with a boy in high school. A month later I was pregnant. When I told the boy, he said the child could not be his. His parents agreed. My own stepmother called me a gypsy slut. My stepfather refused to speak to me. In the end, I ran away and ended up in Montreal. As you can imagine, I was desperate. I had stolen a little money from my parents, but after a week or so the money ran out. I was hungry and desperate when I walked into a Catholic church and asked for help. The priest was a kind man and he contacted the nuns. They looked after me during my confinement. When my daughter, Paulette, was born, the nuns took her from me. I had to sign papers and after that I thought I would never see her again, but I was wrong. Not having any plans, I began to travel. My Roma roots? Maybe. Anyway, I eventually ended up in Rome living with a man who called himself a writer." She let out a sudden shriek of bitter laughter and then continued as if nothing had happened. "When we heard that people were starting an artist's colony in Calcata Vecchia, we came to see and stayed. Two years later he disappeared, but I have been here ever since.

"Then in 1982, I received a letter from Montreal. It was from Paulette. She had traced me down through an organization that helped children find their birth mothers. She was married now to somebody called Daniel Riopelle. We began to exchange letters and pictures. Here, I will show you."

Semiramis got up and opened a chest that stood at the foot of her bed. Héloïse looked at Jean-Pièrre and whispered, "Poor woman." Jean-Pièrre nodded without taking his eyes off Semiramis who was taking papers out of the chest and piling them on the bed. Finally she held up a yellow envelope full of snapshots. She squeezed herself between Héloïse and Jean-Pièrre on the bench, saying, "The light is better here."

For the next half hour, the old woman showed them her pictures. Most were of Paulette alone or with her husband. Jean-Pièrre desperately wanted one of the pictures but, realizing how precious they were to Semiramis, he could not bring himself to ask her. When Semiramis returned to the chest to find her letters, she handed the pile to Héloïse.

"Is this the latest one?" asked Héloïse, holding up a red envelope containing a Christmas card.

"Yes. Christmas of '82. Last one I got from her. She came over to see me the next year."

"May I open it?"

"Yes, yes, my dear."

Inside the card, Héloïse found a picture of Paulette and Daniel, the kind of photograph that people have taken at a studio to send out to friends during the holidays.

"Semiramis, could we take this picture with us? We'll have it copied and returned to you by mail."

"No need. Paulette sent me three copies in different sizes." She looked through her photographs until she located a 5x7 copy of the same picture and gave it to Héloïse. Héloïse thanked her as she tucked it into her purse.

Jean-Pièrre examined the envelope. In the top corner was a sticker with a return address. He pulled out his notebook and wrote it down.

"So why did your daughter and her husband get interested in the *prepuzio*?"

"I had told her about Calcata. In one letter I even told her about the Feast of the Circumcision when the *prepuzio* is paraded through the town in its precious reliquary. She got very interested and wanted to know all about it. Next thing I know, she wrote that she and Daniel were coming to visit me. You can understand how excited I was to be reunited with my daughter after all those years. But our reunion was not a success." She stopped and sipped her tea, overcome by emotion.

"Sometimes that happens," Héloïse told her, "through no fault of your own."

"They stayed for four days, but it was very crowded with all of us here," Semiramis went on. "Paulette thought my birds were disgusting and made fun of finding her mother living in a cave. Her husband, Daniel, hardly said a word. Paulette was full of questions about the *prepuzio*."

"Why was she so interested?" asked Jean-Pièrre.

"Paulette said they had joined a new religion, the Raëlians. They believe that aliens from outer space had met their leader and told him that they had visited a long time ago and created us. She said that Raël – that is the name of their leader – founded their religion in the seventies. Now it is in countries around the world. Have you heard of it?"

"Vaguely," Jean-Pièrre admitted. "I think their headquarters is in Montreal."

"Paulette called it an atheist's religion. I think that, instead of worshiping God, they worship these aliens that they call the *Elohim*."

Jean-Pièrre still looked puzzled. "I still don't see the connection to the *prepuzio*. Do you, Héloïse?" Héloïse shook her head. "It was only after your daughter and her husband left that Don Dario found that the reliquary had disappeared too?"

"Yes."

Jean-Pièrre looked at his watch and could not believe that two hours had passed since he had knocked on Semiramis' door. Standing, he said, "You have been a wonderful help, Semiramis. Thank you."

Semiramis led them back out into the passage and said, "You will tell Eddie about my health?"

"Yes, of course. We owe you so much. If I know anything about Eddie, he will help you all he can, Semiramis."

As they headed back to the bar to find Angelica, Héloïse pointed out a black-and-white poster showing the backs of four men dressed in nineteenth-century costumes pissing against a brick wall. Under the men, three words: *Liberté, Egalité, Fraternité.* The motto of the French Republic.

Jean-Pièrre laughed. "Those French get everywhere."

"And where are we off to now, *mon vieux?*"

"First to find Angelica and hope she is not too drunk to drive. Then, on the road back to Rome and the suite waiting for us at the Spanish Steps. Lydia and Arthur should have checked in by now. We'll see if they have arrived, and then I have to make some phone calls."

## Castel Gandolfo II

Pannychis had just showered in Eddie's bathroom and was still drying her hair when the phone rang and Eddie picked it up. On the other end of the line, Luigi said he hoped he wasn't disturbing them before asking if Eddie would mind meeting the Holy Father in the ornament gardens in an hour. Eddie asked him to wait a moment, covered the mouthpiece of the telephone and relayed the message to Pannychis. "Sounds like a boys only party," she teased, adding, "I want to have a look around the town anyway." She kissed him on the cheek and retreated to the bathroom to put on her makeup.

"Sure. Pannychis has decided to look around the village."

Eddie detected a slight hesitation before Luigi said, "That might be a problem, I'm afraid. She is almost as recognizable as you, and the Holy Father doesn't want to let anyone know you are staying here."

Eddie said he would call back in a few minutes, then walked into his bathroom, put his arms around Pannychis' waist and talked to her in the mirror. "Luigi thinks you might be recognized."

"I'll wear a scarf, my sunglasses and some frumpy clothes," she offered. "What do you think models do in Milan or Paris when we want to step out for a cigarette? You'd be surprised. You can sit next to a table of paparazzi and not get recognized by any of them."

"Wouldn't the fact that you only ordered a lettuce leaf for lunch give you away?"

She dabbed a black spot on the end of his nose with her eye liner. "Idiot." She turned and treated him to a long kiss on the mouth before whispering, "But tell Luigi I'm going anyway."

Eddie knew there was no use arguing. Apparently a Messiah's powers were limited. "O.K. I'll tell him. Maybe he'll provide a couple of Swiss Guards."

"Then nobody will be suspicious."

"Look, he'll be arriving any minute. I'll talk to him."

Pannychis had returned to her room when Luigi arrived. Eddie told him that Pannychis wanted to explore the town, adding quickly that she would be disguised. Luigi suggested a guide, but Eddie knew that Pannychis would not go along with a bodyguard.

Luigi held out his hands and shrugged his shoulders. "All right. I'll get Brother Borromeo to show her the way to the security exit."

Eddie knocked on Pannychis' door and, when she answered, told her, "That outfit works pretty well. What do you think, Luigi?"

Luigi took in the baggy pants, scruffy sandals, oversized sunglasses, large-brimmed hat and her old hold-all, and said, "Very good, my lady. I am surprised at how easily beauty can be buried under baggy clothes. Of course, I am not a man with much experience with women."

"And look. Props," she said, pulling a Nikon SLR out of her voluminous bag. "Can't be a tourist without a camera."

"Looks great. Whoever you are. See you later, babe," said Eddie.

"I'll send Brother Borromeo to show you how to get out of here," added Luigi. "I don't know if I mentioned it, but the Apostolic Palace is bigger that the whole of Vatican City. It's easy to get lost."

"O.K. Send him along. You guys have fun."

As they walked through the endless rooms and hallways, Luigi told Eddie, "By the time you get back to your rooms, you will find that our technicians have installed a new private line and a desk in your room. Here is the number." He passed a card with the crossed-keys and crown Vatican logo embossed in red on the front.

Eddie slipped the card into his pocket. "Certainly can't complain about the service around here."

Luigi, nodding to acknowledge the compliment, opened a door tall enough to admit the tallest of giants, and led Eddie through it and into the acres of ornamental gardens. "Wait," he said after a few steps.

"Excuse me." Luigi pulled out a clean handkerchief. "Allow me." He rubbed the black dot of eye liner off Eddie's nose. "Might alarm His Holiness."

"Might indeed. Thanks, Luigi." Eddie felt that the more he got to know the pope's valet, the more he liked him.

"We even have our own farm," Luigi told Eddie, pointing off to his left as they wandered past a whole series of parterres displaying carefully arranged plants now blooming in a profusion of colors. "A lot of our food, including the eggs and bacon you had for breakfast, comes from there."

They found the pope at the other side of a bell-shaped reflecting pool. He was praying at a small grotto that housed a white marble statue of the Virgin. The pope turned at the sound of their approach on the graveled path and dropped to his knees before Eddie. Startled, Eddie stepped back, took hold of the pope's hands and gently lifted the older man to his feet, saying, "No, no, Pablo. I don't want anybody kneeling to me. Least of all you. I know, most of the time I can't avoid it, but not from you, please, or I'll start in with the 'Your Holiness' stuff."

"I'm sure you can understand how strange I feel Eddie. Ours is a church of hierarchies, of strict forms of address for every level, so it's difficult just to call you Eddie."

"Yeah, I understand. But look at it this way, in the Bible, most passages refer to the Savior simply as Jesus. By the way, my real name is Jesus. It was Joe who called me Eddie."

"Ah, yes, the Spanish pronunciation, Hey-soos." The church's very first pontiff from Argentina nodded. "Eddie," he said as if tasting the flavour of the name on his tongue, "short for Eduardo?"

"No. Actually it's not short for anything. Apparently I used to whirl like a dervish when I was small. 'Like an eddy in the river,' Joe used to say."

Without any conscious decision, they switched to Spanish as they sat down at a rough wooden table under a trellis covered in vine leaves. The morning was getting hot, and the shade from the vines was welcome. Luigi bade them farewell in Italian and headed back inside.

"I love this spot," the pope said, gazing into the reflecting pool. A few flashes of gold under the small patches of waterlily. A golden fish broke the surface for an instant and suddenly the reflected trees began to dance, as the concentric ripples distorted the previously mirrored surface. "How much our lives can change in an instant," the pope said softly. "You know, when I was elected pope, I was terrified. How could I possibly direct the largest church in the world? Me, who started out ministering to the poor in the slums of Buenos Aires. I was even accused once by Cardinal Ratzinger of being a Marxist. I was never really a Marxist, although I did practice liberation theology with my fellow priests. Our belief in a church ministering to the poor brought us into conflict with the church hierarchy from time to time. During the Dirty War, when so many of my countrymen were 'disappeared' by the military, I took courage from the Mothers of the Plaza de Mayo, the mothers who turned up in their simple white kerchiefs with pictures of sons and husbands who had disappeared. They risked arrest, torture, even death but they would march again and again. When the conclave called upon me, I thought of them. Perhaps I could return this great institution to its true place as a church of the poor. Pope Jean-Paul led the way, but he died after only thirty-three days in office. If I have a hero, it is him."

Eddie saw that the old man's eyes were filled with unshed tears and was about to say something when the old man got to his feet and walked back to the little grotto. Eddie watched him go. He returned with a small red clay pot and said, "Come. We will feed the fish."

Eddie walked with Pablo to the edge of the pool. Somewhere in the town below them, a church bell was striking the hour. "Look, here they come." Pablo pointed to the streaks of gold appearing from under the two patches of lilies. Pablo's face was lit by a boyish grin as the fish gathered in front of him, their hungry mouths breaking the surface. "They have trained me." The old man got down awkwardly on one knee and began to drop fish pellets into waiting maws until the water in front of him roiled in a frenzy of golden fish. "Here," he said, passing the clay pot to Eddie as he grasped Eddie's arm to lever himself up. "Your turn."

Eddie, too, fed the fish, enjoying the moment with the old man.

Afterwards, the pope returned the clay pot to its hiding place and they sat again under the vine leaves. "And now it falls upon me to welcome the new Messiah, Eddie," he declared solemnly and reached out his hand to take Eddie's. I am indeed blessed."

Eddie nodded and said, "Then it doesn't matter how many people will think of me as the AntiChrist. I came here for your support, Pablo. God bless you."

Pablo withdrew his hand and gazed into Eddie's startlingly blue eyes. "I will do everything I can to bring about the reforms to liberate the poor, to get my church to allow divorce and birth control, to liberate and educate women. If Pope John Paul had lived, this is what he would have been doing."

"Then let's start today. You are going to Jerusalem on July fifth to an ecumenical council with leaders of the Jews and Muslims."

"You will come with me?"

"Yes. I would like to go to the council and talk to the representatives of all three People of the Book about making this world into the earthly paradise God has always meant it to be."

Pablo gasped at the boldness of Eddie's simple plan. "Shall I alert them that you are coming?" He looked at Eddie whose face gradually broke into a broad grin. Pablo laughed softly. "Of course not." The next moment the pope looked serious and added, "I will have to contact Archbishop Fowler. He is our Papal Nuncio and Ambassador of the Holy See. A word of warning. The archbishop is an old conservative who believes, like some others, that I would do the church a favor by resigning."

"I'll keep that in mind."

"And we must contact the Israeli government too to ensure that the Israeli Defense Force will commit to protecting not just a visiting pope, but also yourself and Pannychis. As I'm sure you know, Jerusalem is not a safe place now. With the Intifadah that started last year, it is impossible to tell when or where the Israelis and the Palestinians will clash. People have been killed on both sides."

"True. Preaching peaceful coexistence might not be what either side wants to hear at the moment. Oh, what time is the meeting with the other religious leaders on Wednesday?"

"Two o'clock, at the King David Hotel."

"I'll turn up there by myself, if that works for you."

"You realize that we will cause quite a stir."

"That's what I came for," Eddie assured him. "Mind you, the whole idea of visiting Jerusalem as the Messiah scares the crap out of me."

"Me too, Eddie. Me too."

*　*　*

Brother Borromeo had led Pannychis through seemingly countless corridors and finally down a long, sweeping staircase, until they reached a nondescript door hidden in a small alcove. The tall monk had not once looked at Pannychis as they walked briskly through the palace, because the sight of such beauty made him nervous. Pannychis may have dressed in the frumpiest clothes she could find, but to Brother Borromeo, it didn't matter in the least. Brother Borromeo even found the perfume Pannychis was wearing to be absolutely intoxicating. During the couple of seconds they waited for the door to open, Pannychis had spotted the closed circuit camera above them. When the door opened by itself, she touched the monk's arm lightly and could feel him shudder.

Behind the door was a suite of modern offices obviously run by the security team. "*Guardia Svizzera*," he told her in a whisper. "Excuse me. One minute, signorina."

"*Ja. Kein problem.*"

While he disappeared into one of the offices, she watched the banks of monitors, many of them quads, watching different parts of the palace. Next to her, two of the operators were moving joysticks to reposition the cameras. One peeked up at her, but when she smiled at him, he became flustered and went quickly back to work.

Brother Borromeo reappeared, accompanied by a large man in a dark business suit who introduced himself as Captain of the Guard, and apologized for making her wait. He nodded to Brother Borromeo, who took his cue and left, aiming a shy smile at Pannychis. The captain led her to a simple, black door. "We are close to the main entrance to the palace here, Signorina Garlande," he told her. When he opened the door, he turned to her and said, "The guards have checked the screens and there is no one around in the piazza at the moment. I suggest you go now. When you return, make sure the area is clear, and then just press this button here." He showed her one of two buttons on a silver console sunk into the stone beside the door.

"Thank you, Captain," she said. "I doubt I'll be gone more than a few hours."

With a slight bow that Pannychis found charming, the Captain pointed to the camera mounted on the console above the buttons. "We'll be watching for you, signorina." And suddenly she found herself standing alone on the black cobblestones of the empty Piazza della Libertà.

To her left, just a few meters past the door, was a low wall. She walked over to the parapet and looked out. Directly below her was a road leading down from the palace towards the lake that she could just see through the trees. On a whim, she decided to take a walk down to the shore. She turned away from the main entrance to the palace, guarded by two Swiss Guards because the pope was in residence. She stopped at Bernini's simple fountain that graced the center of Piazza della Libertà and took a couple of pictures of the palace entrance and then of the fountain with her Nikon. There. Now I look like a real tourist, she thought, pleased with herself. To reinforce her cover, she entered a souvenir shop and bought a couple of spare rolls of Kodachrome 35 mm film. After wandering through a shop full of out-of-style handbags and another selling religious souvenirs, she bought a tiny picture of Pope Urban IX so new, that she was afraid the colors might run.

When she emerged from the store, she saw that the piazza had filled with noisy American and German tourists. More were walking up the Via della Corso.

To escape, she turned down Via Roma towards the lake. Less than a hundred meters down, she found that she could practically see the whole of the lake now, so she stopped into an outdoor cafe called *Il Grottino*. There, she ordered a cappuccino and sat down to take in the view of Lake Albano below. While she was waiting, she got up and walked over to a railing. Almost round, with steep sloping shores, Lake Albano is the deepest lake in Italy, a body of water cradled in the caldera of a volcano. During Roman times, the water often rose and fell mysteriously, as the lava under it moved.

To the west, she could see two brightly-colored boats, shrunk by distance, racing through a line of buoys that had been there since the 1960 Olympics when the rowing events took place here. Just then the waiter arrived with her cappuccino.

To her left, a few cars were parked just before the road began to drop precipitously down to the little railway station. Sitting in the third car, a dusty brown Lancia, were two men. "You think that's the model?" one asked the other.

The fat man in his twenties sitting in the passenger seat reached into the glove compartment and pulled out a small pair of binoculars. After a few moments, he told his companion, "Hard to tell with that fucking hat. Can't really see her face."

The driver, an older man with a neatly-trimmed beard and dressed in a white linen suit, said, "Maybe she's just a tourist."

"Maybe. I'll call Giovanni, give him a description, see if he's spotted her."

The older man handed the walkie-talkie to his companion to call through to Giovanni, who was watching the bottom of the Via della Corso, the road that ran directly into the Piazza della Libertà. Giovanni had not seen a woman matching her description. To be sure, he called the other watcher sitting outside the roman arch on the east side of the piazza. "Been quiet here for the last hour," came the reply.

"Got to be her," said the man with the binoculars. "Ah, there she goes. The waiter just brought her coffee and she's sitting down again. *Figa!* She's still got her hat on."

The man in the white linen suit said, "I'll find out. Wait here," and stepped out of the car. When he reached Il Grottino, he shuffled past her table and sat down at the one beside her where he could see her face. He ordered an espresso and lit a cigarette. "Beautiful view, isn't it?" he said in Italian-accented English.

"Yes."

"Your first time here?"

"In Italy, no. In Castel Gandolfo, yes."

Beautiful and her accent is French. He was sure she was Pannychis Garlande. Twenty minutes later, the news reached Cardinal Achille Silvestrini in Vatican City. When he hung up, the cardinal immediately called Rev. Father Thomas del Sarto.

"As we thought, Eddie Magdalena and his trollop are guests of Urban," the cardinal said, as soon as he got through.

"Could be a huge problem," mused the Black Pope. "I'm guessing that Urban will proclaim him Messiah. When's he leaving for Jerusalem?"

"Wednesday. How close is the professor to finishing his DNA sequencing?"

"He called me this morning. He and his team are so close that he thinks he will have the preliminary results in 48 to 72 hours."

"So we should have the results while Urban is in Jerusalem."

"Yes, Achille. And if he finds a match?"

"You think there is a possibility, Thomas?"

"It doesn't matter what I think. Either there is no match at all, at which time we release the story to the media, or there is a match and ..."

"We bury it."

"But what about the professor and the people working for him?" asked Achille.

"Buffone inducted the boy into the Friends of Santa Croce, the night you were there, did he not?"

"I left early that night, Thomas. I met Marcinkus that evening to try to get him on our side, but he was not interested."

"Still, I'm sure you heard the rumors about our boy, Achille."

"That he got so drunk that he tried to rape one of the dancers? Yes, I heard."

"Exactly. I think the pictures of that night will buy the boy's silence, don't you?"

The cardinal sighed. He hated playing this game, but the stakes had become so important that he had to if they were going to save the church. "Yes. I hope so. And if not?"

"We deny, deny, deny and denigrate anyone who comes forward with the story."

"Let's hope that won't be necessary."

"Now, back to Eddie Magdalena," said the Black Pope. "You sure he's heading for Jerusalem?"

"Oh, he's got to go to Jerusalem. It is the center of the world, not only for us, but also for the Jews and the Muslims. To be proclaimed the Messiah, he'll have to appear there."

"And will Pope Urban proclaim him the Messiah?"

"That's the question."

"If we can get the DNA to him before he commits himself. That might be the answer."

"Yes," agreed the cardinal.

"What if Urban is so besotted by the charisma of this Magdalena, that he goes ahead anyway?"

"Stronger remedies might be needed."

"I'm afraid, I didn't hear that, Thomas. Must be a bad line. Call me when you get the results." The cardinal put the phone gently on to its cradle but only for a moment.

His next two calls were to Cardinal Schicklgruber and Cardinal Buffone. "Time to unleash the press. Let's make this charlatan sweat. By tomorrow morning, the AntiChrist at Castel Gandolfo should get quite a surprise," he told them.

"I think it's important to call a meeting sometime today with the Italian cardinals. If you, Thomas and Alois approve, I'd like to get Xavier to contact as many of them as possible."

"Why get Xavier to set it up?"

"Because, with the pope away, Cardinal Buffone is essentially the camerlengo."

"True. Why just the Italian cardinals?"

"Because they're here in Rome. I have a list of cardinals who are either with us or can be persuaded to condemn Urban. I'll give it to Xavier."

Cardinal Buffone needed no persuading. He noticed that Cardinal Silvestrini's list included most of the Italian cardinals over the age of eighty, many of whom resented the fact that they were no longer permitted to vote in papal elections. The rest of his list contained few surprises.

With a grim smile, Buffone opted for Santa Maria sopra Minerva, a minor basilica located just behind the Pantheon. Just the right place, he told himself with satisfaction, thinking of this church's role in enforcing the doctrine of the faithful over the centuries. The church had long been in the hands of the Dominicans, who also occupied the adjoining convent. The Dominicans, proud of their nickname *Domini canes*, dogs of God, had been at the forefront of the Inquisition, hunting down heresy in all its forms. In one of the convent rooms, Galileo had been condemned as a heretic in 1592.

The meeting would be at 8 p.m., as the church would close to visitors at seven. Buffone called in three priests he felt he could trust and set them to call the cardinals on the list. "Above all be discreet," he told them. "Stress that the meeting is secret for the moment."

When they were finished, two and a half hours later, the priests had confirmed 43 of the 62 Italian cardinals on Silvestrini's list. There might be more attending, as they were waiting for callbacks from seven others. Seventeen of the cardinals who had confirmed were over eighty.

"I think we can expect around fifty. The Carafa Chapel can hold that many. More private than the main church," Cardinal Buffone told the three priests.

Father Benito Ferraro, a noted scholar of church history, agreed. "The perfect place." Carafa had been the given name of Pope Paul IV, Grand Inquisitor of the Roman Inquisition. His tomb is even in Santa Maria sopra Minerva.

"I thought you would appreciate it, Benito," said Cardinal Buffone, approvingly.

## Santa Maria Sopra Minerva

Located just behind the Pantheon at the very heart of pagan Rome, lies Santa Maria sopra Minerva, the church that Cardinal Buffone had selected for his emergency meeting. Built over the remains of a Temple of Minerva, the Roman goddess of Wisdom, Santa Maria sopra Minerva is the only Gothic church in Rome, though the blank white classical facade with its three plain round windows gives no hint of the church's Gothic interior.

In the piazza in front of the church is a low plinth supporting a baby elephant which is carrying the shortest of Rome's thirteen obelisks on its back. The statue, designed by the busy Gian Lorenzo Bernini, has stood there since 1667, and for nearly that long has been dubbed by Romans affectionately as '*il porcino*', the piggy, because of the elephant's rotund body and stubby legs. The official title of Bernini's sculpture is *Pulcino della Minerva*, Minerva's little chicken. Nobody is sure why.

Cardinal Buffone, Cardinal Schicklgruber, and Reverend Father Thomas del Sarto arrived together just as the last visitors were being ushered out of the church at 7 p.m. Several Dominican priests were there to greet them and lead them down the nave with its wonderful blue vaulted ceilings sprinkled with stars, installed on the orders of Torquemada. When they reached the Carafa Chapel, Buffone told the Dominicans, "A van full of plain clothes Vatican security personnel will be here in a few minutes to take care of all entrances to the church."

By 8:15 the chapel, with its Filippino Lippi frescoes, was almost full. Notably absent were Cardinal Silvestrini and Archbishop Marcinkus. The audience grew quiet as Cardinal Buffone, Cardinal Schicklgruber and Reverend Father Thomas del Sarto arranged themselves on three chairs before the altar table with Buffone in the middle. Cardinal Schicklgruber rose first and led the cardinals in a prayer for Divine guidance in these perilous times for Mother Church.

Next to rise was the Black Pope who was furious that Cardinal Silvestrini, by far the most charismatic and convincing figure in the Curia, had avoided this meeting. Oh, he knew why. Silvestrini was worried that this whole thing could go sour and hurt his chances of becoming the next pope. Still, after the last 'amen,' the Black Pope stepped forward and introduced Cardinal Buffone, the Secretary of State, as the most important spiritual leader in Rome while Pope Urban was away from the eternal city.

"Cardinal Buffone has called this meeting at such short notice because of recent developments regarding this latest Messiah. Of course, I refer to Eddie Magdalena who, in recent days, has gained a lot of publicity. We have all watched as his fame grew. Now let us listen to our Secretary of State, the most reverend Cardinal Xavier Buffone."

Excited whispering from the pews as the Black Pope took a seat and Buffone rose. "My brothers in Christ, esteemed members of the Curia, I do not call you here on such short notice for any frivolous reason. I call you here because our Mother Church is in mortal peril due to this newest supposed Messiah, Eddie Magdalena. I'm sure that many of you regard this Eddie Magdalena as the AntiChrist, but around the world many are beginning to worship him as the true Messiah. And now his influence has reached into the heart of the church. At this very minute, we have just learned, he is a guest of Pope Urban at Castel Gandolfo. Urban has gone to great lengths to keep this meeting secret but, by chance, the media has learned that Eddie and his paramour, the French woman, are guests of the Holy Father. The news is spreading around the world as we speak."

Buffone paused and took a sip of water to give the cardinals a chance to absorb the news. Some reacted in shock, others in fury. "I have always thought it was a mistake to elect Pablo Ramirez," one old cardinal told his neighbor. "I would never have voted for him. Surely you remember that Ratzinger slapped him down for his liberation theology."

"What were they thinking electing a pope from South America anyway?" asked his companion, another cardinal who had been too old to vote in the last papal election.

Just as the noise began to get really loud, Cardinal Buffone held up his hands, and the chatter gradually subsided. "Yes, my brothers in Christ, I understand your anger and I share it. We believe that Urban is about to recognize Eddie Magdalena as the true Messiah." Howls of outrage greeted this news. This time the growl of protesting voices lasted longer. "Please, please, hear me out!" Buffone pleaded until the din quieted to no more than an angry buzz running like an electric current through the crowd of churchmen. "As you know, in a few days Pope Urban is going to Jerusalem to chair the Ecumenical Council of the People of the Book. That will involve our Jewish and Muslim brethren. We are convinced that Urban intends to introduce this Magdalena as the true Messiah at the meeting. The very idea is an outrage, an insult and a blasphemy to those who believe in the Lord."

"The man is the son of a whore!" someone shouted from the pews. "Is the pope mad?" asked another.

Buffone seized on the last question. "We may well wonder if the pope has not found the pressures of office to be too great. What other explanation is there? Is that what we are facing here? A pope who is no longer capable of leading our Mother Church?"

Cries of "Impeach him!" and "We need to remove him!"

Shrewdly, Buffone let the anger build before stepping in. "We have no mechanism to remove a pope," he reminded them. "Popes can resign but even that is rare. The last to do so was Gregory XII in 1415 to end the Babylonian Captivity of the Avignon Papacy. I repeat to you that the Curia cannot remove a pope, even one no longer capable of fulfilling his office as the Vicar of Christ." He paused a moment before leaning forward and saying slowly, "But perhaps we can persuade this pope to resign." Cries of approval. "You may think it strange, but in this scientific age we have turned to our own Vatican scientists to find incontrovertible evidence that this pretender, Eddie Magdalena, is not the Messiah he and his followers claim him to be. Our scientists have secretly been comparing the DNA of Eddie Magdalena with that of the Savior himself." Buffone could see that not a few of the cardinals, particularly the more senior ones, had no inkling of what DNA was, so at this point he launched into a brief explanation of Enrico Capelli's research. Reverend Father Thomas del Sarto was surprised and delighted at both how clear Buffone's explanation was and at the fact that he had managed to omit from it both the name of the professor and the source of the Savior's DNA sample.

"The results will be ready within the next forty-eight hours. We are certain that when the DNA comparison proves once and for all that this Eddie Magdalena is not the Messiah, even the most ardent believer will abandon the cause," Cardinal Buffone concluded. "We will immediately pass the results along to the pontiff in Jerusalem and demand his resignation. Finally, we ask you to play your part in this battle for the soul of Mother Church. On your way out, you will see that the Dominicans of Santa Maria sopra Minerva, ever the *Domini canes* dedicated to maintaining the doctrinal purity of our Mother Church, have set up a ballot box and two tables with pens and ballots. There is one simple statement on the ballot: '*As a member of the Curia, I ask Pope Urban IX to resign his office immediately and make way for the College of Cardinals to elect a successor.*'"

"We ask you to sign a ballot and deposit it in the ballot box. We need your support at this, the most critical time in the whole history of our Catholic and Apostolic Church. Pray God you are with us, my brothers." He made the sign of the cross, and without another word led Cardinal Schicklgruber and the Black Pope down the aisle to the tables set up in front of the altar in the main church under the watchful eye of Michelangelo's marble creation, *Cristo della Minerva*. When the trinity had filled in their own ballots, they proceeded to the entrance to watch the proceedings. For the next twenty minutes, the rest of the cardinals filled out their ballots and filtered out of the church. Only three of the cardinals left without filling in a ballot.

"Now we need to pray for just one thing," observed Cardinal Schicklgruber when the last of the gathering had departed.

"That the pope will resign when confronted by the calls from the Curia?" asked the Black Pope.

"No. That there is no match of the DNA."

### Rome Calling

The meeting of the Italian cardinals was still in progress when Angelica dropped Héloïse and Jean-Pièrre at the Inn at the Spanish Steps, shortly before nine that evening. When the desk clerk signed them in, she told them that their friends, the Whiteheads, had arrived a couple of hours earlier.

When the desk clerk passed over the key, Jean-Pièrre noted that it was the same room he had occupied before he had left for Paris and a new life. Turning on the light, he was suddenly overwhelmed by the great gulf that separated his former life as Père Jean-Pièrre from his current life as Jean-Pièrre, lover of Héloïse. And the transition had begun when he had left this room and set out for Paris. Impulsively, he picked up Héloïse, who let out a little yelp of surprise, and carried her carefully over the threshold, "I can't even tell you how much I love you," he said to Héloïse as he kissed her before setting her down on the bed. "It's just that this is the first time we've stayed here together. I guess, in a way, I'm exorcising my celibate past."

"Then, let's do this right," Héloïse said, smiling. "Bring in the luggage while I undress."

After they had made love, they showered together, quickly got dressed and knocked on the door opposite theirs. Lydia answered. After the greetings, Jean-Pièrre told them about the progress they had made in Calcata. "I've got the Montreal address of the Riopelles, and look. Semiramis even gave us a picture." He showed them the picture the Riopelles had sent to Semiramis.

"But why would they want the foreskin?" asked Arthur.

"I have no idea," Jean-Pièrre said. "The important thing is to get our hands on the *prepuzio* so we can use it for our own testing."

"Well done, you two," said Lydia. "Now, let's get something to eat. I'm starving."

They ate at a restaurant just off the Piazza di Spagna. "We've already been in touch with Eddie and Pannychis," Lydia told Héloïse and Jean-Pièrre. "Things are really starting to move along. Looks as if the pope is convinced that Eddie is the Messiah, even without the DNA results. And it appears we'll all be on our way to Jerusalem."

"My guess is that Marie appeared to Pope Urban. She sure as Hell talked her sisters into accepting your new relationship."

"That she did." Jean-Pièrre put his arm around Héloïse.

"The most important thing we have to arrange is getting the other apostles to Jerusalem on the earliest flight," said Arthur. "Apparently Pope Urban already had a visit planned to the Holy Sepulchre on the seventh, so he has asked Eddie and Pannychis to accompany him. Eddie wants the rest of us there too."

"So who will trace down the leads to the *prepuzio*?" asked Héloïse.

"Marc and Jules can handle it."

"And what do we do about Maria Magdalena? I'm not sure it would be a good idea to leave her at our place," said Lydia.

"They'll take her with them," improvised Jean-Pièrre. "You know she is the mother of a Messiah and just might have a part to play."

Pouring herself a generous glass of red wine, Lydia asked, "How are you going to get the picture of the Riopelles to Mahinda and Mark?"

"There is an air express company called DHL that guarantees delivery within 24 hours. They've got an office here. I'll get them to pick up the package tonight. Marc will get it sometime tomorrow."

Arthur was looking thoughtful. "I guess that covers it." He looked over at Héloïse and saw that she looked tired. "Let's call from our room when we get back. That way Héloïse can get a good night's sleep."

"Oh, I'm fine," she told him, trying unsuccessfully to stifle a yawn, "and what about you and Lydia. You must have a bad case of jet lag."

"And it always gives me a case of insomnia. Jean-Pièrre can call from our room, give you a chance to get some sleep."

"If you wouldn't mind."

"Get some sleep," Jean-Pièrre told her when they reached their room. "I'll be back in an hour or two."

From Lydia's room, Jean-Pièrre called the desk to arrange for a package to be picked up as soon as possible. The woman on the desk assured him that the pickup would be within the hour. Next, he asked her to put through a call to Marc Baptiste. He checked his watch – just after six p.m. in Sudbury.

Marc answered on the second ring. After telling him in detail about what he and Héloïse had learned in Calcata Vecchia, he told him that a package would be arriving tomorrow that included a picture of the Riopelles and their last known address. "You and Jules will need to get to Montreal as soon as possible. The Raëlian Headquarters is there."

"What about Maria Magdalena?" Marc asked, hoping they would be leaving her in Sudbury.

"Take her with you. I don't know how, but I think she has a part to play."

"You sure? Might be better if just me and Jules went," Marc objected.

Maria had never said anything about being his birthday present, but her enigmatic smile told him that she had not forgotten the first night they had met.

"Trust me, Marc."

"Sure, Jean-Pièrre, sure. We'll take her."

"Now the second thing, Marc. Can you get the rest of the apostles on a plane to Jerusalem and book them a hotel there?"

"Jerusalem?"

"Eddie's going, and so are the rest of us. He's going to proclaim himself in the Holy City, Marc. Imagine. And we'll all be there. Tell the others that. I'm pretty sure, the pope already acknowledges him as the Messiah."

"Wow! I'll call Mary at All Seasons on the Kingsway. She's always been good. Don't worry about the *prepuzio*. We'll find it. I envy you guys, though."

"Great. Keep in touch."

"Oh, you can count on that."

Jean-Pièrre said goodnight to Lydia and Arthur and took the lift down. At the reception, he handed over the parcel. "It's very urgent. High priority," he told the receptionist. "Do you mind putting it on my bill?"

"No, not at all, sir."

Héloïse was asleep when he slipped in beside her, but Jean-Pièrre was far too full of excitement to fall asleep himself.

\* \* \*

Four hundred kilometers north of Rome, at Europe's oldest university, the lights still burned in the DNA labs even though bells in the surrounding churches had just began to toll the midnight hour. Professor Enrico Capelli had not been in that day because of a summer cold, but he was still awake when the telephone jangled in his apartment. He picked it up on the second ring.

"It's amazing, Enrico, just totally amazing." The professor recognized the voice of Nunzia, his special assistant on the DNA project. "We just got results from the first samples and they are 100% identical. I mean one hundred percent. If the other samples come in with the same results, I think that we have to declare that Eddie Magdalena is the Messiah."

Shit! The Black Pope would not be amused. "You're sure there is no doubt?"

"None at all."

"Have you told anyone else?"

"How many times have you told me how secret this project is?" Nunzia asked him. "Anyway, we have still not got the results from the other samples."

"I'm coming in," he told her and hung up.

When he arrived, he was greeted by Nunzia and the three technicians on duty. "Are you sure there was nothing that contaminated the samples," Enrico snapped by way of greeting.

The excitement felt by the three technicians disappeared in a flash. "There has been no contamination, Enrico. You of all people should know how careful we have been," said Stefano, the boldest of them.

"Does anyone else know of these results?" asked the professor.

"No one," Nunzia told him, feeling close to tears.

"And you all realize that if you mention a single word about this project you could end up in jail." The technicians nodded. "All right. First I want you to stop running the other samples."

Nunzia was shocked. "But that might make them unusable."

"Just do as I say. And do it now!" the professor ordered, the anger in his voice masking his fear. "And as for the other samples, you will say that they became corrupted. Do you understand? All of you?" He waited until each of them mouthed agreement. "Now you will stay here for as long as it takes to contact everyone, and I mean everyone, on the team. Tell them that the results are in and that there is no match. *Mi capisci?*"

He swept out and locked himself in his office, trying to decide whether to call the Reverend Father Thomas and wondering what to tell him.

# Part Twelve: Montreal

## The Raëlian Connection

After the call from Jean-Pièrre, Marc Baptiste set out to book plane tickets from Sudbury to Tel Aviv and hotel rooms in Jerusalem for the apostles.

After double-checking his lists, Marc called All Seasons Travel, located in a strip mall on the Kingsway. The phone rang half a dozen times before the answering machine kicked in and told him that the travel agency was closed. Right, it was after six on a Tuesday night. He hung up and considered for a moment. Yeah, he had Mary's home number in his book of contacts. He found the book in his desk, located the number and dialed, crossing his fingers that she would be home. Mary picked it up on the third ring.

After explaining his urgency, Marc talked her into driving back to her agency and opening up for him. He did a fist pump as he hung up and called Jules. "Meet me at All Seasons. I'll be there in ten."

"Right," said Jules and hung up.

By ten that night, he had booked the apostles out of Sudbury on the 6:30 a.m. flight. They would reach Tel Aviv late tomorrow. Mary had also booked them in to the National Hotel in East Jerusalem just a couple of blocks from Herod's Gate. It was considerably downscale from the King David, but Mary assured them it was clean and comfortable and, most important, had six double rooms available. "How long for?" Mary asked Marc, covering the mouthpiece with her hand.

Jean-Pièrre hadn't told him how long they would be staying. "A week," he guessed.

After finalizing the bookings, Marc and Jules went back to Marc's apartment. From there he called Jean-Pièrre with the confirmation number for the National Hotel and told him, "I booked you guys in for a week. How does that sound?"

"I don't think even Eddie knows how long we'll be in Jerusalem," Jean-Pièrre confessed, "so a week should be good."

By 11:30 Marc and Jules had dropped off the tickets, airport transfers and room bookings to every one of the apostles. "I've booked the airport shuttle to pick all of you up, so be ready no later than five," he told each of them. "Better start packing now. You'll be taking the Air Canada flight out of Toronto, so you won't have to change terminals. Your bags will be checked through to Tel Aviv from Sudbury. Bon voyage."

"I need a drink," he told Jules when they had finished their rounds. "Solid Gold?"

Jules nodded, so for the next two hours they watched the strippers and drank beer. Jules sat watching the girls with a wry smile creasing his face. One or two of them waved to him. Jules had more than once tossed an unruly drunk, and the girls did not forget that kind of gentlemanly behavior.

As he was about to tumble into bed around three, Marc suddenly remembered that he had not called Maria Magdalena. For a second he was tempted to leave for Montreal without her, but then he thought of Eddie and called the Whiteheads' house. Maria answered with a sexy 'Hello' that made Marc suspect that she might be working.

"You alone?" he asked.

"Just me and the entire Sudbury Spartans Football Team."

"O.K., O.K. Sorry to call you so late, but I just got a call from Jean-Pièrre. He wants us to go to Montreal tomorrow for a couple of days. You up for that?"

"Why would I want to go to Montreal?"

Marc explained about the Raëlians run by a former racing car driver, Claude Vorilhon. The idea of the racing car driver piqued her interest.

"What time we leaving, lover boy?"

Marc cursed under his breath and told her, "As soon as the package arrives. Sometime early afternoon is my best guess."

"I'll be ready. Sweet dreams." She hung up.

The courier delivered the package from Jean-Pièrre just before noon the next morning. Marc immediately opened it and spread out the contents on the kitchen table. "He's quite a bit older than her," Marc said, holding up the picture of the Riopelles. "and that goddamn goatee makes him look like some kind of weird poet. Think you'd recognize him?"

"Yeah. Looks like a white dude."

"You mean we all look alike?"

Jules allowed himself a half-smile. "Some days."

"Yeah. Only trouble with you is that you never shut up, Jules."

"You talk enough for both of us."

"Right. You'll recognize him?" Jules nodded. Marc pointed to Paulette. "I'd recognize her. Long black hair. Tiny, thin, kinda cute. We've got their address and phone number. It's a long drive, about six hours, more if we stop for a meal, so we'd better pick up Maria and get on the road."

As they headed out on Highway 17 East, Marc driving with Jules in the passenger seat and Maria in the back, Maria asked, "So why are we going to Montreal?"

Marc hesitated for a moment and then remembered that Eddie had said that she may have a part to play. As they drove through Sturgeon Falls, he began telling her the story of the Holy Foreskin. She listened quietly as he told her about the theft from Calcata Vecchia by the Raëlians.

"Raëlians?"

"A pretty odd group. Jean-Pièrre filled me in." He passed her the package. "There's a picture of the Riopelles in there and their address." Maria looked at the picture for so long that Marc asked, "You know them?"

"No. But I will if I ever meet them. The man has pain in his eyes. He's suffered a lot of what he would call bad luck."

Marc glanced at Maria in the rearview with a new respect. "And the woman?"

Maria was silent for a while and then said, "No, life has been good for her. When was this picture taken?"

"I don't know. A couple of years ago, maybe."

"Then they are no longer together."

"How can you be sure?"

Instead of replying, Maria cracked a window open and lit a cigarette. Marc looked at her again. She must be pushing fifty, he told himself, but she is still one of the sexiest women I ever met. Makes me feel like a schoolboy sometimes. He looked over at Jules. He was asleep, his trucker's hat advertising a Pow Wow on Manitoulin Island pulled down over his face. At least he wasn't snoring.

When they arrived in Montreal, Marc drove around looking for a hotel. The Hotel Place Dupuis had a couple of rooms available. While Marc was checking them in, Maria wandered around the foyer and checked out the bar, even chatting with some of the patrons. When the paperwork was done, Marc handed her a key and they took the elevator up to the fourth floor. Maria caught Marc's eye in one of the elevator's smoky mirrored walls and asked him, "Have you stayed here before?"

"No. Why?"

"Just wondering if you're bi."

"What? Why the Hell would you say that?"

"Because this hotel is full of gays. The gay village is just around the corner."

"No, I'm not gay, or bi." In the mirror he caught a broad smile spreading across Jules' face. "Not that I would mind being bi," he added, glowering at Jules whose grin grew even wider.

As soon as Marc and Jules had entered their room, Marc looked up the number of Paulette Riopelle. Just after 9:30. Still early enough. "I'm gonna call Mme Riopelle, tell her we're from CTV and ask if we could arrange an interview about the Raëlians."

Jules pulled his heavy Betacam camera out of its case, set it on the table under the window and began checking his batteries and spare cassettes while Marc dialed Paulette's number. Naturally surprised at first, she said, "I'm guessing that you tried Raël first and found out he was in Argentina, and somebody directed you to me."

"Yeah," Marc lied. "The woman told us that you were the person to contact."

Paulette readily agreed to give Marc and Jules an interview the next morning and even gave them directions to her condo. "I guess I have an old address," Marc told her and read her the address Jean-Pièrre had got from Semiramis.

She laughed and told him, "Haven't lived there in years."

"She sounds nice," Marc told Jules when he hung up. Next he called Maria's room and told her that they were interviewing Paulette at nine in the morning and wondered if she could amuse herself until they got back.

"In Montreal? You're kidding."

The next morning, shortly before nine, the cab dropped Marc and Jules in Montreal's Old Port. Paulette's building had started life as a warehouse but at some point in the recent past had been converted into condos. When Marc pressed the buzzer next to Paulette's name and announced himself, she immediately buzzed them in. The architect had left the freight elevator in working order, a concession to industrial chic, but had added a couple of modern lifts. "The Riopelles must be doing all right," said Marc as the elevator rumbled its way up to the top floor. You know what real estate costs around here?" Jules said nothing but managed a smiled when Marc added, "Me neither, but I'm guessing a lot."

The door was opened by a petite woman of maybe thirty, dressed in a white kimono-style robe and white mules. Marc introduced himself and, showing her his press pass, added, "And this is Jules, my cameraman."

"Come in, come in," Paulette urged, opening the door to reveal a spacious loft. She led them into a living room featuring floor-to-ceiling windows overlooking the St. Lawrence River. "Make yourselves comfortable," she said. "I'll get us some coffee." With that, she disappeared into an adjoining kitchen. The two men looked at each other and shrugged. Jules walked over to the windows and looked out over the river. Below him was a well-protected marina. To his left, the Jacques Cartier Bridge divided banks of low cumulus clouds that lent their color to the waters flowing under the bridge. Jules heaved the Betacam on to his shoulder. "Great view," he muttered, as he shot a brief panorama.

Marc was more interested in the loft conversion. Shiny ducts crossed the ceiling far above him. The furniture, all tubular chrome and leather cushions, was the same off-white color as the walls. He expected some kind of religious artifacts but could not see any. In fact, the walls were bare, except for three paintings that attracted his attention.

"You like them?" asked Paulette, as she set down a silver tray laden with coffee and *pets de soeurs* on a coffee table.

"Yeah. Especially this snowscape. Reminds me of Lauren Harris."

"Good eye. All three are actually by a painter called Donald Flather.

He was a friend of the group of seven. Cream and sugar?"

"No, just black. Jules likes his with four sugars."

"I like Flather's paintings because they remind me of both Harris and the Group of Seven." She laughed lightly. "And, I can actually afford a Flather."

Both men had crossed and sat on one of the two white couches facing each other across a long coffee table with a white marble top. "Well, I must say I like them, especially the one with the lighthouse."

"It's the Port Atkinson Lighthouse in West Vancouver. Reminds me of Tom Thomson a little."

"Yes. Right now though, I must indulge myself in one of your *pets de soeurs*. My mother made them when I was small. Haven't tried them in ages."

"I baked them myself."

"Good." said Jules, his mouth so full that he sprayed a few crumbs in his enthusiasm.

"Can't take him anywhere."

"Oh, I'm so glad you like them," she told Jules in French.

"Ah, Jules is bilingual, but in English and Ojibway."

Up until now, Marc and Paulette had been conversing in French, but now she switched to English. "Sorry, Jules. I just assumed ..." Jules nodded and sipped his coffee.

A few moments of silence while Jules gazed out the windows at l'Île Saint Hélène across the water. The skeletal remains of Bucky Fuller's

Biosphere after the fire in 1976 was still visible there, a relic of Expo '67. Marc was desperately trying to figure out when to abandon the pretext of the Raëlians interview and tell Mme Riopelle why they were really here.

"So what can I tell you about Raëlianism? It is one of the fastest growing religions in the world." Paulette had made the decision for him.

"Well, actually, Mme Riopelle, we were hoping to talk to you and M. Riopelle about your visit to Calcata Vecchia back in 1983."

The smile left her face, to be replaced by the shadow of fear. "Who are you?"

"Madame, no doubt you have heard of the new Messiah, Eddie Magdalena?"

"What?" She jumped to her feet and Marc, afraid she might flee, stood up too.

"Please, madame, we mean no harm. My colleagues have been to see your mother. She is the one who gave us your telephone number."

Paulette's draw dropped. "My mother. Why would she give you my number?"

"Because what we are after could actually change the course of human history. Your mother believed us, and I am hoping that you will too. Look, let's sit down and start again. I know we are strangers, but you've seen my press credentials. They are real and my name really is Marc Baptiste. You seem like a nice woman, and the last thing I want to do is scare you, so, truce?"

She was peering intently into his face, trying to judge whether to trust him. After a short, tense moment, she relaxed a little and slowly sat back down on the couch. She flinched as Jules got up, but he put up his hands and said, "Just going to look at the view. He's the one good with words. Me, I shoot video."

Marc, too, sat down. And waited until Paulette said, "You say you are from Eddie Magdalena."

"Yes. I was the only reporter on the scene when He arrived."

"And you believe he is the Messiah?"

Marc nodded slowly. "Yes. I do. Especially after the Big Reveal."

Paulette relaxed and even managed a smile. "We Raëlians are vitally interested in him too. In fact, I led a group of seven Raëlians to the Big Reveal and reported back to Raël."

"Really? You were there? And you believe He is the Messiah?"

"It's not quite that simple. Let me explain. I don't know how much you know about us Raëlians, but we believe that extra-terrestrials appeared on earth many years ago and created humanity through sophisticated DNA manipulation. We call them the *Elohim*, meaning 'those who come from the sky.' On December 13th, 1973, our founder Claude Vorilhon witnessed a spacecraft land in a volcanic crater in southern France. The *Elohim* that emerged gave him the task of informing the rest of humanity about them and their involvement in the creation of humankind. In 1974, he founded the movement that eventually became Raëlianism, and changed his own name to Raël, which means messenger of the *Elohim*."

Marc was beginning to wonder where this was going. So far he understood that a long time ago, in a galaxy far, far away ... then Paulette said something that caught his full attention.

"On October 7th, 1975, the *Elohim* returned. This time they invited Claude Vorilhon aboard their spacecraft. He was taken to another planet where he met Moses, Jesus and Mohammad and many of the other prophets who have visited our planet. I am telling you this so you can understand that the appearance of Eddie at the North American watershed, at a time that had been foretold, caught our attention. Raël, in fact all Raëlians, have been following Eddie since that appearance. That's why Raël sent seven of us to the Big Reveal."

"You were really there?"

"Yes. I was one of the seven. I had just been accepted as a Bishop Guide and it was my first assignment. Eddie so impressed us all that Raël called a special meeting where we talked about getting in touch with Him. Raël is convinced that Eddie is yet another one of the *Elohim*. He even stands for world peace, controlling the world's population, educating women, and accepting gays and lesbians just as we do. Add that to the miracles that Eddie performed that night,

**359**

and we Raëlians reported to Raël that Eddie really is a prophet and probably one of the *Elohim*."

"I'm glad you accept Eddie, but that is not why Jules and I are here," said Marc.

"When you sought me out instead of going directly to Raël, I thought you knew that Raël was out of town. Because I am a Bishop Guide, you would have been referred to me. But now I think you're looking for something else."

"What?"

"You're looking for the foreskin of the Savior," she said.

"Yes, madame. We are looking for it desperately. Let me tell you why." Marc's story took a few minutes. He even showed her the notes that Jean-Pièrre had sent him from Rome. "So you see, the *prepuzio* disappeared right after your visit to Calcata Vecchia."

"It was Daniel's idea, but obviously I went along with him. Raël has long been interested in cloning human beings. In fact, lately he has been thinking of setting up an organization called Clonaid to begin the work. When I re-established contact with Semiramis, my birth mother, Daniel was pleased that we had found each other. Not until my mother told us about the *prepuzio* that resided in the church at Calcata Vecchia, did he get really interested. It was then that he got the idea of stealing the *prepuzio* so that we Raëlians could use it to clone one of the prophets. He didn't tell me about his idea until after we landed in Italy. He felt that if he could present it to Raël, he would rise in the movement. You can make fun of me, but I was worried about the morality of stealing such a precious object. He laughed at me and pointed out that if the Catholics had wanted it so badly, they would treat it with more respect. What can I say? It was stupid, but I was so in love, so eager to make him happy.

"When we visited my mother six years ago, we sought out Father Dario's house in Calcata Nuova. When he answered the door, Daniel told him in English we wanted to pay for a memorial mass. It turned out that the priest only spoke Italian. And we didn't. We tried switching to French. He understood a little. The word for 'mass' is almost the same in French and Italian so slowly, with much use of sign language, we managed to get across to him that we wanted to pay for a mass. He was delighted, so we filled out the form and handed over the money. He was showing us to the door when we asked him if he could take us to the church so that we could see the famous *prepuzio*. He laughed and indicated that the *prepuzio* was now in his safekeeping. By the time we met him, Father Dario had begun to celebrate nearly all his masses in the new church in Calcata Nuova. I suppose he was worried that, since the church in the original village was empty most of the time, someone might steal the *prepuzio*.

"He beckoned to us to follow him and went into his bedroom to get it. He was a little drunk, I think, and although he had pushed the door shut behind him, it did not close all the way. As we stood outside the door, it began to swing open of its own accord, and Daniel and I could both see that Father Dario was retrieving a shoebox from his bedroom closet. The shoebox even had a sheet of paper glued to the top describing the contents as the '*Santum preputio* property of Padre Mignoni.' Sure enough, it contained a gold reliquary decorated with two angels. He even opened it and showed us the small white silk pouch than contained the *prepuzio* and the tiny scroll attached to it by a red ribbon. '*Praeputium Iesu Christe*' he told us, pointing at the scroll. He had to repeat it a couple of times before we realized that he was quoting the Latin message on the scroll.

"Anyway, over the next couple of days, we learned that Father Dario spent a lot of his spare time in the bars of Calcata Vecchia. One day we watched until he went into a local bar. Knowing he would be there for some time, we hurried up to Calcata Nuova. Stealing the reliquary was almost too easy. 'They deserve to lose it,' Daniel said, when we found that the Father had not even locked his door. We were in and out in less than a minute and hid the reliquary in my mother's cave until we were ready to leave. When we got back to Rome, we wondered how to get it back to Canada. After asking around, we were directed to an antique dealer who, for a couple of hundred U.S. dollars, authenticated the reliquary and shipped it to our address in Montreal."

"And where is it now?"

Paulette shook her head. "I don't know."

Marc leaned forward and looked at her. "You don't know?"

"Daniel knew that Raël was interested in cloning and wanted to give the reliquary to him. You have to understand something about Daniel. He is much older than I am and he had tried and failed at several careers: folksinging, professional wrestling, smuggling cigarettes out of Akwasasne. In a way, he saw the Raëlians as his last chance to succeed at something. He was almost fifty when he joined Raëlians, so he felt he had to make up for lost time. But he was charming. He was always broke, though, borrowing money and rarely paying it back. Anyway, he saw the reliquary as a miraculous gift that was going to take him all the way up to the position of Bishop Agent. I tried to tell him that Raël would never accept such a holy thing, especially since it had been stolen. He asked me how Raël would ever know, and I said I would have to tell him. That night we argued. In the end, he beat me. After grabbing the box that held the reliquary, he stormed out of our apartment. I never saw him or the reliquary again." Her voice had begun to break and she was breathing in short, sharp breaths, trying to keep the tears at bay.

Marc rounded the table and put his arm around her. "I'm sorry for what you went through, Paulette. May I call you Paulette?" She nodded, not trusting herself to speak.

After she had calmed down a little, he said, "Would Raël know where Daniel is?"

Paulette shook her head. "Daniel never appeared again."

"And you don't keep in touch."

"No, I never saw him again. And that's fine with me."

"And he's not in the phone book?"

"During the purification ceremony when I became a Bishop Guide just over a year ago, I finally told Raël about Daniel having the *prepuzio*. Raël chided me about the theft, but the next day he came to me and said, 'I'd like you to see if you can find Daniel. I'd like to talk to him about his idea of cloning one of the prophets.' The first thing I tried, of course, was the telephone book. He was not listed, but I called every Riopelle in the book anyway. No luck. I looked for him for a week but couldn't find him."

"But Raël might know something," Marc proposed in desperation.

"He is in Argentina at the moment. He won't be back for two more weeks."

*Merde!* Marc thought for a moment, but nothing came. A movement caught his eye. Jules, who had been listening, said, "Maybe you could think about his habits, things he liked to do. His favorite bar. Was he a Habs fan? Did he gamble? Marc needs to get to know him better."

Marc looked at the big man silhouetted against the windows. That was probably the most he had heard out of Jules in the last week. And Marc could have hugged him.

"Yeah, anything, anything."

For the next hour or so, Paulette told him as much as she could remember about Daniel. "So you doubt he would have left Montreal?" said Marc at one point.

"No, no. He is a separatist. Believes that Québec should be sovereign, ruled over by the '*pure laine.*'" Jules turned from the window and looked at her, puzzled.

"'*Pure laine*' means 'pure wool', Jules," Marc explained. "It means the early French settlers, the old families. A Québec ruled by them would not be kind to English Québecers or even French-speaking immigrants."

"Daniel hardly speaks any English and is devoted to both the Habs and the Expos," Paulette explained.

"A sports fan."

"Oh yes. Even if he had no money, he would still find enough cash to buy seasons tickets to the Montreal Canadiens and the Expos."

"Are the Expos playing here?" asked Jules.

"I have no idea," Paulette confessed.

"Got the paper?" asked Marc.

"Sure." She got up and came back with that yesterday's copy of *Le Devoir.*

Marc grabbed it and flipped through it until he found the sports pages. "Hey, they're playing the Houston Astros here tonight," he announced. "Did you ever go to the games with him?"

Paulette nodded. "Yeah, when we first got together. He always bought the same seats. I can't remember the numbers, but the seats were up the first base line."

"How far up?"

Paulette furrowed her brow in concentration. "Just a few meters past first base. Aisle seats, three or four rows up."

"That's great. And you really want to help us find him?"

"I'll help you for the sake of Eddie. What you do when you find him is up to you, but I don't want to talk to him again."

"You have my word, Paulette. I think we need to go to the game tonight. When you went with him, did he usually go early enough to catch batting practice?"

"Yes. He said that watching the players in batting practice, he could get a feel for who was going to perform well in the game."

"So we'll have to get to the ball park early."

"Yeah. We usually got there about 6:30."

"And do you remember what gate you used to use?"

"No, but I can find it."

"Can you think of anything else, Jules?"

"We need copies of this pic." He pointed to the Christmas picture of Daniel and Paulette. "And maybe four more people to cover the gates on both sides of the one you two used. They'll each need a picture."

"Good point. Could you get some of your Raëlians to cover the other entrances? They'd need to have joined since Daniel left."

"I'll arrange it."

Marc rose and gave Jules a slight nod to indicate that they were leaving. "Good meeting you, Paulette. We'll see you at around five thirty, O.K.?"

"Fine. I'll arrange for a couple of people to cover the other gates. They'll meet us at the Big O."

"That'll work out fine. Thanks, Paulette. You're a gem."

Marc was feeling wired, because now they had a plan. Or at least the sketch of one. "How will you get the *prepuzio* back, once you've found him?" Paulette asked.

Marc had been asking himself the same question and had yet to come up with an answer. "We'll think of something, won't we, Jules? Is there a bar or coffee shop near the stadium where we can meet you?"

"Yeah. A small coffee shop called Youppi's just across from the Big O." Jules put his betacam back in its case and headed for the door. Marc, feeling that he had established a connection with Paulette, put his hands on both her shoulders, feeling how tiny she was, and kissed her lightly on both cheeks, as is the custom in Québec. In her ear, he whispered in French, "Thank you so much for helping us out. I'm looking forward to tonight. *À bientôt.*"

After she closed the door behind them, Paulette thought about Marc. A good looking guy, smart, funny. And when he had switched back to French, he had used the familiar '*tu*' not the formal '*vous*.' For too long, she had immersed herself in her work, she told herself. Maybe it was time to date again.

\* \* \*

"So where the Hell is she? We've got to leave in less than an hour." Marc complained, not for the first time. Sprawled out on his bed watching the news on TV, Jules feigned interest in a story from the Philippines about Ferdinand Marcos being in critical condition.

They heard Maria fumbling for her key to the room next door a few minutes before they were due to leave. Marc crossed to their own door and listened. "It's her."

"Give her a couple of minutes to unwind."

"But we're going to be late."

"So we'll be a couple of minutes late. You want her to do you a favor, right?"

"Yeah."

"Then don't go see her when you're all pissed off. As Nakomis, grandmother of Nanabush, once said, 'You can catch more flies with honey than with vinegar.'"

"That proverb first appeared in *Poor Richard's Almanac* in 1744," cried Marc in triumph at finally catching Jules making up an Ojibway legend. Pure coincidence, he would have been the first to admit, that he had done a major essay on Franklin's annual publication as a journalism student at Carleton.

Jules just looked at him deadpan and said, "It had been told to him by an Ojibway woman."

Marc laughed. "You are one crazy bastard! But you're right. We'll set up a honey trap for the mysterious Daniel. Don't worry. I'll be on my best behavior with Maria."

"Am I taking the camera?"

"No, I don't think we'll have any use for it."

"Then pick me up when you've talked to her."

When Maria opened her door, Marc said, "We need to talk." Quickly he filled her in on the progress he and Jules had made. "So you see, we're hoping to find him at the ball game. I don't know how right now but we'd like you to get close to him so we can find out where he lives. We hope he has the reliquary at his place. Otherwise we're fucked. So you see we need your, ah, your expertise."

"Nice to be popular. Sure, I'll do it for Eddie's sake. You say this guy beat up his wife? What if he gets to be a problem?"

"I'll make sure that Jules and I are within shouting distance. If that's not possible, we'll have to come up with another plan."

Maria smiled at him and reached out to stroke his cheek with the back of her hand. "Well, if he's as polite and respectful as you, Marc, we won't have a problem at all." She moved into his body space so close that he was able to smell mint on her breath. "How much time we got?"

"What?" The stirring in his loins embarrassed him. Man, she's the mother of the Messiah, he chided himself. Get a grip.

"No time? Then wait here while I dress. I just bought an outfit that will be great."

"We're running a little late."

"Then we'll just have to be a little later, won't we? Stay here while I change." She scooped up a couple of her new purchases and swept off into the bathroom. She emerged dressed in a black bustier trimmed with blood-red piping, over tight leather pants and a pair of black kitten heels. Her raven-black hair was swept up into a French twist. "So what do you think, Marc?" Maria asked, as she twirled in front of him.

"Stunning!" Marc said, wondering whether to ask her to tone the outfit down, but how would he bring that up. "What man could resist?"

"Then let's go. Don't want to be late." She picked up her large purse and strutted out the room leaving him to pick up Jules and follow her to the elevator.

Paulette was already sitting at a table in Youppi's when Marc and the others arrived. She waved and motioned to the two people with her to make room. "Here are your copies of the pictures." She handed one to each of them. Marc glanced at his and saw that she had cut herself out of the original image and reduced the picture of Daniel to a more pocketable 4x6 print. She introduced her two fresh-faced companions as Greta and Violetta. When Marc introduced Maria, he watched the two younger women's eyes widen.

"It should be easier to spot him now before the big crowd arrives," said Paulette.

"Yeah," agreed Marc. "Paulette. You'll need to be out of sight but close enough that we can find you if any of us spots Daniel."

"Sure. We were just over there. There is a ball cap seller not far from the three gates we need to cover. I'll hang around there. If anyone thinks they spot him, buy a ticket at whatever entrance he takes, watch where he sits and see if he's with anyone."

"O.K. Let's do it," said Marc.

Less than twenty minutes later, Greta found Paulette and said, "I think we found him. Violetta bought a ticket and followed Daniel into the stadium." Steeling herself, Paulette walked to the stadium gate. With Greta, she emerged from the concourse into the vast expanse of the stadium. Violetta was standing at the top of the stadium steps waiting for them. First base was at the bottom of the aisle. Already the batting cage was out and players were beginning to hit long balls.

Without a word, Violetta led them down until they were standing at the aisle just above the tier of seats next to the field. Being careful that Daniel was not looking their way, she pointed carefully to an aisle seat three rows up from the fence. Same seat, but this time Daniel was alone. Paulette recognized him immediately and the sight triggered a dry, sour taste in her mouth. Older, of course, and a little heavier. He had grown a full beard. Afraid she might be spotted, she said, "I'm leaving. No way I want to see him. Find Marc and the others and tell them to get seats somewhere behind Daniel. Tell Marc to call me tomorrow. After that you're free to go. Thanks for the help. Good luck." She left hurriedly.

Marc, Jules and Maria spent the evening seated in the section above and across the aisle from Daniel. The Expos scored six times in the second inning and four in the fourth much to the delight of the home-town fans. Maria was bored to death. After the fourth inning, she turned to Marc and told him she was grabbing a cab back to the hotel. "When you find where he lives, call me."

"What's the matter with her?" asked Jules, as he watched her disappearing up the aisle.

"Not a fan."

During the seventh inning stretch, the two men instinctively bent over their programmes as Daniel passed within a meter on his way up to the aisle. "What the heck are we hiding for?" asked Jules.

"You're right. He doesn't know us from Adam."

A few minutes later, Daniel passed them again carefully cradling two beers on the way to his seat. "That's his fifth and sixth beers," Marc pointed out.

"'Cause they close the bar after the seventh inning," Jules said.

"Oh yeah? The man's sure got a bladder on him."

Daniel started to leave after the Expos scored two more runs in the bottom of the eighth. Marc and Jules were a few paces behind him as he exited the stadium. "What if he takes a cab?" asked Jules.

"We'll have to hope that there's another cab available, and tell him to follow that cab. Always works in the movies." Despite the weak joke, Marc was terrified that either they would lose Daniel or he would spot them.

Enough people were leaving early that they had no trouble following their quarry. Instead of taking a cab, Daniel walked briskly east along Rue Viau towards the river before turning south on Hoshelaga. On the left was a small place called Brasserie 99 which advertised '*écran géant et repas*', big-screen TV and meals. In the window, decals of the Habs and the Expos. Daniel crossed the road and disappeared into the bar. "Make sure he doesn't come out. I'm going to walk back to that phone box on the corner and call Maria."

When he came back, Marc found Jules a few meters down from the bar and still on the opposite side of the street. "She'll be here soon. Let's go inside and grab a table not far from Daniel." The interior was dark. A couple of guys playing pool, a small stage with a 'Karaoke' sign, signed pictures of Andres Galarraga and Tim Raines on the walls. Less than a dozen customers. Daniel was sitting alone at a table in a dark corner. Above him on a small shelf, a television showing a news program. Marc and Jules sat down two tables away and ordered a jug of draft. When the waiter returned with their order, he asked them in French, "You guys going to sign up?"

"For what?" asked Marc.

"It's karaoke night."

"Not me. Jules? Want to sign up for karaoke?"

Jules looked at him and gave a slight shake of his head. The waiter moved on and deposited a quart bottle of Molson's on Daniel's table. The waiter obviously knew Daniel, so Marc guessed he was a regular. "I guess I don't have to ask, Daniel," said the waiter and handed him the sign-up sheet.

The bar was beginning to fill up, mostly with Expos fans. "Who knew Québecois liked karaoke so much," said Marc. A couple of minutes later, the overhead lights dimmed and two parcans came on to light the tiny stage. Like most karaoke bars, Brasserie 99 had a core of regulars. One of them was a plump, middle-aged woman dressed in faded jeans and a T-shirt, with a blonde dye job that was showing gray along her part. Marc recognized Gilles Vignault's *Mon Pays* from the instrumental intro. The song had become an anthem for the Québec separatists. Marc liked the song and was worried that the woman would butcher it, but she had a voice that a seraphim might have envied.

"*Mon Pays, ce n'est pas un pays, c'est l'hiver ...*"

By the time the singer was finished singing that her country 'is not a country, it's winter,' Marc had a lump in his throat. The crowd leapt to their feet and applauded. Marc looked over at Daniel who was on his feet and even shouted out, "*Vive le Québec libre!*", long live a free Québec, which sparked another round of applause.

As people resumed their seats, Marc waved to Maria who had just entered the door. She looks hot, Marc told himself, as she threaded her way through the now-crowded bar. When she reached their table, she kissed Marc on the cheek and waved to Jules.

"You didn't tell me it was karaoke. I love karaoke. Where do I sign up?" she asked.

"Ask him." Marc pointed at the waiter who had just appeared at her elbow. Maria ordered a Pepsi and signed up. Marc glanced at the list. She was in twelfth spot. Could be a long night.

The next few singers were of more uneven talent as is typical at karaoke bars. Ten minutes later, Daniel's number came up. The karaoke regulars applauded as he made his way to the stage and announced that he would sing *Les feuilles mortes*. Marc knew it only in the English translation as Autumn Leaves. To the accompaniment of a solo piano, Daniel teased out the melancholy lyrics and managed to make many in the room recall their own losses over the years. When he was finished, the applause reached new levels and continued until he reached his own table.

When Maria's name was called, she strode confidently through the tables and jumped lightly on to the tiny stage. After checking the list, she chose the only song that was in Spanish, *La Bamba*. Although she was sure the lyrics on the screen would be in French, she knew the Spanish version by heart. After the first verse, Marc leaned over to Jules and said, "Hey, she can really rock it out."

As she swung into the second verse, Maria began to salsa. With the line, "*Yo no soy marinaro*, (I am not a sailor) *soy capitain* (I am the captain), she seized the wireless mike off its stand and began dancing into the audience. To his surprise, she grabbed Marc, and he tried his stumbling best to keep up with her. With her back to Daniel, she winked at Marc, spun around and grabbed Daniel's hand, almost spilling his beer. He got up and danced a heavy-footed Latin rhythm opposite her. Just before the end of the song, he stopped and shook his head. "Look at those hips," he yelled to the crowd. "No way, I can keep up with that." Spinning away from him, she regained the stage without missing a beat and finished the song. During the applause, she pointed to Daniel and clapped.

While the next act was called, Maria went over to Daniel's table and introduced herself. Because Maria spoke almost no French beyond 'Voulez vous coucher avec moi?' and Daniel's English was broken at best, they spent the next little while listening to the other performers and stumbling through conversations heavy on body language. Nevertheless, Daniel couldn't believe his luck. Just before midnight, Daniel asked, "You like come mon appartement?

"Sure. Why not? But right now I have to find the femmes. I need to piss."

"Pisser? Is same in English?"

"If you say so. Hey, write down your address and phone number before I forget."

"Addresse? Mais oui." He ripped off the tongue of his empty cigarette package, scribbled his address and phone number on it and handed it to her. Then he looked puzzled. "But you coming with me, no?"

"Yeah. Now where do I piss?"

Daniel pointed to a corridor on the other side of the bar. "À gauche." As she passed Marc, she whispered, "Follow me."

Outside the toilets, she passed Marc Daniel's address and told him, "He's taking me back to his place. Wait ten minutes and follow."

"You gonna be O.K.?" Marc asked, not liking the way things were shaking out.

Maria stroked his cheek. "Nice that you're worried about me, but I'll be fine. I've been looking after myself for years."

"O.K. but be careful," he agreed reluctantly, pretty sure that she would do what she wanted to anyway. He glanced at the address and noticed an apartment number, 313, and guessed Daniel lived in an apartment block, probably on the third floor. "If the building has a door where you have to get buzzed in, leave it open if you can."

"If I can."

"*Bonne chance!*" Marc ducked into the men's toilet as Maria went back to her table. When he emerged, he was just in time to see Maria leaving on the arm of Daniel.

Marc was too impatient to wait very long, so he and Jules left shortly after to find a cab. Daniel's building was a brick three-story building in the suburb of Longeuil. Making sure he was not observed, he walked into the foyer and checked the inner door to the lobby. Locked. Damn.

"Just start hitting buttons. Say you've lost your key," Jules suggested.

It worked. The voice behind the fifth button buzzed him in. They took the stairs to the third floor and found apartment 313. Marc listened at the door but could not hear anything. "I guess we'll have to wait in the stairwell."

Three hours later they heard the click of heels along the hall. Peeking out, Jules saw Maria arriving at the elevator. "Come on," he said and stepped silently into the hall and proceeded down to the elevator. They stood next to Maria pretending not to know her until they all entered and the doors closed.

"How did it go?" Marc asked.

"Sorry I didn't prop the door open. Didn't have a chance."

"Don't worry about that." The elevator door opened and, to Marc's surprise, there was a cab standing outside the main door. "You called a cab?"

"Sure. You think I'm hiking back to the hotel?"

Maria climbed into the cab and gave the driver their address. Jules got in the front. As they pulled away from the curb, Maria looked into her purse and with great care pulled out a white silk bag with a tiny scroll attached. "Is this what you're looking for?"

Impulsively, Marc hugged her.

Not until they all sat around in Marc's room an hour later with drinks out of the minibar did Maria get around to telling them what had happened. "It was a bachelor's apartment, all right. Crap everywhere. But there was a glass cabinet. The reliquary was in there, not even hidden. Anyway, I insisted on having one last drink and slipped a roofie into his."

"A roofie?"

"Rohypnol. It's what we used to call a Mickey Finn. I always carry some in case of trouble. I gave him a really small dose, because he had been drinking. The beauty of it is that it may be months before Daniel realizes that the foreskin is missing, because roofies also cause amnesia. Pity."

"Why?"

"Because Daniel may never remember the greatest orgasm he ever had."

After a meal provided by room service, the three of them left for Sudbury. They got in just after dawn. Marc had done all the driving so, although he was tempted to call Eddie with the news about the foreskin, he decided to wait until tomorrow.

After he had worked out the six-hour time difference, Marc waited until after noon in Italy. When he heard Eddie's voice on the line, he said, "How are things going there?"

"Fine, fine. Good to hear from you. I hope it's good news."

"Oh, yeah. I think so. We've got the foreskin." Marc went on at length about their detective work, emphasizing Maria's role before concluding, "Now what do we do with it?"

"You realize you'll need my DNA too?"

"Right ... That's another problem."

"And one that, for a change, I anticipated. I left a washcloth and a toothbrush in a sterile plastic bag in the bathroom at Lydia's place. You'll need to collect that. Are you back in Sudbury?" Marc said they were. "Call Chief Sawchuk. I think he might do us a favor. Use your charm and ask him if he can arrange to pass your samples on to the

RCMP. They have a new lab that can do the analysis."

"O.K. We're on it. By the way, your Mom says hi."

"Tell her thanks, and my thanks to all three of you. Great job. Don't hesitate to call again any time, O.K.?"

"O.K. Take care of yourself, Eddie. I've been watching the news. Lots of crap going on there."

"We'll be careful. Bye, Marc."

# Part Thirteen: Italy

## Castel Gandolfo III

In the Swiss Guard security complex at Castel Gandolfo, Helebardier Maggi detected some unusual traffic coming down from Rome on the Via Appia. He checked the time: 9:18 p.m. Traffic on the Via Appia was usually light at that time of night. Camera N-7 was located just south of the Ciampino Airport. He counted nine cars and a TV broadcast truck. Thirty seconds later, the same line of cars was picked up on Camera N-5. At the same time, another line of cars was picked up on N-7, also heading south. Ciampino Airport is only five minutes to the north of Castel Gandolfo. Helebardier Maggi called over Hauptmann Hans Zoss, the officer on duty, and pointed to his screen. "A lot of traffic heading this way, sir."

Hauptmann Zoss checked the location of the camera: N7. "Coming down from Rome," he noted. "I think our secret is out. Block the three entrances to the Piazza Libertà," he told Feldweibel Gessner. "And throw up a cordon at the Via Appia exits. Don't let anyone into town until I give the order. Send Helebardier Solberger to alert His Holiness and Herr Fuseli. Better still, go yourself and take Solberger with you."

"Yes, sir," said Gessner, and hurried off to secure the palace and alert the pope.

Hauptmann Zoss looked back at the screens. More vehicles were approaching. Quickly he called for roadblocks at the entrances to Castel Gandolfo. Two minutes later he noted with satisfaction that one of his vehicles had reached the most northerly exit, and two of his men where setting up a roadblock with flares and spike strips. "Patch me through," he ordered. He could see one of the men at the exit stop and put his hand to the earpiece of his transceiver. "The story is that the road has been closed due to a traffic accident. We should be able to open it in about an hour." The trooper acknowledged and went back to work.

Already two of the three entrances to the Piazza Libertà had been blocked by vehicles. A squad of Guards, dressed in camo and toting MP-5s rather than their medieval partizans, had formed up at the top of Via della Corso.

The pope had been about to say his evening prayers when the guardsmen arrived. He immediately instructed Feldweibel Gessner to stay with him while Helebardier Solberger alerted his valet. "And tell him to ask Eddie and Pannychis to join us here as soon as possible."

Ten minutes later, the pope, his valet, Eddie and Pannychis and the two Swiss Guards were gathered around a large TV set up in Clementina Hall. The television was picking up the Rome RAI station. The excited announcer was telling the TV audience that media around the world had just received an anonymous tip that "Eddie Magdalena, and the famous model Pannychis Garlande, had been discovered in a most unexpected location: the Apostolic Palace in Castel Gandolfo. Secret talks seem to be taking place between Pope Urban IX and Eddie Magdalena, regarded by many as the AntiChrist. Does the new pope intend to recognize Eddie as the Messiah? Stay tuned for further breaking news." Not surprisingly, no names were appended to the announcement, just a mysterious group calling itself 'Concerned Members of the Curia.'

"So how did they find out we were here?" asked Eddie, shaking his head.

"It doesn't matter," said the pope. "The media is arriving as we speak, and we must decide on a course of action now."

Eddie was impressed. "You're right, Pablo. Obviously whoever put the story out is trying to embarrass the papacy. Pannychis and I don't want to cause you any more grief, so best we get out of here. Luigi, can you get someone to pack our bags."

"Certainly, but where will you go?"

"To Jerusalem. We were heading there anyway. We'll just be a day earlier than planned."

"Would you like me to book you into a small, discreet hotel?" Luigi asked.

Eddie grinned. "No, *mio amico*. It's time to come out of the closet.

Book us into the King David. Time to press some flesh, Pablo. The apostles will be arriving in Jerusalem very soon to join us."

"I'll book you into the King David Hotel," said Luigi and hurried away. "I will also call in a few favors, Eddie, and get you on your way."

"What a guy! He's an absolute gem, Pablo," Eddie told the pope.

"Yes, yes, he is. Look, Eddie, you can stay," said the pope. "We'll meet the press together."

"I thought I detected a steel spine under that cassock," Eddie said and risked gently hugging the old man who, after his initial surprise, smiled up at the big man. "I think that the first time we are seen together should be at the Ecumenical Council in Jerusalem, along with the imams and the rabbis. The time is not yet right for the Second Coming, Pablo."

Scenes on the television showed crowds in major cities around the world, filling squares with rival factions, foes and supporters of Eddie Magdalena. In some cases, police were keeping order with water cannon and rubber bullets. The pope shook his head in dismay. "Such violence from those who claim to love God."

"*Merde!*" Pannychis jumped up, startling the pope. "*Merde!*" She put her hand on his arm and said, "I'm sorry, Pablo. I think this whole thing is my fault." Eddie looked at her curiously and waited for her to explain. "When I was out today, I stopped at that little restaurant just a few meters down the hill, because it has a great view of the lake. Well, I ordered a cappuccino and a few minutes later, a man in a white linen suit and Gucci loafers came in, pushed past my table and sat down. He said something to me about the lake, quickly drank his coffee and left. I didn't think anything of it at the time, but I watched him walk away down the hill and get into a car with another man. They left immediately. I think they have been watching the palace. When they spotted me, they probably weren't sure, so the man in the white suit was sent into the restaurant to check me out. Remember I was wearing that big hat that covered one side of my face?" Eddie nodded. "That must be why he pushed past my table before he sat down. It was the only way to get a clear view of my face. I have been so stupid!" She was on the verge of tears. Eddie hugged her to him.

"Hey, not your fault. Strange how our first instinct is to blame ourselves when some son-of-a-bitch – ah, sorry Pablo – screws us over."

Pannychis nodded. "It was because I was trying to think of some way to get us out of here without being seen by the paparazzi, that I even thought about the man in the white suit. Anyway, I think I might have an idea."

Just then, Luigi reappeared. "I have chartered you a flight with AntonAir, a private company that we sometimes use. There is a Citation III jet waiting on the tarmac at Ciampino Airport. It's fully fueled. The pilot has already filed a flight plan to Tel Aviv and should have you in the air half an hour after you arrive."

"You're a miracle worker, Luigi," said Pannychis, feeling relieved.

"At Tel Aviv, you'll find Father Benedetto in the arrival hall. You can trust him. He and I have been friends since the seminary. He'll be holding up a sign that says 'Acme Holy Sepulchre Tours' and he ..." Eddie surprised Luigi by starting to laugh. "What is it, Eddie?"

"A fan of the Roadrunner cartoons, Luigi?"

Luigi began to blush and muttered, "Since my childhood, Eddie."

"O.K. Sorry for the interruption." But he had succeeded in lifting the tension that had begun to permeate the room.

"Anyway, Father Massimo Benedetto. He'll take you to the King David where I have booked you a suite on the third floor. His Holiness will be staying on the floor above when he arrives."

"Wonderful, my son," said Urban.

"Amazing. You just keep surprising me," Eddie told him.

"But we still need to get to the airport without alerting the press," Pannychis reminded them. "Are we getting there by helicopter?"

"No, signora. Everyone would hear it. And Ciampino is so close that the paparazzi lined up along the Via Appia would even be able to see where it was landing."

"O.K. Then d'you have a car with tinted windows here?" she asked Luigi.

"Yes, yes. A Mercedes. Black, of course."

"And a motorcycle. Doesn't have to be very big."

"I have one," volunteered Feldweibel Gessner. "A Ducati 851 Strada."

"A Ducati?" Eddie asked. The Feldweibel nodded.

"Designed by Fabio Taglioni, no?"

"Yes."

"Would you mind lending it to us, Feldweibel?"

"It would be an honor, Eddie."

"How far to the airport from here?"

"About ten kilometers."

"Hah! We'll be there before they know we've gone."

"What about our luggage?" asked Pannychis.

"Can it follow us with the luggage of your entourage?" Eddie asked the pope.

"Of course, of course."

"Hey, I'm going to need my makeup kit, shoes and a change of clothes, but I can fit them all in my bag. And I'll grab the passports." Pannychis was just about to return to their room when a thought stopped her. "Remember Brother Borromeo?" she asked. Eddie nodded. "He's about your height. A lot skinnier but they'll only see him through the tinted windows. We will also need someone to be me. Do you have anyone around my height, Luigi?"

Luigi thought for a moment before saying, "Yes. Sister Anna. She is as tall as you and a fine-looking woman."

"Do you think she would be willing to wear the clothes I wore this afternoon?"

"We can only ask."

"Now here is what we'll do."

When Pannychis had laid out her plan, Eddie said, "Should work." He looked at his watch: 10:09 p.m. "Better get going, huh?"

"Yes. The guards up on the Via Appia won't be able to hold the media back for much longer," Luigi reminded them.

"One last thing. I'd better get hold of Marc and Jean-Pièrre and tell them what we're up to. Give me a few minutes." Eddie strode off to use the telephone in his room. When he returned, he told Luigi. "I talked to Jean-Pièrre, but I couldn't get through to Canada. Could you call after we've gone and let Marc Baptiste know what's happening, give him our room number at the King David?"

"Of course."

Ten minutes later, Feldweibel Gessner walked Eddie and Pannychis to his beautiful red Ducati and handed Eddie the keys. Eddie agreed to leave the bike at the AntonAir hanger where Gessner would pick it up the next day. "First we have to get clear of the paparazzi," Eddie told him. Gessner nodded and favored the couple with one of his rare smiles, as he handed over two red helmets with full-face visors.

"Perfect. We should be able to pass as paparazzi, huh?"

"Wait," said Pannychis. "Luigi made these up just before he left." She reached into her bag and pulled out two stickers, each with the logo of RAI uno TV, the Italian broadcaster. She stuck one on the front of each helmet. "That should fool anybody."

Eddie laughed, jammed on his helmet and gave a thumbs-up to Luigi, who was standing a few feet away in the darkness. Eddie mounted, and Pannychis got up behind him. As the Ducati started with a satisfying roar, Pannychis pulled her Nikon out of her bag, quickly attached a long lens to its bayonet mount and leaned it on Eddie's shoulder.

"You really do look the part," called out Luigi, but with the roar of the Ducati and with their helmets muffling sound, neither Eddie nor Pannychis heard him. Two Swiss Guards saluted them as Eddie took the Ducati through a Roman arch into the Piazza della Libertà. Eddie waved back. "Is that the chase car?" Eddie asked, pointing to a black Mercedes parked at the top of the Via della Corso. Eddie had to shout to be heard.

"With Brother Borromeo and Sister Anna? Yes. Flash your lights and then follow it to the road block at the Via Appia."

Eddie nodded, flashed his hi-beams and steered the bike around Bernini's fountain, feeling out the bike as he negotiated the cobblestones of the square. The Mercedes ahead of him began to move.

When they could see the lights of the roadblock ahead, Eddie pulled the bike over so that it was hidden behind a police van and waited as the Mercedes drove on. Eddie signaled a guard in the van who immediately called ahead to the roadblock just as the Mercedes reached it. Quickly, the guards moved the flares aside and directed the wave of paparazzi through the barrier towards Castel Gandolfo. At the same time, they cleared a path out to the Via Appia for the Mercedes. Cries of recognition as several reporters thought they recognized Eddie and Pannychis in the back seat of the Mercedes.

Many of the media vehicles tried to turn and follow the Mercedes. Three cars piled into each other, blocking the road behind the Mercedes. The TV remote truck got stuck across the road. Car doors were flung open, and suddenly the road was filled with cursing reporters. Less than twenty vehicles managed to get turned and give chase to the Mercedes.

Taking advantage of the confusion, Eddie threaded the Ducati through the chaos. If any gave it a glance, Luigi's RAI stickers and Pannychis' camera with its long lens propped on Eddie's shoulder deflected any suspicion.

Eddie turned north on the Via Appia and stayed at least 500 meters behind the taillights of the traffic ahead. The Mercedes drove past Ciampino Airport at a good pace, a tail of media vehicles following. The plan was to drive the Mercedes into Rome and pull into Domus Sessoriano, the monastery at Santa Croce in Gerusalemme, where Brother Borromeo and Sister Anna would stay the night. As instructed, Eddie avoided the main gate to the Arrivals Hall at the Ciampino Airport and found the small entrance to the AntonAir hanger. They were met by the airline's own security people and hustled on board the Citation III where they were greeted by Captain Lampedusa.

"Looks like the Vatican travels in style," observed Eddie, looking around the cabin. This Citation III was designed to carry no more than eight passengers, and so the individual grey leather seats were arranged around a small table.

"I get the feeling, though, that this is not Urban's style," said Pannychis.

"Welcome aboard. Please fasten your seat belts," the male flight attendant said. "We have clearance to taxi, so we should be in the air in a few minutes."

"Thanks, Luca," Eddie said after glancing at the man's name tag. "You're welcome, sir. It's an honor to have you both aboard."

As Captain Lampedusa began his take-off roll, Pannychis reached out and squeezed Eddie's hand. He looked at her gratefully but did not begin to relax until the Citation reached cruising altitude and the attendant returned to take their drink orders. Eddie ordered a double scotch, Pannychis a whiskey sour.

## The Annunciation

Because of the fierce storm blowing in from the Adriatic, Nunzia found herself alone as she leaned into the wind, head bowed against the blowing sheets of rain that were sweeping across the Piazza Maggiore. Gratefully, she slipped into the shelter of the Basilica of San Petronio, the largest church in Bologna. Last night professor Enrico Capelli had turned her triumph at finding a perfect DNA match into a tragedy, by forcing Nunzia and her team to lie about the results. The more she thought about it, the more she was sure that denying the divinity of Eddie Magdalena was a mortal sin. After a sleepless night, she had dressed and set out into the stormy weather to go to San Petronio and make her confession. On weekdays, she knew, Father Giancarlo Venditti heard confessions between six and seven in the morning for the sake of people on their way to work.

Because of the weather, there were only two older women waiting outside the confessional. First, Nunzia knelt in one of the pews and prayed fervently for guidance until it was her turn to enter the twilight world of the confessional.

With a slight grating sound, Father Giancarlo opened the tiny veiled window that separated them, and she began, "*Mi benedica, Padre, perché ho peccato ...*" Bless me, Father, for I have sinned. A good Catholic, Nunzia had been to confession little more than a week before, so ignoring her few venal peccadillos over the previous few days, she launched into what was really bothering her. "Father, I work at the university as a DNA technician. For the past couple of weeks, we have been working on a most important secret project." Father Giancarlo was suddenly wide awake. Nunzia told him about the DNA sample comparisons that she had been analyzing. "At first we were not sure we could get uncontaminated data from the *santissimo prepuzio* ..."

"Wait a minute, my child," Father Giancarlo interrupted. "How did you obtain the DNA samples?"

"I was told that someone stole Eddie Magdalena's DNA in Canada and it had been brought here to our lab. The Savior's DNA?" She stopped, thought about it, and decided she did not dare reveal the origin of the *prepuzio*. "I'm afraid I cannot reveal that to anyone, Father. I'm sorry, but I think if they find out I have told you, they might kill me."

"Go on, my child."

"Last night the first results began to come in. The two genetic sequences were absolutely identical. It means that Eddie's DNA is the same as our Savior."

Father Giancarlo's jaw dropped. "Then He really is the true Messiah."

"Yes."

"There can be no mistake? No margin of error?"

"No, Father. None. Like our Savior, Eddie Magdalena is the Son of God."

"*Madre di Dio!* Has the Holy Father been told?"

Nunzia dropped her head and burst into tears. Father Giancarlo had recognized the woman kneeling beyond the wall as soon as he had opened the veiled grate, and was now wondering whether to let her know. Yes, he decided finally. "Are you all right, Nunzia?"

"Yes, yes, Father."

"Then just proceed at your own pace. Was there anyone else waiting to confess?"

"No. I was the last."

Father Giancarlo checked his watch. Confession time had ended a few minutes ago. "Then take your time, my child." He heard her blow her nose and then take a couple of deep breaths before continuing.

"The Holy Father has not been told yet. In fact, last night I was asked, no, ordered, to stop the other test samples and destroy the results of the positive one we had just run. Just by telling you, Father, I could go to jail. The authorities, I don't know who they are, but they are from the Vatican, didn't expect the samples to match. In fact, the secret analysis was meant to discredit the new Messiah. They plan to tell the Holy Father that there was no match."

"But he must be told the truth!"

"I have been sworn to secrecy, Father. I feel safe telling you because priests cannot violate the secrecy of the confessional, but I dare not tell anyone else."

"Nunzia, my child. No one can hold you to a vow that is sinful. On the other hand, I can see that you might be in a great deal of trouble if these people found out that you were the source of the leak."

"But what should I do, Father?"

Father Giancarlo thought about her predicament for a few moments before he said, "You are quite right. I cannot talk about anything that happens in the confessional, but it is vital that someone informs the pope. Now let me absolve you and I'll meet you in the sacristy behind the altar. Go through the door on the left. I'm going to give you a penance of a *Padre Nostro* and ten *Ave Marias*. When you have finished, come and see me. Try to make sure no one sees you. Dominus noster Jesus te absolvat ..." When he had finished the post-absolution prayer, he made a small sign of the cross, opened his door and peered out. The church, thankfully, was empty and he walked briskly up the long nave and crossed behind the altar.

After her act of contrition, Nunzia looked around and saw that, except for an old woman lighting a candle, she was alone. The woman was back near the entrance and had her back to Nunzia. Nunzia had known and trusted Father Giancarlo ever since she had landed her job at the University of Bologna. He was the main reason she was determined to continue to attend San Petronio even after she moved to another apartment next month. Her second reason was that she loved the church itself and secretly thought of San Petronio as her oyster; its ugly, unfinished facade hiding a lustrous Gothic pearl of pink marble columns holding up its vaulted ceilings. She had fallen in love with the church on her first visit.

Father Giancarlo was waiting for her in the sacristy. When she entered, he directed her to a chair and sat down opposite her. "You seem to have been through a lot already, Nunzia," he began. She nodded. "And I feel humble that you are trusting me with the secret you have been keeping."

"I couldn't sleep, Father, so I came really to ask you what I should do."

"And you have been brave to do so, but first I need to know what you want to do with the information. Do you want the Holy Father to learn that the results were falsified?"

"He is the Vicar of Christ, Father. I hear that Eddie Magdalena is staying with him in Castel Franco. He must be told."

"Contacting the Holy Father is not that easy," Father Giancarlo cautioned.

"I know, Father. But I thought you might know a way."

"Then you want me to become involved?"

"I don't know who else I can turn to."

"Then leave it with me, my dear. I will try to contact the Holy Father. I will tell him of the fraud being perpetrated here."

Looking as if a weight had been lifted from her, Nunzia sat up and even smiled. "Please. I would like you to do that, Father."

"Then I'll find a way. I do know the pope's valet. I will try to contact him at Castel Gandolfo. And I will keep your name confidential, of course. You said that the authorities, as you called them, are from the Vatican."

"Yes. At different times Cardinal Buffone and Reverend Father Thomas del Sarto visited our lab to see professor Capelli. He is in charge of the project."

Father Giancarlo made a mental note to imply that his information came from Capelli, not his parishioner. "And do you mind if I mention them?"

"No, no. I feel better now that I have told you, Father." Nunzia rose followed by Father Giancarlo.

"Then go home. Say nothing to anyone about this. I swear one way or another, the Holy Father will learn of this."

When Nunzia had gone, the priest went over what he had learned.

Would he be in danger if 'the authorities', as Nunzia had called them, learned of his role? Just last year, he had read David Yallop's book *In God's Name*, where the author had argued quite persuasively that Pope Jean-Paul I had been murdered. Could these people be those same members of P2, the secret masonic group, that Yallop had accused? He shuddered at the thought. He could, of course, pass the information on to the Cardinal of Bologna, Giacomo Biffi, hoping that he would make it public. Biffi was a conservative, but he opposed freemasonry. On the other hand, the man despised homosexuals, feminists and even the ecumenical movement which Biffi believed would weaken the church. He could not be sure how the cardinal would react. No, he would contact Luigi Fuseli himself.

After several phone calls to his contacts, Father Giancarlo finally found out the number to reach the Apostolic Palace and dialed it. The call was answered by one of the Swiss Guards on duty. Father Giancarlo explained that he had an urgent need to get hold of Luigi Fuseli about a family matter. The guard asked the nature of the emergency, but Father Giancarlo told him it was intensely personal. While he waited for the call to go through, the Father hoped that Luigi still remembered him from the time, long ago now, when they both had worked for the church in Venice.

"Here is the Holy Father's luggage, Brother Borromeo," Luigi said, indicating the three suitcases and the two suit bags. "My bags are already downstairs. We have to leave for the helipad in half an hour."

Just then the phone rang. Luigi answered and was surprised to hear the voice of Archbishop Paul Marcinkus reminding him that the chopper would be stopping briefly at the Vatican helipad to pick him up. Luigi had been surprised, as he should have known that Marcinkus was coming to Jerusalem, but he gave no sign as he agreed to pick up God's Banker. Then he remembered that the big man had twice saved the lives of a pope. During a visit to the Philippines in 1970, Marcinkus had overpowered a Bolivian painter who had tried to stab Paul VI, and again during a visit to Portugal, he had saved yet another pope, John-Paul II, from a Spanish priest who tried to kill him with a bayonet. Obviously the Holy Father had decided to take the archbishop along as an unofficial bodyguard. "Glad you're coming, Paul," Luigi said as he hung up.

Five minutes later, just as Luigi was checking his list and looking around the papal apartments to be sure that he had not missed anything, the phone rang again. Luigi picked up the receiver and said, "*Pronto.*"

"Luigi, it's Giancarlo Venditti. It's been a few years."

Luigi had never been particularly close to Father Giancarlo but had found him a pleasant, dedicated priest. "Yes, of course. It has been a long time. Look, Giancarlo, I am just leaving for Jerusalem with the Holy Father for the Ecumenical Conference. Give me your number and I'll call you when we get back."

"Then I'm so glad I caught you, Luigi. I have something to tell you of utmost importance. I have just learned that some powerful players at the Vatican have secretly run a DNA test on Eddie Magdalena. They compared his DNA to that of a sample they somehow obtained of the Savior's DNA. Their hope was to discredit the Messiah, but the results came in last night. A perfect match. Eddie Magdalena is the Messiah, Luigi. But these men intend to falsify the results to discredit Eddie Magdalena and Pope Urban. I imagine they are probably informing the media as we speak."

"Do you have any names?"

"All I know is that Cardinal Buffone and the Black Pope are involved." Silence. "Luigi? Are you there?"

"Yes, yes. I must go, Giancarlo, but I'm grateful for the information and will inform His Holiness."

"Strange world we live in, eh, Luigi?"

"Strange indeed. Now I really must go. His Holiness is waiting. Once again, *grazie mille, Giancarlo. Arrivederci.*"

Instead of hurrying out to the car, Luigi sat down and thought about the enormity of this betrayal by a segment of the Curia. Two porters tapped on the open door to take the rest of the luggage. The polite tap startled Luigi, who had been lost in thought. "Take the rest of the suitcases," he told them, and tell the driver that we might be leaving a little late. "I'll come down to the car when we are ready."

He closed the door behind him and went to the bedroom where Pope Urban was taking a nap before beginning his travels. When he had delivered his news, he noted that the pope did not appear particularly surprised. "So the Gang of Four has finally revealed their true nature," the pope observed. "Time to fight back." He pointed to the telephone. "Get me Cardinal Silvestrini, Luigi."

"Yes, Your Holiness. But first, I had better get Cardinal Buffone to tell your pilots that we will be delayed."

"Of course, Luigi, of course. Not Cardinal Buffone though. He is part of the problem. No, no. Call Pierre Savoie, our travel coordinator, and let him make the arrangements. Tell him ... no, just tell him we'll be late. Why is not his problem but ours."

After Luigi had called the papal travel coordinator, he called Cardinal Silvestrini. When he had the cardinal on the line, he handed the phone to Pope Urban and whispered, "Shall I leave you alone, Your Holiness?"

As the pope took the phone, he shook his head vigorously before saying pleasantly, "Hallo, Achille. We are starting to hear reports that some members of the Curia have secretly been matching Eddie Magdalena's DNA with that of our Savior, so I thought I had better call you, as you always seem to have your finger on the pulse of the Curia."

"Your Holiness, I'm flattered that you think me of such importance. It is true that many of the Curia, especially the senior cardinals, are worried that we are treating this latest so-called Messiah as if he were the real thing. That is probably why a few of the cardinals, I don't know who, have arranged for the DNA test. They are worried enough about what they see as the greatest threat to our Mother Church since the Reformation. They probably feel that if there is no match, it will prove that Magdalena is yet another false prophet."

The pope took a deep breath in an effort to control his temper. "And if there is a match?"

Cardinal Silvestrini permitted himself a small dismissive laugh. "Well, Your Holiness, the latest rumor I heard is that the preliminary results have just come in. From what I hear, Eddie Magdalena is no more likely to be the Messiah than Vico, your gardener."

"Vico has more love in his heart than many of the Curia, Achille. So let me get this straight. There is no chance that Eddie is the Messiah."

"None at all, Your Holiness, none at all."

"And what do you intend to do with this information, Achille."

"I? It has nothing to do with me, Your Holiness. I just try, as you said earlier, to keep my finger on the affairs of Mother Church. If I were to make an informed guess though, I think the results will be released to the press in the next day or two."

"To what purpose?"

"To prevent Magdalena from being formally recognized as the Messiah, Your Holiness. Such a thing would be a catastrophe."

"Achille. If a word of this surfaces before I return from Jerusalem, I will see that you are transferred to the farthest jungles of Papua New Guinea."

"Ah, then let me tell you of another rumor I have just heard. Last night there was a meeting held at Santa Maria sopra Minerva. The notice for the meeting was very short, so only cardinals who were in or close to Rome were able to attend. Nevertheless, about sixty members of the Curia have signed a petition to ask you to resign. That petition, I understand, will be on your desk when you return from Jerusalem."

"Popes do not resign, Achille," the pope said, bristling at the cardinal's triumphant tone.

"It is not unknown, Pablo. Rare, but not unknown."

"Who called the meeting?"

"My sources didn't tell me."

"Thank you, Achille. You have been most helpful." Pope Urban's hand shook as he put down the telephone. Luigi handed him a glass of water. When his anger began to subside, the pope crossed to his prie-dieu and prayed for guidance. Luigi watched him anxiously.

When he was done, Pope Urban levered himself up, feeling older than he ever had before. "Please, Luigi, one last phone call. Call Buffone. It must have been Buffone who called the meeting. As Secretary of State, he has the right to do so when the pope is not available. He should be in the papal apartments."

A couple of minutes later, Luigi had Cardinal Buffone on the line and handed the telephone to the pope. "Ah, Xavier. I hear that you called a meeting last night at Santa Maria sopra Minerva, the church of the inquisition. I'm sure you found such a place appropriate for challenging a sitting pope."

"Whoever told you that is a liar!" Buffone roared.

"Cardinal Silvestrini? Or was it Cardinal Schicklgruber? Or even the Black Pope himself? Which one, Xavier?" He could hear the cardinal breathing heavily on the other end of the line.

"Your Holiness ..."

"Look, Xavier. I am leaving for Jerusalem, but when I get back I want to see your resignation as Head of State. I will be appointing Cardinal Raoul Maldonado to replace you."

"Of course, you would choose another Argentinian. You are leading the church to its ruin, Pablo, and I pledge to use any means to stop you. You will be sorry."

There was no reply to that, so the pope hung up. Luigi felt like applauding. "Come, Luigi. We have a date in Jerusalem."

# Part Fourteen: Jerusalem

## Once in Royal David's City

"Holy Fuck!" Colleen O'Mara, correspondent for the *Irish Times*, suddenly felt as if she had won the lottery. She had been sitting in the Arrivals Lounge of Ben Gurion Airport for the last two hours with nothing to do but listen to her Walkman and try to talk herself out of lighting yet another cigarette to punctuate her boredom. At airports all over the world, other bored reporters were waiting, waiting and hoping for the AntiChrist/Messiah to arrive.

Colleen had taken over the Jerusalem beat four months before when the previous *Irish Times* correspondent, James Sweeney, had been seriously injured. He had been hit by two plastic bullets fired by the Israeli Defense Force as they were trying to quell a storm of rock throwing by young Palestinians during the Intifada that had started just over a year ago.

Earlier today, Colleen had been covering a clash between the IDF and another group of rock-throwing Palestinian boys, just outside the Dung Gate near the Western Wall. She had been standing with the boys, taking pictures, when the IDF started to fire tear gas canisters. The boys had scattered while she, weeping profusely, had ducked into the Old City and found her way back to her apartment in West Jerusalem. There she had quickly stripped off her military-style fatigues with the word PRESS sewn on to the left pocket, put them in a plastic bag and taped it up to contain the gunpowder smell of tear gas. The bag she tossed out on to her tiny balcony. After scrubbing herself in the shower, she looked at herself in the mirror. Her flaming red hair, pale face and freckles, attested to her Irish heritage. Right now her red-rimmed eyes almost matched her hair color. She opened her medicine cabinet, found the liquid Maalox. An old Jerusalem hand had told her it helped relieve the symptoms of tear gas. She squirted a few ccs into her toothbrush mug, added warm water and began to slowly massage her eyes. I should carry some with me, she chided herself. Within a few minutes, the burning began to ease. She patted her eyes dry. Now, what do you wear to meet a Messiah, she wondered, as she looked at the meagre offerings in her closet. She finally selected a sober green dress that she felt complemented her complexion and put on a pair of patent leather high heels.

Colleen recognized the woman first. She had seen her in person, years before in Paris. Pannychis Garlande. And her companion, the big guy with a carefully trimmed beard, had to be Eddie Magdalena. Jesus, Mary and Joseph, he is even better looking in the flesh! The scar, she thought, made him look like a friendly pirate. He seemed even bigger than he appeared on television.

Gotta get a shot, she told herself. Pulling her Canon EOS out of its case, she followed the famous couple. They stopped for a moment as they reached the public area and scanned the few people who were holding up signs. Colleen moved closer and took a couple of candids. The sound of the shutter caught Eddie's ear and he turned and looked right at her. Colleen waved tentatively, feeling like a fool. Eddie surprised her by beckoning her over. Nervously, she approached the big man.

"You're the press, right?" said Eddie.

"Yes. *Irish Times.*"

"Guess you won, huh?"

"Won?"

"You found us. Congratulations," Eddie said with no hint of irony.

Colleen took a deep breath and asked, "Why are you in Jerusalem, Eddie?"

"Jerusalem is the center of the earth for three of the largest religions of the world."

"Jerusalem is a dangerous place right now though."

"Yeah. I've been warned." He turned to Pannychis and added, "We're hoping to stay out of the trouble and maybe see if we can persuade the Israelis and the Palestinians to give peace a chance."

"Bringing peace to Jerusalem would certainly count as a miracle in my books." She turned to Pannychis. "I saw you in Paris a couple of years ago. Lagerfeld's fall collection."

"Oh, the one where Linda Evangelista fell on her ass at the end of the runway."

"That's right. I remember."

Losing interest in the conversation, Eddie looked over at the signs and spotted 'Acme Sepulchre Tours.' The sign was being held aloft by a bony middle-aged priest. The priest had obviously spotted them and nodded when he caught Eddie's eye. Eddie waved and said to Pannychis, "There he is. The guy with the Acme sign."

"Oh, right. I see him. I'm afraid we have to go, ah ..."

"Colleen. Colleen O'Mara."

For a moment, Eddie said nothing, just gazed into her eyes. She had the odd feeling that he was looking into her soul. "Look, Colleen," he said, "It's just after dawn and Pannychis and I need some sleep but, if you like, we'll give you an interview later in the day."

Colleen trying hard to conceal her surprise, said, "That would be wonderful, Eddie. What would be a good time?"

Eddie looked at Pannychis. "How's two sound?"

"Two is fine."

"There you go, Colleen. We're staying at the King David."

"I'll be there at two, then. It's been wonderful to meet the two of you. Thanks so much for this. I'll be filing right away."

"Great! We need the world to know that we have come to the holy city of Jerusalem. See you soon." As Colleen hurried away, Father Giacomo Benedetto arrived and introduced himself.

During the forty-minute drive from Tel Aviv to Jerusalem, Father Giacomo called the King David Hotel on the limousine's radio phone to alert the staff to the imminent arrival of Eddie Magdalena. "Just to make sure they are ready for you," he explained to his charges, before reiterating Colleen's warning that these were perilous times in Jerusalem. "East Jerusalem and the West Bank are the most dangerous areas right now." He urged them to avoid going out, especially without an IDF escort. Eddie thanked him for his concern but was not sure whether he would follow the priest's advice.

As the pink limestone facade of the King David came into view, Father Giacomo said, "You must be tired. I'll let you sleep for a few hours before I bring the papal nuncio, the most reverend Archbishop

Benjamin Fowler, to meet you. He is the Ambassador of the Holy See here in Jerusalem. What time should I tell him?"

"One?"

"I'll let him know."

When the limousine arrived at the main entrance to the King David, uniformed staff opened the doors and took Pannychis' overnight bag, the only luggage they had with them. The concierge, a Palestinian in his sixties with a magnificent white handlebar mustache and a twinkle in his eye, welcomed them to his hotel. "Call me Khaled, my dears. I am at your service at any time, day or night. I'm sure you will enjoy your stay." With that he conducted them through the revolving doors, along the red carpet under the lotus blossom chandeliers, to the front desk. While Eddie accepted the keys, Pannychis was taking in the magnificent art deco lobby painted in various shades of grey.

The concierge and a porter accompanied them up to their adjoining suites on the third floor. The spacious suites were joined by a double door and both had balconies with a view of the walls of the Old City. Khaled pointed out all the amenities and once again emphasized the fact that he was responsible for their happiness, day or night.

As the concierge and the porter were leaving, Eddie reached into his pocket. He had no shekels, so he offered Khaled a handful of lira notes worth, he hoped, at least $20 US. Khaled graciously declined the gratuity. "But I do need to know how you like to be addressed, sir."

"Just Eddie's fine."

"And I'm Pannychis, Khaled." She took his hands. "I know you will look after us well."

When the door closed behind the concierge and the porter, Eddie smiled at Pannychis. "You know that guy would take a bullet for you now."

"Well, let's hope it doesn't come to that." Pannychis opened the doors that separated the two suites and said, "Luigi still seems keen on preserving my virtue."

"Oh, you mean the double suite? He did make sure we'd be comfortable. Look, I could do with breakfast. What do you think?"

Twenty minutes later, they heard the clinking of a trolley, followed by a soft knock on the door. Pannychis opened the door and let out a scream, as she jumped back in surprise before calling for Eddie. The room waiter bore an uncanny resemblance to Elvis. Eddie emerged at a run from the bathroom, but stopped when he saw the Big Guy wheeling in a trolley laden with shiny stainless steel domes, a coffee pot, a jug of orange juice, plates and cutlery.

"It's O.K. It's O.K. It's the Big Guy," Eddie said.

"Hallo, Son. I thought we could have a talk over breakfast."

"Sure. This, as you know, is Pannychis."

The Big Guy just oozed southern charm as He made a polite bow to Pannychis. "Didn't mean to scare the crap out of you, ma'am. Glad to meet you at last. I've heard so much about you."

Eddie had told her about his meetings with the Big Guy and that the Big Guy's choice of a human persona was Elvis' twin brother, Jessie Presley. But it is one thing to have heard about a deity, another thing to meet a Supreme Being in the flesh, if flesh it was. Instinctively she curtsied and was immediately sorry as she saw that both God the Father and God the Son were trying hard not to laugh.

"You are one of the most beautiful creatures in My entire creation, Pannychis. I am honored to meet you. Eddie's been keeping you to himself for far too long."

Pannychis' bewilderment quickly dissipated as the three of them settled themselves around a table in front of the French windows. "I enjoyed your escape from Castel Gandolfo," the Big Guy told Pannychis.

"So did I, as a matter of fact," she told him.

He pointed over her shoulder where a woman in a white uniform stood waiting to serve them. Where had she come from? Pannychis guessed that she must be Marie.

In a soft, low husky voice, Marie said, "Pleased to meet you, Pannychis. You are the right companion for Eddie. I'm so glad he found you."

After breakfast, Marie sat in the chair opposite Pannychis. "You want me to leave?" asked Pannychis lightly. "After all, I do have an entire suite to myself. It's no trouble."

"You just stay put," said the Big Guy. "When the scribes write the new gospels, your name will occupy a place of honor." He picked up the pot of coffee and poured a third cup for each of them. Pannychis quickly did the math in her head: nine cups plus one for Marie after she sat down, so ten cups. About eighty fluid ounces. Sixteen ounces to a pint made ... that small pot had held at least five pints of coffee. She reached out and picked up the pot. Still full. She felt someone watching her. When she looked up, she saw the Big Guy wearing a bemused smile. He winked at her and said, "Now, you've already got appointments at one and two today. And with me barging in like an uninvited wedding guest, you'll be hard pressed to get any sleep. Don't worry. This brand of coffee will keep both of you alert until tonight. Then you will sleep the sleep of the just. Trust me."

Pannychis took a sip of coffee and decided she had never tasted better. In fact, the trouble with coffee, as we all know, is that its taste is but a pale imitation of its aroma. This brew delivered all the taste that other coffees merely promised. In fact, three cups was a new record for Pannychis. "Yeah. If coffee really tasted this good, people would kill for it," said Eddie.

"And we sure don't want that, Pannychis." The Big Guy tilted his chair back. "Killing each other in great numbers doesn't even do much to dent the world's population. Maybe I should have cut out male orgasm in the beginning, but I needed the numbers to kick start intelligent life on this planet."

"Ah, let's hope life here is intelligent enough to buy into the earthly paradise I'm trying to peddle," said Eddie.

"We don't have much time, so let's get started." Eddie was startled by such abruptness from the Big Guy. Did he have doubts about their success in Jerusalem? "Your apostles, most of them anyway, will arrive later this afternoon. They should make it to the National Hotel at around five or so. The National is in East Jerusalem. Not the safest part of town right now. But how would the travel agent have known that? Anyway, you're thinking of visiting the Church of the Holy Sepulchre with them." Eddie nodded. "First you want to walk the Via Dolorosa, stopping at the stations of the cross along the way. The last ones, as you know, are in the Holy Sepulchre itself."

"That's the plan," Eddie acknowledged, reaching out and taking Pannychis' hand.

"And Pope Urban will be following the same path on Friday."

"Right. I see the problem. We'd be upstaging him," said Eddie, getting the Big Guy's drift. The Big Guy nodded. "Instead, I'll call the National Hotel and leave a message for Jean-Pièrre. We'll meet them later and have a meal together."

"A last supper? Just don't knock over the salt." The Big Guy laughed at his own joke.

"And tomorrow, we'll visit the West Bank instead. See the Church of the Nativity in Bethlehem."

"Ah yes. Birthplace of Jesus. Seems like only yesterday. But you should make sure of your own safety. If you're going to the West Bank, the IDF cannot protect you. They might send a couple of plain clothes Mossad agents. Still, the Palestinians over there might just take to our message. What do they have to lose, huh? Oh, one last thing, and then I'll leave you two lovebirds alone."

"The timetable for Friday."

"Yes. The timetable for Friday, July seventh. Pope Urban will follow the Via Dolorosa, praying at the stations of the cross. His tour will end at the Church of the Holy Sepulchre. He will be accompanied by Archbishop Benjamin Fowler, Ambassador of the Holy See and Archbishop Paul Marcinkus."

"The one nicknamed 'the Gorilla'?"

"One and the same."

Pannychis gave the Big Guy a puzzled look. He smiled at her and explained, "The archbishop is a big guy. He's also saved two popes from assassination."

"Which is why Archbishop Marcinkus will be traveling with Pope Urban. The gang of four are planning to stop the pope from recognizing you at all costs. So, in my own way, I persuaded the archbishop he needed to get out of Vatican City for a few days. I need him by the pope's side."

"Saving a third pope?" asked Eddie. "He's just the guy to do it."

"Let's hope so. By the way, We're seeing Archbishop Fowler here at one o'clock."

"Bit of a crusty old son-of-a-bitch. Not one of your fans. Not a supporter of the present pope either."

"Good to know."

"After they have prayed together with the monks in charge of the Sepulchre, all except Pope Urban and the archbishop will walk in procession to the Jewish Quarter. Because of their ages, the pope and the archbishop will exit the Old City by way of the Jaffa Gate and be driven around the walls to the Dung Gate. Once the procession arrives, they will rejoin it at the entrance to the Wailing Wall. There, the pope will meet the two senior rabbis in Jerusalem: Rabbi Avraham Weisel, leader of the Ashkenazi, and Rabbi Mordechai Moisel, leader of the Sephardi. He will don a white kippa and pray with them at the Wailing Wall. Finally, the rabbis will join the papal procession and together they will proceed outside the walls and make their way to the Golden Gate. They'll meet you there at exactly seven p.m."

"So we'll start down from the top of the Mount of Olives around five?"

"Should be fine. Don't forget that halfway down the road beside the Jewish cemetery, you'll stop at the Garden of Gethsemane and the Church of the Agony next door. From there you can see the walls below you. When you see the pope's people coming north along the wall, your procession should begin the final part of the descent. The police will have blocked traffic to the entire block. After you leave Gethsemane, don't stop for anything. It's very important you remember that."

"But the Golden Gate is blocked."

"And there's a Muslim cemetery in front of it, too, put there by the Ottomans. Don't worry. I'll make the rough places plain."

"Wait." Pannychis held up a hand. "Why is that gate blocked?"

"Ah yes. According to Jewish legend, the *Shekhinah* or Divine

Presence used to appear there, and when the Messiah appears, he will enter by the Gate of Mercy, the old name for the Golden Gate. When Jesus entered the Holy City on Palm Sunday, he too came by way of the Golden Gate. It's mentioned in Ezekial."

"That doesn't explain why the gate is sealed."

The Big Guy laughed and said, "Well, Pannychis, Sulieman the Magnificent bricked the gate up in 1541 after he heard the legend. He wanted to make sure that no Jewish Messiah would be able to enter the Old City there and fulfill the prophecy."

"And it will be open? Just like that," asked Eddie.

"Hey, I may not be omniscient but I do a fair imitation of omnipotence once I get going. Leave it to me, but whatever else you do, don't stop after you leave Gethsemane until you are through the Golden Gate. You haven't seen it yet, but the entire hillside of the Mount of Olives is covered by Jewish graves placed so close to each other that not a single blade of grass grows there. Why? Because when the Messiah comes, He will pass through the Golden Gate. According to ancient Jewish lore, all the graves will open and their occupants will be the first into Paradise."

"Really?"

"Hey Son, don't believe everything you read. When you get to the Golden Gate, the papal procession will wait while you pass through and then follow you into the large square around the Dome of the Rock. The Dome of the Rock sits on top of the ruins of the first and second Hebrew temples, so the entire compound is sacred to all the religions of the Book. As you approach the Dome, you'll see a long dais with chairs set up in front of the smaller Dome of the Chain. The chairs are for your people and the leaders of all three People of the Book. There, the two chief imams of Jerusalem will greet you. Pope Urban will speak first and announce you as the true Messiah. At that point, you will step forward and deliver your message of peace and good will. The sanctity of this, the holy of holies, and the presence of the leaders of each of the religions of Abraham should ensure your safety."

"Should?" said Eddie. "Then you can't be sure."

"Free will, Son, free will. That and the Lorenz equation. In a non-mechanistic universe there are always elements of unpredictability."

"The Lorenz equation?" said Pannychis.

"The butterfly effect," Eddie explained. "Edward Lorenz came up with it in the 70's. He discovered that the tiniest of inputs, like the random flapping of a butterfly, could alter the predicted path of a hurricane."

"But that should not happen this time," the Big Guy assured them. "The IDF and the Jerusalem police will keep you safe from the effects of the Intifada."

"It's the butterflies, that haven't flapped their wings yet that worry me," said Eddie. "Maybe I should leave Pannychis back at the King David to keep her safe".

"No! Whatever happens, I'm going to be there," said Pannychis.

"You see? She's ready. And you, my Son. You're about to change the world. How does it feel?"

"Like I'm facing the biggest ordeal of my life."

"And you are. This is your destiny, Eddie. Grasp the nettle firmly and it'll work."

"Yeah." Eddie said, nodding slowly and putting his arm around Pannychis. "We're ready, aren't we?"

"We are."

The Big Guy smiled and got down to business again. "After the greetings of the imams, Pope Urban will introduce you as the Messiah. Keep the message simple: You want to see a New Jerusalem arise. By working for world peace, by controlling the population growth that is choking the planet, by educating women and ensuring their equality to men, by curbing the escalating problems with clean water and air, by tackling the warming of the planet and by ensuring that the poor get a fair share of the world's wealth, these humans can make this blue marble into an earthly paradise." He paused. Eddie said nothing. "You still look worried. Well, that's to be expected."

The Big Guy had been watching as the anger rose in his Son and was not surprised when Eddie burst out, "I remember what happened to Jesus. Why not save Him? You're omnipotent and you couldn't even save your own Son. Just like King David. Oh, he got a hotel named after him but he couldn't save his own son, Absolom, either, could he?"

God had the grace to look slightly embarrassed. "Jesus had to die to fulfill the prophecies and, most of all, so that he could rise again, conquer death."

"You know, most of the Jews, especially the rabbis, even those who believed and followed him, rejected him as the Messiah because he died. According to the Jews, a true Messiah must live for eternity."

Pannychis put her hand on Eddie's arm. "Easy, Eddie, easy."

"Kicking against the pricks," said the Big Guy. "Shows spirit. Look, Son, I know you are afraid. Who wouldn't be? But if you succeed, the people of the world will be launched into a new era of stewardship upon the earth, the earthly paradise I promised."

"And I will have Marie with me," Eddie said, more to himself than to anyone else.

"And me," said Pannychis. She kissed him lightly on the cheek as he lowered his head into his hands and gave a ragged sigh. His eyes were welling with tears when he sat up again and took her in his arms. "I've found true love during this journey. You are more precious than life itself. I'll do it for you ... and for Joe.

"And you'll succeed."

But even You can't be sure, thought Eddie, "If this fails, will it be your last try?" he asked.

"I won't know until we see what happens, but my feeling right now is probably not. I know if these humans keep following the same path to destruction, I won't be watching the prolonged death throes. I'll turn my attention somewhere else."

A long silence. Eddie was profoundly moved as he felt God's sorrow. For what seemed like an eternity, the Big Guy stared out the window at the Holy City and the golden dome that dominated it. "You remember what Jesus said after he had been dying for nine hours in such pain on the cross? 'Oh God, oh God, why hast thou forsaken me?' I had to let the prophecies take their course, so I did nothing, nothing. Those words will haunt me forever."

To Eddie's amazement, Pannychis rose, crossed to the Big Guy and put her arm around Him. He looked at her gratefully. Marie, the Holy Spirit, slowly rose and put her arm around him, too. The Big Guy was touched. "Thank you, ladies."

Eddie and the Big Guy worked on the details for another hour before the Big Guy left with the room service trolley and Marie dissolved back into Eddie.

The phone rang while Pannychis was in the shower. Eddie picked it up and was surprised to hear Khaled's voice. "I hope I'm not disturbing you, Eddie, but the Ambassador of the Holy See in Jerusalem is here to see you."

Eddie glanced at his watch. Noon. He wondered why the archbishop had arrived so early, then he thought of an explanation. "What time is it, Khaled?" he asked.

"One p.m."

They must have crossed a time zone flying from Rome to Jerusalem. "Does he have a priest with him?"

"Yes, Eddie. The priest says that they have an appointment. Should I send them up?"

Eddie hesitated for a moment, listening for the sound of the shower. Silence. "Sure. And why don't you send up a few munchies and some coffee, so I can entertain them."

"Consider it done, sir."

"Oh, and thanks for the heads-up, Khaled."

"You're welcome, sir."

Eddie crossed to the bathroom. He could hear Pannychis humming quietly to herself. "Two clergy on their way up," he told her through the door. "You want to meet them?"

Pannychis opened the door and said, "From what Pablo and your Father said about this Archbishop Fowler, I think I'll retreat into my own suite... unless you really want me here."

"No, *ma chère*. Relax. I'll get rid of them before that reporter arrives."

Pannychis emerged wearing a white hotel bathrobe and kissed him on the cheek. "Good luck," she said as she closed the connecting doors.

Archbishop Fowler did not take more than a few seconds to reveal his choleric nature. When Father Giacomo made the introductions, Eddie said, "Pleased to meet you, Your Grace" and offered his hand.

The old archbishop looked at Eddie icily, ignored the proffered hand and rasped, "His Holiness is arriving tomorrow, so I am very busy, but I have been ordered to see you, so here I am. You claim to be the Messiah, Mr. Magdalena, but all I have seen so far are a few conjuring tricks."

Eddie smiled. "Whoa! Did somebody get up on the wrong side of the bed this morning? Let's get something straight. I do not claim to be the Messiah." The old man looked momentarily to have lost his bearings. "God made me the Messiah. I really had no choice. If I had been offered the job, I would have turned it down."

"I understand you have more or less persuaded His Holiness that you are the Messiah, Mr. Magdalena, but many in authority in the church do not share that view."

"I am not surprised that many are skeptical, Your Grace, but that does not alter the truth." A knock at the door. "Ah, refreshments. Why don't you two make yourselves comfortable over there." Eddie pointed to the table in front of the doors to the patio and opened the door. Taking the room service tray from the waiter, he set it on the table and offered coffee and an arrangement of delightful little cakes.

The archbishop and Father Giacomo remained standing in the middle of the room. "As I believe I told you, I don't have the time. Anyway, I am here to welcome you to Jerusalem and, according to His Holiness, you are to receive every courtesy from my office. Now, if you'll excuse us, Father Giacomo and I have a lot of work to do before the Ecumenical Council."

With that, he looked towards the outer door, a signal to his priest, who immediately sprang into action and opened it. As Father Giacomo closed the door, he caught Eddie's eye and gave a slight shake of his head to indicate his disapproval of his archbishop's behavior.

Glad I don't have Father Giacomo's job, Eddie told himself. The door between the suites opened and Pannychis peeked out. "They're gone?"

"Oh, they're gone all right. What did you hear?"

"The sound and the fury of a miserable old man."

"Pretty accurate. But he did manage to welcome us, or at least me, to Jerusalem. The archbishop must have just eaten. He didn't even glance at the cakes, and they look delicious. Can I tempt you?"

"Don't you dare! You know I have to keep my weight down."

"Sorry. We'll offer them to the reporter. Need some fresh coffee, though."

"Won't be as good as the last blend."

"You're right. That was definitely heavenly."

"This Irish reporter will be here in just over a quarter of an hour," Eddie warned Pannychis, as he set his watch to the right time.

"Then I've just got time to change." And she disappeared into her own suite. Eddie smiled. Ready in only fifteen minutes? Hmmm. But she proved him wrong by emerging less than ten minutes later in a simple white shift and plain leather Manolo Blahnik sandals.

Colleen O'Mara reached Eddie's door at the same time as the room waiter. Her first comment was to Pannychis: "My God, you look amazing. How do you do it?"

"Thinking good thoughts. Come on in. That green dress really complements your coloring."

"Thank you." Colleen said, feeling like a teenager in the presence of a rock star.

Pannychis directed the waiter to the table on their patio. "We'll have our coffee out there."

"Wonderful view," said Colleen politely, as the waiter left.

Pannychis nodded. "I love that big minaret. Do you know what it's called?"

"Oh, it's not really a minaret. It's called the Tower of David or Jerusalem Citadel. Those are the walls of the Old City in front of it. Have you and Eddie not been to Jerusalem before?"

"No. How long have you worked here?"

"Just over four months. Enough to know my way around. And my Arabic is not bad. I was filing from Damascus for two years before that."

"You like it better here?"

"Oh, yes. Damascus is a beautiful city, but here it's easier to get a drink, except in East Jerusalem, and the men don't look on me as prey whenever they see me on the street. My Hebrew, though, is not so good, but getting better."

"I can't wait to get a good look at the Old City," said Pannychis. "Look. Let me set you up with a fixer. I know a couple of young Palestinians I can trust. Would you be interested?"

"Interested in a fixer? Of course." Eddie, who had managed a quick shower, now joined them. "Sounds like a great idea. Actually, I was hoping you could work for us too. Only for a few days."

Colleen could not believe her luck. The biggest story in the world right now was hers. "Of course. I'd be delighted."

"Then that's settled," said Pannychis, picking up the coffee pot and pouring.

The phone rang yet again. Eddie was tempted to ignore it but knew he could not. Should have told Khaled to hold the calls.

A voice he did not recognize announced she was calling from the main desk, and asked would he mind if she sent up the Eli Schlechter, Minister of Public Safety and Aaron Krupke, Chief of Police for Jerusalem. "Sure." Eddie had expected that the police would contact him soon but the presence of a minister, too, indicated that the Israelis were taking his presence seriously.

"The minister of public safety and the chief of police are on their way up," Eddie told the women.

"I'd better leave then," said Colleen.

"Not at all. Why don't you and Pannychis wait in the other suite? I'll come and get you both when the coast is clear.

For the next two hours, Eddie discussed his plans with the minister and the chief of police, but he stopped short of revealing his plan to lead his followers into the Dome of the Rock compound through the Golden Gate. The minister explained that praying was forbidden there, except for Muslims. "We support the ban in order to keep the peace."

Eddie readily agreed to the prayer ban. He was impressed by the security they were willing to provide. The two men representing the Israeli government were polite but betrayed no hint as to whether they believed he was the actual Messiah. Well, Jerusalem had had more than its share of Messiahs over the centuries. The minister objected to Eddie's intention to visit the West Bank, saying that he could not guarantee Eddie's safety there. When it became obvious that Eddie was not about to back down, Eli Schlecter, Minister of Public Safety, softened his stance and offered to send in four undercover members of the *Yamam*, the special police counter-terrorism unit.

The minister and the chief shook hands cordially with him, as they left. The chief stopped briefly and said, "Eddie, I understand you haven't left the room since you arrived, so maybe you don't know what's happening on the other side of the hotel." Eddie looked puzzled. "We've had to put up a police cordon to prevent the crowds from pushing into the hotel. You might want to go down and address them. We've set up a platform and a mike for you just in front of the hotel entrance. There are at least ten or twelve thousand people out there. If you had your windows open, you could probably hear them."

Eddie passed the information along to Pannychis and Colleen. "There were lots of people there already when I arrived," reported Colleen. "I didn't mention it because I assumed you knew. Sorry."

Eddie looked at Pannychis. "Ready to face the music?"

"Your people are my people, Eddie."

Eddie crossed to the French windows that led on to the large balcony and opened them. Rising above the traffic sounds, they could hear the unmistakable chant of "Eddie! Eddie! Eddie!"

# Part Fifteen: Rome

## Friends of Santa Croce

Despite the gloomy atmosphere in Saint Helena's Chapel, the four clergymen were in good spirits. Cardinal Buffone, who had called the meeting, had not been able to attend the first meeting of the Gang of Four as he had been keeping an eye on the Canadian apostles visiting Pope Urban. Like the others, he was a member of the Friends of Santa Croce, and felt Saint Helena's Chapel in the bowels of Santa Croce would be the perfect place to announce his good news.

On the table was a selection of traditional *pinzimonio*, crudités made of sliced carrots, radishes and fennel, and a loaf of *pane napolitana* from the Renella Bakery in Trastavere, so fresh that it filled the chapel with the heavenly aroma of bread just out of the oven.

In front of each place was a crystal tulip glass, a plate, and a small bowl containing Ligurian olive oil, extra virgin of course, with a dash of sea salt and freshly cracked pepper. Because Cardinal Silvestrini did not drink, his place was graced by a bottle of his favorite *acqua minerale* and, next to it, a saucer holding fresh lemon slices. Damned teetotaler, thought Cardinal Buffone, because he was most proud of the bulbous, unmistakeable bottle of Picolit Cru, the famous grappa produced by the Nonino family that held pride of place on the table.

"I have much to tell you," Cardinal Buffone announced, "but first a toast to our diligent efforts to save Mother Church from the actions of this rogue pope." The four men raised their glasses.

"He reminds me of the excesses that Pope John Paul wanted to inflict on our traditions," said Cardinal Alois Schicklgruber.

"Yes, indeed," agreed Buffone.

They drank, and Reverend Father Thomas del Sarto and Cardinal Schicklgruber were fulsome in their praise of the Picolit Cru. The conversation turned to other worthy aspirants to the grappa crown, until the Black Pope quoted Mario Soldati, the Italian writer: "If wine is poetry of the earth, grappa is its soul." Cardinal Silvestrini sipped his mineral water before looking ostentatiously at his watch and saying to Buffone, "I have an appointment in just over an hour, Xavier, so perhaps you could give us a hint of your welcome news."

Cardinal Buffone had been pouring another round for the three drinkers. For a moment he pursed his lips and seemed about to give in to his famous temper. Then he made a conscious effort to pull his face into a smile. Holding up his glass in Cardinal Silvestrini's direction, he toasted, "To the next pope!"

"Let us not forget, it takes the entire Curia to elect a pope, Xavier. And I really don't have much time, so please, your news."

"Ah, yes. You are right, Achille." Buffone downed his grappa and reached for a slice of bread to dip in his seasoned olive oil. "The time to celebrate is after the victory, not before. First, you should know that our friend left Chicago a couple of days ago." The others knew that 'our friend' meant Gino Carbone. "He flew into Tel Aviv last Friday. Before he left, a package arrived at my villa. I knew it was coming so, as instructed, I did not open it. Instead I made sure it went into the diplomatic bag destined for Archbishop Fowler, our Ambassador of the Holy See in Jerusalem. It will reach Jerusalem today."

"You don't know what it is?" asked Cardinal Schicklgruber, incredulously. "Is it heavy? How big is it?"

"I'd rather not know, Alois." Buffone flashed a grim smile. "I believe the phrase is plausible deniability."

And a clean conscience in the confessional, thought Silvestrini. At the same time, he admitted to himself that he, too, needed a dose of plausible deniability. To that end, he should leave before any more revelations about Carbone where discussed. So he deftly changed the subject. "Xavier, I really am pressed for time, so may I propose that you three discuss Signor Carbone later."

With grudging admiration, Reverend Father Thomas del Sarto saw what Silvestrini was up to but did not object. After all, if the man was to become their next pope, he needed to distance himself from even the whiff of scandal. "Yes, Xavier. We should discuss the DNA evidence from the professor's lab before Achille has to leave."

Despite his reluctance, Cardinal Buffone could only agree. "Yes, of course, Thomas. We have to be sure that your Professor Enrico Capelli is willing to stand in front of the press and swear that there was no

DNA match. Can we count on that?"

"Oh, yes indeed. As a good Catholic, Enrico knows his duty."

"What about the members of his team?" asked Cardinal Silvestrini.

"We have offered each of them a large bonus for their work, on condition that they swear to keep the actual results forever secret. Already seven of the nine had signed non-disclosure agreements. I'm sure the last two will pose no problem."

Buffone beamed. "There you are, Achille. The final report will prove that this Eddie Magdalena is no more a Messiah than Anita Ekberg is flat-chested." Polite laughter.

"Anita Ekberg? You're dating yourself, Xavier," chided Cardinal Schicklgruber with a rare chuckle.

"Please, my friends, we need above all to be serious," said Cardinal Silvestrini impatiently. "The question really is, when do we send out the press releases? You say that two of the team have yet to sign the non-disclosure agreements, Thomas?"

"Yes, only two. I understand the only reason they have not signed is that neither has been to work for the past couple of days. They both have summer colds."

"Then I suggest that once you can assure us that the last two members of the team have signed, only then will we send out the press releases."

"It will be done by tomorrow, Achille. You have my word," promised the reverend father.

"Good." He stood up, and looked at the recycled statue of Juno that had been given a wooden cross and made to stand in for the absent mother of Constantine. "I must leave you now. You have done well so far, my friends. We must keep the pressure on for at least the next couple of days." He stopped beside the Black Pope. "Let me know, Thomas, the moment you have the last two signatures."

"Yes, of course, Achille."

A brief silence after Silvestrini's departure before the others found their voices again. "I don't think Achille needs to worry," Cardinal Schicklgruber grumbled. "If Carbone does his job, the DNA results will not matter."

"Ah, yes, let me bring you up to date about Carbone," said Buffone, offering around the grappa again. "At his request, we found him two people to assist him. They come from Palestinian families but were both raised in Algeria. Fifteen years ago they joined Hamas." He reached into his pocket, pulled out a small notebook and opened it. Two small black-and-white pictures fell into his lap. He picked them up and passed them to the Right Reverend Thomas del Sarto, who looked at them briefly before turning them over and reading the names on the back.

"Kamel Zidani and Nassim Hamidori," he read and passed the pictures on to Cardinal Schicklgruber who looked at them and said, "They don't look Palestinian."

"That's the idea, Alois. They have grown up in France. Both are fluent in French. At Carbone's insistence, we are assigning the three of them to the Latin monks at the Holy Sepulchre. The cover story is that they are monks from Marseille. Last week, we recalled three of our Latin monks. Three monk's habits and the mysterious object in the diplomatic bag will be waiting in a suitcase at the Office of the Holy See in Jerusalem. Tomorrow, after they pick up the suitcase, they will join the monks at the Holy Sepulchre. Gino assures me that they will be ready for the pope's visit."

"Let's pray that all goes well on Friday," said the Black Pope as he rose to go.

"Well, after Pope John Paul's unfortunate demise, we know that Carbone is good at what he does."

"And what if he talks?"

"He knows how long the arm of P2 is, Thomas. I'm sure he won't forget what happened to Roberto Calvi."

"Ah, yes. Found hanging under Blackfriars Bridge in London," said the Black Pope.

"And the case was never solved, was it?" asked Cardinal Schicklgruber.

"Precisely." And all three members of P2 nodded, satisfied that they had done all that they could to rescue Mother Church.

# Part Sixteen: Jerusalem

## Apostles' Arrival

Because of the last-minute booking and his need to secure eight seats, Marc had not been able to book a direct flight for the apostles from Toronto to Jerusalem. Even getting eight people out of Sudbury proved a problem. Marc's travel agent, the veteran Mary Deeth, had to book three of the group on to a later flight out of Sudbury. Luckily, both flights would arrive in Toronto in time for the entire group to make the next flight. From Toronto, Mary had managed to book them all through to Jerusalem, but with a four-hour layover in Zurich where they would have to switch to El Al to get into Tel Aviv. Even then they were delayed and did not get into Ben Gurion Airport until 10:15 p.m. The four apostles coming in from Rome had arrived in late afternoon.

The Canadian pilgrims did not check into the National Hotel until almost midnight. Nirvana, the pretty, diminutive Palestinian woman on the desk, welcomed them warmly with the news that their companions had arrived some time ago and were staying in two rooms on the fourth floor. Mahinda called Lydia from the desk and learned that Eddie had already telephoned from the King David. She told Mahinda to drop into their room when everyone was settled, and they would call Eddie and Pannychis.

With remarkable efficiency and good humor, Nirvana signed them in and arranged for the luggage to go up first in the small elevator. She told Mahinda, "You know, Dr. Rapasinghe, I have been waiting for you. My shift was finished at six, but I have stayed to make sure that you and the other companions of Eddie Magdalena receive our very best service."

"Thanks so much, Nirvana," said Mahinda. "It's been a long flight and we are tired. Do you have a restaurant?"

"Yes, of course. Just the other side of the entrance, there is a snack bar and a full restaurant. The restaurant closed a couple of hours ago, but I have made sure at least one of the cooks has stayed to feed you."

"Bless you."

"Where can we get a beer?" asked Claude.

"I'm afraid we do not serve alcohol here. There are a few places in the Old City where you might find alcohol, but they will all be closed now."

"Thanks," said Claude. He turned to Alphonse Ouimet and Thomas LaRue. "It's going to feel like a long stay."

"Rest assured, we will do everything we can to make your stay as pleasant as possible, Mr. Bissonnette."

While the others were settling in, Mahinda visited Lydia's room. Lydia immediately called the King David. "The others finally arrived," she told Eddie. "Great. We were getting a little worried. Hey, we were going to take you out to supper, but it's getting very late and you must be tired."

They arranged to meet at noon the next day, at the National. "I was going to take you guys into the West Bank to see the Church of the Nativity but everybody tells me that would be crazy with the Intifada going on, so why don't we come over around lunchtime and we'll have a look around the Old City. How's that sound?"

"We'll be ready."

"Deal. I'll call before we leave. A lot has happened already. I don't suppose you caught our appearance in front of the King David. Lots of TV cameras there. Huge crowds too. Pretty friendly. We'll talk about it tomorrow."

"Sure. I'll just pass the phone around so those of us in my room here can say 'Hi.'" When Eddie and Pannychis had talked to everyone, Eddie said, "Sweet dreams from both of us. See you tomorrow."

The cook, a tall Palestinian with the usual two-day beard growth, and his boy assistant, welcomed the travelers. They had already pushed some of the tables together so that the group could sit with a good view of the television mounted in the corner. "I am afraid all we can offer you is microwaved lasagna and salads," said the cook. "To drink we have tea, of course, and Coca Cola."

They assured him that anything would taste great at this point. The travelers were so tired that there was little conversation. The boy climbed onto a chair and twisted the dial on the old TV. A moment later, he beamed and said, "English! " Polite applause as he jumped down and disappeared into the kitchen. The apostles watched the television while the boy brought out the salads, a basket of flatbread and a bowl of the inevitable hummus. After a minute or two, Eddie appeared on the television in front of the King David Hotel speaking to a huge crowd. A sudden silence in the room. On screen, Eddie talked about the New Jerusalem that would result if we all respected each other, loved each other and worked to control the dangerous growth of the earth's population.

Cut to a woman journalist doing a standup. "Celebrities, kings, princes, and captains of industry have all stayed at the famous King David Hotel. Today, we can add the man who claims to be the Messiah, Eddie Magdalena. With him is his equally famous companion, the supermodel Pannychis." A still of the couple filled the left side of the screen. "His message is a timely one: save the planet from ourselves through curbing the population of the planet and establishing a New Jerusalem." In the background, chants of "I have been Eddified!" followed a burst of applause. A few scattered shouts of 'AntiChrist!' "It will be interesting to see how successful Eddie Magdalena is, but most of the crowd here seems to be enthralled by his message."

As the news moved on to the next item, the apostles cheered. No longer travel-weary, they were proud of their part in Eddie's success and felt ready to die for him if necessary.

As the lasagna arrived, Claude whispered to Alphonse. "Now if they only served beer."

### Under Cover of Darkness

Across town, just after one the next morning, a white cube van drew up in front of the Embassy of the Holy See. A short heavy-set woman dressed in a niqab alit from the passenger side. She was followed by a tall man wearing a suit and an open-necked shirt. Quickly and quietly they walked around the side of the building out of the light. The woman knocked lightly on an unmarked door. It was quickly opened. The tall man ushered the woman inside and said to the old priest who had opened the door, "We have come from Gino." His accent was French.

The priest nodded. He had been expecting them and now held out his hand. The tall man took his hand in the grip of a third degree mason by pressing his thumb down hard on the old priest's second knuckle in the Jachin grip.

Satisfied, the old priest pointed at a large soft-sided suitcase sitting under a table. "When you are finished, let yourself out." With that, he left them alone, closing the door behind him. Quickly, the stranger stripped off the niqab, revealing a man in his thirties. He was Kamel Zidani, a French Muslim who had been born in Algeria. He had once been a welterweight of some skill. Opening the suitcase, he tossed a dark brown monk's robe to his companion, Nassim Hamidori, and quickly slipped one on himself.

After knotting their rope cinctures, they slipped on the sandals supplied. They deposited the clothes they had just discarded into the suitcase on top of a third monk's outfit, a bottle of Jack Daniels and a plain hickory walking stick. The stick had arrived in the diplomatic pouch from Rome. Zipping up the suitcase, Kamel Zidani gestured to his companion to put up his hood.

Waiting in the van, Gino Carbone lit a cigarette to calm his nerves. He hated working with accomplices at any time, especially people he did not know, but he needed them to carry out the plan.

He had been told by his Vatican contact in P2 to arrive at a juice seller's stall located in the Old City near Herod's Gate. There, he must occupy one of the two plastic tables set out on the cobblestones. His contacts had arrived just after three p.m. As had been prearranged, they each identified themselves as members of P2 by placing their thumbs between Carbone's first and second knuckle in the Boaz grip used by apprentice masons.

Carbone nodded to himself as the two Palestinians reappeared carrying a suitcase.

"Everything O.K.?" asked Gino Carbone as the two men climbed back into the van.

"Sure," said Nassim Hamidori. "You have the cane?"

"Yeah."

"And my robes?"

"Don't worry. We have everything. Praise Jesus!"

Kamel Zidani laughed, but Gino cut him short. "Don't be such a fucking dickhead! I won't insult your religion if you leave mine alone. Got that?"

Nassim said, "Hey, he didn't mean anything."

"You guys are getting paid a lot of fucking money. Just keep your mouths shut, O.K.?"

"O.K., O.K."

"One last thing. The only languages I want to hear from you are English and French. Not one word of Arabic, even in your sleep."

"Yes, Gino. You've told us this many times. I think we can remember," said Nassim wearily.

"Make sure you do." Gino reached into the suitcase and pulled out the bottle of Jack Daniels and the cane. He cracked the bottle open and took a swig before offering it to the two Arabs. Both declined. Gino smiled sourly and took another pull at the bottle. Hard to get booze in East Jerusalem," he said, as he stuffed the bottle back into the suitcase and grabbed the cane.

"How does it work?" asked Kamel.

"The trigger is in the handle," Gino explained. "I made it myself. The Bulgarians invented it back in the early seventies. Used it to kill some writer in London. Look." He held up the cane to show the rubber stopper on the bottom. "See that central ring?" Both men nodded. "The needle penetrates the rubber, injects the poison and then retracts. Death is not instantaneous. But unless you know what the poison is, the subject will be dead before anyone can analyze it."

"What is the poison?" asked Kamel.

"The less you know, the better."

"But won't an autopsy find it?" asked Nassim.

"Remember the death of Pope John Paul I?" Nassim nodded, although he did not know anything about John Paul's death.

"No autopsy then. No autopsy now. Cardinal Buffone will follow the same game plan as Cardinal Villot did back in '78."

In less than an hour, the three newly-minted monks arrived at Saint Savior's Monastery outside the Old City. The monk who opened the door was not surprised to see them. "The Custos is waiting for you," he told them, referring to the Franciscan Custodian of the Holy Land, Francis Lumet. The abbot introduced them to the eleven other monks and then told them all to form up in a procession. At that time of the morning, the streets were deserted. The monks proceeded quietly through New Gate and disappeared into the unlit cobblestone streets of the Old City. A few of the monks looked up at the stars that broke up the darkness above them. One of the new monks walked with a pronounced limp. Luckily, he had a sturdy cane with a rubber stopper, useful on the slippery cobblestones.

## The Last Supper

"Make sure those cases go as well," said Luigi, pointing to the suitcases of Eddie and Pannychis. The monks were carrying the luggage out of Castel Gandolfo for the flight to the Holy Land. When Luigi had checked that everything was in order, he went to inform Pope Urban.

"The cars are ready, Your Holiness. I received a call from Rome. Archbishop Marcinkus is already waiting at the Vatican helipad."

"He must be eager to get out of town," the pope observed.

"Yes. I believe he longs to return to his roots in Chicago, Your Holiness."

"Well, Tel Aviv will have to do for now."

The first rays of sun were just beginning to color the horizon when the eight-seater Agusta helicopter landed in Rome. The burly archbishop climbed aboard. Immediately after his luggage had been stowed, the chopper was in the air again and flew back to Ciampino Airport. There, he was greeted by the pope and his personal staff, before boarding the same Citation III that had flown Eddie and Pannychis to Tel Aviv. At the last moment, an attendant rushed up the steps with an armful of early editions of Roman and international newspapers.

During the uneventful flight, Pope Urban used the time to catch up on the news and renew his acquaintance with Archbishop Paul

Marcinkus. Marcinkus had just resigned as Head of the Vatican Bank, the IOR, but still retained his position as Pro-President of Vatican City. "Looks like Eddie Magdalena's making out all right in Jerusalem," the archbishop told the pope. He passed over his copy of *il Messaggero*. Over a large picture of Eddie addressing the crowd outside the King David was the lead headline: "*Eddie Magdalena Greeted by Adoring Crowds in Jerusalem*."

"Same message as *la Repubblica*," commented Pope Urban, pleased at the coverage.

"And you believe this Magdalena is the real deal, Holy Father?" asked Marcinkus in his usual straightforward manner.

"Yes, I do, Paul. What about you?"

"At first I was skeptical, Your Holiness, but lately I'm beginning to think he might be." He laughed. "Mind you, many in the Curia are convinced that if you recognize him tomorrow, you will destroy the church."

"Is that what you think, Paul?"

"No. The church survived Martin Luther. I'm sure she can survive Eddie Magdalena. Besides, all I want to do with my time left is to move back to Chicago, back to my roots, Your Holiness. Believe me, I've had enough of Vatican politics."

Urban laughed. "Me too, Paul, me too. But you did insist on coming to Jerusalem."

"Yes, I did. To tell the truth, I was beginning to feel as if I had become the ghost of the Vatican. I needed a change of scene."

The two men were silent for a while, until Archbishop Marcinkus picked up a copy of *U.S.A. Today* and told the pope, "The biggest story back in the States is that Oliver North just got a three-year suspended sentence for his role in the Iran-Contra Affair." He shook his head. "I predict that Reagan will pardon him within a year."

"Forgiveness is a virtue, Paul."

"Sometimes." The pilot came on to warn them that they were beginning their descent. As they fastened their seatbelts, the archbishop leaned over and said quietly, "Your Holiness. One of the reasons I came along is that I think you may well be in need of protection. I suspect there is a plot to assassinate you, and I, for one, intend to see that doesn't happen."

Pope Urban looked at him curiously. Like everyone in Vatican City, he had heard the rumors that Marcinkus had been seen near the papal apartments the night that Pope John Paul died. But he did not think the banker had had a part in his predecessor's death. "Then I cannot have a better man at my side, Paul. After all, you do have a track record."

"I'm a lot older now, Your Holiness. But there's still some life left in this old gorilla."

The Citation landed at Ben Gurion at 9:14 a.m. The day had dawned bright and sunny, as it had every day since May 16th. The dry hot spell would not break until October 6th.

From the airport, Luigi called Eddie at the King David and told him that His Holiness would be there in just over an hour. His Holiness would then take a short nap, so that he would be fresh for the Ecumenical Meeting with the leaders of the Jewish and the Muslim communities. On the pope's behalf, Luigi invited Eddie and Pannychis to a private lunch in His Holiness' suite after his nap. Eddie told Luigi that they would be delighted and was about to hang up when Pannychis said, "Ask him about our luggage." Eddie did and assured her it was on its way up.

The Israeli government had provided two limousines and a motorcycle escort for the forty-minute trip from Tel Aviv to Jerusalem. Shortly after the pope's convoy left the outskirts of Tel Aviv, it passed Egged bus 405, the express bus between Tel Aviv and Jerusalem.

This morning the red-and-white bus was crowded as usual. Sitting right behind the driver was a twenty-eight-year-old bearded Palestinian. A resident of the Nusseirst Refugee Camp in Gaza, Abed al-Hadi Ghaneim had not been to Gaza in weeks. Usually he worked at the Carmel Market in Tel Aviv, but today he had a personal reason for taking the Jerusalem bus. As he looked out the window at the desert landscape scudding past, his mind filled with bitter memories of his best friend Radwaan, lying in a Jerusalem hospital, paralyzed in a confrontation with the IDF. Today he would avenge not only his friend but all Palestinians living under the yoke of the Zionist oppressors. When he had seen the motorcycles, he had worried that the police were about to stop the bus. Not until the motorcycle escort passed out of sight did he relax a little, but only a little. As the bus began the long climb into Jerusalem, it had just passed the Abu Gosh Junction. There, the ground beside the highway fell away steeply into a gorge.

At 11:45 a.m., Ghaneim wiped the sweat off his palms and whispered "Allahu Akbar" as he got to his feet. The bus was traveling around 100 kph when he lunged towards the driver and grabbed the steering wheel. For a couple of terrifying seconds, the driver, Moshe Elul, wrestled for control. Stalemate, then Ghaneim managed to brace his foot against the dashboard and wrench the wheel to the right. The 405 bus crashed through the metal barrier and went airborne over the cliff. Ignoring the screams of his fellow passengers, Ghaneim yelled exultantly, "Radwaan! Radwaan!" The bus crashed into a boulder before tumbling down the ravine, shedding bodies as it went. When it reached the bottom of the hundred-meter drop, the bus caught fire and burned many of the remaining passengers to death. Ghaneim, although injured, survived the crash. The driver too would survive with relatively minor injuries, but sixteen of his passengers did not. Twenty-seven others were injured, many severely.

The pope and his entourage had just been escorted to the front desk at the King David Hotel when they heard the first news reports of the tragedy. At this point, it was being reported as an accident with many lives lost. Luigi noted that the pope's eyes were welling with tears. He left Father Javier Ramirez, the pope's personal confessor, to finalize the rest of the details, telling him, "Those four bags need to be delivered to Eddie's suite, Javier. I'm going to escort the Holy Father up to his suite."

Taking Sister Ana with him, Luigi gently steered the distraught pope up to his suite. There, the Holy Father collapsed to his knees in front of the portable altar that had been installed for him. Luigi waited until the pope was deep in prayer before telling Sister Ana to stay with him. "I'm going to tell Eddie we have arrived."

He found Eddie and Pannychis watching the television coverage of the bus crash. "I just left the Holy Father," Luigi told them. He is very upset about the accident. The bus must have been behind us on the way from Tel Aviv."

"The media's just reached the scene," Eddie said, pointing at the television. "There are some rabbinical students helping the wounded." A line of cars had stopped along the highway, their occupants helping with the rescue. Luigi sat down with Eddie and Pannychis. When news came that the authorities had closed the highway until further notice in order to land helicopters to transport the wounded, Luigi left to return to the pope's suite. He needed to find out whether the Ecumenical Council scheduled to take place later in the afternoon would be canceled. An hour later, he called Eddie and told him the Council had been moved back until July 8th. "His Holiness wonders if you would be able to take a late lunch with him here," Luigi concluded.

"Of course we would. Be there in a few minutes."

Pannychis held out her hand for the phone and told Luigi, "Thanks so much, Luigi. Our luggage finally arrived."

Over lunch, they talked of the tragedy of Egged bus 405 and watched the live feed coming in from the crash site as helicopters landed on the roadway and transported the injured to various hospitals in the area. Already some reporters were beginning to refer to Abed al-Hadi Ghaneim as Israel's first suicide bomber, although he had survived with only minor injuries.

"I will hold the injured in my prayers. I will pray also for Abed Ghaneim. He too has suffered," said the pope, after the television had returned to regular programming. "But now we need to talk about tomorrow. We have just received the news from the Minister of Religious Affairs that my visit to the Holy Sepulchre and your procession from the Mount of Olives will be allowed to take place. We're not the Israelis' only problem. The Maccabiah Games at Ramat Gan Stadium in Tel Aviv are slated to run another week. The Israelis are enormously efficient at times like this."

Eddie nodded. "I'm sure they are, but with this bus crash on top of the ongoing Intifada, Jerusalem seems to be turning into a powder keg."

"Then we must trust in God to protect us."

Eddie thought of his last meeting with the Big Guy. The butterfly effect? "I guess we don't have any choice, Pablo."

"No, Eddie."

A sudden thought struck Eddie. "Is this your first time in Jerusalem, Pablo?"

"No. I was here some years ago, just after I became a cardinal. When I stepped through the door of the Holy Sepulchre, I could feel the presence of our Savior. Not surprising, I suppose, as the church is central to our faith, but," the pope put his hand on Eddie's and said, "I'm going to tell you something I've never told anyone else. I've always wondered why the holiest place in Christendom needs to be so ugly."

Eddie and Pannychis laughed, surprised. "Ugly?"

"Perhaps I have been spoiled now by the beauty of the basilicas in Rome. But even then, I found the place a disturbing rabbit warren of chapels and clashing architecture. Many fine mosaics are all but hidden by the hundreds of votive lights hung everywhere.

"I had to remind myself that this is the place where Jesus died on the cross and was buried. Still, it was hard to ignore the noise and constant cameras flashing."

"So you're not looking forward to your visit tomorrow?" asked Pannychis.

"No. I very much want to go back. The church should be quieter tomorrow. I just worry about the monks."

"The monks?" asked Pannychis.

"There are six denominations of them, including our own Latin Monks, the Franciscans. They bring shame upon such a holy place by fighting among themselves. Such unchristian behavior has been going on for so long that in 1853, Sultan Osman II proclaimed a firman called 'The Status Quo of the Holy Places' to protect pilgrims. It did not have the desired effect at the Holy Sepulchre. There, the fighting still goes on. And while they fight, nothing gets repaired or even moved. You must have heard of the immovable ladder."

Pannychis looked at Eddie, who nodded slowly. "Tell us about it," she prompted.

"Well, when you enter the courtyard in front of the church, you see a simple ladder propped up on the roof, under a window. It is in the Armenian section of the church and no one knows who put it there. So now no one dares move it. It has been there for at least a hundred and fifty years."

"Didn't the Ethiopian monks cause a stir around twenty years ago?" asked Eddie.

"That's right. In 1970, they lured the Egyptian Coptic monks down from the roof and seized the area known as the Monastery Deir el-Sultan. The Ethiopian monks then built a series of leaky mud huts where they live to this day."

Eddie noticed that the old pope was beginning to tire and said, "May the monks find in themselves the peace that passeth all understanding, at least during your visit, Pablo."

"Thanks, Eddie. I'll see you at the Golden Gate at exactly seven p.m." The pope stopped and thought for a moment before asking, "Why seven? Is there some significance? I have noticed that numbers have played a part in your arrival, Eddie."

"Ah, you mean the number 165321062533."

"Yes."

"I'm sorry, Pablo, there is a reason for the number seven, but I cannot divulge it at the moment."

The pope nodded, not at all annoyed by Eddie's refusal to answer. The world of religion is full of mysteries. "At least tell me what you told the minister about your plans."

"I told him I would lead the people down the Mount of Olives and join your ecumenical procession near the Golden Gate, and then together we will enter the city. Since the Golden Gate is sealed, he assumed that we would enter through the Lions Gate. I did not confirm or deny but still, a lie of omission."

"Yes."

"Anyway, we'll have some supper together later. Right now, I have to get in touch with the apostles."

When they got back to their suite, Eddie called Jean-Pièrre and told him that the Ecumenical Council had been postponed. "What do we do now?" asked Jean-Pièrre.

"There are roadblocks all over Jerusalem and the IDF is warning people to stay off the streets. We'll have to stay in our hotels."

"Some of the others, particularly the Dionne sisters, are upset. I know you can't get over here, Eddie, but your people could really use a pep talk."

Eddie thought for a moment. "Look. Is there a restaurant near you that might be open tonight?"

"Yeah. There's one upstairs on Salah al-Adin, the street that leads to Herod's Gate in the Old City."

"Ask the desk to call and see if they will open around eleven. If the roadblocks are down by then, we'll get a ride over to your hotel. Tell him there will be thirteen or fourteen of us."

"The last supper?" asked Jean-Pièrre, only half in jest.

"Let's hope not."

They passed the afternoon in a kind of limbo. Alphonse was sure that time had stopped. The civilian chief of police of Jerusalem, Aaron Krupke, had given Eddie his card and urged him to call at any time. When Eddie got through, he was not surprised to find that Krupke was at the site of the 405 bus crash. He asked for Krupke's assistant. He was put through to Inspector Isaac Toledano, a chubby, usually jovial man with a shock of white hair. He had been fully briefed about the presence of Eddie Magdalena. When he had received the assignment, he had said, "So Isaac gets to draw the short straw again. Who gets the pope detail?" When he learned it was Inspector Marion Peres, he threw up his hands and said, "Peres, really? Who let her out on the street?" The official government position was to protect not only His Holiness Pope Urban IX but also Magdalena and his followers during the unrest.

Inspector Toledano agreed to transport Eddie and Pannychis to the National Hotel. He assigned four officers in two unmarked cars to pick them up. The officers would wait outside the restaurant until Eddie wanted to go back to the King David.

When he called Jean-Pièrre back, Eddie learned that the Palestinian proprietor of the restaurant, Ali Sirhan, had agreed to open at 11 p.m. "Apparently he needed to get police permission, and was surprised that they agreed so easily," Jean-Pièrre said.

"We'll see you at the restaurant at eleven. Do you need transport?"

"No, the restaurant is only a hundred meters from the hotel. We'll walk. See you at eleven, Eddie."

"Wait. What's the name of the place?"

"Kiwi Fried Chicken."

"You serious?"

"Yeah. Looks a lot like a KFC and serves great fried chicken. Apparently Ali had to change the name when the American company came after him about copyright."

The restaurant on Sala al-Adin Street had no picture of the colonel but did advertise fried chicken using the traditional red-and-white motif of KFC franchises. Every other business on Sala al-Adin Street was in darkness. Rows of half-inch steel shutters secured with large padlocks testified to the likelihood of trouble.

At the top of a narrow flight of stairs, Ali and his ten-year-old son, Ahmed, greeted Eddie and Pannychis, with solemn bows. Pannychis reached out and shook the boy's hand. Ahmed looked embarrassed but pleased at the same time. Ali said, "Welcome to my humble eating place."

The apostles stood up from the long table set up under the windows overlooking the street and shouted greetings. They had saved a seat at the head of the long table for Eddie, and another on his right hand for Pannychis. On the other side of Eddie sat Lydia and Arthur.

"Blessings," Eddie said. "You have moved me more than I can say." He looked at Alphonse and Thomas LaRue sitting at the other end of the table. Eddie noticed that Alphonse was playing with one of the salt shakers. He caught Ahmed's arm as he hurried past and whispered in his ear. The boy nodded and quickly whipped the salt shakers off the table. Alphonse handed his over reluctantly. "No sense taking a chance," Eddie told his apostles. "Now, do we have to order?"

Lydia told him that the ordering had been done. "Unfortunately, we can't have wine because, well, this is East Jerusalem, but Ali assures me that we have plenty of soft drinks."

"And water?"

"Yes. There's plenty of bottled water in the cooler."

"No, no. Ali, *sadeqi*. Please bring glasses of tap water for all of us." Eddie turned to the others. "Jerusalem water is potable."

Ali nodded and bent down to whisper to his son. The boy was off in an instant and soon was back with the first tray of water glasses.

When everyone had a glass, Eddie raised his own. The others did the same. "Let's drink to making the world a better place."

People clinked glasses. Alphonse looked at the water in his own glass and was disappointed that it did not seem to be turning into wine. Then he tasted it. It was wine, a fine white. Cries of shock and pleasant surprise as the others made the same discovery.

"A chardonnay from Bourgogne, 1984. I thought, you know, white with the chicken. Besides, I want to make it clear that this is not my blood." He picked up a round of pita from the table. "Nor is this my body. Unlike Jesus, I'm hoping to survive tomorrow." Baskets of crispy chicken began to appear, with some kind of home fries.

"Eat, eat, my friends," urged Ali. "It is good to have the Messiah under my roof. It honors Allah, praise be upon Him."

"Thanks, Ali. Praise indeed be upon Him. And blessings upon you, too."

The food was good. "Better than KFC," said Claude, quite an admission for him.

When the plates had been cleared away, Eddie urged Ali, his son Ahmed and the cook to join them. "Yes, Eddie. I will get my brother Karim."

He came back with a very large man in a sweat-soaked undershirt. Karim's face creased into a broad smile as he hugged Eddie to his breast. "You like my food, Eddie?"

"Terrific. *Shukran*, Karim," said Eddie, thanking him.

Eddie had hoped that tonight would be a chance for everyone to relax and forget the morrow. And the evening unfolded like night-blooming jasmine. The Dionnes made a fuss of the boy. Karim found friends among Claude and Alphonse, although he spoke but a few words of English. At one point, the sound of shots and breaking glass filtered up from the street below. Several people got out of their seats and looked out the windows, but the street below was deserted except for the two parked cars. "Intifada," guessed Claude. "Palestinian kids probably attacking the cop station just down the street."

When they finally left the Kiwi, it was after two. The four plainclothes cops were wide awake. Eddie thanked them for waiting. Eddie and Pannychis said their goodbyes and watched as the others walked off into the darkness towards the National Hotel. As their echoing footsteps died away, Eddie turned to Pannychis and they shared a long, lingering kiss. "Whatever happens tomorrow, we have each other tonight, babe," Eddie told her.

"When we get back to the room, let's get started on the New Jerusalem then," she teased.

"Yes, indeed."

As they got into the lead car, the thought 'Father, oh Father, let this cup pass away from me' surfaced in Eddie's mind, but he pushed it back into the depths.

## House of the Holy

Wajih Nuseibeh, Keeper of the Key to the Church of the Holy Sepulchre, took his job very seriously even though the salary was only few shekels a month. Every morning he left his house before four in the morning and walked through the narrow cobblestone streets of Jerusalem's Old City. He had been taking this walk every day since he was fifteen when his father, Yacoub Nuseibeh, had passed the key to him.

The Nuseibeh family had been Keepers of the Key since Suleiman overran the crusaders and took possession of the Holy Sepulchre. As a favor to Richard the Lionhearted, he promised to keep the church open for Christian pilgrims. Not trusting the resident Christian monks, Suleiman had passed the key to the Nuseibeh family, good

Muslims originally from Medina. And the key has been passed down from father to son until the present.

These days, the Keeper of the Key had become a mostly ceremonial office. When he unlocked the main doors, Wajih Nuseibeh was signalling that the world's pilgrims could enter the holiest church in Christendom. The monks, on the other hand, came and went through the rear entrance.

Darkness still reigned when Wajih Nuseibeh walked past the shuttered shops of Souk el-Dabbagha. A flight of steps led him down to the courtyard of the Holy Sepulchre, lit by a sliver of moon. From the final few steps, Wajih could just make out the silhouettes of the Holy Sepulchre's two domes and its truncated belfry. As he approached the door, he noted the immovable ladder perched on a ledge above it.

Because today the church would be visited by Pope Urban, one of the Franciscan monks had been chosen to open the door. Surprisingly, it was one of the new French monks, Brother André. Under his new kafir name, Kamel Zidani had quickly become a favorite of Abbot Francis Lumet. Yesterday, Brother André had caught an Armenian monk listening to the conversations of the Franciscans in the Chapel of the Apparition at the north end of the church, and had laid out the unfortunate brother with a single blow. Abbott Lumet had been impressed. The new American monk, Brother Gabriel, the one with the limp, congratulated the former boxer, too.

Brother André crossed himself as he passed the Stone of Anointing. At the door, as instructed, he waited until he heard a call from outside. When it came, he looked through the loophole, identified Wajih Nuseibeh, even though he had no idea what the Muslim looked like, and then pushed a small ladder through a porthole beside the door.

Outside, Wajih propped the ladder up against the door and, being careful not to touch the door itself, pulled the long, ancient lock towards himself and inserted a twelve-inch-long cast iron key. Deftly as always, he opened the lock and the door was pulled back. Wajih stepped inside and inhaled the familiar odors of sacred incense and ancient mold that oozed from the very pores of the church. He was greeted by Abbot Lumet.

"You must be eagerly anticipating the visit of Pope Urban IX," Wajih said to the abbot.

"Yes. It is a great day for us Latin monks. But first let me introduce you to our new monks." He introduced Gino Carbone and his two accomplices by their aliases.

None of them aroused any suspicion in Wajih Nuseibeh who had always tried to see the best in people. "And we've already met," he said to Brother André, who avoided eye contact.

"Come let me show you around. And then, perhaps, we can offer you an early breakfast." Wajih agreed to a quick tour but begged off the breakfast because he had an early meeting with the imam of the Omar Mosque. The Omar Mosque, next door to the Holy Sepulchre, was where Wajih prayed to Allah.

Several of the Franciscans were cleaning up along the route the pope would take. Wajih and the abbot mounted the curving stairs to the right of the main entrance to the place where the Savior had died, the hill called Golgotha. As they visited the places of Jesus' nailing to the cross, His death, and His descent from the cross, they passed several Armenian monks. Wajih wondered why every single Armenian monk scowled at the two visitors to their area. The Armenians were obviously upset about something but then, when were they not. Wajih hoped fervently that there would be no trouble during the papal visit.

As they descended the back stairs into the Katholicon, the large area controlled by the Greek Orthodox monks, Wajih was greeted by one of the older monks he had come to know over the past decade. They exchanged a few pleasantries before Wajih checked his watch and said he was due at the mosque and would have to leave. On his way out, Wajih, who knew most of the monks by name, noticed that the Greeks, too, had two monks he had not seen before. Greek Orthodox monks always look impressive in their long black robes and flowerpot hats, but these two were enormous. Wajih wondered if the Greeks were bulking up in order to throw their weight around.

"Will you be back, Wajih, for the pope's visit?" asked the abbot.

"I wouldn't miss it for the world," Wajih replied as he stepped out into the dawn light that was beginning to leak into the courtyard.

∗   ∗   ∗

"… so I ask you to remember, we are all our brothers' and our sisters' keepers. Why educate women and treat them as equals? Look around the world and you'll see that those societies that condemn women to nothing more than domestic chores, are mired in poverty because half of their citizens are denied full participation in the economy. Such societies struggle with too few holding the wealth and too many mouths to feed. Equality, education of women and state-sponsored birth control will bring the world's population under control." Some angry shouts from the large crowd. Instead of ignoring them, Eddie responded, "Some of you disagree, but I seem to hear only male voices. But Pope Urban IX agrees with our aims. He has even pledged to me that he will be re-examining the *Humanae Vitae* encyclical put out by his predecessor, Paul VI, the encyclical that forbids birth control under any circumstances."

Upstairs in his suite, Pope Urban IX was watching Eddie on the live feed. Far from reacting with alarm at this point, he nodded his approval. He and Eddie had discussed this speech over breakfast and the pope himself had told Eddie to reveal his support. "All I ask is you wait until we reunite this evening and proceed to the Dome of the Rock. There, I will tell the world that you are indeed the Messiah we have awaited for so long. I will also reveal the secret of the DNA match before the gang of four puts out their big lie."

"Then we can't fail," Eddie had said cheerfully, and added in jest, "What could possibly go wrong?"

"Before we left Castel Gandolfo, we had gained permission to visit the Dome of the Rock. The Jordanians control the whole area. The minister, Ali Bey Abbasi, had granted permission. We checked yesterday with Minister Abbasi and the Jordanians are still ready to welcome us to the Dome, but not to the Al Aqsa Mosque."

"No problem. Only Muslims are allowed into the Al Aqsa Mosque anyway."

"The only caveat: no prayers, but even the Israeli government forbids prayer there in order to keep the peace. I told him we agree."

"I guess your diplomats did not mention which gate we will be using to enter," said Eddie.

The pope replied with a smile, "The subject never came up."

On the TV, one of the cameras began to pan over the crowd. Bigger than yesterday, the pope observed. A good sign. The feed switched back to a medium close-up on Eddie, who had just finished talking about the urgent need to clean up planetary pollution and control carbon emissions to prevent the world from getting warmer. Now he turned to the growing income gap between rich and poor. "In many countries, including my own, the rich have already built walls around themselves in gated communities. Just two examples: In Columbo, Sri Lanka, the rich live in an area called the Cinnamon Gardens. All their large houses are surrounded by high walls topped with broken glass and razor wire and are guarded by people who cannot afford to live there." Silently he thanked Mahinda for this information.

"In California, USA, just south of San Francisco, I once worked briefly as a security guard for a gated community called Pajaro Dunes. The place is crawling with security because many of the richest people in San Francisco and San Jose own the most fanciful holiday places there that you can imagine. Elaborate faery castles, medieval dungeons, even treehouses. And, no one lives there full time; most of the properties are occupied for only a few days a year. Pajaro Dunes and the Cinnamon Gardens are just two of the pleasure prisons that the rich are building for themselves around the world quarrying the stones from the birthright of the poor, the dispossessed."

"Until those with wealth and power realize that not until they raise up the poor, can they themselves live freely. When we feed the poor of the world, we should ask for their forgiveness. Only then will we build a truly just society and make poverty a seven letter word ..."

Eddie finished his speech by urging everyone to love his neighbor, whatever his or her color, religion or country of origin. "The struggle for the New Jerusalem will be long and hard, but men and women of goodwill who love God must succeed, or a last judgment will be upon us. God will not appear to reward the good and punish the others. No, the judgment will involve everyone on the planet for a span of years, as exploding populations become unsustainable, resources fail, and starvation walks upon the earth. 'And I looked and there before me was a pale horse! Its rider was named Death, and Hades was following close behind him. The Four Horsemen were given power over a fourth of the earth to kill by sword, famine, plague, and by the wild beasts of the earth.' It's up to us to take back our planet!"

Thunderous applause and cries of Hallelujah echoed off the walls of the King David. When the noise finally died down, Eddie invited everyone to meet him later in the afternoon at the top of the Mount of Olive to start the procession towards the promised land. Meanwhile, young volunteers from many faiths went through the crowds passing out votive candles and white T-shirts. On the front: 'Join Us to Build the New Jerusalem' in English, Arabic and Hebrew. On the back: the name 'Eddie Magdalena' with a sketch of the Messiah. There was something uncanny about the portrait. The eyes seemed to follow the watcher.

Later that afternoon, Pope Urban, accompanied by Archbishop Paul Marcinkus, Luigi and Father Javier Ramirez, arrived at Eddie's suite to say their goodbyes. "Whatever happens," the pope said, "we have lived to meet the Messiah."

"The feeling is mutual, Your Holiness," Eddie assured him.

"Apart from Eddie, you are the most beautiful human being I've ever met," agreed Pannychis. She planted a kiss on the pope's cheek, shocking Father Ramirez in the process. "Go with God, Your Holiness."

A knock on the door. It was Father Giacomo Benedetto announcing that the transport was ready and that Archbishop Fowler, the papal nuncio, was waiting downstairs. Just as the pope's entourage was leaving, Archbishop Marcinkus took Eddie aside to assure him, "I'll do my best to see the pope comes to no harm, Eddie."

"Then he could not be in better hands, Archbishop," Eddie said.

When Eddie closed the door, he said, "Good to hear that Marcinkus is acting as bodyguard. Unlike some of his predecessors, this pope really believes in a church for the poor."

"He does indeed."

Eddie did not need to turn around to guess whose voice that was. "Here to give extreme unction?" he asked.

"No, not at all," said the Big Guy. "You look terrific in that white linen suit, Son. Looks good with your tan. And Pannychis? She doth teach the torches to burn bright."

Pannychis shook her head. "You are the most shameless flirt."

"Just trying to uphold the reputation of the King of Rock and Roll, my darlin'." The Big Guy put an arm around each of them and gave them an affectionate squeeze. "Now go out there and knock 'em dead. And don't forget. I'll be watching."

## The Holy Sepulchre

Few motorized vehicles are permitted in the narrow cobblestone streets of the Old City. Most of those are small delivery trucks supplying its restaurants and bazaars. Even deliveries are usually off-loaded near one of the gates onto small green handcarts maneuvered by muscular Palestinians. Another problem is that the Old City, built on seven hills, is filled with steps. Each of the handcarts has a small, scruffy tire on a chain that hangs on the back between the handles. If a heavily laden cart begins to run away, the operator throws out the tire and jumps on it to slow it down. Many of the steps feature two lumps of asphalt placed an axle span apart, to aid drivers or handcart operators navigating their way into the heart of the Old City.

The pope had intended to arrive at the Lions Gate in the north of the Old City by two p.m. at the latest. The police and the IDF had closed off Sultan Suleiman Street, which ran along two sides of the Old City walls. A crowd of Christians had gathered on the road around the Lions Gate. Because the Intifada had scared off many tourists, the crowd was more sparse than usual, but it still delayed the papal vehicles enough that they arrived at the Lions Gate over twenty minutes late. As the small bas-relief lions (some claim they are actually leopards) looked down from the top of the gate, Jerusalem police supervised the switch into three small white Lancia convertibles for the trip through the narrow streets of the Via Dolorosa, the Way of Sorrows. The Via Dolorosa is the route followed by Jesus, the route that he had half-carried, half-dragged the pendiculum, the cross-piece of the crucifix that all the condemned had been forced to carry to their own crucifixions. The route from the Savior's condemnation by

Pontius Pilate (the first station of the cross), to the last five stations located in the Church of the Holy Sepulchre, is a winding road.

Before the open cars walked two choir boys: one carried a plain brass cross and the other a pole with the papal sign, a crown over two crossed keys. IDF troopers walked beside the two open cars, followed by the small crowd of Christians singing hymns. Several followers even dragged crude wooden crosses that they had rented from the Franciscan Monastery that housed the second station of the cross: the scourging of the Christ.

The pope, Luigi, and Father Javier Ramirez, the pope's personal confessor, occupied the first vehicle. The second vehicle was occupied by Archbishop Fowler, Ambassador to the Holy See, and Archbishop Paul Marcinkus. In the third vehicle sat Inspector Marion Peres, supervisor of the pope's security for this visit with her special assistant, Staff Sergeant Jacob Torres. Tall and thin, Inspector Peres had been the first woman to reach the rank of inspector. She was an expert on counter-terrorism but had almost no experience on the street. This assignment would give her the field experience to climb the next step in her career. Her assistant, Staff Sergeant Torres, was a war-hardened veteran. He wore an earpiece that kept him in touch with the six-member Rapid Response Team already in position at the Holy Sepulchre.

From time to time, the inspector glanced up at the roofs to check that the IDF snipers were out of sight. She had assured her superiors that the pope's security would be carried out as discreetly as possible.

At each station of the cross, the pope would lead a prayer. The procession took an hour and a half to reached the Souk el-Dabbagha where the pope and his staff had to leave the cars. Walking down the steps into the courtyard of Holy Sepulchre, they were following in the footsteps of Wajih Nuseibeh.

When Pope Urban IX and his companions reached the doors, he turned back to the crowd and, after reciting the Pater Noster with them, gave them the papal blessing, "Urbe et Orbi," the City and the world. Many of the pilgrims fell to their knees. Some even wept while others, overcome by the excitement and the heat, had to be attended to. A line of IDF soldiers had quietly cordoned off the church doors.

Although the Holy Sepulchre would be closed for at least the next hour, very few of the people crowded into the courtyard left, despite the heat.

When he entered the Holy Sepulchre, Pope Urban was greeted by Archbishop Fowler, Abbot Francis Lumet and the small band of Franciscan monks. They were standing in front of the Stone of Anointing, a red marble slab in the place that Jesus had been laid out for burial. After the formalities, Archbishop Fowler led the way up a steep set of stairs to the right leading to Golgotha, the place of the crucifixion. Inspector Peres and her assistant hung back at the top of the stairs. Her six-person Rapid Response Team was positioned along the route the pope would take. All were in civilian clothes and carried a standard issue Glock 17 in a shoulder holster under their suit jackets.

Constable Elazar Bassano was positioned in the darkness of the Chapel of Adam, directly below the place of the crucifixion. Through the door, he could observe the area between the main doors, now closed, and the Stone of Anointing. When the pope and his companions passed to his left to ascend the steep steps up to Golgotha, he was puzzled by the fact that one of the new Franciscan monks had remained behind. As he watched, the monk raised his hood and, leaning heavily on his cane, limped over to a wooden bench just to the left of the main doors. The bench was in shadow and, even better for Carbone's purposes, it faced the back stairs that the pope would descend in a few more minutes. Seating himself there, Carbone propped his cane against the wall. Carefully looking around, he noted two Armenian monks in their distinctive pointed hats, behind the Stone of Anointing. They were standing under the eight votive lights that hung above it. Four tall Greek Orthodox monks were standing next to a massive column at the edge of the Rotunda.

Only the two Armenian monks were in Carbone's line of sight, and they were turned away from him, waiting for the pope's party to reappear down the back stairs. Unable to see Constable Bassano, Carbone concluded that no one was paying him any attention. Just as he was beginning to relax, his cane clattered to the floor. "Son-of-a-bitch," Carbone cursed under his breath. As he reached for it, someone beat him to it. Looking up, Carbone saw the smiling face of Wajih Nuseibeh. Where the Hell had he come from? One of the main doors was slightly ajar. He must have come in that way.

Wajih held out the cane to the monk and said in French, "Here. You'll be needing this, brother."

"*Non capisco,*" Carbone replied. "Italiano or English."

"Ah, I thought you three new monks were French," Wajih said, switching to English.

"Only the other two. I'm from the States."

"Ah, I see. I was just saying that you'll need your cane."

"Oh, thanks," said Carbone, hoping that the Keeper of the Key would just go away.

Wajih sat down next to Gino Carbone. "Bad hip?" he asked, sounding concerned.

"Yeah. Sometimes I just have to sit down."

"My uncle is the same. You can tell it hurts him with every step, but he never complains."

"Yeah," said Carbone, trying to end the conversation. Both were silent for a few moments. When the old monk had started talking to the Keeper of the Key, Constable Bassano had decided that he did not pose a threat.

"I was delayed and missed the pope's arrival," said Wajih Nuseibeh. Carbone nodded but said nothing. Wajih did not notice the snub. "Are they upstairs at Golgotha already?"

"Yeah." Carbone could feel the anger building inside him.

"I'm in time for the visit to the tomb then." This time Carbone said nothing. Instead, he focused an icy stare on the meddling Muslim. This time Wajih noticed the rudeness of the new monk and got up. "I think I hear them starting down. I'm going to find a good vantage point in the Rotunda. Will you be all right here?"

"Yeah, yeah. I'll be fine." As Wajih Nuseibeh moved off into the Rotunda, Carbone silently cursed Archbishop Paul Marcinkus. His presence in the pope's party had been an unpleasant surprise. Marcinkus would recognize him immediately.

Carbone's original plan had been for Kamel Zidani and Nassim Hamidori to create a diversion at the narrow entrance to the Edicule, the small freestanding chapel in the Rotunda, the site of Christ's tomb.

The Edicule sits almost directly under the largest dome of the church. The Edicule's outer walls are crammed with a jumble of styles with odd ornaments, cornices, paintings, strangely contorted columns and, since the British ruled Jerusalem, steel bands to keep the crumbling chapel from tumbling into a pile of ancient rubble. The flat roof of the little chapel is decorated with a small onion dome supported by four small columns.

When Pope Urban stooped to navigate the low arch leading into the Edicule, Carbone had intended to press his attack. Given the well-known volatility of the monks, Carbone was sure that the cops would react to the diversion but not Marcinkus. He would stay with the pope. Carbone's mind worked furiously. Soon he felt he had a solution. The final part of Pope Urban's visit to the Holy Sepulchre was to take place in the Franciscan Chapel of the Apparition. After that, the procession would ascend the steps leading up to the roof which offered a much better chance of escape. Now he had to get a message to the two Hamas agents, but how?

The Keeper of the Keys had been right. The pope and Archbishop Fowler appeared at the bottom of the stairs behind the Stone of Anointing. During a brief ceremony, the pope, like almost all Christian pilgrims, knelt and kissed the stone slab where Christ's body had been anointed before burial. The Franciscans were ranged behind him with their Custos, the papal diplomat and Archbishop Marcinkus. Inspector Peres and her assistant had moved though the two massive crusader's pillars that led into the Rotunda. Staff Sergeant Jacob Torres listened to his earpiece for a moment and then whispered to his tall inspector that the monks seemed to be on their best behavior. Inspector Peres stooped down and said quietly, "It'll be a minor miracle if they stay that way." The sergeant nodded and suppressed a smile.

After a brief prayer, Pope Urban rose and the procession began to move towards the Rotunda. Carbone peered from the shadows as they passed. Bringing up the rear were his two Palestinians. He gave a slight wave of his cane to catch their attention. Kamel Zidani noticed and nudged his neighbor, Nassim. The two men held back while the others disappeared into the Rotunda and then crossed to Carbone. The inspector and her assistant were just about to follow the procession when they noticed the two monks cross to Carbone. Constable Bassano noticed, too.

Out of the corner of his eye, Carbone noted that he was being watched and said to his approaching brothers, "This hip is bad today. Give me a hand." As the two Palestinians helped him up, he thanked them and, leaning heavily on Kamel, he began to limp slowly towards the Rotunda.

Deciding that the three monks were nothing to worry about, the inspector and her sergeant turned and walked towards the Edicule. Constable Bassano continued to watch the monks from his hiding place in Adam's Chapel.

"Change of plan," Carbone hissed. "We're not making our move until we reach the roof. Too many cops around. Listen. I want you, Kamel, to attack the big archbishop when I signal, so keep your eye on me."

"He's old," said Nassim, a trace of contempt in his voice.

"And he's twice as tough as you, asshole." Christ, he hated working with these Muslim pricks. Carbone took a deep breath to suppress his anger. "Anyway, your job is to pick a fight with the Ethiopian monks. They're the black monks that live on the roof. For now, I want you two to stay with the rest of the monks. I'll wait for you in the Chapel of the Apparition. Got that?" The two Palestinians nodded. "Then let's move."

When the two French monks helped their companion to enter the Rotunda, they saw that the pope was about to enter the Edicule, site of the final station of the cross. There the Savior's body had spent three earthly days before his glorious resurrection.

The air in the Rotunda was by now so heavy with the smell of frankincense smoke from the censers, that the shaft of light from the center cupola appeared almost solid. Nassim and Kamel had no trouble disappearing into the throng of Franciscan monks. Carbone moved silently behind a phalanx of Greek Orthodox monks in their kalimavkions, their tall black, brimless hats, before disappearing in the direction of the Chapel of the Apparition.

As Carbone had predicted, Cardinal Marcinkus stood guard at the entrance to the Edicule as Pope Urban ducked through the low entrance. On one side of the narrow passage was a burial bench of marble for final preparations of the body. The pope crossed himself as he passed through and into the burial chamber. After a prayer of thanksgiving for the crucified Savior, Jesus, and, for Eddie, his reincarnation as the Messiah, the pope ducked his head again and was helped out of the low archway on the other side by Archbishop Marcinkus.

Next, the procession moved on to the Chapel of Saint Helena on the other side of the Rotunda. This chapel, controlled by the Armenians, is reached by descending a short flight of steps. The walls on either side are decorated with hundreds of small crosses carved by Armenian pilgrims over the centuries. The *titulus crucis* that now graced the relic collection at Santa Croce in Gerusalemme had been discovered here.

The Chapel of the Apparition belongs to the Franciscans. Carbone knew he had at least ten minutes to wait because, after the visit to St. Helena's Chapel, the pope was scheduled to visit the smaller Chapel of the Finding of the Cross. That chapel lay behind St. Helena's and was hung with many votive lamps.

From the Chapel of the Apparition, the pope would ascend another flight of steps on to the roof of the church. Apart from a short occupation by Coptic monks, the Ethiopians had lived on the roof in squalid conditions since they had been kicked out of the church by the Ottoman rulers centuries ago. Their sin? As the poorest religious community, they had not been able to afford the tribute demanded by the Ottomans. Instead of leaving the Holy Sepulchre entirely, they had moved on to the roof, carried in mud from the Kidron Valley and built the primitive huts that they still occupy. At night they creep back into the darkened church and clean up the debris that falls from the crumbling walls and ceilings.

Pope Urban had insisted on meeting the Ethiopian monks and had even arranged for a few of them to accompany him on his visit to the underground cavern that contained the Cistern of St. Helena, the place where she had discovered pieces of the true cross. After that he was scheduled to proceed to the Dung Gate where he would don a kippa and pray at the Wailing Wall with the two chief Rabbis of Jerusalem: Rabbi Avraham Shapiro, Chief Rabbi of the Sephardic; and Rabbi Mordechai Eliahu, Chief Rabbi of the Ashkenazi. Then the pope and the rabbis would proceed out of the Old City through the Dung Gate and along the walls to join Eddie and his followers near the Golden Gate. Cardinal Buffone was counting on the fact that, when Carbone killed the pope, the act would destroy Eddie's plan to be recognized as the true Messiah. Desperate times, desperate measures, Buffone had told himself when he had contacted Gino Carbone again. Sounds of voices and footsteps accompanied by the clinking of censers.

With a start, Carbone realized that the pope's visit to the Armenian chapels was finished. Hurriedly, he ascended the stairs. When he reached the roof, he looked around. Two tall black monks were watching him from the shade cast by one of the primitive huts. He nodded, and both monks smiled back at him. Carbone, making sure his hood shielded his identity, looked into the open doorway of the next hut. Its only furnishings a rope bed and a battered chair. Most important, the small dark room was empty. Carbone stepped inside.

Following the altar boys who held aloft the large bronze cross and the papal insignia, the pope and Archbishop Fowler led the procession on to the roof. There, the pope stopped and walked over to the two Ethiopian monks who had been watching Gino Carbone. He took their hands in his and offered a blessing. As he turned to go, Kamel approached the two Ethiopians. As he passed the first mud hut, he glanced through the doorway and was surprised to find Gino staring back at him. Gino whispered 'Now!'

Kamel looked back. Everybody seemed to be looking at the pope. He made eye contact with Nassim and nodded. Nassim walked up to the nearest Ethiopian monk and, without any warning, smashed his fist into the man's face, sending him staggering back. The other monk shouted and snatched up a broom. Nassim pulled out a knife. Carbone could hear the sound of running and pressed himself back behind the doorway out of sight. Despite his age, Archbishop Paul Marcinkus was the first to reach the two fighting monks. With a single blow, he knocked Nassim to the ground so that the knife he had been holding skittered away across the roof. Suddenly, Kamel hit Marcinkus from behind and sent him reeling. The other son-of-a-bitch, Marcinkus told himself as he managed to get his breath. Then with a roar, he swung around to confront the new foe. Most of the other Franciscans rushed to join the fray. On the other side, one of the Ethiopians began ringing a tocsin, and suddenly a dozen or so Ethiopians seemed to appear out of nowhere.

Carbone peered out the door of the hut. Everyone seemed occupied so, walking with the usual limp, he joined the pope and Archbishop Fowler. Inspector Peres and Staff Sergeant Torres had stepped in front of the pope, not realizing that the danger to the pope's safety was now standing behind him. "Get the pope and the others off the roof," she ordered Torres. "Have two of our men escort them down into St. Helena's Cistern. They'll be safe there." Sergeant Torres nodded and turned to order two of his men to lead the pope's people off the roof.

Everyone else was watching the melee. Realizing that, at this precise moment, no one was looking in his direction, Carbone swung his cane until it lightly touched the pope's ankle. He triggered the hypodermic. The pope, puzzled by the small prick, looked at his ankle. He could see no damage and assumed he had been bitten by some insect.

Archbishop Marcinkus got to his feet after Kamel's attack and seized the brass cross that one of the altar boys was holding, ripping it out of the boy's grasp. Turning, he located Kamel and swung the cross with all his might, catching the ex-boxer under the arm. He heard a rib crack and was getting ready to swing again when Nassim hit the archbishop from behind, sending him to the ground.

Nassim helped the fallen Kamel to his feet and said to him in Arabic, "Lean on me. We've got to get away from these kafirs."

Kamel said, "I think the bastard broke my rib. Where's Carbone?"

Nassim took a quick look around. "He's leaving without us," he said pointing down an alley on the other side of Saint Helena's Cistern.

"Follow me." The husky former boxer set off at a shambling run.

Nassim ran beside him, shoving an Ethiopian monk out of his way.

Carbone had kept walking, no limp now. Suddenly Kamel caught up to him and grabbed his hood from behind. Shouting, "*Ibn el sharmonta*" son of a bitch, he swung Carbone around before hitting him hard in the face. Carbone went down with Kamel on top of him. A vicious right to the throat silenced Carbone by crushing his hyoid bone. Carbone let out a frantic gurgle as he began to suffocate on his own blood.

Cardinal Marcinkus joined the security detail around the pope. When Kamel pulled off Carbone's hood, the archbishop pointed at him and yelled, "Stop that bastard!"

Constable Bassano thought the archbishop was pointing to Carbone's attacker. Pulling his Glock 7, he raced across the roof. Nassim saw him coming and pulled Kamel off the prone Carbone. On an impulse, he picked up Carbone's cane as the two men ran. When Bassano reached the lifeless body of Carbone, he stopped and fired a single shot at the retreating Palestinians. Kamel crashed to the ground, a bullet hole between his shoulder blades. Nassim kept running until he reached the maze of alleys behind the church and disappeared, still carrying the murder weapon. When he could run no more, he stopped and leaned against a wall. Quickly he shed his monk's robes and lobbed them over the wall into a small garden. But he could not make himself part with the cane.

When his breathing became more regular, he walked through the Old City, even taking the time to stop at a juice seller's stall and buy a drink. An hour later he passed through Herod's Gate and disappeared into the narrow streets of East Jerusalem.

On the roof of the Holy Sepulchre, order had been restored by Inspector Peres and her security detail. The pope assured everyone he had suffered no harm, as he allowed himself to be led by Torres' men towards Saint Helena's Cistern, the place where the pieces of the true cross had been found. The pope, the two archbishops, Luigi and the pope's confessor walked the 200 meters to the entrance and carefully descended the worn stone steps into the water-filled cistern. Their voices echoed off the limestone. The pope began a last prayer, but before he was finished, he began to sway. Luigi caught him and made him sit on one of the stone steps.

"What is it, Your Holiness?" Luigi asked anxiously.

"Just a little faint, Luigi," the pope assured him. "I'll be all right in a minute."

But he was not. Within another few seconds, the pope lost consciousness, and Luigi raced up to the attendant and told him to call 100, the emergency number in Jerusalem. "Tell them the pope is ill. Send an ambulance immediately."

"The streets of the Old City are too narrow. You will have to get the pope to New Gate," the attendant said, as he picked up the phone.

"Then make sure the ambulance is there when we arrive."

Turning to two Ethiopian monks, seated on the stone floor, the attendant directed one to go downstairs and see if he could help. The other he sent out to find something to act as a stretcher for the pope.

Luigi waited for a moment while the attendant made the emergency call before hurrying back to the others. As he reached the top of the stairs, he could hear voices approaching from below. He looked down the narrow staircase just as the tall Ethiopian monk appeared carrying the pope in his arms. Luigi stepped aside to give him room. The other Ethiopian monk had run back to the mud huts of Deir as-Sultan, their improvised monastery on the roof of the Holy Sepulchre. Now he arrived at the outer entrance carrying an old door and a couple of ratty blankets. Between them, the two monks gently laid the pope on top of the door and put one blanket over him and another under his head. Meanwhile, Archbishop Fowler tried to show he was in charge by issuing a stream of instructions. The monks, who only spoke basic Arabic and Gamo, an obscure language even in their own country, ignored him. When the monks were ready, they lifted the door and carried it out into the late afternoon sunlight. The others followed.

And so it came to pass that Pope Urban IX was transported to the Augusta Victoria Hospital operated by the Lutherans. The hospital existed to give the best of modern medicine to Palestinians, often on a pro bono basis. Since the start of the Intifada it had been full to overflowing with the influx of wounded. The pope was rushed into emergency where he came under the care of a Dr. Tawfiq Hassan and two Palestinian nurses.

Waiting nervously for news were Luigi Fuseli, Father Javier Ramirez,

Archbishop Fowler, Archbishop Marcinkus and the Franciscan Custos, Abbot Francis Lumet.

"I'd better inform the Vatican of the bad news," said Archbishop Fowler and excused himself to find a telephone.

Cardinal Buffone answered on the second ring. Fowler filled him in on what had happened at the Church of the Holy Sepulchre, while Buffone made the appropriate sounds of shock and sympathy.

"What's the prognosis?" asked Buffone after Archbishop Fowler had finished.

"The doctors seem to believe that Pope Urban has had a heart attack."

"Keep me informed," said the pope's Secretary of State. "I will be flying in to Tel Aviv as soon as we can get in the air. We'll bring a full medical team to help care for His Holiness. Call me when you have any new developments. And thanks for this, Benjamin."

Less than an hour later, Dr. Hassan, the attending physician, appeared in the waiting room. "Pope Urban has asked for Father Ramirez." The pope's personal confessor rose, a stricken expression on his face. Dr. Hassan put up his hand to fend off the stream of questions. "Please, please. The Holy Father is receiving the best of care. We will inform you when there are any new developments. At the moment, the pope seems to be resting peacefully, but he is very weak." With that, he beckoned to Father Ramirez and led him out of the room.

After the pope's confessor had gone, the room lapsed into a gloomy silence. All the clergy knew that Father Ramirez had been summoned to perform the ceremony of Extreme Unction, a ceremony usually performed when the patient is near death.

Just over an hour later, Dr. Hassan returned, his face a mask of solemnity. He was accompanied by a tearful Father Javier Ramirez. Dr. Hassan looked at the pope's confessor who began, "The Holy Father... The Holy Father..." before breaking down completely and being led to a chair by Archbishop Paul Marcinkus.

Dr. Hassan took a deep breath and said, "Pope Urban IX passed on at seven p.m. My staff and I are extremely sorry for your loss." Addressing the Archbishop Fowler as Ambassador of the Holy See in Jerusalem, he added, "Please let me know what arrangements you wish to make. Once again, the whole medical team is grieving for your loss."

Luigi burst into tears and Father Javier Ramirez lowered his head into his hands. "What did he die of?" asked Archbishop Marcinkus.

"We would need an autopsy to determine the true cause of death," the doctor admitted.

Archbishop Fowler said, "Thank you, doctor. What you can do for us is see that the body is ready for transport. The Vatican is sending an aircraft. If there is to be an autopsy, it will be in Rome."

"What do you mean, 'if there is an autopsy'," Marcinkus challenged. "How else can we tell how he died?"

"The decision is not mine, Paul," said Archbishop Fowler. He knew of Marcinkus' nickname 'the gorilla' and felt physically intimidated by the towering churchman.

"Of course not, Benjamin. You'll leave it all up to that bastard, Buffone. And we know what he'll do. He'll claim that it is against the church's practice to hold an autopsy on a pope. Cardinal Villot claimed exactly that back in '78 when Pope John Paul died. What's more, he got away with it. Better see your confessor, Benjamin."

"How dare you!"

Marcinkus got to his feet and stood over the unfortunate archbishop. "Just give me a fucking excuse." Archbishop Fowler shrank down into his chair while Luigi and Father Javier pleaded with Marcinkus not to make a scene. Marcinkus turned on his heel and stomped out of the hospital. He desperately needed a cigarette.

### The Mount of Olives

By five p.m. the pilgrims from the National Hotel had already arrived at the top of the Mount of Olives. Like the hospital, the Mount of Olives in the al Tur neighborhood stands atop the north-south ridge that overlooks the Old City and the Dome of the Rock. With little traffic moving around the Old City, Jean-Pière heard the siren of the pope's ambulance and guessed, "Probably some poor Palestinian kid injured in the Intifada."

"Probably," agreed Claude, who had heard the siren, too. Until Eddie and Pannychis arrived with their security detail a few minutes later, this explanation was accepted by the crowd of people in white T-shirts who were already beginning to gather on top of the Mount of Olives.

After acknowledging the cheers from the crowd, Eddie approached Lydia and said, "Can you gather the apostles together? Bring them to that lookout over there." He pointed to a curved parapet overlooking the white marble expanse of the Jewish Cemetery and the Old City walls on the other side of the Kidron Valley.

"O.K." Lydia could tell that the news was not good. "About five minutes?"

"Sure. Oh, and bring Colleen as well." Eddie turned away and consulted with Inspector Isaac Toledano, head of his security detail, about closing off the small area while he talked to the apostles.

"Sure, Eddie," Toledano told him.

When he had gathered the apostles, Eddie wasted no time delivering the news: "The pope has collapsed and has been taken to hospital. We don't know what's wrong, but it means he will not be joining us at the Golden Gate. The news came over the police radio while we were driving over."

The apostles, especially the Dionne sisters, took the news hard. Eddie held up his hand and the flurry of questions ceased. He looked over at the crowd above them. Some had noticed the raised voices. He waited for a moment to see if Marie would give him any advice on his next move. Silence. "Let's hope the pope is on the way to recovery," he told the apostles. "Obviously he won't be meeting us on the way to the Dome of the Rock. He was going to reveal the true results of the secret DNA test conducted by the Vatican and then introduce me as the Messiah." Eddie shook his head. "The best laid plans ..."

Alphonse spoke up first. "I know I screwed up at the Vatican, Eddie, but I'd walk into the fires of Hell for you."

A chorus of voices pledging their faith came from the others. The reaction of the Dionne sisters was summed up by Annette: "We are with you until the end, Eddie."

"If there is an attack, we will stand in front of you," added her sister, Émilie The others voiced their agreement.

Pannychis said simply, "I didn't come this far to miss the end."

The lump in his throat silenced Eddie for a few moments before he opened wide his arms and said, "From you wonderful people, I expected no less."

Eddie hugged each one in turn before walking back to the crowd waiting above. He gave them the same news but added, "After his appearance at the Holy Sepulchre, the pope was going to join the chief rabbis at the Wailing Wall. After praying with him, they would have accompanied him to the Golden Gate. I doubt that will happen now. Without the support of the Jews and Christians, I can't predict how the Muslims will receive us at the Dome. Remember the Intifada is still on and tensions are even higher after the bus crash yesterday. Things may turn dangerous. If any of you want to remain here, I will understand. You don't have to say anything. Just stay here when Pannychis and I set out for Gethsemane."

The crowd behind the small police cordon erupted with shouts of "We're with you, Eddie." Eddie led the apostles back into their midst. Someone yelled, "Why not ride the camel down, Eddie?" He was referring to the camel that appeared most days on the Mount of Olives. The two Palestinian boys that looked after her gave rides to tourists.

Eddie laughed. "No, I don't think so." But it gave him an idea and he called Colleen over. "Look. Could you find the boys with the camel and see if they have a donkey."

"A donkey?"

"Yeah. Jesus rode a donkey along this route down to the Golden Gate and into Jerusalem on Palm Sunday."

"Right. I'll see what I can do." She nodded to her fixer, Ismael Hawadi, and together they plunged into the crowd and disappeared.

Over the next half hour, the crowd swelled until Eddie estimated that there must be three or four thousand. If not for the Intifada and the tragedy of Bus 405, the numbers would have been even larger, Eddie realized. He was heartened to see that quite a few Palestinians were wearing white T-shirts. He even spotted a quartet of Ethiopian monks about a hundred meters down the road.

As the time to set out approached, Eddie thanked everyone and offered his blessing. To his surprise, the people right in front of him began to kneel. Like a slow motion stadium wave, the crowd behind these people knelt too.

"I love you guys!" Eddie began. "You are the reason we are here ..." and then he stopped. People were rising and clearing a path for two Palestinian boys and another young boy wearing a kippa. The trio was leading a sturdy white donkey through the crowd. When they reached Eddie, the Jewish boy handed him the bridle. "We did not have a donkey, Eddie," said one of the Arab boys, "but we asked Avraham if we could borrow his. Her name is Miriam."

"Then I thank you, boys. And whether you call Him *Jahweh*, Allah or God, the Big Guy thanks you, too." He raised his voice so that it would carry. "Now, it is time. Let us descend to Gethsemane and then to the Golden Gate, the gate that Jesus used to enter the city. One day people will ask where you were on this the seventh day of the seventh month at the seventh hour. And you will tell them proudly that you were setting out to create the New Jerusalem."

Dressed in his white linen suit, Eddie mounted the white donkey and, with Pannychis walking beside him and the apostles just behind, he turned Miriam's head towards the narrow road that bordered the massive Jewish Cemetery. Behind him he could feel the weightless presence of the Holy Spirit and was comforted by her presence. "Don't worry, Eddie," she whispered in his ear, "I've got your back."

At almost the bottom of the mount, Eddie turned left on to the path that led past the Garden of Gethsemane to the Church of the Agony. The small garden was surrounded by a simple wooden fence. Eddie opened the gate and walked in along a gravel path. Gethsemane, except for an abandoned wheelbarrow, looked much as it had when Jesus tried to rouse his disciples. Sunbaked and grassless, the ground around the ancient olive trees was relieved by a few flowers and low bushes. Somehow the arid landscape exuded a feeling of serenity, an oasis from the troubles of the greater world outside.

Eddie stopped near the solitary well and waited while the crowds gathered along the surrounding fence. When the white-shirted pilgrims bowed their heads as if to pray, Eddie said, "Prayer may be a salve for the soul but only Muslims are allowed by Israeli law to pray in the vicinity of the Dome of the Rock. To keep a semblance of peace among the three People of the Book I urge you to respect the ban. Now, behold. Before you is the Garden of Gethsemane where Christ and his disciples spent their last hours before the agony and crucifixion. Before we finish our pilgrimage, you must visit the Church of the Agony here." He gestured to the basilica that had been built over the rock where Christ had prayed before his arrest. "I need a few minutes alone, my friends, to talk to God before we finish our mission. When I am ready, Pannychis will come for you and we will finish our journey." With that, he turned away and leaned one of his hands on the rough bark of the nearest olive tree. When the sounds of shuffling feet had gradually dissipated, Eddie looked around. Only Pannychis stood outside the gate. He crossed to her.

"Meeting with the Big Guy?" she asked.

"Yeah. I'm guessing, if I sent a messenger to ask the Oracle at Delphi whether it was safe to go on, she would tell me to get the Hell out of here."

"What do you want of me?" Pannychis asked, a catch in her voice.

"Just wait with me. I can't do this without you."

A chaste kiss and Eddie turned away. Pannychis' gaze never left him. Eddie had stopped at the well with his back to her. For a moment she thought that she detected a flickering shadow by his side. The Holy Spirit, she was sure. And she was sure that the Big Guy was there, too.

The Big Guy held out a wooden chalice to his Son. Eddie took it and drank thirstily. The water was cool and refreshed him. As Eddie went to place the empty cup on the top of the well cover, the Big Guy held out his hand. Eddie passed Him the simple wooden cup. "Something stronger?" asked the Big Guy. "Jesus always preferred wine. If you look inside the cup, you can still see the tannin stains from the last supper."

The Big Guy laughed at Eddie's look of surprise. "You mean this is actually the Holy Grail?"

"Lends a nice touch of continuity, don't you think?"

"Yeah." Eddie reached out and took the cup again. It was brimming with wine this time. He took a sip and had never tasted anything remotely like it. "It's wonderful," he told the Big Guy as he finished the wine. Handing the cup back, Eddie said, "Our plan seems to be in tatters."

"You've got this far, Kid. Don't worry. I promised some divine intervention and you'll get it. Don't forget Jesus ..."

"How can I?" Eddie held up his palms to show the scars of the stigmata inflicted by his own mother.

"True."

"And let's not forget what happened to Jesus. Crucifixion and death."

"Ah, but three days later, he rose again from the dead."

"Is that what you have in mind for me?"

"Mysterious ways, Eddie, mysterious ways." The Big Guy smiled and added mischievously, "I'll give you a hint. Ask Jean-Pièrre about *la Strega's* avian companion. Lydia, I'm sure, will see that I've borrowed an ancient Chinese myth about eternal love."

Eddie nodded slowly. "So that's why we have to be at the gate at exactly seven."

"Seventh hour of the seven day of the seventh month. When the numbers align, something wonderful will happen. And don't forget, unlike the many pretenders who have claimed to have Me on their side, you really do."

Eddie had begun to feel light-headed. A wave of fear seized him, and for a moment he wanted desperately to turn away. Marie stroked his cheek and said, "It's your destiny, Eddie."

"Listen to her, Son. She has the wisdom of Pallas Athena and the compassion of St. Francis."

Eddie nodded and said wearily, "It will be done."

"Go in God's love, Eddie," said the Big Guy. "By the way, when you turn around you'll see that the path to the church is filled with baskets of olive twigs. Let each of your followers take one to show they come in peace."

Eddie turned and saw that over a hundred bushel baskets had appeared in piles along the path to the triple-arched entrance to the Church of the Agony. When he looked back, the Big Guy had gone. As soon as the Holy Spirit melded back into Eddie, Pannychis walked up and embraced him from behind. Without turning, Eddie held her hands in his and told her what had just happened. When he was finished, he looked at his watch: 6:40 p.m. "Time to go," he said.

"I'll tell them you're ready," Pannychis said and set out for the church.

The apostles joined Eddie first, while the others were picking up their olive branches and lighting their candles. "What kind of bird did *la Strega* have?" Eddie asked Jean-Pièrre.

"It was a magpie, Eddie," Jean-Pièrre told him, surprised at the question.

"Its name was Deneb," added Héloïse.

"Is there some kind of myth about Deneb?" asked Eddie.

Lydia, the astronomer, said, "Yes, there is. Deneb is the brightest star in Cygnus. We can see it with the naked eye. The Chinese tale is about the stars Deneb, Altair and Vega, known as the summer triad. Two lovers, Altair, a celestial princess, and Vega, her peasant lover, are separated by the river formed by the Milky Way. Once a year, on the seventh day of the seventh month, Deneb provides a bridge of magpies so that the lovers can meet. The journey is often seen as the passage from the human to the divine."

"And we're to reach to Gate at seven p.m." Eddie raised his voice so that the host could hear. "Whatever happens, do not stop until we are through the gate, not for any reason."

An excited buzz coursed through the crowd while the procession reformed. Eddie mounted Miriam, turned in his saddle and, with an upraised fist, yelled, "To the gate!"

The pilgrims now held up their tiny olive branches as they descended into the Kidron Valley. The road between them and the Golden Gate held only police vehicles, all with wire riot screens over every window. Uniformed police officers were standing around in small groups.

A troop of IDF soldiers stood at ease across the middle of the road.

As Eddie reached the road, the unit of the IDF formed up in two columns and took up positions across the road, so that the pilgrims could march between them. Up the hill, a crowd of boys from East Jerusalem was beginning to form. Some gathered rocks while others taunted the police. The police, riot shields held fast, moved in battle rhythm towards them.

Once Eddie and his followers reached the far sidewalk, the IDF platoon was expecting to fall in behind the procession as it turned right and headed along the ancient wall to the nearest entrance, the Lions Gate. But Eddie and Pannychis had barely started across the four-laned highway when the skies filled with so many birds that they blocked out the sun. "Magpies!" some yelled.

Just then the earth began to move. Many cried out in fear, but others urged them to keep going. People reached out to help each other as the earth lurched under them. But none of Eddie's followers stopped or turned back. The cops heading for the Palestinian boys stopped, uncertain. The Old City wall with its double-arched Golden Gate lay dead ahead. The earthquake, first large one since 1927, was shaking the wall so hard that it seemed to the approaching procession to be blurred and out of focus. Rocks hurled by the boys started to hit the road beyond the pilgrims and skitter across the pavement.

The road began to fracture on either side of the procession. As Eddie neared the middle of the road, the chaos of black-and-white Magpies began to descend, provoking screams from the crowd. Now a few dropped out and tried to make it back against the flow, seeing safety in the heights of the Mount of Olives, but not many. The birds brought a daylight darkness over the pilgrims whose candles now glowed brightly in the hollow passage created by the magpies flying in tight circles around them.

To help calm the crowd, Eddie started to sing Amazing Grace at the top of his lungs. Behind him, the Holy Spirit added a soprano counterpoint. The song spread along the procession. A million magpies muttering hoarse hosannas turned the divinely simple tune of Amazing Grace into a complex quodlibet that seemed to quicken the shaking of the stones that filled the Golden Gate ahead of them. Above the crashing and grinding of the earth, the old hymn could be heard even in the Old City beyond the walls.

Suleiman the Magnificent had sealed the Golden Gate in 1541 because, according to Jewish lore, the Messiah would enter Jerusalem by this gate. Later, a few Muslim graves were erected in front of the gate for the same purpose. Now the earthquake was breaking the stones blocking the gate, and they began to crash outwards on to the graves, smashing them flat.

At this point, the pilgrims could hear yelling in Hebrew from the other side of the tunnel of magpies. The police and IDF had been caught by surprise. Unable to penetrate the thick screen of magpies, they were reduced to screaming orders to the pilgrims, demanding that they turn and follow the sidewalk running along the outer wall to the Lions Gate.

Eddie ignored them and led his flock through a screen of trees and over the Muslim graves. The way had been made smooth by the earthquake, and the magpies had stalemated any attempt to interfere.

"Thanks," said Eddie looking skyward as Miriam, Eddie's ride, walked through the right of the two arches in the gate into the darkened gatehouse behind it. As the gatehouse filled with pilgrims, some of the Muslims there prostrated themselves in fear, but others ran in panic up the stone stairway that led to the lookout on top of the gate. Eddie and Pannychis passed the towering pillars inside the gatehouse until they came to the doors leading into the Old City itself. The two sets of green double doors had been flattened by the quake.

The quake stopped as suddenly as it had begun. Behind him, Eddie could hear the cries of 'Hosanna!' echoing off the ceilings. When he reached the final flight of steps ascending into the courtyard of the Dome, Eddie dismounted from Miriam. Handing the reins to Avraham, the Jewish boy, he took Pannychis' hand. At the top of the steps, he stopped for a moment, overwhelmed by the sight of the Golden Dome and, in front of it, the much smaller open structure called the *Qubbet al-Silsilah*, the Dome of the Chain. There he could see, for the first time, the dais set up in the shade of the dome. There were chairs for the pope, the chief imams, chief rabbis of Jerusalem and their aides. All empty. For Eddie and the leaders of the three People of the Book, a large marble table had been placed on the dais. In the middle of the altar-like table was a microphone. A heavy chain hung from the center of the dome directly behind the dais.

Behind him, pilgrims poured into the courtyard, filling it. Eddie and Pannychis led the way on to the dais. At a nod from Eddie, Lydia led the apostles up to join them. While they were waiting for the crowd to settle, Jean-Pièrre volunteered his help: "Eddie. Since the pope is not going to be here, would you like me to introduce you?"

"I can't think of a better man for the job, Jean-Pièrre."

Against a backdrop of the westering sun burnishing the real gold that covers the sacred Dome, Jean-Pièrre stepped forward and signaled for quiet. Behind the vast crowd, he noted that the Old City walls were lined with magpies as far as he could see.

What he could not see were gangs of Heredim, ultra-orthodox Jews from the illegal settlements, arming themselves and rushing towards the Golden Gate in a fury at this desecration of the site of the Second Temple. Nor could he see the Palestinians gathering on the walkway crossing above the Wailing Wall, some with sticks, others with molotov cocktails and a few with guns. There was even a small knot of fundamentalist Christians, led by the Reverend Jerry Lumpass, who were making their way towards the Golden Gate from the Christian quarter of the Old City, some still dragging the crosses they had rented from the Franciscan monks. With a thunder of wings, the magpies rose into the air and blocked the dissenters approaching from all directions.

A deep breath to calm his nerves, and then Jean-Pièrre began, "And the prophet Ezekiel said, 'Afterward he brought me to the gate even the gate that looketh toward the east: And, behold, the glory of the God of Israel came from the way of the east: and his voice was like a noise of many waters: and the earth shined with his glory.' Here at the Dome of the Chain, we stand at the center of the world, the omphalos, for the People of the Book. Solomon the Wise hung this chain for a purpose. Today in courtrooms around the world, witnesses swear on the Bible to prove their words are true. But, in ancient times, Solomon had witnesses hold this chain. If a witness lied, lightning would strike the dome above us. It would then electrify the chain and kill the false witness." Jean-Pièrre reached behind him with his right hand and, taking a firm grasp on the heavy chain, he lifted it above his head. "Well, let me be the first witness. I swear to you all that Eddie Magdalena is the true Messiah." The chain seemed to pulse with a faint blue light for a couple of seconds. The crowd watched spellbound as, one by one, the apostles each put a hand on the chain and repeated the oath. Gradually the crowd found its voice, and a great roar built until at the last Pannychis put her hand on the chain and said, "I too swear this man is the Messiah that has been foretold."

Eddie stepped up to the microphone and thanked them all. Beyond the walls surrounding the courtyard of the Dome, a babble of angry voices shouting in many languages. What else could go wrong, Eddie asked himself. The familiar whisper of his own familiar, the Holy Spirit, breathed in his ear. "Only God knows." Not the most comforting news.

Eddie was just about to address the sea of faces below him, when the whole area was hit by an aftershock even more powerful than the initial quake. A crack appeared under the dais splitting the flagstones and widening rapidly with an ugly, ripping sound. No longer supported, the center of the dais with its heavy marble table, began to sag.

The apostles scrambled desperately to save themselves. Half a dozen of them managed to escape the dais, only to find that the earth beneath their feet continued to writhe and buckle. A thick curtain of stone dust rose from the pit obscuring Eddie, Pannychis, Mahinda, Colleen and Ismael Hadawi. Eddie had thrown his arms around Pannychis, as an ominous base rumble rose in counterpoint to the shrieking of tortured rock. Before Eddie and Pannychis could jump clear, a gaping hole several meters across opened up beneath them. The risers that had made up the dais began to slide into the dark pit, followed by the marble table, now splintered into shards by the stresses placed upon it.

Cries of panic everywhere as the crowd dropped their candles, and those closest to the expanding pit pushed back towards the steps down to the Golden Gate. As suddenly as it had begun, the ground stopped moving. The only sounds now were of sobs and cries of fear and pain. When the dust began to clear, the crowd discovered that no one seemed to be badly injured. A miracle? Perhaps.

Then people began to notice that the dais had disappeared into the yawning maw in front of the Dome of the Chain. Jean-Pièrre took stock. His heart sank as he realized that Eddie, Pannychis, and Mahinda had disappeared. Someone else was missing. For a moment his mind was blank, and then he realized that Colleen and her Palestinian fixer, Ismael Hadawi, had also gone.

The muster of magpies rose in a great crowd and formed an avian river that flowed west over the Dome and the Wailing Wall into the setting sun.

Within minutes, IDF soldiers began flooding into the courtyard to restore order and tend to the fallen.

With the magpies gone, angry mobs of Christians, Muslims and Jews were arriving at the walls surrounding the courtyard. Inspector Isaac Toledano directed the IDF forces to form up in lines between the rival factions. Slowly, behind their riot shields, the police gained the upper hand. Inspector Toledano saw the apostles milling about the remnants of the ruined dais and ordered his men to form up into two flying wedges. Giving the fresh pit a wide birth, the two troops of soldiers pushed their way forward until they reached the Dome of the Chain and rescued every apostle they could find. Jean-Pièrre pleaded with the police to let him stay to look for Eddie and the others that were missing, but Inspector Toledano said, "No time. The situation is too dangerous. We're leaving now!"

Out on the street, Inspector Toledano commandeered a trio of police vehicles. All had metal grilles over all their windows. The bewildered apostles were ushered into the vehicles. Inspector Peres assured them that their hotel would be put under police protection. Lydia was indignant. "We need to know what happened to Eddie."

"Of course. But it's too dangerous here. Don't worry. We'll keep you up to date, I promise. Here." Toledano handed his card to Lydia. "That's my home number on the back. Feel free to call me at any time. But right now, my officers need to secure the area. Please try to understand."

In the second vehicle, Annette said in her native French, "What about Eddie and the others. We can't leave them."

"We don't have a choice," said Héloïse, taking Annette by the hand. As the three SUVs turned up the street towards the National Hotel, they passed the police station across from Herod's Gate and slowed to a halt. A hostile crowd of Palestinians was blocking the road ahead. The lead driver called on his radio for reinforcements. Rocks began to slam into the grates over the windows, scaring the occupants badly. The vehicles started moving forward at a slow crawl. Except for the drivers, none of the others had ever seen such hatred. Jean-Pièrre recoiled as a boy, no more than ten or eleven, spit on his window, the small face twisted by passion.

"Tear gas!" warned the drivers. "Cover your mouths!"

A squad of IDF troopers had rounded the corner and were firing canisters at the crowd. One or two of the braver boys picked up canisters and hurled them back. The melee only lasted just over a minute but seemed a lifetime. As the road began to clear, the police vehicles sped up. More soldiers were forming up in front of the National. The hotel staff, all Palestinians, led the shattered apostles into the restaurant and fed them tea and genuine sympathy.

The wonderful Nirvana comforted them for the next hour, before she directed staff members to take them up to their rooms. It was going to be a long night.

### Sede Vacante

Mere minutes after the pope's death, Cardinal Buffone received another call from Archbishop Fowler. "It is my sad duty to inform you, Your Eminence, that His Holiness has just died within the last few minutes."

"A tragedy for every member of our holy mother, the Church," intoned Buffone. "The last estimate we had from Alitalia was that the plane they are providing will be ready in another two hours, but now that the pope is dead we will have to make further arrangements. We probably won't arrive in Tel Aviv until sometime in the early morning hours."

"We will be waiting at the hospital for your call."

"Leave everything as it is until we arrive. Anything else I should know?"

"Archbishop Marcinkus has taken it badly. He accused us of being accomplices in the death of Pope Urban."

"Us?" Buffone was aghast.

"Yes, he mentioned your name too, Your Eminence."

"Don't worry. I'll deal with him. Where is the pope's body now?"

"I think it has gone to the morgue."

"Send someone to stand vigil over it."

"Yes, Your Eminence. Oh, and the doctor refuses to enter a cause of death on the death certificate without an autopsy."

"It's none of his business!" Buffone said, before realizing he was shouting. "As if the Vatican wants a Jew signing off on the death of a pope. I'll be there as soon as possible." What was the man's first name? Suddenly he remembered. "You have done well, Benjamin. *Dominus vobiscum.*"

"*Et cum spirito tuo.*"

When he had hung up, Buffone allowed himself a moment of self-congratulation. He had just become camerlengo, and during this period without a pope, the period of *Sede Vacante*, the Empty Chair, he was in charge of the church. After a few moments, he picked up the phone again and began to make a series of calls, first to the other members of the Gang of Four and then to the papal press secretary to put out the news. Next, he called the Alitalia representative and told her that several rows of seats would have to be removed to accommodate the coffin.

The woman at Alitalia, her voice choked with emotion, promised to make the arrangements but warned him that the alterations would push back the take-off time by at least two more hours.

After he had finished making arrangements, Cardinal Buffone, acting as camerlengo, ascended to the papal apartments accompanied by two Swiss Guards. The guards waited outside while Buffone entered. Cardinal Villot's actions as camerlengo after Pope Paul's death in 1978 were fresh in his mind. Villot had removed some damning documents from the lifeless hands of Pope John Paul. Those documents have never been seen again. Buffone searched the drawers in the pope's bedside table and found some notes for the speech that Urban had planned to give at the Dome of the Rock. The notes confirmed the Gang of Four's belief that the pope was prepared to commit the church to recognizing Eddie Magdalena as the true Messiah. He read on and was appalled to learn that Urban had intended to give out the actual results of the DNA tests. Not only that: another document listed almost all the members of P2. His own name was near the top. There were other papers that he did not have time to read, so he tucked the whole sheaf into his soutane and hurried out.

"Seal the apartments," he told the two Swiss Guards as he closed the door.

"Yes, Camerlengo," the senior man responded.

When he reached his own quarters, his telephone was ringing. Reverend Father Thomas del Sarto was on the line. "Did you hear the good news?" he asked.

"I'd hardly call it that," Buffone chided. "The death of a pope is always a sad time for our Mother Church and I am sure ..."

"No, no. Of course the death of Pope Urban is a tragedy for us all," said the Black Pope solemnly. "The news I have is about the so-called Messiah. He's disappeared. Turn on your television, Xavier."

And that was when Cardinal Buffone learned of the earthquake in Jerusalem and its effects.

## Notes from Underground

"Hold on to me!" Eddie shouted to Pannychis, as the risers beneath their feet began to tip slowly into the pit. The marble table had already disappeared, and now Pannychis clung to Eddie as they began to slide down the risers towards the blackness below. Eddie looked up as they passed out of the light and saw Mahinda clinging to the long cloth that had covered the table, but it scarcely slowed his fall. After a few feet, Eddie and Pannychis hit a sloping pile of rubble, but even here there was no purchase, and they began to slide with the moving rock down into yet another chamber. Behind them, Mahinda groaned in pain, as he landed on the rubble amid a shower of the decorative candles that had been sitting upon the cloth runner from the marble table. He too began to slide with the rubble that was pouring into the lower chamber.

Eddie and Pannychis scrambled clear of the rock slide and felt their way through the gloom, until they came to a wall of giant carved stones. As soon as they looked around, they spotted two people lying motionless at the edge of the rock slide. Gingerly, they picked their way to the other survivors and, despite the brown stone dust that covered them, they recognized Colleen and her fixer, Ismael. Pannychis felt Ismael's wrist for a pulse. As she did, he opened his eyes and looked at her in complete confusion. Colleen suddenly sat up and began frantically brushing stone dust out of her thick, red hair. "Holy fuck! What the Hell happened!" she asked Eddie as he helped her up.

"Earthquake."

"There's somebody else over there," Colleen told Eddie, pointing to a spot out of the pale stream of light coming though the hole above. All Eddie could see were four or five white sticks, folds of gold brocade and one Reebock running shoe. When he got to the spot, he found the shape of a figure wrapped in the cloth that had covered the table. Five of the tall candles lay scattered around. Two were still in their gold candle-holders. Starting at the running shoe, Eddie pulled back the yards of fabric and found Mahinda staring at him wide-eyed.

"You O.K.?" Eddie asked.

Mahinda sat up and tried his limbs. "I seem to be."

"How are Colleen and Ismael?" Eddie called to Pannychis.

"Shaken up, but otherwise they seem O.K. too."

The ground began to move again but not so savagely as before. "Let's get away from the rock slide. There might be more." And there were. As the five of them helped each other over to the far wall, a last shudder ran through the rocks, triggering another fall of rubble. The noise was deafening. Instinctively they covered their ears and began coughing as the fresh dust filled the chamber. "Cover your mouths!" Colleen yelled.

The rubble poured down the fresh shaft for another few minutes. When it finally stopped, the five survivors were huddled together in pitch darkness. The only sounds now were the creaking in the fractured stones and the ominous sounds of dripping water from at least two directions. No one moved for some minutes, until Colleen said, "I can feel cold air flowing in from the left."

"So there must be a passage that way," said Pannychis.

"This pitch dark is scaring the bejesus out of me."

"Me too."

"Wait." Colleen said, a note of excitement in her voice. "Fiat lux," she added triumphantly as she flicked her Bic. The tiny light illuminated the five survivors enough to clean the worst of the dust off themselves. It also revealed that dust hung heavily in the air. And then the lighter got so hot that Colleen dropped it, and they were plunged into stygian darkness again. "Where the Hell is it?"

"Here!" said Pannychis.

"Pass it to me, please," said Mahinda.

Pannychis lit the lighter and passed it to him. "What do you want it for?"

"I'm going to look for those candles." As he moved away with the light, Ismael lit his own lighter.

"Thank God for smokers!" said Pannychis.

Mahinda had already found two candles and lit them. Colleen and Ismael went to help the search. "Is this any use to us?" asked Colleen holding up the end of a microphone cable. "I grabbed it on the way down. It's still running up into the hole above."

"Yeah, pull it down if you can," said Eddie.

"It might pull down the rest of the rubble so be careful," said Pannychis.

A slight tug did release a few large chunks of masonry, so Colleen stopped pulling. Without a word, Ismael began scrambling up the sloping rubble, ignoring the warning cries to be careful. When he had reached as high as he could, he pulled out a pocket knife and sawed through the cable. He coiled the mike cable and tossed it clear.

Pannychis caught it.

When they had found three more candles, they looked for other survivors in their cavern, but there appeared to be none. Slowly, led by Mahinda with one of the candles, they began to shuffle towards the slight breeze that they hoped would indicate an open passage. They found their way into another chamber but could go no farther when they found several large stone blocks tumbled in front of what looked like the outlines of a gate. "Have you ever been in the tunnels that run along the Western Wall?" Eddie asked Ismael.

The slightly-built boy's face creased into a broad smile. "I'm a Muslim," he said as if that explained it.

"He means that the tunnels are in the Jewish quarter, so Muslims don't go there," Colleen explained, "but I visited the tunnels when I first arrived in Jerusalem. The main tunnel runs north and south."

Eddie nodded. "Does this archway ring any bells?"

Colleen shook her head. "Sorry."

Eddie was silent for a moment while he examined the pile of masonry. Soon he located a stone shaped into a gentle arc. Then he climbed a little higher and found another one carved in mirror image to the first. "You wouldn't have recognized it because these dressed stones were blocking this entrance. Look." Stooping, he picked up one of the curved stones that must have weighed at least thirty to thirty-five kilos and held it up to the top of the arch. "This one goes here. Now stand back." Everyone retreated and Eddie flung the stone on to the floor of the cavern, where it exploded with a loud bang. Two screams penetrated the small opening at the top of the arch. "There are people on the other side of this wall. Come on. I think we can clear a large enough hole to make it through. The tunnel must be on the other side."

For the next two hours, they toiled at removing the top blocks. Despite Eddie's impressive strength, progress was slow after he had cleared the smaller blocks. The larger ones were just too heavy. It was the boy, Ismael, who came up with a fresh idea. "Why don't we use the cable?" he asked. "Wrap it around the blocks one at a time. If you can push, the rest of us will pull on the cable."

"I can see why you selected him as your fixer, Colleen. Let's take five and then we'll give it a shot."

The others gratefully agreed, and sat themselves on several of the blocks scattered over the floor of the cavern. Colleen pulled out a pack of cigarettes and offered them around. Ishmael and Pannychis each accepted one. "I didn't know you smoked," Colleen told her.

"Not very often. But ask any model what the best appetite suppressant is." She held up her cigarette. "This. These are strong though."

"Yeah. I like them strong. They're local." She held out the blue pack of Monte Carlo cigarettes.

While the others were resting, Eddie used the time to try to make sense of what had just happened. Had the Big Guy set him up? No sooner had he formed the question, than the familiar voice of his familiar whispered into his inner ear, "He knew it was a gamble, Eddie. But He could see that the media was beginning to turn against you. The best chance was to go now."

"When the Holy Father was rushed to hospital, it all fell apart," said Eddie softly.

"And there was the Intifada, and the terrible bus massacre yesterday."

"So what now?"

"There is chaos right now up there. The Israelis will have a warrant out for your arrest, for violating the law about praying at the Dome."

"But there was no praying. I made that clear."

"Old habits die hard, Eddie. The shouts of 'Hosannah' by the crowd could be called a prayer."

"What happened to the other apostles?"

"They have all survived, Eddie." A sigh of relief from Eddie. "You five are the only ones missing. Right now there is a standoff between the Palestinian Authority and the IDF about attempting to rescue you and the others."

"So what do I do now?"

"You're doing just fine, Eddie. The Big Guy is testing you and, so far, He feels pleased to call you his Son."

Eddie nodded, not really convinced. He was exhausted. If he could just stretch out on the ground, he could sleep for days. But there was work to be done. Wearily, he pushed himself to his feet and asked, with more enthusiasm than he felt, "Everybody ready?" Murmurs of assent. "Then let's do it."

The first candle was on the point of guttering when they had finally cleared a triangular hole at the top of the archway. One by one they scrambled through and dropped to the floor of the tunnel on the other side. Eddie was the last one through. As he landed, they heard women's voices speaking Hebrew, to their left. Mahinda lit a fresh candle and took a few paces in that direction. He came across three women huddled together on the floor.

"Any of you speak English?" he asked.

"I do," said a pretty blonde of about eighteen. "My aunt also speaks some English, but my mother only speaks Hebrew."

The oldest of the three women seemed afraid and broke into Hebrew. The young blonde seemed to be reassuring her. The third, a woman of imposing size, put her arms around the oldest one and rocked her gently. "My *ima* is worried that you mean us harm, but I assured her that you, too, are lost."

"Indeed we are, oh my goodness, yes," said Mahinda. "Do you know where we are?"

"Yes, of course. We come down here into the tunnel almost every day. We pray in the niche back there across from Warren's Gate."

Her mother began to talk rapidly again. When she was finished, the blonde woman stood up and said, "She has been terrified by the quake, especially after the lights went out. Where did you find the candle?"

"Oh, back there." Mahinda pointed vaguely back the way he had come. "Look. I'll show you if you like. My name is Mahinda. Pleased to meet you."

"I am Ruth and this is my mother, Naomi, and my auntie, Shoshana."

"Come with us. I'm sure you can help us find a way out."

Mahinda was about to make the introductions when they reached the others, but he hesitated when he saw that the three Jewish women showed no sign of recognizing Eddie. Eddie noticed Mahinda's problem and introduced himself simply as Ed Magdalena.

"This is where we were when the earthquake began," said Ruth. "When the shaking started and the blocks began to fall out of Warren's Gate..." She pointed to the arch where the others had entered the tunnel. "... we ran down the tunnel. Then the lights went out and we stayed where you found us." She pointed to the little alcove just along the wall. "This is where we pray for world peace every day. It is the closest place to the Holy of Holies."

"That would be the Second Temple under the Dome of the Rock," said Eddie.

"Yes."

"We are so glad to have met you. We had no idea where we were."

He turned to Mahinda. "I lit another candle while you were away and explored that way. It's blocked by a rock fall about thirty meters away."

"Then we must go north," said Ruth, "but the tunnel comes to an end at the Struthion Pool. She surprised Eddie by putting her arm through his and leading the way. Once, they stopped in their tracks as a smaller tremor shook the tunnel. Soon they could hear the sound of rushing water ahead. Ruth stopped to listen. Looking worried, she said, "I've never heard running water here before. Not far ahead the Hasmonean Waterway crosses the tunnel, but it was bricked up ages ago. It has been dry for as long as anybody can remember. There should not be any sounds of water."

"We'll be all right. Don't worry, Ruth."

The tunnel began to slope down as they approached the pool, so that eventually they began to splash through water. By the time they reached the waterway, the water was almost up to their knees, and the current was making walking difficult. Ruth's mother began to whimper but Auntie Shoshana comforted her.

Eddie and Mahinda held their candles high to assess the situation. "That is the Struthion Pool," said Ruth. "It means the Sparrow Pool. It was originally above ground, but Emperor Hadrian covered it and now the Convent of the Sisters of Zion is up there." She pointed up at the vaulted ceiling. "The sisters put up the wall there to keep visitors out."

The pool was a large one and now it was not only overflowing, but the water coming down the Hasmonean Channel was racing through it, creating the unaccustomed turbulence and a strong current. Mahinda peered closely at the wall that rose on the other side of the pool. They appeared to be trapped. Then he saw it, a patch of darkness in the wall itself. The wall that the sisters had had erected had been breached at one point by the quake.

"My mother wants to go back," said Ruth. "There's no way out here."

"Where is the convent in the Old City?" asked Eddie.

"On the Via Dolorosa at the Ecce Homo Arch."

Suddenly Colleen knew exactly where they were. "That's the second station of the cross."

"It will be dark up there now," mused Eddie. "Ismael. If we can get out through the convent, can you get us out of the Old City to some safe place?"

"No problem," the boy said confidently.

"O.K." He called Pannychis over, and together they walked a few paces back up the passageway. "I have figured a possible way across, but I need you to divert the attention of the Jewish women while I give it a try."

Pannychis readily agreed and looked around her. There were a couple of large dressed stones poking out of the water just ahead. "I'll tell Ruth and her aunt to bring Mama back here where she can sit down."

"Great idea. Let's do it."

While Pannychis shepherded the three Jewish women back along the passage, Eddie told Mahinda, Colleen and Ismael that he was going to try to cross. Ismael immediately volunteered to make the first crossing.

"Can you swim?" asked Eddie.

"Well enough." Ismael did not look him in the eye.

Eddie liked the bravery of the little guy, but said, "The current is going through the pool at a pretty fast clip, Ismael. I appreciate your courage but you'd be swept away. I'll go, but I need everyone's help. Hand me one end of the mike cord." Looking mystified, Ishmael held it out to Eddie. "Now find a rock to anchor the other end."

Ishmael located a large stone near the edge of the pool. Its bottom half was under water, and water spilling out of the Struthion Pool was running over it in a steady stream. "How about this one?"

Eddie reached under the water and tried to lift it, but it was too heavy even for him. He called the others over. "Get on the side away from the pool, everyone except Ismael. When I say 'Go!' We'll all push the rock so it lifts on this side. I want you to be ready with the cable, Ismael. When the stone lifts, you'll need to get the cable under it. We won't have long, so be quick."

"Sure, Eddie," said the boy, proud of his leading role. "Watch your fingers, though." Ismael nodded. "Ready? Go!"

Even with Eddie pushing with the others, the stone would not move at first, but then it began to inch up. Ismael ducked under the water. "Come on! Come on!" grunted Eddie, knowing they could not hold the rock more than a few more seconds. Suddenly Ismael surfaced and gave a thumbs-up. The others dropped the rock back in place.

"Look!" said Ismael pulling on the cable with all his might.

"Great job!" said Eddie, coiling the rest of the cable. It seemed long enough to stretch across the pool, but he could not be sure.

"O.K. Colleen and Ismael, I'm going to walk on the water. It's the only way across."

"What?" from Colleen.

"No time for questions, Colleen. I've never done this on water moving this fast, so wish me luck." Colleen wanted to know more, but wisely held her peace.

Eddie looked up at the vaulted ceiling of the tunnel and muttered, "All right, Big Guy. Not much else has gone right, so let's not fuck this up." No reply. He got the feeling that even Marie was holding her breath.

Looking a lot more confident than he felt, Eddie climbed over the flimsy railing and started across. The water seemed to skid along sideways under his feet, and he had trouble negotiating the first few steps. Then he figured out the balance and began to move forward by executing crossover steps like a skater. Steadily he played out the cable as he went. For a good few seconds, nobody breathed.

Two minutes later, he was across and peered through the hole in the wall that cut the pool in half. There was just enough light for him to see that the pool on the far side was still. In the dim light, he could just make out steps leading up into the convent. Finding one of the fallen stones, he pulled the cable to him, making sure to leave some slack. A last look into the inner chamber told him that there was a ledge that traversed the other side of the wall, just wide enough to walk single-file around the pool to the steps on the far side.

Getting back across to the others was easier now, as he could use the cable as a guide. "That was amazing," Colleen told him.

"You really are the Messiah," said Ismael, awe in his voice.

"That's what I've been trying to tell everybody."

Eddie carried each of them across, starting with Ruth. He needed her on the other side to reassure her mother as she made the journey. Naomi closed her eyes firmly as Eddie picked her up. She prayed loudly in Hebrew all the way across. The burly Auntie Shoshana was the biggest challenge, but at least she showed no fear. "Too bad you're not a Jew," she told Eddie as they reached the other side. "I'm looking for a husband for my daughter."

"Afraid I'm already taken, Auntie."

By the time they had relit the damp candles and edged their way along the ledge to the steps, a couple of nuns were waiting to greet them like the refugees they were. The younger one recognized Eddie and said, "You're the one who claims to be the Messiah."

"Oh, you can be sure there is no doubt about that," Colleen assured her.

At the top of the staircase, Eddie addressed them all in a soft voice. "I only ask you one thing: please do not mention you've seen me for the next three days. Can you all promise that?" Everyone, of course, did.

Colleen asked the nuns, "We're at the Ecce Homo Arch near the Lions Gate?"

"Yes. This is the Ecce Homo Monastery and I am the abbess here," said the older nun with a German accent. "You are all welcome."

"Thanks, but we shouldn't stay," said Eddie.

The abbess smiled warmly and said, "I'm afraid you don't have a choice. Because of the unrest and the earthquake, there is a curfew. It started four hours ago."

"What time is it?" asked Pannychis.

"Almost one in the morning. Please be as quiet as you can. We have guests staying here. Sister Janelle will take you up to the roof, and we'll bring food and drink and bedding. Come. You must be exhausted. The sisters will pray for guidance and see if we can find a way to spirit you away when they lift the curfew at dawn."

## Arrival of the Camerlengo

Delays resulting from removing seats from the Alitalia flight and finding a suitable hermetically sealed, metal-lined casket meant that Cardinal Buffone and his entourage did not reach Ben Gurion Airport in Tel Aviv until six a.m. Israeli daylight time. Despite the early hour he was greeted by Shimon Peres, Vice Premier of Israel. To an explosion of flashes, the vice premier expressed Israel's condolences for the tragic loss of a beloved pope and a pledge of any assistance the cardinal might require.

A few minutes later, Cardinal Buffone and his aides were whisked off to Jerusalem. When they reached the hospital, Buffone, mindful that Archbishop Marcinkus was probably still in the waiting area, asked the driver to take them directly to the entrance to the morgue. There he was met by Dr. Tawfiq Hassan, attending physician, and Dr. Mal Evans, Director of the Hospital. Buffone instructed his staff to wait upstairs and told the director of the hospital that he needed to go directly to the morgue. This morgue, like morgues everywhere, was cold and smelled of disinfectant. Buffone shivered as the morgue attendant pulled out the drawer containing the remains of Pope Urban IX.

"I need to be alone for a few minutes."

"By all means, Your Eminence," said Dr. Evans. "Just press that button over there when you're finished."

"Thank you, Doctor."

When the doors swung shut, the cardinal turned and stood looking down at the dead pope for a few moments. Then he reached into the leather briefcase he had been carrying, pulled out a red velvet presentation case and placed it on the cold steel of the morgue drawer. Opening the case, he took out the small ornate silver hammer and performed the traditional ceremony when a pope dies. Three times he tapped the pope gently on the forehead with the hammer and called out his baptismal name, Pablo Ramirez. When no answer came, he wrestled the papal ring off the pope's cold finger. Cardinal Buffone placed the ring on the stainless steel drawer and smashed it to pieces with three blows before he put the hammer away. Such destruction was made necessary by the fact that each papal ring is individually designed, so breaking it ensures that it cannot be used to forge papal documents. After carefully gathering up the fragments of the ring and placing them in a velvet bag he had brought for the purpose, he thought of kneeling to pray, but a quick look at the polished concrete floor told him that it was still wet from previous use. Instead he pulled out his Roman Missal and recited the prayer for a deceased pope.

When he was finished, he bent down and kissed the pope lightly on the forehead. "May you awake in Heaven, Pablo. Please forgive us. I'm sure you understand by now that we had to save our Mother the Church."

He straightened up and pressed the button. Immediately, the morgue attendant appeared. "Prepare the body of Pope Urban for transport," Buffone ordered and strode out of the room feeling a mixture of triumph and guilt. I must see my confessor when I get back to Rome, he reminded himself. When he joined the tired group in the waiting area, he was relieved to see that Archbishop Marcinkus was not there.

"Where is he?" he asked Archbishop Fowler.

Fowler shrugged. "Nobody knows. A couple of hours ago, he left to find a telephone and didn't come back."

"He caught an early flight back to Rome," said Luigi.

"Hmm. They are preparing His Holiness' body for transport, then we can make our way back to Ben Gurion," said Buffone.

"Did they issue a death certificate?" asked Luigi.

"No. The Jew in charge said he could not issue a death certificate without an autopsy. I told him that, according to tradition, the Vatican does not do autopsies on the representatives of St. Peter, but he was adamant. Damned stiff-necked race."

"Actually, Dr. Hassan is a Muslim," said Luigi mildly. "And there are precedents for doing an autopsy on the remains of a pope."

"Listen, Luigi, I don't need any lessons on protocol from the likes of you." With that dismissal, he turned to the others and said briskly, "In the meantime, I have to make some calls."

The first call was to the brothers Signoracci, the embalmers that the Vatican had used for decades. Ernesto answered, and Cardinal Buffone gave him instructions to meet his plane at Da Vinci Airport. The pope must be embalmed immediately.

"Let me convey how saddened we are to lose such a fine pope, Your Eminence," said Ernesto.

"Yes, yes. Someone will call you about an hour before we touch down."

"I will be there with my brother, Arnaldo, Your Eminence. I trust you have the death certificate."

"Don't worry. I'll send a Vatican physician with you to establish the cause of death."

"Certainly, Your Eminence."

The next call was to the Vatican Hospital where he asked for Dr. Taddeo Salmonelli. When he was told that the doctor would not be in for another hour, he identified himself and ordered Dr. Salmonelli to meet the plane. Buffone knew very little about Salmonelli's skills as a physician, but he knew the one thing that was of paramount importance: the good doctor was a mason.

The last call was to Cardinal Schicklgruber. The two discussed various matters of protocol and decided that the earliest they dared to hold the conclave was in fifteen days. "If some of the cardinals from abroad can't make it, it won't be such a bad thing."

"Certainly not, Alois, certainly not."

When Cardinal Buffone returned to the waiting room, he was informed that the funeral cortege had been formed up. He was to ride at the head with Shimon Peres, since Prime Minister Yitzhak Shamir was still out of the country.

The new camerlengo quickly reviewed the plans he had set in motion. With Urban IX deceased and the false Messiah disappeared, everything seemed to be going according to plan. And in fifteen days, the Conclave of Cardinals would convene and, by the second or third ballot, the white smoke would appear in the sky over the Sistine Chapel, indicating that Cardinal Silvestrini had become Pope Sixtus VI. Within another year, many of the reforms of Vatican II would be struck down, and the church would once again bargain with the rest of the world from a position of power. Amen.

## Early to Rise

The Convent of the Sisters of Sion was a rabbit warren of narrow staircases, unexpected nooks and curious crannies. Sister Janelle, using one of the candles supplied by Mahinda, led Eddie's group up a series of cramped stairways, until they emerged on to the rooftop patio.

"We have some cots that we'll bring up," Sister Janelle told them.

"Can we help?" asked Colleen.

"No, no. Most of our guest rooms are occupied. If they happen to open their doors, they'll only see us sisters. Just wait here. I'll be back with some of the others. Just make yourselves comfortable."

As Sister Janelle was about to leave, Pannychis put a hand on her arm and said, "Sister, one more thing. Could you bring a bowl of water, a razor, some sharp scissors and some soap. When the sister looked puzzled, Pannychis explained, "It's to shave Eddie, make him less recognizable."

"Ah yes, of course." She smiled. "The razor might be a problem. I'll borrow one from one of our male guests."

The others had wandered over to the parapet and were looking down into the Via Dolorosa directly below them. The Way of Sorrows was in darkness because of the angle of the crescent moon, that was imparting a soft white glow to the rest of the Old City.

"Tonight the Old City must look much as it did a thousand years ago," said Colleen wistfully.

"True. Most of these buildings have been here longer than that," said Pannychis, sitting down beside Colleen at one of the tables scattered around the rooftop.

After a few moments, Colleen reached across and placed her hand on Pannychis' hand. "You know who lived here in Christ's time?" Pannychis shook her head. "Pontius Pilate. This is where he condemned Jesus and freed Barabbas."

Pannychis sighed and looked across at the Dome of the Rock gleaming in the moonlight with a pearly opalescence that was no longer golden. She turned to see where Eddie was. He was standing apart from the others, his back to her, his head down. Suddenly, the sight of her lover combined with the tensions of the day rose up in her, and she began to silently weep.

Colleen rose, put her arm around the taller woman and said, "He'll be all right."

"How can he be after what happened today?"

"He is still the Messiah. Nothing can change that. Look at the way he led us out of earthquake zone. I know that no one will ever convince me that he is not the Messiah."

"I think he feels betrayed. Like Jesus," said Pannychis. "Maybe God has a sick sense of humor."

"We don't know the outcome yet. Maybe this was meant to be. Ah, the nuns are back."

The nuns had appeared with cots, blankets, pillows and food. Everyone pitched in to set things up. Soon they were hungrily devouring the plain food and bottled water. Sister Janelle, herself, had brought up the shaving materials for Eddie. "I met Father Duhamel downstairs. This is his razor," she explained to Pannychis.

As Sister Janelle was leaving, Colleen, ever the reporter, asked, "Any news of the Holy Father?"

Sister Janelle's eyes immediately filmed with tears as she said, "The Holy Father has died." With that, she hurried back down the staircase, while Colleen stared after her, stunned.

The night air was pleasantly warm, and many of the exhausted group fell asleep almost immediately after they had eaten. Soon, the only people awake were Eddie and Pannychis. As she started shaving off Eddie's beard, Pannychis asked, "You know where Ismael is?"

"I got a chance to talk to him and Mahinda while we were setting up the bedding," Eddie said. "Ismael has an idea to get us out of Jerusalem. Mahinda will help, too."

"How?"

"A lot depends on the nuns. Ismael's downstairs talking to them now. He's hoping to borrow a couple of habits large enough to fit us."

"I may be a clothes horse, but that would be a new fashion, even for me."

"How do you think I feel?"

"And Mahinda. He'll help us get a plane out of Tel Aviv?"

"No, no. Out of Cairo."

"Cairo? How do we get there?"

"I wish I knew. Now let's get some sleep, my love. Morning will come early."

"Early? Sister Janelle told me the first Muslim call to prayer is about four a.m."

"The *adhan*? Yeah, always much earlier in the hot weather."

"Mmm." Pannychis looked at his face critically. "There. Looks good. Even makes you look younger."

They talked on in whispers for a while, about Pope Urban and their immediate future, before they too dozed off in each other's arms.

At four in the morning, the silence was shattered by the voice of a muezzin issuing forth from a scratchy speaker atop a nearby minaret, calling all Muslims to prayer.

Before Eddie was fully awake, Ismael was at his side. "Boss, we should let the Jews leave first, and then get ready."

"O.K."

"Did the nuns find any habits tall enough for us?" asked Pannychis.

"We won't know until they come up."

Pannychis nodded before getting up and stretching. "What's he saying?" she asked Ismael.

"It's the morning call to prayer. It starts with '*Hayya alal-fatah*', 'Come and flourish.' Then he says, 'Prayer is better than sleep' which proves he is a Sunni like me."

"Why?"

"The Shias don't use that phrase."

They said their goodbyes to the three Jewish women. "Can you ladies keep a secret?" Eddie asked as he hugged each of them. "I ask only that you don't mention meeting us for the next three days. After that, it doesn't matter.

"Of course," said Auntie. "We will even swear it if you like."

"No. You agree. That's enough to me. Go with God, Auntie."

"You know, Eddie, when you appeared in that tunnel dressed all in white, I thought God had answered my prayers."

"You were praying for the Messiah?"

"No, for a husband for my daughter. She's almost thirty."

Eddie laughed. "I'll tell you this. If you keep your word, and I'm sure you will, I wouldn't be surprised if you don't find that prospective husband under a nearby Chanukah bush."

Sister Janelle arrived just after the Jewish women left. She carried two habits over her arm. She ushered Colleen, Ismael and Mahinda down to a room off the next landing where a breakfast awaited them. She handed the first habit to Eddie who regarded it dubiously. "I'm still not sure it's long enough Take it over there and turn your back. I'll come and help you when I have finished here." Eddie took the mysterious black and white pieces of the habit and drifted over to look one last time at the Dome of the Rock. The moon had set so the Dome was in shadow, but beyond it he could see the Mount of Olives. The streetlights were twinkling atop the ridge. Eddie did not know that one of the distant buildings with lights in its windows was the Augusta Victoria Hospital where the pope's remains still lay.

"Look." At the sound of Sister Janelle's voice, Eddie turned around and saw Pannychis dressed as a Sister of Sion.

"Quite a transformation," he told her. "I guess it helps that you grew up Roman Catholic."

"You need to keep your eyes lowered when you are walking," said Sister Janelle. She handed Pannychis a wet cloth. "Better take your makeup off."

Pannychis scrubbed her face and readjusted her wimple. "There. O.K. now?"

"Perfect," said Eddie.

Sister Janelle looked at her critically before nodding. "Now you." She took the habit from him and held it up to his shoulders. It was at least five inches too short. "Wait here. I have an idea." She took the habit from him and disappeared down the stairs.

While they were waiting, Eddie said, "I'm glad the sisters wear the traditional habit. What's your nun's name?"

"Sister Martha. Named after the Virgin Mary's sister. It's the name of the nun who donated the habit. Sister Janelle told me that Sister Martha is Dutch."

"So that's why it fits so well. The Dutch are the tallest people in the world."

Sister Janelle was back with a priest's outfit. "I forgot about Father Duhamel. He is as tall as you, Eddie, but not so broad shouldered perhaps. "Try it on."

A little tight around the shoulders, as the sister had predicted, but not a bad fit. The others filtered up from breakfast and were impressed by their disguises.

"It surely helps that you shaved, Eddie," Colleen told him. "You look like a new man. And look at you, Pannychis. You look to the manner born."

"God be with you," Pannychis said in a soft voice.

"We really need to leave," said Ismael. "It will start to get light very soon. Over breakfast, we decided that these two," pointing to Colleen and Mahinda, "will get your passports, money and credit cards from the King David. Mahinda will go to the National, and Colleen will go first to her apartment then to the King David. Could you give her your key, Eddie?"

Eddie handed over his key. "We'll meet you outside the King David."

"Right," agreed Colleen.

"You and Mahinda will fly out of Tel Aviv to Cairo. Lucky that Egypt is the one country in the Middle East that gives landing rights to planes out of Israel."

"And us?" asked Pannychis.

"Don't worry," Ismael told them. "I will be your fixer."

"And he's damned good at it," said Colleen.

"Anything else?" asked Eddie.

"Just that it's time to leave."

"Where are we going now?" asked Pannychis.

"Ismael is going to smuggle us into the West Bank as members of an aid organization. From there he will take us through the secret tunnels that lead into Egypt."

"I know a man who can make you new passports from the originals," said Ismael.

"Colleen and I will head to Cairo and buy plane tickets for you to get to Sri Lanka," said Mahinda.

Suddenly, the penny dropped for Pannychis. "This is connected to the Buddhist dates in the computer message about the Second Coming."

"Yes. But even I don't know exactly what the connection is. Yet," Eddie confessed. Marie had remained silent on the subject. "Let's hope we're heading to a better fate than the one Jesus knew was coming when he left this house."

## On the Third Day

So far God had not said a word. Recalling the Christ's last words, Eddie whispered bitterly, "My God, my God, why have you forsaken me?"

The only answer came from the Holy Spirit, Marie: "He has not forsaken you, Eddie. He will appear when you least expect it." An answer that explains nothing, thought Eddie. Pannychis reached out and squeezed his hand. She was rewarded with a sad smile.

Taking advantage of the last hour of darkness, Ismael led his party through the deserted streets of the old city, until they reached Herod's gate. There, the fruit sellers were already beginning to set up their stalls. "Here we part," said Colleen.

Eddie nodded. "We'll see you in two days at the airport in Cairo. What the Hell day is it, anyway?"

"Saturday, July 8th. We'll look for you on Monday morning, starting at 9:30. Mahinda and I will take turns standing outside Departures Hall One for ten minutes, every hour on the half hour," Colleen told him.

"You've been wonderful. Safe travels," Eddie told Colleen.

There were tears in Colleen's eyes as she hugged him and Pannychis. "I hate goodbyes," she said.

Eddie, Pannychis and Ismael watched as Mahinda and Colleen crossed the road and walked past the battle-scarred police station, before disappearing towards the National Hotel, their first stop. The first rays of the sun were beginning to brighten the city as Ismael led two unusually tall Christian clergy along the outer walls, until they came to the entrance to Hezekiah's Cave.

Two middle-aged Palestinian men sat smoking at a table just inside the door. They greeted Ismael with friendly banter. After a short conversation in Arabic, one of the men rose and closed the outer door with a clang that echoed through the vast cavern. The electricity had just been restored, and the ugly sodium lighting gave the weeping walls of rock an eerie malevolent glow that intensified the shadows. The only sound, apart from their own footsteps, the constant trickle of running water.

Curious, Eddie walked down some crudely carved steps until Ismael stopped him. "Better stay here, boss," he said. "We'll be leaving as soon as Abdul borrows his brother's van."

The older and heavier of the two strangers said, in heavily accented English, "The Jews have started a rescue effort at Qubbat As-Sakhrah."

"The Dome of the Rock," explained Ismael.

"Yes. The rescue effort will be abandoned later today. The Palestinian Authority has called on all Palestinians to come and protect the sacred ground. Already a huge crowd has gathered and is threatening the rescuers and the squad of IDF. Doesn't seem as if you people will be rescued today." With that he laughed, but no one joined him. "My people are looking for you, too. They want to charge you with sacrilege and with causing damage to a holy shrine."

"But we had nothing to do with the quake," protested Pannychis.

The man rattled his worry beads and nodded towards Eddie. "He claims to be the Messiah. Who else are we to blame?"

Eddie looked at Ismael, a question in his eyes. "Husam and Kadar will not turn you in, boss. They are family," Ismael told him.

Just then a scruffy white tricycle delivery truck pulled on to the wide sidewalk outside the cave and stopped at the gate. On the side was painted 'Hassan's Fresh Fruit' in English and Arabic. "Wait here," said Ismael, as he opened the gate and leapt up the few stone steps. He joined the driver at the back door of the enclosed cargo box and together they began to unload empty vegetable crates. A few seconds later, Ismael beckoned to Eddie and Pannychis, and they hurried out and climbed into the back of the truck. The cargo space became even more cramped when Ismael piled in on top of them, and the driver began stuffing empty cases in front of them until they reached the low ceiling. Without a word, he slammed the door. The first jarring thump came when the truck bounced off the sidewalk and into the traffic. The tiny engine whined under their weight as the driver accelerated. "Do we have far to go?" asked Eddie, as he maneuvered Pannychis' knee out of the small of his back.

"Not far to the first stop. We're meeting Colleen and Mahinda outside the King David Hotel. They will have retrieved your luggage and papers. We'll need your passport, credit cards and money.

When they stopped near the hotel, the door opened again and Mahinda helped the driver jam in their luggage. "See you in Cairo," he said as he handed them their papers and money. "Good luck!"

"Wait!" yelled Eddie as Mahinda was about to close the door. "Did you pay our hotel bill?"

Mahinda looked surprised. "No. The Vatican booked your suite, did it not?"

"Yes, I guess it did."

"There you go. At this moment, we are all broke. Don't worry. The Vatican can afford it."

The door slammed again and they were left in the hot darkness. Half an hour later Pannychis asked, "Are we there yet?"

"Two more hours at most," said Ismael cheerfully. "We are crossing into the Gaza Strip. The driver makes this trip every day, so the Jews almost never check him, especially on the way out of Israel." The phrase 'almost never' gave Eddie and Pannychis scant comfort.

By the time they reached the Israeli checkpoint, the heat in the small cargo space was almost unbearable, but all three of them bore it in total silence. As the windowless van lurched to a halt, they could hear voices outside in both Hebrew and Arabic. Two minutes later they were on their way. Almost an hour passed as they bounced over bad roads before they stopped again. "Lunch," announced the driver as he ripped open the door and flooded the cargo space with blinding sunshine.

They spent the day in a small apartment in Gaza. Someone took their pictures and left with their passports.

Just before nightfall, the passports were returned. Eddie had not told anyone that he could understand most of the Arabic spoken around him. That way, he had decided, if they did mean to betray him and Pannychis, he would know. But all that day, he heard nothing to alarm him. In fact, the nameless Palestinians who fed them and found them a place to rest, treated them with warm hospitality.

That night Pannychis and Eddie said goodbye to their fixer, Ismael, and piled into an old Fiat 500. They headed south until they reached the border crossing in the dusty desert town of Rafah. There, they were handed over to two hard men who blindfolded them and led them into one of the secret tunnels into Egypt. Once inside, the blindfolds were removed and Eddie was surprised to see how large and well-made the tunnel was, with lighting disappearing into the distance. At the other end of the tunnel, they emerged into a desert *wadi* and hiked to the nearest road. There they were met by another car and driven into Cairo.

Outside Departures Hall One at Cairo International, they were reunited with Colleen and Mahinda. "Come. You must be hungry," said Mahinda. "Let's find a table at the Sakara Cafe. It's got great food and we've got nearly three hours until our flight."

Over a meal of lamb shish kebab, tabouli and fattouch, they talked quietly about the nightmare of the past couple of days. "We know that poor Pablo passed away," said Pannychis, "but otherwise we haven't seen a newspaper or a TV since Jerusalem."

"A lot has happened in the last couple of days," began Colleen. "The Israelis have called off the search for us at the Dome. Apparently there was a huge standoff with the Palestinians, who accused the Jews of sacrilege. They said they would take over the search, but they have brought in earthmovers and sealed the whole area of the Dome and the Al Aqsa Mosque. I think they will just fill in the caverns under the collapse. The big news, of course, is the death of Pope Urban and the coming election of the new pope."

"Who's favored to win?" asked Eddie.

"Cardinal Silvestrini."

Eddie sighed. "You know I won't be sorry if I never see the Middle East again."

"I can't say I blame you. Look, Eddie, I'm a journalist and I'll be going back to Jerusalem to cover the Intifada. I'd like your permission to tell your story."

"Sure. Why not?" agreed Eddie. "Just don't tell anyone where we've gone."

"Of course not."

"And make sure Lydia and Arthur know we are safe. They'll tell the rest of the apostles."

At the gate leading into the security area, they all hugged the diminutive Colleen.

"By this time tomorrow, we'll be in Sri Lanka," Mahinda said.

Exhausted, Eddie looked at him and managed a weak smile. "Serendip?"

Mahinda nodded. "The Arab name for Sri Lanka. You will see. My country is a little Eden, a teardrop off the coast of India."

"Except for the civil war," Pannychis pointed out.

"Yes. We Sinhalese and Tamils must learn to live in peace."

"Maybe we should have started there, instead of trying to bring peace and joy to the whole planet."

And on the third day after the disaster at the Dome, they landed in Colombo, Sri Lanka, and stayed that first night at the Intercontinental Hotel, right on the sea. The concierge recognized them and called The Island, a paper so often in trouble with the government that it was regularly starved for money. Because of this, The Island had a loyal following, even though it tended to publish in an odd jumble of typefaces. By the time a reporter turned up at the hotel three days later, Eddie, Pannychis and Mahinda had already taken the rackety old train up into the hills to the holy city of Kandy.

"Do you have a picture of them?" the reporter asked hopefully. "No, but I am sure it was them."

"Why do you think they would have come to Sri Lanka?"

"I don't know."

"And they are not staying here now?"

"No."

"So where did they go?"

"I don't know sir."

The reporter snapped his notebook shut. "It's old news anyway." He slipped the concierge a few rupees, just to keep him sweet. "Let me know if Elton John ever turns up. I like his music."

# Part Seventeen: Aftermath

## Papal Conclave

Despite the heat wave hovering over Vatican City, huge crowds rushed to Rome to mourn Pope Urban IX during the four days his body lay in state in St. Peter's Basilica. He was dressed in a simple white soutane and a white alb. Over these inner garments a red chasuble, the color of papal mourning. His vestments were complemented by a white bishop's mitre on his head and red shoes on his feet.

The great wave of grief washing over Vatican City crested with the funeral that took place on the fifth day. Following tradition, the College of Cardinals announced the *Novemdiales*, the nine days of mourning before they would enter the Sistine Chapel to elect a replacement.

During this period, the Italian media began to ask questions about the death of Pope Urban. Dr. Taddeo Salmonelli, the Vatican doctor that Cardinal Buffone had called from Jerusalem, had pronounced the cause of death as a brain aneurysm. Trouble was that such a diagnosis could not be confirmed without a full autopsy. Questions from the press about embalming the pope before an autopsy could be performed were getting louder.

When reporters learned that Dr. Salmonelli had never met the pope while he was alive, many asked why the cardinal had not called Dr. Urban's personal physician, Dr. Ignacio Rojas. Buffone had claimed that he had not been able to get hold of him.

Reporters had begun to compare the death of Urban to the mysterious death of Pope John Paul, eleven years earlier. In both cases, the body had been immediately embalmed. Both had died just over a month after taking office. Both had been ready to take the church in a more progressive direction as the second millennium approached. Both had been popular popes who wanted to return the church to its role as champion of the poor, against the objections of a significant number of the College of Cardinals. When pressed about the rush to embalm the late pope without an autopsy, Cardinal Buffone had explained that the Holy Church's traditions did not condone cutting into the body of God's representative on earth.

Luigi Fuseli found that he had become invisible under the new camerlengo. With the papal apartments sealed, Luigi, despite being a layman, managed to move into the Domus Romana Sacerdotales, the priest's residence within easy walking distance of St. Peter's. Père Jean-Pièrre had stayed there during Vatican II. During the four days of Lying in State, Luigi was treated as just another person in the crowd of clerical mourners. Feeling impotent, he watched as the Gang of Four moved to take charge of the ceremonies and, beyond that, of the Holy Mother Church herself.

As the nine days of mourning began, Luigi came down for breakfast and was flipping through a copy of La Stampa when he came across a curious article about the Sedevacantists. This group of conservative Catholics believes that all popes elected since Vatican II are heretics for embracing the heresy of modernism. They claim that since the rites of the One, Holy, Catholic and Apostolic church had been radically revised and modernized during Vatican II, the church is no longer Catholic. As he sipped his espresso, Luigi speculated idly that the goal of the Sedevacantists was not so different from that of the Gang of Four. Both wanted to turn the clock back. Maybe the Gang of Four were all closet Sedevacantists. It was well known that those espousing this doctrine usually kept their sympathies hidden. The more Luigi thought about it, the more it seemed to make sense.

All day he thought about the article, but it was not until he was watching the TV coverage that evening that he saw something that pushed him to act. The newsreader was talking about Ladbrokes, the famous British bookie. Ladbrokes had just posted their odds on the papal election candidates. Top of the list was Cardinal Silvestrini at 3-1. Buffone was listed at 35-1 and Schicklgruber 75-1.

The next morning, Luigi began to make discreet phone calls to cardinals he trusted, with the message that Cardinal Silvestrini was a secret Sedevacantist. By the seventh day, he had received fourteen calls from churchmen he barely knew, telling him the rumor circulating about Silvestrini. Even more telling, thought Luigi, was the fact that Cardinal Silvestrini had begun to deny the rumor. As the old adage has it: gossip is never fatal until someone denies it. For the rest of the period of mourning, Luigi checked the newspapers every morning until he found Ladbrokes odds. The odds on Silvestrini's election remained steady for the first few days at 3 - 1 but on the morning of the eighth day of the *Novemdiales*, the odds had dropped to 5 - 1. On the ninth day, Luigi's heart leapt as he opened La Stampa and discovered that on the eve of the conclave, Ladbrokes estimated Cardinal Silvestrini's odds at only 18 - 1.

The next morning at ten a.m., the cardinals gathered in the Basilica for the *Missa pro Eligendo Romano Pontifice*, the mass for the election of a pontiff. After the mass, the College of Cardinals formed up in the Pauline Chapel and walked in procession to the Sistine Chapel chanting "*Litaniae Sanctorum*," the ancient litanies of the saints. In the midst of the crowd, Luigi Fuseli watched as Cardinal Silvestrini passed. Luigi thought he detected a hint of nerves from the usually urbane cardinal, but he could not be sure. Perhaps that is what I want to see, he admitted to himself.

As soon as the last cardinal entered the Sistine Chapel, the order "*Exeunt omnes*" was given and everyone who was not a cardinal was ushered out. Swiss Guards then locked and sealed the doors from the outside. All the cardinals had been sworn to secrecy, and the Chapel itself had been swept for electronic bugs numerous times in the last two days. Some of the newer cardinals gazed up at the world's most precious ceiling, where Michelangelo's *Last Judgment* played out, but most of the 137 cardinals present just got down to business.

Three cardinals were selected as scrutineers to count the ballots and make sure that they matched the number of cardinals. If the numbers did not match, the ballots would be burned without being counted. Each cardinal received a ballot that said '*Eligo in Summum Pontificem*', I Elect as the Most High Pontiff.

The balloting took place in near silence as each cardinal wrote his choice, disguising his handwriting, and folded the ballot twice. When the ballots had been collected, each was checked by two scrutineers in turn before they were turned over to the third scrutineer, who pierced each ballot through the word '*Eligo*' with a needle and thread, adding them to a long string so that they could not be counted twice.

After the first ballot, Cardinal Silvestrini had dropped to twenty-fifth place, but no candidate had attained the required two-thirds majority. The string of first ballots was burned in the small stove installed for that purpose. Wet straw was added to make sure the smoke that emerged from the chimney outside was black.

The balloting went on for three days, but after the two ballots on the first day, it was clear that Cardinal Silvestrini would not become the next pontiff. On the eighth ballot Cardinal Roland Kieffer from tiny Luxembourg received 98 ballots, more than enough for a two-thirds majority required.

A huge roar rose up from the crowds in Vatican Square as the white smoke rose from the chimney on the roof of the Sistine Chapel. All eyes turned to the balcony of St. Peter's Basilica. A few minutes later, the Cardinal Archdeacon in charge of the Conclave emerged and told the waiting crowd, "*Habemus papam!*" When the cheers subsided, he added, "He has chosen the name Pope Urban X."

The important thing about Cardinal Kieffer, to the few who really knew him, was that he was a humble man who intended to reform the church. His mentors, he told the crowd, were Pope John Paul and Pope Urban IX. Then he gave the traditional papal blessing: *Urbe et Orbi*, blessing the eternal city and the world.

No one was happier at the defeat of Cardinal Silvestrini than Father Tito di Belmonte. When the new pope was announced from the balcony of St. Peter's, he used the last of his strength to take his sister's hand and rasp, "We have won, Anna. Thank God ... and Eddie Magdalena." Later that evening, he slipped into a heavy sleep. When Anna checked on him around midnight, the old priest had died. Anna's grief was tempered by the slight smile on her brother's face.

# Part Eighteen:
# The World Moves on

When the earthquake had pitched Eddie and his followers into the stygian darkness on July 7th, 1989, it precipitated a series of aftershocks that changed the lives of everyone involved.

## Colleen O'Myra

After Colleen had said her goodbyes to Eddie, Pannychis and Mahinda, she had flown back to Tel Aviv, where she took a taxi to Jerusalem and the National Hotel. Afraid to leave the hotel, the apostles had been waiting, bewildered and anxiously wondering what to do. Colleen did not arrive until after eight o'clock in the evening. She was surprised to find Nirvana still on duty at the desk.

"Working the late shift?" Colleen asked her.

Nirvana flashed a tired smile and said, "I should have finished hours ago, but I worry about Eddie's people. They are lost without him."

"Perhaps I can help. I have some news that should cheer them up." Colleen checked the restaurant. It was closed. "Could you call their rooms and ask them to come down? We'll use the restaurant to meet, if that is all right."

"Yes, of course. I will turn the lights on. Let me make the calls."

Colleen waited until all nine of them had arrived, before telling them that Eddie, Pannychis and Mahinda were all right. The Dionnes burst into tears. Alphonse and Claude high-fived each other. Arthur and Lydia hugged each other in relief. Colleen went on to tell a compressed version of their escape from the Dome of the Rock but did not reveal the destination of the three fugitives. "I can let you know when the three days are up. My God, that's tomorrow."

The conversation gradually switched to more practical problems. "The hotel is still being paid for by the Vatican, but I'm sure the new regime will stop payment if they think of it. As for the flights home, I think you are on your own."

"We'll pool our resources," said Lydia. The others nodded agreement. Soon there was a pile of traveler's cheques on the table and several credit cards.

"Héloïse and I will go to the travel agent around the corner and book flights for everyone," Jean-Pièrre assured them.

Two days later, Pierre and Héloïse flew to Paris. The others flew back to Sudbury.

## Bus 405

The attack on Bus 405 by Abed al-Hadi Ghaneim on July 6th, that left sixteen dead and seventeen injured, had been the first act of the tragedy that had befallen Eddie's message of love at the Dome of the Rock. Bus 405 was attacked again on September 9th. A young Palestinian stabbed the driver, Shlomo Assor, in the stomach and chest, but the driver managed to stop the bus and survived. Passengers subdued the would-be assassin until police arrived. Just over a week later, on September 17th, Egged bus inspectors arrested another Palestinian carrying a brown plastic bag holding a large commando knife and prevented yet another attack on Bus 405. On October 18th, 2011, Abed al-Hadi Ghaneim, who had been given sixteen life sentences, was released, along with 1,026 Palestinian prisoners, in exchange for Gilad Shalit, a captured IDF soldier.

## Ismael Hadawi

On the third day after the quake, Colleen filed a story about Eddie's escape to the *Irish Times*. The front page was almost entirely devoted to the mysterious death of the latest pope and the preparations for the papal enclave. The Eddie story appeared on page four. Colleen's book on Eddie, called *Millennium Messiah*, appeared eighteen months later and garnered only modest sales.

She still used Ismael as her fixer, and they had become friends. In September of 2000, the Second Intifada broke out, with bitter fighting that lasted for five more years, with a death toll of over 3,000 Palestinians and 1,000 Israelis. During this Intifada, waves of suicide bombers that killed many Israelis led to the building of the barrier around the West Bank. Ismael was guiding two American journalists through one of the markets when a suicide bomber detonated his bomb, killing all three of them.

One of the few signs of co-operation, even hope, among the major religions is Wajih Nuseibeh. Through both Intifadas and several conflicts between Gaza and Israel, he has remained the Muslim Keeper of the Keys to the Holy Sepulchre to this day.

## Archbishop Paul Marcinkus

In 1990, the Italian court dropped the long-standing arrest warrant that had largely confined Archbishop Paul Marcinkus inside Vatican City. He had quit as Head of the Vatican Bank the previous year, and now he resigned his post as Governor of Vatican City and quietly returned to his beloved Chicago. When asked by a reporter in Chicago about the scandals at the Vatican Bank, he said, "I may be a lousy banker, but at least I'm not in jail."

The Gorilla had saved the lives of two popes, but his failure to save Pope Urban IX still rankled. Feeling his age, he moved to a retirement home in Sun City, Arizona, where he lived in a room overlooking the golf course. Father Chink, as his parishioners affectionately called him, died on February 20th, 2006, aged eighty-four.

The many obituaries that followed his death gave mixed reviews of his career, but even the most negative had to admit that the Gorilla was a man whose like would not be seen again.

## Sudbury Apostles

Except for Jean-Pièrre and Héloïse, the apostles returned to Sudbury and, for the most part, tried to pick up the threads of their lives. But something indefinable had changed. They had only spent a couple of weeks with Eddie, but the experience had marked them all. The Dionne sisters felt that, without Jean-Pièrre, they would never again be comfortable attending St. Gabriel Lalemont, so every week they turned up at a different place of worship. Roman Catholicism now seemed too narrow a road for them. One week they would visit a local mosque, another a synagogue, another one of the many protestant denominations. Eventually, the sight of the four elderly sisters treading through the snow towards any of the churches, synagogues, temples or mosques in the area, was greeted with great warmth. After a year or so, they began to see that the different religions could get along quite well on a local level. Perhaps coming back to a place like Sudbury after such a life-altering experience had allowed the sisters to really see the place for the first time.

When the sisters had been born, Sudbury had been a city blighted by the pollution from the smelting of ore, to such a degree that much of the vegetation had died. The earth that remained had been poisoned, and many of the lakes had become so acidic that no fish could survive. During their childhoods, there had been days when the sulphurous air had been so toxic that the children of the town had been kept indoors with the windows closed tight, for days. But even before they had met Eddie, the regreening of Sudbury had begun. First the 1,250-foot Superstack had been built to disperse the fumes from nickel smelting. Then, for years, work crews had spread out over the dead landscape, planting trees and hardy plants, and adding lime to the acid soil to neutralize it.

Not until they returned from Jerusalem did the Dionnes really notice that the regreening of Sudbury had sweetened the air, cured many of the acid lakes and created new virgin forests. "Eddie was right," said Cécile as they set out for the mosque on Churchill Avenue. "Paradise was here all along."

"We just had to remake it ourselves," said her sister Annette.

Every year on the summer solstice, the Survivors of the Second Coming, as they came to call themselves, piled into Claude's bus and he drove them out to the erratic where Eddie had appeared. There, they set up tents and barbeques before gathering around a fire that cast flickering shadows on the erratic where Eddie had been discovered. The reunion had been suggested by Lydia after she and Arthur had each received a postcard. According to the caption, the picture was of Sri Pada, also known as Adam's Peak, a sacred mountain in the center of the teardrop island, Sri Lanka. Each card contained a handwritten note from Eddie. When the cards had arrived bearing no stamp or address, Lydia had called around to the other apostles, and to Marc and Paulette. Every one of them had received a postcard.

At that first reunion, many of them read out the messages. Alphonse and Annette had declined, feeling that their messages were too personal. Over the years, these messages from Eddie told them about the life he and Pannychis were living in Kandy. The local Sinhalese felt honored when, on February 21st, 2006, Eddie had renamed himself Marpa, after the great Buddhist translator. When Pannychis had asked him why he had picked that name, Eddie had told her that Archbishop Marcinkus had died the day before. "His secret name in P2, the masons in the Vatican, had been Marpa. Marcinkus had done his best to save Pablo, so by taking his masonic name, I can honor him too."

Eddie and Pannychis moved into a comfortable old house across Kandy's artificial lake from the Temple of the Tooth. In the mornings during the dry season, they sat on their veranda, drank plain tea and ate hoppers, small thin pancakes shaped like bowls, with *lunu miris*, a mixture of red onions and spices.

The civil war between the Sri Lankan government and the Tamil Tigers had already been going on for six years, with atrocities on both sides, when Eddie and Pannychis had arrived. Pannychis had established a fashion house, employing local Sinhalese and Tamils to make, sell and model her designs. For years, on the runways in Paris and Milan, her tall black models dressed in bright tropical colors showed that haute couture could happen outside the fashion houses of Paris and Milan.

Eddie was soon fluent in Sinhalese and Tamil tongues. He and Pannychis would always attend the annual expositions of Buddha's Tooth, sealed within its seven nested vessels. At these times, buses would fill the town with pilgrims who would line up around Kandy Lake for hours, for the merest glimpse. With the monks, Eddie set up a charity called 'The Peace Option' to minister to the orphaned children on both sides and work for peace. And finally, in 2009, peace came when the government troops decidedly defeated the Tigers and united the country.

Lydia had not been sure how the first reunion of the apostles would turn out. She worried that the only thing they had in common was the intense two weeks they had spent with Eddie. She need not have worried. What they really shared was a need to talk to the only other people who had shared their journey. Those who had tried to tell their friends about their pilgrimage to Jerusalem had found misunderstanding or even ridicule. So every one of them had jumped at the chance to talk to the only people who truly understood how profoundly they had been affected. Jean-Pièrre and Héloïse had flown over for the second reunion and had continued to come almost every year.

Always a highlight of the reunions at the erratic was Lydia's talk about the wonders of the night sky. By the third or fourth year, every one of the apostles, even Alphonse, could point out the summer triangle, three stars visible to the naked eye: Deneb, Altair and Vega. Afterwards there would be a short silence, punctuated in most years by the cry of a whip-poor-will. Then someone would recall the mass of magpies that had shielded them first from the IDF, then from the religious mobs that threatened them, as the earthquake struck. Sometimes the mood was nostalgic as one or another longed for the chance to see Eddie just once more. At this point, Lydia would set up her telescope and distract them with the sights of the Crab Nebula or the spectacular whorl of the Andromeda Galaxy.

Over the years, as e-mail and then Skype became commonplace, Lydia, Jean-Pièrre and Héloïse, and Mahinda had kept in touch. None of the others had a computer, so Lydia took it upon herself to keep them up to date on the news from Paris and Kandy.

When they had met for the twenty-fourth time, in 2013, the mood was sombre. In the brief span of two months, all four of the Dionne sisters had died. Émilie went first, followed twelve days later by Annette, then Cécile and last of all Yvonne. The others had organized themselves to keep a vigil as each of them faded away. Jean-Pièrre and Héloïse had not come because Héloïse was undergoing chemotherapy for breast cancer and was too weak to travel.

Alphonse managed to brighten the mood briefly when he was looking through the telescope at Messier 12, a star cluster full of binary stars whirling around each other in tight orbits until one destroys the other. Suddenly Alphonse saw a streak of light cross the lens and said, "I saw a flash."

"It was a meteorite. We all saw it," Lydia told him, "but seeing it through the telescope is very, very rare. You should make a wish."

"Don't tell anyone or it won't come true," said Claude, the bus driver.

The others began to tell each other that the streak of light reminded them of Eddie's arrival from the sky.

At first, Marc Baptiste had little to do with the other Eddifieds, because he was spending all his spare time in Montreal with Paulette Riopelle. He had also started a new job as Liz Tyler's Public Information Officer. All of the Eddifieds were invited to Marc's wedding to Paulette in the summer of 1992.

In their spare time, Marc and Paulette worked with Jules on their pet project. They had invested the remainder of the money that had poured in to support Eddie in Water Works, a project to bring clean water to every native reserve in Canada. "Paradise now!" was their slogan.

Maria Magdalena had returned to Madame Souci's. When the old Madam became too infirm, she turned over the Sans Souci whorehouse to Maria. She made Eddie's mother promise that she would keep up the house's high standards and look after her 'ladies of negotiable affection.' With her new responsibilities, Maria only got intimate with clients when she felt an urge. Her main exception was Alphonse. At least one Saturday night a month, she would see Alphonse and play the Blessed Virgin to his penitent penis. Afterwards, he no longer rushed to the St. Gabriel Lalemant for absolution. Eddie had told them to work to create an earthly paradise, and his sessions with Lisa (he still used Maria's pseudonymn in the House) made him happy in anticipation, in action, and in recollection. An orgasm induced by Eddie's mother? What could be more heavenly?

# Part Nineteen: Sri Lanka

## Twenty-five Years Later: Apotheosis

No wind means that the snow that has fallen in large flakes overnight has settled gently on to the winter-bare tree branches. Like pencil sketches of themselves, the trees around frozen Ramsey Lake stand silent and still. Behind them, the dawning sun tints the few clouds in watercolor pastels of pink and baby blue. The sight takes Lydia's breath away as she opens the curtains. Soon the first breezes will destroy the perfect snowscape by stripping the branches bare. We treasure beauty partly because it is not eternal, she tells herself. Not for the first time, she wishes she could paint, but even Lauren Harris could only paint an interpretation. Despite the fact that everyone seemed to have a camera phone these days, no reproduction by any means could capture this scene. "First day of spring next week," she mutters to herself with a smile. Most northerners are ready to curse the winter by this time and hope it will just melt away, but for Lydia this brilliant snowscape is the earthly paradise Eddie had talked about.

When the coffee is ready, she opens the front door. A single set of footprints in her driveway. The papergirl has already delivered the Globe and Mail for March 16th, 2014. A breath of cold air leaps in when Lydia closes the door. Clutching her robe to her, she crosses to the kitchen island and pours herself a coffee. A glance at the headlines: War in Ukraine. Obama Imposes Further Sanctions. Suicide Bombing in Damascus. Rob Ford, Toronto's crack-smoking mayor claims, "I am not a criminal."

She closes the paper and slides it across the table. Turning towards the French windows, she looks out over the lake beyond her snow-bound deck. Already a chill breeze has sprung up and the trees are beginning to shed their snow. Arthur will grumble about the late snowfall. To him it means he will have to shovel the driveway. Last year she had suggested that they get a snowblower, but he had refused. "It's one of the few exercises I get since I retired," he had explained, "That and curling at the Idylwylde."

She hears him now shuffling down the stairs and pours him a coffee. At that moment two white envelopes drop through the mailbox announcing themselves by soft slaps on the hardwood floor. "I'll get it. Here. Drink your coffee. It's a lovely morning."

"Hmmm," Arthur says, looking out at the new-fallen snow.

"Letters from Eddie," Lydia says, coming back to the table with the two white envelopes. "There's one for you and one for me. No addresses. Just like the postcards we get from him every year."

Arthur goes to the door and looks out. "Well, someone delivered it. There's a set of tracks up to the door."

"That's the papergirl's. There would be two sets of footprints."

"Hmmm." Arthur returns to the table and sips his coffee. "Mysterious."

"Ways," she answers automatically.

"You think these are letters from the Big Guy this time?" Arthur looks at the envelopes with renewed interest. "Same writing as on the post cards. Fine cursive writing with a fountain pen. Eddie's handwriting. Who else even knows how to write like that any more. The kids just text all the time on their iPhones."

"I think it's charming," says Lydia.

The envelopes contain invitations to join Eddie and Pannychis in Kandy for the twenty-fifth anniversary of their first meeting with Eddie at the erratic. "And plane tickets," says Lydia, waving hers in the air.

After breakfast, Lydia calls Jean-Pièrre and Héloïse. They too have received invitations. Héloïse is feeling better; her cancer is in remission. "Then you'll be meeting us in Kandy?" asks Lydia.

"As long as Héloïse is fit to travel," Jean-Pièrre tells her. "It'll help that the plane tickets are first class. It's a long journey. Even farther for you people."

"They're first class tickets?"

"Ours are. I just assumed ..."

Lydia picks up one of the tickets. "You're right. Makes me feel like a princess."

Lydia spends the next couple of hours calling the others. Marc and

Paulette cannot go because their daughter is graduating from McGill Medical School.

"Ask Eddie what I should do with the holy foreskin," Marc says.

"You still have it?" asks Lydia, surprised.

"Yeah, it's in a safety deposit box at the Royal Bank on Durham Street."

"Really? I'd forgotten all about it."

"Jules and I had decided to ask Chief Sawchuk if he could get the RCMP lab to test its DNA. But after the debacle at the Dome, we thought we'd better hang on to it."

"I'll ask Eddie what we should do with it," Lydia assures him.

One last call, and she is hesitant about making it. Maria Magdalena had rebuffed Lydia's early attempts to keep in touch. But she is Eddie's mother, Lydia tells herself as she dials the number.

Maria acknowledges that she has received the invitation, but although she would love to see her son again, she cannot make it. "I have to be in Ottawa at the end of June. You probably remember that the Supreme Court struck down Canada's prostitution laws on December 20th but the damned Tories have a year to come up with another repressive law. I'm on the executive of the SPOC, the Sex Professionals of Canada, with Terry Bedford, so I have to be there for the big rally. But let Eddie know I was thinking of him."

"Sure will," says Lydia as she hangs up.

## Brown's Upper Glencairn Bungalow

Jean-Pièrre and Héloïse touch down at Colombo's Bandaranaike International Airport on Thursday, June 19th. Mahinda, Eddie and Pannychis are waiting for them under a backlit sign that claims 'Air Lanka: No other airline gives you a taste of Paradise.' After a joyful reunion, Eddie says, "I'm sure you two could use some rest, so Mahinda has booked us all rooms at the Galle Face Hotel on the waterfront. The others are due in tomorrow morning. Sleep in as long as you like. We'll pick up the others in the morning and come back for you. The hotel even has free wi-fi. All the modern conveniences. Oh, and aircon, of course. I'm sure you find it hot here."

Pannychis says, "33 Celsius today and humid."

"Oh, Sri Lanka is always humid," Mahinda admits, "especially now. It is monsoon season here and in the hills."

"It is very hot," Héloïse admits.

Pannychis had been at her mother's side in Paris a few months before as Héloïse underwent chemo. She is looking a little better, Pannychis tells herself. "It is very hot, *maman*. Don't worry. Tomorrow we are driving up into the hills. Up there you might even need a sweater in the evenings."

The next morning, the Sudbury contingent arrives. Everyone piles into the battered white minivan and the Land Rover, borrowed by Mahinda from the Institute of Fundamental Studies in Kandy.

On the winding drive up into tea country, Arthur, with his peculiar sensitivities, notices something has changed in Eddie. True, they are all a quarter of a century older but it is something else, something he can't quite put his finger on. Not until the vehicles stop for refreshments at a roadside stand a few kilometers south of Kandy does Arthur realize what it is. Arthur had always been the only apostle to see the Holy Spirit clearly. Only now does he realize that he has always felt her presence, even when she was within Eddie. Now, she seems to be absent, and that disturbs him.

When Eddie excuses himself and walks into the jungle for a piss, Arthur follows him. While the two men are watering the base of a strangler fig, Arthur says, "It seems to me, Eddie, that the Holy Spirit is no longer with you."

Eddie says nothing until he has squeezed out the last drop and is adjusting the sarong he is wearing. Finally he turns to Arthur and says, "That's right. The others sometimes caught a glimpse of her but you, Arthur, you always sensed her. And, as usual, you're right. As soon as Pannychis and I had settled in Kandy, Marie appeared to both of us. We had been sitting on the veranda of our house, looking out into the garden and beyond that the lake and the Temple of the Tooth. Marie had appeared in her nun's habit at our table. Even Pannychis could see and hear her clearly. She talked to us for quite a while about what we'd begun to call 'The Disaster at the Dome.' She told us how impressed the Big Guy was about how we had handled the situation. I was still bitter about the Big Guy dumping us in the shit, not to mention that we had accomplished absolutely zip. 'Only the passage of years will reveal what truly happened that day,' she told us. 'You don't need me any more. Without me, you will be able to live normal lives. But I will return when the Big Guy sends me.' Well, she returned briefly at the vernal equinox and told me to invite the surviving apostles to Sri Lanka. Apparently the Big Guy needed us again. That was why you all received the tickets and the letters. Then she disappeared again, but she assured us she will be back when we all meet the Big Guy again."

"We're here to meet the Big Guy?"

"That's right."

Some hours later, they arrive at Brown's Upper Glencairn Bungalow, in the hill country above the tiny village of Dickoya. The handsome single-story mansion, once the home of a British plantation manager, is surrounded by hillsides full of tea plants where Tamil women pluck the leaves as they have for generations. Sitting at more than 4,000 feet, the bungalow was once a place for the British to escape the heat of the coast. Here the air is temperate enough that the British had no trouble growing the roses that are still a feature of the bungalow's ornamental gardens. From the gardens, there is a spectacular view of Sri Pada, the conical peak sacred to Buddhists, Hindus, Christians and Muslims. Now a small hotel, the bungalow has five guest rooms, so Mahinda had booked the entire place.

That night after an excellent supper, Eddie pours himself another glass of wine and leads his guests out into the twilight garden. "Magical," murmurs Lydia as she looks out across the mist-covered valley at Sri Pada, now glowing in the last rays of the setting sun.

"Like a tongue of Pentacostal fire," says Jean-Pièrre. Others nod agreement.

"That's where we are going tomorrow," Eddie tells them. "Mahinda has agreed to act as our local guide. He's going to tell us about the mountain. When he's finished, I'll give you an idea of what we've planned."

"We're really going to meet the Big Guy?" asks Alphonse.

Eddie laughs good-naturedly. "I can always rely on you to get right to the point, Alphonse. I'll say more about that when Mahinda's finished."

The sun sets quickly in tropical latitudes, so by the time Mahinda points to the magic mountain, darkness has fallen but a sliver of moon has risen and is making the mist in the valleys seem to emit a ghostly glow. Towering above the mist, Sri Pada is darker than the sky, except for a ribbon of lights stretching up to the very top.

"Sri Pada means 'beautiful footprint' in my language. We believe it is the footprint of the Buddha. The Christian Portuguese and the Muslims call it Adam's footprint, but it has many other names. It was recognized as a holy place in Lanka's *Mahawamsa* as early as 140 B.C., and again in the *Ramayana*. "Unlike the site of the Dome of the Rock and the Second Temple, which have been soaked in blood for centuries" – several of the pilgrims shuffle uncomfortably at the memory – "Sri Pada has always been a sanctuary for all faiths. Tomorrow we will ascend to the Buddhist monastery at the top where we will see the footprint itself."

"How high is it?" asks Thomas.

"About 2,200 meters."

"What's the elevation of this place?" Jean-Pièrre asks.

"Around 1,200 meters."

"So we're going to climb over a thousand meters? Tomorrow? We're not in the first bloom of youth, Mahinda. I'm not sure most of us would survive. And you know that Héloïse has been ill."

"Yes, yes, but Eddie assures me we will have no trouble. There are steps all the way to the top, and we will take our time."

Eddie realizes it is time for reassurance. "I promise every one of you that you will find it surprisingly easy tomorrow."

Héloïse assures them that if Eddie says not to worry then she, for one, has no reservations about the climb. For a few minutes, the pilgrims discuss it among themselves before appointing Lydia as unofficial spokesperson. "We are with you, Eddie, no matter where you lead us."

Eddie's eyes well with tears. Pannychis takes his hand. "He loves you beyond imagining," she tells them, "and I, for one, don't really know what awaits at the summit, but I believe it will be something wonderful."

"Won't there be other people going up at the same time?" asks Claude.

"No. Signs have been erected today closing the path to other pilgrims due to weather. We are in the monsoon season up here, and torrential rains sometimes make the mountain dangerous, so closing the path for forty-eight hours will not seem odd. Very few risk the climb during the monsoon anyway."

"Then let's go in and get a good night's sleep. If you can manage it, my love, then I, for one, can't wait to go up," says Jean-Pièrre.

"I'll be fine," says Héloïse and means it.

"Better bring some rain gear and a sweater," Eddie says. "Oh, someone should let Marc know that the safety deposit box in his bank is empty."

"So where is the *santissimo prepuzio*?" asks Jean-Pièrre.

"The Big Guy transferred it to the Temple of the Tooth in Kandy. There it shares pride of place with Buddha's Tooth."

"But what about the annual exposition of Buddha's Tooth?"

Eddie smiles. "The monks never open the seventh sealed jar that contains the tooth itself."

"Then no one will ever see it."

"Exactly. Marie told me the Big Guy wanted to keep it close. Just in case."

### Ascent of Sri Pada

Late the next evening, Eddie and the others pile into the vehicles for the thirty-three kilometer drive to Sri Pada. Taking the Hatton path, the pilgrims walk under the red and yellow ribbons streaming in the wind from the great Makhura Gateway. Just as they begin to climb the ancient steps, they are surprised by a sudden tropical downpour. While it lasts, conversation is almost impossible, so they shelter under a kithule tree. A few minutes later, the rain stops as suddenly as it began. Eddie shrugs and says, "Rainy season. The four biggest rivers in Sri Lanka originate here on Sri Pada. That's a lot of water. Sometimes when the rain comes, water rushes in torrents down these steps."

"Then what the Hell are we doing here?" Claude mutters.

"A fair question, Claude. The Big Guy assured me that the rains will clear as we ascend," Eddie tells him, knowing that Claude is not the only one remembering the unpleasant surprises leading to the Disaster at the Dome a quarter of a century before. "A word of caution. This is the off-season so you'll see that, especially on the lower slopes, the jungle has begun to reclaim the paths, as it does every year. So watch for tangled roots, fallen palm leaves and so on. If you see any movement on the path, stop. It might be a green pit viper. Oh, one last thing. Land leeches. Mahinda has a good supply of Deet. The leeches hate it."

"I fucking hate leeches," says Thomas LaRue.

Mahinda passes out bottles of the powerful insecticide. "I import it from Canada through the internet," Mahinda explains.

Eddie's forecast is right. Within the first few minutes, Thomas lets out a terrified yelp. "I got them sons-o'-bitches on my arm. All I did was brush against some wet leaves."

Mahinda nods. "That's all it takes." Deftly he puts a tiny drop on each of the three leaches on Thomas's arm. One by one, they shrivel and drop off.

"Wow. I love this stuff," says Thomas.

Within the first hour of their climb, the rain clouds clear. They can see few stars because of the lights along the path, but they are cheered by the emergence of a crescent moon above the summit. When Eddie asks if they would like to stop to rest, the pilgrims all decline.

"I can't believe I have so much energy," says Héloïse. The others agree.

"Let's wait until we reach the Sama Chattya. It's a white stupa built by Japanese Buddhist monks," Eddie suggests. "We can eat the sandwiches the cook made for us."

So they set out again in good spirits. As with those pilgrims who set out before them, whether to Canterbury, Santiago de Compostella, or the Ka'aba, Eddie's followers filled the time with talk as they climbed the steps.

"Why 1989?" asks Arthur suddenly, as a band of cloud moves up from the valley and begins to shroud the path in a pale mist. "Why not the millennium? It was only eleven years away."

Eddie nods. "Dates are slippery, Arthur. You're talking about eleven years, but what about the eleven days?"

"Yes, Arthur what about the eleven days?" agrees Lydia, the astronomer. "When we switched over from the old Julian calendar to the Gregorian one we use now, eleven days disappeared, never to be seen again. There were riots in England with mobs shouting, 'Give us back our eleven days!.'"

"And here in Sri Lanka, Arthur, the millennial year was 2544 in the Buddhist calendar."

"1989 was a special year," Jean-Pièrre says. "The USSR fell apart. Tiananmen Square. An earthquake struck the Dome of the Rock."

"Another stopped the World Series in San Francisco, same year," says Claude, a baseball fan.

"Didn't Khomeini die that year?" says Lydia.

"And politicians were just beginning to take climate change seriously," says Héloïse.

"Yeah," says Eddie, "finally everyone is taking it seriously, but remember there is a greater threat to global wellbeing. The population explosion. Since we got internet access at the Institute of Fundamental Studies, Mahinda has been monitoring the population growth over the years. Tell them what you have you learned, Mahinda."

"Certainly, Eddie. Twenty-five years ago, on the day we first met, there were more than five billion of us on the planet. Today, the world population stands at over seven billion."

"Then the population is growing faster than ever," says Arthur, a note of disappointment in his voice.

"Well, yes and no, my good friend. Yes, the population has grown by around two billion in only a quarter of a century, but the growth has slowed. Eddie appeared during the slack tide of population growth. 1989 was the year the annual population increase began to shrink. The increase in 1989 was still ninety million but almost every year since Eddie's appearance, fewer people have been born. This year the population will still rise, but only by about eighty million."

"But it's still getting bigger," Jean-Pièrre points out.

"Yes. But today there is less famine in the world than at any time in our history."

"But how long can we keep it up before a huge die-off happens?" asks Jean-Pièrre.

"Let's wait until we get to the top. The Big Guy must have an answer," says Eddie. For a time, they climb in silence.

"Well, we've done our part," says Alphonse after a time.

"What do you mean?" Lydia asks.

Alphonse suddenly looks shy as all eyes turn to him. "Well, how many of us have kids?"

"That's right." Jean-Pièrre looks at Alphonse with a new respect. "Héloïse had Pannychis before she met Eddie ..."

"And Arthur had Bartholomew before he met me," adds Lydia.

"Not that we've seen him in over a decade," says Arthur gloomily. "Not since he decided not to keep in touch with us."

"Yes, Dear." She pats his arm sympathetically. Arthur rarely mentions Bartholomew any more, but the hurt will never leave him. "The only one of us with more than one child is Mahinda. He's got those four lovely girls."

Mahinda nods. "Only the younger two are still at home now. Nevinka is at JPL doing post-doctoral work in aerospace engineering. This spring, my wife Anusha and I moved our second eldest, Lakmini, to Birmingham, England. She is studying at the Shakespeare Institute there."

"I'm glad to hear they are doing so well," says Lydia.

Mahinda sighs. "Anusha and I have been married exactly twenty-two years today," he says in a soft voice that betrays his great love for his wife.

"Ah, you decided to marry on the summer solstice," says Lydia.

Mahinda shrugs. "The astrologer approved."

"Whenever someone in Canada puts down arranged marriages, we tell them how happy you and Anusha have been."

"How the years have flown by. As we get older, we realize how short our lives are." Nods of agreement. "We went through some bad times during the civil war, but in the last few years Sri Lanka has really lived up to its claim that it gives one a taste of paradise."

"Would you ever consider living anywhere else?"

"Oh my goodness no. This island has wrapped itself around me like that." Mahinda points into the darkness beyond the path lights at a huge strangler fig caressing its dying host.

When the ghostly white stupa, Sama Chatiya, looms out of the darkness, the pilgrims sink gratefully on to the rough steps and revive themselves with the sandwiches and water they have carried up with them.

Arthur picks up a piece of rock and examines it closely in the beam of his flashlight. "Finding any fossils?" asks Mahinda.

Arthur laughs. "Hardly."

"What's so funny?" asks Claude.

"Oh, this." Arthur says, tossing the rock to him. "This metamorphic rock is Precambrian. Metamorphic and Precambrian. No chance of fossils."

"Right. Now I get it." Claude tosses the rock back.

"We geologists try to avoid taking too much for granite." Mahinda groans. Arthur turns to Claude and tells him, "And now you've heard the two oldest jokes in geology."

Claude holds out his hand for the rock again and Arthur passes it to him with the flashlight. "What's special about this lump?" he asks.

"Well, remember where we first met?"

"At the erratic."

"Right. All the rock in that area is Precambrian, worn smooth by glaciation."

Claude peers closely at the rock in his hand. "Doesn't look like this. Our hills are smooth and round. They don't feel like this either."

"That's right. But believe me, they are exactly the same rock. That piece in your hand is garnetiferous gneiss, metamorphic rock with lots of garnets in it. See those reddish protrusions?"

"Yeah."

"Those are garnets."

"Eddie appeared to us on the erratic," Mahinda explains. "And here, on the other side of the world, the rock is the same. But you are right, Claude. They don't look the same at all. Here in the tropics, hot weather and pounding rain breaks down the rock and liberates the gems inside."

Eddie walks over and says, "The clouds are moving in above us." He points up the path where heavy mist has already closed visibility down to no more than ten meters. "We'll be on top in just over an hour if we leave now. That way, we'll be in plenty of time to see the sunrise." And so they set out again.

One last twist in the path and they break free of the clouds. Fifty meters farther up, they stop and look out in awe at the flat clouds glowing white below them. The lights of the temple and the shelters on the summit are clearly visible, too. They quicken their steps and, a few minutes later, they arrive at the small plateau on the summit of Sri Pada. Somewhere, a muffled bell is tolling slowly. Sitting in the full lotus position before a candle surrounded by lotus blossoms, is a monk with a topknot. In saffron robes despite the cold, he radiates serenity.

Following Mahinda's lead, the others raise their hands and put them together in a *wai* and bow to the venerable old monk. "What should we call you?" Arthur ventures.

The monks favors him with a seraphic smile and says, "You can call me Sid, Arthur."

Eddie suddenly throws back his head and laughs, startling the others. "It's Him, Arthur. It's the Big Guy."

The monk nods and hums a couple of bars of 'Love Me Tender.' "When in Rome and all that. Good to see you all again."

"And I'm guessing that's Marie ringing the bell."

"Sure is, Son. Now gather around, people, I've got some very important things for you to consider, and we don't have much time." The pilgrims form a semi-circle around the old monk. "Come here and sit by me, Son." Eddie sits at the Big Guy's right hand. A moment later, amid gasps from the others, Marie emerges from behind the temple, still dressed in her grey nun's habit, and sits on the Big Guy's left.

"I can see her," Alphonse says, his eyes big with surprise. Sounds of delight and shocked agreement from the others.

"Yes, now you can all see her, not just Arthur," says the Big Guy.

## God Only Knows

"First thing. It's great to see you all again. You have been very patient. I know, I know, it must seem like a long time. Twenty-five years. All I can say is that, to me, it seems no more than a nanosecond.

"Let me take you back to what you have been calling the Disaster at the Dome." He looks at each of them in turn. "I just have to say that you guys were so brave. I still find it hard to believe how well you handled that. You were all wonderful. Thank you from the bottom of my heart!"

Eddie can see that everyone is moved by the Big Guy's thanks but, at the risk of spoiling the mood, he asks the question that has been on his mind for the past quarter century: "Did you cause the earthquake?"

For a few seconds, everyone present seems too tense to breathe. Finally, the Big Guy smiles and slowly nods. Eddie holds up his hand to stifle the murmurs of discontent. "All part of the plan?"

The Big Guy sighs. "Remember we talked about chaos theory, the butterfly effect? The fact that tiny, even insignificant effects can, in combination, have a vast influence on future events and make it very, very difficult to predict how that same future will evolve? Not surprisingly, most predictions about coming times appear laughable when that time arrives. Well, let me tell you that even a God in such a non-deterministic universe, is unlikely to predict outcomes with unerring accuracy.

"Hey, what I'm trying to tell you is that I did cause the earthquake, but it was a decision made at the last possible moment. The Intifada was, of course, a factor, but the crash of Bus 405 the day before your visit to the Dome pushed the enmity between Jews and Arabs to a new level. And the murder of poor Pope Urban was the final straw ..." Suddenly everyone was shouting at once. The Big Guy stared at them until the last voice died. "Yes, he was assassinated. I felt that with Bishop Marcinkus by his side – he'd already prevented the assassination of two popes – and a well-trained detachment of Israeli police, Carbone would not be able to find a way. But there is always a moment. Carbone found his moment but died a few seconds later at the hand of one of his own accomplices, Kamel Zidani. Zidani died with a police bullet in his back. The other accomplice, a Palestinian Muslim who had been living in France, is the one that interests us. His name in those days was Nassim Hamidori. More about him in a moment.

"With the dying pope out of the picture, your meeting with the other leaders of the People of the Book was never going to happen. The two chief rabbis of Jerusalem were waiting for the pope to reach the Wailing Wall. When they heard the news from the Holy Sepulchre, they were outraged and called for Jews to join them in marching onto the grounds of the Dome of the Rock, the site of the Second Temple of Israel. That temple lies under the Dome, except for the Western Wall.

"The Muslim leaders of the Sunni and Shia sects felt betrayed, too, when they received the news. Immediately they had withdrawn from the Dome area to raise a force to oppose the new Messiah. Even the fundamental Christians were approaching along the Via Dolorosa.

"So ... the earth moved. And thanks to Eddie, the IDF, and the Jerusalem Police, all of you survived, bruised mentally and physically, but unbowed."

While the Big Guy had been talking, Marie had risen and drifted from view behind the small temple. Now she emerges carrying a large brass tray and sets it down in the midst of the company. "Plain tea," she says.

A pause while Marie fills the teacups and hands them out. For a few minutes, while the pilgrims sip the warming tea, they talk among themselves about the notable events of the past twenty-five years: 9/11, the ill-advised invasions of Kuwait and Iraq, the market collapse of 2008, the bitterly disappointing results of the so-called Arab Spring and now the rise of Daesh, who are sweeping through Syria and Iraq, leaving a trail of tears, blood and desolation.

"Not a quarter century of peace on earth or good will towards your fellow creatures," the Big Guy comments as they finish their tea. "Every attempt by western democracies to fix the Middle East has made the chaos worse."

"And yet nobody tried the solution that Edward de Bono proposed," says Eddie.

The Big Guy breaks out in a huge grin, shaking his head. "De Bono's proposal was certainly one of the least damaging. We'll never know if it would have worked even though the U.N. championed it."

"Who's this de Bono guy?" asks Thomas LaRue.

"He's a famous thinker, Thomas," Eddie explains. "Writes shelf loads of books, especially on creativity. Came up with the term 'lateral thinking.' In 1999, the U.K. Foreign Office called him in to try to solve the perpetual crisis in the Middle East. De Bono told the committee that one of the basic problems of the area was that all the bread was unleavened. Unleavened bread has no zinc. The lack of zinc makes people irritable. De Bono reasoned that since Marmite, the yeast extract that the Brits eat on toast, is full of zinc, the west should ship it by the case to the Arabs. The U.N. is rumored to have seriously considered his idea but never carried it out."

"Pity," says Thomas. "Who knows? Might have worked."

"Certainly wouldn't have done any harm," agrees Jean-Pièrre.

"Well, at least it produced a great headline, Louise Jury's piece 'De Bono's Marmite Plan for Peace in the Middle Yeast,'" Eddie tells him. Polite laughter.

God clears his throat and everyone subsides into silence. "Earlier I mentioned Nassim Hamidori."

"The guy who got away after they killed the pope," says Alphonse.

"That's him. Because of him, I think that mankind still has a chance to set up an Earthly Paradise." The Big Guy can see that the pilgrims are puzzled, but he certainly has their attention. "For a few years, he worked with Hezbollah sending rockets into Israel. Then he dropped out of sight, but three years ago he resurfaced as a member of ISIS, using an Arabic name meaning 'the Killing Cane.' He has become one of the most ruthless commanders of Daesh, who are striving to revive the Islamic Califate. Based in Ramalla, he has committed such atrocities, that his very name strikes fear. You may have seen one of his videos. He is usually carrying an apparently ordinary hickory cane but there is nothing ordinary about it at all. It is the cane that Gino Carbone used to kill Pope Urban and he uses it to taunt his victims before killing them.

"You must understand that this man would not have followed this life path if he had not taken on the job offered by Gino Carbone. The experience that day helped to radicalize him further. Now he is one of the greatest war criminals in the Middle East, and helps the Califate control large swaths of Syria and Iraq.

"At the moment, a dark cloud of evil has settled over the Middle East, but from this great evil will eventually come a great good. Already boatloads of refugees are fleeing into Europe. Over the next few years they will flood into Europe in the millions. What are these people bringing with them? These are the educated people fleeing, and they bring skills to Europe and eventually North America. The western democracies have grown old, their birthrates too low to sustain their population. They need this infusion of youth, energy and ambition. In turn, the refugees seeking a better life will eventually assimilate into western societies. Their women, many of whom are already educated, will become equal members of their adopted societies and will have fewer children. There will be lots of problems, of course, but in little more than a century, the world population will stabilize and an earthly paradise will take its first tentative steps.

"So you see, the Disaster at the Dome was not the disaster you have always thought. If you people had not gone to Jerusalem to support Eddie, the world might have taken a different, more dangerous direction." The Big Guy puts his arm around Eddie and Marie. "So you see, you've all played your part in establishing the New Jerusalem. But because your time on the world's stage is so brief, none of you will experience it."

"Like Moses," Eddie says softly.

"Like Moses," the Big Guy agrees. "So I am offering all of you immortality." The Big Guy puts up his hand against the sudden flurry of questions. "Wait. Let me quickly explain. I have already talked about this with Eddie and Pannychis. They have accepted. Your journey to this point began twenty-five years ago in a season when caterpillars had overwhelmed the landscape where you live. And now you have crossed the seas and come to Sri Pada, to the mountain of the butterflies. If any or all of you decide to join Eddie and Pannychis, you have the next two hours to decide."

A quick whispered exchange between Héloïse and Jean-Pièrre and then Héloïse says, "We will come."

"Oh, yes," cries Jean-Pièrre. "We will come."

"Where will we be going?" asks Alphonse, sounding not a little confused.

"We will be going to a planet inhabited by some of the most pleasant bipeds you'll ever meet. They will welcome you like the long-lost cousins that you are. The inhabitants, a long-lived people called the Arthurians, refer to their planet as 'Avalon', but I usually think of it as 'Camelot' because the weather is so temperate. Oh, to help you make up your mind, let me tell you that those four lovely Dionne sisters are waiting there for you to join them." He shrugs and adds, "Marie insisted."

The Big Guy rises and the others follow him up a few steps into the small temple that houses Buddha's footprint. There, Eddie and the others contemplate the large stone outline in silence, until their minds are emptied and each is filled with a tranquility that passes all understanding. One by one the pilgrims choose their fate, but before anyone can announce their choice, Marie says, "Now we need to look to the East. The sun is about to rise."

They follow her out to the parapet. With heart-stopping suddenness, the sun rises above the horizon and floods the mists in the surrounding valleys with its rays. Then the butterflies appear flying in strings, like decorated kite tails. Up through the mists they rise, battalions of painted sawtooths, yellow-and-white with a fringe of gold, tigers in brown-and-white, fluttering fritillaries, painted ladies and red admirals. Soon they cover the temple and the outer shelters and even land on shoulders and palms.

"Where's the Big Guy?" Eddie asks Marie.

"Gone on ahead," she tells him before leading the pilgrims to the west side of the small plateau. "Look there." she points to the perfect triangle which is the shadow of Sri Pada projected by the new sun on to the canvas of clouds below so that, by some optical illusion, it seems to stand before them. Mesmerized, they all watch the triangle shrinking as the sun gets higher.

Just then, a kaleidoscope of butterflies flutters up and the pilgrims are engulfed by their gentle chains. Mahinda hears the unmistakable voice of the Big Guy saying, "Second star to the right and straight on 'til morning." And then the butterflies rise towards the crescent moon until they become a dot in the brightening sky, and then even the dot disappears. Silence descends on Sri Pada and Mahinda finds himself alone.

Going back into the place of the footprint, he says a prayer before stepping out and looking off to the west. As he starts down, he pulls out his cellphone and calls his wife. When she answers, he says simply. "I'm on my way home."

He is halfway down the mountain before he realizes that there is no cell phone coverage from the top of Sri Pada. He smiles and quickens his pace.

*Fin*

www.ingramcontent.com/pod-product-compliance
Lightning Source LLC
Chambersburg PA
CBHW061029030726
47504CB00002B/307